WALKER'S COVE

a Romance

Suzannah Ellingwood Walker, age seventeen, on her wedding day.

WALKER'S COVE

a Romance

SET AMIDST THE WAR FOR INDEPENDENCE

1765–1777

E. P. WALKER

Any resemblance between the non historical characters in this book to those both living and dead is intentional, for they are my ancestors.

For information or comments, please write to:
David E. Murphy
Walker House Publishing
P.O. Box 95
Rockport, MA 01966

ISBN 978-0-9964307-1-5 (hardcover)
ISBN 978-0-9964307-0-8 (paperback)
ISBN 978-0-9964307-2-2 (ebook)

Library of Congress Control Number: 2016905243

Printed in the United States of America

To Katharine Fearing Loring

with love from your cousin

"She made home happy, and was all the world to her own . . ."

To Francis Ellingwood Abbot

"Love was the light . . . without you I would be nowhere . . ."

Ainsley Walker, 1772–1857

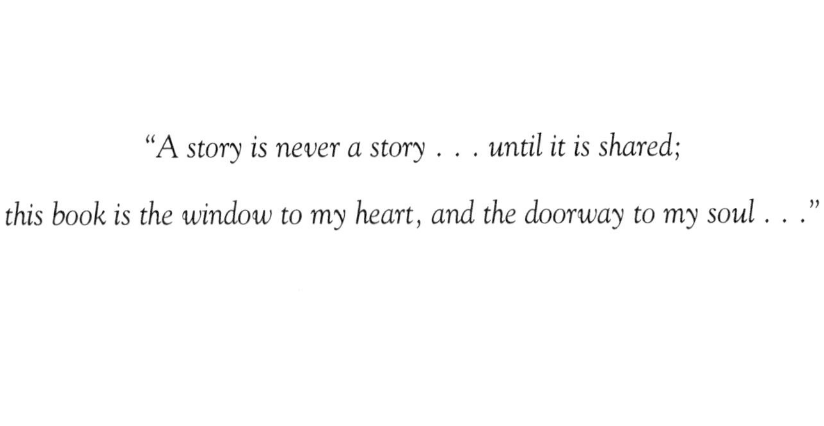

"A story is never a story . . . until it is shared;

this book is the window to my heart, and the doorway to my soul . . ."

With Grateful Thanks

For the assistance so generously given him during the course of writing *Walker's Cove*, the author is deeply grateful to:

Helen Phillips Walker, thank you for being my mother, and passing down the rich heritage of the Walker genes and ancestry. Little did we know . . .

Francis and Katharine Abbot, without whose gentle inspiration, the chronicle of *Walker's Cove* would still be unwritten.

Joslyn T. Pine, my tireless and wonderful editor, who deserves the credit for this novel's virtues, and is in no way to blame for its faults.

Susan M. Dagostino, my dear patient long-suffering wife, for standing by me all these years as I left you in literary widowhood. You had more faith in your husband's ability than he did.

Frances Elizabeth Lewis, who began the pink and white carnation tradition that carries on to this day.

Quincy S. Abbot, my distant cousin and the brother I never had. You are my soul mate and trailblazer, your unwavering guidance made this novel possible.

Betsey Wells Farber, thank you dear cousin for listening and sharing Katie through our common heritage. Through this novel, I now fulfill a sacred promise I made to her so long ago . . .

Shifting Trade Winds

here are many folk who call the seaside village of Walker's Cove "charming and quaint," while others call it "remote and isolated" . . . but I call it home. It is here that three generations of my family have lived, worked, married, raised children and died. Our family name is Walker, and I, James Walker, am the second in line to bear the name of my father, whose father Richard, founded Walker's Cove at the height of his powers, a mere one hundred years ago.

My grandfather Richard Walker, a "blacksmythe, clocke and gonne maker," was born in Surrey, England in 1673. After learning his trades at the hands of several blacksmiths and clockmakers, he undertook an apprenticeship to a fine London gunsmith. There, he perfected his skills in the manufacture of high-grade fowling pieces, muskets and pistols. While he believed that a "well rounded" tradesman during economic trouble or war could earn a good living from any one of these occupations, he knew a blacksmith would always be in demand.

Being an adventurous man, my grandfather left England, sailing for the Colonies on the ship *Elizabeth*. He was immediately attracted to the bustling harbor of Boston, a thriving hub of commercial activity, where he set up his first smithy. There, the merchant ships and shipyards were in constant need of spikes, mast and barrel hoops, house nails, pulley pins and decking nails. The carriage trades required wheel hoops, axles, axle nuts, pins, horseshoes and saddle rings. The taverns and homes needed cooking utensils, fireplace pokers, door hardware, kettle braces, firedogs, sconces and all manner of other odds and sods. Because of Richard's talents, the quality and variety of his goods, as well as their timely delivery (importing such necessities from England usually took a great deal of time), he made a very good living and quickly became noticeably wealthy.

Soon after his business became well established, Richard was admitted as a freeman—or a full citizen of Massachusetts—about the same time that the Royal Governor's administration took notice of his success, hounding him for levies on certain products of his manufacture, as well as for the privilege of residing there and carrying on his business. After ten years of punitive tax disputes, and with honest business deals becoming as scarce as feathers on a fish, he decided to flee from Boston's tax collectors and unabashed hustlers. He sold his business and sought a new place to live and work, far from the aggravation, taxation, accusations, swindling and pervasive religious intolerance he'd experienced.

Heading north, Richard found an expanse of land nestled in the sheltering arms of a small, isolated cove. Upon discovering that the only inhabitants were the native Abenakis who summered there, he quickly befriended them; forging arrowheads, fishhooks, knives and hatchets, and tridents for hunting and spearing eels in the rivers and marshes. In time he fabricated other tools and items that were useful and necessary to take a living from the land or sea. By trading honestly with the Abenaki people for land, pelts, game meat, crop foods and knowledge—especially in the ways of the woods—Richard became greatly respected and admired among them.

After a while, some of the sea captains who had patronized his business in Boston reacquainted themselves with Richard. Through word of mouth, they discovered his new location, and they were anxious for him to process their smuggled pig iron, copper, lead and even gold. Needing forged iron, pewter, brass goods and occasionally gold ingots, these men did not wish to "legally" import them, due to the Royal Governor's fees, taxes and endless bureaucratic delays. The scrap metal business thus began to thrive at Richard's smithy; and because all the transactions were hidden from the prying eyes of royal officials and their agents, his new enterprise helped foster a flourishing free trade center, which became loosely known as Walker's Cove.

As the years drifted by, other settlers, mostly tradesmen, farmers and seafaring folk, came to Walker's Cove to live. In fact, the demand for forged goods became so great that Richard eventually returned to Boston to obtain the materials to build a larger smithy—taking on two Abenakis as temporary journeymen. With their support, Richard began to forge heavier items suited for industrial use. When at one point he was asked to coin silver shillings, which involved dealing with the dreaded government bureaucracy, he flatly refused the job with no regret.

During this period of intense business activity, Richard was severely injured in an accident. He was taken aboard Captain Josiah Wheeler's trading vessel to convalesce, where he was nursed by the captain's daughter, Rebecca, whom he later married. By the time my father, James Walker, was born in 1714, Walker's Cove had grown into a close-knit community of sixty-three inhabitants—all helping each other survive.

As the village continued to thrive, its residents eventually pooled their labor and resources to construct a large, sturdy wharf, which

allowed heavier vessels to berth there. It thus accommodated the offloading of bulkier shipments more efficiently than if they were transported piecemeal by water to and from the shore. Since almost all the goods manufactured or grown in Walker's Cove—whether from Richard's forge, the cooper, the woodwright, the broom-maker, or the farmers and fishermen—were quickly bought up by the merchant captains and travelling peddlers, the wharf was always buzzing with activity.

While Captain Wheeler helped keep the trading brigs coming to Walker's Cove, Rebecca, now Richard's wife, kept both the account books and the large house Richard had built. Here they could provide lodging for his father-in-law and his crew when they were forced to wait out the tides or the weather, or when they just wanted to tarry for a friendly visit. Eventually, the couple welcomed paying guests, until Rebecca found herself in the unexpected role of innkeeper—and they prospered because of it.

My father James never had any siblings, which was more a matter of fate than a lack of love between his parents. In fact, the situation was something of a cross to bear for my grandfather, who wished to have five apprentices for his forge, and three chambermaids to help with the inn. So it fell upon my father to become the sole heir to the family business . . . and from the tender age of nine years, he began wielding his first hammer and pumping his first bellows. Working together, the two made the forge a great success.

When engaged in the smithy, Father always felt he was slaving over Vulcan's fires. He much preferred the relatively tranquil work of creating clock movements upon a clean, solid bench. It wasn't long before he became a better clockmaker than his father. At the time there wasn't much demand for clocks themselves—but there was for clock movements, which could be sold in Boston for excellent commissions from some of its wealthiest residents.

At the age of twenty-three, when Father agreed to trade one tall clock to Portsmouth innkeeper Silas Rennsdale for one bull, two milking cows, three pigs, and an assortment of hens and roosters, he got more than he bargained for. For when he arrived at the inn to deliver and install the clock, Silas was not there to receive him—but his daughter Ainsley was.

By the time she was eighteen years old, Ainsley Frances Rennsdale had become the toast of Portsmouth. She had taken an active role in helping her father manage their inn and tavern, the Mariner's Rest, since the age of eight. Ainsley's mother, a good woman named Frances, was known for her kindness, and she was also a gifted soothsayer. Tragically, Frances had died young giving birth to another child when Ainsley was only four. During those long and busy inn-keeping years, Silas honored his wife's memory and never remarried.

So it was that Ainsley lost her childhood to the Mariner's Rest, as she became the very essence of its fine reputation for hospitality. She was also well versed in the art of bartering and other matters pertaining to commerce, like dealing tactfully with the drunken behavior of all too many of the patrons.

Over the years, many a seafaring trader arrived at the place, boasting that he could outwit the "Belle of Portsmouth." Indeed, they would sit—smug with confidence—at the trading table opposite the pretty Ainsley, only to leave with an empty purse and a bad case of intestinal fermentation.

In any event, it was Ainsley who admitted my father to the room where the tall clock would be installed. While James was engaged in that activity, Ainsley leaned in close to observe the inner workings of the timepiece, which she apparently regarded with great veneration. She explained to him that she had never seen the innards of a clock before, and would consider it a particular favor if he would educate her in the mechanics of clockwork. This he did . . . and by evening's end, his student was entranced.

Father courted Ainsley by traveling to Portsmouth every weekend to see her. During his visits, they would walk the long crescent beaches holding hands, and between kisses, carry on long conversations: about clocks, trading, inn keeping and cooking, and the obnoxious behavior of men in general and her customers in particular. From what she shared with James, it seemed as if Ainsley knew what people felt about things without having to ask—which gave her the advantage in her dealings with the traders. She once told me she knew my father's feelings for her long before he really knew them himself. She called these sensations "heart feelings"— this clairvoyance apparently an inheritance from her mother—and they always proved true.

It wasn't long before Ainsley and James became affianced, but Silas Rennsdale delayed the posting of their marriage banns. Father had to beg his permission to allow my mother to travel to Walker's Cove to meet her future in-laws, and Silas would not agree until they could arrange for a chaperone. Finally, it was decided that Ainsley's closest childhood friend, Fanny Johnson, would accompany her.

When Richard and Rebecca met Ainsley for the first time, they were immediately charmed by her poise and maturity; so much so that Father prevailed upon Eben Thatcher—owner of the local dry goods store—to give Ainsley and Fanny room and board. As the courtship continued, Eben and his wife grew so fond of the girls that they offered them paid positions: Ainsley as store hostess and Fanny as inventory clerk.

When Rebecca learned of her future daughter-in-law's flair for running the Mariner's Rest, she approached her about helping out at their inn. Ainsley was agreeable to the idea, and was soon working in conjunction with James and Richard, managing the purchase and distribution of all food and spirituous liquors, which included obtaining the best quality rum for the lowest possible price, and serving up potent mixtures of ale, rum, flip, grog and mulled cider. She also cooked, cleaned and made beds. The inn thrived under her direction, and gradually Rebecca let Ainsley run the entire enterprise. Ainsley had fully returned to her old trade of inn keeping. Rebecca was content to become the helpmate, and the role suited her well, especially in light of her advancing age.

During the following winter, Ainsley and James were finally betrothed. Rebecca purchased a magnificent custom built organ from England to be played at her son's wedding. It had a gleaming black walnut case, custom fitted with two manual keyboards consisting of large ebony keys nestled among smaller white ivory keys. These were laid in two manuals, one staggered above the other. There were ten stops for changing the timbre of the many pipes, of which there were two ranks of fifteen each.

It was installed in the little church at Walker's Cove, the only church in the area to be graced with one. But as fate would have it, the new organ was first played not for a wedding, but for a funeral. Shortly before the momentous occasion, Richard was killed in a freak accident—thrown from his horse on the icy wharf. The entire village filled the church, along with the sea captains who were then in port, to honor the founding father of Walker's Cove. My grandfather Richard was the first person laid to rest in the little cemetery overlooking the cove. The year was 1745.

GRANDMOTHER REBECCA WAS never the same after my grandfather's burial; she seemed to have lost her will to live. My mother Ainsley always said she died of a broken heart—she claimed to "feel it." But Rebecca was ever silent upon the matter, never revealing her secret grief. The winter after Richard's death, she succumbed to a fever; and despite the frozen ground, she was gently laid to rest beside her beloved . . . Grandfather's hand-forged shovels being used to dig her grave.

Not long after the funeral, Mother and Father were finally married. They had planned to make their nuptials a quiet and private affair, but because of their recent bereavement, in an outpouring of love and support, the entire village attended the ceremony.

Mother continued inn keeping until she became pregnant with me. After that, she gradually curtailed her responsibilities until just before I was born, when she closed the inn altogether. Father carried on with his clock making and blacksmith work.

To transform the inn into a proper home, modifications had to be made. The great room was divided in two by constructing a new wall. A central chimney and new fireplaces were added on both sides, creating a parlor of generous proportions on one side, and a capacious winter kitchen on the other.

I was born in the upper right chamber of our house, "Mother's room," which had four large windows. After a successful delivery, Doc Brown handed me to my father, announcing proudly, "Jim, you have a healthy son!" As it turned out, it seems I was lucky to have been born at all, since Mother never conceived another child—much to her ongoing regret.

Ours was a very happy and loving home, and I have a treasure trove of fond memories from my youth. For example, during the heavy snows of winter, I recall scampering in the chill air to my parents' bedroom, where we would all frolic on the warm bed together, having pillow fights and playing hide and seek beneath the blankets. Later, on such a day, the three of us might make molasses candy in the bright and cozy kitchen.

I also remember that long stretches of my boyhood were spent in harmless deviltries with my friends in the village. They were the sons of sailors, soldiers, farmers, fishermen and boat builders—a diverse sampling of occupations and financial means. Those who were the poorest wore their poverty and hardship behind smiling faces, for we all got along on the common ground of friendship, and we were happy to share whatever we had to survive harsh times together.

My closest friend was Jonathan Barrett, the son of a Walker's Cove farmer. When his parents died in a cholera epidemic, as did so many of our other townsfolk, his aunt Rhoda stepped in to raise him. Jonathan was a very cerebral individual—not at all well suited to a life of farming. But he came naturally to the role of mastermind for our boyhood adventures. In our younger days, we often went down to the wharf to play pirate ship: we would design and build magnificent "ships" out of old oil barrels and scraps of rope we found there—or that were "donated" for our amusement. The sailors, who dubbed us "the wharf rats," were ever-present when schooners were berthed for cargo exchange. They frequently sat with us, spinning yarns about their adventures at sea. They even encouraged us to build a working raft and offered advice.

When I was not bound to my father in the clock shop or smithy, Jonathan and I spent endless days entertaining ourselves outdoors. When we were older, my apprenticeship actually contributed to our play, since sometimes I would forge nails, spikes and hasps so we could build our seaworthy raft out of scraps of lumber nailed to barrels. One time, a sympathetic ragman donated enough pieces of cloth so that we could have a sail—after Mother spent a week sewing them together. The result was eight feet wide and twelve feet long—an engineering triumph for two twelve-year-old boys! It became our floating base of operations for fishing, sailing, swimming, exploring, or just lying quietly in the warm sun. While we drifted across the cove, the seals were our constant companions, barking and peering at us with curious but wary eyes.

Nathan Whipple, a nephew to old Mrs. Whipple who lived next door, was a frequent guest on our floating fortress. He was expert at wielding an eel spear, assuring us of a large catch by day's end. Eventually, he became our honorary cook. To help enhance his natural talents, I made him a high quality eel and lobster spear with an extra-long shaft, so he could snatch his prey from the shallows without even getting his feet wet. In return, his aunt brought her business to our smithy. We repaired the odds and sods in her house that had broken, such as firedogs, firebacks and door hinges; and—when Father thought I was good enough—I made her a cooking crane and clock jack as a fitted pair.

The raft figured importantly with another friend of ours: yellow-haired Rebecca Damon, a very sweet and pleasant girl whose dog was almost swept out to sea by the departing tide; that is, until Jonathan and I rescued it on our raft—after which she kissed me as a reward. Later, she attached herself to Jonathan rather than to me, which was fortunate, because after the kiss I always felt somewhat uncomfortable in her presence.

Jonathan and I kept our little craft in good condition, and with it, we discovered a secret place inside Walker's Point where we docked within its protective crescent. It thus became our rendezvous point from the time we were twelve, until Jonathan left Walker's Cove for Harvard at the age of seventeen.

What happy, golden days those were! Father's clock and forge businesses continued to prosper, and all in all, we were a busy lot. The schooners and barks were our lifeline to prosperity, and yet we remained distant enough from cities like Boston to avoid bureaucratic entanglements—which dovetailed perfectly with my grandfather Richard's original plan.

A New Neighbor

hen a full moon casts a haloed blue into the sky's deepest regions, the folks here call it Midnight Blue. It occurs but once or twice a year, and on those special evenings, something good happened if one wished upon the first star sighted.

Sitting alone at Walker's Point, diligently searching the heavens for that first star, I wondered what to wish for. When I finally sighted it in the southwestern sky, I suddenly realized I had everything a young man could want. I had a wonderful father who was skilled in three trades, and an empathetic and loving mother, who instilled in me kindness and character, and taught me about the inner secrets of the human heart. I was blessed with good health and a safe home to live in, and two trades to ply.

Still, I found that life, as a seventeen-year-old in Walker's Cove, was often very difficult. In many ways I was happily ensconced in my niche, but something was definitely missing: I was starved for companionship. My closest friend, Jonathan Barrett, like so many of my others, had left Walker's Cove for better opportunities elsewhere. Currently, he was attending Harvard College, leaving me alone and friendless.

Yes, companionship was definitely what I lacked.

Since old Mrs. Whipple, our next-door neighbor, had become infirm, she'd gone to live with her daughter. A new family had purchased her house and would soon be moving in. Seeing a potential there for friendship, I decided to wish for a new friend, someone my age with whom to share my leisure activities, and so I uttered my secret wish: "I wish upon the first star of Midnight Blue for a

companion . . . someone to share happy times, adventures, wander-
ings and delightful discoveries . . . to perhaps become the best and
dearest of friends. This is my only wish." As I gazed intently at the
star, I noticed its brilliance increase as though acknowledging my
wish; but then, just as quickly, it seemed to return to its normal
glow. Closing my eyes I whispered, "Thank you."

The sudden clanging of a captain's bell interrupted my thoughts.
It was Mother's signal to me to come home. As I headed back, it
was with a buoyant step and a lighter heart—as I harbored the hope
that a new friend was on the way to the Whipple house.

When I was nearly home, the delicious aroma of burning spruce
laced with vanilla, betrayed the presence of a fire in our summer
kitchen—Mother was making custard. Next to her affections, her
toothsome custard made my world just right.

When I appeared at the kitchen door, she smiled at me and said,
"You've been to the point."

Kissing her cheek, I replied softly, "Yes, I have. You know I like
to enjoy the company of my thoughts in the stillness there."

"Indeed, you do," she replied, a spoon to her lips as she sampled her custard. Satisfied with the taste, she put the spoon aside
and moved closer to kiss my forehead. "Jim, you're a *special* young
man . . . as good as Heaven makes!" While I grinned sheepishly,
she tousled my hair and then retrieved her spoon.

My father's voice suddenly echoed, "And Ainsley, my dear, you
are *also* as good as Heaven makes!"

When he appeared in the doorway, he beckoned her to him and
clasped her in a long, tender embrace. After exchanging several
affectionate kisses, they held hands before they reluctantly broke
apart. After so many years of marriage, it charmed me to see their
love still burned like new. I hoped the same blessing would someday
befall me.

"Did you make a wish on Midnight Blue?" Mother asked me.

"Yes, I did," I replied, surprised that she'd guessed it.

She added gently, "May it come to pass, then."

Mother already knew what I'd asked for because we could sense each other's feelings; we were often able to communicate our feelings without words—merely by a glance. I gave her a quick kiss on the cheek before heading upstairs to my room.

Then I heard Father call out behind me. "By the way, Jim, our new neighbors will be moving into Mrs. Whipple's house tomorrow."

"Really? I didn't know it would be so soon." I replied, recalling my wish.

"Yes," he said, "and as I've already told you, my dear old friend Sam Ellingwood has purchased the property. He's a very interesting and talented fellow—a superb furniture maker who'll be making clock cases for us. We might even form a partnership to increase our selling opportunities—particularly in Boston."

"Now why would such an exceptional furniture maker move to Walker's Cove?" I skeptically asked.

"He wishes to dwell among folk of his own persuasion."

"Persuasion?"

"*Political* persuasion," Father clarified.

"Oh, you mean that business in Boston . . . and the unrest with the King?"

"Precisely, Jim. He's a peaceable man who wishes to live out his years without being pestered about his loyalty to the king, or his beliefs."

"I don't like the weak-headed king," I said flatly. "Does he?"

"No, he has no use for him either. His shop is in Roxbury, but he grew up here—right next door in the Whipple house. So this is a kind of homecoming for him." He smiled and then looked bemused, perhaps recalling fond moments from his youth.

I knew that my father had felt abandoned when his best friend moved to Boston at the age of eighteen to be a furniture maker. With Sam returning, they would renew their friendship, which was my wish granted—in a way. I was disappointed for me, yet glad for him. "I'm happy for you, Father," I said with an involuntary pang of regret. "Good night."

"Thanks, son, and good night. Oh yes, and remember we have to mill out brass for clock movement plates tomorrow."

"Yes, sir, I know," I said as I mounted the stairs to my bedroom.

Opening a window to let in some fresh air, my eyes were drawn to the heavens. The stars resembled fallen embers upon God's hearth. I noticed that the star I'd wished upon was now flickering with exceeding brilliance. Inhaling deeply of the scent of pine mixed with the salty sea breeze—which to me was like the breath of life itself—I felt I could live to be a hundred. Still contemplating the light from Midnight Blue as I settled into my bed, the ocean's gentle lapping at the shore—was the last sound I heard before I fell asleep.

THE FOLLOWING MORNING I woke to a cacophony of sounds: horses' hooves, wagon squeaks, teamsters yelling and cursing, all peppered with the thumping and banging of great heavy objects. The atmosphere outside was like that of a loading dock, and I thought perhaps we were receiving a delivery of brass from Boston. Not wanting to miss the excitement, I sprang out of bed and bolted to the open window to regard the commotion below. There I observed a beehive of human activity as men unloaded wagons and maneuvered bureaus, bedsteads, clothes, wardrobes, chests, cookware and unfinished furniture—*lots* of unfinished furniture—into the Whipple house. While I dressed quickly, I counted eleven wagons in all—one complete house consisting of eleven wagons' worth of goods. And all this belonged to the Ellingwoods!

After splashing some water on my face, I hurried downstairs to investigate, and was surprised to see our house full of people I didn't know. Each had a tumbler, glass or mug of Mother's hot spiced cider to wash down her feast of pumpkin pie and baked apples, which she'd set out on the dining room table. A large, heavily muscled man immediately caught my attention. Although he was seated in a chair, I could tell he was easily over six feet tall, broad in the shoulders and thick in the waist—though by no means fat. He wore ancient buckskin breeches, a poorly woven shirt that was liberally peppered with stains, and despite the warmth, a capacious multi-pocketed tinker's coat. Set directly before him on the table, were several glasses and tumblers of cider and a half-dozen baked apples.

I stared in goggle-eyed disbelief at the sheer quantity of victuals before him. When he looked up and saw me staring, he bellowed, "By God, don't *you* look like your mother! Must be the hair and face. The rest is your father." With a big smile, he stood up and offered his ham-sized hand in greeting.

"Who are you and what is all *this?*" I asked, looking around at the crowd of folks in our house.

"Well, young feller, I'm Zebulon Galletin Hawkes, and I *organized* this here move! Ol' Sam Ellingwood, he promised us food, drink and a fee of thirty pieces of eight for our services." Leaning in closely, as though to share a secret, he hoarsely added, "I mislike my damned name, so you can just call me Zeb."

Although we'd finished speaking, I couldn't take my eyes off him. He returned to his seat, picked up an apple, and after squeezing it so hard it dripped over his plate, he pushed it into his mouth whole. Chomping on it as a horse would, he then chased it down with a tumbler of cider that he swallowed in one gulp. Seemingly the cider wasn't enough, because after an extended belch, he held up the empty tumbler and yelled to my mother, "Hey, Ainsley, you got any damned *rum* hereabouts? This drink could sure use a kick in the bunghole!"

Although he seemed rude crude and indelicate, I sensed there was something unmistakably endearing about him. In response to his summons, Mother brought over a small keg of rum, and as she placed it before him, she told him almost in a whisper, "This is the end of the old Essex stock . . . so make it *last.*"

Zeb didn't waste any time as he tackled the bung with a large knife that mysteriously appeared from thin air. I watched in spell-bound fascination as this giant of a man picked gently at it, worming it out of the hole with the unbridled enthusiasm of a small child. Suddenly he roared, "Hey-ho! Here she is!" He tipped the barrel slightly to nearly fill his tumbler with the coveted brown liquid. He then added the cider, and drawing a poker from the fire, he thrust it into his mixture. The liquid rumbled and hissed furiously as he bellowed, "Hey, Ainsley, you got any damned *butter* hereabouts?"

Butter was a precious commodity in our house, used only for baking and spreading on bread. Nonetheless, Mother volunteered a small ball of butter for Zeb's tumbler—and he put the whole of it in, watching it melt with gleeful anticipation. After taking a deep draft, he banged the tumbler on the table. "*Damn!* Even Sam Adams can't get rum like *this!* Mrs. Walker, this damned village needs a tavern again. You have a great-sized house and it would be the only tavern for *fifty* miles!"

Slapping the keg affectionately, Zeb passed it to his men and continued his plea. "Ainsley, with a product like this, they would travel fifty miles just for *it*, let alone your turkey pies and venison stew!" Smacking his lips and nodding, he declared, "Yup, I can taste those potatoes even now! What say you, dear old Ainsley?"

"*Old?*" Mother blushed in surprise. With a hand fluttering at her throat, she answered reluctantly, "I shall take it under consideration, but my tavern-keeping days are *over*, Mr. Hawkes!"

Choking on his drink, Zeb exclaimed, "Mr. Hawkes! Mr. *Hawkes?* What in hell is *that?* Anyway, you were pretty damned good at tavern keeping, if my memory serves! Did you not keep the Mariner's Rest in Portsmouth?" he added with a twinkle in his eye.

"Yes, I did for some years, but it was my father's tavern, not mine."

Setting his tumbler down, Zeb said thoughtfully, "Well, your father had a hell of a trader in *you*, my good lady, almost as famous as Sarah Gooding!"

With a look of surprise, my mother replied, "Ah yes, I remember her well. She had her own sloop, while I had to wait for business to come to me."

Zeb raised his tumbler to Mother. "Yup, she did, but that made you sharper. I would love to see the two of you in action, competing against each other."

Mother smiled. "In that case, I would have those beaver coats of hers, and she would have my clock."

"Really, now how do you know *that?*" Zeb asked, as he put down his drink and belched again loudly.

"Because we had an agreement. But I left the inn to work here, be a wife and tend *this* tavern. The trade never happened, the deal was never done."

"Well, I'll be *damned!*"

Patting his massive shoulder, I heard Mother say as she leaned in, "This place was once a very busy tavern—but that was many years ago. I'm a married woman now; perhaps when my son is out of the house, I may reconsider the idea." Her expression betrayed a flicker of regret.

Observing her downcast eyes, Zeb earnestly replied, "You really ought to, Ainsley—you really ought to. You were the best!"

Then Mother added with a wistful smile, "Many times I truly miss those days of boundless activity, Zeb . . . housewifery can take its toll in tedium, but it does have its own rewards."

"You need to talk to your damned husband about converting this place. Hell, it's plenty big . . ." Smiling broadly, he continued, ". . . and you can get your rum from your old pal at a steep discount."

Zeb turned away then to yell to his crew, "Hey fellers, listen up! Let's toast one of the finest tavern-keepers and traders I ever knew—to Ainsley Rennsdale Walker!"

Lifting their tumblers, glasses and mugs in unison, they all roared, "To Ainsley Rennsdale Walker!" and drank their spiked cider down.

As I observed their exchange, I wondered how Mother ever came to know Zeb, but apparently he was a vital link to the liquor supply of a tavern-keeper.

At that moment, my father entered the room, and when he spotted Zeb he blurted out, "Well, God alive! Look who we have here! Zebulon Galletin Hawkes!"

Crushing my father in a bear hug, Zeb exclaimed joyfully, "It's great to see you, Jim; *damn*, you look swell. Married life agrees with you! And you have a fine strapping boy here—looks like his mom, don't he?"

"Damned good thing, too!" Father retorted, bringing a laugh from both.

When he spotted the keg on the table, Father remarked, "I see your nose for *rum* is still as sharp as ever!"

Zeb broke wind with a forceful grunt before proclaiming proudly, "Yup, can't fool *me*!"

Just then, the front door opened to reveal another large man with enormous forearms. He bellowed, "Hey Jim, where are you? I need you to lend a hand to this bureau!"

"*We* will get that!" Zeb answered. "Come on, men, we need to get finished here."

The rowdy group hustled out together, leaving Mother's parlor and sitting room littered with empty tumblers and mugs.

The man who had summoned my father approached me, reaching for my hand. He shook it hard with an unintentionally forceful grip. "Hi son, I'm Sam Ellingwood. I'm your new next-door neighbor."

"Glad to meet you, sir."

Sam was about six feet tall, but he wasn't heavyset like Zeb. His highly arched brows—which lent his face an expression of perpetual surprise—framed his kind blue eyes, while the aristocratic shape of his nose suggested he was to the manor born. Up close, his forearms were indeed sinewy, strong and thick. If he was a furniture maker, he certainly showed the signs of being one. His general demeanor indicated a person easy to please and one anxious to please others as well.

Sam turned back to Father, and slapped him fondly on the back. Then they looked each other over to detect any unusual changes since they'd last parted. Apparently satisfied with what they found, they left the parlor for the kitchen to greet Mother, who met Sam with exuberant hugs and kisses and delighted exclamations.

After I recovered from my surprise at this sudden burst of familiarity, I decided to step outside and take a peek through an open window of the Whipple house. The interior was bustling with activity as everything was being brought in and set in its place by the movers. I saw splendid pieces of furniture: highboys, tables, chests and chairs. But what I admired most was a rocking chair of *very* unique design. It had no real rockers attached, and yet it looked as if it would rock—*somehow*. Since everyone was inside the house at this point, I decided to investigate further, coming around to the front door for a better view.

While standing at the open doorway, I encountered the most enchanting sight of my life. Standing before me was a small girl, not five feet tall, just rounding into womanhood. Although she wore a comely blue bonnet, it didn't hide her soft golden-brown hair, which framed her face in graceful waves, and fanned out across her shoulders and down her back in a most pleasing manner. But it was her eyes that captivated me most. Her large gray-blue eyes were wondrous—warm, sympathetic and soulful. Her youthful innocence shone through those divine windows. She seemed as pure and gentle as an angel, a winsome, dainty little angel—delicate beyond measure—with smooth creamy skin as flawless as a newborn babe's.

As she met my gaze, she gave me the sweetest smile, and during that moment my heart was inexplicably and irresistibly bound to her. I also felt a boyish burning that possesses every young fellow approaching manhood, as I realized I had just experienced a newfound joy.

We stared at each other for a silent awkward moment, until I finally cleared my throat and found my voice. "Hello there . . . ah . . . I'm James Walker, your new neighbor!"

Her face lit up with another winning smile, as she gave me a charming curtsey and replied in a light, silvery voice, "Hello there, I am Suzannah Ellingwood, *your* new neighbor!"

"Neighbor!" I thought, "why, this is God's littlest angel!" I knelt down on one knee, and looking into her beguiling face, I innocently asked, "Are you an *angel?*"

"Why no, not yet at least!" Suzannah replied merrily, glancing over each shoulder for telltale wings. "I'm in my fifteenth year and my father is Samuel Ellingwood. He is your father's friend."

Still in a dreamlike trance, I vacuously replied, "Yes, I know."

Suzannah placed her delicate hand upon my shoulder to bid me rise, and as I did, she said, "I'm the youngest daughter and the only one remaining at home."

"You mean there are *more* of you?" I asked nonplussed, imagining her stunning beauty multiplied.

"I have four sisters: Lydia, Jenny, Katharine and Sarah. They are all married."

"My gosh!" I exclaimed, thinking of their fortunate husbands.

"Five girls! Think of my poor father." Then, as she started removing her bonnet, she added, "Would you like to come in and see the entire house?"

I'd seen plenty of it before while doing chores for Mrs. Whipple, but to keep this sweet creature in my presence, I'd do anything. "Sure," I answered eagerly, "lead the way!"

Suzannah led me through all the rooms in the house, now furnished with pieces built lovingly by her father's own hand. During the tour, as she described the rooms and the furniture, I treasured the warmth in her facial expressions, and memorized her kindred smiles. As we entered the old great room, I admired some old repairs I'd done when I was fifteen: one to the old fireback, and three others to the firedogs. These were my very first blacksmith projects.

The unusual rocker was in the great room, which Suzannah referred to as the parlor. As she stirred about the room, the rustling of her dress conveyed a soothing air of domesticity, reminding me of Mother. When she noticed some clods on the floor tracked in by the workmen, she picked up a small corn broom that stood before the hearth, and swept the debris onto a sheet of tin that she dumped into the fireplace. As she busied herself with this task, I followed every movement of that lovely hair. I couldn't help but feel a profound fondness and reverence for her—to me she was absolute perfection.

Returning her attention to me, she sighed prettily. "This house needs *so* much tending!"

"Well, it would probably be wise to wait until the men are gone before you begin a thorough cleaning."

She nodded brightly. "You are right! That is *exactly* what I will do!"

Just then, my father and Sam Ellingwood entered the room, the latter remarking with obvious pleasure, "Well, well, well . . . getting acquainted I see. So I guess you two have met already."

"Yes, sir," I replied.

"Yes, Father, we have been having a delightful tour," Suzannah chimed in.

"Oh, really?" my father said, teasingly. "Well, Jim, don't forget to show her the secret stairway near the chimney."

My face flushed hotly when I looked over at Suzannah, and she asked me in a soft voice, "And what *other* secrets does your heart hold, Mr. James Walker?"

To cover up my embarrassment, I hurried over to a wooden panel beneath the mantle and wiggled a nearly imperceptible latch. In a few seconds, the left side panel swung open to reveal a hidden stairway behind the massive center chimney.

"My goodness gracious!" declared Sam as he peered up the stairs. "All my life . . . I never knew it was there! The old place is full of surprises, isn't it?"

Looking directly at Suzannah I boldly affirmed, "Indeed it is, sir, indeed it is . . ."

As the four of us were exploring the hidden stairway; we were interrupted by the loud clanging of a bell.

Father explained, "That's our dinner bell. Ainsley uses it to call us in from the clock shop behind the house."

Glancing toward Suzannah, I reluctantly affirmed, "Yes, that is the dinner bell . . . we are being summoned home."

As we headed back to the parlor, I heard Father musing aloud. "Hmmm, I wonder what's on the table . . . Sam, why don't you folks take a break and join us?"

"Well, I appreciate the invitation, but I figure we still have a few hours of work yet, and I do have to get Zeb and the boys out of here."

"Well, some other time then?" Father asked eagerly.

Sam's eyes twinkled as he patted my father's back. "You bet, Jim, *count* on it! I will have Fanny call on Ainsley."

"I'm looking forward to it." Placing his arm around his friend's shoulder and giving it a firm squeeze, Father said, "It's great to have you back, Sam."

Sam's eyes started to tear up. "Well, it's great to be back! Fanny is very pleased too."

"She's a wonderful presence here . . . as are *you*, young one!" Father suddenly exclaimed, tweaking Suzannah's nose with his thumb and forefinger. At first, she feigned annoyance, but then smiled sweetly at him.

I guess it was evident to my father that I couldn't take my eyes off her, because the next thing I knew he started poking me in the chest with a finger as stiff as a marlinspike. "Hey . . . wake up, James—let's go before Mother bends a poker over our heads!"

"Goodbye, Suzannah . . ." I said, reluctantly relinquishing my gaze.

In a soft hushed voice, she murmured, "Goodbye, Jim—and thank you for coming over. I'm sure we'll be great friends."

"Indeed . . ." was my heartfelt response, as father grabbed my arm and pulled me toward the door.

I could hear Sam calling Zeb Hawkes as we left the house. After we crossed the road, I looked back to catch a final glimpse of Suzannah . . . but she was already gone.

OUTSIDE OUR BACK door I could smell the molasses and beans on the dinner table. There was also roast pork and sweet potatoes freshly dug out of the ashes, and everything was served up piping hot.

When Father sat down at the table and Mother placed the bean pot before him, he rubbed his hands in gleeful anticipation. Gently prying off the cover, he delicately worked the ladle through the thin crust, releasing the heavenly aroma of beans, sugar, molasses and onion. He filled a plate with three heaping ladles of the mixture, and then laid a thick slice of pork over it. A sweet potato on the side was the finishing touch to this meal fit for a king—or queen, as it was in Mother's case.

My mouth watered furiously as I tried to wait patiently, since I was always served after my mother and before my father.

As we began to eat, Mother smiled at Father and asked, "Well, dear James . . . how is your old friend and playmate?"

"They are still getting organized, Ainsley, but they will be quite happy when they are settled," Father replied, forking a piece of pork dripping with bean gravy into his mouth.

Mother looked thoughtful. "I'd like the Ellingwoods to come to dinner sometime soon . . . just like the 'old days,' before they moved to Boston."

"Yes," Father agreed, "soon, darling. You shall let me know when to extend an invitation."

Not wishing to be left out, I immediately asked, "Can Suzannah come, too?"

In reply, they both turned toward me at once—wide-eyed in stunned silence.

After putting his fork down and dabbing his napkin to his lips, Father smiled and calmly answered, "Why . . . *yes*, of course—if you wish it."

"Oh, I *do*, indeed!" I replied enthusiastically.

Mother, fidgeting with her napkin, smiled knowingly and said, "My little boy is smitten . . ."

"He is *not!*" I protested, embarrassed and infuriated that she could always see into my heart.

"Jim," Mother said evenly, "please do not be so proud and deny what you know to be true . . ."

"I'm *not!*" I hotly retorted, knowing I was rapidly losing ground.

"What did she say to you—for you are surely taken with young Suzannah."

"I don't know that she said anything, Mother; it's not what she says . . . it's that she is beautiful . . . like an angel!"

"Oh, she undoubtedly is," Mother agreed, and then added teasingly, "but if you cannot remember what she said, perhaps you weren't listening. Too busy talking, my dear?"

"No, Mother. I was looking . . ."

"Oh, looking!" she declared, cutting me off playfully.

My face downcast, I fell silent with hurt and shame: my heart had been laid open, fully exposed to be made sport of. Then Mother gently touched my cheek with her fingers, and when I looked up at her, I saw that her eyes were now sorrowful and sad, as were Father's.

"Why do you both look so sad?" I demanded weakly. "*I'm* the one who is hurt."

Mother rose and stood close to me, leaning over to drape an arm around my shoulders. "Dearest son, it's something we parents go through, to see our children reach another milestone in life, gradually leaving us behind—one step further into the sacred past— and one step closer to the inevitable end."

She paused, thoughtfully, before continuing. "I tell you this both as a mother and a dear friend, for you are a man now, with manly feelings of tenderness for Suzannah Ellingwood. If you both choose, your friendship will nourish your hearts and bind your souls, and may lead to a lasting communion that will satisfy your hearts' desires."

Now it was Father's turn. "I agree with your mother, and we apologize for teasing you. We never wished our only child to leave our nest someday—and we are still in denial of that time, Jim. Meanwhile, know that we are *here* for you, and we will try to guide your heart as it leads you where it will."

I felt relieved somehow. For that measure of support was indeed a precious comfort to my newly fluttering heart, now budding with feelings for the little angel next door.

Mother sat down again, and we all returned to our meal.

After a while, Father spoke. "Let's have the Ellingwoods over sooner rather than later, Ainsley."

"In that case, I will speak to Fanny tomorrow," Mother softly replied, winking at me with a moistened eye.

Is She the One?

The next day it rained. When I awoke that morning, I found a note from Father beneath my chamber door: he and Mother had gone to church with the Ellingwoods. Still in my nightclothes, I went downstairs to the parlor and sat before the fire. Relaxing in Father's high-backed chair, I listened to the rain, its soothing pitter-patter echoing through our empty house. At this time of year, it was a warm rain—the kind that always brings fog to Walker's Cove.

Sitting alone, I couldn't help but ponder my feelings for the lovely Suzannah. In so doing, I became restless and fretful, until I finally rose, only to gaze forlornly out the window at the Ellingwood house. As I watched the rain flow in tiny rivers down the glass, yesterday's events filled my thoughts. I remembered the first moment I laid eyes upon Suzannah, feeling grateful that she lived next door—and then doubly grateful that it didn't rain yesterday. What if it *had* rained and I had never met her? What would have happened if she'd met another young man first—like the dandy, Moses McBride, who could sweep a lady off her feet by the wink of an eye and a tip of his tricorn? But against these troublesome thoughts, I remembered those mesmerizing gray-blue eyes. Oh, and her pretty white teeth peeking out so adorably behind her sweet girlish smile . . .

A lightning bolt flashed, immediately followed by a fierce explosion of thunder. Suddenly, the rain came down more intensely. As it bounced furiously off the windows, the Ellingwood house vanished in a watery haze, and my thoughts turned inward once again. Would she, I wondered, ever care for me—the awkward Walker boy next door? Mother's comment at dinner yesterday, "My little boy is smitten," echoed in my heart. Was she as smitten with me as I was with her? I relived the images of yesterday's encounter over and over, seeking any hopeful sign that my feelings for Suzannah were requited. Then I envisioned her in the present, standing silently before her own rain-swept window—and if so, was she thinking of me?

So absorbed was I in my reveries—compounded by the sounds of thunder and driving rain—I didn't hear Mother come in through the kitchen. Nor did I hear her footfalls as she entered the parlor or the rustle of her dress, or see the empathy in her face for her son, knowing he was experiencing the first bittersweet awakening of love.

She came up behind me and leaned in to rest her cheek softly against my arm. Reaching for my hand, she gently entwined our fingers and tenderly murmured, "You're thinking of *her*, aren't you?"

In stony silence, we contemplated the faint image of the Ellingwood house through the rain. After a long moment, she turned me toward her, seeking an answer to her question.

Looking down, I replied guiltily, "Yes . . . your heart is as correct as ever."

"Yours are the worrisome thoughts of an eager young heart," Mother continued.

"Yes," I said, still looking out toward Suzannah's house, although I still saw nothing.

She kissed my cheek and softly said, "In romance, a man's heart is quicker to love than a woman's, because she must give herself totally and completely—and that takes time. Don't worry, son, Providence is kind, and if the pull is strong, her heart will follow yours. So put away your fears, and enjoy the friendship and good times that are bound to come. You are both younglings, only two years apart. There is time and room for love to grow." Then, as she tousled my hair she added, "Tomorrow I'll make custards, but you must go to Thatcher's in the afternoon and get some of the fixings. I'll prepare a list."

Custards were my favorite comfort food, and Mother knew that good words and good custards would chase away my worries. I smiled at the prospect of things to come, yet there was still a great trepidation in my heart, for all these feelings were new to me—uncharted waters. Mother was my heart's compass on this journey, but despite her encouragement and soothing advice, I felt my anxiety increase measurably . . . for where would it lead?

The Voice of an Angel

fter the soaking rains of yesterday, the shadows of this evening seemed softened, and the air was warm and pleasant. Winnie and I were returning home on foot from Thatcher's, carrying the ingredients for Mother's custards. Because Winnie liked to munch on roadside delicacies, and since neither of us was in much of a hurry to get home, I freely obliged her desire to explore. Spotting some wildflowers growing in profusion in front of the church, she moseyed over with her head lowered, her nose nudging the ground to investigate.

As I approached the church, I abruptly decided that Mother's custards could wait, for I heard the sound of organ music playing. Whenever I heard that instrument, I always thought of my grandmother Rebecca. However, this melody was unfamiliar—it was a slow sweet tune, like a lullaby. Tying Winnie to a post near the front door, I went inside to get closer to the soothing tones of the pipes. While I stood there listening, I saw a notice indicating that the service on Sunday morning would feature a new singer: ". . . whose talents everyone may find favorable to their hearts and dispositions." This was God's house, where a rebirth of faith took place every week—and all that was needed was this enrapturing music to understand why.

I wondered what song was being played and who was playing it, so closing my eyes I thoughtfully listened. The softness of the music resonated within me, transporting me as though I was floating on a cloud—to a dimension beyond that of mere existence. When the organist changed octaves, I suddenly heard a voice— a gentle, clear *female* voice unlike any I'd ever heard before. Its clarity pulled deeply at my soul, and seemed to whisper, "Come hither with me . . ."

Feeling compelled to discover who possessed this angelic voice; I quietly closed the door behind me and dropped the latch. Treading softly as I entered the main chamber of the church, by the dim candlelight, I could see the waist high pew boxes lined up on either side of the chamber, each with a small door opening to the main hallway in the chamber's center. On each door was the family name of its owner. Grandmother's organ was located on the right side of the transept, and the pipes were located on the left side. From my vantage point, I could see part of the organ, but not the organist. The delicate voice continued to float and echo within the church walls, in a language I had never heard before.

Quietly moving forward from the deepest shadows, I surreptitiously approached the organist's platform from the side. I was then *stunned* to see Suzannah Ellingwood—playing the organ and singing.

Moonbeams drifted through a nearby window, illuminating the image before me, highlighting Suzannah's hair and making it appear golden. She was perched daintily upon a red and gold velvet pillow, clad in a pink linen dress with a delicate white sash around her waist, tied in a large bow in the back. Completely mesmerized, I took a few tentative steps toward her. Suzannah was so absorbed in her music that she didn't notice me. The deep soft lows of the delicate melody entwined itself around my heart, and as her tiny fingers worked the keys without looking down at them, her voice soared effortlessly to the rafters, leaving me with goose bumps. As I floated on a level of ethereal bliss, I heard myself whisper, "My God . . . she *is* an angel . . ." I didn't know what Heaven was like, but if it consisted of music like this and a voice like hers, I could not wait to get there.

I then realized how fortunate I was to have this gifted young woman as my *neighbor*! Against that, an excruciating pang of inadequacy enveloped me, for I was humbled and awestruck, and felt somehow unworthy to even *know* her. I bowed my head, thankful at least I was privileged to have met her and—despite Mother's confidence—I determined then and there that Suzannah Ellingwood

was *far* beyond my humble reach. When I asked silently, in the semblance of a prayer, "How can I ever be worthy enough to deserve God's littlest angel?" I received no discernible answer.

Feeling disconsolate now, I prepared to leave—hoping to recede quietly into the shadows . . . and perhaps out of her life. While slowly backing into the darkness, I fell over an unseen lectern and its bible, knocking them over with a clattering crash. As I too hit the floor, the noises echoed through the church and suddenly the music stopped. Stunned, I lay there holding my breath, hoping that if all remained silent, she would resume playing.

Suzannah rose, stepped down from the platform and reluctantly started down the aisle. She called out: "Reverend Metcalf? Is that you?"

Overcome with dread that she might find me, I remained where I was, motionless and silent. Then, I heard her footsteps come to an abrupt halt.

"*James?*" she exclaimed, as she stepped closer and kneeled at my side. "James Walker, is that you?"

With my eyes closed to feign injury, I pretended to emerge from unconsciousness, but didn't speak.

"James! It *is* you! What's happened? Why are you here?" Then her gifted hands were upon my cheeks, turning my head from side to side as she examined me, anxiously looking for signs of any injury.

"Yes, it's me," I confessed at last. "I was looking for the reverend— is he here?"

"Why no," she replied. "I thought you were him. Let me help you up, James." Taking my hands in hers, she gently tugged me into a sitting position, and as I stood up, brushing off the dust I imagined had clung to my clothes, I shyly whispered, "Hello again, Suzannah Ellingwood."

She curtseyed adorably, such that I thought my heart would burst. "Well, James Walker, it is nice to see you again. It seems you are still full of surprises!" She laughed as she walked to the lectern and righted it, returning the ponderous bible to its platform.

"Suzannah?" I said, my heart racing.

She looked at me sweetly with those heavenly gray-blue eyes and softly answered, "Yes?"

"You have a *beautiful* voice . . . a gift from God, I truly believe."

Smiling, she said, "Why, thank you, Jim."

I was thrilled to the core of my being—she called me "Jim"! "How long have you played the organ?" I finally asked, struggling fiercely against my strong desire to touch her.

"I have played since I was ten years of age . . . I learned how to play in Boston."

"You are a gifted musician, and I felt privileged listening to you play."

"How lovely of you to say so, Jim. I enjoy it very much. My first instrument was the pianoforte—it's my true love."

"I see . . ." I said, groping for the right words and not finding them. "Suzannah?"

"Yes, Jim?" She said my name again, and my heart rejoiced.

"Perhaps I could listen to you play some more?"

"Of course!" she exclaimed happily. Gently taking my hand, she led me to the first pew box, opened the door and bade me sit. This I did, but when she turned to leave me, she couldn't, as I still held her hand. Turning to face me, she blushed while admonishing, "Jim . . . I cannot play if I haven't *both* hands."

"Oh, yes . . . sorry . . ." I stammered, gently releasing her.

"I'm not," she replied, smiling at me again while she closed the pew box door.

After resuming her pillowed seat, Suzannah started to play a song similar to the first one—and she looked straight at me while she sang. Her eyes glistened in the moonlight as the deep bass of the organ, accented by the delicacy of her voice, literally moved me with a warm physical resonance. This time her heavenly voice went straight to my heart as she sung. At that moment our hearts seemed to connect, as if it were love I was hearing now . . . and not only did she move my soul, she was simply enchanting. While I listened, I began to perceive her anew as warm, friendly and approachable— not unattainable, after all. I felt as if she were serenading *me*.

I dared to hope I had found someone—a girl no less—who embraced my friendship with tenderness, grace and caring. Furthermore, she understood my delicate boyish feelings. Remembering my wish on Midnight Blue, I decided that with the arrival of the Ellingwoods, perhaps Father and I both had found what we were so desirous of—true, loving friends.

When Suzannah finished her performance, she seemed entirely satisfied with it. I gave her a hearty round of applause, and she stood and bowed graciously. Then she blew a small whistle, the signal for the organ pumper to quit his bellows, and approached me in the pew where I was still sitting.

"What type of music is that?" I asked. "It's *glorious* . . ." As she sat beside me under the candlelight, I admired the flecks of warmth in her eyes.

"It's called Gaelic."

"Is that the same as Latin?"

"Not at all, Jim. Gaelic music comes from the mountains and hills of Ireland, Scotland and Wales. It is sometimes referred to as music for the soul because it's so ancient, harkening back to the Druids perhaps."

"Indeed. And the words—are they also Gaelic?" I asked, thinking about how their ethereal sound filled my heart.

"Indeed, they are," she said as she gazed out the window at the moonlit darkness. Then she turned and looked straight into my eyes, and all I could do was squirm under her scrutiny. Sensing my discomfort, she continued, "Gaelic is a soft and delicate language, with none of the harsh guttural sounds of so many others."

"Like Greek and Latin?" I inquired.

"I'm speaking more of the Teutonic languages," she explained.

"Well, I definitely agree that Gaelic is an exceedingly pleasant language. Although I don't understand it, it still means something to me. Or, perhaps it's just the way you sing it, Suzannah."

She laughed and patted my hand lightly. "You certainly know how to compliment a girl!"

When her eyes held mine for another long moment, I felt a stirring within me, as though my heart had wings. Attempting to overcome my awkwardness, I then suggested, "It's getting late, Suzannah—might I escort you home?"

"Escort?" she repeated, quizzically.

"Yes," I explained, "I have Winnie outside waiting for me." As her face fell, I saw an expression of dismay.

Then she looked up and tentatively asked, "Who . . . is Winnie?"

"I'm sure she would love to meet you, so come outside with me so I can introduce her."

Suddenly she seemed distant. "I'm sorry, I feel awkward . . . I don't know if I . . ."

"Now, Suzannah, please, I insist. And I assure you that I have only honorable intentions."

She regarded the door apprehensively for a moment and said, "Very well then . . ."

As we approached the doorway, I tapped the notice that was posted nearby. "The congregation is very lucky; wait till they hear the special treat that is in store." Then I gently took her arm and led her outside.

She stood at the entrance looking vulnerable and uneasy. "Where is Winnie?" she asked.

"Right here."

Looking around the empty portico, she retorted, "Jim, are you trying to vex me? All I see is a *horse* . . ."

When I saw the obvious confusion in her eyes, I apologetically replied. "Yes . . . *that* is Winnie!"

"A *horse?*"

"Yes . . . a horse, and a good one, too!" I added boastfully.

With the dawn of understanding, Suzannah began to giggle, and then laughed in short silvery peals that were delightful to hear.

Pretending not to comprehend the significance of her laughter, I examined Winnie perfunctorily and said, "What's so funny? She's not *that* silly looking, is she?"

"Oh, dear Jim, not at all . . . not at *all!*" she declared, obviously relieved, as she stepped closer to Winnie and gently patted her nose. "So *you* are Winnie! I'm so happy to meet you, dear lady."

Winnie lifted her head and seemed to nod her tacit approval of Suzannah's words.

I suggested then that she ride Winnie home, while I would walk along beside them. She agreed, and as we went, we talked of Winnie, wildflowers, the stars, the moon, the ocean, Walker's Point and music . . . all the way home.

After we arrived at Suzannah's house and said our goodbyes, she lingered outside her front door. Bursting with happiness, I turned back repeatedly to wave, and as I rounded the corner toward the barn, she finally went inside.

I had good friends my entire life, but none gave me the feeling that Suzannah did—she had utterly captured my heart. And tonight, despite the lack of Mother's custards, all was right in Walker's Cove.

THE HOUSE CALL

he weeks passed quickly after the Ellingwoods settled into their home. During that time, Mother was so eager to see Mrs. Ellingwood—Fanny, as she called her—that she went over every day to help her unpack, arrange and decorate the house. Whenever Mother spent the entire day there, like today, I tended our kitchen fire in her absence. I also had to lay the dough and peel potatoes for her pork pie, which we were having for dinner.

Since I was also busy in the shop with Father, I had no time to visit the Ellingwoods, which was especially hard for me, being desirous to see Suzannah again. Leaving the shop just before noon that day to retrieve a fritter for lunch, the aroma of roasted pork hooked my nose and led me straight to the kitchen, where I was surprised to see Mother, busily engaged in making her pie.

"Well, you're the last person I expected to see here today," I declared, surveying the ingredients she had arranged neatly on the counter.

"Fanny is *completely* settled!" Mother proclaimed joyously. "Suzannah was a major help to us, Jim—she is so well organized."

"Well, that's good. Does that mean we get our cook back?" I asked, delighted to be spared kitchen duty. "I shall have to personally thank Suzannah for returning you."

"There's no need for that, Jim. Fanny gave me a ready excuse for you to visit Suzannah for as long as you wish—today."

I was stunned. "Today?" I repeated stupidly, not believing what I'd heard. "Suzannah?"

"Indeed, wouldn't you know . . . Fanny needs to have her clock set up and working . . . she says she can't bear to be without it. I would ask Father, but I knew you would have a stronger interest in this mission than he would." Kissing my cheek and patting my hand, she lowered her voice to whisper, ". . . and *she* is waiting."

I could feel my heart throbbing as this thrilling news jolted it from its slumber. I would finally see this beautiful angel once again.

"A perfect opportunity seems to have presented itself," Mother commented as she kissed my cheek. "Providence is definitely with you, Jim—I can feel it."

That was all the encouragement I needed, since Mother's heart feelings were always correct.

"I'll go over as soon as I can gather my tools," I replied breathlessly.

As I was leaving for the shop, I heard Mother giggle as she resumed her work, sweetly sighing something resembling, "Ah . . . young love . . ."

Back at the shop, I told Father about Fanny's clock, whereupon he suggested I take the so-called emergency kit, which he kept in an open toolbox already supplied for the purpose. I grabbed it and left in a whirlwind of clattering excitement. As I hastened my pace, I heard Father call out, "Jim, please pay attention to *both* faces!"

As I APPROACHED the Ellingwoods' door, a shadow inside the window rose and floated toward it. Suddenly the latch was thrown, and when the door opened, there stood Suzannah as I remembered her from our last meeting—positively radiant.

"Welcome again to our home," she said in greeting, flashing me a dazzling smile and raising her eyes to mine. My heart pounded so relentlessly that I inadvertently relaxed my grip on the toolbox, dropping it on my foot with an audible crash. When a searing pain shot through my tender instep, I started hopping repeatedly on one foot to ease the pressure on the injured one.

Soon Sam came over to investigate the cause of all the noise. To my chagrin, when he caught sight of me hopping, he started clapping his hands and stomping his foot in time to it.

Suzannah stamped her own foot and angrily warned, "*Father*! What are you doing? Can't you see he's in pain?"

Sam froze in mid-motion to ask with surprise, "Pain? I thought James was teaching you a dance step!"

"Don't be silly, Father. Perhaps you should drop some tools on your foot to see how it feels. Rest assured, you would *not* feel like dancing." She followed up her reproach with a disarming smile . . . that immediately solicited an apology from her father for making sport of my distress. I dismissed it awkwardly with a blithe remark: "Tools of the trade, you know . . ."

Suzannah offered herself as a support—draping my arm over her shoulder—to help me to the sofa. When she touched me, an immediate burst of tenderness shot through me, a warm feeling of contentment I'd never experienced before. Leaning on her shoulder, I was able to hobble toward the sofa in the parlor, where a small fire burned feebly in the large fireplace. I was somewhat reluctant to sit, since I didn't wish to remove myself from her comforting softness. But constrained by a sense of propriety, I finally did sit, still entranced by how wonderful she felt.

Sam's remarkable rocker sat in front of the fireplace. He was indeed a gifted cabinetmaker, and almost all the furniture in the Ellingwood house was of his hand, including their tall clock. Father told me Sam had once made several Roxbury style clock cases that were superbly finished. Each of them was fitted with one of Father's tall clock movements, and one resided here; the others were given to Sam's daughters as they married and made their own homes.

As Suzannah gently massaged my throbbing foot, she gave me a sweet lingering look, as though waiting for me to speak. That look was so compelling, so hauntingly lovely and so beautiful to behold, my heart raced as I struggled to find something to say. Then my cheeks flushed with embarrassment as I coughed instead, smiled awkwardly and finally managed, "Thank you for your kindness, Suzannah, I feel much better now." Then I reached for my shoe.

Apparently satisfied that I was recovered, she left the room to find her father. Following her progress down the hall with my eyes, I breathed a heavy sigh, and then limped back to the foyer to collect my fallen tools. When I returned to the parlor, I sat gingerly in the large rocker, and was astonished to find that the slightest movement on my part caused it to *glide* rather than rock. Being curious as to its operation, I leaned over the arm to see how it was constructed.

"It's the lever action that holds the secret to the glide . . ." said a voice from the parlor door. It was Sam, of course. As he strode in, he added, "I'm deeply sorry for making sport of your injury."

I rose and we shook hands. "How *is* your foot?" he asked wryly.

"Swelled up a bit, but still ticking!" I replied, offering a feeble joke.

"Good!" he said, patting my shoulder. "I'm glad you're here, Jim. Our Willard clock is in need of repair. Not only that, but Fanny would like it moved to the parlor."

"Yes, sir, I'll have a look at it straight away."

He led me into the dining room where the clock awaited me. "That boy prodigy, Simon Willard won't be coming to these parts any time soon, and my wife's day begins and ends with this clock." It was one of Simon Willard's one-day timepieces, the design copied from an English bracket clock.

"She winds it every morning, doesn't she?"

"Yes, just before refreshing the fire," Sam affirmed.

I set my toolbox down, pulled a piece of clean oilcloth from it and spread it over the parlor table. First removing the hood of the clock, I brought it over to the table to examine its movement. As I set out the case parts, Sam sat in his rocker, and taking up a small magnifier, began examining some of the clock case joinery.

"Are you finished with your apprenticeship, Jim?"

"Not yet, sir. I will be finished with it this September."

"That's excellent news. There is a need for a man of your talent around here. I do hope you'll stay in Walker's Cove."

"I believe I shall." I replied. "This place contains my whole world."

Once I had everything arranged on the table, I pulled up a chair and began to examine the movement's wheels and pinions, rocking the train back and forth with my index finger. They seemed in good order, but the pivots were dry as a puffball. "All it needs is oil," I remarked, "but I will check for wear and scoring on the pivots . . . after all, if you could give me the perfect oil, I could give you the perfect clock."

"Ah! Spoken like your father, the clockmaker. And speaking of your father, did you know that we were best friends when we were boys? Always together."

"I know that, sir," I said with a smile.

"Your father is very special and very dear to me. He saved my life once."

I nearly dropped my tweezers in surprise and looked up at him. "Really?" I was astonished beyond words that Father had never mentioned it.

"Yes, we were both fourteen years old . . ." He leaned back in his rocker and closed his eyes as he recalled the incident. "It was during the winter of 1728, and we were skating on the marsh pond. We'd had a very frigid winter that year, and the ice was exceptionally hard.

"After skating, we came in to warm up and your father sat where you are right now—at that very table—to indulge in hot cider and a piece of my mother's 'great cake.' Ah, we were delighted to have it, and as a thank you for her kindness, he volunteered to fetch some wood from the barn.

"Well, we buttoned ourselves up once again and took a small sled and headed over to get it. On the way we passed the knoll overlooking the marsh river, which we saw was frozen from bank to bank. Mind you, this was the river that fed the pond, and *never* had this happened before, so it was indeed a matter of considerable excitement to a boy of fourteen. I thought it would be a great adventure to cross the river on foot—just to say we did it, in the manner of boastful boys.

"Your father advised against it; but being an impetuous soul, I challenged him to a foot race across the ice. He still refused, so I dared him to come out with me. 'Sam, *don't* do this!' he screamed at me as I ran toward the center. I taunted him, saying, 'Come on,

Jim, it's easy! I *dare* you!' And although I kept taunting your father, he still refused.

"Thinking I would easily make it to the opposite bank and back, I pressed on without him. Suddenly, there was a loud cracking sound that stopped me in my tracks—the ice had cracked all around the spot where I was standing, like jagged lightning bolts.

"The fear of death overcame me and instinct told me to flee. I took only two steps before the ice caved in. Upon the instant, freezing water swallowed me up. As I came to the surface gasping and flapping my arms in the freezing water, I heard your father screaming, 'Sam! Sam!' and heard his steps pelting across the frozen river.

"My clothes were starting to freeze and became solid, heavy with ice. They restricted my movements and dragged me down as I screamed desperately for help, trying in vain to reach the edge of the hole. It was when my feet became numb and I started to lose feeling in my hands that your father got to me. He had stopped about ten feet from the edge, pushed the sled toward me and yelled frantically, 'Grab the sled, Sam! Grab the *sled!*' But it was out of my reach. Next, he removed his coat and untied the rope from the sled. As he did so, he kept screaming, 'Keep moving, Sam, don't stop *moving* or you will die!' He then tied one end of the rope around his empty coat sleeve, the other to the sled, and gradually pushed the sled toward the hole. It seemed close enough to me so that I could attempt to grab at it twice, but I missed it altogether.

"So your father lay down on the ice, aimed the rear of the sled at the hole, and shoved it with all his strength. The tip of the runner settled just over the edge. 'Grab it, Sam, for God's sake, grab it! You *must!*'

"I was starting to lose consciousness, but with one last desperate grab, I found the runner. My hand wrapped around it, frozen in position like an iron knob. Your father kept yelling at me to keep moving, but hold onto the sled, as he stood up and tried pulling me out of the hole. But with all that weight opposing him, he couldn't gain a foothold on the slippery ice. Finally, he got down on his hands and knees and using his knife as a pick, he literally crawled his way across the ice, away from the hole—with me in tow.

"When he thought we were safe, he loaded me on the sled and rushed to bring me back here. I was mostly frozen when we arrived, and I was placed before this very fireplace to thaw out. Gradually—little by little—the feeling in my arms and legs returned.

"In the end your father was wise . . . while I was reckless. He saved my life, Jim. And that is a debt I can never repay, even if I live to be one hundred." Pausing thoughtfully, he shook his head and gave a heavy sigh before he added, "You seem to have the same wisdom and good sense as your father—along with the heart of your mother."

Our attention was diverted by a delicate rattling sound. Suzannah was bringing in a tea tray from the kitchen, laden with cups and saucers, a teapot and biscuits. As she passed near me, she smiled demurely and winked. "Mother thought you could use something warm after a frozen tale such as that!"

Sam rose, "Thank you, Suzannah, and tell your mother I owe her a kiss."

While I sat gawking at her, she poured our tea and quietly withdrew to the kitchen, my thoughts trailing along behind her.

Observing me closely over the rim of his teacup, Sam remarked, "She is the last and the best of the litter."

"Yes, sir, I've heard it said that one always saves the best for last." That said, I returned my attention to oiling the pivots.

"Yes, indeed—it certainly seems so. When she was little, she would always hold my hand as though it were God's." He smiled as another memory flooded in. "Although her heart was very new, she could trust it with what was true. For never was a child so cherished as she was. Even at that tender age, she would ask, 'Will you love me forever, Papa?' My answer was always the same. 'My dear little Suzannah,' I told her, 'although sometimes I get mad, and sometimes I get sad, my heart *always* belongs to you!'"

"Those are certainly memories worth treasuring," I remarked, setting down the container of oil and taking a sip of my tea. "I sense much goodness in your daughter. Of course, I can see you are a very fine father." And I meant it—honestly and sincerely.

"Only because of yours . . ." he replied, setting his cup down carefully on the saucer.

As I started reassembling the clock, Sam sat down next to me at the table. When he spoke, his tone was confiding: "Jim, Suzannah is my youngest, and she is very special. We feared for her life because she was born so small, and it was like a miracle to us when she survived. Although small in stature, when it comes to matters of the heart, she's capable of a great generosity of feeling. This gift was confirmed by your own mother as being real and genuine."

I felt awkward and yet honored that Sam was sharing such personal thoughts about his daughter with me. All I could think to say in response was, "She also has a lovely singing voice."

"Another gift." Sam smiled with satisfaction at how well I'd borne him out.

There was silence for a while as I worked, and then Sam started up again. "We were older folk, Jim. Fanny was well beyond her childbearing years when she unexpectedly found herself with child. Suzannah was born when her mother was thirty-nine. There *is* something unique about my youngest daughter."

"Do you think she is an angel?" I asked him in all seriousness.

He looked at me for a long moment before he answered. "Your mother is the closest thing to an angel in *this* world. Surely she'll be one in the next, too . . . just ask my wife." After stretching himself like a cat, he added, "We're delighted to be settled into our old home again—especially with Suzannah. This has been a difficult transition for her, but I believe her new friendship with you has made a big difference—it's raised her spirits considerably."

Fit to burst with joy at his words, I grinned sheepishly. "Thank you, sir; with gratitude and respect, I thank you."

Sam stood and placed his hand upon my shoulder. "When you're finished here, come join us for dinner."

"Oh, I can't, sir," I replied, though I desperately wanted to say "yes." I was thinking of Mother cooking our own dinner at home.

"But I *insist*! It is the least I can do for my dearest friend's son."

"In that case, sir, I'd be honored to accept." I decided that my parents would understand that I couldn't possibly refuse in the face of Sam's insistence.

With that matter settled, I resumed my work on the clock. A little while later, I heard the sound of laughter and animated conversation coming from the dining area. Closing the parlor door so to focus on the clock's ticking, I had just hung it and achieved an even beat when the door opened behind me. I turned around to see Suzannah silhouetted in the doorway.

"Jim," she said softly, "it's time to come inside for dinner. We have some very special guests who are joining us . . ." Then, with a mischievous smile she added: "You just *might* enjoy their company."

I grinned shyly and followed her to the dining room, where an abundance of food had been set out in fancy dishes on a long rectangular table. I could feel myself growing hungry at the sights and smells that assailed my senses. When I next looked up, I was startled to see my own mother and father come in through the kitchen door.

"Well, I'll be . . ." I declared: surprised to discover the identity of these "very special guests."

Sam, in a conspicuous show of gallantry, escorted Mother to the table, saying, "Mrs. Walker . . . allow *me* . . ." as he pulled out her chair. Then he strode over to the head of the table and pulled out the chair of honor for my father, adding, "Mr. James Walker, it's my great pleasure to serve you."

Following suit, I pulled out Suzannah's chair, and she occupied it prettily, saying, "Thank you, James."

While Fanny added some finishing touches to the table, Sam threw a few logs onto the fire. Then he saw his wife to her chair, before seating himself at the other end of the table across from Father. When he noticed I was still standing, he said, "Jim, sit—*please*," gesturing toward the only empty chair, directly opposite Suzannah.

And there I sat, feeling awkward as I gazed stupidly at Suzannah, who looked back at me through those arresting gray-blue eyes.

Then she abruptly made a silly face by wrinkling her nose at me—like a rabbit—and I couldn't help but laugh.

Crooking my little finger, I wiggled it back at her.

She, in turn, smiled at me with happy eyes, and then bowed her head slightly as a girlish blush suffused her cheeks with pink.

At that moment, Sam tapped his glass and announced a prayer of thanksgiving. I was deeply touched when he ended with the words, ". . . and bless James and Ainsley Walker . . . our old neighbors and dearest friends . . . and bless O Lord all those present . . . whose young hearts are true to their own."

When Mother flashed a knowing look that went from me to Suzannah, I coughed to cover my embarrassment. But Suzannah seemed to bask in her father's blessing, gazing at me silently, conveying her tender feelings for me with her eyes.

I was enormously grateful to receive this subliminal message from my little angel, and in light of it, I recalled Sam's earlier comments about her mystical powers and wondered what others she possessed. But right now it was enough for me to know that the sunshine in Suzannah's soul lit up our friendship.

After I acknowledged her apparent affection for me with a broad smile, she raised her pinky finger, crooked it and wiggled it back at me.

"She loves to play!" I thought happily as I smiled at her again, causing her to stifle a giggle.

Clearing her throat, Fanny sternly announced, "I think all secret signals should be put aside while we are at the dinner table."

Suzannah and I both felt caught, so we stopped exchanging glances and finger signs. Instead, while Sam proceeded to dish out the helpings, we stoically observed the adults, with as serious an expression on our faces as we could muster.

During our meal, I felt positively jubilant—for Suzannah had infused me with a lighthearted buoyancy that made me smile . . . and I hadn't smiled since Jonathan Barrett left Walker's Cove for Harvard.

UPON FINISHING DINNER, we remained for an after-dinner treat: apple pie and tea. Afterward, everyone repaired to the parlor to relax before the fire and catch up on times gone by. But after a while, the conversation took a brief turn toward the present, as Fanny dwelt upon her excitement about having the Willard clock running again. That inspired Sam to vacate his rocker and bid Father to sit there instead, as he regaled him with technical details about its construction. Then I overheard Mother and Fanny chatting about Mother's inn-keeping days, followed by stories about their children, mutual acquaintances and favorite recipes.

Thus were Suzannah and I left isolated together on the corner sofa. After a protracted period of silence, Suzannah's eyes lit up with excitement as she was clearly struck by an idea. "James, would you like to see my pianoforte up close?"

Happy to please her, I instantly replied, "I'd be delighted!"

Rising from the couch, she took my hand and led me over to the pianoforte. With my heart beating like a trip hammer, we sat cozily, side by side on its bench. As Suzannah showed me how to play simple notes, she gently guided my fingers over the keys, and my face burned at her every touch. The lessons and soft banter continued while she played and occasionally hummed along with the music, and once more I became acutely aware of how talented she was. The hours flew by.

When the tall clock struck one bell in the dining room, my mother jumped up declaring, "Oh Fanny . . . we've done it *again!*"

Fanny then affirmed, "Some things never change, Ainsley dear."

It was one in the morning, and all six of us had been so pleasurably engaged that our visit had lasted almost seven hours—while mine was almost ten!

"We haven't done this since we were newlyweds!" Mother added, her eyes sparkling with happiness.

"Well, Ainsley, let's get some sleep, and plan another one of these wonderful nights soon," Fanny suggested.

"We surely will," Mother said as she hugged Fanny; and then she did something I'd never seen her do before: she kissed her friend goodbye on both cheeks and added, "It's so wonderful having you back!"

Fanny, tearful now, snuffled and replied, "God be with you, dearest Ainsley—and may He keep us all healthy and together."

"Amen!" declared Father, hugging Sam to his heart.

After these overwhelming displays of affections, I was frozen with fear about how to say goodbye to Suzannah. "Should I hug her? Surely not *kiss* her!" I wondered to myself. But since there was a deep and undeniable feeling in my heart that needed further expression, I took a deep bow and awkwardly announced, "Thank *you*, Suzannah . . . you have pretty hair . . ." I stopped in mid-sentence when I realized what I'd said, feeling like a complete dolt.

But to my surprise, as if I'd said exactly what she'd wanted to hear, she curtsied back and smiled at me sweetly. "And thank *you*, James . . . you are a true gentleman and friend. I hope to see you again soon."

Still embarrassed I said nothing in return—I just managed to eke out a weak smile as I picked up my toolbox. And with my eyes riveted to her lovely abundant hair and cherubic face, I slowly backed away toward the open door. When I turned around, I crashed directly into the doorjamb with my tools, spilling them onto the entryway floor for a second time in the same twelve-hour period.

This time all three Ellingwoods helped me collect my tools and recover my honor, bidding me a kind-hearted farewell and laughing heartily in the process.

When we arrived home, Mother and Father retreated to their bedchamber, and I prepared for bed.

A few moments later, Mother came in and stood beside me. With the flat of her hand she gently rubbed my back, letting it come to rest upon my shoulder. "Suzannah has an abiding fondness for you," she softly murmured.

"How do you know that, Mother? Did she tell you?"

"In a manner of speaking," she replied mysteriously.

"So what do I *do?*" I asked, uncertain about how to handle myself in the situation.

Kissing my forehead she then tousled my hair and brightly said, "Just be friends."

"Friends?" I repeated, thinking of activities like hunting and fishing. "But she's a girl!"

Placing her hands upon her hips, Mother boldly challenged, "And what is wrong with *girls?*"

Realizing that I'd offended her gender's sensibilities, I hastened to reply, "Nothing—absolutely nothing!"

Poking my chest with her index finger, she playfully declared, "You wished for a *friend* on Midnight Blue, did you not?" Looking down in guilt, I knew Mother was correct . . . for along came Suzannah.

Mother lifted my chin and with moistened eyes softly whispered, "Trust me James . . . she will be *more* than just a friend . . ."

Kissing my cheek, she smiled benevolently and headed for the door. Upon its threshold she halted, turned, and over her shoulder coyly whispered, "Good night and sweet dreams, dear son of mine."

She gently shut my door while softly humming. I listened quietly as her tune faded away, finally ending with the clack of her bedchamber's latch.

I drifted over to the window and stared at the stars shining like diamonds in the evening sky. Admiring their beauty and inhaling the fresh sea air, I changed into my nightclothes and lay on my bed, reflecting upon my evening with Suzannah.

While musing happily upon my visit, I suddenly felt a palpable stirring within my heart. Instinctively, I rose and returned to the window. Looking toward the Ellingwood house, I noticed Suzannah was at her window, too, with a candle in her hand. I could see by the dancing shadows on her face that she was looking at the stars, as I had been earlier.

"Odd coincidence . . ." I thought, but *was* it really?

A few moments later, she finally turned away and the candlelight disappeared. As it did so, something in my heart also darkened, as though the light of my life had suddenly departed . . . like
that flickering candle across the way . . .

A Visitor

ecause our shop was busy with clock jack orders from Boston, I didn't see Suzannah for several days following that memorable visit. Those days passed like weeks as business took precedence over everything else. While my thoughts struggled to return to Suzannah, Father's constant surveillance of my work interrupted them. Working in the rear of our shop, he measured the depth of the wheels, pinions and pivots, and marked the plates for drilling. After he drilled them, he would bring them to the front, where I would cut the wheels, pinions and pivots. In the course of our labor, Father was always fretting about being on schedule, as he piled up the drilled plates for me to fit with wheels.

On this particular day, we'd been in the shop but two hours when I heard a gentle knocking at the door. Putting aside my file and brass wheel, I got up to see who was there. The next thing I know, the door opened from the outside, and standing before me was the exquisite form of Suzannah Ellingwood.

Looking up at me, she exclaimed, "Oh . . . it's you!"

"Aye, new neighbor—what brings you here this fine summer morning?"

She giggled, while peering up at me adorably. "I was looking for your father, actually. Your mother wishes him to come to our afternoon tea and open house for Father's business."

"Oh, I see," I replied, trying to hide my disappointment.

Looking past me into the recesses of the shop, she asked, "Is he here?"

She wore a floral scent that reminded me of the wildflowers in Richardson's fields; Richardson being our largest farmer, whose fallow lands between plantings went to tall grasses and wild flowers, which Mother harvested for our home. Realizing I could stand there and admire her loveliness forever, I overcame my shyness, cleared my throat and said, "Would you like a tour of our shop? Father is in back with his depthing tool."

"*Depthing* tool?" she repeated quizzically.

I bowed to her and declared, "Welcome to the Walker shop of clockery!"

Placing her dainty foot upon the threshold, Suzannah stepped inside, and looked around goggle-eyed at the various tools and clock movements at different stages of production. Undaunted by the noisy medley of ticks and tocks, she stopped at my bench to carefully examine a variety of wheels I had recently cut and filed. Holding one in her hand, she said, "Your skill is a gift, is it not? Not everyone can do such meticulous work."

"Oh, I don't know about that . . ." I replied sheepishly, and then added, "I bet you can cut a wheel as well as I can."

"Oh, I think not!" she replied sweetly.

"Well, let's see about that!" I challenged, gently taking the wheel from her hand and holding it before her eyes.

"See the teeth?" I asked, looking at her and not the wheel.

"Yes . . ." was her soft reply.

"Each tooth is actually a point on the outside edge of a circle." Taking up the index wheel of the tooth-cutting machine, I displayed it alongside the cut wheel. "Can you see a corresponding pattern between the two wheels?" I asked.

She studied them while I admired her gray-blue eyes, marveling at their serenity. Finally, pointing to the fifth set of holes in the index wheel, she said, "I think *this* is the row that is closest, yes?"

Stunned by her acuity, I exclaimed, "My gosh, Suzannah, you are a natural-born clockmaker! Indeed, that is *precisely* the row I was using when you came to the door."

As she flashed me a radiant smile, I couldn't help but notice once more how unusually beautiful her teeth were—so uniform in shape and brilliantly white—unlike those of most people.

"Well, let's see . . ." I said, tearing my eyes away from her face in order to reattach both wheels to the cutting machine. Suzannah stood on her toes and leaned over the bench to carefully observe what I was doing. I lined up the index with the wheel turned to a blank spot. Taking an edge file, I cut down toward the center of the wheel, thus creating a new tooth.

After she watched me re-index and cut another tooth, I handed her the file. "Would you like to try doing one?"

"Oh, no, I couldn't possibly do that—this is a man's work. A woman could never do it as well as a man."

"Who says?" I countered.

"Well . . . it . . . it would not be . . . decorous," Suzannah replied feebly, lowering her eyes.

"Nonsense!" I retorted. "A woman's touch blesses everything!"

Her eyes seemed to search my face as she repeated, "Everything?"

"Yes," I said, gently touching her hand so she'd open it to hold the file. Suzannah's skin was so soft, warm and delicate to touch, that I suddenly felt a rush of heat across my face. I lay the file gently across her palm, placing her forefinger along its top and her thumb along its side. Positioning her hand with the file in it upon the rim of the wheel, I then said, "Now . . . pull back and apply light pressure while doing so."

She did, and the file bit into the brass, sending tiny shavings to the bench. Relaxing her grip she moved the file up, then pressed down and drew it back with another stroke. Looking up at me expectantly, my heart raced when her eyes met mine. "Shall I carry on?" she inquired.

Bewildered by their depths I then stammered, "Yes . . . please do . . . about fourteen more strokes."

"Very well," she replied, returning her attention to the wheel. Carefully pulling the file across the wheel blank *exactly* fourteen times, she created a deep slot that was perfectly square at the bottom. "Now, what do I do next?"

"We'll move the index wheel one hole forward and you can file another slot." So saying, I moved the index wheel one hole and placed the file upon the rim of the wheel blank. "Now . . . proceed exactly as you did with the last cut."

Focusing intently on the wheel blank, Suzannah began to draw the file back in smooth, even strokes. After she'd finished, she asked to do more, and I happily obliged her. Indeed, she seemed to have the makings of a great clockmaker—so I guided her all the way around the wheel.

"I like the idea of creating something permanent," she remarked after we'd finished.

"Permanent?" I repeated.

"Yes," she said. "This thing I've created with you—it will be part of something beautiful and treasured for as long as someone cares for it."

"Yes," I replied, feeling unaccountably awkward. "I suppose there is something in what you say."

Suzannah looked at me meaningfully as she added, "And so it is with life."

As I pondered her words, I saw new qualities in her—degrees of depth and introspection I hadn't noticed before. But this revelation didn't help me form a reply.

Then a reprieve in the guise of my father entered the front room. He was so focused on a partially disassembled movement in his hands that he was, at first, totally oblivious to Suzannah's presence. "Jim, I think perhaps the second wheel of this time side needs to be . . . Well, well, well! Look at the beautiful flower that graces our shop today!"

"Good morning, Mr. Walker." Suzannah said demurely, still holding her file at the ready.

Father, bowing before her, raised his eyebrows and asked merrily, "And are you, dear girl, my newest apprentice?"

Suzannah's face turned a bright red as she glanced from Father's face, to her file and back again. "Well—I think not, but I . . ."

"Suzannah made this wheel!" I interjected, holding it up for his inspection.

Father took it without saying a word, and held it between his thumb and forefinger, studying the cuts carefully for their placement and uniformity.

"I see an old pattern here," he remarked, handing the wheel back to me.

"An old pattern?" I asked as I examined it—totally lost on his meaning.

"Yes. I will explain someday . . . or better yet, perhaps your mother shall—she knows the old pattern by heart. And so my dear Miss Ellingwood, to what do we owe the pleasure of your company in our boring old workshop?"

"I came because Father and Mother request the presence of you and Mrs. Walker at the occasion of our special tea this afternoon."

As she talked with Father, Suzannah looked to me like a picture of perfection: her face, her hair, her dress . . . and oh, that silvery voice! She was such a winsome little thing, yet she possessed a vigorous intellect and the wherewithal to tackle anything. "Imagine— a female clockmaker . . ." I blurted out, tapping Suzannah's wheel.

"Indeed!" Father replied, adding mysteriously, "Just ask your mother about that someday."

The movement bells began striking—noontime was upon us. Suzannah, alarmed by all the noise, gave an involuntary start. By the time the echoes of the final bells faded, her fright had turned to fascination. While the pendulums were still swinging, she stooped to carefully observe one particular movement. She watched its escapement with a focused intensity for several minutes.

"Remarkable . . ." She softly uttered. "How does it work?" she quickly asked, looking up to me for an answer.

"Oh, boy . . ." Father mumbled under his breath as he left to resume his depthing of arbors, pinions and wheels.

Suzannah repeated, "How does it work, Jim? What makes it *go?*"

"Well, let me show you," I said, delighted she'd asked.

When I offered her a stool so she could sit comfortably, she daintily gathered up the folds of her dress to settle herself on it. I took a simple timepiece movement and placed it on the table before us. I knelt on one knee so my face was level with the table surface, then carefully placed the movement at a right angle across the open jaws of the vice.

"Everything starts with gravity," I explained.

She lowered her elbows onto the table to more closely observe the movement, and I noticed those large gray-blue eyes gazing through it to meet mine.

"If I drop this weight, what happens?" I asked, trying to keep my mind on the subject at hand.

"It falls to the floor!"

"Exactly! A clock is nothing but a device to control the weight drop."

"Yes," she mused, looking at the movement. "A controlled drop device . . ."

"That's right. And we determine the *rate* of weight drop by making wheels with varying numbers of teeth in them. We can speed up the weight drop by using fewer teeth, or slow it down by using more teeth. This gives us a rough estimate of marking the time of day, but the pendulum provides the precision."

"Yes, it seems to break the weight fall into finely measured steps," Suzannah remarked, eyeing the escape wheel and pallets. She examined their action by twiddling the escape wheel, forcing the pallets into motion. Then she added, "The force placed upon this anchor thing controls the pendulum swing through this piece here . . ."

"Yes," I replied, astonished at how quickly her mind had grasped the concept of clock escapements, solely through her powers of observation and deduction. Clearly, she was intellectually gifted.

Silently holding one finger before her, I placed the weight upon the pulley and hung the pendulum in the chops, threading it through the crutch. Giving the winding arbor a turn or two with the crank, I said, "Now—give it a push."

She gave the bob a sideways push with her forefinger, setting the works into motion. As the device began to tick, Suzannah slowly lowered herself from the stool—like a cat watching a bird. She crouched down so her face was level with the ticking movement. Cocking her pretty head from side to side, she silently scrutinized the motion as if she were in a trance. She was again touching the pallet anchor with her forefinger when the front door opened to reveal my mother.

Surveying the scene that greeted her, Mother said, "My heavens, I have just stepped back in time!"

Unaware of her presence until she spoke, Suzannah snapped out of her reverie. "Oh . . . greetings, Mrs. Walker."

"Good morning, Suzannah. Are you learning about wheels and pallets?"

"Oh, so you know clockmaking, too?" Suzannah inquired, sounding surprised.

"Well, I'm married to a clockmaker and live with another, but many years ago . . ." She broke off in mid-sentence, seemingly lost in a distant reverie.

"Yes, Mrs. Walker? Please go on," Suzannah said expectantly.

"When I saw the two of you with *this* . . ." Mother replied, pointing to the movement still ticking on the vise, "well, it awakened sweet memories." She crouched down to watch the motion of the works, then dreamily added, "Such *wonderful* memories . . ."

Now all three of us were gazing at the ticking movement when my father returned unobserved. When he cleared his throat to get our attention, we all stood and dutifully faced him.

"It seems I keep getting *new* apprentices . . . each more beautiful than any I ever had before!"

He kissed Mother and placed an arm around Suzannah. "And how *are* my lovely apprentices on this fine day?"

Mother looked up at him and smiled. "*We* are just fine . . . and *you* have to prepare for tea at the Ellingwoods." Then she tweaked Father's ear and softly kissed his cheek.

Observing the kiss, Suzannah smiled at me shyly. I blushed in return, feeling uncomfortable in the face of it. I didn't know what, if any, meaning was attached to it, but it was a look I wouldn't forget anytime soon.

Father turned to me. "Jim, why don't you close up here, and I'll escort our two lovely apprentices back to the house."

"That would be most welcome," cooed Mother. Then, to Suzannah, "How would you like to help me prepare tea breads for your party? Your mother tells me you're an excellent cook."

"I should love to," Suzannah replied, her eyes bright with enthusiasm.

Father linked arms with Mother on one side and Suzannah on the other, and the three headed out.

I put away all the files, save the one Suzannah used. I then swept up the brass filings and other scrap materials, and dumped them into the reclaim bin. When I got to Suzannah's tiny pile of brass filings, I left it untouched, without knowing why. Finally, I gathered it up and poured it into a small piece of paper, folded it securely and wrote the date—August 3, 1765—on it. Then I hid the packet high up on a cupboard shelf—to preserve it without really knowing why.

When I returned home, I found Mother and Suzannah in the kitchen, preparing to bake tea breads for the Ellingwoods. Suzannah was mixing the dry ingredients in a bowl and Mother was cutting up the fruit. Since I felt entitled to a bit of a respite now, I sat down at the table to watch them work. Their sudden familiarity with each other had struck me as odd at first, but it didn't take me long to realize that a natural bond had sprung up between them. Without words, they worked in tandem together, able to simply intuit the next step of any collaborative endeavor.

When Suzannah reached the stage of coating the inside of the tea bread tins with flour, I stood up and approached her. "Is there anything I can do to help? I feel like I should do *something*."

"Baking is a woman's job!" Mother declared.

Suzannah looked up at me with a wry smile, and I knew she was thinking of her comment earlier about clockmaking being a man's job.

Then Mother added, "Stick to clockmaking—or perhaps you could mend the firedogs in the parlor."

"But the firedogs in the parlor are fine," I protested.

Mother then shook a little flour from her fingertips at me, saying, "Well . . . then shoo! *Out* of our kitchen!"

Some of the flour landed on my shirt, leaving some telltale streaks. When I glared at Mother, somewhat astonished at her behavior, she giggled like a child, picked up some more flour and flicked it my way, repeating, "Shoo! *Shoo!*"

Observing this exchange, Suzannah kept her eyes down and busied herself by layering a portion of dough into each tin. But I noticed the corners of her mouth twitch and finally turn up as she unsuccessfully tried to stifle a laugh.

Suddenly, with a resounding splat, a small ball of moistened dough hit me straight in the center of my forehead—where it promptly stuck. Feeling pitiable, I stared at my mother for a long moment, and then at Suzannah for another. Feigning anger—as I slowly wiped the dough from my face—Mother started giggling again and covered her mouth to hide her mirth. When I heard Suzannah laugh with her—that did it. They were not going to make sport of *me!*

Grabbing a quantity of loose flour from the table, I smiled sweetly as I held my arm above Mother's head and dusted her hair with it.

She, in turn, gleefully gathered up a whole handful of flour and hurled it at my face. I ducked, and when I looked up, I saw that it had landed on Suzannah's beautiful golden brown hair, which was now speckled with white.

Suzannah looked at Mother, who stood there aghast. She nodded to Suzannah, who seemed to know what she was thinking. Then, with mischievous grins on their faces, the two grabbed handfuls of flour and attacked me, shouting as one, "Get him! *Get him!*"

The two pummeled me so thoroughly that great billowing clouds formed in the air, covering us all with a thick white residue. We were screaming and laughing, with nary a care . . . until my father entered the room.

"What is *this!*" he demanded, peering through the floury haze.

We were instantly stunned into silence. Finally, Mother warned him haughtily, "*You* stay *out* of this!" and nonchalantly tossed a remaining handful at him, powdering his freshly barbered face and neatly combed hair.

Rising to the occasion, Father suddenly gave chase to Mother, who scrambled over to the kitchen table for fresh ammunition and tossed it in his face. He stopped in his tracks, looking like a ghost, and then began to chase her around the table, my mother squealing with delight as she declared, "Suzannah, get him! *Get him*! He's a *ghost*!"

Suzannah hesitated, but I did not. This time I grabbed a hand full of flour and tossed it at Father, hitting him squarely on the chest.

He paused to survey the damage, and then scooped up his own hand full of flour, a very large one at that. Father couldn't suppress a laugh as he prepared to throw it.

As I backed away from him, I warned, "Now, Father, be *nice* . . . and put that flour *down!*"

He let it fly.

I ducked, but still caught a tiny powdering on my shoulder as I heard the remains of it land on something with a loud *floof*! I straightened up to gloat at him—since he'd mostly missed me. But when I turned around and saw Suzannah behind me, I realized that she had been the recipient of father's flour bomb.

My jaw dropped. We had ruined her dress.

Suzannah mimicked my action by letting *her* jaw drop. Holding her hands out in a helpless gesture of surrender, she put one hand over her mouth as she began to giggle. First one or two coquettish bursts . . . until she began to laugh uproariously.

Mother went over to Father and carefully dumped an entire cup of flour on his head as punishment. "*That* is for the *women* in this house!" she announced, triumphantly waving her empty cup in a victorious gesture.

Suzannah clapped her dusty hands excitedly, and in a show of solidarity called out, "Yes—one for the *women!*"

Father slumped into the nearest chair, hunching over with shame at his resounding defeat. The sight of him caused Mother to start laughing again. Her laughter was contagious because it started Suzannah off again, and then Father—and finally me. We couldn't look at each other without pointing and bursting into more gales of laughter . . . until the back door opened to reveal Fanny Ellingwood.

Fanny looked like Fanny, but Father found her irresistibly droll because she alone was not covered in white. As she stepped into the white haze of our kitchen, she addressed a whitened figure with penetrating blue eyes. "*Aiiinnnsley*—is that *you?*"

On the instant, in unison, we all roared with laughter—that is, all except Fanny. She backed away, then looked at Father and declared, "*You* look like you've seen a *ghost!*"

Now we laughed even harder at her unwitting reference to what had started us off.

But Fanny was not amused.

Father finally managed to gasp, "Well . . . *I* have!" pointing to Suzannah, who was no longer laughing, but instead had a worried expression on her face—evident despite her whitened features.

Sympathizing with Suzannah and wishing to curb Fanny's anger, we ceased our cachinnations and quieted down.

Fanny spoke to us in a scolding tone. "Well . . . did *anybody* here get an invitation to *tea* this afternoon? From the look of things, I must be in the wrong house!"

"Why, yes we did!" Mother assured her.

Fanny turned to her and said, "Ainsley Rennsdale Walker . . . you really take the cake!" Looking Mother up and down with a critical eye, she added anxiously, "You *are* coming, are you not?"

"Of course, we'll be there, Fanny—and we'll bring the tea breads we baked specially for you."

"Looks to me like you're *wearing* the tea breads!" Fanny quipped as she crossed her arms and frowned at her friend.

Mother looking crestfallen, gave Fanny her most appealing sad-eyed expression, until Fanny's frown slowly dissolved and gradually turned to laughter. "This is the silliest thing I've ever seen in my life. You really know how to have fun, *but what a mess!* Will I see you all in *one* hour?"

"Absolutely, resolutely!" Father promised.

Addressing her bewhitened daughter, Fanny sternly warned, "Suzannah, you need to tidy up in time, so come along young lady!"

Suzannah, giving me a worried look, nodded obediently as she went to her mother's side.

When the door closed behind them, I turned to Mother and nervously asked, "Do you think she will get in trouble?"

After a thoughtful pause, Mother answered with a touch of humor. "I think not, son—especially since this was a family effort!"

I placed my arm around her shoulders and kissed her floury cheek.

"Hey—" Father protested as he stepped over to Mother and draped his arm around her—"that's *my* territory!"

Mother kissed him and said, "Oh, Jim, stop being such a fop and get yourself cleaned up. There's plenty of water in the barrel."

The Escape

The barrel Mother referred to was a contraption suspended above what looked like an oversized roofless
privy. Within, there was a changing and drying area
fitted with pegs for clothes and towels. This was adjacent to the
bathing area, where as its name "the barrel" indicated, was in fact
a large barrel that collected rainwater, with a smallish bung in the
center of the lower face. Below that hung a large concave tin pan
about two feet in diameter, punched with hundreds of tiny holes.
When the bung was pulled, the water flowed through the holes,
cascading upon whoever stood or sat below it—giving the effect of
a gentle rainstorm. The barrel would enable us to clean up and get
to the Ellingwoods in short order.

Since the enclosure allowed for total privacy, in warm weather
Mother and Father used it together, bringing a fresh change of
clothes with them. I always wondered what other activities went
on in there, as I often heard Mother giggling or making cooing
sounds, and sometimes even letting out a sharp cry. At all events,
they were together under the barrel at least once a week, sometimes
twice, staying until the water ran out. If we needed to use it again
right away, we would replenish the barrel with well water. Mother
always encouraged me to use it, since she was fastidious about our
personal hygiene.

After washing away our white mantles and donning fresh clothes,
we manned corn brooms and wet rags to restore the kitchen to
its former spotless condition—in less than an hour. While Father
and I retreated to our rooms to put some finishing touches on our
grooming, Mother remained in the kitchen, cutting up slices of tea

bread. She stacked them onto pewter plates, which she covered with clean kitchen cloths, as was her custom. The cloth served not only to protect the tea bread from flies, but also from "sticky fingers" lurking in the kitchen.

I heard a knock on my door, and it was Father. "Are you ready, Jim?"

"Not quite, but let's go," I replied, anxious to see Suzannah.

I finished running a comb through my hair as the parlor clock struck three bells. We all reassembled in the kitchen, my father and I each taking one plate of tea bread to bring to the Ellingwoods.

Once we arrived, Father knocked on the front door, and to my surprise, it was opened by a lovely looking lady I'd never seen before. She looked to be about twenty-five, and was an adult version of Suzannah, complete with gray-blue eyes that lit up at the sight of us. She threw her arms around Mother, exclaiming, "Well, good afternoon, Ainsley!"

Mother met this greeting with a hug of her own. "It's wonderful to see you again, Lydia."

My first thought was, "Mother *knows* this person?"

Lydia escorted us into the parlor, where an exquisite sideboard was laden with a full tea service, cakes and scones; to which our tea bread would soon be added. After we partook of the refreshments, we found ourselves surrounded by small groups of people engaged in lively conversations.

At my request, Mother introduced me to our escort—Lydia Ann Barrett. As I'd surmised, she was indeed Suzannah's oldest sister, born in Walker's Cove, before Sam had moved to Boston, which is why Mother was so familiar with her.

Lydia had come from Boston specially to help her mother prepare for this occasion.

I soon remembered that the Ellingwoods were hosting this "open house" to promote Sam's newly relocated business among the merchants, traders and townsfolk. Since Sam had made most of the furniture in their home, it became a showcase for his fine craftsmanship.

"A masterful stroke of advertising," Father remarked, as we strolled through the rooms looking at the fruits of his labor.

When we passed through the parlor, I saw the Willard clock I'd repaired mounted over the fireplace looking very impressive indeed, with the calendar, seconds dial and moon phase indicator all functioning. Since it had a fairly small dial, I found it difficult to read the time at a distance, so I stepped closer to see that it was 3:35.

Father stood alongside me to get a better look at it too. "Willard is just a boy, but he does good work for one so young."

"Yes, I agree. But what if the dial were larger, so it would be easy to read; and what if it *sat* on the mantle or a table instead of hanging on a wall?"

"You may have something in the notion of a larger dial," Father replied. "Perhaps we should try out that idea someday."

"I think we should do it sooner," I persisted. "It would appear to the customer that he's getting a bigger clock for the money, without us needing to make a bigger clock movement."

After a thoughtful pause, Father agreed. "Let's try out that idea soon. Perhaps I can even get Sam to build the case."

Turning away from the clock, my eyes were drawn once more to Sam's rocker. When I pushed it lightly, it moved back and forth within its fixed frame. Although I'd seen it several times before, it still struck me as being the most ingenious apparatus I'd ever encountered. Seating myself in it, I felt how remarkably smooth and pleasing it was, enhanced by the addition of two plush cushions tied in place—one on the seat, the other on the backrest.

"I think Fanny made those recently," Father commented, poking at the cushions. As he wandered off to refill his teacup, someone pulled him aside to discuss an order of clock jacks for shipment to Boston.

Meanwhile, I remained in the rocker, resting my head gently against Fanny's pillow. Closing my eyes, I became captivated by its gentle motion, and despite the noise of the crowd, I was soon lulled into a blissful state of drowsiness . . . and the downy comfort of deepest sleep.

A PERSISTENT TUGGING at my sleeve interfered with my slumber, and I heard a soft voice say, "Jim, wake up. Are you *so* tired? Would you like some of this tea to help you wake up?"

My eyes fluttered open to see Suzannah's pretty face. I didn't speak, but I thought the word, "angel." Realizing I'd been asleep, a glance at the Willard clock told me it was 4:23! I had slept nearly an hour in the rocker. I sprung up and bowed to her in total humiliation, stammering, "I'm *so* sorry, Suzannah! I didn't mean to fall asleep here. I merely sat down and it just happened."

Looking at me with an expression of great warmth, she offered me a slice of tea bread on a small plate in one hand, and a cup of tea in the other. "I see my father's rocker has claimed another victim. Wouldn't you like these refreshments to invigorate yourself?"

Suffocating with embarrassment and eager to flee, I replied, "I think perhaps some fresh air would be better."

Carefully setting her plate and cup upon the sideboard, Suzannah gently pressed my arm and whispered, "Then let us *both* escape this tedium!" She immediately headed to the front door with me following a few steps behind her. She opened it, and stepping into the walkway leading to the street, she eagerly motioned for me to follow.

As we walked alongside each other under the sheltering trees that bordered the path toward the village center, she slid her eyes toward mine and said coquettishly, "So, James Walker . . . another surprise."

"Surprise?" I said quizzically, feeling like a perfect dolt.

"Why, yes! Mother didn't know the Walkers engaged in *flour* fights," she said, stifling a laugh.

"Well . . . ah . . . so did I neither," I sputtered, not yet fully awake.

Suzannah looked at me suddenly with a serious face. "Hmmm . . . 'so did I *neither*'?" she repeated incredulously.

"No . . . I mean . . . yes . . ." But mercifully, I stumbled over an exposed tree root, saving me from any further explanation. After recovering my balance, I hastily added, "I guess *this* will teach me not to fall asleep in other people's houses in broad daylight!"

"Oh, James, don't even think twice about it," she assured me. "You can fall asleep in Father's rocker any time you want."

Since we'd stopped momentarily, I gazed directly at her face to better read her meaning . . . and saw honesty, innocence and sincerity there. Searching the depths of her eyes, I nodded and softly replied, "I shall take that under advisement."

"Do the Walkers have flour fights often?" she asked with a sweet giggle, as we resumed our walk.

Adopting a tone of exaggerated seriousness, I said, "We usually have at least one or two a week, save when whitened flour is expensive . . . then we have at least three a week, because we don't know what to do with all our money!"

"Mother was perfectly astonished when she found us in such a state." Then she added gleefully, "And do you remember the way she said 'Ainsley' to your mother? I thought I would burst!"

"Even funnier was Mother's straight-faced silence!"

Suzannah couldn't suppress a dainty little laugh, almost childish in its delivery. She was always trying to stifle her mirth, but was very transparent in doing so, which made it all the more endearing.

"Actually, we have *never* had a flour fight before—but we have had water fights," I volunteered.

"Water fights?" Suzannah sounded bewildered by the idea.

"Oh, yes," I replied, "especially in summer when it's so hot."

"Oh, please tell me about them!" she begged.

"Well, on hot summer days we all go down to Walker's Point and—"

"Where *is* Walker's Point?" she interrupted.

In answer, I pointed vaguely in its general direction. "It's down there . . . by the old beech tree, just at the end of the trail."

"James, take me there! I would love to see it."

At first, I hesitated, for Walker's Point was a sacred place to me. I didn't relish sharing my secret hideaway with anyone. But then I reasoned, if Suzannah was to be a friend, friends do share secrets, do they not?

"Very well then, I will. But what about the open house—won't you be missed? Will your father come looking for you?"

"I think not, Jim, since Father pretty much lets me do as I wish—within reason. Besides, he knows you."

"*Knows* me?" I repeated, amazed at her innocence. "He just met me three weeks ago."

"But he knows you're a trustworthy friend."

I let her words quell my fears as we headed toward the old beech tree, where a serpentine path led us to the outcropping of Walker's Point. We stood on its rocky base, which jutted out into the sea like a slanted question mark. From its hooked end, one could see in all directions.

"Let's go to the end!" she said with excitement, her voice barely audible above the breakers' roar.

Feeling the saltwater spray us, I looked down at her feet and warned, "You'd better be careful, Suzannah—leather shoes are slippery on wet rocks. And I don't want you to ruin a good pair of shoes in addition to a dress today!"

"Fear not, O noble gentleman! I will be careful—I can do it," she replied undaunted, thrilled by this chance for adventure.

I therefore led us on a path that was safest for a girl's leather shoes to navigate, finally arriving at the tip of the question mark, where we were two lone figures, looking out at the wide expanse of open sea. I pointed to the inside curve of the question mark—which formed a protected cove of sorts. "There are usually seals in here, Suzannah." As if on cue, a dark bullet-shaped head popped up from the surface of the water and barked at us.

"Look at *that!*" Suzannah exclaimed, delighted by the sight. "Can we get closer?" she asked, breathless with excitement.

We carefully inched our way to the water's edge, where the seal watched as Suzannah kneeled to approach it. When she slowly raised her hand in the seal's direction, it barked at her several times, but it didn't move. "Come . . . come over here, I won't hurt you. My name is Suzannah . . . and I'm your new friend. Please come over to see me," she said beseechingly, while wiggling her fingers.

I doubted the seal would move toward her—but then, lo and behold, it did! It swam back and forth as it came closer, evaluating this delicate creature in the blue pastel dress. A mystical connection seemed to exist between the two, as it drew near to where she kneeled at the water's edge. While I stood behind her, quietly observing her entreaties, I noticed her golden brown hair glinted and shimmered in the sun as it flowed across her back . . . and I was irresistibly drawn toward her, as was the seal.

Heaving itself upon the rocks the seal flopped down next to Suzannah, and from brimming eyes, watched her and waited. Slowly extending her little hand toward the animal, Suzannah touched its nose. Finding no fearsome elements about the girl, with nostrils pulsating and whiskers twitching, the seal nestled its wet snout in Suzannah's palm. When she scratched its chin with her free hand, it started to whine and turn its head to the other side, while Suzannah continued to scratch.

I never saw the like of it before—there was something truly magical about my little neighbor. Now, as I watched in amazement, Suzannah was petting the seal's head, tickling its belly and causing it to roll onto its side, holding up its front flipper to be scratched. As she did so, her eyes lit up as she looked over her shoulder at me. "I wish I could take it home with me and have it as a pet. It seems very fond of me, and it's so adorably cute!" Turning around, she tenderly caressed its underjaw and squealed, "*Wook* at deez *bootiful* eyes!" The seal groaned in pleasure as it completely surrendered itself to Suzannah's attentions.

I cautiously stepped around to the other side of the seal, and taking care not to frighten it, I sat down beside it. Slowly extending my hand to gently rub its stomach, it stretched out full length between us, flippers high in the air as if to signal its happiness.

As the waves crashed around us we three remained, and I silently envied her talent. "Suzannah—you certainly have a way with nature's creatures," I said admiringly between the hissing of the waves.

"I love animals, and I love nature . . ." she explained, "and animals do seem to gravitate to me."

"Well, seeing is believing," I replied, nodding toward the seal, which was still on its back.

Perhaps a bit embarrassed by my effusive adulation, Suzannah changed the subject. "How long has your family lived here? Is their presence here the reason it's called Walker's Cove?"

I'd never had to relate my family history before, and the idea embarrassed me, as though it entailed bragging about my own people. But nonetheless, coughing to assuage my nervousness, I pressed on to please Suzannah. "My grandfather came here to avoid the royal tax collectors and religious zealots in Boston. They were pressuring him for money and trying to impose their rules and beliefs, while he felt it was his right to live as he wished."

"Just like Father . . ." she murmured dolefully. "Some things never change—not even after a hundred years!"

"That's partially true, Suzannah. But your father isn't a victim of *religious* persecution, he's a victim of *political* persecution."

"Yes, I know . . ." she admitted sadly. Bowing her head, she stopped scratching the seal, and looking up with a hurt expression, she lamented, "But it split up our family. We had lived together in Boston for years. It was the promise of a thriving business there that drew Father from Walker's Cove twenty years ago."

"Yes, I've heard that from my father."

"We were all born in Boston, save for Lydia," she continued.

"Everyone liked the city, then?" I inquired, secretly dreading she would return there someday—and our friendship would be lost.

"Not so much liking the city itself, but we were all together and happy in one place. One by one, my sisters married . . . and now I'm the only fledgling left in the nest—and I'm afraid."

"Of what?" I asked gently.

"I only wish for my parents' happiness and safety," was her heart-felt reply. "I shall do all I can to make their final years good ones."

"I commend you for that." I softly replied, and was impressed by her altruism, especially considering her tender age. I felt it echoed in some ways my own situation. "I feel as you do about my own parents, perhaps even more so because they are all I have. You see, I'm alone—I have no brother or sister. You are very fortunate to have four sisters."

"I know I am," she said, casting her eyes downward.

I knew she was feeling awkward because I had no siblings, but after a pause, she smiled again. "I'll devote myself to the role of being the final nestling, and try to be all I can to them."

"You're a very special person, Suzannah. You honor yourself and your parents . . ." I trailed off as I was suddenly struck by the painful thought that I might never become part of her life.

As if she sensed my feelings, she looked directly into my eyes and said in a soft caressing tone, "Jim, you have brought such comfort and happiness to me as my new neighbor and friend, welcoming me with an open heart. It's because of you I feel at home now in Walker's Cove—and especially here at Walker's Point."

I was delighted by the unabashed expression of her feelings and how special she made me feel. At the same time, I was embarrassed by my physical attraction for her, which seemed improper. Finally, I couldn't sit still any longer and stood up to stretch my legs. She got up too, and when she faced me, I finally managed a reply, albeit a feeble one. "I'm also happy you are my neighbor, Suzannah. I have never known a girl very well before, but I'm glad you came here with me—and I'm glad we're friends. Now . . . ah . . . let me show you a tidal pool."

We picked our way carefully across the rocks together, until we came to the tidal pool where my family bathed and engaged in water fights. At high tide, it became populated with all kinds of sea life that were fascinating to observe. While Suzannah searched for signs of the creatures that dwelled there, a woeful howl from our new friend rent the air, imploring us to return—which we did.

Suzannah sat down first, and when I sat beside her, she moved closer to me, so that our sides were touching. A sudden wave of heat flushed my entire face as a new kind of thrill surged through my body. Then I held my breath . . . silently praying that Suzannah wouldn't notice my thoroughly unsettled condition.

But she sat there unperturbed, petting the seal, glancing around the point and out to sea. "So, Jim, you were telling me about your grandfather . . ." she reminded me.

"Well, as I said earlier, he left Boston to come as far north as he could at that time. For weeks he tramped through the woods with nothing but a pack, a musket, a knife, and the desire to be away from zealots and people who vexed his brain.

"He befriended some Abenaki Indians who took him to their camp and showed him all the best places to hunt and fish. The land and the water provided all he needed to get along, after a fashion. He learned the basics of the Abenaki language and became a skillful hunter and fisherman.

"Despite that, he still wished to settle on his own land and carry on his trade with a new smithy. When he realized he was too far removed from civilization to support a smithy, he found an area close enough to Boston to do business—but far enough away to ensure the independence of his trade *and* his spirit."

I paused briefly and Suzannah just smiled. When I remained silent, she brightly said, "Carry on—I'm listening . . ."

"Well, he found a congenial place where he decided to build a cabin with the help of his Abenaki friends. They helped him cut down the trees it was made from. The cabin stood where our own house stands today. The stream that now runs through Richardson's fields was a quick mover, so he decided to build a small sawmill beside it.

"Several trips to Boston were required to secure the tools and parts needed to build his forge, his cabin, and the waterwheel on the stream. While in Boston, he spread the news of his relocation among his old customers. Once everything was in place, my grandfather was able to make ironware, mostly for himself or to trade for other necessities. From his new smithy came hammers, pincers, nails, awls, saws, pliers, adzes, files, chisels, traps and even muskets. Many of these items he bartered with the Abenakis for skins, furs, canoes and buckskin clothing.

"Soon his old associates sent their schooners and brigs to the little cove. Once they saw the smoke from the smithy, the trading began. Newcomers would also come ashore to investigate. Grandfather welcomed them and traded with them, too. The word eventually got around about the 'Man Hermit' in the cove who was a skilled smith and honest trader.

"Thus our little cove became known as Richard Walker's Cove, or just Walker's Cove. By and by, as other merchant captains heard about Grandfather, one of them—Josiah Wheeler—arranged to take most of his products and sell them in various ports south of Boston. They eventually built a thriving business together, and my grandfather was constantly in want of enough time to produce his goods.

"To relax body, soul and mind, he came to this very spot to gaze upon the ocean. He loved to breathe the bracing salt air, hear the sea gulls' cries and the ocean whisperings—and he even slept on the rocks like a seal.

"In fact, it was on a day very much like today, in the warmth of the sun, that my grandfather fell asleep on this rocky point. In the midst of a deep slumber, he was suddenly awakened by a sinister growl. He sat up and dismissed the sound as something he probably dreamed. Suddenly a crushing weight slammed into his back, and one of his arms was savagely clamped in a needle-like vise. The impact threw him forward into the sea—right over there." I pointed to the approximate area in question.

"While standing in the shallow water, Grandfather tried to determine what caused the searing pain in his left arm. It was then that he saw a pack of five adult wolverines staring at him from above. Anticipating a meal, their jaws dripped with saliva and their eyes flashed death to their prey. My grandfather knew they were ready to pounce on him, water or no. He also knew they smelled blood—his blood—for his left arm bled heavily from the initial bite, so he knew he was running out of time.

"Grandfather's only weapon was a small patch knife he kept in his belt. Keeping his eyes riveted on the pack's leader, he reached slowly for the weapon with his right hand. Once he had it in his grip, he lunged at the lead wolverine, wrapping his wounded arm around the beast's body while driving the knife deeply into its stomach, laying it open upon the rocks . . ."

Suzannah grimaced, and I stopped to spare her any further distressing details, but she urged me to continue.

"The other wolverines went into a frenzy, tearing viciously at the legs and body of the dead animal, while also snapping and ripping at Grandfather. He sliced blindly into the haunches of a second wolverine, disabling it. The remaining three then attacked the wounded beast with the same fury as they had the first.

"While they were thoroughly immersed in cannibalizing each other, grandfather reasoned that it was a good time to escape. So he hobbled away toward the top of the point, turning just in time to see one of the wolverines launch itself through the air, hitting him squarely in the chest. Both fell onto the rocks, with the beast atop Grandfather.

"The snarling demon snapped viciously at his neck, but narrowly missing it, sank its jaws instead into his shoulder. Screaming in agony, Grandfather got a solid grip on his knife and in desperation, drove it into the wolverine's neck, the force of the blow snapping the blade. Mortally wounded, the beast howled in pain while my grandfather struggled to push it off his chest and into the open sea."

When I paused for a moment to ensure I hadn't upset Suzannah, I saw she was too spellbound by the story to react, so I hastened to continue.

"Although bleeding heavily from numerous wounds, Grandfather staggered to his feet and stumbled over to the top of the point. At the sight of him, the two remaining wolverines ran off. He then fell to his knees as he started to lose consciousness, hearing what he thought were human voices before he passed out.

"It was at that moment Captain Wheeler and two Abenakis arrived at the site of his struggle. From the smithy, they'd heard the howls and shrieks of what sounded like predators in a feeding frenzy, and feared for Grandfather's safety since he was nowhere to be found."

Suzannah seemed to be in a trance . . . her gray-blue eyes were wide as saucers and her rapid breathing was audible. "Are you all right?" I asked her, waving my hand in front of her face.

She nodded, saying, "What a story! Did your grandfather survive the attack?"

"Yes, he did," I replied. "After all, I am here as living proof! Shall I carry on?"

"Yes, please do!"

"Where was I . . . ?" It was easy to lose my place, having Suzannah as my captive audience to distract me.

"You were saying that the captain and two Abenakis came to rescue your grandfather," she reminded me.

"I remember now. The Abenakis and Captain Wheeler carried Grandfather back to the smithy. And using what medical knowledge he'd acquired as captain, Josiah proceeded to sew up the rents and tears on my grandfather's body. Since he was near death and needed constant tending, Captain Wheeler's men brought him aboard his vessel, where he was nursed by Rebecca, Wheeler's daughter."

"Oh, and let me guess," exclaimed Suzannah, "he married the captain's daughter!"

"Why yes, Suzannah, he did!" I said, laughing at her obvious enthusiasm for the idea.

"Oh, Jim, I wish we had a romantic tale like that in our family," she said wistfully.

Since I couldn't think of a suitable reply, I finished the saga. "The word got out among the Abenakis about Grandfather's great courage in the face of overwhelming odds, and so granted him the exclusive right to hunt and dwell here. They also decreed that the point would henceforth be known as Walker's Point—because his lone spirit had defeated singlehandedly five wolverine spirits—and it would now be sacred to him alone."

Suzannah looked up at me as she declared, "What an *amazing* story!" When our eyes met again, I looked deeply into them, and thus mesmerized, I couldn't speak.

Silence reigned for a time, until I noticed that the sun was very low in the sky. "Do you like sunsets, Suzannah?"

"I love sunsets," she said, glancing westward. "I've loved them since I was little, but it was difficult in the city to see them very often."

"I suppose it was—what with all the buildings in the way."

"Yes, Jim. But I'm sure they'll be even more beautiful here over the water where there is a clear view westward."

When I turned to face west, Suzannah did likewise, scooting up beside me. Once again our sides touched, sending a jolt of warmth racing across my face and chest, while my heart palpitated wildly. But a few moments later, once we were settled there, I felt overwhelmed by feelings of peace and contentment.

As we contemplated the horizon, a dark gray band of clouds gradually covered the sun. Above it, a brilliant yellow glow of sunshine remained, while below it the sky shone an iridescent pink. Fanned by the gentle westerly breezes, we remained lost in thought as we observed the changing shapes and colors of the sunset—that is, until we were startled by something wet and wiggly forcing its way between us. It was our little seal, which we'd totally forgotten. Laughing, Suzannah affectionately draped an arm across its back— as did I. It sniffed and twitched its whiskers, but it stayed right there as we watched the sun sink out of sight.

Suzannah tugged at my sleeve and murmured softly, "Thank you, Jim . . ."

"For what?"

"For everything you've told me and shown me. In four short weeks, I've learned *so* much about your village, about my house, about your family and—" she paused to flash me a heart-stopping smile before adding—"about flour." She finished by stifling a giggle.

I looked down at her tenderly as I said, "Welcome to Walker's Cove, Suzannah."

Then, she said somewhat hesitantly, sounding more serious than before, "Thank you again . . . for being such a kind and caring friend, Jim."

Nearly choking with gratitude, I struggled to answer. "The pleasure is all mine. And I'm very happy you are here . . . with *me*, Suzannah."

Looking up at me with moistened eyes, she pursed her lips to beat back a whimper . . . then simply smiled.

At that moment, I felt my wish on Midnight Blue had indeed come true, for my loneliness, like winter's ice in spring, was starting to melt and gently float away—chased by the warmth of Suzannah's smile.

THE CHALLENGE

Because of the heavy demand for roasting jacks, door hardware, muskets and clock movements, Father and I were confined to our shop, and so occupied, the summer months flitted by. Sam experienced a similar demand for sewing tables, candle tables, ladder-back chairs, elaborate mirrors, and a variety of other small pieces of furniture. Suzannah was kept busy serving lunch and refreshments to the workers in Sam's shop—as an inducement to work extra hours.

Consequently, Suzannah and I saw each other barely once a week—usually in church on Sundays. I was motivated to attend not to ask God for anything in particular, but rather to admire my little angel, especially when she sang and played Grandmother's organ. After the service, because of our busy schedules, my parents and the Ellingwoods revived an old tradition: they alternated hosting Sunday dinners, first at our house, and then the Ellingwood's. These weekly gatherings enabled us to share news about business, events in Boston, Portsmouth and Walker's Cove, and finally, to catch up with each other.

In the hours after church and the Sunday meal, Suzannah and I spent precious time together at Walker's Point. We relaxed and discussed our thoughts and feelings, our adolescent doubts, as well as our likes and dislikes. If we couldn't figure out the solution to a problem we were having—usually involving our parents—we both talked to God, who, in our little world, was personified by Nature.

As summer turned to fall, I could see the value of our friendship meant as much to Suzannah as it did to me. This increased my happiness tenfold, for I could readily tell just by how she looked at me that she preferred my company above all else. We were fortunate, too, that throughout this period of mutual discovery, our parents supplemented our experience with their loving guidance and encouragement. I always kept in mind Mother's advice about enjoying the friendship and good times, and how a woman's heart was slower to love than a man's. So I hesitated pursuing Suzannah as anything more than a friend—not unlike what Jonathan Barrett was to me. But I knew she was a very different kind of friend, with whom I had much more in common—and whose special glow filled my heart with joy. She was like a dear second self who harmonized perfectly with my first self . . . and life with Suzannah became an ever-present pleasure.

ON A DANK rainy October day in the clock shop, I was engaged in doing the dreaded depthing work. But in the midst of marking distances between arbors on a new movement plate, I would frequently stop to savor the most memorable moments of my past summer with Suzannah: when her eyes radiated happiness, when her abundant hair was loosened by the wind and caressed her face—and especially when her smile morphed into a kindred glance.

I was still at my bench when Mother entered and quietly closed the door behind her. Her hair was wet with rain, as was her dress. As she stood over me with a quizzical expression on her face, I removed my lens and looked up at her expectantly.

"Dear sir," she announced with an air of formality, "we have a guest who requires an audience."

"Who is it? Do they wish to buy a clock?"

"Perhaps someday," she replied evasively, "a *potential* customer, perhaps. But right now there's play afoot"—and she broke into a giggle that reminded me of Suzannah's. "So will you put those things aside, and kindly tend to your guest?"

"Very well, if you insist," I replied half-heartedly, relinquishing my magnifier and tweezers. "But I am busy today, in the middle of depthing wheels, which I'd wanted to finish before day's end," I said as I reluctantly removed my apron and headed for the door.

At the threshold, Mother kissed my forehead and held me in a long embrace.

"What brought this on?" I asked, touched at her sudden outpouring of affection.

"I love you, James. It is a mother's privilege, you know."

"Why yes, I know . . ." I replied softly as she placed her arm around my waist, and we walked leisurely through the rain back to the house.

Entering the parlor, she whispered loud enough for me to hear over the fire's spit and crackle, "Go on . . ." as though I were taking my first steps.

It was then I noticed a figure sitting on the sofa, silhouetted against the firelight. My heart leaped when the head turned and I beheld Suzannah's exquisite countenance. Her hair lovingly caressed her face and cascaded over her shoulders, its sheen glinting in the parlor firelight. She had woven carnations in her hair, and their sweet aroma enveloped me as I came closer, and when she looked up at me. I nearly swooned before her.

"I thought because it's raining, you might like a visitor to keep you company. I've brought some games with me," she said softly, as if she didn't want Mother to hear. As she started arranging her game board, she added, "Would you prefer a game of Draughts, or Fox and Geese?"

"You choose. I'm honored that you came here, Suzannah. But I thought your time was not your own these days."

"Well, Father gave me today off . . . it's my birthday."

I didn't know the exact date—only that she was born in October—so I was mortified that I had no gift to give her. Not knowing what else to say, I offered, "Well then, let me be the first to welcome you to your sixteenth year, Suzannah!"

Just as I finished uttering the words, Mother returned with an enormous apple cinnamon cake, liberally dressed with milk frosting. She placed it on the table in front of Suzannah. It was freshly baked and the aroma of sugar and cinnamon made my mouth water.

Raising her eyebrows in surprise, Suzannah asked, "Why, Mrs. Walker, what is *this?*"

Mother clapped her hands three times, and at that moment, the Ellingwoods, my father and a dozen mutual friends poured into the room, yelling "*Surprise!* Happy Birthday!"

Suzannah stood up with her hands pressed to her cheeks, her mouth open wide with astonishment. As she looked around at all our faces, she wept with joy and gratitude. A chorus of three huzzahs rose up before her, ending with a robust round of applause.

Mother handed Suzannah a knife, and cheered on by the group, she cut the cake and distributed portions to everyone. As Fanny served up the hot buttered rum, mulled cider and tea, Father added more wood to the fire to counteract the especially damp chill. Finally, everyone was ready to eat, drink and socialize.

Suzannah, meanwhile, carefully laid out the game chips on the squares of the board. Draughts was a favorite game among the Boston populace, but we'd had little exposure to it here. So I listened carefully as Suzannah explained it to me.

"It's a lot like chess, Jim. Every move opens up untold possibilities and closes untold others. So it's wise to keep a few different moves in mind when playing, as there would be no quarter for anyone who is captured."

"Captured?" I repeated.

"Indeed!" She continued, "The object of the game is to capture all your opponent's chips, or move your chips so your opponent's final chips are in a position where he can't withdraw. That's called the end game—similar to checkmate."

The game of chess, which I had occasioned to play with my friend Jonathan, had always befuddled me. I was never quick to analyze the moves necessary to my survival on a chessboard. The game was Jonathan's forte, and I was a faithful and willing victim, ever rising to his challenge for an inevitable defeat. Jonathan's aptitude for the law went hand in hand with the fact he could store so many chess moves in his head, whereas I barely got by with one. If by a stroke of luck I got the better of him, he would wriggle free with a number of countermoves I couldn't possibly have envisioned.

"These two back rows are called the king's row." While pointing out the two rows on the opposite ends of the board she then continued, "You can only move diagonally, and you must use the white squares. If your chip gets to my kings row, I place a chip on yours and you then become a king."

"Swell!" I replied excitedly, "and what does *that* get me?"

Placing a chip on another, she illustrated the kingly moves. "A king moves backward *and* forward, but still only diagonally, and only on white."

"Sounds simple enough," I remarked, as Fanny pressed a mulled cider into my hands.

As I stumbled through our first game, Suzannah thrashed me soundly. We played several more times, and on each occasion I was badly beaten.

Then the taunting began as Doc Brown came by. Seeing nearly all my chips stacked on Suzannah's side, and only four of hers on mine, he suggested I take a tutorial on the fine art of strategy.

After my fifth resounding defeat, Doc pulled up a chair next to mine, and hunching over the board, took on Suzannah for the next game. I watched with admiring fascination as this young girl trounced Doc in the same manner as she did me.

Afterward, I placed a sympathetic arm around Doc's shoulders, gave him a tankard of buttered rum, and suggested we both needed a tutor.

By this time, several other guests were watching, all of who wanted to challenge the undisputed champion. Thus our company became divided as Suzannah had her backers and her opponents had theirs. One by one, each suffered a resounding defeat. The only difference was in how long it took Suzannah to dispatch her victim.

The last and best of Suzannah's challengers was her own father, who was himself a seasoned player of Draughts. The afternoon faded into night as we all huddled around the table, completely absorbed in this Herculean match between the two Ellingwoods—which had gone, so far, nearly three hours, with a fairly even exchange of chips.

We had eaten all the cake and drank most of the rum and cider, but not one soul left the house—all eyes were riveted on the game.

Sam was good, far better than any of us, for he thoroughly analyzed his every move—and even several moves ahead—as he tried to determine what Suzannah's new strategy might be. Now, after almost ten minutes of deliberation, he moved a chip to take two of Suzannah's, shouting, "Hah! How about *that* for a master's play, dearest daughter?"

Suzannah looked into her father's eyes and asked warily, "Are you *certain* of your move, Father?"

Sam's smile disappeared as he reexamined the board intently, and after a few minutes replied, "Yes, I think so." Leaning back in his chair, he smiled smugly and taunted her, "Top *that* one, birthday girl . . ."

No sooner had the words escaped his lips than Suzannah said coyly, "Very well, Father . . ." And taking up her king, she made a single move that captured Sam's five remaining chips—including two kings.

An admiring roar of approbation went up among us as we all marveled at Suzannah's stunning victory. She had contrived to set a trap for her father, maneuvering her chips into position, and then sacrificing two of them in order to capture all his remaining ones in a single move.

Sam, feigning tears, stood and held Suzannah to his heart. As he did so, he announced, "I'm honored to present my daughter with a special gift for her special day, one intended to last a lifetime." He motioned us over to the parlor fireplace as Mother and Fanny refreshed our drinks, and then clapped his hands three times. The signal summoned two men, who came in through the front door carrying a large chest covered with a velvet blanket. They placed it in front of Suzannah.

Sam raised his glass and declared, "As the last of a long line of losers at Draughts today, I hereby bestow the title of champion upon my worthy daughter!"

We all gave a rousing cheer, and during its ebb Sam continued, taking a more serious tone this time. "Suzannah, this is *your* day. We are here because we love you and want to celebrate you and your abiding presence in our midst—for which we thank God. As a token of my love and affection, I've built a hope chest for you, to contain not only your hopes, but also the treasures of your heart . . . the things that represent your future, your loves, and most of all, dear daughter, your dreams. Keep them safe, and never lose sight of them." As he set down his glass, Sam seemed to be choking back tears—real ones this time.

We cheered some more as a tearful Suzannah reached up to hug her father, who held her tightly to his heart and then gestured toward the chest. "Well, have a look now."

When Suzannah drew away the blanket, everyone in the room gasped to behold what looked like a gleaming jewel. It was a chest made of highly polished mahogany, with glistening brass support hinges, lock and carrying handles inlaid seamlessly into the wood surface. The convex lid was adorned with a large inlaid ivory "S," etched in lamp black to create the effect of shadows, giving it a dimensional quality. All around the "S" numerous silver wire inlays radiated intricate representations of flowers with leaves and tendrils. Framing the letter and its embellishments was an oval herringbone inlay about an inch wide consisting of hundreds of alternating sections of ebony, holly, rosewood and birch. Underneath the oval, inlaid in a script of curly maple, was Suzannah's birthdate—October 18, 1751—a date I surely would never forget.

As the chest reflected the firelight, its beauty silenced us all. But finally, we bestirred ourselves and moved closer to examine its magnificent artwork.

"Sam, you have outdone yourself!" Father said, clapping his hand heartily on Sam's back. "I have seen this work done by the great masters in Philadelphia and Boston, and yours is in every way the equal of theirs. I'm damned proud of you."

Sam took my father's hand as he said, "Coming from you, Jim, that is indeed a very high compliment—and her reaction, my greatest reward."

The workmen came and rewrapped the chest and took it to Suzannah's chamber. There, it would have the enviable company of Suzannah's hopes and dreams, and become a silent witness to all she did.

Sam continued to receive compliments from each guest as they prepared to leave. And before venturing into the blustery October night, they kissed Suzannah and wished her many happy returns on her day. Not long after, the Ellingwoods thanked us profusely for hosting the party, bade us goodnight and returned home.

When I retired to my chamber, I reflected on Suzannah's wide-ranging accomplishments, which now included a mastery of the subtle strategies of Draughts. Apparently, her brain was the equal of my friend Jonathan Barrett—he who was at Harvard! The more I mulled this over, the more I doubted myself and felt unworthy—there was no way I could measure up to her.

I felt much the same way when I came upon her in the church, playing the organ and singing like an angel. Despite how much I yearned for her, in my anguished mind—I felt now as I did then, that she was better off without me.

REDEMPTION

In my solitude, I speculated upon what might have been. But my mind kept damning me, insisting Suzannah was beyond my reach, that I shouldn't waste any more of my time or hers. Yet my heart cried out in protest, for her friendship meant the world to me, nurturing my happiness and making my life worthwhile. Now life without her could only be pointless and drab.

I didn't even try to sleep, but sat upright on the bed in a state of fevered agitation, torn by the ambivalence between thought and feeling. Which would rule, and why was I feeling so insecure? I was never insecure about Jonathan, when he constantly defeated my best efforts in chess and showed himself possessed of other talents I lacked. But then, of course, I wasn't trying to *win* his friendship—it was a fait accompli. What drove my doubts about Suzannah most involved her being a girl, and the potential of our relationship now and in the future.

When my chamber door creaked open, I knew it was Mother. She sat down next to me on the bed, and I turned toward her. "I sense turmoil within you, Jim." She softly said. "What happened tonight? Why do you have misgivings about Suzannah?"

She was her usual clairvoyant self, but she still amazed me with her insight. "After her victories at Draughts, I felt like I knew nothing and she knew everything—that she has an intellect far superior to mine."

"And what determined that for you?" Mother asked.

"When she beat her father at Draughts. She is *smarter* than her father! I'm nearly eighteen and look how far I am behind him, let alone Suzannah."

Taking my hand, Mother grasped it affectionately and softly explained. "Sam said he yielded to her superior *play*. Do you think *he* feels inferior to his daughter?"

"No, but against that he is endowed with a gift—you saw the chest he made!" I retorted.

"And you also have talent," she declared, poking a finger into my chest. "I will *never* forget the look on Suzannah's face when you were showing her how the clocks worked. She *envied* you, Jim! Don't you remember you had to convince her that a woman could cut a clock wheel?"

"Yes, I remember."

Giving my hand an encouraging squeeze, Mother added, "Jim, we are all endowed with certain talents, and as such we complement each other by using them for the benefit of ourselves and others. It's a noble trait in human nature that we love those on whom we can confer a kindness; and in so doing—we become interwoven through our hearts and our talents. Joined together thusly, we succeed in life.

"Look at your father and me," she continued. "Your father is a blacksmith, clockmaker and tavern-keeper—albeit a reluctant one. I was an innkeeper and trader with all the attendant responsibilities of running those businesses. Our talents complement each other. Your father knows so much more than I do, yet I love him more than life itself—not for his talent or his knowledge, but for his pure heart and for his love."

Gently lifting my head with her finger beneath my chin, Mother softly said, "You are so much like your father . . . you have a strong sense of mind and are very sensitive in your heart, but always remember, Jim, the greatest gift that God has given us is the capacity to love; and while I understand your feelings regarding Suzannah's talents, look into her *heart* . . . because that's where you'll find you are more than equal."

Tousling my hair, she kissed my cheek and stood up to leave. "Keep this in mind, Jim: that if you die without a particular talent or kind of knowledge, it won't matter; but if you die without knowing *love*, you are wholly deprived."

With that and a parting kiss, she left the room, and once again I sat alone, this time pondering her words . . . and damning myself for being so foolish.

Silent Night

It began snowing today, not a frozen, wind-driven snow, but a floating snow, soft and continual, drifting down slowly to rest in the still white silence of a winter's night. "How appropriate," I thought, staring out the parlor window, "to be blessed with the soft white touch of His angels' wings."

Our house was very warm and quiet. Father had fallen asleep before the fire's intense heat, I sat at the table making inventory lists by candlelight, and Mother was preparing the winter kitchen for Christmas baking. This would be our first Christmas with the Ellingwoods living next door, and Mother hoped we could celebrate the holiday with them. She was invigorated by the prospect, as she went back and forth briskly from the kitchen to the parlor numerous times, collecting ingredients and cooking tins, checking her recipe ledger and the like.

At one point, she came over to where I was sitting and settled herself beside me. She then tenderly laid her hand upon mine—always a sign she had something she wanted to say.

"What do you think about the idea of inviting the Ellingwoods over here for Christmas Day?"

I smiled immediately, thinking of my little angel, Suzannah. "That would be wonderful," I whispered softly, so as not to wake Father. "Do you think they will come?"

"I believe so," she replied, her brilliant blue eyes sparkling merely at the thought.

"Well, I know I'd like that."

"Then I'll ask Fanny right now to find out if they'll come."

While she was donning her bonnet and shawl against the cold, Mother turned to me and said, "I'll be right back." But as she reached out to open the door, we suddenly heard a loud knock. "Who could that be at this time of night?" she exclaimed.

I got up from the table and stood beside her, in case there was trouble afoot. "I'll open the door," I said, bracing myself for the unknown. Imagine my sense of relief when I found Fanny and Sam Ellingwood standing at the threshold, all bundled up and lightly covered with fresh snow.

"Well, my heavens, what a coincidence!" Mother declared, beckoning the Ellingwoods inside with great enthusiasm. Removing her bonnet and shawl, she added, "I was on my way out to pay *you* a visit, Fanny!"

"Imagine that! The heart feeler still has sharp skills," Fanny remarked as she stood on the braided rug in the doorway, shaking the snow off her coat and stomping the residual ice from her shoes that the boot scraper missed.

Father finally woke up, and managed to make his way over to the door, albeit sleepily. He took their coats and hung them on the hooks of a nearby wall rack, and invited them into the parlor.

When Fanny greeted me, she fumbled in her large bag and handed me a warm bundle wrapped in cloth. "Suzannah is at home baking tonight, James, but she sends her warm regards—and this."

As I unwrapped it, the enticing aroma of cinnamon and pumpkin suddenly scented the air. My mouth watered as I beheld a perfectly formed loaf of freshly baked pumpkin bread. Touched by Suzannah's thoughtfulness, I softly asked Fanny, "Will you please give your daughter my heartfelt thanks?"

Giving me a sly look, Fanny replied, "Of course, I will. Suzannah thought you would enjoy something that has the flour on the *inside*."

"Will I *ever* be able to rid myself of that flour fight?" I asked in jest.

"Of course not, James Walker!" she replied with a smile, looking meaningfully at my mother.

Pointing to the bread I was holding, Mother said, "I have some salted butter, made fresh today, that will be very tasty on that;" then to the Ellingwoods, "You folks make yourselves comfortable before the fire, and I'll put the kettle on. So, Jim, would you mind sharing your newfound riches?"

"Of course, I will."

We settled ourselves in the parlor chairs, and Mother served Suzannah's pumpkin bread with her butter. The womenfolk had tea and the men had hot buttered rum.

"Suzannah certainly has a talent for cooking!" Mother noted, savoring her first bite.

"I must say she enjoys it very much," Fanny replied.

Licking the crumbs from her fingers, Mother declared, "I *must* have this recipe, Fanny! This is wonderful, and I'd love to make some before our pumpkins are gone."

Smiling with pride, Fanny said, "Oh, Ainsley dear, please ask Suzannah for her recipe directly, since I'm sure she would feel flattered to hear your praise. Just don't tell her I ever said so."

Mother nodded agreeably, and helped herself to another slice.

Father got up and stoked the fire so the heat fanned out and penetrated deep into our bones, making us feel cozy and secure. Then he retrieved a very old bottle of wine and five crystal glasses from the hutch. Since the crystal was used only for special occasions, I decided this must be one of them. The wine label indicated a 1736 vintage, and Father explained it was a gift from Sam's father when he and Mother were married.

Sam, upon seeing the bottle, was speechless . . . and his eyes moistened as he watched my father cut the wax from the top. Father handed him the bottle and a corkscrew. "Pull the cork, Sam . . . I would be honored . . ." Sam carefully pulled the cork and handed the bottle back to Father. It almost seemed a religious act as Father accepted it and reverently placed it on the table. He let it breathe for a few moments and then poured a small amount into each glass. Silently, he passed one to each of us, and then held his up to make a toast.

"Welcome back, Sam and Fanny! How precious these evenings will be if we're permitted to pass them together. May God bless this house and all those within. May He bestow His blessings upon

Suzannah and her sisters, too; and may we all love and cherish each other for this Christmas . . . and all those to come. In the name of our Lord, amen."

We all raised our glasses and repeated, "Amen."

After the toast, Mother tearfully embraced Fanny for a long while, and Father and Sam did likewise. From the constriction in my throat, I knew I was witnessing something very special, for there was a natural evenness and familiarity between these four friends . . . as though never a secret was kept from the others, or hearts ever betrayed. Every touch was a loving touch, and it was so magic and subtle to observe, Nature herself seemed to bless their special bond. I could readily see it was not about work or the travails of life that brought us all together this evening. No . . . tonight we were celebrating the hearts and souls of loving friends, finally coming "home" after an absence of many years.

So we retired to the parlor, where Mother brought out cheese, hardtack, and the rest of Suzannah's wonderful bread. Long into the night, we sat cozily before the fireside, chatting amiably about deep friendships . . . and as the snow deepened outside in winter's icy darkness, we all remained safe, warm and totally protected from her withering grasp.

The Sleigh Ride

t was about two weeks since our memorable Christmas with the Ellingwoods—and our last significant snowfall. But when I peeked out of my window on this morning, I saw that we'd had another.

Unlike last time, the aftermath of this storm blessed us with a clear and bright sunny day. In fact, the brilliance of the sun's rays reflecting off the snow was so intense that it forced me to look away for a moment. The day promised to be warm, as long as there were no chill winds stirring. I watched as a pair of snow rollers, one behind the other, passed in front of our house attempting to flatten the blanket of snow. But it still looked at least a foot deep, as the horses struggled in it up to their withers.

My stomach grumbled as I stretched and began to think about breakfast, for there was something about a fresh snowfall that whets the appetite and excites the spirit, so I hurried downstairs to the kitchen. When I arrived at the bottom landing, my nose was immediately assailed by an assortment of olfactory delights: apple pie, cinnamon bread, molasses and beans, pumpkin spice cakes and fresh baked bread. Following the aromas into the kitchen, I saw Mother standing at the table, dressing an apple pie crust with a layer of cinnamon sugar.

"Well, good morning, dear son of mine! And what do you wish to do today?"

"Today would be a great Suzannah day!"

"A *Suzannah* day?" she repeated thoughtfully. "Then why don't you take her for a sleigh ride to Richardson's fields. The snow is perfect for it, and Winnie needs a run."

"What a good idea!" I agreed enthusiastically for more reasons than one: I was secretly relieved at the idea of not being trapped in the smithy or the clock shop.

Gently patting my shoulder, Mother said, "Suzannah is such a heart treasure, Jim—go ahead and show her a grand day out!"

"Yes, she is rather splendid," I affirmed.

"She is more than that, Jim, *so* much more. Did you know she also possesses scholarly gifts?"

"What do you mean by *that?*" I was somewhat dismayed by this new turn in the conversation, recalling as it did the night we played Draughts and Suzannah outshined us all—and most especially me.

"About three weeks ago, when Father and I were at the Ellingwoods, Suzannah was in the midst of studying Milton's *Paradise Lost.* On her parents' prompting, she recited a whole section of it after only one reading. She can also read and recite Latin, and make calculations in long division and complex multiplication as easily as if she were doing simple addition. Plus, she has the most beautiful handwriting I've ever seen. She has it *all*—heart, head, hand and health!"

After she'd said her piece, Mother handed me a large slice of pumpkin bread and added, almost as an afterthought, "And she is so fond of *you*, Jim. Don't let her get away."

"But I don't *love* her yet, Mother," I protested, not ready to share my true feelings. "I think she's a lovely girl, although a bit *young*."

"Suzannah is sixteen years old, James, and that is the perfect age to form a steady acquaintance," Mother retorted. "Remember what I advised last summer? My advice is still the same—become friends at first, *enjoy* each other's companionship and find interests in common. The rest will take root naturally, and your love will blossom." She tousled my hair, kissed my cheek and resumed her pie making.

I finished eating my pumpkin bread, and then headed out to the barn to fetch Winnie.

We hardly ever used Winnie, save to occasionally pull our wagon or our sleigh. She was more of a family pet than a work animal. Mother had first developed a special affection for her when she was a filly possessed of an exceptionally gentle disposition. So she decided that when Winnie was older, she could haul felled trees and split wood, and do some light plowing—but no more than that.

During the summers, Mother frequently rode Winnie in the open fields of Richardson's farm, which was Winnie's favorite spot to graze—sweet grasses and wild flowers were abundant there. William Richardson always said that Winnie had the sweetest breath this side of Walker's Cove, horse or human. I always took his word for it and never tested his assertion.

On entering the barn, I saw Winnie lazily munching some hay supplied by Richardson's farm. When I opened her stall, she stepped forward and nuzzled my cheek with her soft lips. I was always struck by how soft, warm and supple a horse's nose and lips were, and how comforting it was to pat and press them to my cheek. She knew something was hidden inside my coat, since her nostrils were twitching and she sniffed loudly while poking into its recesses.

"Very well, Winnie. I do have treats for you," I admitted, laughing, holding out two apples I retrieved from my right pocket. She crunched them up immediately and was soon eager for more. So I produced a carrot, another apple and finally some sugar. Winnie loved sugar, but it was a costly and key ingredient in Mother's kitchen, so I only took modest amounts of it infrequently. Thus fortified for her mission, I installed Winnie's bridle and harness, and backed her up to the old red sleigh.

We had a second sleigh for hauling freight, and a flatbed wagon, but we had owned this particular sleigh for as far back as I could remember. It could hold four passengers, two in the front seat and two in the backseat; I say backseat, but in reality it was the small cargo area in the rear. Since it was built for speed, the sleigh was relatively light and low-slung, with runners made of wrought-iron scrollwork. The seats were of tooled black leather fastened and trimmed with brass rivets. They were very plush and comfortable

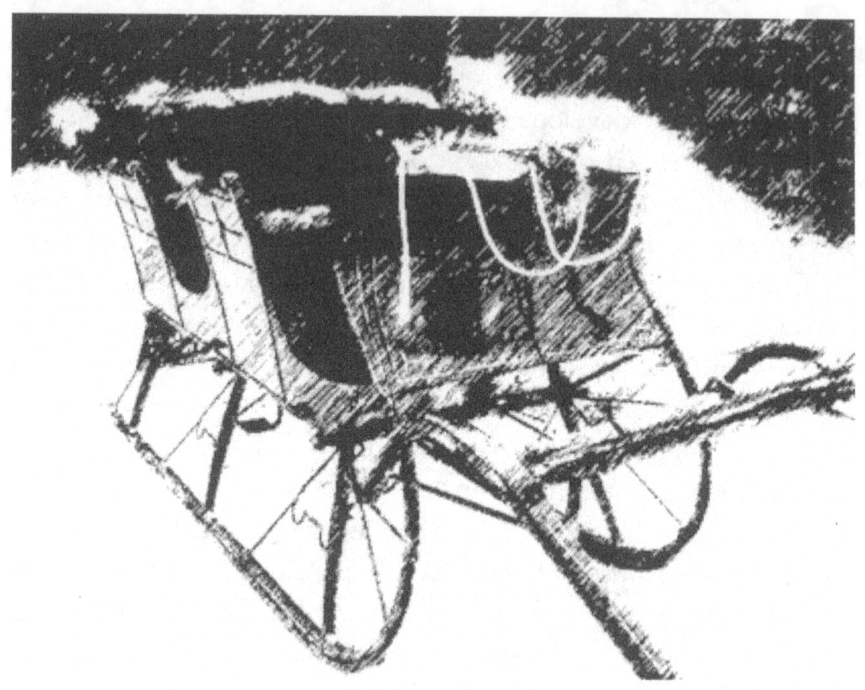

even for extended trips because they were mounted on leaf irons; the flexing of the leaves made the ride a smooth one.

Wide leather belts bolted to both seats strapped in the occupants securely. It was Father's addition because he tended to drive her fast and furious; they ensured that passengers would not pitch over the side when the driver or the horse became too frisky. Father courted Mother in this sleigh, and as such, Mother said it would always remain in our family, to be passed down. The fact that she encouraged me to take Suzannah out in this family heirloom lent a deeper meaning to the innocent adventure.

After harnessing Winnie, I stood for a time looking over the rig with great satisfaction. It was indeed a pretty sight to behold—red, with black trim and fine gold detailing. With Winnie attached, it seemed to be going fast just sitting still. At thirteen hands, Winnie was the perfect size for this sleigh, and they fit very well together. Turning toward me, she tossed her head and tapped her hoof several times, indicating she wished to be off.

After checking her harness one last time, I led Winnie into the snow. She twitched her ears, sniffed at the frosty air, and searched my coat in vain for another apple. Lastly, I placed the whip securely in its slot, knowing that while I might crack it in the air, I'd never use it *on* Winnie.

Leading Winnie on foot, I stopped in front of the Ellingwoods' house, and almost simultaneously, the door opened and there stood Fanny in the doorway.

"Well, well, well . . . my *gracious*!" she exclaimed, looking over my rig.

Judging by her show of surprise, I thought I'd forgotten my breeches, or committed some other transgression. As I could find nothing amiss on my person at least, I inquired politely, "Is there something wrong?"

"Oh, dear me, *no*. But that *sleigh*, it brings back so many memories!"

"Memories?" I asked, perplexed.

"Oh yes," she said dreamily, clasping her hands tightly together. "*Sweet* memories, my dear James." Turning around to face the open door, she called out, "Sam, oh Sam, come *see* this! You *must* come!"

Holding Winnie's harness, I waited patiently, feeling like a dutifully bound coachman awaiting his lordship.

Sam's anxious face popped out from the doorway and after rubbing his eyes, he stared at me without saying a word for a full minute; then: "Well I'll be *damned*! It's the same *one*, Fanny, the same *one*!"

"What am I missing here?" I finally asked, not grasping the significance of all this amazement.

Putting her arm around her husband, Fanny smiled. "You are missing *Suzannah*!"

Sam disappeared into the house for a few minutes, and then emerged to approach the sleigh, now wearing his shoes, with both on the wrong feet. Undeterred, he hobbled ape like around the sleigh, examining it carefully, and then burst out triumphantly, "It *is*! By God, Fanny, it's still here! Come! Come look!"

With a shawl thrown over her shoulders, Fanny came out into the snow and stood next to her husband, both focusing intently on the rear seating area—poking each other and giggling like children. Sam brought his wife closer to him and pointed to a spot on the back of the front seat. There, carved into the wood, were two sets of initials: J+A W, and below those, S+F E, then the date, DEC 17, 1736.

"You mean you owned this rig?" I asked Sam.

"Hell no, your father owned it—we were both married in it!"

"Married in a *sleigh?*" I asked incredulously.

"Well . . . not exactly . . ." Father interjected from the Ellingwoods' doorway, reminding me by his presence that he'd preceded me here to discuss clock cases with Sam.

Finally, I lost my patience and demanded, "All right! What is the secret between you, Mother and the Ellingwoods here?"

"Oh! No secret whatsoever," he declared.

"No! None at all!" echoed Sam.

"You see," Father said as he stepped outside and gave Winnie a fond pat, "your grandfather Richard built this sleigh and gave it to me for my eighteenth birthday—but I never could afford a horse. Sam here had a horse, but no wagons or sleigh. So, being the kind of friends we were, we combined our riches: sometimes he would borrow *my* sleigh and sometimes I would borrow *his* horse!"

They smiled broadly at each other and said practically in unison, "It sure fooled and impressed the ladies!" Then they both laughed heartily at the images conjured up by the recollection.

Now that I was finally in on their secret, I joined their cachinnations without knowing exactly why.

"You see, Jim," Father explained, "I courted your mother with this very rig, and Sam courted Fanny with it, too. It wasn't until we all had to use it to attend the same Christmas party that the girls *finally* knew our secret."

At this point, Suzannah appeared in the doorway, her curiosity aroused by all the commotion. "Oh, it's you, Jim!" she said happily.

Then, stepping outside, she examined the sleigh, wide-eyed with admiration. "This is *beautiful!*" she gasped, fingering its gold detailing. Winnie turned her head toward Suzannah and nuzzled her shoulder, snorting affectionately.

Nearly whispering I said, "Suzannah, I thought you might like to come for a ride . . ."

"Oh, Jim, of course—I would be delighted! I'll just get my things and be out shortly." Then she called out, "Mother, where is my heavy coat?" as she disappeared into the house.

Sam turned to Father, "Well, James, the tradition *continues.*"

Indeed it does, Sam," Father said beaming, "and now our secret is finally out." Addressing me, he added, "Sam and I married on the same day because we were all such close friends. And this sleigh is the same one we used to drive us all to the church—except Winnie, of course, was not the horse."

I looked at him, astonished. "Well, I'll be damned!"

Draping his arm around my shoulder, with a wistful expression he confidentially advised, "So, you see, Jim, this sleigh has great sentimental value to your mother, me—*and* the Ellingwoods. Take good care of it . . ." and nodding toward the Ellingwood house, he finally added, "and make it a sentiment to that young lady in there also."

Lifting his arm, Father slapped me on the back and said, "So where are you headed?"

"Richardson's fields."

"Good idea. When you get to the hayfields, let Winnie run— really work her!"

"Consider it done."

"That's my boy, give Suzannah a thrill!" he said encouragingly, slapping me on the back once again. "When I used to take your mother on sleigh rides, I drove so fast that she used to call me a daredevil."

Just then, Suzannah reappeared at the door. "I'm ready!"

I helped Suzannah into the front seat, and when I was seated next to her, I fastened the leather strap across her dainty waist, cinching it securely.

"What's *this* for?" she asked, looking down at the strap.

"Just leave it in place, and wait and see." I replied while strapping myself in beside her. When all was secure, I looked into her wondrous eyes and softly asked, "Ready?"

She nodded sweetly.

When I cracked the whip, Winnie startled, jolting the sleigh and snapping our heads back, and then started off at a fast gallop. Before we left our street, I heard my father shout to Sam, "That's my *boy!*"

As we rounded the corner next to her house, Suzannah shrieked, grabbed the seat rail with one hand and my coat sleeve with the other, hanging on for dear life. Next, Winnie bounded diagonally over the road and rocketed behind the Ellingwoods into an immense field riddled with troughs, bumps and rolling hills.

As Winnie gathered speed, the rushing wind caused Suzannah's hair to be blown straight back, giving her the aspect of an angel in flight. Then the sleigh dropped suddenly from beneath us as we tore across some ridges, lifting us in the air for some brief thrilling moments. My hat blew off and I hollered with delight when clods of snow flew by us from Winnie's churning hooves . . . we were literally flying. The sleigh rebounded and we were bounced—laughing and squealing—every which way on our seat.

Winnie heeled suddenly to the right, so that our path was bordered by a row of snow-covered evergreens whose overburdened branches grazed Suzannah's side of the sleigh. She screamed with delight as they dumped their newly collected snow straight into her lap and into the foot well of the sleigh. I was struck dumb by the sight of her: her eyes large as china saucers, the morning sun glistening in her disheveled hair, and the expression of unalloyed joy on her face as her peals of laughter rang out with total abandon.

As Winnie sped ahead, I tried guiding her gently to the right with the rein. Instead, she bolted right, and our bodies were thrown to the side so that Suzannah was nearly on top of me—and the careening motion kept her pinned there. Oh, how wonderful she felt, clinging tightly to me and screeching with excitement! As Winnie jumped a small brook, the sleigh became temporarily airborne until it landed on the opposite bank with a resounding *foof*! It was an indescribably exhilarating experience for both of us.

Winnie picked up speed again, bolting straight ahead toward a thicket of haystacks left over from the October harvest. She managed to zigzag through the stacks, tossing us from side to side. As I caught precious glimpses of Suzannah in varying degrees of excitement, I realized that Mother was right all along, of course—she was *indeed* a treasure!

Winnie had just flown past the last haystack and headed instinctively for the path that led to Richardson's fields. As we flew by his barn at a full gallop, we saw William Richardson emerge to see what all the noise was about. As soon as he stepped down onto the ramp from his barn, we tore across it, *barely* missing him, but showering him with clods of mud and snow.

"Damn it, Jim Walker—slow *down*!" he yelled, but his words fell on deaf ears as the unstoppable Winnie pressed on, across the wooden bridge and on into the woods that led south back to the cove. We continuously bounded over large fallen branches, throwing the sleigh up a good half-foot, then bouncing it down again, making our ride an endlessly thrilling one.

"Oh, Jim—you are *so* daring!" squealed Suzannah.

"It's not just me," I called back. "Winnie has spirit and she likes to run free, but rarely gets a chance!"

"Yes, I can see that she's a fine horse," she returned breathlessly.

As we continued to thump along the wooded path, I stole admiring glances at the sweet bundle of happiness sitting next to me. She, in turn, occasionally beamed secret smiles my way, and when she caught me ogling her, she would giggle mischievously, sending my heart soaring with elation.

When we emerged from the woodlands, the sun was exceedingly strong; and because there was no wind, it was almost warm. As we trotted along at a leisurely pace, I suggested we head back to the village.

"Oh, but Jim, my sisters—that is, all but Katharine—are coming today, and if we return now, I may have to cut our ride short . . . and I would rather *not* do that."

As she looked at me imploringly from beneath her fluffy bangs, I couldn't take my eyes off her, for never had a face captured a man's soul like hers did mine at that moment.

I slowed down as we approached the village trough so Winnie could stop for a refreshing—albeit icy—drink. While we waited for her to finish, we exchanged greetings with passers-by who were unusually exuberant: spirits often ran high after a snowfall.

I reined Winnie in when we left the village center to prolong our time together. All too soon we arrived at the Ellingwoods, where I pulled Winnie up to the front door, champing at her bit. Puffing and blowing, she looked back at us, tossing her head several times in frustration, for she wanted to be off again.

As we were unfastening the seat straps, Suzannah pulled at my sleeve. "Jim?"

"Yes?" I said, turning to face her.

Suddenly, she threw her arms around my neck in a frosty hug. "That was *so* thrilling, Jim! Promise me we can do this again. *Please?*"

I felt awkward putting my arms around her to reciprocate, and as I did so, she squeezed me even tighter. I reveled in her softness. When she pressed her cold cheek against mine, seemingly eager to linger in my embrace, my heart beat faster. Rebecca Damon once hugged me when I rescued her dog from the flood tide two years ago, but this hug was different—it was a new and intoxicating experience.

Finally, drawing away, Suzannah held my gaze with her soulful eyes, and I felt my willpower yielding . . . but to what? I wondered.

Suzannah brightened and said, "Guess what?"

"What?"

"I think we should prepare a basket of food and go out again for an *afternoon* trot! I'm sure my sisters won't mind if I'm not gone for too long."

I yielded instantly. "Since that's the warmest part of the day, and the sun is especially strong today, I think that's a *great* idea!"

I dismounted, went around to her side and lifted her down. She was as light as a feather, and her waist was perfectly fitted to my grip. Looking into her expectant face I said, "I'll see what fixings my mother has, and you see what yours has. Let's meet again in two hours and see what we've collected for your basket."

She was a perfect picture of happiness as she declared, "Then we'll pack it and be *off*!"

Stunned by her radiance, I could only nod and stare at her face haloed by the sunshine.

She gently patted my cheek. "Go on now . . . and find another hat. I don't want you catching a cold!"

At that moment, the front door opened to reveal Lydia and Sarah, apparently delighted to see us. Suzannah waved goodbye to me, then flew into the house laughing and giggling with her sisters.

The Trot

Sighing at her departure, I gave Winnie a pat and said, "Let's go home, girl, we have work to do." Basking momentarily in the unusual warmth of the sun, I felt a lover's buoyancy welling inside me, prompting an involuntary smile and a lively bounce to my step . . . and suddenly; I had a much softer view of the world around me.

As I led Winnie across the street toward home, Jonathan Barrett met me in his sleigh going the opposite way. As he pulled up, I called out, "Hey, Jonathan, how are things at Harvard College? I do hope you are *behaving* yourself!"

We clasped hands as he dismounted, and we embraced each other warmly. As we separated ourselves at arms length to look each other over, he then said, "I had just arrived earlier yesterday morning . . . and my aunt Rhoda began talking about you. She mentioned that you and Suzannah Ellingwood are attached. Is that true?"

I was astonished at first, but then, on further reflection, not really surprised. Rhoda Barrett knew everything about everybody in Walker's Cove. "Well, I suppose you'll have to ask Suzannah that question," I said, shaking his hand warmly in greeting.

"Indeed . . . but I see I'm a few moments too late for that!" he remarked, having glanced into the sleigh and noticed a tiny glove upon the front seat.

"Oh my!" I said, following his gaze. "I'll have to return that."

"Oh no, Jim! I wouldn't do that if I were you," Jonathan countered. "This is an instant heart treasure, is it not?"

I picked it up and placed it carefully in my coat pocket. "Yes—as a matter of fact it is, Jonathan."

"Ho! Then it *is* true!" He exclaimed in his best lawyerly voice.

"Well, it is true . . . in my heart at least," I affirmed wistfully, realizing I was caught in the act.

"I understand," he replied, reaching over to pat my shoulder. "Your heart wishes for more than what it sees, correct?"

"Well, yes, Jonathan, but I feel like Suzannah returns my affections. She makes me *very* happy."

"Excellent!" my friend exclaimed, slapping his hands together gleefully. "You are in *love* . . . and I rest my case on it!"

"No, no," I argued, "not yet."

After remounting his sleigh, Jonathan looked down at me and said, "Jim Walker, some sage advice from your lawyer friend . . . never deny the truth in your heart."

"But, Jonathan, heart feelings are not the law," I retorted.

"Oh yes, they most assuredly *are* the law—the law of God. Accept her, my boy, and good luck and good health to both of you!"

"Thank you, Jonathan," I replied, feeling humbled. "You will be a good lawyer someday."

Jonathan smiled. "Why, thank you, James! When I'm ready to start my practice, I'll be sure to purchase a Walker-made clock for my office."

As he pulled away, I yelled after him, "With an Ellingwood case!" He acknowledged my words with a wave of his hand as his sleigh glided off.

I forgot to ask him about his relationship with Rebecca Damon; and as he faded from sight, I wondered if I would ever see him again. It seemed to me that once folks left Walker's Cove for the big cities, they seldom returned. In my heart I wished him well, and hoped that I would hear news someday soon about his marriage to dear Rebecca.

After I guided Winnie into the barn and settled her in her stall, I brought her a bucket of water and a bundle of hay. Next, I planned to raid the kitchen to see what culinary delights I could filch for Suzannah's basket. Tapping the snow from my boots before I entered, I was confronted first by intense heat, and then the sight and exquisite aroma of freshly baked cinnamon fritters, topped with a thick layer of sticky milk frosting. I nearly held my breath as I placed my thumb and forefinger around the one closest to me, being careful not to disturb the hardening layer of frosting. I lifted it to my lips and bit into it—it was still warm and tasted heavenly.

Suddenly I heard a sharp cry. "CAUGHT!" Mother said as she stood at the kitchen door pointing at me.

"Dead to rights!" I added calmly, chewing slowly to savor the soft cinnamon dough mixing with the flavors of the milk frosting and bits of apple. I swear there is nothing better tasting on earth, save for Mother's custards.

"How was your sleigh ride?" she asked, as she lined up some fritters that needed frosting.

"Suzannah is magical, I think."

"Indeed!" she exclaimed, stopping what she was doing to cross her arms defiantly and stare at me in wonder. "Now, *that* is a term I've never heard to describe the female sex!"

I quickly looked down to avoid her eyes, adding softly, "She is special, Mother. And she's a sweet and gentle friend. Do you think she likes me as well?"

Mother came toward me and kissed my cheek, then smiled dreamily. "In my reveries, I see you chasing the rainbows over her heart. I also see, James Walker, her little fairy feet, walking directly into your unsuspecting soul! You are well matched, and I know it in here"—she pointed to her heart—"that there is more than enough to bind your destinies."

Mother's pronouncements were music to my ears, especially since I was beginning to feel less awkward around Suzannah. Her vibrant nature put me at ease and melted away my feelings of anxiety and self-consciousness. She was a joy to be near, and a welcome release from the dull routine of my work life.

"By the way, we are having another trot this afternoon."

"Oh, really?" Mother said, as she mixed a new batch of milk frosting.

I glanced around the kitchen. "So what can I take with me? We're packing a basket."

As she put the bowl aside, Mother observed, "My, my, you *are* having a good time today." On the counter, she laid out a large kitchen cloth and placed on it a variety of small molasses confections, some dried and sugared blueberries and cranberries, some fritters, a few slices of spice cake and cinnamon-coated, dried apple slices. After tying the corners of the cloth together, she retrieved a small wooden cask and filled it with hot mulled cider, saying, "This will keep your hearts war . . . ah, the chill at bay. And if you leave it in the sun, it will remain warm." Then she picked up her bowl and handed me a spoon.

"What's this for?" I asked in bewilderment.

"The Ellingwoods!"

"What? A spoon?" I said, still baffled.

"No, James, *not* the spoon, you need to earn your keep."

"Oh?"

"I'd like you to coat eight fritters with a nice thick layer of milk frosting."

"Are you making a gift of these?"

"Yes, your father and I are going to the Ellingwoods this afternoon for tea—*and* to hear news about Boston."

"Boston?" I asked.

"Yes, Lydia, Sarah and Jenny are visiting, and Fanny came by to ask us to tea, so this is a proper hostess gift." Handing me a pewter tray, she instructed, "Line up eight fritters on there and I will add some spice cakes between them for good measure."

I took a large scoop of frosting and layered the first fritter with a thick coating, spreading it over the tops so it formed little rivulets that dripped partway down the sides. After stopping a runaway rivulet with my finger, I licked off the residue. Mother tapped her spoon sharply on the table in warning: "Do not touch *anything* until you wash your hands. These are intended for our *guests*, so let's keep them free of your fingers. Remember, James, that hand was last on Winnie's rump!"

Feeling like a little boy again, I went to our dry sink and applied warm water from the kettle to my hands. As I washed them, I asked nonchalantly, "Mother, what does a young man talk about with a girl?"

"You mean a young man who is courting? One who is *attached?*"

"It's funny you say that. When I encountered Jonathan Barrett today, he used the same word regarding Suzannah and me."

"Oh, dear," Mother said with some dismay. "It sounds like Rhoda had a tea and spread the news."

"*What* news?" I asked, suspiciously.

"That you and Suzannah spend much of your free time together. People see you, and it's natural for them to think you're attached."

"Rhoda is a busybody!" I said flatly, feeling rather annoyed.

"Oh, Jim," she laughed, "it's just talk and it's harmless. Never be afraid to admit the truth of what's in your heart."

"Jonathan said the *same thing* to me—were you all at the same tea, perchance?" I asked somewhat facetiously.

"No, I think not, James; we're both showing an interest in you, and we're glad for your happiness. Young love is irresistibly romantic. And many of us relive those times in memory through our children's experience of it."

"I guess I understand . . . you're remembering your courting days with Father . . ."

"Yes. No matter how old the body, love ages like a fine wine. It never gets stale if properly kept, and cherished memories help keep it that way."

I smiled while I dried my hands, and turning toward her, inquired earnestly, "Well, wisest of all mothers, now that we're . . . ah . . . well, getting to being more than just friends . . . what shall I say about different things, and how shall I say it? We have never discussed anything at Walker's Point other than Nature's beauty, her life in Boston and my life here."

Mother sat down at the table with a sigh, resting her chin on her hand, a pensive expression on her face. "I would ask her a question about her likes and dislikes that she will have to answer. Then you find something in her answer to expand on; if not, then ask another question. After a while, you'll find yourself engaged in a conversation you can take in any direction you like."

"What did you and Father say in your first romantic conversation?"

She closed her eyes as she recollected the moment, and said with a wry smile, "I asked him how a clock worked, and the rest is history—twenty years of it!"

"But I'm too shy to ask her directly about much of anything, let alone her feelings."

"Then write her a letter. Girls *love* to receive letters. Give it to her when you take her home this afternoon. She'll answer you, I'm sure of it."

"Very well," I agreed. I left the kitchen immediately, thinking I better get started right away. There wasn't much time if I were to give her a letter this very day. Later I realized I'd thoughtlessly abandoned the task of frosting, but I suspected that Mother would forgive me in view of my current state of distraction.

From the secretary I procured paper, a quill and a bottle of ink, and wrote:

January 7, 1767

Dear Suzannah,

How can I know if we have a true friendship, and how can I know the way it should feel?

Your friend, Jim Walker

When the ink was dry, I carefully folded the letter into quarters. Lastly, I wrote her name on it and slipped it inside her glove, expecting that when I returned it, she would surely find the note. "Oh, for you to be a faithful messenger . . ." I whispered, and then placed it in my pocket.

Returning to the kitchen, I fetched Mother's bundle and the keg, and headed for the back door.

"Have a good time, Jim," Mother called after me, "and please tell Fanny we'll be there in one hour."

"I will," I said, and quietly closed the door.

Winnie had finished her hay and drank nearly all the water. I noticed that she'd quickly picked up the scent of my bundle, twitching her nostrils and poking at it with her nose. Holding it away from her, I grabbed the reigns as I climbed aboard the sleigh to head back to the Ellingwoods.

When I knocked on the door, Lydia opened it; she smiled and then scrutinized me for what seemed like a very long moment. If she had spoken her thoughts aloud, I suspected she would have said, "You and Suzannah are attached and I know it." I certainly hoped she approved of me, for I felt she was judging my character by what I said and did.

"Hello, Lydia," I said sheepishly. "I've come to see Suzannah."

Lydia's face lit up as she looked over at Winnie and the sleigh, then back at me. I recalled from our first meeting that she resembled Suzannah in face and figure—but that she was taller, and older, of course. "Quite fetching," I thought, "for a married lady of Boston."

"Come in, James. We've heard so much about you and your sleigh."

Lydia had a free and easy manner that made her seem warm and approachable; she was not a stuffed corset like so many other Boston women I'd met. I followed her into the parlor, where I saw Sarah and Mrs. Ellingwood sitting. I delivered mother's message first, and then added, "Mrs. Ellingwood, did Suzannah ask you for any sort of victuals today?"

"Why yes, she did, James. She's with Jenny in the kitchen."

As I headed toward the kitchen door, it opened suddenly and there before me stood Suzannah, her eyes wide with surprise.

"Jim."

"Yes."

She opened her arms and hugged me briefly, sending a tidal wave of heat and joy to my face. Lydia and Sarah nodded in approval.

After releasing her I said, "I have a stash of goodies waiting in the sleigh, Suzannah."

She looked elated. "Oh, that's wonderful! I'm bringing some, too."

It did my heart good to be around someone who was always *so* happy!

Suzannah led me to the parlor where Sarah and Fanny were preparing the tea—arranging cakes and tea bread, and stoking the fire. She retrieved her coat, and as she turned toward the door she hesitated. "I seem to be missing a glove," she declared, looking all around in a vain attempt to locate it.

I reached inside my pocket, saying, "I almost forgot . . . I found this in the front seat of my sleigh . . ." When I pulled out the glove, the note flew out and landed on the floor, directly in front of Sarah.

"Well, what have we *here?*" Sarah said as she picked up the note and examined it. She turned it over and upon seeing Suzannah's name, held it up for Lydia and Jenny to see. In unison they said, "Ooooh, a *letter!*"

By now, I was thoroughly mortified and wished only to melt into the floorboards. Since I couldn't, I stood by in helpless agony, unable to say or do anything as they gathered around the note, speculating excitedly on the contents.

Finally, Fanny, God bless her, broke up the hen party. "Ladies! *Ladies!* It's as though you never left home! You're all being very immature, mocking your little sister like that and denying her the dignity and respect she deserves!"

All three backed away, stifling giggles, as Fanny imperiously took the note away from Sarah and handed it to Suzannah. "This is for *your* eyes only!" Shooting the three girls a scathing glance, she added pointedly, "*And* it's private!"

Feeling mollified that Fanny had put her daughters in their place, I wondered if it had always been this way for Suzannah during her youth. In any event, my little angel looked at the note, turning it over in her hands, and then glanced up at me with what I would describe as a loving countenance. "I shall put this in a special place . . . where no one else will see it." She hurried upstairs to her room, and returned in no time.

I thought, she is beautiful, and her sisters are beautiful, too. So overcoming my shyness, at least momentarily, I made a bold request. "Suzannah, will you take a place by your sisters on the sofa? I should like to see all four of you together." She did so, and as they all smiled at me expectantly, I spoke my thoughts out loud. "Four out of five are here, and oh, what a canvas you would make! I shall never see so much beauty in one place again 'til I get to Heaven!"

As the four of them giggled with embarrassment, I went over to each one, bowed and then kissed their hands. When it was Suzannah's turn, I lingered over that kiss, which led her sisters to ooh and aah appreciatively. They were obviously pleased that the youngest among them was being courted.

Suzannah got up and curtsied politely, saying, "I'm ready to leave when you are, Master Walker."

Lydia, who was as playful as Suzannah, waved daintily at me. "Have a lovely outing, James!"

Then Jenny piped in, "Oh yes, please *do* enjoy the sunshine."

Turning her reddened face, Sarah simply covered her mouth and giggled.

Suzannah and I finished packing the basket in the kitchen, and when she suggested we bring liquid refreshment, I told her about Mother's keg of cider.

"That's so thoughtful of her, Jim. Well then, let's be off."

I nestled the basket on the rear seat floor beside the keg and then lifted Suzannah into the front seat. She smiled so radiantly that I felt positively elated. I climbed in beside her, and when she immediately moved closer to me so that our bodies were touching, my heart skipped a beat.

"Where shall we go?" she asked excitedly.

I yelled out, "Winnie! Where shall we go?"

As if on cue, Winnie began to pull us toward the wharf in the village center, while Suzannah waved happily to the passers-by. When we approached Thatcher's dry goods store, Suzannah asked if we could stop there so she could buy a paper of pins for her mother. "Of course," I said as I pulled up alongside Thatcher's. "Winnie and I will wait here for you until you're done."

I dismounted to help Suzannah down; and after placing her gently onto the snow; I looked up into the anxious face of Rhoda Anne Barrett.

"Good afternoon, Miss Barrett," Suzannah cooed sweetly, and knowing her reputation as a busybody, teasingly added, "Aren't I lucky to have a strong, handsome escort like James to drive me about town?"

Rhoda gasped, "My gracious, I would say so, indeed!"

Suzannah excused herself and headed into Thatcher's.

I noticed that Rhoda looked flustered, so I changed the subject. "I saw Jonathan earlier today. Is he planning to stay a while?"

"Why, yes . . ." she said hesitantly, "I believe he plans on a longer visit than usual." Now her attention seemed focused on the sleigh. "Is that your father's?" she inquired.

"Yes, it is."

She looked at it more closely. "Isn't it strange, but I seem to recall a sleigh just like it that belonged to Sam Ellingwood."

"Well, it kind of did," I said, being purposely vague so as to confuse her. She silently strutted around the sleigh, examining it with a jaundiced eye, as a hen looks at a new pile of feed. As she did so, I awaited her next inquiry with no further comment.

My uncomfortable silence was mercifully broken when Suzannah came out of Thatcher's. She smiled at Rhoda and said, "Miss Barrett, I do hope we shall see Jonathan and Rebecca while he's here visiting." I'd mentioned Jonathan to Suzannah—and Rebecca as well—in at least one of our many talks.

"Oh, I'm certain they would enjoy *your* company, Suzannah," Rhoda remarked drily.

"I meant as *two couples*," Suzannah clarified with surprising assertiveness.

Rhoda, her mouth agape, glanced from Suzannah to me and back to Suzannah.

Taking my cue from Suzannah, I lifted her carefully into her seat and repeated, "Yes, two couples," with a broad smile. "So please, Miss Barrett, let them know we're available any Saturday afternoon."

Suzannah then put a finer point on it. "The four of us can have tea at either my house or at Rebecca's."

Rhoda watched me reoccupy my seat and Suzannah nestle close beside me. "Very well, then. Good afternoon to you both," she said tersely, while her eyes remained riveted on us as we drove off.

Suzannah giggled. "That little tidbit of gossip will keep tongues wagging at the next Barrett tea party!"

We laughed as we headed down the path to the Olsen shipyard. An unfinished vessel was on the ways, its talon-shaped ribs clawing at the sky. I wondered if old Jens was around. He had come here from Norway and was an expert ship-builder. His boats and small sloops were stronger and more durable than any other—and he had no difficulty in taking down the king's best trees for his use, all marked with the broad arrow. He was a strong, wiry fellow who still ran the show—helped by his two sons who were now in the business with him, carrying on a long-standing family tradition. As we passed by the yard, I stopped to read the name on the stern of the ship being constructed on the ways—it was *Sunrise*.

Suzannah was silent for some moments, before she asked, "Why do men refer to ships and all manner of boats as 'she'?"

"Well, Suzannah, I guess because sailors are basically at the mercy of the sea and all its vagaries. The boat is like a protective mother, housing the men in a symbolic womb, safe from all outside calamities. See how the ribs form two hands joined at the bottom?" I held up my own hands to mimic the position. "It's like being in a mother's hands that enfold and protect, associating her with survival on the sea."

She nodded her understanding.

"I hope to have a ship someday, Suzannah."

Patting my arm, she said, "Perhaps you will, Jim, perhaps you will"; and for some reason, continued to regard the skeleton of the ship with an anxious countenance.

"Are you alright, Suzannah?" I asked.

"Yes," she said, her voice nearly a whisper. "But I have a *feeling* . . ." then she waved it away.

"*Sunrise* . . ." I said, urging Winnie onward. And thinking of its beautiful connotation, I added, "What a sweet little name for a ship."

Winnie trotted on, and there at the rise was the ancient beech tree that marked the path to Walker's Point. Despite the deep snow, Suzannah insisted on tromping over to the tree. She looked at it almost worshipfully, and then stepping back into the sunlight, she observed, "The sun and lack of wind will warm the rocks on the point. May we bring the basket there?"

This we did, and we found the rocks were indeed warm and dry, the snow melted by the sun's heat. Suzannah spread her blanket, and we carefully arranged the basket's contents on it so we'd be looking out to sea.

As Suzannah marveled at a fritter, I said, "Nature is so beautiful, isn't she?"

"Yes, she is, Jim. Even though I've been on outings many times before, everything here seems new, especially with you to enjoy it with me. I'm so pleased we like the same things."

We ate, drank and chatted all afternoon about little things . . . things probably meaningless to others, yet so important to young hearts. Then we took a break and sat cozily together on the point, silently watching the sun drift toward the west. The seals barked and hawked below, imploring us for food, as did the sea gulls. We tossed bits of food their way and laughed as they scrambled frantically for the tasty morsels.

We were having a thoroughly delightful afternoon—until I took a bite of the last fritter and something warm, heavy and wet landed on my head with a resounding splat!

Suzannah heard the sound and looked up at me, smiling sweetly at first, until I saw her eyes widen in amazement before she began to laugh uncontrollably.

How I loved to hear her laugh! She had an infectious, silvery laugh—unlike any other. But I was totally mortified when I finally put my hand on my head, and it came away covered with a white, gelatinous goo, speckled with hardened bits of green matter. Gawking at my hand in embarrassing disbelief, Suzannah doubled up in ecstatic uncontrolled laughter.

"I have to go home . . ." I said hesitantly, ambivalent about putting an end to our outing.

Suzannah, sensing my embarrassment, hurriedly packed up the basket, but was unable to suppress her short bursts of tittering.

Between these bursts, she took a breath to declare, "I think you need—some hasty restoration, Jim!"

After cleaning my hands in a freezing tidal pool, I took up the basket and started back to the sleigh, still feeling totally humiliated.

Suzannah caught up to me, and threaded her arm around my waist. With her eyes on mine, she cheerily said, "Don't fret, Jim. It would take a great deal more than bird droppings to ruin our lovely afternoon for me."

Looking into her reassuring eyes, I could see how much she cared for me.

Before I lifted her into the sleigh, she firmly held my hands at her waist. My heart thrilled to her touch and beat faster. Once seated beside her, I cracked the whip and began to laugh—first silently to myself, then out loud. When Suzannah heard me, she began to laugh too.

By the time we trotted into town, tears were rolling down our cheeks. Gliding down the main street, the sound of our laughter caused passers-by to wonder what was going on with Jim Walker and Suzannah Ellingwood. Their bewildered expressions caused us to laugh even harder. We were still at it when we arrived at the Ellingwoods' front door.

"Oh, Jim! I've laughed so much my stomach hurts!"

Then I was at it again—and so was she, until the door opened to reveal my mother, Mrs. Ellingwood and Suzannah's sisters filling the doorway with anxious faces.

When Suzannah saw their worried expressions, she pointed at them and redoubled her cachinnations. A few minutes later, she finally managed to calm herself enough to dismount from the sleigh. Wiping away her tears of laughter, she took her basket and still breaking up, blindly stumbled into the house.

I sucked in enough air to say, "Home, Winnie!" As we pulled away, gales of laughter exploded from within the Ellingwood house, and of course I knew why.

Guiding Winnie into the barn and after tending to her needs, I went immediately to the kitchen to heat up some water in a kettle to wash my hair. After stoking the fire and removing my shirt in preparation for my ablution—a loud thump came from the front door, as though a horse had accidently kicked it.

When I opened the door, a block of wood was laying in the snow with a string tied around it. Looking about, and not seeing anyone, I picked it up and found a letter attached to the string. The block was made from a finished piece of curly maple, so I knew from whom it came and brought it inside.

Sitting at the kitchen table by the firelight, I carefully unfolded the note. Written in an exquisite penmanship was the following message:

January 7, 1767

Dear Jim,

You ask how you will know if we have true friendship, and how it should feel.

Listen to your heart . . .

Your best friend,
Suzannah Ellingwood

Tween Time

After supper, with everything tidied up for the evening, we retreated to the parlor and our favorite places: Mother to her rocker with her needlework, Father to the sofa with his account book and me to the other rocker, opposite Mother. While I rocked, my eyes rested idly upon her, busy with her needlework before the warm fire. For us, this was tween time, a time set-aside at day's end to be together for relaxation, conversation or quiet reflection before we retired for the night.

Laying my head back, my recollections of my day with Suzannah drifted across my mind as if in a sweet dream, inducing me to close my eyes and savor every moment. She was so beautiful that I couldn't help but smile when recalling the lively expressions on her face, or the kindred glances we exchanged so often. I was even enchanted by her name because it was such an endearing one and suited her so perfectly. Because it was spelled with a "z" rather than the ubiquitous second "s," it thus became uniquely hers.

Suddenly I felt inspired—perhaps impelled is a better word—to rise and seat myself at Father's secretary. Taking quill and paper in hand, I commenced writing her name over and over. With each attempt I made the script more elaborate by surrounding the letters with delicate embellishments like shading and ornaments.

Noticing my assiduous scratching at the secretary, Mother's curiosity finally got the better of her. Laying aside her needlework, she approached the desk to see what I was writing. After a short period of silence, she murmured, "You are quite taken with her, aren't you?"

Surprised, I looked into her eyes and replied, "Yes, Mother, I *do* fancy her indeed!"

Drawing up a chair, she sat beside me and gently placed her hand upon mine, forcing me to stop writing. As I turned my face to hers, she looked into my eyes and asked, "Do you spend wakeful nights thinking of her?"

"Ever since I met her, my day begins with her name in my heart and ends with it in my prayers," I confessed.

Mother squeezed my hand lovingly. "You are my heart's *true* son, for yours speaks to you early in this courtship. Jim, may this relationship be blessed!"

"She is constantly in my thoughts, Mother."

"As she *should* be, Jim," adding, "Is *she* happy?"

"I believe there is no happier girl in Walker's Cove."

"Ah! But is she happy because it's her nature, or because you made her so?"

"My sincerest hope is that it's *both*."

She closed her eyes and pressed her fingers to her temples, furrowing her brow in intense concentration. After a minute or two, she smiled and announced, "Both!"

"How do you know?"

"She told me."

"When?"

"Just now."

I looked at her in befuddlement. "Mother, how do you do that?"

"We can sense feelings without speaking words. It's a gift. Our hearts feel the questions and answers. I can't explain it other than by saying it *is* a gift, one that we would have been burned for less than a hundred years ago. I believe this is how angels become guardians, for they must accurately sense the heart feelings of their charges. I believe only angels possess these powers."

"But you're not an angel, nor is Suzannah, though I believe she is."

"I know, Jim," she replied, patting my hand gently. "Sometimes God works in mysterious ways for His own reasons. As I said before, Suzannah *is* very special."

Intrigued by all this talk of mysticism, I asked, "Does she *know* you asked her this?"

"No, I can *feel* her happiness," she replied while tapping her heart. "It's there and it's genuine!" Then, looking at me sympathetically, she lovingly ran her palm across my cheek and with moist eyes, whispered, "My little boy is truly growing up . . ."

Feeling her warm hand upon my cheek, my throat constricted as her sweet smile faded into the watery depths of her tears. I stood, as did she, and we embraced. "You are sad, Mother . . ."

"Yes, my dearest child, but it's a sadness every mother expects."

"I have this sense too . . ."

"Indeed, you do," she replied, placing her hand on my heart. "I feel it in you and around you, Jim. Remember, my mother also had it."

I then held her again and whispered, "And yet . . . I sense your feelings are bittersweet."

"Yes, they are."

"Why?"

"Like your father and I have mentioned before, it's the circle of life coming 'round to completion. We will see you leave this house someday, marry, have a home of your own—and then children will come . . . and the circle continues. My work is nearly done. You are a young man now, ready to sail your own little ship upon the sea of life. That you have fair winds and following seas are the loving wishes of your mother."

"Thank you for those wishes . . ." I replied, holding her tighter. Tears welled in my eyes as I added; "I shall keep them in my heart evermore."

She then looked up at me and sighed. "I only regret, dear son, that you haven't a sister or brother to go through life with."

"Do not regret that, Mother . . . you have more than made up for it by being the very soul of motherhood all my life."

"Thank you, Jim. Such a compliment is the highest a mother can ever hope to receive."

"Your place in Heaven is assured," I replied, "or I will have something to say about it!"

Suddenly realizing how late it was, I released Mother and called out, "Good night, Father!" across the room.

"Good night, son," came his preoccupied response. "And God keep you!"

His blessing startled me, for it seemed to indicate he was listening to my conversation with Mother. Then he rose from the sofa and came over to us. "Should you wish a partnership, Jim, I am ready—and you will be sole proprietor of the tavern."

"What tavern?"

"We are going to convert this house back into a tavern."

When he saw the astonished look on Mother's face he said, "I can feel hearts also, perhaps not as good as you two—but I know your mother misses keeping a tavern, so a tavern we shall have . . ."

Covering her mouth to choke off a sob, she threw herself into Father's arms. "I'm the happiest woman in Walker's Cove!" But then she turned to me and through tears of joy knowingly added, "*Except* for Suzannah Ellingwood!"

I delayed my departure upstairs to watch as Father clasped Mother to his heart, holding her tightly in his arms. Despite their almost embarrassing intimacy, I remained before the fire to admire their passionate kisses and impetuous affection for each other. I couldn't seem to break away as Father lifted my mother off the floor, twirling her around and setting her down gently for another lingering embrace.

How did that feel—to love so deeply, tenderly and consistently for so many years? I envied their great love and hoped someday I would enjoy its equal with my dear little Suzannah.

Striding over to the secretary, Father sat down, took the quill in hand and declared, "Well, son, let's see what Mother needs to get this tavern going!"

Mother sat next to him, nervously fingering her hair and letting it cascade below her shoulders. She was, in spite of her forty-seven years, a very attractive woman both in face and figure. I remember stories Father had told of Mother's fending off unwanted advances while keeping the Mariner's Rest. I suspected she would have to do the same again now, despite her age.

Father centered a sheet of paper on the desk, dipped the quill in ink, but hesitated when he noticed my handiwork—the sheet with Suzannah's name scrawled all over it.

"Hmmm . . . someone is either in love . . . or is practicing the fine art of penmanship."

Seeing my face redden, Mother quickly saved me. "As a matter of fact, he is practicing his . . . ah . . . serifs," she explained.

Raising his eyebrows skeptically, he repeated, "I see . . . serifs, indeed." Then he looked at me and smiled. "If you could only be this diligent when drilling clock plates!"

"Oh, but Father," Mother chided, "it gives him a little pleasure, and besides, don't you think that such a skill could be applied to clock plates, too?"

"I suppose so," he replied. Then pointing to my sheet he declared, "But this is for love, not clock plates." His eyes twinkling, he patted my shoulder affectionately. "May it be as you wish, James—you have my blessing."

"Thank you, Father."

He finally began to write, saying, "Now, let's make an inventory list for Mother's tavern . . ."

The Beech Tree

ecause of that list and the numerous preparations it set in motion, the winter flew by. Every evening, hunched over the dining room table, my parents sketched dozens of plans detailing how our house should be changed. Within our new great room—to consist of tables, chairs, wall decorations, candle sconces, new windows and new fireplaces—Mother wanted to seat fifty people. She also decided what would be required for her expanded kitchen.

Since twenty years had passed since they'd kept a tavern or dealt with any of their former business associates, my parents depended a great deal on Sam's advice as well as his contacts in Boston. He suggested that the best price for sturdy furniture could likely be had from his business partner there. Sam would accompany them to Boston to help arrange meetings with the Boston tradesmen he knew, so together they would select the goods and services Mother needed.

It was also decided that my parents would stay with Lydia in Boston for the duration of their trip, perhaps a month or more, while Sam would return alone to Walker's Cove after paving their way. This was an especially fortuitous arrangement since Lydia's husband, Richard Barrett—whom the family called Fay—was a lawyer. Born and bred in Walker's Cove, he was also Rhoda's brother and Jonathan's uncle. As such, he offered to provide legal advice for any matter that might require it, and volunteered to create and review Mother's proposals and vendor contracts. Upon her return as proprietress at a later date, they would execute and place down payments on the accepted vendor contracts.

It seemed that Mother had a role in mind for Suzannah in the tavern, so she wished to have her along when she actively solicited vendors. Mother wanted her to meet them and become familiar with the negotiating process, as well as educate her in what was needed for such an enterprise. Their plans included a meeting with the silversmith Paul Revere regarding pewter and brass utensils and other cookware needs, while Father would take Sam and Richard to visit the Willards at their clock shop in Grafton.

After they left, my time was monopolized by work, so that for the remaining days of winter and on into the spring, I practically lived in the shop. I became the sole provider of our income—at least temporarily. Fortunately, Mother had made arrangements so that my solitary life was leavened by welcome visits from Fanny. She assisted generously with cooking, cleaning, washing and companionship.

During the long winter nights, we had many conversations about Suzannah over Fanny's tasty dinners. For some reason, I found myself more comfortable discussing my feelings with Fanny than with Suzannah. Perhaps because Fanny was very much like Mother: approachable, gentle, loving and serene. Then again, perhaps I was secretly hoping that she would disclose to Suzannah those special little things I couldn't say to her directly.

Mother's informative letters reported their progress, and it seemed as if the reestablishment of our tavern was coming to pass surprisingly quickly. Naturally, Fanny and I were delighted to hear of it. Then the bittersweet moment arrived when Mother sent a letter announcing their return in two weeks, while Suzannah and Sam would remain *another* three. It was Sam's idea to seize this rare opportunity to visit with all five daughters at once, without any business distractions impeding him. So it was with stoic determination that I labored on further into spring, patiently awaiting Suzannah's return.

I WAS VERY thankful and delighted when my parents returned. There was much joy in our reunion despite Mother's perpetual state of nervous excitement, which was of some concern to us. Even Fanny's best efforts to calm her were to no avail—the tavern had become the new center of her life.

The requests for proposals had been drawn up and submitted to the vendors by Richard, and all we had to do was wait for the replies. After construction began in August, Mother planned to return to Boston, and stay with Lydia and Richard. During this final phase, she and Richard would review the proposals and award her business in each category to a select few. In addition, Richard would assist her in preparing legally binding contracts.

Meanwhile, our house remained full of carpenters and contractors, measuring, estimating, agreeing and disagreeing as to what kind and how much material would be required to lay a new foundation, build a new cellar, a new privy, new chimneys and the like—in sum, what was required to make all the modifications necessary for the transformation. Wishing to avoid all the confusion, I remained sequestered in the clock shop . . . and my life without Suzannah dragged on.

THE TALL CLOCK struck six bells in the midst of a beautiful April morning. Since Father had accepted an order for five clock jacks from Thatcher's store, I needed to get to work early, drilling and fitting pillars to five sets of plates. I walked down the hallway quietly, so as not to make the floorboards creak. As I passed by my parents' door, I thought it strange to hear no stirrings from their chamber. So I peeked in and was surprised to find the bed made and the room unoccupied. It was then I recalled that Father had mentioned that he and Mother were expecting a special shipment; but I didn't know when the vessel was due to arrive at the wharf—perhaps it was today. In any event, I went off to work alone.

As I approached the shop, I noticed that the morning spring air had a sweet fresh scent. To further enjoy this fragrance, I opened the window overlooking my bench. There I worked alone all day, and not once did I see either of my parents.

It was late afternoon when I finished the clock jack plates and found myself hungry for dinner. In high spirits because of my accomplishment, I left the shop and headed toward the house. As I entered the kitchen, I stopped dead in my tracks . . . for before the fireplace, totally absorbed in account books and journal entry papers, sat Mother *and* Suzannah.

"Well, *this* is a surprise!" I exclaimed happily.

As they both looked up, Suzannah beamed at me with one of her radiant smiles, making my heart jump.

Mother hastened to explain. "We met Suzannah and Sam at the wharf this morning, Jim. I'm in the process now of teaching

Suzannah how to keep the accounts for a tavern. Oh, and you might be pleased to know that she has agreed to work for us—that is, once we get everything in order. For now, she will be my apprentice, and she'll be here every day to grace us with her company."

Astonished—and thrilled—at hearing this wonderful news, I didn't know what to say.

Then: "Ah! Beauty and brains times *two*!" came suddenly from behind me, as Father stepped into the room and gave Mother a tender kiss.

Suzannah flashed me another smile and I could resist no longer. "Would you like to accompany me to the point and watch the sunset when you're done, Suzannah? It's such a fine day for it."

"I would *love* to . . ." Then, somewhat timidly, she said to Mother, "Do you object, ma'am?"

Mother closed her account book and smiled. "Of course not, we can carry on with this anytime," and glancing my way, she softly added, ". . . after all, sunsets will never wait."

Taking Suzannah's shawl, I held it open to wrap it snugly around her, thus savoring her softness.

Before we stepped out the door, she turned to smile prettily at Mother. "I shall return on the morrow, ma'am."

Mother, who was packing away the account books and papers, said cheerily, "Your lesson will be waiting. Have a good time—and be careful taking her on the rocks, Jim! Oh yes, and there's no need to call me ma'am, Suzannah."

"What shall I call you then?" she asked innocently.

Mother approached her and after gently stroking Suzannah's hair, she softly replied, "We are *all* family here, Suzannah . . . so just call me Ainsley."

Her eyes brimming with happiness, Suzannah smiled and softly affirmed, "Very well . . . Ainsley."

As soon as we were outside the door, Suzannah hugged me so tightly it almost hurt. Hand in hand, we ran across the way and down toward Walker's Point. Suzannah was behaving like a puppy—full of life and eager to please and play, and I was positively overjoyed at having her back.

When we reached our landmark, the ancient beech tree, she attempted to embrace its girth—which she could never do, it being nearly eighteen feet in circumference. Undaunted, she simply remarked, "I don't remember this tree being so large! It must have been here since the days of the pilgrims."

Looking at its gnarled and knobby trunk, I said, "Probably since before the Abenakis. I suspect this tree was probably here before man put his first little foot on this land."

As we gazed up into the intricate network of branches that stretched ten feet in all directions, the easterly breeze caused the rusty brown leaves to murmur softly like whispered secrets . . . perhaps about the two younglings below.

Suzannah stepped back from the tree to admire it anew. "It will probably be here forever!" she remarked, emphasizing its sturdiness with a strong push.

"Only if some fool doesn't cut it down for firewood." Fingering the gray bark, I mused aloud, "I wonder how many lives were lived since this was a sapling?"

"It has become the tree of life of Walker's Cove, hasn't it? Here since the beginning . . . a silent witness to all," Suzannah said thoughtfully.

"Indeed, it does seem to symbolize life," I replied, pointing to the branches. "Growing in all directions from one common bond, Suzannah. I wonder how many air castles have been built beneath this massive canopy?"

"Ah! *Air* castles!" she repeated softly. "And what have yours been like, James Walker? Tell me some of your favorites!"

I took her hand as we strolled to the point. "While alone all winter, my air castles have been puffy little clouds of daydreams, drifting aimlessly about my whims and thoughts. Sometimes, a swift moving shadow will chase them away—clearing my entire dreamscape—then I drift on to build the next . . ."

"What a pretty description. And what are they usually about?" she asked.

"Oh, the usual: duty, work, love and the future."

"Love and the future?" she repeated.

The beech tree at the path to Walker's Point.

I thought, "Oh, she's a quick one alright!" and then said, "Yes," looking away from her.

"Do your air castles include a special person?" she hopefully inquired.

"Sometimes," I replied evasively.

"Who?" came the direct shot across my bow.

"When I was young, it was always Mother and Father because they were all I had."

Looking up at me expectantly, she said very low, "But what about now? Who are they about now?"

"They are about you," I confessed, finally looking into her eyes, and with weakening knees I courageously added, "*all* of them."

Throwing her arms around me and pressing her cheek to my chest, she earnestly said, "Oh, Jim, may they *all* come true. You touch me so deeply!"

After she released me, we continued walking toward the point. When we'd settled down cozily next to each other in our customary spot on the rocks, Suzannah sighed deeply at the familiar sight that greeted us. "I love to watch the sunsets. The pinks and grays and whites are never exactly the same color—each sunset is so unique."

"Just like people," I observed.

"Yes," she said, and then added very softly, ". . . special people,"

A burning wave shot through me, for I knew she was sending me a message. I looked into her gray-blue eyes and pausing to muster all my courage, I softly reaffirmed, "Special people . . . like *you*."

"Me?" she asked, feigning surprise.

"Suzannah, I've never had a friend like you, ever!"

"Do I bring you happiness?" she inquired sweetly.

"Yes!" I replied fervently, and looking out to sea, added, "Even when you're away."

Beneath the sea gulls' cries and the breakers' crashing in rhythmic syncopation, the setting sun made a crimson path that enveloped us in its rosy glow. Returning my gaze to her, I then confessed, "I've missed you, Suzannah, and having you back is a great comfort to me—to have you around me, around our home—and I'm very happy about your apprenticeship, too!"

Threading her arm through mine, and clasping her hands together, she said softly, "You make my heart sing, Jim . . ."

As I gazed at her face, upturned to mine, I felt a strong urge to kiss her . . . our first precious kiss. But feeling cowardly, I spoke instead. "Suzannah, will you be my friend—for life?"

Pulling me closer by our linked arms, in a loving voice she softly replied, "For always and forever, Jim . . . for as long as life is!"

My heart flooded with love at that moment because my little angel made me feel so wanted. "We *are* attached, aren't we, Suzannah?"

"In more ways than you think, Jim." she replied, reassuringly squeezing my arm.

The sunset's reflection in her eyes took me to a place I'd never been before—and I felt choked with emotion.

"Do you have hope about us, too, Jim . . . about our future together?"

"Yes, Suzannah," I said. "But I feel like it's a child's hope—an innocent hope, if you will."

Taking my hand, she paused for a moment as if to collect her thoughts, and embracing my hands tightly within hers, she then continued. "Jim, I believe one's heart feelings radiate like a star: and certain hearts can exchange these feelings without words, and through them we find that hope, and build that air castle, or that little rainbow . . . and thus we recapture our childlike belief that everything will be fine, that it's spring again; and along with that comes a renewal of spirit, of soul and of hope."

"Yes, Suzannah, I absolutely believe you, because for years I've felt those feelings between myself and Mother."

"Your mother and I also exchange these feelings—we know each other's hearts full well. I don't quite understand how it happens; but I know these feelings are honest and true, so I just accept them as part of my nature."

"What else do you believe in?" I asked, anxious to know more.

Lowering her eyes demurely, she confessed, "I believe the spring air is God's breath upon the earth. When it combines with the water, new life appears and flourishes everywhere. Because of all this, I shall never mourn the death of winter."

"I understand what you mean, Suzannah." I motioned toward the coastline, and then upward to higher ground and the nearby farmlands. "Just look at the seal pups, the spring gulls, even the farm animals, the trees and the raspberry bushes!"

"Yes, Jim," she agreed, laughing at my enthusiasm and taking my hand to give it a good squeeze.

I drew her closer, so we were pressed to each other's side.

Then a thought struck her, and she inquired merrily, "Did you know your mother and I went for an early morning walk today?" I shook my head no, as she continued, "We spoke of my apprenticeship, and we stopped and listened to the birds. We noticed that the river bordering Richardson's fields is wide and deep. We could see the morning dewdrops on the shrubs we passed—your mother called them angels' teardrops . . . such a pretty way of saying it."

I fear I must have looked bored, because she patted my hand and added, "I'm sorry to speak too much of these girl things, but they're close to my heart and I wish you to share them,"—and looking directly into my eyes—she whispered, ". . . because they are *me*."

Suzannah held me spellbound—by her wisdom well beyond her years, and by the depths and sincerity of her words and touch. Gazing into her beguiling gray-blue eyes, I floated upon her rapturous cloud of gentle comfort . . . for I was falling deeply in love with my lovely, gifted, "friend for life."

WITH THE MOON lighting our way, we headed home, stopping briefly at the beech tree. We stood there looking at it silently for a few minutes, holding hands in a way that we hadn't before.

Suddenly, I was inspired by an idea and retrieved my pocketknife. "To commemorate our decision to be friends for life, I shall carve our initials upon this tree . . . *our* tree."

Giggling shyly, Suzannah squeezed my hand and pressing her cheek against my arm, cheerfully said, "Very well, Mr. Walker, let's tell the world we declare it for life!"

As I began to carve our initials into the soft gray bark, she affectionately rubbed my back as I slowly pronounced, "For as long as life is . . ." and cut the following:

JW+SE FRIENDS 4 LIFE
APRIL 17, 1767

"A fitting tribute!" she declared happily.

"Indeed!" I replied, quite proud of my work. We stood back and admired the carving with satisfaction before leaving, and as we walked toward home, I took her hand and squeezing it warmly, earnestly said, "Thank you Suzannah."

"For what, Jim?"

"For being you . . . what you said on the point was so special and meaningful to me."

Looking up at me she softly replied, "That's so nice to hear, Jim."

It was all too soon thereafter that we found ourselves standing at her front door. I wanted to lift her chin and kiss her, but damning myself for the lack of courage, I knocked hesitantly, because I didn't want to leave her.

Sam opened the door almost immediately, and declared, "Good evening, James! I see you've brought something *home* to me."

"Yes, sir . . . it's getting late."

"Well, little one," he said to Suzannah, "I haven't seen you since early this *morning*!" Draping his arm around her shoulders, he humorously added, "I don't know whether you belong to me or to the Walkers!"

As he herded her through the door, Suzannah flashed me a look that clearly said, "The Walkers!"

❨ 135 ❩

The Girl Who Came to Stay

ur spring was followed by a perfect summer, with one glorious day after another filled with a pleasant warmth and brilliant sunshine. The sea breezes wafted a fresh saltwater aroma into the village center, so that no matter what else was happening in their lives, everyone in Walker's Cove felt invigorated and friendly.

On one such day, Mother had just served a hearty breakfast of sausage, eggs and apple fritters, when we heard an urgent knocking on the rear door. Father, in the midst of cutting his sausage, rose and strode toward the door, curiously asking, "Now who can that be at this hour—and at the rear door no less?"

Opening the door, he found Sam Ellingwood standing there wearing a very worried look. "Sam, what in hell happened to you?" he asked while slowly escorting him to a chair at our table.

"Is Fanny unwell?" Mother hastily inquired, while placing a hot apple fritter before Sam. Getting no response, she gently added, "I feel how deeply troubled you are, Sam. What's happened?"

Looking up at her with eyes full of sorrow, Sam whispered, "Joshua Lane is dead, Ainsley . . ."

"Oh God, no!" Mother gasped, covering her mouth in shock.

I didn't know who Joshua Lane was, but judging from the expression on Sam's face alone, I would have guessed he was his father or brother.

Even Father was stone silent until I finally asked, "Who is Joshua Lane?"

Sam stared at me blankly and seemed unable to speak.

Father explained. "He was Sam's business partner, who was in the process of fulfilling Mother's furniture order for the tavern. Joshua was also our middleman for Boston-made clock cases. *And* he was our distribution agent for clock jacks and movements. But more than that, Joshua Lane came from Walker's Cove, and was like a brother to Sam and me—similar to you and Jonathan Barrett, save our relationship spans decades."

Still standing near Sam, Mother leaned down, wrapped her arms around his shoulders and whispered softly, "I am so sorry, Sam. Is there anything we can do to ease your burden?"

Graciously patting Mother's hands, he gratefully replied, "Ainsley . . . Jim . . . Fanny and I must go to Boston right away to settle my business affairs. A great deal of my money was tied up in Joshua's business, and my claim relates to Joshua's estate because he never married. I don't know when we'll return, as the courts may be slow to hear my case . . . we may be gone a long while."

"Of course," Father said reassuringly. "But what can we do to help?"

His eyes wet with tears, Sam turned to address Mother who had resumed her place at the table. Placing his hand warmly upon Mother's, he humbly said, "Ainsley . . . Suzannah loves you, and since she is now your apprentice, do you suppose it would be asking too much if she could stay here with you until we return? I can't leave her alone at the house—and yet I cannot have her with us for months while we liquidate a business."

Mother took his hands and squeezing them, sympathetically replied, "Of course, Suzannah can stay with us. She is like a daughter to me, anyway, and it would give us the welcome opportunity to be a family of four." She paused, and glancing at me with a knowing smile, Mother then added. "There is plenty of love here for Suzannah, Sam. So, no fears my dear friend! You and Fanny do what must be done with an easy mind. Suzannah will stay here with us and we'll cherish her like you and Fanny do. I'll keep her busy learning all about tavern-keeping too."

"That's wonderful news," Sam said, looking considerably relieved. "God bless you, Ainsley, you're an angel. We plan to sail on tomorrow morning's tide—if that's acceptable to you?"

Father interjected here. "We can haul Suzannah's trunks whenever they're ready, Sam. Just say the word, and we'll come get them." Then he added, "Oh yes, and if it will help, why don't we take you and Fanny and your luggage down to the wharf in the morning?"

"Thanks, Jim. That would be very helpful. It seems I'm in your debt once more."

"Nonsense!" countered Father, patting Sam on the back to quell his misgivings. "This is what friends are for. We'll drop by your house later on to pick Suzannah's things up."

"Thank you all!" Sam said with a grateful smile.

Pouring him a cup of tea, Father said, "Now, Sam, I insist you join us for some breakfast. It'll make you feel even *better!*" Turning to Mother he asked, "So how *is* your little apprentice coming along?" It was obvious to me that he wanted to change the subject for Sam's sake, and he knew Mother would catch on.

"She is just fine, a brilliant girl who will be mistress of her own tavern in short order. She actually out-traded Josiah Wheeler last week!" Mother exclaimed, warming to the topic.

"Really?" Father said quizzically, pretending not to know the story already. "How did she do that?"

"Remember the lead you couldn't find in Boston?"

Father nodded.

"Well, it seems our old friend Jens wanted to trade a wagonload of sheet lead to Josiah Wheeler in exchange for four coils of deck rope he needed for the rigging of his new schooner—you know, the *Sunrise?* Josiah had no rope, but Suzannah heard about Jens' offer, and managed to find five coils of surplus rope on an outbound Providence bark while it was still anchored at the wharf. The captain—Wilkins, by name—was eager to get rid of it since he needed the space for his cargo of lumber and corn. He told Suzannah that if she would arrange to have the rope removed from the hold that very day, she could have it in exchange for a loaf of pumpkin bread, a piece of blueberry pie and a pint of spiced rum when the tavern opened.

Suzannah persuaded Eliphalet Wheeler and Noah Clemmens to remove the rope immediately, and deliver it directly to Jens, who, in return, gave her ten shillings *plus* the scrap lead. So expending *nothing*, Suzannah received ten shillings hard money, and," turning to Father, "you have 300 pounds of lead sitting by the smithy—less the one shilling Suzannah paid for the hauling!"

"Damned *smart* girl!" Father remarked, beaming at Sam, who wore a smile so broad, he hardly resembled the downcast man who had knocked at our door an hour before.

Mother was shaking her head in disbelief as she added, "And to think she's all of *sixteen* years old!"

"Wait until she is twenty," Father said. "She will buy and sell us *all*!"

When we arrived at the Ellingwoods just past noon, there were two trunks waiting in the parlor ready for the trip to our house. They were small and delicate, and weighed very little, like their admired owner, who would now be—at least for the time being— my adopted sister.

I felt ambivalent about this new wrinkle in our relationship: on the one hand, she would always be near me, and that was indeed a blessing. So I was eager for her to get comfortably settled so we could spend more time together.

On the other hand, how would her presence affect my feelings toward her—or more importantly, her feelings toward me? Being in such close proximity might breed contempt, possibly alienating her affections at a time when they should be growing stronger, as they had been till now. The idea that our relationship might be harmed by this new arrangement caused a gnawing ache in my stomach that lasted all afternoon.

When I brought Suzannah's trunks upstairs, I saw that Mother had expertly prepared the guest room for our special visitor: it was all ready for her to take up residence. The thought of her living on the other side of my chamber wall put me in mind of the custom of bundling . . . but my thoughts were interrupted by the sound of a musical "Jim?" from downstairs, accompanied by the trip-trapping of little feet upon the floor . . . unmistakably my little angel. Hearing the outside door close and Suzannah calling out my name again, my face burned with anticipatory blushes as I answered, "I'm up here—with your trunks!"

I watched her climb the stairs until she finally stood before me, looking angelic and radiantly beautiful.

"Here is your . . . ah . . . *bed chamber*!" I excitedly stammered, as she entered the room. While admiring her beauty, I caught a delicate aroma from the flowers she'd woven through her hair.

Suzannah surveyed the entire room before suddenly turning to catch me staring at her, totally entranced. She smiled and softly said, "Jim, this is *so* beautiful. Your mother is very kind to make a home for me."

"Well, I hope you're comfortable uh . . . here. We, uh, want you to feel at home . . . and, ah, *I* want you to feel *welcome*."

Giggling at my adolescent stumbling to welcome her, Suzannah's disarming smile finally put me at ease. She moved closer, and stood on her toes looking up at my face. For a long moment she said nothing, then finally whispered, "Thank you, Jim! You are *still* full of surprises!"

"You are more than welcome, Suzannah. My chamber is next door if you need anything. Take your time to look around and settle in. Mother has emptied the highboy for you. This house has not been an inn for twenty years, so now is as good a time as any to make it so again. I'm very pleased that you're its first guest . . ."

With a deep curtsey, Suzannah quipped, "Well now, how shall I pay for my room and board, o' master innkeeper?"

"Just be your wonderful self, and learn your lessons well!" Mother's voice echoed from the bottom of the stairs.

Suzannah's eyes snapped wide open, as did her mouth, which she covered with a slap of her hand. Pleasantly mortified at being overheard, she winked at me and slipped into her chamber with a bang of the door.

❦

During the following week I still had trouble believing that Suzannah and I were living in adjacent bed chambers—just a few inches away! But since we were so near, we couldn't resist devising a secret code to communicate with each other by tapping on our common wall. Long after bedtime, we would tap until the clock struck as late as two bells sometimes; and when we finally went to sleep, we were comforted knowing that the other was so near.

The four of us sat together for every meal, and I felt honored every night by her presence. But for all of us, the first order of business each and every day was work and training.

As a large part of their daily routine, Mother instructed Suzannah in a simple unpretentious manner: about tavern keeping, general trading, selecting and purchasing ingredients, and in particular, the selection, mixing and sale of spirituous liquors. Within a few short months, Suzannah knew almost all there was to know on those vital subjects.

Her first lessons were in managing the kitchen, and learning how to cook the menu items that were staples in most New England taverns. Her training included mastering meals for large numbers of guests, regulating quantities to minimize waste, and creatively reusing much of what remained at day's end.

Mother also schooled Suzannah in the financial side of the business: how to keep accounts, count specie of various denominations and reconcile their exchange rates; and most importantly, how to purchase goods and services, as well as establish and maintain relationships with a variety of vendors. Mother emphasized routines that maximized efficiency and economy in order to make the operation profitable; and shared some important do's and don'ts based upon her own hard experience—like never counting and recording the day's proceeds until after the last patron has left the tavern.

Because of Joshua's death and the new demands it brought to bear on the clock shop, Father and I worked in isolation from morning to night. In Sam's absence, we tried to use his jigs, forms and specialized tools to make our own clock cases. This encroached on our production of brass works, and although the results were adequate, they were not entirely satisfactory. And because we were forced to make relatively cheap clock cases, we had to forfeit—at least temporarily—orders for our higher-end products.

We received letters from Sam and Fanny, who were staying at Lydia's house in Boston. There they would remain until the liquidation of the Lane estate was final. Mother wrote back often and eagerly looked forward to their return. She missed Fanny, especially now . . . and didn't realize how much so until this lengthy absence.

Suzannah's presence in our midst enriched our lives, as was amply demonstrated by how my parents doted on her. On most evenings, we all sat together for tween time, writing letters, talking business, or playing chess. As summer progressed, Suzannah and I grew fonder of each other and her loveliness increased with each passing day . . . so much so that as she approached the age of seventeen, she rounded into radiant womanhood before our eyes.

But not one inch did she grow—just more enticing to me than ever before. Because I was unsure of what to say or do in light of my growing affections, even my bidding goodnight to her in the hallway could become very awkward. Sisterly feelings sometimes crowded out my lover's feelings, and as such, if I treated her like the sister I never had, I didn't feel so uncomfortable. The truth was Suzannah had come to dominate my every thought, hope and ambition. There were times when I was so overwhelmed by her daily presence in our house, that my heart begged relief from wishing her *not* to return home . . . ever.

As part of our new routine, I began escorting her to church on Sunday mornings. Trying not to be obvious, I would sit quietly in our pew, slouched down low with an open bible before my face, peeking discreetly over the pages to catch a glimpse of her sitting alone in the Ellingwood box. Every so often she would glance my way, giving me a smile of such delicious sweetness that I would fumble the good book and drop it with a resounding crash, thus revealing to one and all my true purpose. Everyone in the congregation, especially Reverend Metcalf, glowered my way, annoyed at the disturbance I'd caused. All except Suzannah, whose shoulders shook as she placed a dainty hand to her mouth to smother a silent giggle. Ah! *She* knew!

After church on Sundays we walked hand-in-hand to Walker's Point. Sometimes we had picnics there while we read aloud letters from her parents or talked about nature. We liked tossing mussels to sea gulls and searching the tidal pools for creatures we never knew existed. Through the early autumn, we continued to explore life together, and ours was a bounteous trail of discoveries, including those of the heart. My parents encouraged our togetherness, and partly because we had their blessings, trust, participation and love, our bond strengthened even more.

In October, the Ellingwoods returned to Walker's Cove, their fiscal matters finally settled. Suzannah returned home, and it seemed my life ended with her leaving. My sadness was somewhat relieved when Fanny declared that we were all celebrating Suzannah's seventeenth birthday on October 18th. Not only was she turning seventeen, but Mother declared she had "graduated from school," and was now a bona fide tavern-keeper of the first order.

Sam's gift to his daughter was sending her to Boston to board with Katharine and her husband, Francis, who would tutor her in the most up-to-date business methods. He was a Harvard graduate and an esteemed private tutor, well equipped to prepare Suzannah for her new role.

Anxiously wondering how this trip might change Suzannah, I deeply feared she would meet another man during her stay in Boston—a man far more educated and genteel than I—and thus she might never return to Walker's Cove. If Suzannah did fall into the arms of someone else and married, I thought that she could still be my friend for life; but that rationale would never do—and I wished to somehow approach her with an understanding before she left; but at every given opportunity, my fear was so great, I lacked the courage to do so.

As the day of her departure drew near, my anxiety increased tenfold, for I had suppressed my feelings and concerns for fear of leaving our hearts undone . . . even though we were friends for life. Finally, on the 20th of October, Father woke me early and asked if I would like to drive Suzannah to the wharf to privately say our goodbyes. I readily agreed since this would be my last chance to speak with her alone.

Father went to the Ellingwoods to check on their readiness while I went to the barn. As I hitched Winnie to the wagon, I felt a constant ache in the pit of my stomach from not knowing what to say or how to say it. My instinct was to say little, so as not to expose my insecurities about "my friend for life." As I led Winnie toward the Ellingwood's front door, the morning chill and lingering shadows only reinforced my gloominess.

Father and Sam were waiting and we loaded her three small trunks into the wagon, and when Suzannah emerged from the house, I stood by mutely while she greeted us with beaming eyes and a radiant smile.

Father clapped his hand upon my shoulder, declaring, "Well, son, have a nice ride and we'll see you when you get back."

Sam kissed his daughter, and after lifting her onto the seat, he patted her hand and said, "Now, don't forget to write us—we'll be *expecting* your letters. I love you, sweetheart, and I'll miss you." Then, kissing her once more, he turned to me and declared, "She's all yours, Jim!"

He and Father strode off together, heading toward the comforting warmth of our kitchen—oblivious to the inner torment they were abandoning me to.

When I mounted the seat, Suzannah took my arm and drew herself against me. Looking into my eyes, she murmured softly, "Jim, I can *feel* what's inside you, but have no fear. How can I reassure you that we will be fine?"

I was stunned—she said "we"! But of course, she was a heart feeler, and I realized there was no way to avoid her sensing my turmoil.

"I will miss you, Suzannah," I said, almost in tears. "I miss you *now*, and you haven't even left! I've missed you terribly since you returned home from our house."

When I finished speaking, she simply hugged me. It was a firm and heartfelt embrace. As we held each other, my quiet tears stole into her hair, but I quickly wiped my eyes, for I didn't wish us to part on a sad note.

Father opened the kitchen door and yelled, "Hey Jim, hold her at the wharf, not here! Mind the outgoing tide!" he warned, as he waved us on and closed the door.

As Winnie trotted off toward the village center, we quietly enjoyed the beauty of the autumn landscape, for the trees were now dressed in their full colors. We made a brief stop near our old friend, the beech tree, and silently regarded our carved initials. As we did, a falling leaf twirled slowly to its final resting place, which led Suzannah to thoughtfully ask, "I wonder how many spring days were required to grow that leaf? And then how many days did it hang on the tree? What is its fate now when it falls to the ground? What do you think, Jim?"

"I think it mimics all life, Suzannah," I replied. "Its mother is the tree, and the leaves are her children. For a time in spring they are helpless, and need nurturing and care; then during summer, they grow stronger and almost independent. In autumn, they separate and go their own way—by falling to the ground, I suppose."

Turning to me with soulful eyes, she gently stroked my hair and softly replied, "Perhaps, Jim, they do not fall . . . but rather let go . . ."

Not knowing how to reply, I merely nodded . . . for I had to let go . . . and she knew it.

With her arm circling my waist, she gave me a reassuring squeeze, and we drove the rest of the way to the wharf in silence. The tide was nearly out and someone on board the tethered vessel hollered up impatiently, "Is this the woman we been waitin' all day fer?"

"Yes," I shouted back, "Suzannah Ellingwood!"

"Then move *smartly*, miss!" he tersely replied. "We been waitin' plenty, and the damned tide is nearly gone! We mustn't tarry another minute!"

I hurried to the rear of the wagon and handed her trunks to the sailors on the gangway. As they quickly passed them down the ship's hatch, I lifted Suzannah off her seat and after setting her down, embraced her tightly.

"Our separation will pass quickly, Jim," she said, "and when I return, I will be the *same* girl who left you."

"My heart will follow you, Suzannah," I replied, choking back my tears.

"As mine will follow you, Jim." Gently fingering my hair, she affectionately added, "Keep in your heart the memories of the girl who came to stay, and she will return to you in good time."

Suddenly, without a word of courtesy, one of the sailors brusquely took her by the arm, and the two scampered onto the deck.

As the vessel pulled away, Suzannah remained on deck, looking back at me with those comforting eyes. Surrounded by the crew as they clambered all around her attending to the ropes and sails, I watched forlornly as she became smaller and smaller. When I saw her no more, with my heart in tears, I finally turned away.

HEART TREASURE

he winter after Suzannah's departure was exceedingly busy, for there was a strong demand for clocks and clock jacks from any maker. It seemed that clock jacks had suddenly become a necessity for every kitchen, and their manufacture kept us busier than clockmaking. In the course of her weekly updates about her life in Boston, Suzannah reported that clock jacks were now coveted by all the housewives in Boston—and possibly in the colonies as well—since most peddlers complained they could never get enough to meet the demand. Suzannah noted gleefully that Katharine managed, despite their scarcity, to secure one of our own make, which pleased her greatly.

To facilitate our clockmaking, Sam Ellingwood was now making our tall clock cases, including those of the Roxbury style inspired by the Willards. According to Suzannah, those were the most popular of all our clocks that were being exported to Britain. Not surprisingly, as a result of all this new business, our income grew considerably.

After an exhausting day in the shop, before retiring to my own chamber, I visited Suzannah's old room. I would sit alone on her bed, holding her pillow, and wish she was there with me until my heart ached. After a while, totally dejected, I withdrew to my room to gaze mournfully out the window at the Ellingwood house . . . ever wishing to see the flicker of a candle, or shadowy firelight reflecting off her chamber window. But alas! All remained dark.

During that unforgiving winter, the consoling friend that bound my heart and thoughts was constant labor. Then, on April 4th,

Mother handed me a sealed letter that had arrived that morning. It was from Suzannah and read as follows.

Dear Jim,

Home—April 21st!

Suzannah

I couldn't wait . . .

ON A WARM April afternoon, we met Suzannah, Katharine and her husband, Francis, as they disembarked at the wharf. Her three other sisters and their husbands, who were already in Walker's Cove for the homecoming, came with us. We were in high spirits at being reunited with our darling girl, who we welcomed with an abundance of hugs. In honor of her return, a celebration with family and friends was planned for later in the day; so when we got back the womenfolk went off to the Ellingwoods to prepare an elaborate spread.

After allowing Suzannah some time to unpack and rest for a little while, I whisked her off to Walker's Point to speak with her in private. I had months' worth of thoughts and feelings to share. At one point as we were walking, I turned around to observe our footprints in the sand: first separate, then together, then separate by a wide margin, then together again. I noticed that my prints were the ones that wavered, while the path hers made was straight and true.

"How symbolic . . ." I muttered, feeling a sense of shame about my lack of self-confidence. As I pointed to the pattern, I added sheepishly, "Sort of looks like our relationship, doesn't it?"

Suzannah looked down at our footprints and then out to sea. Finally, after a time, her eyes met mine in a troubled gaze. In a voice barely audible above the ocean noise, she softly asked, "Do you think there's something *wrong* with our relationship, Jim?"

Catching me off guard, I could say nothing—I was too bottled up with feelings I couldn't articulate.

After a few moments of my silence, with a tremor in her voice, Suzannah bravely asked, "Tell me, Jim, what does your heart say?"

Her question inspired me to overcome my inhibitions at last, and express the depth of what I felt for her. I retrieved from my pocket the very first note she'd written to me—after our memorable sleigh rides—and held it before her.

With bright, happy eyes, she exclaimed in a tone of amazement, "You *kept* it!"

"Of course, I did, Suzannah."

"Oh, Jim, that was such a happy time!"

"*Very* happy!" And then I reached down and clasped her to me tightly, rocking her gently in my arms while the water lapped at our feet. As I began stroking her flaxen hair, I told her of my loneliness without her. Then I asked, "Our times together, will they become heart treasures for life?"

"For *life?*" Suzannah repeated, searching my face for meaning.

"Yes," I replied. "For those dreary moments when we're apart, or alone—or perhaps even old?"

With her eyes still on mine, she replied, "Yes, Jim, heart treasures make us who we are. They shape our thoughts, our desires, our feelings, and they will always remain if we want them to." There was a long pause as she gazed out to sea once more, then back up at me. "Jim?" she said softly.

"Yes?"

"I still have your question . . . in my hope chest . . ."

She was referring to my note to her—that elicited the response I now held in my hand as we held each other even closer than before.

We reluctantly broke apart since it was getting late and we didn't want to hold up dinner. As we continued home we held hands and this time when I paused to look behind us, the path of our footprints were in unison. The tide continued to roll in and together we recklessly splashed through its sweeping waters. As we approached the deeper shallows, I stopped to gaze silently into the evening sky. The moon had stolen a silvery path through the wisps

"The moon had stolen a silvery path . . ."

of stray evening clouds. As the gentle breeze softly placed a delicate kiss upon her cheek . . . carrying to me the sweet aroma of her floral essence, I nearly choked at her beauty as I stammered, "What a blessed night, Suzannah . . . because you are here to share it with me."

She looked up at me with those beautiful searching eyes that penetrated into the very depths of my soul. The moonlight illuminated her hair with a halo's shimmering whiteness, and finally choking with emotion, I still managed to continue.

"Suzannah, everything is so new . . . my heart constantly overflows with tender affection and many other warm feelings I can't explain."

"That's perfectly normal, Jim," she said reassuringly, as she touched my lips tenderly with her fingers. Oh, how soft and warm those fingers were! "You will soon be able to speak from your heart . . . all in good time."

"I hope so," I said, not entirely convinced she was right.

Above the ocean's murmur, she proclaimed sweetly, "*I* know what your heart feels, Jim, even though you can't express it. Meanwhile, follow your heart and see where it takes you."

I realized then that she understood, and that she knew of my inexpressible love for her. "How do you know this?" I asked. "What makes you so certain?"

As we started walking again, Suzannah squeezed my hand. "I feel it . . . I sense it . . . *here* . . ." she said, pointing to her heart. "That's how I know it's the truth."

"Yes, I remember Mother saying you can read thoughts."

She stopped abruptly and turned toward me. "No! Never thoughts, James. *Feelings*! There's a difference."

"Well then, what am I feeling now?" I challenged.

"You really wish to know?" she asked, smiling.

"Yes, I do," I said boldly.

Taking my hand in hers, we continued home together as she spoke. "I feel our hearts share a strong and unbreakable bond. We're feeling that cozy heart treasure called mutual affection. That means you are comforted by my presence, and I am comforted by yours.

However, I sense you're troubled because you lack an understanding of your heart's workings, and by your difficulty trying to express it when speaking with me."

Laying her warm palm on my cheek she gave me a look that for a moment—nearly stopped my heart—before she continued. "I *feel* your love, Jim, and I know you feel love's palpable warmth, joy and comfort from that precious seed that's growing within you . . . which bears the possibility of . . . of endless love . . ."

I stopped and turned her toward me. "*Yes!*" I whispered, "*Exactly!*"

"Well then, Jim, let the seed germinate—there's no need to hurry . . . I'm here now, and we're special friends enjoying each other's company."

Holding hands once again, we left the beach and took the road home. When we arrived at Suzannah's front door, I gently caressed her shoulders and turned her face up to mine. The moonlight illuminated her angelic beauty . . . and for a long rapturous moment I felt overpowered by my emotions. Drawing her closer, I brought her hands to my lips and kissed them tenderly. Then, with my heart in my throat, I softly whispered, "Suzannah, can we still be friends . . . for life?"

Laying her palm to my heart, with endearing sincerity she whispered her reply, "For as long as life is . . ."

My eyes filled as I slowly lifted her chin. Closing her eyes in sweet anticipation, she moistened her slightly parted lips and waited. When her hair fell away to reveal her loving look of commitment, I could no longer resist . . . and just as I bent to kiss her, Mr. Ellingwood opened the door . . .

"Well! Come on in you two—it's time for dinner!"

The Prophecy

s we entered the vestibule, we were greeted by mouth-watering aromas from all the special dishes that had been prepared for the occasion. I followed behind as Sam escorted his daughter into the parlor, which was already crowded with people engaged in lively conversation. But once they spotted Suzannah, everyone immediately flocked to her.

One surprise of the evening was that Suzannah's sisters had pre-pared their favorite recipes, as did our mothers. While these culinary delights awaited us, Katharine's husband, Francis, tapped his glass with a knife, to formally announce he had something to say—and at that, we all fell silent. Francis had a very kind face, character-ized by soft, gentle features and large gray eyes. His hair was light brown and thinning to baldness, so he wore a compensatory beard that shifted an onlooker's eye to the lower part of his face. He had a perpetual air of serenity about him that befitted a minister more than it did a private tutor from Harvard College.

As Francis introduced himself, the soothing tone of his voice immediately relaxed his audience, and thus holding their atten-tion, he raised his glass and proudly announced, "Upon this joyous occasion before family and friends, I want to call attention to the brilliant achievement attained by my sister-in-law, Miss Suzan-nah Ellingwood. She was a remarkable pupil whose extraordinary mind has retained all the benefits of my Harvard training. Because she reads so voraciously on her own and retains everything she reads . . ." he then hesitated and raising his hands, he humorously declared, "With Suzannah in my house, I began to feel that my library was totally redundant!"

A burst of laughter followed by applause filled the room as he paused for a breath, then glowingly added: "As such, I am very proud to officially endorse her as eminently qualified to teach any subject whatsoever—even at the Harvard levels."

Amid our gasps of admiration for Suzannah's accomplishment, Francis again raised his glass. "To Suzannah Ellingwood . . . the *finest* pupil I have ever tutored! Huzzah!"

Everyone raised their glasses, repeated "Huzzah!" and added another round of applause.

Francis then turned to Father, "I wanted to tell you that my wife is positively delighted with her clock jack."

Whereupon Father quickly replied, "Well then, Francis, it's my son who deserves the compliment, since he makes all our clock jacks."

Setting his glass on a nearby table, Francis stepped over to where I was standing and shook my hand heartily, repeating, "My wife is very pleased with her clock jack, ah . . . James, isn't it?"

"Yes," I said. "I'm glad to hear Katharine is so pleased with it." Then I added, "Please spread the word if you can . . . as it's good for business."

"Of course, I will," Francis assured me; and gently taking me aside, in low tones he confided, "Meaning no disrespect, dear sir, but are you *certain* Suzannah wishes to operate a *tavern*? Her academic potential is enormous!"

"She does, sir," I answered. "Her intention is to remain here and care for her parents." Though in my heart I believed her desire to be near me strengthened her original plan, I couldn't tell him that.

Fanny rang the dinner bell, proclaiming the feast was ready, and Sam escorted us into the dining room where the table was set with fourteen place settings, complete with silverware, china plates and wineglasses. The centerpiece was comprised of two large vases filled to overflowing with bouquets of wildflowers, freshly picked from Richardson's fields.

Sam led Suzannah to the head of the table, where she daintily sat in her chair. Ah, how lovely and radiant was our guest of honor! I was beside myself with pride.

Served up for our delectation were pickled cucumbers and onions, freshly baked bread with cheese, Brunswick soup, a large ham garnished with apples, cloves and sugar, baked sweet potatoes, mashed turnips, and boiled carrots laced with molasses and butter. For dessert there were gingerbread cookies, pumpkin pie, apple fritters and Indian pudding—washed down with syllabub, spruce beer, flip and ginger beer.

Our dinner ran late into the night, and we parted company at half-past two in the morning, with Mother offering our guest rooms to accommodate Sarah and Lydia and their husbands.

Not surprisingly, we overslept the following day. When Sam called that morning to discuss the plan to convert our home into a tavern, he was met by sleepy guests staggering around our kitchen, splashing cold water on their faces to wake up. Being selfless hosts, Mother and Father resorted to the rainwater barrel outside to rouse themselves.

At last, Sam, Lydia's husband Richard, my parents, and I finally gathered around the table in the kitchen, while Sarah and Lydia made breakfast. Sam had brought his drawing tools that he used to sketch initial plans for the exterior grounds, the cellar excavation and the structural expansion. Sam also created a detailed list—accompanied by line drawings—for the interior design as envisioned by Mother.

Not wishing to give up her parlor, the expansion of the house provided for a new "great room," twenty-four feet wide and thirty feet deep. There would be a twelve-foot-wide fireplace in the great room, on the inside twenty-four-foot wall, equipped with ovens, cranes, clock jacks and serving grates to keep food warm and the room well heated.

By day's end, incorporating ideas and guidance from everyone present, Sam had completed a set of preliminary plans for the clearing and milling of trees, the excavation of a new cellar and foundation, and the architecture of the great room and the façade of the house. From that he would develop a final set of plans—to be approved by Mother—that would include any additional design modifications that might arise in the interim. He would make one set for my parents, one for the construction crew, and keep one for himself.

Now Mother could schedule her next trip to Boston. There, with Richard, she would award and execute her contracts for the purchases of glass, flooring stone, furniture and the other items that appeared on her growing list of necessities.

Sam insisted that the felling of trees and preliminary foundation work must begin immediately—while the ground was still soft—so that by winter, the framing, fireplaces, chimneys and exterior walls would be in place, thus sheltering us from the cold while the carpenters worked on the interior. My parents agreed, and the word was given to proceed.

In a few weeks, Sam would oversee a crew of lumberjacks, wood-wrights, teamsters and oxen as they disembarked from the ship and trundled up the wharf of Walker's Cove. He led them to their destination, which was our two houses, since they would room with us, and the Ellingwoods, until all the work was finished.

Their first task was to find suitable trees in the King's Forest to fell, and then drag them to Sam's shop by oxen, where they would be milled to the specifications on Sam's plan. Then the finished lumber would be put aside for the carpenters, who were due to arrive three weeks hence.

From the finished lumber, the carpenters would assemble the framing. The excavators, meanwhile, would dig the foundation for the expansion space, and set the large granite blocks that would support the great room addition. Bricklayers had been hired to build the new chimneys and fireplaces that would follow once the foundation was done. In exchange, all the workers would receive free room and board, plus a stipend in hard money as their wages.

The highly anticipated tavern construction had officially begun.

Our home soon became a beehive of activity. Mother and Suzannah were practically chained to the kitchen, preparing meals for the work crew. They decided it was the perfect opportunity to sharpen their cooking skills for large numbers of guests, as well as test new recipes for the tavern menu. As for the spirits, they spent entire weekends making drinkables of various potencies, including hot buttered rum, ginger beer, spruce beer, syllabub, flip, grog, and finally blackstrap, which was a dubious mixture of watered-down rum with a touch of molasses for flavor.

Because Suzannah was pressed into active kitchen service, I saw little of her during construction. Every morning about four, she and Mother would begin preparing breakfast, followed in no time by the noon meal, which entailed picking fresh herbs from the garden and rummaging in the old root cellar for other ingredients they might need. They worked tirelessly until the evening, when the dinner bell was rung for the men to come and eat, and beyond, when it was time to clean up and prepare for the next day's meals.

They followed their plan to develop a menu, and showed off their cooking skills to the nonplussed workmen who greeted their tasty fare with a great show of gratitude. They were served pumpkin muffins, apple pies, apple fritters, pumpkin fritters, rich porridges, pickled cucumbers, salted pork, pork pie, mutton pie, venison and moose stew, venison pie, potato and fish chowder, corn chowder, broiled eel, baked cod, baked beans, breads of various sorts, and finally the poorest and cheapest of all, rummage stew, in which squirrel, rabbit or raccoon was used as the base meat, accompanied by potatoes, carrots, turnips and onions.

Later in the evenings, Mother and Suzannah relished the opportunity to collapse onto the sofa, and discuss the comments they received from the work crew. By exchanging ideas about specific suggestions, they would frequently modify their recipes, and made notes accordingly in their recipe ledger. Also, whenever she had the opportunity, Mother would give away some of the leftover food to passersby or visitors to the village center, soliciting their opinions and suggestions for improving her recipes.

One day, while the men were outside eating during their break, I went to the kitchen for a tin of hot chowder and a piece of bread to dip into it. The truth is I wished to keep company with Suzannah while I ate, because although she was often near, I missed her. While I waited for her to appear, Mother ladled out my soup. As she was handing the bowl to me, Osgood Lovejoy, our town cobbler and letter carrier, appeared in the doorway.

"Fine day, Ainsley, what say, Jim . . . got a letter here!" he greeted us cheerfully, placing a letter from Boston on the table, next to the large kettle of chowder.

"Well, good day to you too, Osgood!" she replied amiably, picking up a clean tin to fill it with chowder. "How are Mildred and the children?"

"Oh, all are swell, Ainsley. We can't wait for your tavern to open."

After ladling the soup into the tin, Mother offered it to Osgood. "I should like your opinion of this chowder, Osgood . . . and please be honest."

Osgood looked at it, and then up at my mother, searching her face as he asked, "Ainsley, I should like to give this to a needy visitor from the wharf—would you mind?"

"Why, no. Who is it and where is he?" Mother said.

"It's a *she!*" Osgood declared triumphantly, as though his wife just had another child. Then he went outside and promptly returned with a woman clad in soiled rags.

Behind me, I heard a sweet voice I recognized as Suzannah's gasp in dismay, "Oh, dear me . . ."

The woman who entered behind Osgood shuffled about the room with a tottering gait. She looked to be destitute, apparently carrying all her earthly possessions in a well-worn and begrimed leather bag. She was about seventy years of age, if not older, her posture slightly stooped, so that she appeared to have no neck whatsoever, and was obliged to turn her entire torso to look in a particular direction. Under coarse bushy eyebrows, her tiny deep-set eyes peered out at us quizzically as if to ask: were we friend or foe?

Mother escorted her to a chair at the table. "Dear lady, would you like some hot chowder and bread? You look like you haven't seen a morsel in a fortnight."

"She was stowed away on the *Winston*," Osgood explained.

"The *Winston?* Is that a British ship?" inquired Mother.

"Indeed it is—and they didn't want her, so they threw her off!" Osgood replied angrily.

"Well, we shall see about *that* . . ." Mother said indignantly, grabbing her cloak and throwing it over her shoulders. After asking Suzannah to see to our guest, Mother headed out to the wharf in a furious huff.

Suzannah gazed sympathetically at the old woman as she gave her a plate of bread and a tin of hot chowder.

The woman peered up at her benefactress and whispered, "Tank dee, dear childt."

Suzannah stepped back and said hesitantly, "I am Suzannah . . . this is James. What is your name and where do you come from?"

The woman started consuming the chowder greedily, but stopped for a moment to answer. Beaming a toothless grin at Suzannah, she replied, "I am Lyuba . . . and I come from far avfaye."

"We heard you stowed away on a British ship," I observed, "but your name and your speech are not English."

"Yes, I hide indt der ship . . . alones by der barrels in der holdt, to go to Boston colonies," she explained in halting, broken English.

"But why?" asked Suzannah. "Do you have a family there?"

The question was greeted by silence as Lyuba finished eating all her food before resuming her story. "No . . . no fambly dere . . . but I am a soodseyer for der copper penny. I come to Boston to get bedder life . . . I giff yoo der future fer diz foodt . . . yes?" She paused, hungrily eying the soup kettle and the remaining bread that sat enticingly nearby.

I prepared another generous serving of chowder and bread, as I replied, "Very well, tell us our future. Here is some more food to keep body and soul together." I felt sympathy and admiration for this brave old soul, who was so desperate for a better life that she would hide in a ship for the span of an ocean crossing—about two months!

Suzannah smiled at me, pleased at my generosity. And once Lyuba had finished, we sat down at the table beside her.

Reaching into her large bag, she first withdrew a wooden stand that she placed upon the table, followed by a sphere of some sort, heavily wrapped in cloth and about the size of a sixteen-pound shot. When Lyuba removed the covering, Suzannah gasped in surprise, for there before us was a large clear ball, apparently of pure rock crystal, which she placed gently on the stand. It rested on a trio of buttons to prevent it from rolling.

I looked at Suzannah to glean her reaction, and she gazed back at me in wide-eyed wonder. The crystal ball possessed a mystical quality in its center and was beautiful to behold, and neither of us had ever seen anything like it.

Lyuba proceeded to polish the ball till it shone; and then after placing both hands upon it, focused her eyes on its center, as if searching for something lost within. "Place your handt upon mine," she commanded Suzannah abruptly.

My little angel gave me a fearful glance, and then with the shadow of a smile, complied wordlessly with Lyuba's order.

"Now, Chamess, put your handt upon my uddher handt."

I did so half-heartedly, believing that her performance smacked of fakery of the highest order.

Lyuba stared intently into the ball for some time, until she gave a sharp little cry and pulled away, but without loosening her grip on it. At that point, she seemed to enter a trance-like state, uttering incomprehensible words that sounded foreign to me and were frightening to Suzannah. And then it came . . .

"O, I see der bitter fates of life pursue dee, Chamess Vocker . . . duringk dark timess aheadt. In der future, I see dark nights to come vhence feverish slumberss and spectral shapess crowdt drearily upon die soul. Dere iss alvayss a morningk after der darkest night . . . yet dere comess again . . . der returning night of Death . . . ovf coldt-hearted cheerless pain and ruin. Broodingk fear shall haunt die dreamss youngk one . . . for die Death Angjel comess to dee witt a coldt caresss . . . und woos dee to die gravfe. Der beloffed figgure of die muddher . . . fadtes from my vishion as mist upon dee vahter . . . leafing die soul consciouss off notting. It iss only vhen lofe iss lost foreffer . . . only vhen dee inexorable vorldt of Death separates a fambly by trowing it upon der sea of fadte, sometimess into der eternal darknesss off der gravfe itselff, do you den feel and miss dee abidingk affectionss off a fambly member. You, Chamess Valker, vill bee destinedt to recall wit sighs of rependtance, dose reproachful vords or passionate outbreaks dat shall haunt die heardt wit misgiffingkss and sorrowss. You vill remember effery rendt und tear in der fabrick off die life, undt hide die bitter disappoindtmendt in Death. In dee darknesss off die soul, you shall call up bidder tearss for dat spirit off die lost member; crying for help ven none can safe dem. Death leffels dee holy capacity off dee liffing angjel, und destroys die vission off vhat life shouldt be, und deliffers a cruel stroke ass to vhat it really iss . . . und yet . . . I see hope for die future. Success becomess you . . . und lovfe bintds you bofe to become pillarss off great strengdt. Die housse shall not fall, Chamess Vocker, yet dere iss much death und destruction to come. Dee future iss cloudy . . . I see a venching grip upon die soul, Chamess Vocker . . . budt dere remainss a rainbow . . ."

Then, turning her wizened, careworn face toward Suzannah, Lyuba gasped out a sudden revelation. "You . . . *you* are dee guardtian angjel, who keepss dee rainbow gloving und shimmeving wid dee colorss off life, hope and lofe. Your vill is strongk for vone so small . . . und your heardt . . . a most powerful strengtdt it hass."

When Lyuba released her grip on the sphere, we all sat back in our chairs.

"Cheery old gypsy, aren't you?" I said sarcastically, and then wished my words hadn't sounded so harsh.

Shaking her head sadly in response, the old woman added a warning. "None shall alter der vayss off der Fadtess. Do vhat you vish young Chamess Valker, budt keep diss angjel"—she paused to place her hand upon Suzannah's arm—"at your sidte . . . for you shall *not* surfife widhoutd her."

Then Lyuba carefully rewrapped the sphere and returned it along with the stand to her bag. "I am sadk my childrendss, budt you shall see difficuldt timess aheadt . . . budt dhere iss hope . . ."

Her face softened as she gave Suzannah a wistful look, and then suddenly turned to me. "*She* is der liffingk angjel, *belieff* in *her* . . ." And with that, she got up and shuffled out the door.

After Lyuba was safely out of earshot, I said to Suzannah, "What do you make of all that? Did I hear her say I'm bad luck?" I was left feeling quite distressed by the old gypsy's words, and I hoped Suzannah could calm me, tell me I was imagining things.

In reply—with a hand to her throat and a frightened expression on her face—Suzannah simply looked up at me and said nothing.

"Surely you don't believe her!" I exclaimed vehemently, feeling my heart begin to break.

Again, silence, as Suzannah rose from the table and turned her back to me, slowly walking toward the fireplace. Then I heard the word "No" uttered, barely audible, and saw her head bowed as though she were brooding. She had been profoundly shaken—my heart could *feel* it—and inwardly I cursed myself for having this "sense" my mother made so much of, for now it gave me nothing but aching torment.

Thinking to comfort her, I picked up her shawl and going over to where she stood, I tenderly placed it over her shoulders. She looked up at me with a distressed expression and formally said, "Thank you." Then I watched helplessly as she headed toward the door, never raising her head, and left without another word.

A crushing blow collapsed my stomach, as I felt a hollow, gnawing sensation at my very core. Not because of the prophecy, which was indeed disturbing, but because of Suzannah's coldness and distance. It was as though I had suddenly become too loathsome for her to be around.

"It's over, isn't it?" I thought to myself in a panic. "She's gone and now I have *nothing*! My best friend—evaporated like sea smoke in the hot sun."

Feeling totally dejected, I went into the parlor and slumped down onto the sofa, my head in my hands as I tried to comprehend what exactly Lyuba had said to inspire such trepidation in Suzannah, who was usually so unshakable and wise beyond her years.

I felt sick and dispirited by the black curtain of destiny that had abruptly darkened my brightest dreams . . . and now all seemed irretrievably lost.

MOTHER FOUND ME on the sofa in a state of utter desolation, poking mournfully at the small fire. She sat down beside me and gently placing her arm around my shoulders, she softly asked, "And what burdens your soul tonight, dear son of mine?"

"That old woman—Lyuba—she told my fortune, and it did not go well . . ." My voice tapered off as I wiped away tears, until I was ready to continue. "Suzannah barely spoke to me after she heard it, and then she walked out—she went home! I think she is gone, Mother, frightened away by that gypsy."

Mother closed her eyes a moment, fell silent for a few more, and then said firmly, "No, you are still in her heart, now *more* than ever. I sense her great desire to protect you, *not* to get away from you, James. Her heart is yours just as before, but now she knows there will be difficulties to overcome . . . *together.*"

At first I was speechless. When I finally recovered myself, I repeated "*Together?*" in disbelief.

"Yes, of course. She is devoted to you, James, never forget that or take it for granted. With each passing day, you are growing closer . . ."

Mother paused thoughtfully after that, gazing out the window at the sunset, then at the Ellingwood house. When she found the words she was looking for, she said, "Life is seldom easy and often filled with challenges. Soothsayers may indeed be correct, at least sometimes, and if so, you can prepare for the future they predict to avoid the entanglements that might otherwise await you. You and Suzannah are stronger together—and fear not, she will always love you, James, no matter what happens. I believe your destinies are joined in this life."

Mother's words were like a balm on my soul, quieting my raging doubts. I tried to recall what Lyuba had said that so stirred things up, but couldn't except in the broadest detail, so I decided to dismiss her from my mind. What it came down to was, she handed me a bag of hokum in payment for my generosity and compassion, and I would never see her again.

Sensing my relief, Mother tousled my hair, saying, "Lyuba has continued on to Boston because I paid her remaining passage. But remember, Suzannah will be back here tomorrow, so you needn't worry that she's gone from your life. I still have some last-minute packing to do for my trip to Boston tomorrow, but I think I'll have enough time to make warm custards for dessert tonight."

That put the finishing touch on the whole affair for me—my miserable mood was now replaced by one of good cheer. How thankful I was to have Mother as my heart's guiding light. Hugging her gratefully, I wondered what I would do without her keen wisdom and tender concern.

THE LONG JOURNEY

was jolted awake by a loud thumping and banging below me, as though an exceedingly restless horse had been led into the parlor. When I remembered that Mother's departure for Boston was imminent, I realized that the noises were probably associated with preparations for her trip. So I rose immediately to offer my assistance and to share our goodbyes.

I drifted downstairs and peeked into the parlor, where six lighted candles and a crackling fire revealed two large trunks that were about to contain dresses, shoes, parasols, coats, mittens, gloves, and most noticeable of all, silver and gold specie. I had no idea we were so wealthy until I saw the several large bags of coin on the floor that would soon be nestled among Mother's clothes.

"Good morning, dear son!" was her joyous greeting. Mother looked alert, bright-eyed, and more energized than I think I'd ever seen her. And yet, when my eyes wandered groggily to the tall clock, I was astounded to see it was 3:47 in the morning!

"Good morning to you too, Mother," I said, rubbing away the slumber from my eyes. And then as I surveyed the sheer quantity of items destined to accompany her, I added, "I didn't realize you were going on such a long trip."

"Well, James," she explained, as she was filling the first trunk, "the deals I'm expecting to transact do *not* always happen instantly. The bargaining table is where one lives until the deal is done. So I expect to be at least eight to ten weeks in Boston."

Father entered the room just then with a bundle of female unmentionables, stockings, and strangely enough, a pair of small leather boots. He offered sheepishly, "Just in case it snows . . ."

Mother stopped what she was doing to approach Father and entwine her arms about his neck. "Ah, my dearest husband . . . preparing me for *any* contingency?" she purred, as she pressed herself seductively against him, and planted a perfunctory kiss upon his lips that soon grew into something more passionate.

Father dropped his bundles on the floor so he could fully return her embrace, until Mother, laughing and squealing with pleasure, wriggled free.

Peppering his face with little kisses, she warned, "Now, Jim, playtime is done for now, but there will be plenty more when I return, so back to business . . . James!"

After Mother withdrew from his embrace, she turned to grasp my hand and pull me over to the sofa. When we were seated, she put her head close to mine and whispered, "My heart senses you are sad, James. Is it because I'm going away?"

"No, Mother. I was just thinking about how close you and Father are, and hoping that I have the same kind of marriage—someday."

"Indeed?" she asked, her eyes widening at my unexpected reply.

I felt at that moment that I'd never looked so deeply into my mother's eyes before. Now that I did, I think I saw what Father saw: two beautiful pools of dark blue that radiated love, kindness, comfort and security. I had the same feelings when I was with Suzannah— I felt safe.

"You are thinking of Suzannah, aren't you?" Mother asked softly.

"Yes. I hope to have with her what you have with Father."

Drawing her arm to embrace my shoulders, she replied, "I believe you shall, James . . . my heart feelings tell me so. You and Suzannah will share an everlasting love."

For some reason, I looked up at Father then, who nodded his assent. But I already knew it was the truth—I could feel it deep inside me.

Mother abruptly broke the spell when she rose and demanded, "Now where did I put that ledger book?"

As he watched her scamper off in search of it, Father smiled contentedly before he turned to me. "Well, Jim, this first trunk is full. After Mother checks it, let's get it into the wagon."

A few minutes later, Mother returned with her ledger book and started reciting the contents of trunk number one—item by item. Once everything tallied, Father closed it up and secured the straps, cinching them tightly.

Grabbing the handles, we lugged the trunk outside to the wagon, where Winnie waited patiently in the bitter darkness. As the cold wrapped me in its unforgiving arms, I shivered and found it difficult to breathe; but I still managed to help Father lodge the trunk in a space behind the seat.

As I made some final adjustments, Winnie looked at me forlornly, her soft nostrils covered with ice crystals. Her gaze evoked in me an unexpected sense of loss at the realization that the life and light of our home was leaving.

Trepidation surreptitiously wormed its way into my heart as I reflected on my mother, Ainsley Rennsdale Walker, innkeeper and trader of long ago, returning to the vibrant world she truly loved and clearly missed. She now flew about the house as if suffused with an aura of magical energy—taller and stronger, her eyes brighter, her voice louder and more authoritative. I couldn't help but wonder if my "old mother" would ever return. Would her roles as wife and mother be lost in the press of her new responsibilities?

It then occurred to me that Suzannah's presence in our house at this time of great change was indeed a blessing and a solace to me. Her apprenticeship had successfully groomed her as a reliable, intelligent partner at the trading table, in the kitchen, and with the account books. Mother's lifelong dream had already yielded that rich reward, and hopefully there would be others—though none so precious as that to me.

I returned to the parlor and began to pack the remaining bundles in the second trunk. The first item was a small but heavy object wrapped in green velvet. Curiosity got the better of me, so I opened it up and was surprised to find two exquisite portrait miniatures, one of Mother and another of Father. They were mounted in a gold case that closed like a book to protect them from harm. Mother looked young, *very* young, and Father, it seemed, was but a boy. They were indeed a beautiful couple. I soon realized that the miniature portrait of my mother was an exact duplicate of the painting that hung above our parlor fireplace.

So absorbed was I in my discovery that I didn't hear Mother enter the room. By the time I felt her presence, she was already kneeling beside me.

"That will be yours, when your father and I are gone."

"Gone?"

"When we are no more, James—when we are dead."

I stared at her wordlessly—the word "dead" struck fear into my heart.

Mother stood up and bid us sit on the sofa together. "I want you to have this keepsake as a permanent reminder of who and where you come from, James. Someday you can show your own children this likeness of their grandparents when they were married." She leaned down to take the open case from me and lovingly ran her finger over Father's face. Then, with shimmering eyes, she whispered, "Not one moment would I give back to God . . ."

As Mother's eyes watered with tears, an innocent flush crept slowly across her face—as if she were a youthful maiden caught unawares with her lover. Then she smiled and gently dabbed her eyes with her finger. "My poor mother died when I was only two years old, so having a mother was a part of life I never knew. I have wished my whole life I could remember her face—to pray to, to talk to. I suppose that's why I insisted we have these miniatures done, since I didn't want what happened to me—to happen to my own children. These—and this tavern—shall be our legacy to you.

"Your father and I are married almost twenty-one years, Jim, and we are heart treasures to each other. Never have we exchanged a harsh word, or lost the passion, kindness and closeness of love. Father would never admit it, but he is a true romantic. Last week he confided to Sam Ellingwood a secret wish that the two of us share: which we will do everything in our power to make happen. And I know if it did happen, Jim, my life would be complete."

"I'll remember your words, Mother," I softly replied, placing my hand upon hers. "But what is this wish?"

"Ah! My dear son, I cannot divulge that secret, but in time, it shall be revealed."

Although I looked at her quizzically, I was nonetheless certain that the wish involved me.

After closing the case, she pressed it to her heart. "Although I'll be away from Father in Boston, I'll have his loving presence with me." Then she carefully rewrapped the case and placed it in the chest, adding, "I want *us* to have a thriving tavern. This has been my dream for my entire married life."

"Very well," I replied, "then it will be the best tavern twixt Portland and Boston, especially with you and Suzannah in charge."

"Ah, Suzannah, a sweet loving flower; she has nestled herself in my heart as though she were my own daughter. She will be a daunting trader and an elegant proprietress. With her at my side, our tavern-keeping business will thrive."

She grew silent and gazed into space for a time, then turned toward the window that faced the Ellingwood house, whispering, "I will . . ."

"You will what?" I asked.

"Oh, nothing, James. I was just thinking out loud."

But I followed her gaze through the frosty panes into the early morning shadows, and saw a flickering candle in Suzannah's window.

Mother breathed deeply and sighed.

"What's wrong, Mother?"

"Suzannah was very loving when we were saying our good-byes . . . and she seemed somewhat troubled as she expressed her wish for my safe return."

"Aha! And you replied, 'I will,' through your heart feelings?"

Nodding silently, Mother looked out at the Ellingwoods' again and noticed that the light in Suzannah's window had gone out.

I decided I would ask Suzannah someday about the heart feelings she and Mother had shared.

Father clumped in with his heavy boots, declaring, "Well, if everything is packed, are we ready to go?"

Mother looked at me with moist blue eyes. "Come with us, James. I want us all together on the wharf."

While Mother went off to gather up a few small items she'd carry on her person, Father and I loaded the second trunk into the wagon.

Finally, we were aboard, sitting three across, all ready to go, until Father abruptly dropped the reigns and shot me a beseeching look. "Jim, trade places with me, please," he said as his eyes darted from me to Mother.

"Very well," I said, as I dismounted and came around to the driver's side of the wagon. Once I was situated, I took hold of the reins.

Father took my place on the passenger side so that Mother was sandwiched between us. He held her around the waist with one arm, took her left hand with his free one, and pulled her snugly against him. When they were nestled together to his satisfaction, I could readily see that Father had her in the right position to be held, hugged and kissed, because his hands were free of the reigns. I could sense his happiness—the same happiness I felt with Suzannah next to me.

I smiled to myself as I barked, "Let's *go*, Winnie!"

As we made our way toward the wharf through the spitting snow, my parents chatted, giggled, kissed and held each other close. They also discussed in detail the wide range of items Mother would need to purchase and have shipped back home for the tavern. They remained deep in conversation until we approached Walker's Point, when Father asked me to stop. The sun was peeking over the horizon and we could hear the white caps crashing angrily against the rocks.

Father dismounted and went to the back of the wagon to retrieve a loose bundle. He rummaged through it until he found what he was looking for. Walking back over to Mother, he took her hand and guided her gently to the ground.

"Now, my little Ainsley . . . close your eyes and open your hands."

This she did, while I watched with curiosity. He placed a small box in her hands and curled her fingers around it. "Open your departure gift, dear," he said, his voice barely audible above the roar of the breakers.

Despite the cold, Mother was able to open it without much effort. After peering into it, she delicately drew out a slender golden chain, and then promptly burst into tears.

I leaned in closer to see why the gift had evoked such heart-felt emotion. At the bottom of the chain hung a large gold-framed cameo set against a background of deep blue—*precisely* the blue of Mother's eyes. As the newborn sunlight graced the cameo, it revealed a carved ivory portrait of my father—as he then appeared—rendered in the finest detail.

Mother, her mouth agape, examined it minutely, and words seemed to fail her. She was like a child, spluttering, "Oh . . . my dear . . . James . . . so precious . . . I . . ."

Father lifted the cameo gently from her hands, and opened it using a nearly invisible latch. Inside was a clear crystal, beneath which lay a large lock of his hair. Behind the cameo itself was yet another crystal, protecting a tiny paper that displayed in his writing:

> *Ever faithful,*
> *Ever together,*
> *Ever more . . .*
> *Your loving James.*

Mother collapsed in tears and flung herself into Father's arms. He swung her around as their lips met, seemingly locked together for an eternity, while she sobbed into his kiss.

As I sat in the wagon contemplating my parents, I saw what love brings at its zenith. It was as though their love was born yesterday, instead of twenty years since. With it they had built a castle of eternal strength, greater than the universe itself. If I fol-lowed their lead and mustered the courage of my convictions, I would build a castle of my own with that dear girl across the way. It was then I realized that my air castles—my youthful dreams and reveries—were the basis of what could become my own fortress of love.

Finally, they broke apart, and Mother turned around so that Father could fasten the chain at the base of her neck. Then he stepped back to admire both his treasures, while Mother held the cameo in her hand, gazing dreamily at his likeness carved in ivory. Then she draped her arms around his neck and said into his ear, "James, I wish you near my heart *always* . . . and never shall this be removed to my last breath."

With moist eyes Father replied, "Ainsley, I love you beyond death itself. It's my prayer God deliver you safely home . . . to us."

Another deep kiss sealed their words, and then quick as a fox, Father had her back in the wagon seconds before he climbed up beside her. Once again in the middle, Mother put one arm around Father and the other around me, and she declared to the rising sun, "My heart bursts with love for the two wonderful men in my life! There is nothing greater I could ask for!"

Now it was my turn to speak. "Let's go, Winnie!"

In high spirits, we lurched forward into the sun's brilliant rays as we again headed toward the wharf. As we rumbled across its timbers, we were astonished to see Fanny and Sam awaiting our arrival. Once the wagon stopped, Father jumped off and helped Mother down, so they could greet the Ellingwoods immediately. After the couples embraced, they walked together toward the pier while I backed Winnie up to the loading ramp. I wondered idly why Suzannah wasn't with them, but recalled that she and Mother had already said their farewells the previous day.

The departing schooner was anchored in deeper water, the morning sun silhouetting the deckhands that looked like giant spiders in the rigging. As I climbed off the wagon, a strange little man with a thin body but enormous arms quickly approached me. He had an accent I'd never heard before, and judging by appearances, not one sound tooth in his entire jaw.

"Ho labbie! Ese be goon oop?"

"Oop?" I repeated.

"Aye, ese goon oop?" he asked again.

I paused for a moment to more carefully consider what he said; suddenly understanding he was referring to the trunks, I replied, "Yes, both go on board," pointing to the schooner in the harbor.

He stepped off the wharf into a large whaleboat, and then lifted up his muscular arms to receive the trunks from me.

Handing him Mother's trunks, he carefully placed them in the boat.

"Thank you," I said, looking at him appreciatively.

Suddenly I felt a pair of arms tighten around me and turned to see Mother dissolved in tears. "I don't like leaving everything I love behind!" she sobbed.

Fanny, who was standing nearby, handed her a handkerchief. "Now, Ainsley, you'll be back from Boston in no time, with your business successfully concluded. And when you return, we shall celebrate the tavern with a big welcome home party, just for you."

Sam chimed in, "I will watch the boys, Ainsley. They'll come to no mischief!"

Mother hugged Sam, kissed Fanny, then me, and lastly, Father. It was another passionate embrace, embarrassing me in front of the Ellingwoods. I coughed loudly, hoping to turn their attention away from the spectacle, but to no avail. Mortified, I continued to watch as they remained locked in each other's arms, oblivious to all, their lips and bodies still pressed together.

Fanny leaned over to me and whispered sympathetically, "This is *nothing* compared to their wedding day. Now *that* was a public display never to be repeated!" She smiled at me and rolled her eyes in mock dismay. "Indeed," she continued, "that kiss is still referred to as 'The Kiss' by those still here to remember it!"

"I'm sure . . ." I said feebly, wanting to drop out of sight.

Mercifully, the fellow who'd taken the trunks scurried up a rope using only his arms, and landed on the wharf near us. Clumping up to my parents in his hulking sea boots, he tersely bellowed, "Ere ye done? Ut tide evin noo. Otto eve noo!" Seeing no response to his warning, he boldly jabbed Father's ribs with a finger the size of a belaying pin, shouting, "Ut guhl be *goon* noo, boyoo!" It did the trick—my parents finally broke apart.

"Farewell, darling," Mother whispered to Father as he effortlessly lifted her into the boat. "Big Arms" clambered into the boat after her and grabbed the oars. Then, reaching over with one hand, he deftly pulled a rope, and the boat was magically free of the wharf, heading toward the waiting schooner.

Mother—standing ramrod straight in the stern, her lithe figure silhouetted by the morning sunshine—waved and blew kisses until we could no longer see her.

As the whaleboat disappeared around the starboard side of the schooner, the four of us stood in silent reflection. Sam finally put an arm around Father. "We have a nice fire going at home, and Suzannah has some good things prepared for breakfast. Why don't you boys come over for a while?"

Looking expectantly at Father, I thought that breakfast and a hot fire sounded very appealing. The thought of Suzannah serving it made it even more so.

Father didn't answer Sam, but continued to look forlornly out to sea. The schooner had cracked canvas and was under full sail for the open water. Seeing no sign of Mother on deck, I replied for us both, "We graciously accept your invitation."

"I thought you would," Sam said with a twinkle in his eye.

With some impatience, I poked Father. "Well, shall we head along?"

Despite all the talk of breakfast, his eyes were still trained on the distant schooner. It was now moving fast with the cold winter winds, which compelled us to finally turn away; but before we did, I heard Father utter clearly for all to hear, "May God go with her . . ."

Changes

On the return trip home, as we followed behind Sam and Fanny in their wagon, Father was silent. I could tell that his mind and heart were still with Mother on the high seas. How could I blame him? I felt the same way when Suzannah left for Boston and stayed the entire winter with Francis and Katharine.

"You know, I felt the same way last year, Father," I offered in an effort to console him. Turning toward me, he nodded his understanding and smiled.

I patted his shoulder and added, "Don't worry, Mother knows what she's doing. It won't be easy not having her around—but now we'll have *Suzannah* and *Fanny* to look after us!"

Father snorted with humor, as older men often do when a disagreeable situation is met with an amusing, but unsatisfactory solution. "You're right, son, and you've chased away my dark mood. What a good man you are—and I am damned proud of you!"

As I stopped the wagon in front of our barn, I slapped him on the back. "Thank you for that, Father. Now, from one proud man to another . . . let's *eat!*"

Jumping down from his perch, Father said, "I'll be in the parlor, Jim. Meet me there after you put Winnie up, and we'll head out to the Ellingwoods together."

Working alone in the stable, my own trepidation at Mother's departure continued to bubble up to the surface, but I kept reminding myself that we were not alone. We were with friends who loved us.

As we walked toward the Ellingwoods, I asked Father, "Do you have a preference for what type of tableware Mother chooses for the tavern?"

"No, none whatsoever." He paused thoughtfully and continued, "This is Mother's dream, Jim, and I'm sure she will choose something sturdy, good looking and long wearing." Then he added, "Perhaps after placing forks and knives on the tables, she can train the sailors to eat with a civilized air, rather than grabbing and tearing at the food with their fingers like savages."

I was surprised to hear Father express himself so bluntly. I don't think I'd ever heard him say anything like it before. "I didn't think you cared about such things. Why do you say that?"

"Your mother and your grandmother didn't like the manners of the old days much. The patrons of our original tavern were mostly an uncouth lot. Knowing your Mother as I do, I'm sure she'll want to run a clean, reputable and congenial place of business. Remember, Jim, we will need to court repeat business, and to do that, we will need to be known for good food, good spirits *and* for the good company at Walker's Cove tavern—and nothing less."

Looking at me with a serious expression, he then continued. "Mother and Suzannah will hold to very high standards, and because of that, our patrons will want to return. Many of the old-timers still remember the Mariner's Rest, and Mother's association with it, which will give us an important head start." Pointing toward the Ellingwood home, he added, "Suzannah will be a great asset to our business. We are very fortunate to have her, Jim."

It pleased me to hear this, of course. I observed that Suzannah had kept her sweet girlish ways, while developing into a tigress at trading, a masterful cook and a shrewd provisions manager. Because of these attributes, I was thankful she would have such a significant role in determining our success.

Father knocked on the Ellingwoods' front door, and left it open for me as he was let in. As I followed behind him, I smelled the usual enticing aromas that spell home . . . burning spruce, a touch of spiced rum and mouth-watering cinnamon. All made it feel as though Mother was actually here. We shed our coats eagerly, and made ourselves comfortable on the sofa near the parlor fire to recover from the bitter morning cold. Sam sat down in his rocker and just beamed at us, probably enjoying the same welcome sense of relief and warmth that we were. As Father and I sat there contentedly, we breathed in the intoxicating odors from the kitchen, which served to heighten our appetites.

Suzannah glided in to greet us, looking radiant in a blue dress and white apron. She approached me at my place on the sofa, stretching out her arms and hugging me tight. Smelling deliciously of cinnamon and sugar, her body felt so incredibly warm—probably from being overlong near the kitchen fire—that her embrace made me feel as snug as an infant nestled in its mother's arms. Her daring flabbergasted me, for she did it before Father and Sam as though they weren't even there.

When she finally broke away, she took my hand and tenderly pulling me up, encircled her arm about my waist and guided me into the kitchen. There, a blazing fire enveloped me with its penetrating heat amid the stronger aroma of cinnamon and sugar. I saw a large table whose every inch was covered with steaming plates of the food that scented the air.

Fanny looked pleasantly surprised by my sudden presence. "Well, James, I hope you're hungry for breakfast!" She gestured toward the banquet that was laid out before me, adding sweetly, "I believe your mother would say the same, would she not?"

"But you invited just Father and me for breakfast, Mrs. Ellingwood— not an *army!*" was my teasing reply, as I took in the sights and smells of pumpkin bread, apple fritters, sausages, eggs, pancakes, molasses, cider, tea—and a touch of rum for us to add to the cider against the cold. There was also an apple pie for dessert, sprinkled with dried blueberries.

Suzannah removed serving dishes from the hutch, and handed them one at a time to her mother who piled heaping portions on each.

Saying nothing more, I sat quietly in a chair, content to observe Suzannah help her mother with the preparations. Listening to their delightful chatter by the morning flames, I noticed Suzannahs's voice had a gentle earnestness in its tone . . . a particular honesty and meaning that could never nurture the slightest thought of guile.

While stirring a cauldron suspended on a fireplace crane, Suzannah threw me a lingering glance so flushed with honesty and glowing hope, it burned into my brain with never forgotten memories. So mystical and dreamy did my thoughts become, I forgot about breakfast altogether; until I abruptly came awake when I heard the booming voice of Sam Ellingwood. "Well, now, I would say it is time to put the feedbags on *these* horses!"

Father trotted in behind Sam as he entered the kitchen, and the two men seated themselves at the table. But Fanny chased us all into the dining room, where Suzannah had already started setting out the food.

The table was decked out in all its finery, and was far more elaborate than a typical everyday meal at the Walkers. There was a fine linen cloth with an openwork lace trim draped over the table. Each setting consisted of matching china plates, rather than the pewter ones normally used for breakfast. There were also delicate porcelain teacups painted with pink flowers and green leaves resting on matching saucers. The knives and forks were placed on linen napkins embroidered with a colorful floral design. It was evident that we were regarded as guests of special significance, and this was the Ellingwoods' way of expressing it—or should I say Suzannah's way?

At all events, we enjoyed a long and pleasant breakfast, mingled with enthusiastic talk about the tavern. After we'd finished and the dishes had been cleared away, Sam carefully laid out his newest set of drawings before Father and me, so we could review the finer points of the structural conversion. These included a detail of the front—the South Elevation—and an enormous chimney on the center left. The windows that faced south would be enlarged to allow in more sunlight, thus burning fewer candles during the day. What candles we did burn would be installed in mirrored wall sconces to reflect more light. And the huge fireplace would provide warmth at night, as well as illumination. All the ideas about how to maximize light came from Mother.

Suddenly, I felt a gentle arm thread its way around my waist. It was Suzannah, of course, who pressed closer to me to view the drawings. "Gosh, the tavern is going to be beautiful, Jim."

In reply, I put my arm around her waist and squeezed, and then she, in turn, playfully pressed her hip against my leg. My face flushed as I squirmed from the physical sensations that ran through me.

Fortunately, Sam caught my attention as he started talking about the mechanics of the construction. "First, we'll need to construct three bents just for the addition . . ."

"What is a *bent*, Father?" Suzannah interrupted.

"A bent is a frame consisting of interlocking timbers that form a truss," Sam replied. "These will define the cross section of the expansion space. We will then build upon the bents by filling in the connecting beams and joists," he added, indicating a drawing of the expansion space, with all the posts, bays and bents labeled, and the various joints that would be needed at all the junctions."

"Oh, now I see how this all fits together," Suzannah exclaimed happily.

As I contemplated the drawing, I made a mental note of the names of the joints: dovetail tenons, knee brace joints, mortise and tenon joints, and tusk tenons. Each was numbered, and the corresponding numbers were located on the drawing's frame junctions.

Sam turned our attention to another drawing that showed a different building, the style similar to that of our new tavern but containing five doors with designs cut into the wood: two with a blazing star, and three with a crescent moon. "This is what I call a Pennsylvania inn—commonly known as a privy!" Sam said with enthusiasm as he held it up so we could get a better look.

Suzannah looked bewildered, as did I.

Sam, noticing our confusion, cleared his throat to explain. "For those who are unfamiliar with the signs, the crescent is for the *women*, and the star is for the *men* . . . and the structure should be embowered far back from the tavern itself," Sam said as he sniffed suggestively, but said no more.

Fanny, who'd just finished in the kitchen, came in at this point in our discussion. She looked at the drawing and remarked, "Well, at least you gave the womenfolk an ample number of seats!"

"Indeed," replied Sam, "especially generous, considering most of the patrons will be men!"

"Well, thank you, kind sir!" Fanny replied, sarcastically, tapping his nose lightly with her index finger. "You should be glad that *men* don't have to wear petticoats!"

The excited chatter over the drawings continued until a knock came at the door. Outside was a small crew consisting of carpenters, excavators and shipwrights who had arrived for a meeting that would soon commence in the parlor.

I sat in as the plans were distributed and carefully reviewed, followed by a discussion of what would be expected in the way of their services and when. It was decided that the work would begin the following day. The expected chronology was as follows.

First would come the excavation for Mother's new ground cellar with a bulkhead, which would connect to an integrated well shaft, which would in turn be incorporated into the expansion space. This arrangement would provide ready access to food and water under one new roof *and* in one cellar, making it unnecessary to venture outdoors for either necessity.

In tandem with the cellar excavation, a new foundation of granite blocks would be laid, which would support the new expansion space. Constructing the bents would come next, which would then be raised and supported on the granite blocks. Because our forge had no floor, it would be moved so that the new privy pit could be easily dug there, and the privy itself constructed over it. The clock shop would thus remain in its present position because of its wooden floor.

Once the meeting was concluded, Father and I stayed on at the Ellingwoods, since we were invited to stay for dinner. Then, at last, we returned to spend our last night in the place that we called home. Starting tomorrow, it would be transformed into a tavern.

Before retiring for the night, Father came to my chamber and sat on the bed. "Jim," he said, looking out the window toward the Ellingwood house.

"Yes, Father?"

He put his hand on my shoulder and his eyes met mine. "I know this is a big change for you, son. It was a big change for me too, when I was about your age—perhaps a little older—and watched as my home was turned into a tavern. As construction progresses, your childhood memories will slowly be stripped from the old home you love, but they can never be taken from your heart. Remember, the sorrow that may oppress you now is not for the lost memories, but for the *reminders* of them. The memories themselves will always remain—your mother and I promise you that."

"Thank you, Father," I murmured as he reassuringly patted my shoulder and left, gently closing the door behind him.

When I was finally alone, I lay awake—thinking about our "new life" and all the changes that were taking place. My boyhood home was slipping away . . . and Father was right . . . there were so many memories to hold so dear—and as silent tears rolled into my pillow, I clenched my blanket and helplessly wondered, "What would this new life bring?"

As I LAY in bed still half asleep the next morning, I vaguely heard the sound of picks and crowbars imbedding themselves into terra firma. As I came awake, when I heard the clanking of shovels against rock followed by human grunts, I knew that construction had begun.

I sprung out of bed, dressed quickly and practically flew downstairs to the kitchen, when I suddenly felt crushed by the realization that Mother was not there! No loving greeting, no fire, no cinnamon, no sugar, no fritters.

As I stepped outside the back door, the freshly dug trenches for the foundation hinted at how huge this addition would be—our tavern was going to be enormous.

A musical "James, come on over for breakfast!" greeted my ears, and I could see Fanny at her back entrance, waving frantically in my direction. As I headed toward her, Father approached me wearing his leather apron, which meant he was already working in the forge.

"Jim, as soon as you finish eating, come out to the forge," he said with a note of urgency in his voice. "We need to make as many nails as we possibly can before we have to move it."

"I'll be there soon," I said. So this was it, I thought, knowing that the conversion would begin with the excavation for the new foundation and the forging of the first nails.

When I arrived at Fanny's back door, I was greeted with a welcome blast of warmth from the kitchen fire. Breakfast consisted of the same fare as yesterday—and was just as good—accompanied by a tin of cider laced with rum to stave off the morning cold.

Suzannah, looking exceptionally lovely, breezed by me with a loaded plate. "Good morning, master blacksmith. You'll need to eat hearty to swing your hammer today."

"Indeed, beautiful one!" was all I could muster. She stopped abruptly to turn around and with a loving look she asked, "You *really* think me beautiful, Jim?"

Despite the loud clanking sound of the tools outside, I could only whisper, "I do!"

Then, almost as an afterthought, she set the plate she was carrying before me. "Jim, you take this one, Noah can wait a little longer . . ."

I sat down and picked up my fork. "You are too good to me, Suzannah!"

At that moment, I thought she would kiss me, so I waited patiently in eager anticipation. But Fanny suddenly appeared in the room and told Suzannah to make haste and serve the workers, depriving me of that special pleasure.

Father had the forge blasting. That morning three enormous bundles of nail rods had been delivered. Hammering away, he yelled to me above the noise. "I'm glad to see you, son. I'm making two-inch nails, and I need you to make three inch and four-inch nails. That last bundle there is for five-inch-long spikes. Sam wants to use dowels, but would like spikes for extra strength on the sills. We need to finish them before they start demolishing the walls and moving the forge. We have about a week."

Having received my orders, I donned my apron and thrust my first nail rod into the coals. After securing my favorite two-pound mallet, I withdrew the orange rod and hammered the end point. Then I dented it at three inches and shoved it in the nail header. I snapped the rod off in the header and peened over the protrusion above the header face to form the nail head. Finally, I dipped both into a bucket of water, since the shrinkage caused by cooling loosened the finished nail from the header.

All the while, Father kept up a running commentary without missing a stroke of his hammer. "Sam has one pit saw and two pole saws rigged outside his shop for the heavy timber—the sills and summer beams and such, which are being dragged up now. They have broad axes to start the heavy work, and will lay the finished pieces behind Sam's barn."

Give a man enough work to do, and it seems he forgets his life outside it. Relentlessly pounding away, side by side with Father, I didn't think about Suzannah, Mother's absence, or the fate of my boyhood memories for even one moment that day—and the kegs of nails filled up. It felt good to be a pair of second-generation father-and-son blacksmiths, engaged in a common goal for the betterment of our family.

NIGHTS, AFTER A day at the blazing forge, begged for sleep—and that's just what we did. Often we were even too tired to eat dinner with the Ellingwoods, welcoming only a kettle of hot water and a wash up before bed to relax our aching muscles. But many times we were pleasantly surprised by an unexpected visit from Suzannah, who brought us baskets of food and read aloud from her letters from Mother about her progress and her adventures in Boston.

On Sundays, we quit work early and went to the Ellingwoods' for supper. There, during tween time, we relaxed in their parlor: me in Sam's rocker, Father in an armchair and Sam at his table, revising his drawings to reflect the current stages of completion. Invariably, Sam's rocker lulled me to sleep, an occurrence for which I was now famous in the Ellingwood house.

As fall settled in, Sam became concerned about getting the new addition enclosed before it was too cold or snowed. But our routine changed little as the bents were pieced together, using dowels and our freshly made spikes. As the existing structure was disassembled, almost all the materials were saved for reuse in the new one.

The weeks flew by and the foundation stones were laid, the basement and water well excavated, and the brick for the well shaft was in place. The next stage was to build the living areas above the great room: a new twenty-by-fourteen-foot bedchamber for my parents, with a yawning fireplace centered on its inside wall, and six additional guest chambers, fourteen feet square. This would bring the total number of guest rooms to nine.

Amidst our labors, the snow finally came, and the cold encouraged all of us to work as quickly and efficiently as possible so the walls could be closed.

Meanwhile, Mother wrote to us weekly, while Father anxiously anticipated her letters. She was enjoying the company of Lydia and Fay, but the many signs of unrest between the Tories and freedom seekers made Boston a hotbed of dissent. Despite the political turmoil, Mother managed to place orders for the tables and chairs, pewter ware, mirrored sconces, and the dozens of cooking utensils and other items that were deemed necessary for the tavern. Father kept a record of everything she listed in her letters, since he would use it to reconcile the quantities when they eventually arrived.

Mother also mentioned that she and Lydia had the pleasure of meeting Simon Willard, the clock-making prodigy who was becoming the great master of his trade despite his tender age. He and his brother, Benjamin, had a small shop on the family farm in Grafton, which they worked in addition to making clocks. Mother said his tall clock movement was equal in quality to Father's best efforts, and perhaps a bit more robust. Lydia had written separately about Benjamin's musical tall clock—she had seen it and heard its music—but said the price was beyond the means of most ordinary folk. She added that having now seen the competition, she was comforted by the thought that we were embarking on a new business!

Not surprisingly, Father scowled when I read what Lydia had written.

"Perhaps it gives us a standard to measure up to," I suggested. "Remember the clock I oiled at the Ellingwoods' house? That was a work of art, Father. Willard took a poor one-day movement and gave that clock a striker, a calendar and moon phase mechanism, all in one elongated case, which added the illusion of greater size and sophistication. That was the one I thought would be better with a large dial."

"Yes, I remember when you worked on it, Jim, but when I saw the movement itself . . ." he sighed gustily before he continued, ". . . let's just say that boy is a talent to be reckoned with!" He paused and then added, "Perhaps blacksmithing and tavern-keeping *are* best for our future, as Lydia suggests." And he left it at that.

I pressed on and read Mother's final paragraph to Father. "Even if the undercurrent of general unrest wasn't a constant shadow upon my visit, I can scarcely wait for the closest opportunity to be nestled once again with those I love."

How that line made us smile . . .

By the time winter's full force was upon us, the façade of our tavern was done. The new windows and fireplaces were functioning properly and were beautiful to behold. In their light and warmth, we laid floors of wide yellow pine, free of knots. It filled the rooms with the wonderful aroma of freshly cut wood, which could conceivably inspire any man to build something—*anything*—so long as he can inhale its perfume while doing it.

We had less time to spend socializing with the Ellingwoods as we fitted the new fireplaces with jacks, cranes, firedogs, kettles and hooks—the items Mother specified before she left. Father, Sam, Fanny and Suzannah outfitted the new chambers with furnishings, and I helped the carpenters complete the plaster walls in the new kitchen and great room. It was our hope to have everything ready by the time Mother returned, and we finished just before Christmas.

It was Saturday night, the 23rd of December, when Father and I retired to the Ellingwoods'. We had a warm and cozy dinner that night as the four of us planned a celebration for Mother, who would return as soon as she could book passage. Comforted by the soothing tick of the Willard clock, I stretched out in the rocker, gazing through the window at the winter darkness, savoring these moments before the fire with Suzannah so near.

The wind had begun to swing into the northeast, bringing snow and ice pellets with it. I heard the pellets tapping lightly on the panes as though asking permission to enter. I shivered as the thought of them made me cold, and drew closer to the fire to ward off the sudden chill that seized me. Meanwhile, Suzannah set a tray upon the side table laden with pemmican, cheese, tea bread, tea and hot buttered rum for all of us to enjoy.

As the snow piled up outside, we were happily engaged in discussing the festivities for Mother's homecoming. Her recent letters indicated that because of the tensions in Boston, finding a ship was very difficult. It had become necessary to first bribe a captain to make it worth his while to chance seizure by the British, which few had the appetite to do at any price. Mother also informed us she had hired a scullery maid, one Dimmis Sexton, who would return home with her. Mother wrote that Dimmis would happily work the kitchen and great room, assisting with cooking and serving.

As I contentedly chewed a stick of pemmican, the fireside talk turned to Christmas Day. Sam and Fanny insisted we celebrate the holiday there, because it was unlikely Mother would be home by then. I continued to relax before the hot fire and drift away while Suzannah, wrapped snugly in a blanket, cuddled beside me on the floor. Laying her cheek upon my leg, she entwined her fingers within mine, seeking to gain my attention. I gently squeezed her hand in acknowledgement, and when she looked up at me, her hair fell back, revealing her angelic face before the firelight. With my heart fluttering at her loveliness, I softly whispered, "How much Heaven can I stand in one lifetime?"

With loving affection, she softly replied, "As much as you desire . . ."

At such a response I became lost in her warm and soulful eyes . . . she was so beautiful and comforting, and as I lovingly stroked her fluffy hair, playing with the curls at its ends, I felt an overwhelming contentment that never came upon me before now . . . a relaxing secure feeling that told me, "This is how love is *supposed* to be."

Our mutual reverie was broken when Fanny and Sam started discussing a piece of lace they wanted to use to adorn the sideboard at Christmas. Sam thought it a bit too yellowed, and suggested that it be starched and ironed.

Suzannah hastened to voice her objection. "Lace is never starched or ironed, Father! I can wash it in sugar and water, then in milk, which will stiffen it and give it a creamy color. We can then lay it out before the fire to dry, and it will be fine."

Fanny rose and ferreted through a drawer in the sideboard. She removed a square of fabric and held it up to let it unfold. It was a large rectangular piece of lace, with delicate patterns stitched within its borders.

Suzannah rose to examine it closely, as did I. I had never seen such exquisite needlework before. As Fanny draped it across the sideboard to show its detail, I noticed it fit the surface perfectly.

"Where did you get this?" I asked, wondering what gifted hands created it.

"My mother made it when she was a young girl," Fanny explained. "It was just before her wedding, when she was so stricken with rheumatism she could barely move. Weary of being idle, she was determined to make this lace to occupy herself. She told me that because she'd lost the use of her fingers for work such as this, she only had strength enough in them to set her needle and then pull it through . . . with her *teeth* . . . and this is the result."

After pausing for a moment to let us study the lace more closely, Fanny continued, "Mother used it for this sideboard after she married, and now it's mine. It was mother's wedding gift to me when Sam and I were married—and Suzannah, *you* shall have it when you are married."

Suzannah hugged Fanny, exclaiming as she did so, "Thank you, Mother. I feel honored that you've kept this for me."

At that moment, a fierce blast of wind suddenly rattled the east window, nearly shattering it with an unbridled force. The sound distracted Father, who remarked, "Listen to that wind!" He seemed to be the only one of us who noticed the storm outside had intensified to such an extent.

It was Sam's turn now to become aware of the extreme weather when he saw ice crystals forming on the windows. He suggested Father and I remain there overnight—and since it would be exceptionally cold in the upstairs chambers, all of us could sleep in the winter kitchen. There, the fire would be easier to maintain, he explained, by feeding it with wood stored in the summer kitchen, thus avoiding trips outside to dig it out of the snow and ice.

With her eyes shining at the prospect of a possible night of bundling, Suzannah volunteered immediately to go upstairs and retrieve quilts, blankets and pillows for everyone. But as she approached the stairs, her pace slowed and she paused awkwardly. Covering her heart with her hand as if she had suffered a blow, she staggered forward and fell heavily upon the balusters.

"Suzannah—are you all right?" I said as I rushed over to her.

Before I had a chance to lend her support, she managed to lift herself off the balusters, and with slow uncertain steps, approach the east window. Staring into the stormy darkness, she again slowly clutched at her heart. Shaking her head in disbelief, she sharply gasped, "Oh, no . . . this cannot *be*. Dear God, *no* . . ." and collapsed to the floor with a sickening thud.

Shadows in a Mirror

Sam was at her side in a heartbeat, and I right behind him. Together we lifted the unconscious Suzannah from the floor and gently settled her on the sofa. By the golden glow of a lantern, we all watched as Sam placed his ear to his daughter's chest, listening intently while we held our breath. Finally, he lifted his head, exhaled deeply and then declared, "Her heart is beating . . . and she's breathing . . . thank *God*."

Fanny went over to Suzannah and tenderly grasped both hands in her own. Clearly alarmed, she said, "She is as cold as the ice outside, Sam. We need to get Doc over here . . . *now!*"

I stood by helplessly, gazing at my little angel's lovely features in repose, still wondering what caused her sudden collapse. Why did she cry out, "Oh, no!" as though she'd been frightened?

Fanny sat with Suzannah while Sam went to fetch more wood for the parlor fire, thinking warmth was her most urgent need right now. When he left the room, my anxiety for Suzannah peaked, and I whispered to Fanny, "*I'll* go and fetch Doc."

"Thank you, Jim . . . and *please*, tell him to *hurry!*" she replied, patting my hand and looking very worried. "Nothing like this has ever happened before."

As I was preparing to leave, Father came up behind me and said, "Take Winnie, Jim. The snow is already deep and a horse will get you there faster." Then he handed me a pierced-tin lantern, already lit with a candle, to help me find my way to the stable.

When I opened the door, the wind gripped it like a sail, knocking me back violently into Father and covering us with hurtling snow and ice pellets.

"Go . . . Go!" Father yelled as he pushed me outside, shouldering the door shut behind me.

As I held up the lantern—miraculously, the candle stayed lit—and stumbled through the snowdrifts toward the stable, I could smell the spicy scent of the Ellingwoods' fire coming from their chimney. The storm swirled and wailed around me like a recalcitrant child, ever reminding me of who wanted to be in charge.

Nearly out of breath when I finally reached the stable door, I forced it open and slipped inside to be greeted by Winnie's welcome nuzzle. She looked almost a ghost of herself in the lantern light. As I rigged her to the sleigh, I felt she detected my sense of urgency, for she was anxious to be off.

A fear of darkness cannot be fully felt until one is forced to dwell in it. When Winnie pulled us to the open road, obliterated by the night and the storm's snowy depths, I felt a moment of terror and was uncertain of where to go. The whirling snow blinded me intermittently, and the ice pellets pummeled me with a fury that seemed determined to beat me down and defeat my efforts. But knowing the trees as I did, and able to glimpse them at intervals, I used them as a guide to position us in the right direction.

When I yelped, "Let's go, Winnie!" by instinct she knew where to go; but pulling the sleigh was a struggle, for the snow was up to her withers and the sleigh was bound by its floor. But finally, thanks largely to Winnie's valiant effort, we made it to Doc's house.

I jumped from the sleigh and landed in a snow bank up to my thighs. But I managed through a sheer effort of will, to launch myself out of it. In retaliation for my freedom, the storm lashed my face with ice pellets that felt as though a hundred needles were pricking me. After throwing my lap blanket over Winnie to shield her from similar agonies, I flattened myself against Doc's door, pounding it with my fist so violently, that it began to hurt. Repeated poundings finally yielded a flickering light in the window, hazily outlining the grizzled features of Doc Brown observing me, wondering I am sure, what lunatic was at his door on such a night as this.

The door swung open and I stumbled into the room, propelled by the furious wind. Wedging my back up against the door, I pushed it closed, using my legs for leverage. Hearing the latch finally click into place, I looked up, and in the flickering candlelight, found myself greeted by Doc's fearsome countenance. He looked like a demon trying to decide what level of hell to consign me to, evidently for waking him up. As he came more fully awake, he squinted his eyes and said, "My God—Jim *Walker*? What terrible thing has happened to bring you here on such a night as this?"

"Something is wrong with Suzannah. She lost consciousness and we can't wake her . . . we're frightened, Doc."

Placing his candle on a nearby table, he retrieved a blanket, his coat and his medical case, and then hopefully asked, "You got a horse?"

"Yes, Winnie is outside with the sleigh."

Without another word, Doc put on his coat and boots, and into the storm we went. The ice pellets stung us so we had to cover our faces, and with some difficulty we managed to climb aboard; once settled in, Winnie took us back the way we came. Except for the sleigh's turnaround, the return trip seemed much easier; because Winnie retraced the previous path she had trampled into the snow. So we arrived at the Ellingwoods' in half the time it took us to get to Doc's.

While I threw my blanket over Winnie and led her into Sam's barn, Doc thumped loudly on the front door with his boot and was let in by Sam. A few minutes later, I let myself in, accompanied by whirling snow and ice pellets skittering along the floorboards. Sam helped me wrestle the door closed against the wind, and told me that Doc was already in the parlor attending to Suzannah.

Fanny helped me off with my coat and put it near the fireplace to dry, as she kissed me and whispered, "Thank you *ever* so much, Jim. You can't know what worry you have saved this poor mother!"

Too overcome with emotion to speak, I could only take Fanny's hands in mine by way of reply.

"Come," she said, leading me into the parlor, where Doc was bent over Suzannah, assessing her condition.

Sam appeared a few moments later. "From a very grateful parent and friend!" he said as he held out a cup of buttered rum to me.

He'd prepared one for Doc as well, which he placed on a table near the sofa.

After some time, Doc pulled up a chair and sat before the fire with outstretched hands. When he'd warmed them sufficiently, he picked up his cup of buttered rum and took a few quick sips. Finally, he said, "I reckon she is *fine*, Sam."

I could hardly believe my ears as Doc continued before anyone else could speak. "Nothing wrong with *that* girl—not in *the least*. What I would like to find out is *why* she fainted, but she is the only one who can tell us that."

"Well, Doc, when do you think she will decide to wake up and tell us?" Sam asked, in a slightly sarcastic tone.

Doc rose, and ignoring Sam's caustic remark, patted his shoulder reassuringly. "Well, Sam," he replied, ". . . *now* is as good a time as any, I suppose . . ." and reached for his medical case. He then retrieved a bottle filled with powder and a small silk bag, and pouring a little of the powder into the bag, he thoughtfully sniffed its contents. Seemingly satisfied, he quickly tied it closed and brought it over to Suzannah. As he did so, there arose a stench the likes of which I had never known, filling the room with a piercing, penetrating odor.

"What is *that?*" I blurted out, pointing to the little bag.

"It smells *terrible!*" my father added, holding his nose.

"This here is called devil's dung," replied Doc.

"*Devil's dung!*" I repeated, now holding *my* nose. "For God's sake! What's that?"

Proudly dangling the little stink bag before us, Doc cheerfully announced, "Good for almost anything that ails ye! Good for coughs, colds, sore holes and pimples on the backside! Great for the digestion too . . . why, intestinal fermentation is totally *cured* by this miraculous powder! By Jove, just a few judicious snorts will even cure over-imbibing in buttered rum!"

Despite this enthusiastic endorsement, I could only look on with concern as Doc knelt beside Suzannah, gently waving the little bag beneath her nose. Suddenly her nostrils began to twitch, and then instantly flared as they rejected the odiferous powder. Her eyes suddenly popped open and she choked, coughed and tried to sit up, pawing at her face to rid herself of the invasive stench.

"Well, I'll be *damned!*" Sam declared, impressed with Doc's little stink bag of cures.

As Suzannah sat up, she looked at our anxious faces until she noticed Doc standing nearby, staring at her intently.

Doc then kneeled and turned her toward the fire, and while wrapping a blanket around her, gently asked, "How do you *feel*, Suzannah?

Suzannah, staring into the flames with a distant look, replied in a ghostly tone, "Doc, I *felt* something . . . a violent disturbance to my heart, as if it was being squeezed by an unknown force . . ."

"Your *heart?*" he repeated, raising his brows. "What did you *feel?* Was it *pain*, Suzannah?"

Raising her eyes to meet his and then her father's, she vacantly replied, "No, Doc . . . it was . . . a *cry* . . . a sudden cry . . . rather, a *desperate* cry . . . for *help*."

We were all stunned by her words and mystified as to their meaning.

"Can you feel that *now?*" asked Doc, leaning toward her with concern.

Suzannah closed her eyes and pressed her fingers to her temples. While she concentrated her efforts on finding an answer, the storm outside raged on, mocking our hopeful silence.

Finally, after several minutes had passed, she turned to Doc and sadly admitted, "The feeling was *strong* and it *shook* me, but I can't feel anything now . . . save emptiness." She rose and stood alone before the mirror, searching her image for an answer. "Something important has been lost . . ." she gravely uttered, "I feel a dear shadow . . . flitting *by* me . . ." Turning from the mirror, she stepped slowly—almost cautiously—toward the east window, and added the haunting words, ". . . gone from me now . . . and *forever*."

Draping a loving arm around her daughter, Fanny held her close and helped her back to the sofa.

Sam poured her some tea, while Doc returned to his chair, observing Suzannah's every move as he resumed his questioning. "No *heart pains*, Suzannah?"

"No—not the kind you mean," she softly replied, while helplessly shrugging her shoulders.

Doc, satisfied with her recovery, rose to return the little bag to his case. Father then tactfully changed the subject. "So Doc, what *is* that powder, anyway?"

Cinching the strap on his case, Doc casually replied, "*Ferula Asafoetida*—that's the botanical name for it. Some call it devil's dung, stink powder, giant fennel or hing-ting. It's one of the most valuable medicinal herbs there is." Raising his eyebrows, he bragged delightedly, "Can *cook* it too—it tastes like leeks . . . and the folk in the Far East use it to spice their food!"

I nearly gagged at the thought of *any* food tasting like asafoetida smelled; but at all events, it was certainly effective in arousing Suzannah from a dead sleep.

After settling her daughter on the sofa, Fanny had left the room and now returned from the kitchen with warm pumpkin bread. As Sam replenished our tea and buttered rum, he asked Doc to spend the night, an invitation he readily accepted.

After Sam loaded more wood into the fireplace, we all stretched out to warm our bones before its penetrating heat. Despite its comforting warmth, what happened to Suzannah constantly nagged at me; for such a "feeling" as she described is surely of some consequence and should not be ignored. However, as the evening deepened, I dismissed this passing shadow of hers, letting my anxiety wane as she now felt nothing, and her heart feelings were ever true.

The night had been turbulent in many ways; but now that we were together before the friendly flames, all seemed safe and well.

THE GRAY HAVEN

s the storm outside continued raging, we were lulled into a sluggish drowsiness by Sam's buttered rum, Suzannah's pumpkin bread and a *very* hot fire. Father tried valiantly to stay awake in Sam's rocker, but his fluttering eyes surrendered to the elixir of sleep that always accompanies its motion.

I was seated on the sofa with Suzannah who, after having nestled herself in the crook of my arm, had quietly fallen asleep, such that I was obliged to remain sitting up—my head bobbing continuously as I drifted in and out of slumber. During these hazy moments, I observed Fanny and Sam asleep on the sofa opposite, having drawn a blanket around themselves because they were farthest from the fire.

Suddenly, I found myself working away at my clock bench, drilling two massive plates of clock brass. I had drilled the first pivot holes when the bit broke abruptly and became wedged in the back plate. When I attempted to tap it out with my finger, it would not move. Using my brass hammer instead, I began to tap away at the bit shaft, but for some strange reason I kept missing the shaft and hitting the plate instead, resulting in a loud *bink*. I resolved to take better aim at the shaft with the hammer, but no matter how I tried to strike it, I would always miss.

As my sense of frustration grew, the exercise became one of circular absurdity—the more determined I was to hit the shaft, the more I would miss it, banging harder and harder upon the brass plate until the sound overwhelmed me. It finally became so loud that I shouted, "*Goddamned plate!*" . . . and found myself staring into the bed of glowing embers in the fireplace. Looking around the room, I realized I was not working, but *dreaming*. Then I was startled to hear the same metallic sound I'd heard in my dream . . . coming from the direction of the Ellingwoods' front door.

Still half asleep, I gently loosened my arm from Suzannah and nearly stumbled as I went to open it. Throwing the latch, I was met by a snow-encrusted Eben Thatcher with shovel in hand. He burst in, and I forced the door closed behind him.

"Jim, where are Sam and your father?" he asked with a breathless urgency.

Somewhat put out with him for his insistent banging, I answered reproachfully, "Right here, Eben—and damn it, everybody is *asleep!* Why are you here *now?*" I demanded. "And what's the shovel for?"

"For God's sake, Jim, we must *hurry!* A *ship* is breaking up in the damned cove, just below the *point!*"

Suddenly, Sam was beside me, already wrestling with his coat. He too must have been awakened by Eben's efforts to rouse us. "A *ship*, Eben? In *this* weather?"

"A three-master, Sam—or what *was* a three-master!" Eben exclaimed. "Wheezer Hutchinson got some folks down on Walker's Point, but we can't see the wreck much or get near it. We can *hear* it breaking up though, and there is debris *everywhere*, floating into shore. Might'n there be some folks out there who need saving?"

"God help 'em if there are!" Doc replied ominously, hastily donning his overcoat and grabbing his medical case to join the rescue efforts. "What with the darkness, the waves and the cold, they haven't much of a chance."

His pronouncement filled me with a chilling sense of doom.

Suzannah and Fanny were now awake; scurrying around looking for scarves, gloves and anything else they could find to protect us from the storm.

As I was throwing on my outer clothes, Father appeared at my side dressed and ready. "Jim, you bring Winnie and get the sled, some rope and any shovels you can find to the point—and *hurry!*"

As he, Doc and Sam followed Eben into the darkness, I closed the door, and Suzannah immediately rushed over to embrace me. Silent, her gaze alone conveyed a profound distress, until I felt her whole body shudder. Then her lips moved to form words, but she couldn't seem to get them out. Finally, her voice trembled as she said, "Jim, I'm sick with worry . . . with a secret *fear* . . . oh, Jim . . . it's . . ." Suddenly tightening her arms around me and burying her face in my chest, Suzannah burst into tears.

Another harsh bang on the door was followed by Father's commanding voice. "*Jim, we need to go . . . now!*"

I'd never felt so torn as I weighed the urgency of the situation against abandoning Suzannah when she needed me most. For to leave her now, when she was so clearly anguished, was abhorrent to the very core of my being.

"*Jim*, we *need* you!" came from outside the door—this time it was Sam.

Furious at my predicament, I gave Suzannah a gentle push to free myself from her tearful embrace, and without a word opened the door and left.

Trundling through the snow toward Sam's barn and feeling sick to my stomach, I hurled blistering epithets at the storm as my heart broke for Suzannah—and I dared not look back—for fear she'd never forgive me for what I'd done.

AFTER STOWING THE rope and shovels in our sled, I guided Winnie toward the front of the house. Doc, Sam, Father and Eben climbed aboard. As we approached the cove below the point, the driving winds nearly pitched us off the sled and into the drifts, but somehow we managed to hold on. When I heard what sounded like cannon shots coming from the shore, I brought Winnie to a halt.

As we listened to the great concussive bursts, Sam yelled, "Is someone signaling with a *cannon*, Eben?"

"No, Sam, those are the *waves* smashing on the *rocks!*" Eben screamed above the hellish roar of the wind. Then, almost as an afterthought, he hollered to me, "Jim, drive the sled behind the lee of the point. We'll unload over there."

"Will do!" I called back, as Winnie pulled us behind the rocks, thus providing merciful relief from the wind.

Gliding into our shelter, we saw the seas heaving with enormous swells the size of a house, hurtling themselves at the rocks with deafening booms that pressed our ears with pain. They seemed determined to smash everything in their path, and not God himself could end their seething destructive power.

When we scrambled to the seaward side of the rocks, we spotted a knot of men along the shore—lit by lanterns—frantically working their picks and shovels, trying to extricate something tangled in their midst.

"There they are!" cried Eben, and as he led the charge toward the men we followed him, equipped with our shovels and rope. Suddenly he stopped and pointed out to sea, *"There* she is! By *God,* there she is!" he anxiously screamed.

Standing silently, sheltering our eyes from the flying ice pellets, yet straining to see against the coming grayness of dawn, we beheld the distant silhouette of a three masted schooner. She was stranded upon the leeward side of the sandbar, just beyond the cove's protective crescent. The winds lashed her with a fury of freezing sleet and snow. Ice had heavily weighed her topmasts, and through that wind-driven strain, we saw they had been carried away. Now three jagged stumps stubbornly remained—a last act of defiance against the unrelenting storm. The waves battering her side had driven her sideways into the bar, embedding her keel in the sand, while her deck was exposed to the ferocity of the open sea. The sound was sickening to hear: hollow thudding followed by splintering wood as the maniacal sea rushed in, ripping her insides apart. It was a sound I would never forget.

Ezekiel Wilford approached us hollering, "Glad to see ye here. We managed to get a signal fire going down shore . . ." and as he watched the hulk beginning to break up, he added doubtfully, ". . . in case there might be survivors." Then looking down, he said nothing more.

As he patted Ezekiel's back, Father said, "Good idea . . . one never knows, and . . ." Father's voice was eclipsed by the sharp sound of splintering wood and snapping ropes giving way under tremendous strain.

"There she *goes,*" interrupted Ezekiel, looking sadly out to the wreck, then back to us. "Them's the bones inside her breakin' . . . 'tis her *death* cry . . ." His voice tapered off as the skeletal remains disappeared below the mountainous breakers.

"... Them's the bones inside her breakin' ... 'tis her Death cry ..."

Down shore, the men were gesturing excitedly around something they had found. We hurried toward them to see what it was. They had hauled up a large flat wooden board, thoroughly battered and deeply splintered at one end, but with the gold leaf carving still intact. It read: *Sunrise.*

"Damned to hell!" yelled Elijah Abbot. "*Sunrise* is one of Olsen's ships! No wonder she went down so hard. Ne'er a better ship built than *his!*"

As we stood in reverent silence because we'd lost one of our own, we all wondered, *who was on board?*

After enlarging the signal fire, we thoroughly traversed the entire length of the cove, stumbling over ice encrusted rocks and slippery seaweed. Debris was constantly washing ashore with the violent tides, and like hungry cats, we poked and pawed through tangled spars, masts, boards, barrels, decking and lumber. As the grayness of morning broke upon us, not one salvageable item could we find . . . and although we called out to survivors until our throats burned and our lungs ached, to our great dismay, not one person could we discover . . . living or dead.

At midafternoon, our search party headed back, all of us sad, cold, tired and hungry. Other townsfolk had been arriving steadily since morning, so there was no end of people who wanted to help. Unfortunately the storm raged on, giving our valiant searchers no respite from the hellish ice pellets, heavy seas and unforgiving winds.

Father and I returned to our new tavern. Because it was as cold inside as it was out, I built a fire in the new parlor fireplace—and it did not disappoint. In short order, we basked gratefully before its warmth for the very first time.

As I wiggled my toes before the leaping flames, my thoughts turned to Suzannah and the terrible state I'd left her in . . . when there came a light knock upon our door.

Father raised his eyebrows and looked at me, and I shrugged as I said, "I'll see who's there."

When I opened the door, I was thrilled to see Suzannah, bundled up against the storm and smiling so sweetly that my heart leaped in my chest. I threw my arms about her and pressed her to me for a few precious moments, and then led her inside. After removing her coat—wet with melted snow—I took her hand and brought her to the fireside, so Father could greet our lovely visitor.

I was surprised to find the parlor empty, but I supposed he'd gone to the kitchen to find some food for our guest. As I lay her coat near the flames to dry, Suzannah said, "Thank you, Jim, for being such a support for me yesterday."

"Indeed, Suzannah, it is *I* who should be thanking *you*, dear one! I'm so sorry to have left you in such a turmoil last night . . . I know it wasn't *right* . . ."

"But I understood that it was an emergency. You made the right choice."

"I'm so relieved you see it that way, since it felt awful to leave you right then." I felt a load lift from my heart.

"But before you left, Jim, I was trying to tell you something, but I *couldn't* . . ." she said, taking my hand in hers, and added unhappily, "I wish we had my father's rocker here. I would *love* to be rocked right now . . ."

Threading my arm around her, I drew her to my side as she huddled against me.

"Jim, I've carried a secret fear for a long while, ever since you took me on our first sleigh ride."

Disturbed by her confession and recalling the scene before the mirror last night, I asked anxiously, "So tell me, what has burdened you all this time, Suzannah?"

Facing me now, and looking up into my eyes, she softly said, "The ship we saw, Jim, the one still being built that you wished to own someday, do you remember it?

"Yes, I do. It was the *Sunrise*."

"Well, a pall came over me when I saw it then—it struck *fear* into my heart. I felt misfortune would befall that ship . . . I felt it in my *heart*, Jim. The wreck today . . . it's the *Sunrise*, is it not?"

I stared at her dumbstruck, wondering if Sam had already told her—or had she truly foreseen it?

"Your father gave you the news?" I asked, hopefully.

Looking into my eyes and touching her fingers to my cheek, she whispered, "Father has *yet* to come home, Jim. I tried to tell you this last night, but the words *would not* come . . ." As her eyes filled, she whimpered, " Jim, I was so *fearful* . . ."

A violent banging on the door broke the spell, and its urgency was greater than Eben's had been. After looking at Suzannah in total disbelief, I went to open the door. This time it was our postman, Osgood Lovejoy, who stumbled in panting and gasping. "Jim, we *found* somebody! Sam needs the sled. I will *take* you to him!"

Suzannah and Father came into the great room together, and stood by silently when I asked Osgood to repeat what he'd told me.

"We found a *woman!*" His voice cracked shrilly as he explained, "She's half *froze* but we think she's *alive*, and Sam wants the sled to take her down to Eben Thatcher's place. Doc is already down there waiting, because it's the closest house to where we found her."

"I'll get Winnie ready," I said as I hastily put my boots back on and donned my coat. "The sled is still in our barn, Osgood . . . so wait here and I'll come around."

"Thanks, Jim," he replied. Then, turning to Father he fished inside his coat and pulled out a wrinkled letter. "Oh yes, I almost forgot . . . I had this since last week, but then I took sick and stayed in the house till now. I'm sorry to give you this a tad late . . . but better late than never, like they say." Looking apologetic, he handed the letter to my father.

As Father took it, I tarried, and waiting to hear any news, I momentarily forgot the urgency of my errand. Osgood did likewise, and seemed as determined to hear it as I was.

When Father broke the seal and recognized the handwriting, he announced happily, "Jim, it's a letter from Mother!"

Father read it to himself, his lips moving silently. When they suddenly curled into a salacious grin, I knew the letter contained expressions of amorous desires—as hers to him usually did. Then he smiled broadly, and I took that to mean she was coming home at last. Just as suddenly Father gasped and his smile disappeared. His pupils dilated, his mouth hung open and his hands began to shake. The letter rattled as his fingers twitched in uncontrollable spasms.

As Father speechlessly dropped the letter to the floor, Suzannah whimpered, "Oh, God—*no* . . . No!"

Staring ahead vacuously, Father slumped heavily into his chair, his lower lip trembling and his hands fumbling on its arms.

Leaning forward and peering into Father's face, Osgood gently asked, "Jim? Are you feeling well? What news from Ainsley is so happy and yet so *dreadful?*"

With tears streaming down her face, Suzannah finally blurted out, "She's coming *home,* Osgood . . . on the *Sunrise!*"

Hope and Memory

ll I could do was gasp, "*Mother!*" before fleeing the house and pelting toward the barn. My mind raced as I felt it detach from my body, watching my actions from a distant perspective, as an angel might from above. I saw myself hitch Winnie to the sled faster than I ever had before, and felt miserable for whipping her for the first time ever—such was my haste to find Mother. With tears streaming I approached the house, and didn't care who saw them. Rounding the corner I found Osgood waiting, but Father wasn't with him.

"Your father is with Suzannah!" Osgood explained, and then added, "I'm deeply sorry, Jim . . . I didn't *know* . . ."

But there it was: Suzannah *knew* Mother was on that ship without even reading the letter. She was too frightened to say it. That's why she felt and acted as she did. It all made sense now: Mother was in desperate circumstances and cried out for help . . . and Suzannah *felt* it.

If Osgood had delivered the letter on time, would it have made any difference? No. The hand of fate was raised against Mother when she sent it.

Osgood continued, "Suzannah told me to tell you to do what you must, and she will care for your Father."

"Thank you, Osgood. Now, please come aboard."

He climbed on and we drove to the shoreline at the end of Walker's Cove, where we met a group of men huddled around a prostrate form on the ice. Afraid to look for fear it was Mother, I remained with Winnie and the sled to postpone the inevitable for as long as possible. Finally, waiting another second became unbearable, and I decided to go down there after all.

Eben was there and waved me back, calling out that this was the only survivor so far, and we needed to get her to Doc, post haste. I knew then that it wasn't Mother since Eben surely would have told me if it was. As the men carried her in a makeshift stretcher, they struggled across the ice and seaweed covered rocks. Some tripped and fell, cruelly gouging themselves on the barnacles. Despite the rough going, the lone survivor was never in danger of being dropped.

Placing her carefully onto the sled, they slid her body forward so her head was behind my seat. Eben and Ezekiel sat on either side of her, and Eben signaled me to go.

At the Thatchers', we were met by Doc Brown who asked with some trepidation, "Is she still *alive?*"

When we answered in the affirmative, he and a group of women-folk helped get her inside, while I unhitched Winnie and brought her to the Thatcher's barn. By the time I got to the house, I saw that the woman was settled on the sofa before the parlor fireplace. I could see that her skin was very pale—nearly white. But her hair was blood red, and I had never seen such a color in all my days. To me, despite her ordeal, she was beautiful to behold.

Shooing the men out of the room, the women began cutting away her frozen clothes so that Doc could tend to her wounds. I heard one of the women remark that she was Gaelic, and now the ladies' tongues were all atwitter about the Gaelic woman, who now "resided" in Eben Thatcher's home. I wondered if she would ever gain enough strength to be able to speak, for only she knew the tragic story of the *Sunrise*. But that wasn't possible now, so I left to join in the continuing search, and as we searched, my aching heart took on a more urgent and pressing question: "Where were the others on board . . . and was one of them Mother?"

Several hours passed and we would soon be replaced by a new group of volunteers. When they arrived, I decided to return to Eben's house to ask Doc to examine Father and Suzannah when he was finished there. After I was let in, I approached Doc, who was seated at a table before the fire, scratching away on a sheet of paper. He was making notes about his patient's medical condition.

When he saw me, he stopped. "Jim, I thought your father would be with you. I haven't seen him either time you've come here."

Sitting next to him, I whispered, "*He* is why I'm here, Doc. It seems he's not well . . . on account of Mother . . ."

"*Your mother?*" he exclaimed, raising his eyebrows in surprise.

"Yes. You see Osgood gave him a letter today that was delayed because he was sick last week. It was from Mother, saying she'd be returning home . . . on the *Sunrise*."

Doc dropped his quill and stared at me, his eyes filling with tears. "Heavens, no! Are you *certain*, Jim?" And from my look, he saw I spoke the truth.

Choking back emotion, I explained with great difficulty, "Father is in a stupor, Doc. I think he believes mother is *dead* . . . Suzannah is home with him."

Declaring that he had done all he could for his patient for now, Doc rose and strode across the room to grab his case. He let the Thatchers know that he was leaving with me, but would return later. Popping back into the front room and snatching his notes, he ordered, "Let's *go* Jim!"

Suzannah opened the door to greet us—a welcoming angel in my time of desperate need. To me she personified courage and hope when without her I felt neither. I was also eternally grateful to her for tending to Father while I was gone.

As Doc removed his coat and hung it near the door, he remarked, "The room is quite warm, Suzannah. Is that the *new* fireplace I'm feeling?"

Taking his scarf, she replied, "Indeed it is, Doc, and I think it might be one of the best fireplaces *ever*, as it requires little wood to throw off a great deal of heat." Suzannah's observation was a compliment to Mother, who had masterminded its design.

Suzannah left for the kitchen and returned with two mugs of spiced rum to chase away the chill. When Doc praised the flavor, she smiled sweetly and asked him if he wanted another, adding it was "Ainsley's" recipe.

The mention of Mother's name brought a low moan from Father, who until then had been sitting silently, just as I left him.

Doc took notice of the sound and pulled a chair over to Father. He held a lit candle near his face, waving it back and forth to see if Father's eyes followed it, which they did. Then he declared sadly, "He's been put back."

"*Put back?*" Suzannah exclaimed in bewilderment.

"Indeed, little one," he affirmed. "It means he has set up a defense against what he thinks is coming." Leaning forward, his nose nearly touching Father's, Doc softly asked, "Jim, it's Doc, can you *see* me?"

"Yes . . ." he said, in a tone devoid of feeling.

At that point, Doc explained to us that Father was in shock. "I've seen this before in other men, especially those whose wives have left them, which is the worst kind of widowhood. His wife *lives* . . . and yet is *lost* to him. Your father is suffering the same malady. It's the uncertainty that is paralyzing your father. Uncertainty is *very* distressing . . . especially when it involves life and death."

"But Doc, he's assuming she *is* dead . . ." I protested.

Standing to fill his pipe, Doc added, "She is alive until *proven* dead, or lost at sea in this case. She may be out there in the cold, just like the Gaelic woman was, hanging on until we find her. And if she *is* out there, they *will* find her!" He paused, looking pensive, before he continued.

"Your father's body is perfectly sound, Jim; the trouble is with his heart. His lifelong soul mate is missing. But everyone in this town loves your mother—and if she was on that ship, they will leave no stone unturned in the effort to find her. I fervently hope they do, if only to end this hellish uncertainty for your father . . ."

A loud knock on the door interrupted Doc.

Suzannah opened the door and Eben Thatcher stepped inside.

He regarded Suzannah briefly with an air of discomfort, but then his gaze settled on me. Clearing his throat, he quietly stated, "I have news, Jim . . ." and again looked fleetingly at Suzannah.

"Anything you have to say can be said before Suzannah, Eben, so please go on."

Straightening up, he removed his hat before uttering, "Jim, we *found* her . . . and she is your mother no more . . . in *this* world."

At these devastating words my heart gave up its hope against hope, and crushed and desolate, I sat before the fire and wept.

"We have her in the church," Eben continued, "if you wish to see her . . ."

The Bitter Sepulchre

n the rear chamber of the freezing church, Father and I knelt at the coffin, silently contemplating Mother's pale face. Her sparkling blue eyes were now dark and sunken. Her flaxen hair was dull, lifeless and stringy. Her soft full lips were set in a tight grimace, and her gentle hands had become claw-like from Death's relentless grip.

Outside, the unforgiving storm still howled unmercifully, pulling a cold windswept rain into the frosty winter night . . . and its dreary bleakness symbolized the malevolent permanence of Death. As the church timbers groaned beneath its wind, besieged by morbid thoughts, I continued to stare intently at my mother. So this was Death—and never had the specter of death changed the face of life . . . as it did mine at that moment. Waves of anger and resentment seethed within me, because the one who had sheltered my heart with love, kindness and protection had been violently ripped away, leaving it to drift in utter darkness.

Sorely tempted was I, to defiantly hurl bitter maledictions at God; but I was stunned . . . and so floated into a dreamlike purgatory, where there was no color to my life . . . only the blackness of Death. So I silently prayed, "When would the white doves and angels flutter down and guide her spirit to Heaven?"

But Father, his eyes still wet with tears, interrupted my thoughts as he said woefully, "Son, if you take nothing else from Mother's death, remember to make your loving nights linger, and your goodbyes long and very fond . . . for time, distance and death are the mortal enemies of true love . . . and as you see, death can come at any time."

Then, bowing his head over Mother, with his unwavering gaze upon the face that brought such joy to us, and to so many others, he prayed in a quavering voice. "Dear God in Heaven . . . *Death* hath overtaken our home . . . and now we are only *two* . . ." He then placed his palm upon her forehead and softly continued, "Sleep evermore my darling wife, and rest thy weary head, for darkness falls and life hath ended, to Heaven's gate wilt thou be led . . . Amen."

"Amen," I echoed as I watched him bring his face closer to Mother's. Was he going to *kiss* her? I wondered, extremely distressed at the idea, believing it was a sacrilege.

But kiss her he did—a long loving and heartfelt goodbye, followed by the whispered words, "And now my dearest angel, thy heavenly journey begins . . ." Father rose and seemed to collect himself before declaring, "I must see Reverend Metcalf about bringing Mother home, to sleep there for one last time."

After Father left, I sorrowed alone in the sanctuary of God's church, regretting that I inherited Mother's heart feeling ability. For tonight I had *felt* my father's heartbreak . . . his pain was beyond excruciating grief . . . and I shook with fear as to how he would go on without her.

For some reason I noticed the town bible was unlocked and open on the lectern, now located within the chancery. The ponderous volume, bound in thick embossed leather covers, contained not only religious text; it also contained an informal history of Walker's Cove. Curious, I walked over to examine it, and noticed the volume had been left open to the year 1736—to the page where my parents' marriage was recorded. When I read the entry I saw the name, "Ainsley Frances Rennsdale," which struck me as odd since I'd only ever known Mother as Ainsley Walker.

I reflected on what I knew about her before her marriage: that she was a happy, spirited child, full of fun and mischief, who had lost her mother at the tender age of four. Although she was forced to grow out of childhood very quickly, her resilient nature triumphed over adversity, and she became her father's helper at the Mariner's Rest from the age of eight on. Eventually, by the time she was eighteen, she was known far and wide as the very soul of hospitality there, until she married Father and managed his tavern in Walker's Cove. This all happened, of course, long before I was born. Despite her reassurances to me over the years that all her choices were happy ones, I felt a pang of remorse that I *had* been born—since because of me she gave up the life she loved, devoting herself full time to motherhood.

And now, in attempting to recapture those fond early days, Mother had given her life; not only because she missed the old business; but because she wanted to help our family prosper. She was famous in her time as a superb tavern-keeper, and she wanted to capitalize on that reputation for our sake, and the sake of our village.

WHEN I RETURNED home, I saw that Father had gotten there before me and had readied the parlor as the place for honoring Mother. Sam Ellingwood, Doc Brown and I returned to the church, where we met Reverend Metcalf, and the four of us bore her home on the sled, Winnie leading the way.

Not long after Mother's coffin was laid open before the windows of our parlor, Fanny and Rhoda Barrett arrived. Tearfully, with gentle hands, they lovingly washed and arranged Mother's hair, powdered and rouged her face to give it a more natural color, and changed her dress, which was soiled and torn. Around her upper torso they lay boughs of spruce and pine, mingled with pinecones and holly berries, for there were no flowers to be had in winter. The cameo Father gave her on the morning of her departure still hung around her neck, repositioned so it could be easily seen. The candles were lit and placed to throw a soft light to the farthest corners of the room, and the fire was brought up to ward off the chill.

The transformation seemed almost holy—for in the shadows of the firelight, Mother looked as though she was just napping . . . resting her eyes before greeting her guests.

Reverend Metcalf took me aside, and placing his arm around my shoulder, he spoke in a soft confiding tone. "As you know, James, your mother was widely beloved and highly regarded. During this day of mourning and tomorrow's burial, you will meet many people you don't know. Be sure to honor them nonetheless, since many are making a long and arduous journey to share your grief and sorrow." Affectionately patting my shoulder, he added, "Ever remember dear boy, the victory of the grave is all but inevitable. But against the sting of death comes the breath of new life . . . and love . . ."

As these words were uttered, Suzannah entered the room. I gaped at her in disbelief at such perfect timing. She nodded her head in greeting to Reverend Metcalf, then gazed at me, her eyes overflowing with sympathy and concern. Oh, how I wished to hold her at that moment, to console myself in her warm and loving embrace. But she turned and made her way to the coffin, where she bowed her head, her beautiful tresses falling across Mother's bosom.

I began to approach her to thank her, but when I observed her whole body shaking with smothered sobs, I keenly felt the pain of her loss. Suzannah loved Mother deeply, as a daughter would . . . and now in her own grief, she hovered above Mother like the little angel she was.

The next few hours seemed interminable, filled with an all-consuming grief. Despite our internal agonies, we kept our bravest faces—not for ourselves, but for the endless stream of people who came to honor my mother. Some were traders and sea captains of her acquaintance who also knew both my grandfathers—Silas Rennsdale and Richard Walker. I felt an extra measure of family pride hearing Mother praised as a tough but fair trader and consummate tavern-keeper. And I was surprised to learn that at the Mariner's Rest, she received hundreds of marriage proposals, including from some of the men who mourned her now, who claimed to be after a beautiful and astute young wife to aid their business, rather than to warm their beds.

On reflection, I found it remarkable that of *all* the men who crossed her path, Mother fell in love with a young clockmaker who delivered that tall clock so many years ago. The fact that she and her life long friend, Fanny Johnson, came to Walker's Cove together in friendship, and then stayed on for love and marriage, seemed almost like a fairy tale . . . yet it *had* happened! And if Mother *had* married a rich sea captain or some powerful merchant, Suzannah and I would not be . . . and that thought made me shudder.

AND SO WE buried my mother at Grandmother Rebecca's side. Father had arranged his own burial to be on the other side of Mother—so she would ever be loved and protected by both.

The convocation at Mother's graveside was awe-inspiring. We were deeply touched by the outpouring of love as each person tossed a spade full of earth upon her coffin. When the sepulchral dirt formed a well-packed mound, upon its top we laid a wreath of spruce, trimmed with holly and pinecones. Perhaps the most beautiful gesture of all . . . was when Suzannah tearfully placed a bouquet of dried flowers at its center—directly above Mother's heart. As Reverend Metcalf spoke the final blessings, the gentle wind swung northeast, and a pure white fluffy snow floated from the heavens, covering her grave with the touch of angels' wings . . . so soft, soothing and gentle. In my heart, I believe the angels did this just for Mother . . . and nobody can ever prove to me they didn't . . . and so, in the still white silence we left her—along with the life we knew and loved.

THAT EVENING, BEFORE we parted company for the night, Father and I quietly held each other in a long embrace. The dawning reality of Mother's absence crushed his heart and mine. I whispered, "I love you, Father," but knew it was no substitute for her love. His eyes were wet as he whispered back, "I love *you*, son . . . and I love *her*, who is no longer with us . . ."

At first I looked away because I didn't know what else to say. My father seemed like a little boy lost, and there was nothing I could do to restore the sweet life we had in her presence. But then I remembered something he'd said at the church yesterday, and so

I repeated it back to him: now we were two, but we still had each other. He seemed to take some comfort from my words as we solemnly retreated to our respective chambers; but later that night, in silent tears I lay in bed thinking about Father. He was alone in there . . . she was alone outside . . . and his soul was starving without her.

Quietly rising to check on his welfare, the last thing I saw that night—was my poor desolate father, holding her miniature to his cheek . . . crying himself to sleep in her empty pillow.

A New Direction

ince Mother's body was found on Christmas day, Fanny and Sam would not hear of us spending the holiday time by ourselves, so during the following week we stayed with the Ellingwoods.

After a lengthy discussion over their dinner table one night, Father determined that he would honor my Mother's fondest wish: he would proceed as planned and open her beloved tavern. It would mean curtailing his activities as a clockmaker and blacksmith to devote himself full time to tavern keeping, just as grandfather had. He also pledged to never remarry, for his love for Mother was forever—and he was absolutely certain he would meet her in Heaven. So despite the common practice of remarrying for practical reasons, he knew he could never betray his heart . . . or hers.

Amidst all this talk, I wondered how we would fare without Mother's leadership and experience, without her winning ways and good common sense in all things. I thought about Suzannah too, who we needed more than ever now; who would be burdened with a much weightier role than she had before, as she would have to navigate without Mother's gentle guidance.

But in the course of that week we had some unexpected news. We learned more about the woman who survived the shipwreck. Her recuperation was going well, and she spoke Gaelic and the King's English. She informed Doc that her name was Dimmis Sexton, and she had been hired by Mother to serve in the tavern and live upstairs if she wished it. Meanwhile, with the future of our inn then uncertain, Eben Thatcher had kindly offered Dimmis a room and employment after she was fully recovered. Now we had a decision to make: should we carry through Mother's plan to hire her, or let her go her own way?

Since we weren't quite ready to open the tavern, Suzannah offered to visit Dimmis, to get to know her as she imagined Mother had, and to see if she truly belonged in our tavern. When she returned from her mission, Suzannah reported that Dimmis was very likable and possessed a strong faith in God and in her God given abilities. She also played the violin, but sadly her instrument had been lost in the wreckage. Most meaningful of all from Suzannah's viewpoint, was what this hardscrabble immigrant from London had to say about Mother. Despite knowing her only a short while, she had an unshakable confidence in Mother's assurances for a new hope and a new life: for Dimmis had risked everything in her long voyage to Boston, and Mother, seeing that Dimmis was experienced as a cook and a server, and had all the other requisite tavern skills, was justified in offering her a home and a job as her assistant.

The upshot was that Father informed Eben he was welcome to retain Dimmis in the interim, until we came closer to the time when the tavern would officially open. Eben, in turn, was happy to have her in his store, since he had long been in need of help.

I BELIEVE FATHER felt that before carrying on with the tavern, we needed first to heal our hearts—to the extent that we could. And that, at least for me, was very difficult. After Mother's burial, I wished to be alone most of the time, either in the clock shop or at the forge. Being consumed with an iron-willed focus on work suited me perfectly.

Fanny visited often, trying to keep a female presence in our lives. Enlisting Suzannah's help, they would keep house, do our laundry and keep us company. The Ellingwoods generously shared their meals with us—there were two extra settings at the Ellingwood table every day of the week. And the minute we arrived, Fanny would always clasp Father to her heart, hoping to sooth the aching void in his.

Despite such generous empathy, Father and I remained outwardly stoical, hiding our feelings from the Ellingwoods, and worse
yet, from ourselves. And as we mourned all winter, the tavern remained empty, not only of furniture and patrons, but of joy, love and
warmth. Mother's absence was a great chasm that neither Father
nor I could leap over. Indeed, I stood tottering upon its precipice,
knowing I must make the leap to go on with life: yet despite Suzannah's presence, my life could not go on without Mother in it, and
I was completely lost without her.

As time passed, Father and I spent many hours by the fireplace,
sharing fond memories of Mother and speaking endlessly about our
loss. But finally we realized we needed to plan for our future, even
if it was now only for the two of us. We had to know what Mother
had last purchased in Boston, who held the orders and how much
money we owed. After all, our investment in the tavern was taking
nearly all our savings—which had accumulated from *two* generations of Walkers. We also had to be prepared to receive the shipments, by finding out when they were due to arrive.

All of Mother's papers had been lost in the wreck, but in the
course of a conversation at the funeral, Father learned from one of
the mourners that a vendor of imported goods had accepted a size-
able down payment from my mother for pewter and furniture. The
individual in question was well known in Boston as a "Tory"—a
member of a faction still loyal to the crown. The friction between
the Tories and the common folk was considerable, and the knowledge of his political affiliation upset us both, for there was a lot of
money at stake already in his hands.

Father decided he would go to Boston and meet with the vendor
personally to ensure that Mother's order was filled, and that we
would receive the merchandise in exchange for the balance due. He
planned to stay with Lydia and Fay in Boston, which was an especially propitious arrangement since he could call upon Fay for legal
advice. For one thing, Father wanted Fay to help track down a copy
of Mother's original invoice. This would verify that her order was
legitimate. With no record of the sale from her side, the task would
be difficult—especially if the Tory should deny that any such order

was ever placed. What worked in our favor was that the vendor didn't know about Mother's death—or so we believed. Father and Fay could approach him as her representatives, and might thus succeed in finalizing the deal and arranging for delivery. Finally, if it became necessary to seek legal remedies from the crown, Fay could help Father expedite the process.

I was to remain at home while Father was in Boston, and he entrusted me with the work orders that had to be completed in his absence.

WHEN FATHER'S DEPARTURE was imminent, he elected to travel the ninety miles to Boston on horseback—to avoid the sea at all costs. Indeed, I was delighted and relieved when William Richardson loaned him a well trained riding horse. Father would now be safe, and I would still have Winnie for use here.

The morning he was to leave, while we ate breakfast with the Ellingwoods, Father laid out his plans for me to follow in the coming weeks. He then hugged each one of us before he left, and I felt his gratitude for having our support. He was departing on an errand that honored Mother while signaling a resigned acceptance of her absence. His bittersweet tears revealed the inner man I seldom saw, yet knew existed. During those precious moments, I saw what Mother saw—and it was no wonder to me that she could not bear to be without him.

I knew I didn't yet have the strength to move on as he did, which made me especially proud of his determination to see Mother's dream fulfilled. In this singular act of love, Father was also demonstrating a strong commitment to our lives, as—almost four months after Mother's death—he boldly leaped over the chasm.

She was in his heart . . . and watching horse and rider slowly vanish down the road, I prayed to God that *someday*, I would find the strength to follow him.

THE WEEKS PASSED slowly, and I was lonely without Father. During the day, I busied myself at the bench, finishing all the tasks left for me to do—filling the existing orders for clock jacks, and occasionally making movements for peddlers who depended on our prompt service.

At night, I would retreat into my parents' chamber, and lovingly press Mother's pillow to my heart, whispering into it the inner secrets of my soul. I pretended that I was still holding *her*, and crying into *her* soft beautiful hair, just as I did when I was a small boy—but where were the comforting arms that made *everything* better? Night after night I tearfully begged her spirit for guidance and remission from the constant heartache I endured without her.

Yet here I was, alone in this new, empty structure that resonated with the void in my heart. I felt as if I didn't belong here, but rather in a cozy place with a warm fire and the close comfort of a family. But this was definitely not that; so I soldiered on as best I could—by isolating myself with my pain, and keeping busy.

I WAS NOT accustomed to having visitors in the clock shop, so I was rather surprised when I heard a shuffling sound at the front door—particularly since there was a nor'easter raging without. When I looked up from my bench, I saw it was Fanny in the doorway, struggling with the cloak she wore to protect her from the rain. As I put down my tools and rose to greet her, I assumed she was just checking in on me, as was her wont. When she finally stumbled inside, nearly half drowned, she shook out her hair so it lay in natural waves around her shoulders. At that moment, she put me in mind of Suzannah. I had not realized before how closely they resembled each other.

"Well, I wonder if there'll be any rain left for anybody *else* in the world besides *me*?" Fanny remarked as she stood before my fire, drying her hair by fluffing it with her hands.

I watched her wordlessly, lost in admiration for her beauty. With her hair down, Fanny was exceptionally pleasing to behold.

Finally, I found my voice. "Sorry to have gotten you out here in such frightful weather," I offered. "You needn't have braved the elements just to see *me*."

Fanny beamed at me as she said, "Your mother and I had an agreement to look out for one another—and that included our children. When I was confined with Lydia, your mother was my constant nurse and companion—a little angel hovering about the room, tending to every need there was, and while running her own tavern!"

The mention of Mother in her youth brought a smile to my face, for it felt like the first happy thought I'd savored since her death.

"I took the better deal from your mother," she continued, "for I ended up with five children to her one, so she did much more for me than I ever did for her. But now I can make up for that, by helping you in any way I can."

Fanny stepped closer and gently placing her hand on my shoulder, softly added, "Jim, to be alone in life is a *terrible* thing. It makes folks bitter and hard, like poor Rhoda Barrett. I don't wish to see you turn into someone like that."

"I shall *never* be like Rhoda," I replied firmly. "My heart is just the opposite of hers. It yearns for companionship and love." Then, looking directly into her eyes, I softly confessed, "I'm certainly troubled by Mother's loss now, and I try to carry on as Father has, hoping that the pain of her loss will pass. But the pain is still there . . ."

Taking my hand, Fanny sat down on a stool, and motioned for me to sit on the one beside her. As I did so, she placed her other hand on mine, a sweet gesture that brought tears to my eyes; for it was what Mother always did when she had something to say. "Jim, *dear* Jim . . ." she said, pressing my hand lovingly, "please understand that I *feel* your loss, which is perhaps even *equal* to yours! I've known your mother since we were *little girls*! We shared *everything* we had—our hearts most of all, because we *had* little else."

"That miserable old *coot*, Silas! He never let her have a proper girlhood. Most of the time she was busy with her work at the Mariner's Rest. So together we *made* her childhood—and it was easy because we loved each other's company. We played, did our school work, learned to cook and sew—did *everything* together. We made our first samplers when we were twelve, and learned the arts of niddy noddy and spinning at fourteen. We had our first suitors at sixteen. And, as you well know, we were both married together in your father's sleigh . . . at eighteen."

She paused as she rose from her seat and went over to her cloak that was drying by the fire. She retrieved a piece of cloth from one of its pockets and brought it over to show me. I could see that it was densely embroidered with letters, numbers, flowers, birds and other animals. The colors were rich and beautiful, as was the intricate needlework. When I looked more closely, I could see it was Mother's sampler. Beneath the carefully stitched letters of the alphabet and the numerals **1** through **0**, the following verse appeared:

> When life for thee is full of dread,
> Think of flowers in gardens deep,
> And how they give thy weary head,
> A restful peaceful place to sleep!
> Ainsley Frances Rennsdale . . .
> Her Work . . . Dec 24, 1730

"This is yours now, Jim. I've had it for years and years." Laying it upon the workbench, she gently patted it flat. "I know Ainsley would want you to have it."

As I reached over to pick it up, I was mesmerized to actually *touch* something my mother created—some thirty-nine years ago, at the tender age of twelve.

While I examined her handiwork, Fanny gazed out the window at the rain. "Ever remember, Jim, *life* is but the road to death, but God grants us the privilege of making the best of our time . . ." Turning to me and taking my hands gently within hers, she softly added, "Perhaps I might leave you with this little thought: trying to light a warm fire from cold embers . . . is like trying to kindle love from a loveless heart. First there must be life, warmth and *love*. And to love and not *be* loved . . . is *precious* time lost."

Her eyes moist with tears, Fanny kissed my forehead as she prepared to leave. Before opening the door, she winked at me and
announced, "We have dinner at six of the clock. I don't think you'll
be late . . . considering you are a *clockmaker*." The next thing I
heard was the latch close behind her.

I held Mother's sampler while listening to the rain, contemplating the hidden meaning behind Fanny's heartfelt advice. There was
indeed a special depth to her words, for I suddenly realized I hadn't
spent time alone with Suzannah in a very long while; and I knew
I needed to see her sooner rather than later—more than anything.

THE RELEASE

hat night, dinner at the Ellingwoods' was frustrating and awkward, for I desperately wished to be alone with Suzannah. But Sam was eager for news of Father's progress in Boston—asking me in detail about Father's letters—thus making the time that separated us from each other seem interminable.

Fay had located the Tory for Father, and the order had indeed been placed by Mother and was fully documented. Everything would be delivered by ship directly to Walker's Cove in the fall, which meant we would be able to open our tavern before next winter. Meanwhile, Father would tarry in Boston to ensure the quality and quantity of the goods, and oversee the bill of lading when the items were loaded onto the ship. Then he would return home the same way he came—by horse.

As I feared, because the dinner went on so long, Suzannah took me aside and told me that she was too tired to talk then, but suggested an outing the next day to Walker's Point—just the two of us. She promised to bring a basket of goodies. Having fond memories of our days together at our sacred spot, I quickly warmed to the idea with a growing sense of excitement. It was the first time I'd felt that way in months.

THE WEATHER DID not disappoint, for the sun shone brightly in a cloudless sky. As we sat together cozily enjoying our picnic, I felt my sorrow lifting, my burden easing, by just being in her presence again; but for some inexplicable reason, I couldn't share my feelings with her.

The time flew by, until I noticed with some surprise that the sun was already setting. Wisps of the retreating sea breeze whispered through the pines, seemingly begging our hearts to listen. Suzannah rose to pack our remaining food in the basket, pausing to glance longingly at me, and then she let out a deep sigh—as though she had a burden upon her heart.

When I went to her, she turned to gaze at the sunset, a sad, faraway look in her gray-blue eyes. I wished I had the courage to ask her what was wrong, but instead, I pressed the back of her hand with my fingers and drew a circle, and flattened my palm upon it— but still, I could not speak.

After a long silence, she said, "Have you ever considered that death is a constant companion?"

Her question stung me . . . for the pain of Mother's death was foremost in my heart, and while my feelings for Suzannah had been suppressed . . . they still battled against Mother's memory.

"Not really," I replied cautiously. "Although I know it's ever present, especially now. But I try hard not to dwell upon it . . ."

"No, I didn't mean death in *that* particular sense," she said softly. "I mean in our youth, we don't know when we will die. As such, we tend to think of life as an inexhaustible well."

She was right, because my well went dry with the death of my mother.

"Yes, I think that's so," I agreed, adding, "but it saddens me to think of death at all."

"But it should make you think a bit more about *living* . . . for the *future*," she said firmly. This she followed with an exquisite smile that made me feel so hot and foolish, I couldn't look into her wondrous eyes; so shamefaced, I bent down as if my shoe needed attention.

Stepping closer, she stooped and asked, "Jim, how many times will we as younglings remember a certain afternoon of our youth? Or afternoons with your mother . . . or just the two of us together— especially an afternoon like *this* one—so deeply part of our being that we can't conceive of our lives without it?"

"I'll *always* remember every day I spend with you," I said, my eyes still focused on my shoes, and damning myself for not looking at *her*.

Suzannah paused for a moment before she continued. "Perhaps you will think of those days four or five times, perhaps not even that; yet it all seems so limitless because we are *young*. Listen to your *heart*, Jim, and tell me if what I say is true."

She clearly felt the paralyzing conflict that raged within me. While I *dreamed* about Suzannah and needed her solace, I had stiffened my heart against the pain of mother's loss, and thus against Suzannah too. My unspoken truth was that I wished to *run* to her . . . and be comforted by her love. Suzannah knew my feelings better than I did.

She took my hand and together we sat down facing each other; then gently placing her hand on my cheek, she leaned forward so her face was only a few inches from mine. I became lost in her wondrous eyes as they silently reached into my broken soul—and read the pain that was written there. "Although your heart hungers for its *lost* love, Jim, you must turn it toward the *living*. If your soul desires to join another as one, it must first *find* the other . . . and if the love is true, then these two spirits will carry on as one—from this world to the next." Suzannah's eyes filled, and still looking deeply into mine, she softly pleaded, "*Don't* cast your love to the four winds to be scattered . . . to never know a *home*. *Hide* your love, James Walker—*don't* let the cold winds of Death find it . . . *Hide* it . . ." And laying one hand upon her heart, she softly whispered, ". . . *Here* . . ."

Suzannah went silent, giving me a chance to respond. The sea gulls squawked, the seals barked on the rocks below, and I heard the sea murmur as it caressed the shore, "*Tell her . . . tell her . . . tell her!*"

I breathed deeply and whispered, "Suzannah?"

"Yes, Jim?" she said, expectantly.

Finally I managed to blurt out, "I don't wish to be hurt again as I was when Mother died. I couldn't bear the pain. I've been afraid of exposing my heart to *anybody* since that day, for it shook my faith in God and man." When I looked into her eyes once more, and saw in them the love of her caring heart, I *knew* she would cherish and protect what was left of mine, and *always* keep it safe. Overcome with feeling, I reached out to clasp her hands in mine.

"I know your pain," Suzannah softly whispered, squeezing my hands in comfort. "I see how faithful your heart has been in its sorrow and silence . . . but I *feel* your loss and emptiness too, Jim, for I loved your mother as if she were my own."

"Suzannah . . ." I said, choking back tears as my terrible loss finally rose to the surface. "I've been so *afraid* . . . I knew all along you cared deeply . . . but I was frozen with grief, so I withheld my feelings—it has been an *agonizing* silence."

Pressing my hands tighter within hers, she said, "I know you struggled valiantly to say what you did just now. And if you feel any tenderness for me at all, *please* let me help you."

"Why would you want to do that? Why do you still care?" I asked, in a final act of self-renunciation.

"Because I *lo* . . ." and she stopped short.

"You . . . *love* me?" I asked in utter astonishment.

Now it was Suzannah who cast her eyes down, looking at our hands that were still entwined, mine caressing hers, and in between seal barks, she softly whispered, "Yes . . ."

Feeling unmitigated joy, I looked at her for a long moment before bringing her hands to my lips. As I softly kissed them, I felt Mother's spirit touch me, encouraging me to accept all that was offered from this loving girl with the golden heart . . . to finally rest mine within hers. It was then that I gently drew Suzannah closer . . . and she came willingly. And just as the sun faded below the horizon, silhouetting us against the purple sky . . . our lips finally met.

A heavenly warmth flooded my heart as an indescribable sweetness flowed between us, during this, our first sacred kiss . . . and through it and her loving embrace, my pain and grief surrendered to her. In my heart I heard Mother's spirit whisper, "Yes, give unto *her* your heart and soul, dearest son—*love* her—and be *loved* . . ."

Moving her hands slowly from my shoulders to my neck, Suzannah gently interrupted our kiss to say, "I sense that you are now released unto my heart."

I was dumbstruck. "*How*? For God's sake . . . how do you *know* this?"

"Your mother speaks to me . . . through your heart, through your kiss, and through your tears." Touching her forehead to mine, she gazed intently into my eyes. I could see beautiful flecks of green in those heavenly gray-blue eyes.

"My God, Suzannah," I whispered, "You know me better than I know *myself*!"

"I know when your heart speaks to me, even if your lips do not. I know when your heart cries for help. You are gifted with a heart feeler's spirit. I can feel it all around you. I see it in your eyes, I feel it in your touch, and I hear it in your voice. Your mother gave you her blessing to move forward and be released."

"How do you *know* all these things?" I asked in disbelief. "When I heard you sing in church, I thought you were an angel. I was captivated from the first moment I saw you, and doubly so when I heard you sing. I felt that God was speaking to me through you."

"He speaks through *all* of us, Jim. I'm but a girl of sixteen years, who has faith and love, and some sensitivity beyond that of others."

"No, Suzannah, you are not *just* that—you are also *dear* and *special* to me. And you were sent back into my life to relieve me of this unspeakable burden."

"So be it then," she said as she kissed away my tears. "I am here and I shall be all things to you—for *that* is my heart's desire . . . and I'll be your angel too if you need one."

"Oh *yes*, Suzannah," I said breathlessly. "I want you to know I've *always* loved you. But I need your forgiveness now—for I've neglected you far too much since Mother died."

I wrapped her tightly to my heart, and kissed her all over while she held me—rubbing my back and rocking me in her arms as a mother does her crying babe. Her face blurred through my tears as her sweet lips met mine in perfect happiness.

Then, amidst a constant flurry of blissful kisses she said, "Jim, never fear to tell me of your happiness . . . or your darkest fears . . . or your deepest troubles. I will listen to you and protect your heart with mine forever more."

"Suzannah, do you promise?" I begged between kisses.

"I *swear!*" she softly whispered as her mouth gently opened to mine. And as our love, long denied, flowed deeply and warmly between us, I believed her as I never believed anything in my entire life.

Father's Heart Treasure

Boston at Fay Barrett's

My Dear Son,

I am comfortably settled here with Fay and Lydia, and my health is good and I pray likewise for you. Now I have a few words of progress to report.

The horse William lent me is a peaceable but tough-mouthed beast, requiring me to pull exceedingly hard to guide him in the direction desired. Other than that, he is an agreeable companion who delivered me safe to Boston.

Fay and I continue to work successfully with the Tory vendor . . . and all will proceed as normal, but at considerable risk.

There is unrest aplenty down here, for every night the mobs are chasing down Tories and forcibly removing them from their very homes into the streets. Thus expunged, their bodies are covered with hot tar, and the mobs gleefully dump buckets of feathers over their persons, such that they become a sticky, feathered mess, nearly impossible to clean.

Some Tories who have made grievous errors in political judgment (according to the mobs) seem to require further injury by being tied to and ridden upon a rail through the streets, whilst bystanders taunt and jeer at their misfortune.

Fortunately for us, our vendor maintains a very low profile, and Fay says we have a reasonable chance of successfully closing our transaction.

Despite the difficulties and uprisings, it is evident from the talk hereabouts that this action against the King is a terrible road we take. Indeed, we are aware of all the treacherous bumps and bends, for we have been warned. But still we go, for we know where this road will end if we do not go.

Lydia is a beautiful and gracious hostess, and puts me very much in mind of Mother. Tonight she spoke fondly of her old home in Walker's Cove; she said: "Wherever we may live, it is ever our family home— a place to ultimately return to, whether it's joy that brings us back, or sorrow. Collected there are the echoes of generations of voices, witnessed by those sturdy walls. Oh, that they could speak!"

Hearing her fond feelings for home expressed, Dear Son, made me more determined than ever to preserve Mother's wish for our tavern to open.

When I think about Mother, I cannot describe the immensity of my loneliness, save that there is, and always shall be, an unbroken bond between her spirit and mine. Every Sabbath I pray, remembering our favorite moments gathered during a lifetime of love. These moments transcend the world as we know it. And thus, in the still solitude of my chamber, I unfold the delicate piece of cotton cloth, the precious scrap of her wedding dress, so worn and fragile. This fragment is like a picture to me. It is a delicate pink and blue sea moss pattern on a white background. I carry it mainly because I see her face in it—a face of pure loveliness that bears an inextinguishable expression of hope.

Heaven claimed her before my life's voyage ended. Her beautiful form, now laid to rest beside grandmother, is lost to my pillow evermore, but never from my heart. She lived long enough to make a loving home for us all, and may her love-light remain in our hearts as long as we live. For if we tend that light always, her memory shall never pass away. This is the wish of,

Your affectionate father.

P.S. I shall send you a ship date as soon as I have a copy of the signed bill of lading.

Into the Darkness

My Dear Mr. Walker,

It falls upon myself to perform certain duties as an officer of this honorable body of men. One of the most infrequent yet compelling of these duties, is to notify family members of those who have departed this life by natural causes of God, or misadventure by man.

It is indeed, Sir, my sad and humble duty to inform you of the death of one James Walker, who we believe to be your father, a resident of Walker's Cove; clockmaker and tavern keeper. Whilst conducting his business in the Green Dragon, the tavern was raided by His Majesty's troops on Long Wharf. During the ensuing scuffle, your father was accidentally shot with a horse pistol, subsequently dying of his wound. In order to conceal the despicable event from their superior officers, and those who may be inflamed by their malicious misdeeds, his body was taken by His Majesty's troops and unceremoniously dumped into the Harbor.

We who represent the Sons of Liberty, gave chase to the culprits, and conducted a valiant search by boat and swimmers to recover your father's body; but alas, our efforts were in vain.

Please accept my deepest sympathy and regret. These are dangerous times, and I may assure you, Dear Sir, this cowardly act shall not be forgotten or go unpunished—there are dark times ahead.

I shall remain ever your faithful servant in Liberty, and I sorrow deeply for your loss.

Your humble servant,
Samuel Adams

Diary of the Lost

Jan 7, etc.

The most difficult thing to understand is why God, in his great wisdom, chose me to heap these misfortunes upon . . . the loss of Mother, and now Father? He doesn't answer—in my solitary darkness, silence is His only voice.

I am so lost without you, Father! All night, like an animal of the darkness, I restlessly pace the floors, my hands bundled into fists. Sorrow and rage permeate my being. The pages of this diary are dappled with the bitter tearstains of the grief I cannot express in words. I yield to that Power—so when will God's earth receive me? Departed ones, mother of my heart and father of my life, have been taken from me . . . and without them I shall die.

Dear Mother, the crushing reality of Father's death makes me inconsolable in my grief. My life's meaning has been irretrievably lost. Dear Life as I once knew it is gone, departed forever . . . and shall not return, even in dreams.

Mother, I'm a broken man . . . a solitary worldling . . . totally and absolutely alone. I have only your portrait, and within the silence of our home, I feel lost and abandoned. Today I found your comb with strands of hair entangled in its fingers—just as you left them! Oh, the means to touch thy priceless self!

◦❦◦

Happiness has vanished. What made my home a home is now gone. Emptiness is my friend . . . loneliness my parent. My heart has lost the capacity to love.

◦❦◦

In the solitary darkness of exile, I reflect upon the blessed past . . . so plagued am I by our lost moments, I lay my heart upon the cross of resentment . . . and all is hopeless despair.

◦❦◦

I see no purpose to my worthless life. Who will guide my heart? Who will be my mother? Who will dispense fatherly wisdom? Where will the heart talks come from? They are forever gone.

◦❦◦

Father, your wretched son has no future. Our loving home is but a barren edifice where blessed memories dwell, bidding me return . . . to joy, love and warmth. But only in my dreams, Father, or perhaps when I'm dead. My heart cries to you, but is answered by desolate, penetrating silence.

◦❦◦

Rum feeds my seething anger, assuages my emotional pain. Inebriated, I patiently wait for Death.

◦❦◦

Mother, I am a living corpse . . . drunk and devoid of feeling, impervious to pain, bitter with resentment. Consuming jealousy devours my soul. Resenting my neighbors, I wish them all in Hell; for life remains unchanged in their little worlds, whilst I slump at our table totally bereft. My grief is relentless, for Father, for thee . . . and at last for myself.

◦❦◦

Mother, there is no pardon from the omnipotence of Fate. All shall be as fate decrees. The old woman was truthful after all! Yet Fate shall not decree my end, which is in my hands. I shall perish here, among my memories and heart treasures, left where you touched them last, in their sacred places.

Defiantly I mock Fate! This house shall be my coffin—a shrine to my solitude, a memorial to what was beautiful. Rum dulls my pain and blunts hunger's edge . . . Death slowly approaches.

Dear Mother,
     A knock at the front door I dare not answer. I am mourning Father, you, and lastly whilst I can, myself. When they find me, this diary shall tell why I'm gone.
                                        Your loving son, James

The flame of life is gone—from my heart, my soul and my body. No food. No drink, save rum, which I consume to blindness. I do not speak, yet I am called from the door. I remain silent, for I see no earthly purpose.

Loving my parents in their old age . . . such hope is dead . . . like the cold whitened embers of our long extinguished fire.

Like a fallen leaf before winter, my soul has been crushed into tiny fragments, then scattered by the winds of fate . . . and I am nowhere . . .

The spark of life remains, but not the spark of love. A perfect failure was thy son. But dearest Mother . . . remember my boyhood when *golden days were ours? Every day was a path to happiness, and your love, my light at path's end.*

Mother, will I see you when I'm gone? Is there a place where souls dwell in eternal happiness, where heavenly joys make us forget the pain of life? I beg of thee, extend thy hand and help your son follow. Will Father be there? If so, I'm ready, for there is nothing here.

Today I heard a knock upon the door—light and tentative. I dropped my quill to hear and to remain silent, so I shall die in peace. My body stubbornly clings to life. A little longer . . .

Today yet another persistent visitor, but nothing said. I'm not here, I'm not anywhere. I haven't the courage to end my life quickly—my instinct for survival is still too strong.

What day is it? Weak and tired, sleep dulls the pain. Ice and cold numb my senses, yet I hear a mouse . . . is Death this quiet?

My lost father, a heavy snow covers the shutters. The house, frozen and dark, a comfortable tomb for thy son.

In the penetrating darkness of an agonizing cold, I freeze . . . among my memories of you and Mother.

Perhaps soon, sleep will be endless.

A breath of sweetness . . . Suzannah knocked and called out to me. God love her, for I remained silent: she should love another and waste no time on me. Now weak, I was glad I had bolted the door when I still had the strength.

A banging at the door—poor, sweet Suzannah yet again! Such a heart . . . my bittersweet tears are for her and her alone. God sends His angel but she is no longer of my world. Hark, dear parental spirits! Suzannah is gone . . . my heart is at rest.

Mother, your child cries . . . lost, afraid, near death and alone. I beg thee for comfort and succor, but you do not listen, you do not answer.

So weak . . . I can barely write . . . abandonment complete . . . my Death Angel approaches. In my distorted dreams, I await her with open arms . . .

"Jᴉᴍ! Jᴉᴍ! Pʟᴇᴀsᴇ answer me! It's Suzannah! I *know* you're *in* there! Jim, what have you *done? Please* let me in! Come to the door, Jim— I *know* you're here! If you let me *in*, I could *comfort* you . . . I can bring you *home!* You *are* here, my heart *feels* it. You are not *well*, and Jim, you're in *pain!* Oh, *please* . . . in the name of our love open the door! It's *snowing*, Jim . . . I'm *cold.* Open the door for *my* sake . . ."

My eyes opened slowly. What day was this? No, it *wasn't* a dream; it *was* what I thought—an angel's voice crying in despair . . . to *me.* Perhaps I'm dead . . . but no . . . Attempting to stand, I collapse upon a table, sending it splintering to the floor.

"Jim! *Jim! Please* open the door!" the angel called out again.

It was too late. Doubled over in pain, I croaked hoarsely, "No! Go away, Go *away!*" While groaning in abject misery, I added, "I do *not* wish to see you!"

"Dear *God*, Jim, you *are* alive! It's Suzannah! *Please let me in!*" An urgent rapping at the door followed.

As my stomach cramped, I drifted in and out of consciousness. Finally gathering enough strength to sit upright on the floor, I felt drunk, disoriented and confused, and voices seem to come at me as cacophonous echoes. Where *was* I? Is this *Hell*? I wondered.

"Come to *me*, James, I can't get *in*, so *you* must come to *me*!"

In a drunken, half conscious, arrogant voice I angrily answered, "Go *away*, little girl . . . go love *another*! Our fate is *not* together!"

Outside the door there was a stunned silence; then Suzannah burst into tears.

Like a demon possessed with pure hateful vengeance, I drove a stake into that golden heart. "Now, get away from me and leave *me alone*! I wish to die *alone*! You can see me when I'm *dead*! Now be *gone*!"

She frantically wailed, "But Jim, you are not you . . . I *love* you and my heart is *breaking*! Let me *in*! Tell me to my *face* you wish me *gone*! I don't *believe* you! Grief has *poisoned* you, Jim . . . don't let it *kill* you! Don't let it kill *us*! I'm *here* for you! Oh merciful *God*, give me the strength to *open* this *door*!" I heard her clawing on it, frantically, as she added, "*Jim*, listen to your *heart*, and tell me what it *says* . . ."

I drove the stake deeper as the heart of gold bled. "*It says nothing*!" I snarled. "*It's gone—and so are you*! My Death Angel is approaching . . . so *you*, go away, *now*!"

The sound of her desperate clawing gradually faded from the center of the door where it started, and moved downward with agonizing slowness until it ceased at the bottom.

Sobbing uncontrollably, despite the hurt I'd given her, she steadfastly remained at the door's bottom panel. The golden heart was not yet dead. From behind the bottom panel she begged, "Put your *hand* upon the door, Jim, right *here*! You don't need to *open* it!" she entreated while repeatedly striking it with her palm, so I knew where to place my hand.

Despite the numbness in my limbs, I alternately crawled and rolled toward the door, forcing my hand upon it by sheer effort of will when I reached it.

After a moment, Suzannah groaned through her sobs as if she had suffered a blow.

"Oh, *Jim*," she whimpered, "You're frozen and starving! Your heart has been poisoned! I *forgive* your words . . . they are the words of *resentment* and *anger*. Your mother *spoke* to me, Jim! She *sent* me to you! Listen to *her* words through *me*; you *know* I speak the truth!"

"Mother?" I asked in near delirium.

Suzannah, prostrate in the bitter cold, continued to cry while she spoke. "She does not want you to *die*, frozen and alone, nor do I! What purpose would that serve? Listen to *her*, Jim!"

She paused, weeping and sniffling. She was but two inches away, yet I couldn't touch her.

"Jim, I can *defeat* the Death Angel! Remember the prophecy? I am your *guardian* angel! And your mother has spoken to *my* heart to save her only *son* . . . you *know* this is true!"

"Yes . . ." I whispered mostly to myself. Then, as my hand slowly fell from the door, I heard her declare, "Jim, *Jim*! I've lost your touch! Put your hand back on the door—*on the door!*"

I was doubled up in pain as convulsions wracked my body, and I couldn't move.

"The *door*, Jim!" I heard her beg once more.

The pain subsided but I was drained. I attempted to stand, but immediately lost my balance and my head hit the door latch. A searing pain shot through my skull as if I'd been stabbed there and the blade twisted. As I lay prostrate on the freezing floor, I heard Suzannah's urgent plea renewed. "Jim, my dear God, *Jim* . . . touch the *door!*"

It was a struggle, but I managed to bring my hand back up to its former position.

"I *have* you, Jim! I *have* you!" she cried, "and my heart suffers *with* yours. Do you remember the sunsets, Jim?"

I could not answer, but Suzannah pressed on, undeterred.

"I waited for you for many days and built air castles out of our love, but you never came! The sunsets are the saddest part of my day, for without *you*, they have lost their beauty. I feel I have *nothing* now, not even air with which to build my air castle. Have pity on me, Jim. I'm freezing cold out here and I *love* you—but guardian angels are not invincible!"

"Yes . . . I know . . ." I murmured, as I floated back into my dark purgatory.

EXCRUCIATING CRAMPS AWAKENED me as I found myself in an icy pool of blood that held my cheek to the floor. Unable to move my head, I scraped at the skin where it had adhered until I finally managed to free myself. I felt no pain in the process, just a wiry beard and nothing else.

I got to my knees shakily as I tried to remember how I had landed on the floor. In the dim light, I caught a glimpse of my face in the mirror, and saw a mutilating gash across my temple, crusted over with blackened blood. My beard was half an inch long and my eyes were dull and sunken in their sockets. I noticed my breeches were loose because I hadn't eaten for some time, and filthy too because I had soiled myself on several occasions. I was a totally wretched, pathetic piece of human vermin.

Looking toward the parlor window, I reflected upon how— before I sealed my life in darkness—it captured a wide expanse of the heavens by night and an oft-brilliant sunrise by day. That was in a much better world . . . when my parents were alive.

Suddenly, I remembered what had happened. "*Suzannah!* May God forgive me!" I hoarsely croaked as I staggered to the door. Then, mustering what little strength I had left, I screamed "*Su-zan-nah!*" as I unbolted the door.

She lay before me on the doorstep, curled up like a baby and covered with a six-inch layer of snow, looking frozen in death. I noticed her fingertips were torn and bleeding from clawing the door frantically in her desperate attempt to break through to me. The sight of her in such a state—because of *me*—broke my heart.

Sobbing uncontrollably, I kept murmuring, "*No, no, no, no . . .* this cannot *be!* I've killed the one person I have left to me!" I kneeled over her and frenziedly unburied her lifeless form from the snow, gasping out, "My God, *Suzannah*—oh, my dearest one! What have I *done?*" Then, lifting her gently I carried her toward the Ellingwood house.

Panting like a dying dog, my lungs ached for air as I carried her along. My arms quivered and shook from her weight—although I knew she was light as a feather. My legs wobbled and were almost useless, the muscles burning like hot molten lead. I had to stop and rest several times to marshal my strength for the next few steps. When I reached the Ellingwoods' door, I slammed my back heavily against it, gasping desperately for air.

While I stood there waiting for what seemed like an eternity, I finally heard Fanny's voice behind me and turned to face her.

"My *heavens!*" she screamed, horrified by the sight that greeted her. "In God's name, who are *you?*" she said, stepping aside so I could bring her daughter inside.

"*Samuel!* Oh, in the name of *Heaven . . . Samuel! Come down here!*" Fanny called out.

I carried Suzannah into the parlor where there was always a fire, while with bitter tears I whimpered over and over, "I've *killed* Suzannah . . . I've *murdered* your last born!"

Sam hurried into the room wearing nothing but breeches and pulled the sofa closer to the fireplace. After I carefully placed her there, Sam covered her body with a heavy quilt.

"Is she alive or dead?" he asked in a trembling voice.

"I don't know," I replied, "I found her outside my door . . . like *this*. But my heart tells me she's alive."

We all stood by silently, letting Suzannah lay undisturbed for a time near the comforting warmth of the fire. Then Sam bent over her and put his ear to her chest. "She may be somewhat frozen, but she *is* alive!" he declared joyously. Then he turned to Fanny. "Get warm water—not hot—barely *warm!* Get towels, warm clothes, a blanket and a scarf."

Looking at me as he would a repulsive insect, Sam pointed at Suzannah and finally hissed, "*What* is the meaning of *this?*"

My brain wasn't working. The heat in the Ellingwood house seemed to stifle all thought. Finally, I was able to form a reply, albeit brokenly. "She came to me, but I know not when . . . she tried to help me . . . but I was desperately sick and I turned her away . . ." I couldn't suppress the tears that started flowing freely—and I was too stricken with guilt to go on.

I expected Sam to banish me from his home on the spot, but instead he said in a more sympathetic tone, "Come, Jim, sit down and tell me how in God's name this *happened*—and what in Hell happened to *you*? You look like Lucifer himself! Where have you *been* for the last two weeks?"

"*In* Hell," I replied shivering, "but Suzannah saved me!"

At that moment, Fanny returned with an armful of dry clothes and a kettle of warm water. Before she started removing Suzannah's frozen clothes, she looked first at me and then at Sam, and motioned for us to leave the room.

We went to the kitchen and sat at the table, close to the fire. Gazing into the flames, Sam breathed deeply several times to partially release his anger. Finally, he removed the kettle from the fire and said, "Go to the dry sink and clean yourself up, son. This will pass . . . we'll get through it."

His encouraging words warmed the frozen void within me as I felt the first stirrings of hope in my soul . . . an unaccustomed feeling since Mother's death. And it was all because of that loyal, loving—and persistent—girl in the parlor . . . to whom I now owed my life.

The Awakening

am left the house to fetch Doc Brown. Meanwhile, I ate some bread and drank a tumbler of apple cider that Fanny offered me. Despite the nourishment, I still felt groggy and weak from my self-inflicted ordeal.

When Doc arrived he went immediately to Suzannah, who still lay unconscious on the sofa. I remained in the kitchen nearly insane with worry. The minutes dragged on, until I heard a sudden shuffling and banging. I looked up to see Doc in the doorway, anxiety etched on his face. He pulled up a stout ladder-back, thumped it down, and without a word examined my head wound in the firelight.

Leaning back to look straight in my face, he scowled and crossly asked, "What in God's name *happened* to you two?" Not waiting for a reply, he reached into his medical kit to retrieve a needle. "Jim, that cut's deep and needs stitches. I'll try not to hurt you much."

As he cleaned the wound, I declared flatly, "I almost killed Suzannah, Doc."

"Yes, she *is* in trouble . . ." Doc replied while threading his needle.

Wincing at the first stitch, I asked, "How *much* trouble?"

He paused thoughtfully. "How *much* trouble all depends on how much feeling comes back to her hands and feet. That will be the measure of her recovery. Meanwhile, how did all this come to pass, Jim?"

Before I could form a reply, Sam entered the room. "Suzannah is bandaged just as you instructed, Doc. She's still not awake."

"Very good, Sam. Now you can just keep her covered up with a blanket. She's a strong healthy girl . . . and my sense is that she'll be fine."

Glaring at me angrily, Sam said, "*Damn* it, Jim, tell us what happened! Why have you been living like a rakehell?"

No words came, until I remembered the diary. "I kept a record of my lost days—it's at home. I'll bring it here to show you, since it has all the answers."

"Very well, we'll wait," Doc said as he knotted the sutures. "And when you come back, I want you cleaned up and *presentable*. I'm embarrassed to see you in such a state; remember, I saw you on the day you were born!"

I felt deeply ashamed as I walked home, and not only about looking and smelling like a ruined stable. It began to dawn on me why I isolated myself. I was trying to kill off my feelings, shunning those who loved me and unintentionally wounding them to the core. But I realized that all wasn't lost—there were still people who cared about me, like Doc and the Ellingwoods, who were now my family. Feeling a wave of gratitude and lighter of heart, I picked up my diary and trundled back through the snow—with less exertion this time. My body was getting stronger at last.

I found Doc and Sam still in the kitchen, so I humbly set my journal on the table before them. They looked at each other, then at the book, and then at me.

Finally, Sam sighed. "Jim, why don't you get cleaned up first, and then we'll get some more nourishment into that emaciated frame of yours."

He escorted me into the winter kitchen, where Fanny and a hot tub of water were already waiting for me. Without a word, she coldly thrust a clean towel at me and as she turned to leave I softly whimpered, "Thank you . . . I'm so *very* sorry . . ."

She stopped, turned around and looked hard at me from beneath her furrowed brow. "James, I *love* you like a *son* . . . but *this* has broken my heart! Why did you not tell *us* of your pain? Not only are you our neighbor but you are like a *son* to us! You ought to *know* that by now."

Because I hurt her so deeply, all I could do was stand there as tears betrayed my abject misery.

Fanny looked at me sadly then, shaking her head perhaps in regret. "Here I am, a grown woman chastising *you* after all you have *lost* . . . when all you're seeking is comfort from *us*. No, James, *I'm* sorry—forgive me, dear boy."

She came over and hugged me, the first hug I'd had from a mother in a long time . . . and it felt wonderful. My silent tears dampened her neck as I slowly wrapped my arms about her. While pressing her to my heart in a feeble attempt to hide my shame, I held her tightly while she soothingly rubbed my back—just as Mother used to.

Giving me one last squeeze, she let me go and smiled up at me. "I'll check in on Suzannah now, and you clean yourself up. I'm sure she'll want to see you when she awakens. You certainly don't want her to see you looking like *that*," adding, "I left some pumpkin pie and johnnycake on the table for you."

I spluttered helplessly, "I don't know how to thank you . . ."

Fanny placed her palm on my cheek and said in a hushed tone, "Just take *care* of my daughter, James, she *loves* you . . . you're her world."

"Yes, I swear I will," I promised fervently. "Suzannah is a precious treasure to me. She is *my* world. Thank you . . . Mother E."

As Fanny headed out the door, she turned and smiled at me sweetly. "Hmm, Mother E," she softly repeated, ". . . I *like* that . . ."

I BATHED MYSELF and carefully shaved off my beard, then put on some clothes that belonged to Sam. The fit was a bit too long and narrow, but they were a big improvement over the filthy rags I'd been wearing. I tossed them into the fire and without further ado, I rejoined Doc and Sam in the kitchen. I was hungry, but the enticing victuals Fanny left for me would have to wait.

"Well now, who is *this* natty looking fellow?" teased Doc as I entered.

As I sat down, I pushed the diary toward Sam, bowed my head . . . and waited.

They passed it back and forth and discussed certain entries. I didn't listen too carefully to their talk since I was anxious for the final verdict.

Sam was the first to speak to me, as he pointed to the one and only dated entry—January 7th. "It seems you lost track of time during your ordeal."

"Yes, sir, I didn't think it mattered after a while."

Continuing to read, Sam raised his brows and then declared, "Doc, look at *this*!"

Doc leaned over, harrumphing as he read. Then he exclaimed, "My heavens, you crucified *yourself*, Jim. Your bitter feelings about your loss were unknown to all of us who care about you! Why, you told no one!"

"No, I didn't," I replied, "but Suzannah knew."

Reading on, Doc scratched his chin thoughtfully. "Of course you felt abandoned, Jim, but only because you stayed by yourself."

"Yes, but Suzannah knew."

Setting my diary down as if he'd seen enough, Sam looked at me in utter astonishment. "You wished to *die*, Jim? *Why?*"

With my eyes cast down, I murmured, "Having just lost Mother, I felt I had no hope of *anything* after Father's death. So I wanted to regain my happiness by joining my parents . . . and remaining wherever they were."

"But you know, Jim, killing *yourself* wouldn't bring back your *life* with them. You ought to know that!" Sam admonished.

"I do now . . . now that I'm better."

Sam then confided to us that Suzannah was profoundly troubled about my absence. Then turning to me, he added, "*She* would never tell you this, Jim, but she suffered every night she didn't see you. She told us of your loss, your pain, your depression and your desire to die. She *knew* all about it without even being in your presence!"

"Remarkable!" Doc interjected, shaking his head in disbelief.

Sam continued, "When she could tolerate it no longer, she took it upon herself to seek you out. She mentioned a "Death Angel" hovering near your house . . . some such thing. Somehow, Jim, she *knew* you were trying to die and she couldn't let that happen; so unbeknownst to us—she snuck over there in the middle of the snowstorm. She *loves* you son, and I can't blame her. You're a fine and honorable person, just like your dear parents. I'll help you however I can to reestablish your life without them."

"As will I!" echoed Doc, tapping his chest. "That's what the community is here for, son. We support our own, and help each other when we're in trouble. Call it a barn raising for the soul."

Sam nodded vigorously in agreement before he rose and left the room, saying he wanted to look in on Suzannah.

Doc picked up the book and thumbed through it again, until he came to the final entry. "So she was out there *all* night . . . remarkable! The mercury was *seven below*, Jim! You should thank God he looked after her!"

"I do—believe me, I do." I paused to concentrate on holding back my tears.

"As your family physician, I'm prescribing a *cure* for your depression."

"What do you suggest?" I asked, hopefully wiping my eyes.

Pointing toward the parlor he said, "I suggest you show your diary to *her*, so that she may confirm her feelings were *correct* in their sense of your situation."

Doc sat silent for a few moments, furrowing his brows as if he was lost in thought. Then he leaned forward to whisper with some urgency, "If it were not for that *girl* in there, son, *you* would probably be *dead* now! Your parents want you to open the tavern and *succeed*! It is not to their honor that you die by your own hand in a frenzy of self-pity and regret. Look into your heart and tell me this is so."

He sat back in his chair with a satisfied air and waited.

"That's what Suzannah always tells me . . . look into your heart . . ." I murmured.

Doc nodded.

"Yes . . . it's so." The words were no sooner said than I felt a crushing burden lifted from my soul—for Doc had known, just as Suzannah did.

"Now you take this book, and after *both* of you have read it *together*—and talked about it, entry by heartbreaking entry—let it *die* with the past! *Life* is for the living, James! I suggest you take that girl's hand in marriage . . . and *live*! It's what your parents wished for more than *anything* in this world!"

"They *did?*" I said in amazement. "How do you know *that*, Doc?"

Fumbling at the buttons on his waistcoat and repeatedly clearing his throat, he softly confessed, "Well . . . they asked me to keep doctoring long enough to deliver your first born."

At first, I felt guilt-stricken that through my selfishness, I nearly ruined their cherished dream. But as this new air castle began to form, I softly mused "How warm the thought . . . my first born . . ."

"Your mother was *convinced,* that you and Suzannah would be married," he said, relieved the secret was finally out. "She had that same power as Suzannah and thus she *knew*, Jim."

"So *that* was her wish," I said, remembering our last conversation, before she left for Boston.

Doc placed a firm hand upon my shoulder as he said, "Now, I suggest you take care of that young lady in there, and *follow* my advice!"

Snapping the diary shut, he handed it back to me. I tried to take it, but he didn't release his grip. When I looked back at him in surprise, he stared straight into my eyes and raised his eyebrows. "To the *future* then?"

"Yes!" I smiled through tears of happiness, "To the *future*!"

A New Hope

uoyed by my new outlook on life, I went directly to the parlor and sat down near Suzannah. Again, food would have to wait . . . as my hunger was replaced by my burning desire to watch for my angel's recovery.

I reflected on how this sweet creature risked her life to save me from my wretched, miserable self. As I now knew, she had loved me unselfishly since first moving to Walker's Cove. Who would have guessed—when I wished upon Midnight Blue—that someone like Suzannah would ever come my way? That of all the towns and villages in the colonies, she landed here. It did feel like divine intervention, as Mother had said.

My heart fluttered with fear at thinking of what might have happened had we *not* met, and she had fallen into the clutches of some Boston toad, who could never appreciate the beauty of her selfless love as I do!

Impelled by the strength of my feeling, I rose and knelt by her pillowed head. Tenderly stroking her hair, I spoke to her in a near whisper. "Suzannah . . . my dearest and truest friend, my *only* love . . . I can never hope to repay you for your sacrifice. I'm unworthy to even *grace* your slumbering presence.

"But I want you to know that thanks to *you*, my life and my love are renewed. I'm *reborn* because of what *you* have done . . . and I *swear* as God is my judge, *you* are my heart's desire, and I shall *honor* and *love* you until the end of my days. We *shall* be married . . . and we shall go forward together with a new hope, for this is the great gift you've given me. I swear this promise on the souls of my parents—for it was their fondest wish. I *love* you."

Then I delivered to her lips a long tender kiss, and as I did so, I felt *something* pass between us. My grateful tears fell upon her face, and I murmured softly, "Thank you, dear Suzannah . . . *thank* you."

As I gently dabbed my tears from her cheek, my soft ministrations evidently caused her eyes to flutter open. She looked disoriented for a moment—until she recognized her surroundings.

Wishing to have private words with her alone as Doc had prescribed, I forestalled calling in her parents. It was then that she yawned prettily, stretched and looked straight into my face. "I had the most *wonderful* dream, Jim!"

Despite feeling like a miracle had happened, I found I still had the power of speech. "And what was *that*, Suzannah?"

"We were *married!*"

"What does your *heart* say?" I asked, reversing our roles and holding my breath.

"It says I would happily *do* so!" she whispered weakly.

"But first you need to rest and get *well*, my guardian angel! You've been through *a lot!*" I said, caressing her cheeks and then kissing her.

My heart burst with joy as I called out to the Ellingwoods and Doc to come quick. After the three spent some time with Suzannah and amply expressed their huge sense of relief at her sudden recovery, I asked them if we might have some time alone together. I was thrilled when they acquiesced gracefully.

We resumed our talk and gloried in what felt like our newfound intimacy, lavishing affection on each other freely. But at a certain point, Suzannah looked at her bandaged fingers quizzically, until she remembered what had happened. "Oh, Jim—you *opened* the door!"

"Yes, Suzannah, because you opened my heart—when it was completely closed."

As she beamed her winsome smile at me, I held the diary before her.

"What's *this?*" she asked with curiosity, first looking at its leather binding and then to me.

"Let me show you, Suzannah . . ."

ABOUT TWO HOURS later, the two of us were still sitting on the sofa before the blazing fire. Suzannah had snuggled against me: my sheltering arm around her shoulders, her dainty feet toward the hearth, a warm scarf around her throat, and her hair flowing gloriously down her back—just so I could fondle its wavy curls. My remaining hand tenderly clasped her little white fingers, which had lain so temptingly in Sam's bandages.

As we whispered endearments and exchanged soft kisses, the winter wind howled outdoors, totally banished from Love's warm fireside. Indeed, the fire was much *hotter* now than it was before . . . and between kisses, we watched in mesmerized silence as the shadows of its flames magically danced upon the walls, the floor, and the ceiling.

What we did *not* see however, were Sam and Doc standing quietly behind us, nodding to each other in approval as the diary burned . . . consumed by the flames of eternal love.

PINK AND WHITE

ather's death proved a turning point in my life for many reasons. First and foremost, it strengthened my bonds with Sam and Doc. Both men cared for my wellbeing, and as such, our relationships were now built on emotional strength and solidarity of reason.

I particularly remember Doc lecturing me on the occasion of my twentieth birthday. He told me it was time to assume the responsibilities of manhood, and press forward with my life: first, by honoring my parents' wishes through opening the tavern, and second, by marrying Suzannah—which was my fervent desire as well.

During the remaining winter, Sam guided me toward my goal of completing the tavern, helping me draw up detailed plans of all that was in our power to get it "a-going"—as Father was fond of saying.

In late spring of that same year, we had wonderful news—some of it quite unexpected—in the form of a letter from Fay. He confirmed that the items in Mother's order were currently on their way to Walker's Cove from Boston. Sometime after Father's death—but in no way connected with it—the Tory vendor was tarred and feathered, and his home confiscated by the Sons of Liberty. The persecuted individual quickly fled to the safety of Canada, his exact whereabouts unknown.

Fay, feeling under no obligation to track him down in order to pay the outstanding balance, decided that the remainder, some 137 pounds in gold and silver, be returned to me with his compliments—to begin "your new life" as he put it. He closed by offering his and Lydia's help with setting up the interior of the tavern once everything had been delivered.

While composing a letter of thanks to them both for all they had done, I realized more fully than ever, how the Ellingwoods were becoming my new family. Yet I constantly fretted over what people would think about our awkward arrangement: of Suzannah running *my* tavern and not being married to *me* . . . particularly since tavern keeping had been our family trade for two generations.

Bright and early one April morning, I was pleasantly surprised by the arrival of Suzannah, Fanny and Dimmis, who came over to clean and plan the final layout of the great room. Talk of marriage went unsaid, and yet it seemed as if everything was proceeding as Mother had planned . . . but now with only Suzannah and Dimmis running the tavern.

I was very grateful, of course, for I would have been hopelessly lost without their expertise and experience. Having their charming company was incredibly refreshing, and when they left for the night, I missed them terribly—and wished them more in my life.

In late April, the huge order of furniture and other goods finally arrived. Rounding up the number of wagons and horses we needed, Sam also recruited some of the townsfolk to help us haul the furniture from the wharf to the house. There, Suzannah, Dimmis, Lydia and Fanny, would supervise the arrangement, while Sam, Fay, Osgood, Eben and I would do the heavy lifting and placement.

Things were finally falling into place; and looking up at Mother's portrait, I whispered to her, "It's *happening*, Mother. Your tavern will *open* soon, and your dream shall be fulfilled."

By May Day, all the inn's new contents were set up in their proper places. Early on that morning, I sat on my bed, sorting through belongings that were stored in Father's old bedchamber. In a small tin box I found a few silver coins, a bundle of Mother's letters, a lock of her hair, her miniature and her jewelry. What particularly caught my eye, however . . . was that *here* were Mother's rings . . . her betrothal ring and her wedding ring.

Her betrothal ring, which Mother called a "poesy" ring, consisted of a gold band with a blue stone inlaid in its top. It was the same blue color as were Mother's eyes. Engraved on either side of the stone was "Love . . . forever thine . . . is mine . . ." Inside her gold wedding ring was engraved, "James & Ainsley Walker." Although taken by Father as her parting gift on the night of her death, I thought them lost when he died. But no! He kept them among his heart treasures in this box.

As I held the precious symbols of my parents' love in my hands, the blue stone glinted in the sunlight. In its reflections, my eyes moistened as I recalled Father's bitter admonition on that terrible night: to make every minute of life *count*. Choking up at that memory, I took the discovery of her rings as a subtle message from Mother herself . . . and decided to see Suzannah immediately . . . and ask for her hand in marriage.

CLUTCHING THE BETROTHAL ring in my palm, I brushed my hair and pelted to the Ellingwood's front door. Shaking with fear and anticipation, I stood there . . . gathering the courage to ask the girl who saved my life to marry me. Ensuring the ring was secure in my pocket, I cleared my throat, inhaled deeply, and knocked at the door.

When it opened, I was instantly greeted by the fragrance of fresh cut flowers. Suzannah stood before me, looking up with happy loving eyes. She had woven pink and white carnations in her hair. From this floral garland, her hair then parted across her shoulders, with some cascading over her bosom, and some flowing down her back. As I gawked at her in awestruck silence, I nearly swooned as she sweetly commanded, "Oh Jim, please *do* come in!"

Grasping my hand, she drew me into the parlor and stood before the window, where the afternoon sun bathed her in light. Her delicate flowing dress was trimmed with pink ruffles and white lace. Combined with the flowers in her hair, she was nothing less than a little masterpiece, the angel of my dreams. So moved was I by her ethereal presence, that my eyes misted over and my throat began to constrict.

Noticing my expression, she gently caressed my cheek and imploringly whispered, "You *do* like my dress *a little*, don't you, Jim?"

"My heavens . . ." I choked, "indeed, I do . . . the dress and especially the living flower within it . . . *never* have I beheld such compelling beauty."

She blushed with a becoming modesty.

I kissed her hands, and gazing into her wondrous eyes so radiant with love, I could no longer resist . . . and I burst forth in a torrent of words.

"Suzannah, I have faithfully prayed every night since 'then,' that He grant me your precious love. Come to my *heart*, Suzannah, and make your *home* there forever. Let me *love* you and *keep* you and nurture your love. I cannot say there will be no bumps along the way to forever, but I swear I shall *die* if I cannot marry you. And so I ask you now . . . to be my *wife*."

Gathering her in my arms and binding her tightly, I rocked her and rained grateful kisses upon her hair, finally burying my lips among her pink and white flowers. My eyes filled as her arms slowly encircled my waist, and then clamped tightly around me with surprising strength. Overcome by the scent of her hair, her garland, and her answering embrace, I felt myself in a state of ecstatic bliss.

Not wanting to break the spell, I gently lifted Suzannah's chin, and when her lips parted, into them I breathlessly whispered, "My dearest Suzannah, I believe there is a world where hearts are never parted, where tears of sadness never dim our eyes; where nothing exists but love and beauty through eternity . . . and I choose to share eternity . . . with *you*."

And with those words I took her left hand from my waist, and slipped Mother's ring upon her finger. "I *beg* of you, Suzannah, *please* share this journey with me . . . *make* my air castle come true."

Looking down at the ring with her lower lip quivering, and then up at me, she whispered her reply. "I would never make such a journey . . . unless *you* were at my side. I have loved you since we met . . . but you knew it not . . . and so I waited, faithfully believing that Providence would bring your heart to me . . . and now it comes to pass . . . and I shall never love another . . . for I *will* be your loving wife."

As I gently caressed her cheeks she fell silent, her eyes pooling with loving tears. Tilting her head back, her hair fell away as her lips parted in speechless love . . . and she waited.

For me, this was a holy moment . . . and I wanted her more than my own life. I softly kissed each tear stained cheek, and finally, that dear parted mouth. She melted into my kiss, entwining her fingers around my neck so our bodies were closer than they'd ever been before. While my soul burst with unparalleled joy, I whispered in her ear, "My God in *Heaven*, Suzannah!"

"Call me your only love, Jim!" she said breathlessly.

"Oh Suzannah, my *only* love!" I panted, as her mouth once again sought mine.

The feel of her kiss was like Heaven's breath and glorious beyond anything I'd ever experienced. My brain reeled in ecstasy. I couldn't let her go—I would *never* let her go.

Wrapped in each other's arms, we stood silently rocking before the fire, and when the clock bell struck, I gently kissed the top of her head and asked, "How does it feel . . . being betrothed?"

She gazed up at me with a look of pure rapture. "Oh Jim, it's what I've wanted since the day we met. I wish to be all yours, and everything to you for always and forever!"

I brought her ringed hand to my lips and kissed it, and then pressing it to my heart, I confessed, "I love you, Suzannah! I love you *so* much, my heart is *breaking*!"

"Then let it break for love and happiness . . . *never* sadness," she murmured softly, adding in a reassuring tone, "I am in *you*, and you are in *me*, and we shall *never* part, even unto *death*."

"Do you *mean* that, Suzannah?"

"Oh yes, I *do*, like nothing else in God's universe."

"My darling Suzannah . . . I shall *always* be blessed . . . as long as I have *you* . . ."

And so we kissed: a long deep betrothal kiss. But during that sealing kiss, she was so moved she began to cry. She then stepped back, and plucking a flower from her hair, she delicately touched its petals to her tears . . . and as she nestled it in my hair, she pledged a sacred oath. "From love's dearest heart I give to thee your living flower . . . to be your wife and guardian angel . . . and petals of love shall fall upon you . . . for as long as your flower lives."

Her comforting words captured my soul as I instantly vowed, "Then I swear to *God* . . . that I shall do all that's necessary to ensure it *does* live . . . and *thrive* . . ." And looking deep into her soulful eyes, I pulled her toward me. As her lips parted in anticipation, I whispered into her mouth the final words, ". . . and *multiply*."

A New Son

hen a smoldering log rolled from the firedogs onto the hearth, Suzannah broke away from our betrothal kiss, which probably rivaled the legendary kiss of my newly-wed parents that Fanny had remarked upon.

"Jim, the fire needs tending. I really should fix it, but please don't stir." Taking the poker, she attempted to roll the log back, which protested in a shower of sparks.

Seeing her difficulty, I placed my hand gently over hers on the poker. She looked up at me with such an adorable smile, my heart almost stopped.

"Oh, for this moment frozen in time!" I exclaimed.

"Dearest love, in our hearts there are places where time stands still, to ever be *ours* to share. Many, many *more* of these moments will *surely* come to pass."

"Oh *Suzannah*, make it *so* . . ."

I couldn't finish before another kiss was planted sweetly on my lips. Dropping the poker, our arms found each other once more. Pulling away, panting and breathless, Suzannah softly warned, "If the fire isn't *tended*, we shall burn the house down!"

"I know . . . but I think right now *we* could burn the house down without any help from the fire, don't you?"

My playful suggestion served to further inflame her passion. Bringing her lips within an inch of mine, Suzannah murmured her agreement, and what she said next brought a special thrill to me. "Jim, you can't know how a woman's heart *yearns* for certain things. For *mine*, your love is the light that makes your flower live, thrive . . ." while pressing her body urgently against mine, she stood on her toes and echoed my own sacred words, "and *multiply*."

Again, she smothered me with another shower of kisses. I picked her up, twirled her around and set her down in the rocker, bidding her sit and watch a blacksmith demonstrate how to build a fire.

Kneeling by the hearth, I stacked a dozen logs in an **A** pattern and crisscrossed them to provide plenty of air for burning. Almost immediately the flames roared up, filling the parlor with suffocating warmth. I was obliged to stand back as the fireplace snapped and spat enormous flames into the flu and up the chimney.

Suzannah rose from the rocker with a look of concern, but I reassured her there was no cause for alarm as I sat down first so she could nestle in with me. As she rested her pretty head against my right shoulder and looked up into my eyes, she whispered, "Rock me to sleep, my love, so I may dream sweet dreams in your arms!"

I loved having her so close, and we quietly rocked for hours. Eventually, the candles flickered out, leaving only the fire to illuminate the room.

"When we're married, can we *always* rock like this?" she asked, her soulful eyes reflecting the firelight. "Isn't it exciting to speak of *marriage* that way, all of a sudden?"

Kissing the top of her head, I replied, "I've been *married* to you for *years* . . . ever since I first saw you . . . I just never had the courage to *admit* it."

"Really?" she exclaimed, as she giggled with a mixture of embarrassment and glee.

"Yes," I reaffirmed. "From the moment we met . . . for me it was love at first sight."

"But what made you *love* me? I was just a *girl!*" she said in a more serious tone, searching my face for an answer.

"I don't know, Suzannah. The first time I saw you I felt an inexplicable *pull* on my heart. I'd never experienced that before, not with *anyone*. When did you love me?"

Nodding toward the clock, she confessed, "It was the day Father needed the Willard clock repaired."

"Father couldn't come, so he sent his *apprentice* to render the service instead. That was certainly an unforgettable day."

"I remember every detail," she said dreamily. "It was *I* who opened the door to you."

"Yes, you did. Do you remember how I dropped my toolbox on the floor, smashing my foot?"

Suzannah giggled that little girl laugh I loved so much. Kissing her finger, she then touched it to my lips, saying, "I'll *never* forget it . . . speaking of moments frozen in time!"

Because her laughter was so infectious, I had to laugh with her before I could continue. "I jumped around like a cricket in your vestibule, right over *there:* hopping and jumping until your father finally came out to see what the commotion was about."

"Father thought you were teaching me a *dance* step . . . and clapped his hands in time to your agony!"

After breaking out into gales of laughter, we gradually regained our composure.

"How you cared for me then increased your beauty and innocence in my eyes. You revealed the goodness in your heart . . . and as its beneficiary, you made me feel very special."

"So *that* is why you stared and stared at me in the summer kitchen—*after* you repaired the clock!"

"Suzannah, darling, I couldn't help myself! There were constant yearnings in my heart that made me feel hot and foolish around you. When I did the repairs, I deliberately tarried—to peek at your hair, your beautiful skin and those warm, comforting eyes. Whenever you looked at me, somehow I felt safe—totally free of any fear or worry. I knew *then* that this little flower bud would become the precious bloom you are today."

She squeezed my hand to acknowledge her understanding, and lifted her head to kiss me.

"What an adorable sight you are!" I declared. "Ah, sweet dreams *do* come true!"

"Yes, indeed they do," she agreed, "for love makes all things possible."

"My dear wife?" I asked.

"Yes, my husband?"

"I just wanted to hear how it will sound to call you my wife."

"Wondrous joy!" she softly replied.

As we snuggled together near the fire, Suzannah took my hand and pressed it to her heart. There she tenderly stroked it with her thumb. While I stroked hers with mine, I wondered silently, "How could time *dare* be the thief of moments like this?"

WE CONTINUED OUR rocking and noticed with some surprise that the moon had risen, suddenly visible in the parlor window. Suzannah yawned, and then asked, "Jim, after we are married, will you rock me *every* night?"

"I couldn't think of a better way to spend tween time," I replied. "After all, *you* fit perfectly in my lap and *we* fit perfectly in this rocker! We can talk about anything, make plans . . . whatever we want."

"Snuzzle, too?" she asked.

"Snuzzle?" I repeated, unfamiliar with the word. "What is snuzzle?"

"It's my *invention*," she said proudly.

"I see . . . but what does it mean?"

"We are snuzzling *now!*" she explained.

I still wasn't sure what she meant. "Oh, you mean, *rocking?*"

"No, no, no. Snuzzling is a two-word word. It's a combination of *snuggle* and *nuzzle*, and maybe *nestle* too!" she said thoughtfully. "We are *snuzzling* now!"

"I enjoy snuzzling—'tis good stuff!" I affirmed.

Suzannah gave a few more contented yawns as our exciting day was drawing to a close. "My wife to be is getting *sleeeepy!*" I teased, pushing her hair away from her forehead in preparation for a final kiss, adding mournfully, "I must be leaving soon."

"No, Jim, please stay, please hold me and keep me safe. I don't wish to lose a single moment of your love. I don't wish to go to bed *alone*, either," she implored, her eyes sparkling with mischief.

"But, Suzannah, what about your *parents?*" I reminded her, starting to think she was serious.

"They *know* I love you . . . they just don't know we're betrothed yet. So if you stay and hold me all night, you'll be able to talk to Father . . . *first thing* in the morning!"

Needing no coercion, I said, "I shall ask your father then," as I adjusted my arms and she snuzzled her way into a more comfortable position.

"No . . . tomorrow *morning*," she insisted sleepily.

Without moving my body, I got hold of the blanket that was draped over the back of the rocker. Tucking us both in against the night cold, I slouched further into the seat cushion and rocked, watching Suzannah's eyes gradually close.

"How *trusting* for a woman to sleep in a man's arms . . ." I thought, but love *is* trust, and therein lays its hidden beauty.

After tenderly kissing her slumbering lips, before so awake with womanly passion, I then rested my cheek atop her head. Our carnations touched . . . and I kissed the dear hair I revered like spun gold.

How lucky I was to stumble upon a treasure so devout and so good as Suzannah, who wouldn't even *consider* another love from the tender age of fourteen. Yes, love *is* trust in so many ways.

Following Suzannah's example, I drifted off as though I were in God's own featherbed, breathing in the heavenly fragrance of the flowers in her hair. Tonight, all was perfection in Walker's Cove.

THE CLOCK STRUCK six bells and I awoke with a start, and for a moment I couldn't place where I was. Suddenly I realized a bundle of sweetness remained in my lap. I dared not move for fear of waking her, or disturbing our divine position.

Noticing a distinct chill in the room, I looked around and saw the fire had gone out, which is when I saw Sam standing quietly in the parlor doorway.

Totally unprepared for his presence, and worried about his reaction, I managed to say calmly, "Good morning, Sam," while trembling inwardly.

"Well, well, *well*, Jim," was his greeting, and evidently noticing the ring on the finger of Suzannah's hand that rested on top of the blanket, he added, "It seems I have lost one rocking chair . . . *and* my last daughter."

I moved to rise but was confined by my precious bundle—oblivious to our exchange as she slept on undisturbed.

"Oh, no . . . no need to get up," he reassuringly said, striding across the room to add kindling to the fireplace.

Still feeling embarrassed, I desperately tried to explain, "Sir, it's *not* what you think . . ." I feebly protested.

"Oh, it's *not*! He replied angrily. "You mean despite all evidence to the contrary, you *don't* want to marry my daughter?"

Before I could answer, he must have decided to spare me any further distress. With a broad grin, he said, "You are here so often, Jim, I don't know whether you *need* a home of your own. I have *five* daughters, but *four* are out of the house, so I really like having you around."

Then he knelt before the hearth pumping a small bellows to catch the kindling on the firedogs. "I could use a *man* to talk to and get a different perspective, you know . . . then everything wouldn't be from a *female* point of view."

"Yes, sir," I replied, wondering if my voice revealed my huge sense of relief. "I can see how you would suffer from a disadvantage when it comes to a point of view."

"Indeed, I'm *still* outnumbered two to one," he commented sadly while tossing some wood into the fire. Then, turning to face me and observing his sleeping daughter, he added, "It pleases me to see your affections so openly displayed toward my last born."

On firmer footing now, I boldly confessed, "Yes, sir, Suzannah is the living flower of my heart. There she will live and thrive . . ."

Harrumphing first, Sam raised his eyebrows and confidentially added, ". . . and *multiply*? Hmm?"

He had *overheard* us! A hot flash seared across my face and my ears burned, as I wanted to worm my way into the floorboards!

Again, not waiting for a reply from me, he said earnestly, "Jim Walker, I have known your father since boyhood, and I know he could only have raised a *wonderful* son; a good, kind, considerate and sensitive fellow . . . who I've watched grow into a shining example of manhood.

"So it pleases me, son, to see how much you *care* for Suzannah, so much so that your love for her won out over your strong sense of propriety. You chose to risk *my* anger in order to give her what *she* wanted. If you love Suzannah one-*tenth* as much as I love Fanny, I'm well satisfied.

"I know you are betrothed. She has wished it since she was fourteen years old. I'm *delighted* to see her wish finally come to pass . . . *especially* with your mother's ring. Jim Walker, my first son, *welcome* to the Ellingwood family!" He came over and patted me affectionately on the shoulder. "And . . . ah . . . I love your flowers." He humorously added, "*Both* of them!"

"Thank you, sir, and as your first son, I shall do my *best* to honor you."

"I have no doubt you *will*, no doubt whatsoever," he said firmly before he left the room.

At that moment, I felt happiness beyond measure. Because of Suzannah, my new life was beginning—my air castle was, brick by beautiful brick, becoming a reality.

As the fire began to flare, I knew Sam's kindling had caught. A loud pop in the wood startled me and jolted Suzannah awake.

Rubbing the sleep from her eyes, she mumbled groggily, "That *scared* me!" But when she realized where she was, her eyes lit up. She threw off the blanket and wrapped her arms around my neck, crying joyfully, "Oh, *Jim*, you kept me *all night*! You stayed and *snuzzled* me! Oh, I *love* you *so* much!"

In return, I gave her three kisses: one on each cheek and one on her lips.

Suddenly she asked, "If we were snuzzling together all this time, how did you start the fire?"

"I had some help," I said tersely.

"Really, at *this* hour?" she said, sounding puzzled.

"Oh, yes," I said, enjoying her confusion.

"Who was it then?" Suzannah pressed.

"My new father," I replied nonchalantly.

"We must *tell* Father . . . you need to *ask* him for my hand! Please do it *now*, Jim, I want them to know my happiness!"

Hearing the word "father" sent her off on a tangent, since she didn't respond to what *I* had said. But instead of explaining what I meant, I simply said, "They *already* know, Suzannah."

Then, again, she went along on her own track, not seeming to hear me. "My father will be leaving soon, so . . ." But suddenly she stopped, finally realizing who I meant by "my new father."

"You *told* him?" she exclaimed, her mouth open in amazement.

"He already *knew*," I whispered.

"But *how?*"

"When he came into the parlor this morning, he saw us together *and* the ring on your finger. That told him *everything* he needed to know!"

THE WEDDING

ur marriage banns were posted with no objections raised, and our wedding day was set for August 3rd, 1769, when Suzannah would be in her seventeenth year, and I in my twentieth.

Because he was like a father to me, I asked Sam to be my best man. He sheepishly declined, explaining his role was to give his daughter away. But, he added, he would be delighted to honor me in that way if I were *not* marrying Suzannah.

I then wrote a letter to my old friend, Jonathan Barrett, who was still at Harvard, asking him to serve as my best man. But in his reply he explained that as a teacher at the law school, the overseers would not allow him to leave in midterm. He ended his letter with heartfelt wishes for our happiness and an order for an office regula-tor clock, if I was still making them.

Still without a best man, I thought of Doc Brown. Like Mother and Suzannah, Doc had a gift to *feel* hearts, and knew how to heal and care for them too, in the medical *and* the emotional sense. He was also a font of practical wisdom, which seemed to have been acquired through his own life experiences. He generously shared what he knew with young folks like me, who especially needed it. Because of that and his close friendship with my parents, I asked him to be my best man and he gladly accepted.

While I stayed in the clock shop filling backorders, Suzannah and Dimmis prepared the tavern kitchen for cooking and planned the menus. They spent a lot of time outfitting the new cellar, includ-ing ten buckets to draw water from the well that was now located there. Trial runs of the winch—drawing water and foodstuffs up from the cellar to the kitchen—proved successful, and Suzannah was very pleased with its convenience.

In the early evenings, Suzannah reserved solitary time to make her wedding dress. Only when she had finished that task was I allowed to visit with my betrothed and her parents.

Dimmis and I became better acquainted through her closeness with Suzannah. She was very congenial and attentive, as well as unexpectedly refined, possessing both propriety and grace. To me, her most attractive feature was her hair—fiery red and fluffy like Suzannah's— and she *always* wore it down. It contrasted pleasingly with her milky white skin, which was flawless. I could never determine the color of her eyes, for they seemed to change with the light. Sometimes they were a pale robin's-egg blue, but at other times they exhibited a green tint around her irises.

Dimmis also had a very handsome figure. Many of the men in Walker's Cove called her the "tip topper," because she was taller and shapelier than most of the other ladies in our village. I knew she was flattered by their admiration, and I was glad of it, since I felt it might bring some customers into our tavern . . . not only for a pint or two, but also to see *her*.

Mother once recalled to me that her own appearance drew men into the Mariner's Rest; but along with the additional business, came the need to fend off unwanted advances. Dimmis was strong and firm when she needed to be, and I was certain she would have no trouble in such matters.

Dimmis would occasionally mention to Suzannah that besides the loss of Mother in the shipwreck, her greatest lament was losing her violin. She mourned its absence as though it were her child, and so reverently did she remember it, Suzannah had one secretly delivered from Boston as a gift.

It arrived when Suzannah and Dimmis were making final adjustments to the cooking cranes in the kitchen fireplace. As Osgood Lovejoy laid the wooden box upon one of the tables in our tavern's "great room," I witnessed one of the most grateful moments I'd ever seen. Upon opening her gift, Dimmis drew out the violin, and while speechlessly holding its neck, threw her arms around Suzannah, and burst into tears.

As she clutched her tightly, Dimmis gratefully asked, "Suzannah, how can I ever *thank* you? I've *never* had such kindness and love in my *entire life*! *Where* does such beauty come from?"

After gently rubbing Dimmis' back as a mother would, Suzannah brushed away her friend's tears before kissing her cheek and saying, "Dimmis, it comes from within *us* . . . *you* are the essence of kindness and love. And remember, we *love* you, you are *not* in England any longer, you are *home* now, safe and well . . ." And through this tearful embrace, they forged a lifetime bond.

Dimmis, who was orphaned as a child, had never experienced the nurturing love of a parent. She had lived in poverty all her life, and in desperation, with scarcely more than the clothes on her back and a few coins in her pocket, came here seeking a better life. I was damned proud that Mother had chosen *her* for our tavern. I felt *doubly* proud that Suzannah had taken up her plight where Mother had left off: to ensure she would have a decent home, honest work and a new life . . . and thus through the magic of Suzannah's love, Dimmis Sexton was *reborn* in Walker's Cove.

AFTER THAT MOMENTOUS day, my life became more musical. Many times I would drive by the Thatchers' and hear Dimmis playing in her chamber. Just as often, I would visit the Ellingwoods and be treated to a duet with pianoforte and violin. Invariably, the music was transporting. Some selections were from the great European composers, but many were Gaelic folk tunes. The repertoire included slow, soulful and introspective laments of bygone days, as well as pieces with faster tempos, played as though the fiddle was on fire. Whenever Suzannah couldn't keep pace with Dimmis' violin, she would simply stop playing and listen in stunned admiration.

The opening of the tavern had to be delayed since that summer I spent nearly seven days a week singlehandedly making the remainder of the clocks, which would carry me beyond our wedding date. I had to be free of one obligation before being able to fully immerse myself in the next.

Meanwhile, Suzannah and her sisters were busy making all the preparations for our wedding. But every Sunday, just before sunset, Suzannah and I would steal some time to ourselves and saunter down to Walker's Point. While we watched the setting sun from our usual spot, between kisses she would inform me of the week's doings. On our last "unmarried" Sunday outing, she announced she had a wedding gift for me. Then, with barely contained excitement, she told me she and Dimmis had the tavern ready to open—it was waiting only for me. She knew it would come as a surprise, since I had been too absorbed in my activities at the shop to notice all the changes in my surroundings.

In turn, I could only gasp in astonishment and admiration at her accomplishment. So after kissing her tenderly, she snuggled her back against my chest and faced the sunset. She then drew my arms around her, and for the rest of our evening, she remained locked in my loving embrace.

We would silently kiss from time to time, and then she would take my hands and tenderly nibble on my fingers. Through her constant loving affection, there were moments when words became woefully inadequate . . . but our hearts would forever savor . . . and our souls would never forget.

ON THE MORNING of August 3rd, 1769, I awoke from sleep for the last time as a bachelor.

An urgent knocking at the door proved to be Doc, arriving early to help me dress, so that I looked "worthy" of marrying such a special lady as "Miss Suzannah Ellingwood." Doc spoke of her as if she were royalty—which in *my* eyes she was. He noted the church was nearly filled, and there was only one hour remaining until the ceremony. He also reminded me about Mother's wedding ring, which would be entrusted to his care until he turned it over to me during the ceremony.

Suzannah and I had decided to use Mother's wedding band because it was doubly cherished as having belonged to my parents and been a symbol of their love. The Ellingwoods had long ago saved her grandfather's ring for Suzannah to give to her husband-to-be—and that would soon be mine.

Out front, Doc had decorated Winnie and the carriage with ribbons and bows in pink, white and blue. She had three bows attached to either side of her harness, so they would stream in the breeze as she trotted along.

When I had finished my grooming and donned my clothes and presented myself for Doc's inspection, he said, "You look like a pretty natty *fellow*, Jim!" Poking me in the ribs he added, "Hell, are you getting *married* or something?"

I laughed as I quipped, "That's a distinct possibility, Doc, but *you* must get me to the church on time!"

"Your carriage *awaits*, Master James," he announced, bowing gracefully toward the door.

Doc AND I entered the church by the side door, which was Reverend Metcalf's usual entrance. He met us there and invited us to tarry in the sacristy, a small room across from grandmother's organ. The murmur of voices echoed through the church, and leaning into the hall to observe the congregation, I quickly retreated and shivered with fear . . . there were *people* out there, *lots* of them.

Sensing my anxiety, Doc adjusted the collar on my shirt as he declared brightly, "So, young fellow, are you ready to take the *plunge* into *marriage?*"

"Yes, Doc, and I could never have done it without you and Sam. Without you two, I wouldn't exist, and neither would my beautiful Suzannah."

"Ah, yes!" Doc exclaimed, sitting on a chair to adjust my cuffs. "In my older years, I've found that some of the most beautiful things I've ever seen are created by *God*—sunrises, sunsets, the *moon* on Midnight Blue . . . But in all the universe, Jim, there's nothing so sublime as resting one's eyes upon that one beautiful *human* creation . . . *sanctioned* by *God* himself . . ."

"And *what* do humans create that's more beautiful than a sunset?" I asked, laughing in anticipation of another teasing remark.

Lifting his brows, Doc patted my shoulder and whispered, "A *bride*."

Before I could form a reply, Reverend Metcalf, now fully clad in his vestments, came up to us to instruct us on our respective positions at the altar. After we took our places, he stepped forward to take center stage, facing the main entrance of the church. After a flurry of dainty footsteps echoed from there, all became silent. Reverend Metcalf nodded toward the organist.

At that moment, the choir stood, as did the entire congregation. Next, a thunderous crescendo from the organ shook the floor beneath us, as the choir began to sing with a mighty volume so gloriously as to send chills down my back. The sound descended upon the pews, and I was *certain* it resonated to the very gates of heaven—and I felt as if my soul had risen along with it. I thought of Mother and Father then, and wished they could be here with me at my wedding.

As the bridal retinue made its way to the altar, it seemed as though Heaven's angels were passing through the church . . . and most breathtaking of all was the final angel, who, after kissing her father, came over to stand beside me.

Suzannah was beautiful beyond measure, a vision in blue, pink and white. She wore a blue openwork dress, the material light and airy against the heat. Beneath it was a pleated white chemise ruffled daintily at the cuffs, while tiny pink and blue embroidered flowers adorned the edging of the neckline. Most endearing of all to me, because it hearkened back to the day of our betrothal, pink and white carnations graced her hair, which flowed in thick cascading waves across her shoulders and back, and gently caressed her bosom.

I took her hand as we turned to face Reverend Metcalf. When the choir finished the hymn, through his silent gesture the congregation took their seats . . . and the ceremony began.

"A hearty welcome to all of you gathered now before the altar of God. We are here to celebrate and be witnesses to the deepest want, and the greatest gift of the human heart: love . . . and marriage. In *marriage*, man and woman are meant to be all they *can* be to each other . . . a oneness of heart, of soul, and of purpose. In all of God's infinite universe, there is nothing more sublime than when a man and a woman join their hearts and souls together . . . and vow to love each other forever . . . and to build upon that love, a kingdom second only to that of God Himself.

"Between the hearts of Suzannah Ellingwood and James Walker, there is a unity so profound, that their love transcends mere existence and mortality . . . thus opening the holy path from God to man. And what lies at the end of this path? The peace of God's love, the comfort of His presence, and the fulfillment of the soul's capacity to love. For God hath ordained that woman shall draw *life* from man, and give it back as the bearing of children. Look into a newborn's face and *behold* the face of God! And *children*, the greatest gift that love can bring, shall perpetuate this love we celebrate today, as will their grandchildren and great-grandchildren; long after Suzannah and James have embarked on their heavenly journey."

Reverend Metcalf then turned to us, and raising his hands declared, "These words, once exchanged in the presence of God, shall never pass away. And so I say unto you both . . . *love* is the bread of Heaven that satisfies the soul. And at our end, it is the light that illuminates our path unto heavenly peace and everlasting life."

Gently placing his hand upon my head, Reverend Metcalf continued. "Love is the highest service of our lives, and so, James Walker . . . I charge thee in God's holy name to bind Suzannah into the embrace of thy love . . . in body and soul . . . and keep her evermore thine. Doest thou promise to protect her, care for her, and love her evermore as thy wedded wife, in all circumstances and conditions . . . until death do you part?"

My throat ached as I took the ring from Doc. When I turned to look into Suzannah's upturned face, my vision blurred as I took her tiny hand and drew the ring over her third finger, saying, "I do . . . as God is my witness . . . I shall love thee *evermore* . . . my *dearest* Suzannah."

Suzannah, eyes fluttering to chase her welling tears, looked from me to her wedding band and back. Finally, overcome with emotion, she burst out crying and threw her arms around me, burying her face in my chest. Instinctively wrapping my arms around her, I cradled her to my heart, stroking her hair and rocking her gently.

A heartfelt chorus of "Oh's" and "Ah's" emanated from the congregation, while Reverend Metcalf embraced us as we cried—I into her carnations, she into my shirt.

"We still have one vow remaining," he whispered, "so take your time . . ."

Katharine, who was standing behind Suzannah, came forward and handed her a handkerchief to dry her tears. "Remember dear sister, *you* are married but James is *not*. . ." She gave her a kiss and tidied her hair as Suzannah, regaining her composure, faced Reverend Metcalf with a brave and beautiful smile.

Here and there the sound of sniffling could be heard among the guests, as some were moved to tears by the scene they had just witnessed.

Finally, when the room was again silent, Reverend Metcalf, placing his hand gently upon Suzannah's head, continued. "And likewise . . . Suzannah Ellingwood . . . I charge thee in God's holy name to bind James into the embrace of thy love . . . in body and soul . . . and keep him evermore thine. Doest thou promise to protect him, care for him, and love him evermore as thy wedded husband, in all circumstances and conditions . . . unto death do you part?"

I turned to Suzannah and looked steadily into her eyes. As she took my trembling hand, she met my gaze for a long moment. We could only hear the sound of our own breathing—not a soul stirred otherwise. As she slipped the band of gold upon my finger, deep within my being I suddenly felt her spirit *pull* at my very essence . . . and nestle it into her heart.

She then declared proudly in tones loud enough for all to hear, "Oh *yes*, I *do*! I will be your wife . . . *and* your guardian angel!" And looking up at me with renewed tears, she secretly whispered, *"Evermore!"*

Reverend Metcalf's eyes filled as he heard this, and looking out over the congregation, he solemnly declared, "May this marriage between Suzannah and James be blessed with unconditional love, the joy of intellect, the felicity of humor, and the miracle of children," adding triumphantly, "What God hath joined together, no man shall tear asunder!"

Turning us to face the congregation he joyfully announced, "Ladies and gentlemen . . . may I present to family and friends, our *newest* couple, *Mr. and Mrs. James Walker!*"

The congregation rose spontaneously in boisterous applause.

Reverend Metcalf gestured for us to walk down the aisle together, so joining hands we did so while the enthusiastic clapping continued. The organ started up with a Gaelic tune that Suzannah had undoubtedly chosen beforehand, and we must have kissed, shared tears with, or shook hands with every denizen of Walker's Cove, and many who weren't.

As we approached the end of the aisle, Sam came over to his daughter and embraced her, sharing private words from his heart. I saw her tears come again at whatever he said, and she hugged him very tightly standing on tiptoe.

I smiled as I recalled how I always wondered why Suzannah was so short when her father was so tall.

At all events, Sam turned to me and shook my hand furiously. "My last born is in *wonderful* hands! None better! Somewhere, Jim, I *know* your parents are smiling! This was their fondest wish above all others—to see you two *marry*."

With grateful tears, I threw my arms around my newly adopted father, who was now my father-in-law too.

After bidding Sam and Fanny goodbye, Suzannah and I, hand in hand, slowly made our way through the throng until we were outside the church. There, our wedding carriage awaited us, with Winnie regarding us sympathetically. Since she seemed as eager to flee as we were, we climbed in immediately, and waved to the crowd as I barked out, "Home, Winnie!" whereupon, to the huzzahs of the crowd, she trotted off.

Suzannah was now my irreplaceable treasure . . . and to begin our life's journey together, I was finally bringing her home.

HOME

 ently setting down my pink and blue bundle before the door, I threw the latch and let the door swing open. Suzannah peered into the empty house, and looking somewhat apprehensive, she softly said, "This is the first time I'll enter this house as a *wife* . . ." Bowing her head, she then murmured, "Jim, I feel strange . . . as though it's not really *mine*. After all, it belongs to your parents."

"No, Suzannah," I explained, "it belongs to *us*—and they would have wished it so. It shelters many tender and happy memories, which we shall revisit together."

She smiled as she wrapped her arms around my waist, and leaned her head against my chest. As surely as if she had spoken it, I *knew* in my heart that she was remembering the flour fight, the times spent so pleasantly as Mother's apprentice . . . and how fond they were of each other.

"And those *dark* times?" she softly asked, looking into my eyes with a soulful expression. She was remembering that terrible night when she nearly died, right where we now stood.

"We shall *learn* from them," I replied, gently kissing her forehead, "and remember how they brought us closer together . . . and then, we'll let them drift into a sea of forgetfulness."

"While we live and love on . . ." she added with conviction.

Letting that sentiment hang in the air to mark the occasion, I picked up Suzannah once more and carried her into her new home.

I spun her around, while giving her fierce hugs, such that she squeaked several times. Finally, I nipped playfully at her neck while I let her down, and with an air of feigned formality, I proudly announced, "Welcome *home*, my dear Mrs. Walker!"

As she surveyed the home that would soon become a tavern, Suzannah echoed breathlessly, "Yes, *home* . . ." Then she ventured a few tentative steps toward the new parlor where Sam's rocker now resided, a wedding gift from the Ellingwoods. There she regarded Mother's portrait above the fireplace.

I felt a sudden pang of guilt thinking there should never be *two* Mrs. Walkers in the same house, so I offered, "I can remove this if it makes you feel uncomfortable . . ."

"Absolutely *not!*" she sharply rebuked, "She will stay here *with* us . . ." Then her voice tapered softly as she added, "for *all* our days . . ." Drawing closer to the canvas, Suzannah gazed intently at Mother's face. When she closed her eyes and stood there silently for several moments, I felt that *somehow* they were exchanging "heart feelings"—perhaps for one last time. Finally, she nodded and whispered, "I *will*." She looked away for a moment and then back at me, her eyes moist with tears—and I *knew*.

Enthralled by her powers, I asked, "She has given you her blessing, hasn't she?"

Nodding silently, she then turned toward the portrait once more, and tenderly stroking Mother's cheek, she wistfully uttered, "*Home* and *mother* . . . there are no words more sacred . . . to life's tender dreams and associations." Sighing and dabbing at her tears, Suzannah smiled upward at Mother and whispered, "I *love* you . . ." and blew her a gentle kiss.

Overcome with emotion, I encircled Suzannah's waist from behind. Placing her little hands atop mine, we rocked side to side as one, regarding the portrait with love and reverence. After a few minutes, Suzannah turned to me, smiled and softly said, "And thus . . . I begin my first day of housewifery."

THAT DAY THE parlor was not only in disarray, but airless and brutally hot from the intensity of the sun. Apologizing profusely, I

threw open the parlor windows to allow in a breeze. This inspired Suzannah to go about opening every window on the first floor.

Perspiring heavily from her modest effort, she next drew me to Sam's rocker and sat coyly on my lap.

I apologized some more as I mopped my brow. "My poor flower has such a hot and disheveled pot to dwell in—I'm so *sorry*, darling."

Bringing her face up to mine, she delivered a deep, salty kiss. It thrilled me, for it was hungry and daring. Then she placed her hand over mine and squeezed it reassuringly. "Your flower cares *not* for what pot it grows in . . . so long as she gets love, rain and sunshine," Then tapping the center of my chest, she whispered, "from *here!*"

Surprising me with a sudden burst of passion, she nibbled on my ear and pressed her hand against me, until I became aroused. Then she threw her arms around my neck as she panted, "Oh, Jim . . . we are actually married—will you take me now? I shan't wait a moment longer! Can we go upstairs now?"

"As you wish, my angel," I said. Then I warned her, "but you'll find it even *hotter* upstairs!"

In reply, she took my forefinger and put it into her mouth, suggestively feathering it with her tongue. Astonished at her brashness, I shuddered with delight, nodding eagerly as my anticipation grew tenfold.

Suddenly she stopped and suggested thoughtfully, "Then let's *wait* . . . perhaps five minutes?" Then, with a mischievous giggle, she declared, "*I* will finish the house tour . . . then *you* can tour *me* . . ."

Nearly insane with desire, I was tempted to say the house tour could wait; but as she wished, we left the parlor and proceeded to inspect every room. While Suzannah scrutinized everything, she made comments and suggestions, while I took notes and made sketches based on her observations.

"A home should be attractive to the *eye* as well as the *heart* . . ." she declared, "*especially* if it's also a place of business."

"Well, Mrs. Walker, perhaps we should put a little more thought into the aesthetics of our home—*and* our tavern."

"Well, dear Mr. Walker, just remember that happiness of home and heart is *my* job! Such happiness will lend complete harmony to our new lives." I knew full well, of course, that her abiding presence and cheerful goodwill were a wonderful start to that end.

As she looked out one of the kitchen windows, she commented wistfully, "Even the humblest dwelling can be made a home . . . through just a bit of loving care."

Sensing she was thinking of her old home, perhaps even her own chamber, I clasped her tightly and kissed her forehead. As I released her I declared, "Well, darling, this whole house is *yours!*"

She placed a dainty finger in her mouth and continued to look around while I inquired, "So, what *are* you going to do with this place? It seems to need so much."

"I think I will ask my sisters to come visit . . . and help me make curtains."

"Curtains?" I repeated with surprise. "In a *tavern?*"

"Yes, indeed! Lydia, Jenny and Katharine can make curtains, and Sarah can paint beautiful landscapes on the plaster walls, if we'd like."

"Wall paintings would be quite attractive . . ." Then thinking aloud, I continued, "But I would hate to have drunken, besotted fools mess them up by spilling rum, flip or *worse* on them."

"There will be *no* drunkenness in *our* tavern!" came her terse reply.

"It sounds like everything will be in good hands, then."

"Ten of them to be exact!" Suzannah replied brightly.

"Wonderful idea!" I agreed, remembering with affection her sisters' collective fondness for fun and silliness. "Your sisters don't come often enough for my liking," I added, recalling how they teased Suzannah about the first note I gave her—around the time of our memorable sleigh ride.

"No, they don't." She replied wistfully, "I wish they *would* come more often, especially with the tensions afoot in Boston."

"Well, my little bride, I shall leave you in peace to explore your new home. Meanwhile, I'll put Winnie to feed, and then return shortly. Are you *ready?*"

"Of course, I'm ready," she said with a perky nod and mischievous smile.

After a deep kiss I left her; a small but strong little figure; barely
seventeen and a married woman, standing alone on the very spot
Mother stood . . . when I asked her about Suzannah for the very
first time.

WHEN I GOT back, I found Suzannah with a bundle of sheets, ready
to prepare our new bedchamber for the all-important first night. We
went upstairs together into the sweltering heat of the second floor,
and opened every window to let in some fresh cool air.

When I returned to our chamber, Suzannah was already flapping
the blanket over the bed, sending dust motes flying in all directions
through the sultry air. The retreating sunbeams highlighted their
myriad gyrations, and her face dropped as she watched them settle.
With an air of total frustration she exclaimed, "No matter what I
do, I can't be rid of them!"

Watching them twirl and float slowly downward, I took her
blanket and laid it on the bed. "Let's go downstairs until it cools off
up here. Meanwhile, these particles will settle and be gone. Come,
Suzannah, we *shall* return."

She carefully smoothed the blanket with a dainty touch here
and there, and reluctantly left the room to accompany me.

Once we settled ourselves downstairs, she took a seat at the
secretary desk to write a note to her sisters, who were lodging with
the Ellingwoods for the wedding. She thanked them for her wedding gifts, and solicited their advice about our tavern. She closed
with an invitation for them to come and begin decorating—the
very next day!

While she was thus occupied, I ferreted through Mother's heart
treasures, and discovered a letter from my father to my mother that
I hadn't seen before. It seemed that my grandfather Silas was a strict
guardian, seldom allowing Mother to become friendly with men in
general, *especially* customers of the Mariner's Rest.

Judging from the content of the letter, Father seemed to think he outwitted Silas for "The Belle of Portsmouth." The clock's set up and "weekly maintenance to ensure its accuracy" were but a ruse to get by the crafty old Silas and spend time with Mother. So while grandfather got the tall clock, Father got the girl!

"Remarkable!" I said aloud. "What a crafty old fox you were, Father."

Thinking I was alone, from behind me I suddenly heard, "And what a crafty old fox *you* are!" Next, a pair of warm arms came from behind my chair and surrounded me, as I felt her gentle kiss upon my head, and finally, the exquisite softness of her cheek against mine. Whispering in my ear, she sweetly asked, "Rocking time?"

Placing the letter down, I took her hand and led her to the rocker, which was fortunately situated near an open window. I sat on its cushioned seat and Suzannah snuzzled into my lap. I wrapped my arms about my little treasure while she settled her head on my shoulder. As I started to rock and tenderly stroke her hair, I noticed a dreamy expression on her face as she closed her eyes. Feeling her relax, I was overjoyed knowing that we were home at last . . . and she had made it so.

Gazing at the rising moon through the sultry twilight, I saw that it was Midnight Blue. In its honor, I pressed my lips to Suzannah's head, keeping them there for a long, thankful, loving kiss. My thoughts flashed back to that day I remembered so vividly . . . seemingly from a lifetime ago.

She must have sensed the strength of my feelings, since she squeezed my hands and pressed them to her heart.

"Suzannah?"

"Yes, my husband?"

"I have a confession to make."

"I *know* . . ." she replied, and looking up at me with her understanding smile, she added, "Never fear to tell me of your feelings, your hopes, your dreams—and especially your sorrows. I'll be here for you evermore. I'm your wife now *and* your guardian angel."

I lifted her chin to kiss her, saying, "My God in Heaven, Suzannah, how could I ask any more of this life?"

She responded with a deep rapturous kiss that sent me to a sacred place in her heart, where I alone was privileged to be. As the kiss lingered, I prayed silently to Midnight Blue, "Thank you for this most precious of all gifts . . . my loving wife."

When our lips finally parted, Suzannah softly asked, "So tell me, Jim, what does your heart say?"

Kissing the center of her forehead and caressing her head to my shoulder, I gently stroked her hair as I made my confession. "Some years ago, when I was seventeen, I sat alone on Walker's Point. It was a night like tonight—embracingly warm with a very light breeze—and it was Midnight Blue.

"I was lonely and wanting for a companion . . . a *friend* with whom to share good times and adventures. When I saw that first star, I hoped my little wish would be granted, for none of my friends remained in Walker's Cove.

"It was that very night I learned of your father's imminent arrival. Thinking my wish had been granted—but given in error to my father—my heart broke; but I could *never* tell Father about it. On the contrary, I was overjoyed at the news that his boyhood friend would be back in his life.

"But *my* wish was not ignored, after all. For the very next day, I found *you*. Of course, I didn't know at that moment that my wish had been granted. Only later did I realize it; and not only for friendship, but also for love, life and happiness." I paused briefly then to catch my breath.

"There are *thousands* of wives, Suzannah, but *none* are living angels on earth. You may freely deny such talk, but I believe you are of that nature. Mother always said you were unique and special. She was so correct.

"We have been through so much since that day; ups and downs, triumphs and tragedies, even in this very house. Through it all, you remained faithful to me in heart and soul, when you were never compelled to do so, save by your golden heart."

While fingering her wedding band, I struggled to continue. "I wanted to tell you that I shall *never* in this life . . . be able to repay God—or *you*—for the gift of your loving self."

Suzannah's beautiful gray-blue eyes filled with tears, and while the evening breeze blessed us with its cooling breath, she then said, "Remember you told me once that you were saddened because your heart couldn't express its feelings?"

I nodded.

"And I told you not to worry, that your heart would express itself in its own time?"

"Yes."

"My dearest husband, it just did, more eloquently than any angel or mortal could ever hope to hear—and this is not the first time. You are my rock and I am the wave, and I shall forever hold you in love's embrace."

And placing her hands behind my head and pulling my face toward hers, my vision blurred as her loving mouth met mine . . . and I faded into kisses of exquisite tenderness.

Before retiring for the night, Suzannah wished first to unpack her trunks and deliver the note to her sisters. I felt a twinge of disappointment at the idea of another delay, but I was pleased she was so devoted to getting our house in order. Accordingly, we ended our rocking session to arrange our belongings just as we wanted them. When we finished, Suzannah went off to her mother's, while I fetched wood for the parlor fireplace. There, we would resume our rocking in delightful anticipation of the pleasures to come.

I stacked the wood in the fireplace and coaxed the tinder so it finally ignited. A fire was just beginning to flare when I realized Suzannah had still not returned. Overcome with a heartrending anxiety about the whereabouts of my new bride, at that moment a light rustling sound emanated from the back door. Turning to see what it was, Suzannah entered the room with a tear-stained face.

I rushed toward her and immediately asked, "What's *happened*, darling? What's upset you so?"

Looking up at me with reddened eyes she angrily declared, "This is *not* the way to begin a *marriage*, Jim!" And with that, she dashed upstairs to our chamber.

I followed her like a pistol shot and found her lying face down on our bed, sobbing into her pillow. In stupefied silence, I sat beside her and started stroking her hair. Finally, after rubbing her back a long while, she seemed more relaxed, and then I bravely asked, "My God, Suzannah, what have I done? Why is my new bride of a few hours in tears? Do you wish to go home and not be married? Are you afraid? Please tell me, dearest!"

Rolling on her side to face me, Suzannah continued to cry uncontrollably like a child, coughing and making intermittent choking sounds.

"I . . . oh, Jim . . . I'm such a *terrible* bride!" she wailed in abject misery.

My brain was suddenly reeling and I panicked, thinking she didn't wish to be married after all. "For God's sake, Suzannah. What makes you utter such nonsense?"

Throwing her arms around me, she pleaded, "Oh Jim, forgive me, forgive me, find it in your heart to *forgive* me!"

"Of *course*, I forgive you . . . but forgive you for *what*?" I asked, still anguishing about her distress and her abrupt mood change from before.

"I'm a *terrible* bride!" she repeated, shaking her head while the tears kept coming.

Pressing her to my heart, I said firmly, "Suzannah, there is *never* any way you will *ever* convince me that *you* are a terrible bride!" After lifting her chin to kiss her wet lips, I dabbed her face with a clean handkerchief. Then I took her in my arms and added, "Now stop this nonsense and tell me what's in your heart."

After crying into my shirt with muffled sobs, she finally looked up at me as rivers of tears streamed from her pleading eyes. "Oh, Jim . . . I am *sick* . . ."

I stroked her hair tenderly and softly said, "Well, you look fine to me, darling. Where do you hurt?"

"Here . . ." she cried, pointing to her heart.

"But why?" I asked, in my best Doc Brown manner.

Looking up at me as if her heart were breaking, she moaned, "I can't perform my bridal obligations because of my sickness. I'm so *sorry*, Jim!"

Stupidly I asked, "*What* bridal obligations? We are married, you *are* a bride!"

Entwining her fingers in my hair, she pulled me closer, and as if sharing a secret, she whispered in my ear, "You don't understand . . . I have the *womanly* sickness. It comes once a month and is the *bane* of a woman's existence."

Finally understanding her plight, I said, "But you never mentioned it before now, Suzannah."

"Well, *that* is one thing a woman only shares with her mother . . . and her husband—but only when necessary."

I started rubbing her back again, saying, "I see. But how does that affect your heart?"

Threading her arms around my neck she replied, "Because it *breaks* at thinking our wedding night . . . our lovemaking . . . has to *wait*."

As she used the handkerchief to wipe her tears, her face suddenly brightened. "But I have *other* ways I can give to you!" As she reached for my belt, I had to stop her hands. Looking disappointed, she said, "Don't you wish me to make you happy on our wedding night?"

"Of course I do, Suzannah," I said breathlessly, recalling her earlier display of passion. "I wish it more than anything! But darling, I want us to enjoy each other *together*, not one at a time. It doesn't matter if I don't have it tonight. I would rather *wait* until your sickness is done, when there will be no barrier to *your* happiness."

Throwing her arms around me, she declared joyfully, "I have the *best* husband in the world!"

"And I have a living *angel* for a wife . . . I couldn't be more blessed. Now, come downstairs and we'll sit before the fire and snuzzle away our wedding night . . . while eating cake and drinking tea!"

After that, we bounded down the stairs together. Laughing and poking each other, we drifted into the parlor where the fire was well underway—it being an unusually cool night for August. And once again my bride's beautiful eyes shone with unalloyed happiness.

While I sat in the rocker before the fire, Suzannah fetched our tea and cake. Then she eased herself onto my lap, and in between sips and bites, we exchanged long, ardent kisses and caresses. The love I saw in her eyes after each kiss melted my soul.

"You are indeed the most beautiful woman in the world," I whispered into her lips. She replied with a passionate kiss that seemed to last for an hour.

When at last our lips parted, Suzannah asked, "Will you still look upon me with pleasure when I'm an old woman, Jim? Would you love me if my face was wrinkled, and my hair was all gray and stringy with old age? Would you love me if my shoulders were bent and my neck crooked forward? Imagine if you can, dear husband, the vital young girl before you, as an old wasted hag with no teeth, unable to get to the privy or undo her own petticoats!"

"Age can be the enemy of lust and passion for many couples," I replied. "But always remember my little bride, time may erode your youthful beauty, but *never* the beauty of your heart."

As I pressed her head to my chest, I said, "You shall never be too old for me, dear one! And what makes you think *I* would become any more handsome with age? *I* will probably lose my hair, my strength—and perhaps even my *wits*! I shan't have a sound tooth in my entire underjaw, and will end up a drooling, delusional old fool, a mere shell of the man *you* married."

Laying her hand upon my chest, she softly replied, "So long as your heart is *here*, so too will be my love."

As we rocked, a piece of cake suddenly found its way to my lips. This I allowed to be placed in my mouth, whereupon I gently gripped *her* fingers between *my* lips, and suggestively feathering them with my tongue, I withdrew them with a slow and deliberate motion. Suzannah shuddered, moaned and clung to me again for another long and passionate embrace.

We finally decided to finish the cake by dividing the remaining piece in two, and ate our portions . . . never taking our eyes from each other's.

Afterward, holding her tightly, I rocked before the fire, basking in the warm sanctity of wedded bliss. When I bent to kiss my little bride once again, I realized that the cradle-like motion, along with the fireside heat, had lulled her into a deep sleep.

As I placed soft kisses upon her hair and forehead, it was a great comfort to know that even though we couldn't make love on our wedding night, we were well satisfied with God's blessings: for today, "our day," He gave us the gift of each other . . . and *that* we would share . . . now, and ever after.

Day's End

 espite the blazing heat and humidity of the week that followed, Suzannah and her sisters worked tirelessly to put our house in perfect order. Their ceaseless labor made me even more aware of how lucky I was . . . to have my wife . . . and belong to this good and generous family my parents loved so much. Fanny and Sam respected our privacy, and true to their word, treated me like their son.

Fanny brought us all food and drink every day at noon, and we sat around the kitchen table sharing meaningless prattle we enjoyed immensely. Back at work, we laughed often, even at the expense of productivity, at the sisters' comic antics—depicting their fatigue from the heat, or reproaching themselves in an exaggerated manner for careless errors and slips of their brushes, needles and scissors.

At the end of that week, we had our first formal meal together—as an entire family—in the great room. Participating in the camaraderie of the Ellingwoods meant the world to me, for in spite of my sisters-in-law's constant teasing and playful antics, they were always kind, generous and loving to the core of their being—and I loved them for it; for in them I clearly saw where Suzannah got her beautiful heart and disposition.

The Ellingwoods were unique among families, and I knew that when Suzannah's sisters left for Boston, I would feel bereft of their company. I secretly wished that supper would never end . . . for afterward, as my sisters-in-law packed their belongings to tearful goodbyes and numerous embraces, a large lump swelled in my throat and would *not* go away. I felt I had somehow married each and every one of them. The truth be told, my heart broke to watch them leave . . . for now all their endless activity and commotion would be gone, replaced by an empty penetrating silence.

After her sisters returned to Boston, Suzannah and I carried on together. I was usually outside, splitting rails for fences, while Suzannah was inside, putting the final touches on our chamber, and cleaning the great room's fireplace. All day long, the relentless heat would sap my strength until I was totally exhausted.

On just such a day, when the merest exertion produced rivers of perspiration and considerable discomfort, I managed to drag myself back to our front door. As I looked out toward Walker's Point, I saw the sun slowly approaching the horizon.

"Suzannah?" I called into the house.

After several moments she appeared at the door, looking like a drowned chimney sweep: her apron was a mess, her hair was all askew, and her dress was soaked with perspiration. Her lovely face was tired, and her eyes were baggy and blackened with soot. We were both sorely in need of a well-deserved rest.

Reaching for her hand, I declared, "Let's go to the point . . . I've had enough, haven't you?"

Giving me a sooty crooked smile that was totally captivating, I gently pushed her hair aside and again suggested, "Come darling, it's day's end . . . and this was no way to spend your first wedded week." Without a word, she dropped her brush to the floor, removed her apron and placing it on a chair by the door, she took my hand and we left.

We walked down the dusty street hand-in-hand, entertained all the way by melodious birdsong and squalling sea gulls. As we continued on to Walker's Point, she smiled through her fatigue in anticipation of our unexpected respite. Passing the beech tree where I'd carved our initials, we heard the waves crashing power-fully against the rocks. As we clambered across them, Suzannah breathed deeply of the cooling sea air, and the salty mist sprayed us with a refreshing shower.

Walker Tavern after expansion.

Once we arrived at the point, Suzannah sat heavily upon our favorite rocky ledge. Facing west, she lay back and closed her weary eyes, using her forearm to shield them from the retreating sunlight.

I went on to the tidal pool, and kneeled down to dowse my face. It was *so* invigorating! I pulled off my shirt and soaked it in the water, then draped it over my head, thereby removing several layers of sweat and grime. Oh, what a welcome relief!

When I looked back at Suzannah, I saw she was now sitting upright on the ledge, suffering silently in the scorching heat. My new bride was exhausted, overworked and overheated; so I thought of a way to cool her. First, I dipped and rinsed my shirt in the cool saltwater. Wadding it into a ball, I returned to her side and drawing her hair back from her face, I gently mopped her forehead and cheeks and then her neck, removing most of the grime. The relief in her eyes told me all I needed to know.

She put her hand over mine—the one that held my shirt—and guided it softly across her temples and over her delicate ears. She then took it and squeezed it so the remaining water dribbled onto her head. "Feels *wonderful*," she said.

I kissed her tenderly then, and found that she tasted pleasingly of salt and perspiration, but she was still too hot. Returning to the tidal pool to rinse the shirt again, I lost my footing on the seaweed and slipped into the water. Suzannah screamed as I fell in, but since it was only waist deep, I came to the surface straightaway with no harm.

Suzannah, standing above me at the precipice, anxiously asked, "Are you all right? I feared you might *drown*. And we've only been married ten days!"

"I think I can safely say," I replied while vigorously rubbing my chest and face with the cooling seawater, "that I have found *bliss* in this tidal pool!"

"Bliss?" Suzannah asked, looking into it skeptically.

When I looked up to answer her, I noticed she was still perspiring heavily . . . and she looked so uncomfortable in her heavy, sweat-laden dress.

"I lost my shirt, Suzannah! The tide has carried it off!"

"Oh Jim . . . *now* what will you do?" she asked, exasperated by fatigue.

"*THIS!*" I jumped up and grabbed her waist and brought her down with me into the pool, dress and all.

Suzannah screamed, and then laughed uncontrollably as I made certain she was thoroughly dunked from head to toe. Her sopping dress clung tightly to her tiny perfect figure, making her look like a drowned squirrel. Her hair hung loose and being heavy with seawater, she tossed her head to shake off the excess. As she did, I caught two thick locks and kissed them, and looking up at me, she'd begun to shiver, as water dripped from her dainty chin.

I kissed her quivering lips and clasped her wet torso to mine, hoping to provide her with some warmth. As she gazed up at me adoringly, her eyes seemed larger than ever and more intensely gray-blue. Her hair floated freely in the water, and as I played with it, I finally declared, "Well, little bride . . . I guess you're not hot and tired any longer."

She squeezed my waist and finally said, " No, I'm not, darling . . . and I'm *done* now."

"Done?" I repeated stupidly, disappointed that our water play was over.

"We have something else to do now. Remember why we couldn't make love on our wedding night?" she asked.

"Yes, indeed, how can I *ever* forget?" I replied, pulling her tightly against me.

With a lusty smile, she poked her finger into my chest, demanding, "Tonight! *Tonight!* And not *one moment longer!*"

Lifting her chin, I put my arms around her and kissed her deeply. She responded by pressing herself against me with an urgent need. As I fully responded to her pressure, she softly moaned and broke the kiss. Maintaining her pressure, she slowly rotated her hips against me in the water . . . and tilting her head back, she licked her lips and closed her eyes . . . as though savoring an erotic dream.

Fearing I would lose my self-control, I quickly picked her up, and as I carried her back to the ledge, she let out a hoydenish titter. She had sensed my fear and wrapped her arms around my neck as I gently set her down, fanning her dress over its surface to dry. "Fear not, my husband," she softly reassured, "but don't you just *love* a tease?"

"I do, angel, but such boldness . . . in public . . ."

"We were not in public," she replied, "we were in the *water!*"

She snuggled under my arm, giggled and comforted me by softly nibbling on my fingers. As the sun dropped below the western horizon, we cuddled together, marveling as it painted the remaining clouds with pink iridescent hues. Letting out a comfortable sigh, Suzannah squeezed my hand and remarked, "It is so *beautiful* here, Jim, *truly* beautiful."

"I've known no other place," I softly replied, and kissed her hand. "I grew up here, this is my home, yet for so many years I could never share it."

"Well, now you can, for I'm here with you . . . in this, *our* sacred place." Now she kissed *my* hand and then entwined it within hers, her thumb stroking the back of mine. "Jim, you once said your heart *speaks* to you here, is that so?"

"Yes, particularly at this time of day—day's end."

Looking up at me she squeezed my hand once again and asked, "What is your heart saying now, Jim?"

I met her expectant eyes and lovingly replied, "It tells me I'm truly blessed to have you here beside me . . . and I love you beyond *all* else in this life and the next."

She smiled and kissed me with a special sweetness. Then as she rested her forehead on mine, she placed my hand over her heart. "My heart tells me I love you also, *more* than life can hold. My love for *you*, James Walker, knows no bounds, and I shall *treasure* our every moment."

"As shall *I*, Mrs. Walker!" I affirmed, kissing her forehead.

We held each other and whispered endearments, watching the pink glow gradually turn to deep blue, then to purple, and finally to black.

"Come, Jim, it's time we went back. We *do* have a home to return to."

"It was a home once . . . and *you*, dear Suzannah, have made it so again."

"I'm just starting out at housewifery," she apologetically confessed, "and I'm afraid I'm not terribly good at it, so far."

"Nonsense!" I replied. "Your presence alone illuminates my life and our house with endless love," and squeezing her hand I added, ". . . and boundless joy."

As we rose to go, she gave me a demure smile and another deep kiss. Then she took my hand and we headed home.

Although it was late, away from the shore the air remained stagnant, wet and unbearably hot. In the parlor, I slumped into the rocker, feeling fatigued once again. The moon had risen and was visible through the parlor window.

Suzannah came to me, sat in my lap and cozily worked her way into her snuzzle position. Despite the heat and our damp clothes, she felt wonderful in my arms. An unaccustomed sense of security came over me, for I felt nothing could harm us now . . . for we had each other, and we were all we needed. In the candlelight her silken tresses nearly touched the floor, and her eyes glinted like gray-blue diamonds.

As I rocked us slowly, her wedding band glittered in the moonlight . . . and silently reaffirmed, "She is *forever* yours: the eyes, the heart, the hands, and that precious love." Gazing longingly into her eyes, I then whispered, "I *still* can't believe we are really, truly *married*."

Not taking her eyes from mine, Suzannah opened her dress.

"What is this?" I asked mischievously as I stopped rocking.

Laying her head upon my bare shoulder, she kissed my chest and whispered, "Anything you *want* it to be."

"Anything?"

"All your heart desires!" she whispered, leaning her head back and licking her lips in anticipation.

Suddenly, my little Suzannah, all ninety pounds of her, shook off the top of her dress and passionately began to nibble and lick my chest, my neck, my face and my ears. She grasped my head in her hands to pull me toward her.

I saw the erotic sensual look in her eyes, and taking her hand I kissed each finger, one at a time, and placed my hand over her left breast. I could feel her heart beating like a trip-hammer.

"I'm all *yours*," she whispered, "and I *want* you so . . . oh, Jim, *take* me to the *heights!*" She reached her arms around my neck and locked them there.

"Let's go then," I breathlessly replied.

"I'll not wait one more second!" she said urgently, her hot tongue flicking into my ear one minute, her lips nibbling my neck the next.

Finally, I picked up my little wife and carried her upstairs to our chamber and gently set her down on the bed. Shedding the rest of her clothes in a heartbeat, she lay back in all her naked glory, her hair forming a fan around her angelic face. Her girlish figure and pure white skin were inexpressibly soft and warm to touch. I was shaking, *possessed* with love as I lay down beside her, kissing her first on her soft inviting lips, then down her milky neck, until I reached her heavenly breasts.

It was then that she wrapped her legs around me with a sudden urgency, pulling me deeply into her waiting womanhood. I felt caressed and surrounded by her wonderful warmth; and when I reached her softest deepest part, Suzannah gasped, "*Jim!*" and I became delirious.

She bit at my chest and my neck, and then drew my lips to hers and opened her mouth into mine. We were now exquisitely joined as one, and I felt the scorching heat of her womanhood as she pressed it against me, enveloping me, all the while telling me of her hungry, burning desire for me to love her deeply and repeatedly.

In the course of our wondrous lovemaking, I drifted into a reverie of slow sensual motion, where time stood still. Never had I imagined that our sexual awakening would be like this, that we would learn so quickly the secret arts and skills of the marriage bed.

Stopping momentarily to catch her breath, Suzannah was still at the height of her passion when she panted out, "Jim, our bed shall be our Eden . . . for the fruits of love . . . are all ours . . . and *nothing* is forbidden . . . or to be untried . . . Jim . . . *promise* me this . . . *please?*"

Giving me no time to answer, she rolled onto her back, her legs once more embracing me, driving me deeper into our oneness. Moving our hips together rhythmically, I plunged into her softness and she moaned with every bottoming thrust. Her burning warmth drove me to love's highest thrill when suddenly, as I held her in a crushing embrace, my muscles involuntarily tightened. With spasmodic waves of ecstatic delirium, my warmth filled her as our pulsating bodies melted into one . . . and as I moaned, "Oh *God*, Suzannah, *yes*, promises are mine to give you!" . . . on my mother's soul, I meant every word.

Rhoda Barrett's Visit

Once Suzannah and I finished preparing our home for ourselves, we were finally ready to set a firm date for opening the tavern. When the word got out, the townspeople spoke of nothing else, such was their excitement about its revival. Of course, only the older folk remembered Mother as its keeper, and they wondered if Suzannah would do as well.

Suzannah offered Dimmis a place in our home—a private room upstairs—but she declined gracefully, saying she felt quite settled with the Thatchers. She had a particular desire to remain with Mrs. Thatcher, who was elderly and required more care than Eben alone could easily render.

Her decision impressed me greatly. Someone as young as Dimmis, who was twenty-eight years of age, usually sought to marry and have children. But she chose instead to give freely of herself to those in need. She would earn a living at our tavern, but her heart remained with the Thatchers, and I admired her for that.

On several occasions I came upon Suzannah and Dimmis sitting before the fire, exchanging confidences in the gentle tones of Gaelic. How fortunate they were to have their own private language and their music in common too. Now Suzannah had a close friend in Dimmis, as well as a highly competent and trusted colleague in the tavern.

Despite her sterling character, there was gossip afoot in the town about Dimmis having a disreputable past; as a woman of loose virtue. It was even rumored that we'd hired her because her "services" would lure male customers to our doors. I suspected much of this loose talk came from Rhoda Barrett, as it usually did. It reminded me of the times when Suzannah and I first became attached, and tongues wagged about *us*. The talk back then was not so salacious; but rumors of Dimmis' reputation were believed—because she was unknown to most of the locals.

About a month after our wedding, Rhoda Barrett came knocking at our door, a concerned expression on her face. Except for her nephew Jonathan—who was still at Harvard and no longer lived in Walker's Cove—Rhoda was mostly alone in her life, with gossip her only companion. So I couldn't help but suspect that her visit was for the purpose of prying into our affairs for some fresh scuttlebutt.

I decided I would control any discussion that ensued—perhaps even turn it to my advantage. So I invited her in, welcoming her as though her intentions were pure.

"Come in, Rhoda, and please stay for tea. Perhaps a hot cup would lift your spirits."

"Why, thank you, James," she said, smiling as we entered the great room. "I hear you'll soon be opening your tavern?"

"Indeed, we shall!" I said enthusiastically. "Come, let me show you what we've done!"

First, I took her around the great room, which measured twenty feet wide and thirty feet long. It was furnished with twenty square tables, randomly spaced, with two chairs each. We also had forty chairs lined up against the longest wall that could be added as needed to make foursomes or more by combining tables. There were two ovens in the fireplace for the baking of beans, a staple that would be ready to serve at any time. Two large plank tables in front of the fireplace were the serving station for hot drinks, warm bread and tins of cooked food.

The original parlor fireplace had been enlarged so that it was eight feet wide. It housed three small ovens, and one slightly larger for cooking any type of meat, fowl or fish. The ovens were also a good source of heat for the great room. Mother's portrait hung in its place of honor above it.

Suzannah's pianoforte was ensconced in the left corner, out of harm's way. The placement enabled us to take acoustical advantage of the proximity of the joined walls, so the music would be heard

above the din of the patrons' conversations and the loud crackling of the fire. In the right corner was the tall clock Father had made so many years ago for my mother, visible from any vantage point in the room.

Sarah's murals appeared on the rear wall: on the left was a bustling harbor scene with ships at dockside being unloaded; while on the right was a depiction of the village center in summertime, with people coming and going—including Suzannah and me in our wagon, being pulled by Winnie.

Rhoda scrutinized everything, as if memorizing each and every detail for future dissemination around town. Mother always said the best advertising was by word of mouth, and if Rhoda behaved in her accustomed manner, I thought she *might* do us an unintentional favor. But upon hearing her initial remarks, I realized that I might have been mistaken.

"I have never been inside a tavern in my life," Rhoda said drily. Then beneath a scowl, she sternly advised, "And the thought of drink and debauchery is repellent to every fiber in my being!"

"There will be no drunkenness, debauchery or wenching in *our* place of business," I tersely replied. Pointing to Mother's portrait, I looked Rhoda straight in the eye and declared, "This tavern is for my *mother*, whose dream it was to *reopen* it . . . and be its hostess once again."

Rhoda looked up at the portrait solemnly and then at me. "Your mother was an *honorable* woman," she said, her voice much softer than before.

"Yes, she was!" I replied looking up at Mother's portrait. "I would like to think she will keep a diligent eye, and watch over all who gather here."

Nodding, Rhoda approached the portrait and touched Mother's cheek, much as Suzannah did on our wedding day. As she did so, she added in a reverential tone, "Such a perfect face . . . such a perfect soul." Then, turning her attention back to me, she suddenly declared, "I wish you every success when you open, James."

Delighted by her approval, I said, "Please come by some time. We shall serve you well—and it'll be free of charge."

At that moment, Dimmis chanced to come out from the kitchen and stopped dead to give Rhoda a cold stare.

"Good day, Miss Sexton," Rhoda said curtly.

The ill will between the two was palpable.

"Good day to you as well, Miss Barrett," Dimmis responded, pushing her red hair away from her face. She was perspiring heavily from the heat of the kitchen fireplace.

"Dimmis, I was giving Rhoda a tour of our tavern. I'd like to show her the kitchen now, if that is convenient for you."

"I should think so," she coldly acknowledged, while gingerly stepping around Rhoda as though she were a pile of horse droppings. Then, without another word, Dimmis took her shawl, opened the front door and disappeared outside.

Clearing my throat to break the tension, I suggested, "Well then, Rhoda, let's go on to the kitchen now."

As we entered the main kitchen, Rhoda and I immediately felt the intensity of the heat. The new kitchen fireplace was twelve feet wide, and capable of handling up to three fires. It had three ovens that were even larger than those in the great room. Two had clock jacks, which necessitated a wider hearth. Suzannah sat before the ovens and the clock jacks recording their cooking times for future reference. She greeted Rhoda warmly, as was her custom.

Rhoda, in turn, expressed astonishment at the size and complexity of the fireplace. "This is not a kitchen . . . this is a *forge*! You have a fireplace large enough to feed the entire population of Walker's Cove!"

Suzannah rose from her stool, and took Rhoda's hands in a further gesture of welcome. "Well, Rhoda," she explained, "we need to cook a *variety* of foods, *all* at one time, and at different temperatures, which is why we need to test the ovens and the clock jacks, and mark the cooking times."

"But isn't that needless waste . . . burning *all* that wood?" asked Rhoda, indicating the blazing coals.

"Not really," Suzannah replied brightly. "Because we are cooking several meals for several families . . . using *their* food . . . and *their* wood, which is the price in exchange for *our* labor. In turn, we get to test the cooking times for various meals and plan our menu accordingly. The families will come by later to pick up the meals. Dimmis has gone to let the Lovejoys know their meal is just about ready."

Rhoda's expression soured on hearing Dimmis' name. "And what *about* that tavern maid, Dimmis? She is a *soiled* dove! Is it to your advantage to employ her?"

I was startled at such a blatant condemnation of both Dimmis *and* Suzannah's judgment; but, unfortunately, that was typical of Rhoda.

Without saying a word, Suzannah drew Rhoda to the kitchen table and sat her down. When they were both seated she said, "I'm *sorry* to hear you speak such impure thoughts about Dimmis. She is a *kind* woman, *tough* to be sure, Rhoda, but she has *had* to be."

Rhoda sat up straight and folded her arms defensively, while Suzannah continued.

"Ainsley hired her while she was in Boston on business, and she brought her back to Walker's Cove on that fateful voyage. And as you well know, Dimmis was the *only* survivor."

We heard a movement, and then there was Dimmis, frozen in the kitchen doorway, glaring at Suzannah and Rhoda.

Suzannah rose, gently took Dimmis' hand and led her to the table.

Dimmis came reluctantly, and the air between she and Rhoda was thick with hostility. Fearing there might be harsh words expressed, I decided to sit next to Rhoda, while Suzannah sat with Dimmis next to her—so we in fact separated the two women.

Something echoed in my heart from Suzannah . . . a fleeting sense that the enmity between them would soon end. I wondered how my little wife was going to accomplish this, so I watched her every act and listened to her every word.

Suzannah took Dimmis' hand in her own and placed it upon Rhoda's, whereupon Rhoda sharply withdrew hers—but not before Suzannah could stop her. With her hands covering both Rhoda's *and* Dimmis' together, Suzannah began to speak.

"Rhoda Ann Barrett of Walker's Cove, I want you to *meet* Dimmis Sexton, lately of Boston, and London before that. Dimmis was hired by Jim's mother to assist her and me in running the tavern. *Remember* Rhoda, Ainsley *died* trying to make this happen, and if Dimmis was good enough for Ainsley, she is *certainly* good enough for *me*."

Looking into Dimmis's blue eyes, Suzannah addressed her. "Now, *Dimmis*, please tell Rhoda about your past, and your troubled journey to Walker's Cove."

Dimmis regarded Rhoda with a gimlet eye, whereupon Suzannah suddenly cleared her throat, as a hint to behave civilly.

Clearing her own throat, Dimmis exhaled deeply and began her life story.

"Well, Rhoda Barrett of Walker's Cove, *I* am Dimmis Sexton. I do not *know* what you have heard about me, but this is the truth of my life, as I know it.

"Unlike *you*, who are fortunate to have friends and relatives here, I have neither friends, save Suzannah, nor relatives. Mother was a common harlot, my father her one-time customer. They had no need for a wailing, white-skinned, redheaded daughter . . . so my father, who never *married* Mother, left her with child, *never* to return.

"My mother took up residence with a tavern owner named Richard Sexton. He operated a drunken brothel behind his "establishment" in two filthy rooms near the privy. And there she plied the world's oldest trade for the very *muck* of London." Then with a fearsome countenance, she angrily hissed, "Rakes, beggars, thieves and drunkards . . . *just* to keep body and soul together for the two of us!

"We lived by the privy stench so long, I forgot what fresh air was like. Mother was renowned as the best wench on Gin Lane, but she was also a notorious drunkard. Frequently I was left to toddle alone among the Sextons, while she recovered from gin-besotted sex for days on end. She was often so drunk, that the money she received from her customers was stolen back while she lay in a stupor.

"When I was but four years of age, it was a blessing for me that Mother was killed as the result of an argument between two drunken patrons. They couldn't agree who should have her first . . .

for one did not wish the remains of the first customer to soil his pleasure as the next.

"Because they couldn't agree, the first man announced that *none* shall have her, and that said, plunged a knife in her stomach. The two left her alone in the alley to die a whore's death . . . while they went off in different directions to seek new wenches."

When Dimmis paused to collect her thoughts, we all noticed that Rhoda sat in a stunned silence, her mouth open in disbelief. Even I was appalled by Dimmis' story.

"And so," she resumed, while wiping away her painful tears, "I was determined to be *nothing* like her. As an orphan who now had to earn my keep, I became helper, cook and serving maid for the Sexton tavern. I learned all I could about cooking, serving, drinking, slapping, grabbing and groping. I saw and experienced it all in Gin Lane, where people have few morals, where sexual favors and spirituous liquors were coveted . . . *more* than the lives of loose women or *bastard* children—of which I'm certainly one!

"I had no choice in being *born*, Rhoda Barrett, or when and where it happened to me, but I was now alone in the world . . . and I needed to survive. And so I worked and saved a few coins over the long years as I grew up. When I combined those with the few mother had stowed away under the privy floor, I was finally able to buy passage to Boston . . . and a new life.

"The voyage to Boston was almost as bad as Gin Lane, for sailors are the devil . . . always thinking of and with their manhood. By and by, they were pressing me for my services, and so the advances came—oh, those horrid, drunken, thrusting advances— but I refused them all! I have maintained my virtue and self-respect all these years. I'm proud to swear before you and our God, that not one man has passed the portals of my womanhood to this day. And I'm resolved to keep my virtue along that virgin path into marriage.

"So, Rhoda Barrett of Walker's Cove, I've struggled through life's roughest seas and I've cut my share of triumph and tears. Yet through it all, I have worked myself to the bone in hopes for a better future. In every tavern I worked, I pushed the sales hard and the beer and whiskey flowed. The swishing in their bellies and the happiness in their heads provided precious coins that rang into my purse, to further secure my future. And it was Ainsley Rennsdale Walker who gave me a chance for it, for the gift of a new, meaningful life . . . both as a woman and as a soul . . . and now I proudly exult in that freedom as I honor her sacrifice!"

Dimmis stopped, and we all remained silent. The crackling and snapping of the fire emphasized the burning of a past life . . . that Dimmis recalled for Rhoda alone—and surely wished to forget. But the look on her face became a hopeful one as she continued her saga, this time with a more confident and less self-deprecating air.

"And so Rhoda Barrett, my life changed the moment Ainsley Walker came to Boston, when she walked boldly into the tavern where I worked, and asked me if I knew of a good cooking woman. It was then I gave her my *entire* story. We spoke of cooking and tavern-keeping for days, right in her own rooms, we did! She hired me for her tavern, to work with her and Suzannah, and offered me a home with her; but said if I chose not to live with her, then she would find me another.

"And with joy and promises to keep, we sailed happily out of Boston, on the schooner *Sunrise*, Captain Roger Trumbull. Although he could tell by the tint of the sky and the strength of the swells that we would be challenged at sea, Ainsley was so eager to return home—with *me* and her good news—that we sailed anyway, against Trumbull's better judgment."

As though in a trance, Dimmis stared out the window toward the distant sea. Clasping her hands in a frightened manner, in a ghostly voice she eerily recalled the nightmarish details of her ill-fated voyage.

"Late that evening, with the stars out of sight, the thundering gales came a-wailing and the devil's perfect storm swept upon us—with screaming winds that drove the frozen snow . . . until ice encrusted the *Sunrise*. In the face of the storm's hellish fury, we risked our lives to put our little ship on course. And so, laboring mightily, we slipped past death on the outer banks, a hundred leagues to the southeast, *before* her topmast was carried away under the burdens of ice and wind.

"She was now severely wounded; and as the unmerciful waves punished her further, I remember how she *shuddered* and *shook* in defiance. Just outside the cove she rolled and tossed, and suddenly, she listed *so* badly—I thought we would surely perish. In that instant, I saw Captain Trumbull swept off the icy deck . . . along with many of the crew. With no helm, she ripped and tore herself to shreds, and finally broke up just offshore."

After pausing to look at Rhoda briefly, Dimmis carried on in a more normal voice.

"Ainsley and I were tossed into the raging frigid waters, and only the floating hatch cover saved us. We clung to it in desperation as we were tossed about by the monstrous waves, which sent us crashing toward the shore. Our hands and feet became frozen and painful as ice began to cover us from the spray, and our clothes froze solid to our bodies. The silver and gold coins sewn into the hem of my dress, along with the weight of the water and ice, finally pulled me away from the hatch cover. I was rolled and thrashed against the rocks, certain I would perish, and when I suddenly found myself gasping for air, I was on the hatch cover once again . . . *beside* Ainsley. She had pulled me from the grasp of an icy death, and was holding me fast with her one free arm.

"Her final words above the shrieking winds were, 'I have you, Dimmis! Are you *hurt*? Can you hold on?'

"We held fast to each other until a violent wave sent the hatch cover crashing into the rocks, and I saw Ainsley tossed away from me . . . as an angry child would toss a rag doll. She landed hard on the frozen rocks with no further movement. I screamed desperately for her as I struggled onto the large rocks of the point . . . and there I collapsed . . . unconscious until I was found."

Turning to Rhoda, Dimmis' piercing blue eyes now held Rhoda's unblinking gaze, and so, as her voice rose with passion, she drove her point home.

"Rhoda Barrett, Ainsley's last act was to save my life, and I shall never *waste* her precious gift. Aye . . . I'll say *again* . . . that surely the devil was before our mast. And so I ask, if you ever saw that tempest that was a blowing . . . would *you* have ever risked *your* life to come here as I have *mine?* All my life, I have kept my eyes on my sails, and my hands on my gaff . . . and unloaded my prayers unto *God* at every breath . . . and *He* saw me through it, even as I slipped and stumbled on the icy rocks of Walker's Cove! And so I am *here*, where I have found inner peace *and* a better life—because of *her* who forever sleeps in her *grave* down the way . . ."

Dimmis ended with her arm outstretched, her finger pointed toward Mother's burial site on the hill.

Rhoda's eyes were moist, and I could feel in Rhoda's heart that Dimmis' life story would have been fatal, had Rhoda had to endure it. I was also deeply moved by what mother had done as her final act, and the wetness in my eyes revealed that truth. And as Rhoda slowly placed both hands over Dimmis' and squeezed them tightly within hers, she whispered, "Thank you, Dimmis . . . *dear* girl. And if you choose to, you shall *always* have a friend and heart-mate in me."

As they both rose and embraced each other like girlhood friends, Suzannah came over to stand beside me. Threading her arm around my waist, she gazed up at me with her illuminating smile of satisfaction. I was so *proud* of my seventeen-year-old wife . . . for an acrimonious gap that existed between two women through ignorance and callousness, was now firmly closed . . . and I rejoiced in their happiness . . . and in our own.

The Letter

On April mornings the sunlight poured through our east windows with an exceptional brilliance. Combined with the scented air of spring, it can instill an indescribable vigor, an energy that makes one thankful to be alive.

Such energy inspired Suzannah and Dimmis to prepare a sunrise breakfast for the crews from the trading ships. Our ships were not ships of the line, but modest brigs and schooners, whose captains and crews were the lifeblood of our village economy. They provided a vital link between our tradesmen and the bustling maritime centers of the eastern seaboard.

Sailors, ever being hungry, thirsty and tired, enjoyed having our tavern as a haven for quality food, drink and a bed, none of which could be found aboard ship. Our business and our reputation flourished because Suzannah and Dimmis were such fine hostesses and cooks. They piled the plates high and filled the tankards to overflowing. As Suzannah was known to say, "If any soul left our tavern hungry or thirsty, it was their own fault!"

With breakfast over, I ventured downstairs to find Suzannah was gone . . . possibly for a morning walk. The kitchen was still very warm and infused with the aromas of cinnamon, sugar and apple; a sure sign of freshly baked apple fritters. To my delight, I found a tray of them cooling before an open window, still warm and dripping with milk frosting. Rubbing my hands together in gleeful anticipation, I inhaled deeply of their sweet fragrance before seeking out the drippiest one.

I took my breakfast into the great room where I seated myself at one of the tables. I surveyed my surroundings and was pleased to see that everything was clean and tidily arranged, awaiting the next round of hungry customers. The settings consisted of forks, spoons and knives nestled beside large pewter plates; some places lacked those accoutrements since some patrons came only to drink. Most tables had the added amenity of long-stemmed clay pipes for smoking tobacco, whose tips would be broken off for use by the next smoker.

I marveled at how meticulously Suzannah and Dimmis attended to every detail. Mother would have burst with pride to see how efficiently they ran her tavern. I even felt a pang of guilt because our financial prosperity was largely due to *their* efforts, rather than my clockmaking or blacksmithing. However, my guilt would be brief, because once I finished with the few remaining back orders, I would be the head innkeeper.

When I returned to the kitchen, I heard a sudden rustling and a snippet of sweet song, and there was Suzannah coming through the back door, carrying a large bucket of Richardson's milk. Her gray-blue eyes lovingly sparkled when she saw me. Setting the bucket down on the table, she threw her arms around my neck and kissed me long and deep, a kiss flavored with the essence of cinnamon—and heaven.

When our lips broke apart, she whispered excitedly, "Good morning, lover! I can't stop thinking about last night . . . you brought me to the heights *five* times!"

I pressed her to my heart and gazed into her dazzling eyes. "Good morning, little vixen! It was very special, wasn't it? You brought me to the heights *twice!*" I whispered back.

"Five and two!" she squealed, and then giggled delightedly as I picked her up and swung her around—the most precious creature in the world. As I set her down, she added, "I have fritters and milk should you wish some breakfast. And there are sausages in the oven too."

She resumed her song while she poured some milk into a nearby pitcher and placed it on the table. Dipping a spoon into the milk, she sampled it thoughtfully, declaring, "Well, Jim, it's still warm—fresh from Phoebe, the Richardson's cow. She has outdone herself this morning!"

I stood once more before the tray of fritters and took another drippy one, laying it on the plate Suzannah handed me . . . just in time to catch the falling drops of frosting.

"Even *Zeb* uses a plate, Jim . . ." she teased, drawing her dainty finger under my chin and lightly across my cheek—when there was an urgent knock upon the door.

"Who could that be at *this* time of the morning, Suzannah? Or is that Dimmis?"

She licked her fingers and shrugged, "Well, Dimmis wouldn't *knock*, she would come right in." As she sliced her own fritter into bite-size pieces, she added, "So darling, will you please get the door for me?"

Upon opening the door, I was greeted by the smiling face of Osgood Lovejoy.

Osgood Lovejoy was a man who lived up to his name, and was probably doing more to increase the population of Walker's Cove than any other. He and his wife, Mildred, must have gotten lots of *love* and *joy* from each other since they had twelve children, with a thirteenth on the way. A cobbler by trade, he supplemented his income by also acting as the town postman. He would arrive at the wharf early each morning to collect letters broadsheets and occasional bundles from the vessels docked there, and then diligently distribute them to their intended recipients in the village. This service was rendered in exchange for a voluntary token of support for his ever-growing family.

"Come on in!" I said, guiding him inside to a table in the great room. "So, would you like something to drink, Osgood?" I asked, toweling off a mug in anticipation of drawing him some hot buttered rum.

Sauntering in behind me, Osgood took a seat and unloaded his packets of letters onto the table, fanning them out as though they were a deck of playing cards. "Lots of letters today, Jim—*look* at these!"

I instantly recognized the bold swirls of Lydia's handwriting. There were two letters from her: one addressed to us, and one to her father. Picking up our letter and examining it closely, Osgood observed, "Looks like a *thick* one . . . well, it seems to be." Holding it out to me, he dryly added, "From Boston . . . not good, not good . . ."

"It's from *Lydia*," I protested. "What's not good about it?"

Looking at me quizzically, Osgood shook his head as he explained, "Nothing wrong with *Lydia*, Jim—it is Boston!" Handing me our letter and gathering up the others, he warned, "Wait till them sailors come ashore, then ye'll get an earful, methinks!"

I gave him a copper and nodding in appreciation, he merrily doffed his hat and approached the door. There he almost stumbled into the arms of a sturdily built older man who was about to enter. He wore a cocked hat and sported a long coat covered with dry salt spray. After righting himself, Osgood continued on his way without another word.

As the man entered the tavern, a small crowd of sailors behind him hastily seated themselves at the tables. Fortunately, Suzannah had finished her breakfast and arrived in the great room to attend to their thirst and appetites, while I dealt with their leader.

Bowing slightly, he genteelly asked, "Pardon me, sir, where can a man get a decent drink of rum around here? Those infernal lobster-backs have finally done it now!"

Motioning him to an empty table, I invited him to sit.

Once settled, he looked around the room until he finally fixed his gaze upon me. "I have no desire to disoblige you sir, but your New England ordinaries are mostly known for diluted rum, cold tea and poorly cooked chops served with rock-hard rolls! I've also been treated to burnt, dried-out ham hocks, served with weevil ridden biscuits covered with over-salted butter that turned my stomach sour!"

Shaking his head in dismay, he added, "Oh, and let us not forget the appallingly wretched-looking womenfolk who serve them up!"

"I'm sorry to hear of your unfortunate experiences," I replied calmly, while preparing a tumbler of hot buttered rum made from Mother's recipe.

Placing it before him, he tentatively looked into it as if searching for something he couldn't find. Finally, he lifted the tumbler and proceeded to sip from it thoughtfully, rolling the liquid around his tongue several times before he swallowed.

Then, with a sudden smile, he looked at me and said, "This is the *finest* rum I have ever had—*strong* in flavor and *smooth* in the gullet. Hah! What a *treasure*, my dear sir!"

Draining the remainder in one swig, he crushed the tumbler in his hands so it was bent beyond use. I marveled at his strength, thinking him stronger even than Zeb Hawkes, up to now the strongest man I ever knew.

Then he contemptuously hurled the crushed vessel to the floor and shouted, "*That* is a lobsterback's *skull* I just crushed—just like *that!*"

"Well, I shan't give you another until you pay for that one *and* the tumbler!" Offering my hand, I added, "I'm the *keeper* here, and I've not had the pleasure of your name, sir."

Taking my hand with an iron grip, he pumped it once, and stood to secretly utter such that only I could hear. "Henry Wiggins, mate aboard the *Palladium*, one hundred thirty-seven tons, sir!" Pressing a silver shilling into my hand, he quipped, "I trust this shall cover the expense my good man . . . damn their eyes . . . had I a thousand more to give . . . and you, sir, a thousand tumblers to crush!"

Mollified by his generous payment, I introduced myself in turn. "Henry Wiggins, welcome to my tavern. I'm Jim Walker. Have another . . . what shall it be?"

He tossed his empty purse upon the table saying, "You have me at a grave disadvantage, my good fellow. I'm fresh out of silver, keeper Walker!"

Clasping him on the shoulder I bid him sit again. "No charge, Henry, your shilling is good while you're here today. So what may I serve you in exchange for information from afar?"

Lifting his eyebrows in hopeful anticipation, he unabashedly enquired, "Have you flip here?"

"Suzannah makes the best flip ever to pass your lips!" I declared flatly.

"'Tis so?" he asked skeptically. "What's in *her* flip to make it so?"

"Eggs, sugar, cream, ale, spices, molasses, a touch of pumpkin—
and a liberal dose of gunpowder."

"Ye gods, man, *gunpowder?*" he expostulated, rising before me in
a threatening manner.

At that moment, Suzannah placed a large tumbler of flip before
him. Regarding the steaming liquid, he looked at her skeptically, as
though assessing the validity of my claim.

Giving Henry her most disarming smile, Suzannah explained,
"Dear sir, understand that *we*, who must protect our secret recipes,
cannot be as honest as we should. Jim uses the term *gunpowder* to
describe our special *secret* ingredient . . . and I can assure you, Mr.
Henry Wiggins, mate of the *Palladium*, one hundred thirty-seven
tons, *your* secret is safe with *me!* As such, *my* secret shall remain
safe from *you!*" Leaving it at that, Suzannah winked, nodded and
returned to the fireplace.

"How did she *hear?*" Wiggins asked, stupefied. "She is the smart-
est, most *beautiful* tavern girl I've ever come across! Perhaps if she
were thirty-five years older or thereabouts . . ."

I handed him a pipe, and while he stuffed its bowl, I cheerfully
set him straight about the so-called tavern girl. "*She* is the true
proprietress of our tavern . . . my *wife*, Suzannah."

While lighting his pipe, his eyes were trained on Suzannah's
doings at the fireplace kettles. "Another well-kept secret, *indeed!*"
he remarked, giving me an admiring smile.

I laughed and then advised him, "Don't ever trade with *her* if
you expect to capture an easy profit . . . you'll be left without your
breeches."

Henry drank a small quantity of his flip, rolling it over his tongue
to savor the taste like he did with the rum. Placing his drink on the
table, he smiled broadly and said, "*Damn!* Upon my word—what a
drink! So, she is your *wife*, you say?"

I smiled and nodded proudly.

Henry leaned forward to confide, "Well, with all due *respect*,
sir . . . finding myself with no breeches in *her* company, would be
fine by *me!*" Then, laughing heartily, he mused, "Even at *my* age . . .
not that I could follow *through*."

By now the regulars were streaming in, joining the sailors for good food, good drink and good company . . . and the great room soon became raucous with a multitude of simultaneous conversations.

Flitting about like butterflies, Suzannah and Dimmis cheerfully served the patrons. Some didn't eat or drink, but sat about their tables puffing contentedly on their pipes. In the spirit of camaraderie that usually accompanies the act of pipe smoking, many amiably shared their tobacco with total strangers. With the fragrant sleepy haze of tobacco and firewood permeating the great room, the former din became a relaxed drone of endless chatter as folks exchanged stories and gossip.

Excusing myself from Henry's table to help Suzannah and Dimmis, I made my way toward the cooking area. As I did, I overheard snippets of conversations: the words "best rum" popped up on my right, while on my left I heard, "for the black cow I will give . . ." I also heard typical sailor talk like, "aye . . . I been battered by Master Quigley when I worked those waters all me years . . ." Behind me I heard a sneering laugh as a voice declared, "so I *told* the sallow-faced wench to get herself to a *nunnery*, and tell not a soul that she had gone"; and finally, I heard the sweet voice of home, my own dear wife saying, "Oh, Dimmis, can you please serve a tankard of flip to the gentleman at table six? And he would like pork pie to go with it . . ."

Feeling my eyes on her, Suzannah suddenly turned—and when she saw me, her eyes widened. She took my hand and leading me into the kitchen, she jumped up and down like a little girl. "Oh Jim, we are so *busy!*" she reported breathlessly. "We can't take the money in fast enough!"

Picking her up, I held her tightly as I kissed her. "Angel, I have riches in my arms that a king's ransom cannot buy!"

When I set her down, she wrapped her arms around my waist. "Your angel desperately needs your loving!" And with that, she pulled me down for an open-mouthed kiss. When she finished, she said excitedly, "Well, what do you think?"

"I will tend to *you* later, after closing perhaps?"

"But not one moment longer!" Glancing toward the great room, she added, "I will play, if you will serve."

"Good idea!" I said nodding, and grabbed my apron.

AT DUSK, OUR tavern was always a veritable beehive of activity. Zeb was correct when he predicted to Mother they would come, and so they did. As I circulated among the tables to take orders and help Dimmis serve, a clattering of accoutrements, accompanied by a noisy chorus of male voices signaled more sailors had arrived. Dimmis and Suzannah greeted them as they flowed into the great room, dumping their seabags on the floor against the far wall.

As she passed me, Suzannah quipped, "I'm back to serving . . . too busy to play"—and then she was off.

The new arrivals seemed rather a different breed from the sailors we were used to serving. Their primary topic of conversation was Boston. And as their drinks were served and their pipes were lit, the noise level increased tenfold . . . and then the table pounding began.

It seemed that certain words were always punctuated by a ferocious bang of the fist. From one table, I overheard the word "unrest"; from another, "murder"; and from yet another, "Kill 'em all, and send the rest of 'em *back!*"

With all the pounding, I purposely drifted over to Henry's table. "Can you hear what they're saying? What's happening in Boston with the British soldiers these days?" I was expecting an amusing story.

As he pressed his tumbler to his lips, Henry softly confided, "They killed a boy some days ago, Jim. *A boy!* Then they murdered a bunch of our folks on King Street, and they are dead with no reprisal! *None!*"

With my hatred rising as I recalled Father's tragic and needless death, I asked, "Why did they do this? What purpose did it serve to kill a *boy*, Henry?"

The table pounding and yelling grew so loud I couldn't hear Henry's response. A large bell suddenly pealed in urgent tones, and continued until the tavern went silent. In the deafening silence that followed, all eyes were now upon the bell ringer—Suzannah.

Still holding Mother's dinner bell, she scanned her audience to ensure their attention. With a muffled clank she put the bell down and spoke. "I have a letter from my sister in Boston. Here ye, *her* words!"

She removed a folded insert from the letter, which she examined with sudden distress. I watched her with concern, trying to sense her heart feelings, but I could not.

Dimmis helped her up so she could stand on a table, to be better seen and heard. Then Suzannah read Lydia's letter aloud.

My sister,

We have entered into a dark time in the city, for there is much unrest and friction between the king's troops and the citizens. We are forced to quarter troops against our will, and are not recompensed for our inconvenience or obliging kindness.

Every week there are new sores that erupt over tax collections, meanness of the troops, and political side taking, and as such, the chafing continues unabated. The most recent sore to erupt was that of one John Adams, solicitor, defending his majesty's troops against the slaughter of our citizens in the street—fittingly on King Street.

I enclose a broadsheet of the Gazette, and though this happened on the fifth day of March, it is a constant festering sore that Richard says shall not heal. Walking by Water Street on that fateful day, Richard observed a crowd gathering by the customhouse. Inquiring as to what the purpose of the crowd was, he was told a soldier on duty, one John Goldfinch, had not paid a wigmaker's fee, and the wigmaker's apprentice, one John Gerrish, was soliciting before the crowd, calling out soldier Goldfinch for payment on behalf of his master.

This was a supreme insult to the soldier, as unknown to Gerrish, he had actually paid the bill and thus he did not dignify such action with a response. Apprentice Gerrish then went to enlist some friends sympathetic to his master, and returned to again petition the soldier for payment. Once again, no payment and no answer were given to young Gerrish.

The boys then began to pepper the troops with snowballs, in hopes of soliciting a payment to beg them off. Still, there was no reply of any kind.

The noise began to grow, and so did the attending citizens and bystanders, until there were perhaps three hundred in all. The sentries formed themselves into a rank for protection against the snowballs, but Richard noticed the newest arrivals to the scene were holding clubs, and amidst the continued taunting, a soldier was struck by a club. Suddenly the word "Fire" was heard!

A spattering of musket fire resulted in five deaths: three instantly, and two, after a few days lingering.

Dear sister, be ever thankful you and James are safe, for in the end, they killed them all for want of words!

A stunned silence hung over the room.

Looking around at the crowd before her, Suzannah lowered Lydia's letter. She could feel the hostility rising in every heart, and I could feel her fear. She opened the broadsheet and started to read; the tone of her voice chilled me to the marrow.

The remains of the young Snider, the unfortunate boy who was barbarously murdered the 22nd of February last, were decently interred on the Monday following . . . his tragic death and the peculiar circumstances attending it had touched the breasts of all with the tenderest sympathies, only a few excepted, who have long shown themselves to be void of the feelings of humanity.

The little corpse was set down under the Tree of Liberty, from whence the procession began. About five hundred schoolboys proceeded; and a very numerous train of citizens followed. In the estimation of good judges, at least two thousand of all ranks were amidst a crowd of spectators, who discovered in their coun-tenances and deportment, the evident marks of true sorrow.

The pall was supported by six youths, chosen by the parents of the deceased.

Upon the foot of the coffin was an inscription in silver letters, LATET, ANGUIS IN HERBA! *("A snake lies in the grass.")*

Upon this very mournful occasion and during the solemnity that followed, the Sons of Liberty ordered a placard to be affixed to the Liberty Tree, inscribed with the following quotations from the sacred writings, which perhaps cannot easily be misapplied.

THOU SHALL TAKE NO SATISFACTION FOR THE LIFE OF A MURDERER

Suzannah handed the broadsheet to the nearest patron, as with reddened eyes she said softly, "Pass it around . . . to see with your own eyes, the tragic death of an innocent boy."

As the sailor took it from her, the great room was still so quiet we could hear the sound of the breakers on the distant shore. And nobody sat down.

After Suzannah stepped down off the table, she went over to an open window and looked out to sea for a long time. Her eyes never blinked as the sea breeze lightly fingered her hair.

Meanwhile, Lydia's words burned off the page, searing my brain as they echoed, ". . . *and they killed them all for want of words . . .*"

Suzannah turned to address the patrons . . . speaking as if she were in a trance and in the stillness of the moment, all eyes were upon her.

"Darkness shall come . . . for with all this talk, the demons in our souls are rising . . . and will breed a venomous hatred into our hearts . . . and this hatred will be heated until it becomes the defining instrument of Death . . . *war* . . . and so it shall come to pass."

Suddenly Henry Wiggins stood upon his chair, shook his fist and yelled, "There is devil's work afoot! The fiery demon of war is descending upon us! Freedom accords with the dictates of God's nature, combined with man's sense of civility and reason! If liberty does not rest upon God and our morality, then what is there to distinguish it from tyranny, I ask? We need not the egotistical abuse of any man self-endowed with rights beyond God's or ours . . . especially that of a *weak-headed king!*"

The roar of approval was deafening and the table pounding resumed, while many bawled for more drinks. As we frantically refilled the tumblers, another man rose and started speaking over the din.

"Hear ye this, I ask! Must we embrace *violence*? Should we not go forward to stand before our king and bare our souls pledging *loyalty*? Perhaps we could beg him to withdraw his troops—posthaste—so we can carry on with our lives . . ."

The pounding became even louder then, and the bawlers immediately shouted him down. The poor man retreated timidly and resumed his chair. A tumbler of rum was thrust before him with the admonition: "*Here*, weak one, drink *this* . . . it will make you quiet and peaceable . . . then you will be able to *reason* . . . or we can toss you out on your deaf ear!"

During the ensuing laughter, I noticed someone leering at Suzannah before announcing drunkenly, "Why burden our souls with all these moral platitudes . . ." then pointing to Suzannah, "when one may live so *pleasantly* by seizing the few *joys* the world provides."

The great room fell silent, save for the ticking of Mother's clock and the crashing of the distant breakers. The stranger continued to regard Suzannah with a lecherous grin, and focusing on the area of her womanhood, he boldly added, "Upon my soul, little maid, you *are* indeed well trained in the womanly arts—are you not?"

"*Enough!*" I shouted, and jumping up with murderous intent, I started for his table when the words, "*No, Jim!*" suddenly broke the silence . . . it was Suzannah's voice.

Passing me, she headed to his table, while his hooded eyes followed her every move. She patted his shoulder sweetly and placing a new tumbler before him, said, "Now, dear sir, do not get as unsteady on your *feet* as you are in your *heart*, or you shall surely find yourself in the street in short order."

And then, as if on cue, Henry Wiggins, who had already made his way over to the offensive fellow, lifted him straight out of his chair from behind and held him up while he asked me calmly, "So, Jim, how do you want to dispose of this . . . *reptile?*"

Striding to the door, I opened it and said, "Please do us the honors, Henry . . . the farther into the marsh the better!"

And with that, followed by the entire tavern crowd, Henry carried the writhing miscreant across the street, and tossed him onto the slimy banks of the muddy salt marsh . . . home of the bloodthirsty no-see-ems.

Wiping the pungent slime from his face and clothing, the stranger's eyes blazed with a venomous hatred while hissing, "We shall see about this . . . we shall *see* . . ." He then slithered away through the marsh like the loathsome reptile that he was, slapping the no-see-ems as they, and the looming darkness swallowed him up.

I held up Henry's arm in a gesture of victory and announced a free round for all. I was greeted with a chorus of huzzahs as everyone scrambled back inside for their tables.

The commotion seemed to attract more locals, people who were curious about the details and also wanted a pint. Even some womenfolk trickled in, whereupon Suzannah and Dimmis served them ginger tea laced with spiced rum, as their husbands looked on askance but voiced no objections.

The merriment was palpable and everyone was in good spirits when we closed our doors at ten of the clock. We cleaned up but had little to prepare for the following day, since we would be closed for the Sabbath. After Dimmis left, we finally retired to our chamber.

While Suzannah ferreted out my sleeping socks, I lay in bed reflecting on the contents of Lydia's letter. I felt my hatred toward the British rise again because of Father's death. They took him with no provocation of any kind, save to cover their own cowardice. Their murderous act nearly killed me—and I nearly killed Suzannah.

"Suzannah, I *despise* the British for what they did to Father . . ." I spat out bitterly, "and it's like a poison in my system!"

She hastened over to me, handed me my socks and kissed me tenderly. "Let's put all these dark feelings aside, lover . . . and *escape*." Then she kissed me again, this time deeply, hungrily, while she stroked me gently with her hand.

My manhood rose instantly to her magic touch, and without breaking her kiss, she loosened her hair so it fell to the small of her back. Then as our lips broke apart, without taking her eyes from mine, she smiled and dropped her dress to the floor. I looked on in astonishment as I realized she had been *naked* all day—with no chemise or petticoats—just *boldness* and a dress!

Nestling her exquisite nakedness into the bed, she sat up and spread her legs beneath the blanket, fluffed her hair and crooked her finger for me to come closer.

Forgetting the events of the letter, and dropping my clothes to the floor beside her dress, she lovingly wrapped her hands around my throbbing manhood, tenderly squeezing while guiding me toward her.

Moistening her lips and sensing my readiness to release, she briefly paused to lovingly ask, "Darling, can we try for *six and three* tonight?"

No Flowers for Suzannah

n the first year of our marriage, Suzannah continued to be the light of my life. Almost every night I stood beneath the heavens and contemplated the stars, while remembering my mother and father—and the days of my youth. I whispered prayers of gratitude for having my parents as long as I did, and I wondered if they now smiled on their only son and his cherished bride . . . who saved his life. I prayed tearfully that Suzannah's love would never be extinguished, for Mother was correct in every sense: her love was rich, true and healing.

Beside Mother's portrait in the great room hung a likeness of Suzannah in her sun hat and flowers—painted at the time of our wedding. And so the two women in my life remained close: in heart, memory and spirit. I felt it was because of those paintings that the patrons kept their behavior to a high standard; and most gave the "tavern girls"—Suzannah and Dimmis—the respect they truly deserved. One of the biggest treats in store for those not "in the know" was being served food and drink by the proprietress of the tavern. It then pleased them immensely to learn that their server was one and the same with "the beautiful girl in the picture."

Since the tavern opened, Walker's Cove saw more frequent visits by ships laden with foodstuffs, Essex rum, cider—and numerous other supplies ordered by us and other local tradesmen. Sometimes, among our many seagoing patrons, an older ship's captain would come to sit at a table with a pint, fondly recalling stories of Mother at the Mariner's Rest, as well as the proprietress of the former Walker's Tavern. While dismayed to learn of her tragic passing, they found comfort and pleasure in seeing her portrait in its place of honor.

Often while Dimmis and I carried on cooking and serving, Suzannah was in the process of transacting business for us, which she continued to improve upon. As she initiated newer and better deals for us, her trading partners still came away with the highest regard for her acumen, honesty and fairness in wanting all concerned to realize a profit.

Eventually our lives became so hectic that I sometimes yearned for the carefree days when we were courting. But now, as co-proprietors of the family business, we worked like demons from six in the morning until ten at night, except on the Sabbath. So not only were we married to each other, we were also married to the tavern. As such, we had to make frequent adjustments to our daily routine so we could spend time alone together.

Our nightly ritual of tween time evaporated, and moved to Sundays. We still had our rocking sessions, but only after cleanup and preparations for the next day were completed. Often Suzannah wanted to frolic in our bedchamber—or any other suitable place that was convenient to her mood—so at least some of the stresses of tavern-keeping were vented through our vigorous lovemaking. But it was more usual for Suzannah and I to simply drop into bed, wrap our arms around each other and pass out from exhaustion, when my final conscious thoughts were: "Mother, how in God's name did you do it?"

At all events, it took us quite a while to adjust our lives in such a way that favored us a little more than the tavern. And we learned very quickly why Mother closed it when she decided to start her family. I wondered how on earth *I* would ever do it alone, when Suzannah might become with child.

By the time our anniversary approached, the tavern had become a brilliant success, but only due to the tireless labor and attention we all—including Dimmis—lavished on it. So it was that I determined to make August 3rd a special day for my wife of one year. We planned to celebrate it by ourselves, especially since Fanny and Sam were on an extended visit to Boston, house-hopping among Suzannah's sisters.

Taking Winnie, I sauntered off in the early morning to gather the wildflowers that grew in profusion in Richardson's fields . . . flowers for my living flower. To surprise her, I carefully bound them with string and hid them in the barn—in a pail of water so they would not wither overnight. Among them were tiny white ones with yellow centers that grew on delicate stalks. "How beautiful they would look in her hair," I thought, "especially if *I* could place them there."

My other anniversary gifts were hidden in Winnie's saddlebag: an anniversary note written from my heart, and writing papers I obtained through Lydia from the most distinguished stationer in Boston. Suzannah wrote her sisters very frequently, and since there were four of them, she was always wanting for paper and ink. It would also help keep one of our favorite pastimes going: snuzzling in our rocker before the fire, while Suzannah read aloud the most recent of her sisters' numerous letters.

When I arrived at our back door after my quest for wildflowers, I was greeted with deep passionate kisses from my sweet and charm-ing wife. There was also a special meal awaiting me, with custards for dessert. We shared a perfectly glorious evening that culminated in a particularly frenzied session of lovemaking. Suzannah was *ready* before we even reached the stairs to our chamber . . . she choosing the stairs for our first "visit to the heights."

Lately I had noticed that despite her fatigue, Suzannah was always eager to make love—almost excessively so, for she wanted me with her constantly. So we altered our routines to accommodate her, and I was true to my promise: we made love with wild abandon, reckless experimentation and endless variations . . . and nothing *was* forbidden.

Yet after an entire year of marriage, I still found it difficult to believe that such a gentle, soft-spoken enchantress—could be such a bold and brazen hussy in the marriage bed—or anywhere else the mood struck her. What delightful carnal behavior from the demure, angelic little girl that met me at her door a few short years ago!

Knowing I was indeed fortunate in this, I loved her all the more. Tireless and long were the fun filled nights of our adventurous lovemaking . . . and Suzannah would still want more. Then, afterward, my lioness would gently wrap her legs and arms around me and sleep as sweetly as a newborn kitten.

Early on our anniversary morning while it was still dark, I snuck out of bed. Gently drawing the covers over Suzannah so as not to wake her, I quietly stole down the stairs, and headed toward the barn to retrieve her gifts.

I put the stationery on the table and arranged the flowers in a pewter vase in the center, propping the note against it. I then made her a special breakfast of maple johnnycakes, sausages, corn muffins, butter and warm milk. After setting everything out on the table, I went to wake my slumbering wife.

At the doorway to our chamber, I was startled to find Suzannah awake—and standing *naked* before the window. She was looking forlornly toward the morning sun, rising in the east. When she heard me enter she turned to face me.

"Happy anniversary, darling," I said softly, "it's *our* special day, Suzannah. What would you like to do?"

When she let her tresses fall away, in her face I saw not an expression of joy, but of sadness. I rushed to her side and wrapped my arms around her, but she protested, pushing me away. "No Jim, *don't* hold me!"

"What? Suzannah, what's wrong?" She uttered not a word of explanation as I took her chemise from the chair and gently helped her into it. As my heart sank, I took her hand and said, "Come downstairs, Suzannah, I have something for you . . ."

But she would not come.

So I gave her arm a little tug, while imploring, "Come . . . *please* come, Suzannah."

Reluctantly, she followed me down to the kitchen, where she saw the table dressed and ready for "our day."

"For my loving bride of one year!" I announced proudly, indicating what awaited her on the table.

She examined in turn, my note, the papers and the wildflowers . . . and her eyes filled with tears. With a tiny whimper, she covered her mouth, turned around and ran upstairs to our chamber. Stupefied and distressed by her behavior, I sensed there was a secret dread or sorrow that burdened her.

"Of all days . . . *this* day," I thought as I wondered if perhaps a walk to the point would help ease her dark mood—for she was *not* the same woman I went to bed with last night. With my heart in turmoil, I slowly ascended the stairs and peeked into our chamber. There I saw that Suzannah had exchanged her chemise for a yellow dress trimmed with white lace. Although her appearance put me in mind of the sun, her spirits were as far from sunny as they could possibly be.

"Suzannah, shall we go to the point?" I asked.

By way of an answer, she whimpered again; and when I tried to take her hand, she put it behind her back. And so, for the first time ever, we walked *separately* along the road leading to Walker's Point.

I was in agony! What had upset my poor wife today of all days? I noticed as we walked she was still visibly upset, so we didn't talk at all. She still wouldn't take my hand or even look at me. Unlike Mother I could only *feel* her despondence, but could not grasp *why* she felt this way.

Along the path to Walker's Point, I stopped beneath the beech tree, wordlessly taking her hand and pressing it to my heart. She finally gazed up at me, and my heart broke because her eyes were wet with quiet tears that had made little trails down her cheeks.

Kneeling on one knee, I caressed her face with my hands, gently wiping her tears with my thumbs. "Suzannah," I whispered, holding her head so I could search her eyes, "I feel such a heaviness in your heart. *Why* is this so?"

Looking away to avoid the question, she said nothing.

"Suzannah . . . I can't sense feelings like my mother could, but I *know* you're carrying a burden, but I cannot tell why. You *must* open your heart. Tell me the reason you're so sad, dear one."

She turned away from me without a word and went to the beech tree. Standing before its massive trunk, she stared at the love carvings we made in our younger days. Then she rose slowly onto her tiptoes and with a trembling hand, tenderly fingered the scars that composed the word, LIFE.

I stood behind her, watching every move she made, trying desperately to understand what she was trying to convey. Her forlorn little figure looked even smaller and more forlorn before the immense tree trunk.

Placing my hands gently upon her shoulders, I could feel the tension in them. They began to shake as she tremulously lowered her fingers from the carving. Raising her hands to cover her face, she wiped away copious streams of renewed tears.

When I guided her gently toward me and folded her against my heart, she wailed uncontrollably as she'd never done before. I kissed the top of her head and caressed her hair until she slowly put her arms around my waist, and cried all the more. I rocked her to and fro as I always did when she wanted comforting, but she just couldn't seem to shake off her burden.

Still holding her in my arms, I looked up at the carving we'd made in the midst of such joyous happiness. My heart ached at the irony that this sadness should happen *here* . . . on the very spot where four years ago, our hearts soared together on the wings of newfound love.

As I stroked her silken tresses and backed her up gently against the tree, I kissed her ardently and began repeating, "Suzannah, remember I love you . . . *I love you.* You are my wife an *entire year* on this day! Suzannah . . . unburden yourself to your anxious husband! Remember, a burden shared is only *half* a burden. We will bear this *together. Please,* don't shut the door to your precious heart."

She sniffled in my shirt, and then looked up at me with reddened eyes. Suddenly, through lips quivering with dread and heartbreak, she shook her head violently and blurted out words that pierced me to the heart. "Oh Jim, our marriage has been a perfect *failure!*"

I was stunned at this confession! "*What* did you just say? *Surely* I did not hear what I *thought* I heard, Suzannah."

Pulling away from me, tears cascading, she stamped her foot and once again—this time with her fists clenched—hurled these stinging words at me. "Jim, I *love* you with all my soul and heart . . . but our marriage is a perfect *failure!*"

"For God's sake, Suzannah! If you *love* me, how can our marriage be a *failure?* Did I do something to injure your sensibilities?"

I gathered her into my arms again, and for a brief moment she tried to pull away—but I wouldn't let go. She relaxed then and putting her arms around my waist, with her cheek against my chest, she softly asked, "You *do* love me, Jim, do you not?"

Squeezing her tightly I said, "Of *course*, I do . . . more and more every day. You cannot imagine how *privileged* I feel to wake up every day of my life, and see your beautiful face next to mine. You are *everything* to me . . ."

When I paused, she looked up at me with sad puppy eyes and murmured, "Then will you love me *forever* . . . no matter *what?*"

"Of *course*, Suzannah!" I lifted her quivering chin and pulling it toward me, I kissed her: first on her lips, then on her wet cheeks, her forehead, nose tip—and back to her lips. This was one of her favorite displays of my affection. After our lips parted, her pretty white teeth flashed through a half-baked smile. It meant she was coming around.

I picked her up and sat with her in my lap beneath the tree, as easily as cradling a babe. She wiggled a bit to snuzzle deeper in my arms, and once settled released a huge sigh. I then kissed the tip of her nose again which made her giggle.

Deciding now was the time to strike, I calmly asked, "So tell me dearest wife, how is it that our marriage is such a perfect failure? Who said it was a failure?"

She hesitated. "Well, nobody *said* . . . it was . . . a failure . . ." she stammered; ". . . but it *is!*"

Kissing her forehead I gently asked, "And *why* is that? Name *one* reason! Last night on our anniversary eve, you kept me busy most of the night with your wonderful lovemaking antics. So how, my dear Suzannah, is our marriage a failure? We work well together, we hardly disagree—and we can't keep our hands *off* each other!"

With her eyes downcast, she said, "Oh Jim, when you make love to me, I feel so warm, secure, wanted and *very* happy. I love bringing pleasure to you and feeling the deep inner sensations of our being joined. But, Jim . . ."

Her eyes tearful, she suddenly blurted out, "I'm a . . . *barren woman* . . . I'm not bearing your children . . . so you may cast me off as your wife, and I shall accept it . . . because I am *imperfect* . . ." her voice tapered off with a hollow crack, and resumed as barely a whisper, "and you might wish for a *better* wife who is able . . . to bear . . ." and looking up at me with pleading eyes and a quivering lower lip, she whispered, ". . . children . . ."

So there it was. She had laid bare her soul to me to be judged. I, who was totally unworthy to judge anything or anyone, and if I should judge her harshly, she was unselfishly offering to take her pain with her . . . so I might seek another wife.

I was moved by her unspeakable bravery, knowing she would willingly sacrifice all she had in life—just for *my* happiness—and this was not the first time. Such was the courage of her selfless love!

I placed my trembling hands upon her cheeks and sternly announced, "*Suzannah!* There will be *no* other wife!" Then I added, "Suzannah, *never* look down—always look proud, strong and confident . . . for *that* is the kind of wife you *are*! There will *be* no other wife . . . *ever!*"

The look on her face—a silent and sad expression of adoration— melted my heart. Her eyes filled again as she silently nodded her understanding.

Knowing the nature of her bittersweet pain, I felt that now I could comfort and reassure her. Rocking her in my arms I softly said, "Suzannah, my dearest angel . . . *fear not*. I shall love you *forever*, whether you have twenty children—or *none*. It is *you* I want. It is *you* I married. I want to spend my days with *you*, my nights with *you*, and every moment of my life with *you*—even death with *you*. Can you not see that love of body and soul isn't contingent upon the ability to bear children?"

Holding back more tears, she whispered, "But Jim, I thought that is the *purpose* of marriage!"

Tightening my grip around my precious bride, I softly replied, "That is not the *only* purpose. Remember what Reverend Metcalf said at our wedding? We are meant to be all we *can* be to each other . . . not *everything*. Also, in all conditions, correct? God has written no law that demands children be a *condition* of marriage. We are *all* far from perfect!

I lovingly took her cheeks and when she closed her eyes, I tenderly kissed her tears away . . . and then holding her to my heart I solemnly said, "So if the *condition* is that you are not able to have children, I *accept* that. The only condition I *cannot* accept . . . is to live my life without *you* in it! We are together as man and wife— I can't ask God for any greater blessing than that. If He grants us a child, I pray it's a true copy of what I hold at this very moment."

Suzannah nuzzled her cheek to my heart and squeezed my waist. "God has given me the *best* of husbands! I shall *never* forget your words, Jim . . . you have made me whole once again."

"As you have made *me*, dearest bride. Remember, I shall *never* forsake my wedded wife, and besides . . . who are *we* to judge who is perfect or imperfect? That is *God's* purpose. *Our* purpose is to live and love on . . . in an imperfect world . . ."

She kissed my hand, and gently pressing it to her heart, gave me one of her incomparable smiles.

THE MIDNIGHT STROLL

er smile led to a flurry of adoring kisses and many sweet whisperings beneath our tree. These in turn led to uncontrollable giggles and other kinds of foolery; so declaring I'd had enough, I scooped her up in my arms to carry her home.

As I walked along, my little wife's hands were free to plague me. She laughed and tittered continuously while poking and prodding me: playfully pulling my hair, squeezing my nostrils, sticking fingers into my ears, nibbling my neck and pinching my cheeks—all the while daring me not to drop her.

She was wonderful! No joy was ever so rich as ours!

Dusk was upon us when we finally arrived home, and while I stoked the fire, she puttered around the kitchen to concoct an evening treat. While I listened to her happy singing, I settled myself into the rocker feeling quite content. Some time passed before I called toward the kitchen, "Is it rocking time yet?"

As if on cue, Suzannah came out bringing two spoons and a bowl of custard. She nestled into my lap and softly confirmed, "Indeed, it is," adding a little kiss that quickly turned deep and passionate. When we finished, I kissed the tip of her nose and whispered, "I *love* you . . ."

"I love you *more* . . ." she replied with her irresistible giggle.

We rocked and kissed tenderly between mouthfuls of custard that we fed to each other. When it was gone, Suzannah finally settled down with me in the rocker, gazing dreamily into the fire. I watched her study the flames, the firelight danced in her gray-blue eyes . . . and gazing deeply into them, the truth of her love reflected back at me. She loved me unconditionally as I did her, and we *were* indeed as one.

The day's emotional distress invited sleep, but I wished this first anniversary night with *her* to never end. And so we rocked on in loving silence as the candle flickered into darkness, leaving only the fire's glow. When finally that too was gone, Suzannah rose from my lap, gently took my hand, and led me upstairs.

To keep her heart hopeful, our lovemaking sessions became even longer and more unbridled; and whenever her monthly sickness was late, we would daydream together about having a child, even to the point where we considered names. When we could not decide, I finally asked Suzannah if she would name our firstborn female Fanny and our second, Ainsley. For the firstborn male I asked if she would use Samuel, and Richard for the second.

These requests touched Suzannah deeply and she agreed to all, thus bringing us ever closer. I could readily see they gave Suzannah hope—and she was comforted in knowing how strongly I supported her in her secret grief.

During the year that followed, our tavern continued to thrive, keeping us exceedingly busy . . . so much so that Suzannah seemed to have forgotten her sorrow over our childless condition. She flourished in her role as hostess, as her buoyant heart prevailed over her grief and she took comfort from our boundless love for each other.

As tavern-keepers, we were fortunate that Walker's Cove in summer had certain natural amenities that increased our customer traffic. The proximity of the seaside meant that visitors would benefit from the fresh, bracing sea air, and might enjoy viewing the wide variety of seabirds that populated the saltwater marshes, including mallards, black backs, egrets, piping plover, geese and swans. Even during spring, when the morning dew covered the shore grasses with glittering diamonds, the fowl nested there, loitering in the marsh pools until the smoggy mists of autumn . . . when they finally headed south to live in warmer climes.

When crews and passengers alike disembarked from the ships, they were likely to stroll up the road parallel to our splendid seacoast and find at its end our welcoming tavern. Because grandfather had built it at the top of the main street—within view of the wharf looking southward—every passerby would invariably come within olfactory range of our kitchen . . . and thus be keenly drawn by its enticing aromas, making them desirous of food, drink and company.

Often, Suzannah, Dimmis and I would mingle with the patrons, sitting among them to hear news of other ports. If we were lucky, someone would produce a broadsheet from Boston, New York or Philadelphia. Broadsheets provided many accounts of the growing discontent throughout the colonies . . . discontent instigated by the punitive manner in which Parliament and King George had mistreated our people.

Sunday remained our day to be alone together. We walked to church, and on the way home, usually stopped in Richardson's fields. There we would dwell among the wildflowers while, exchanging soft kisses in the summer breeze, we laughed our cares away. We invariably ended each Sunday nestled together at Walker's Point, spending hours talking about trivial things that were dear to us, and then watching the sunsets in silent awe.

Once a week, I took Winnie and our new freight wagon down to the wharf to load supplies and foodstuffs from newly arrived vessels. We would then bring our cargo back for storage in our new cellar, or the old forge, under the watchful eyes of Suzannah and Dimmis. Many of the items I hauled were spices and other ingredients needed for the dishes featured on our menu; but there were also heavy barrels of Essex rum, Boston beers and apple cider. Salted meats, flour and molasses were also routinely transported in barrels, making it easy for Dimmis to inventory them *and* draw from them. Using a rule of Mother's called "first in, first out," this routine minimized the amount of waste due to spoilage.

Despite all the time it took us to learn our new trade, we were happy and content with how well things were going. Suzannah's apprenticeship under Mother paid off handsomely, especially when combined with Dimmis' experience in her "prior life"—as she called it. Thus, on the first anniversary of the tavern—marking the day when Suzannah had announced its readiness to open (as her wedding gift to me)—we gave Dimmis a special gift of appreciation: 250 silver coins, known as pieces of eight. Whereupon she tearfully confided she would remain with us for as long as we wished her to, even if we chose not to pay her at all. The truth be told, we could not have succeeded without her, and Suzannah had come to love her as her dearest friend.

In summer, the heat usually stifled the tavern, and despite the open windows, it was sometimes difficult to catch a cooling breeze. So after closing each night, Suzannah and I sauntered down to Walker's Point in search of a cooling sea breeze. When we returned, we dowsed ourselves under the barrel that still resided behind the tavern, and thus refreshed, we scampered to bed where even greater pleasures awaited.

During that July, I noticed that Suzannah became easily fatigued. This I attributed to the intense heat of her kitchen and the stress of endless work on her tiny frame. As I recalled, it had not been that hot since our wedding day. So after we closed on the sultry eve of our second anniversary, Suzannah excused herself from our walk, saying she was too tired and preferred to rest at home instead. When we reached the front door, I kissed her deeply and reassured her that my walk without her would be brief.

The penetrating quiet heightened my senses as I walked along the moonlit street. The gentle breeze carried the fragrances of lilac, roses, honeysuckle, and even the dusty aroma of oak . . . reminding me of Suzannah's wildflower bouquets in our bedroom. As I passed several houses overlooking the cove, within their windows I saw dimly lit by failing candlelight, fireplace mantels graced with warm homey furnishings: a shelf clock here, a portrait there, some fine pewter plates in another—all, the pride and joy of its inhabitants.

Feeling as though I had surreptitiously intruded upon moments of my neighbors' lives, with a pang of guilt, I hastened silently to the wharf. There, I finally met up with the welcoming sea breezes I was seeking, faint tonight, but an unmistakable presence nonetheless. In the shallows, I heard the tranquil lapping of the water against the hulls of the trading brigs. I stepped closer to observe their gently swaying masts, listening to the rigging slap against them in time to the tide's gentle swells. The tranquility lulled me into realizing how tired I really was; so wishing to rejoin Suzannah, I headed home.

As I turned up our street, so noisy by day, now veiled in a tomb-like sleep, my footsteps echoed in the stillness. Approaching our tavern's doorstep with its two large boot scrapes, I could not help but smile, for inside was my Suzannah.

While I removed the soil from my shoes, the door slowly cracked open and Suzannah peered out, still looking tired and drawn.

"The bed has been warmed and I made some of Grandmother's custards tonight. Will you indulge your little wife in a cup and a snuzzle?"

I started to correct her by saying, "*Grandmother* never made custards . . ." when she interrupted me by kissing my lips ever so tenderly . . . and sweetly murmuring, "Oh yes, she *did* . . ." while delicately holding her stomach.

Dumbstruck with astonishment, as I slowly raised my eyes from her stomach to her face, her eyes welled with tears as she whimpered, "Oh *Jim*, there will be *three* of us in the fall . . ."

I drew her gently to my heart, and wept openly in her hair, kissing the top of her head, her face and her lips . . . over and over again. Against the silence of the night, our cries of joy echoed softly throughout the quiet village . . . while I wondered how could I *ever* deserve such a wife?

A Mother's Love

uzannah immediately wrote her family in Boston with our news. She missed her parents at such a time as this, but she was too distracted by her daily routine to focus on their absence. The first person I told of Suzannah being with child was Rhoda Barrett. Because she had her weekly tea on Thursdays, I expected the entire town to have the news by Thursday evening. Within two days, a constant stream of excited well-wishers came by the tavern to see Suzannah and congratulate us. Meanwhile, as we basked in all this adoration, we had a wonderful summer watching our tiny child grow within her.

What an experience to see that soft maternal glow radiate from my little wife. As her face grew rounder and her body grew pleasingly plump, her sweet girlish figure became almost matronly as her breasts became large and full. I felt obscenely guilty in some respects, because I *admired* her delicate condition, and loved seeing her that way. To me, she was more beautiful than ever before. In our chamber, she would pose nude for me, as though I was a great classical painter; and she enjoyed exhibiting her pending motherhood from various angles, that sorely tempted me to engage in activities I knew we shouldn't.

But that didn't stop Suzannah, and she always had her way with me—after all, I would melt like butter in her loving hands. In the afterglow of our lovemaking, I often cuddled her from behind by threading my arms around her growing midsection; and she would whisper that I was *inside* of her—and *outside* of her—and that was the *best* feeling she ever had in her entire life. Thus overwhelmed with love and gratitude, I would gently stroke her hair, and wrap it around my hands to inhale its floral scent . . . and drift away into a peaceful deep sleep.

Once, during a quiet time after lovemaking, Suzannah took my hands and placed them on her belly. I felt movement there, for the child within was seemingly at play. She giggled sweetly and whispered that motherhood was *so* agreeable to her, that she hoped we would have twenty children . . . whereupon my response was a deep loving kiss . . . and hers was another lovemaking session.

ONCE THE ELLINGWOODS got wind of Suzannah's condition, they cut their trip short and returned to Walker's Cove. They wanted to be a support to their daughter in any way they could, and thus Suzannah enlisted Fanny's help in the great room, and soon the tavern became a two-family business: for the Walkers *and* the Ellingwoods. Under Suzannah's understanding guidance, Fanny learned to work with Dimmis nearly as seamlessly as her daughter had.

As Suzannah grew larger, she gracefully withdrew to the kitchen. There, until the birth, she would continue to cook, monitor inventory and conduct other tavern business behind closed doors. But increasingly, I stood in for her, placing the orders and paying for goods and services. During what we called our "kitchen visits," I would consult with her on certain matters—and also steal a kiss or two—and then apply her advice and knowledge without her having to be present. Finally, Suzannah reached a point where her role in tavern affairs ended, save for cooking, which she still greatly enjoyed.

Although Dimmis and Fanny were now the tavern hostesses, I still helped them out. I was familiar with our regular patrons and their preferences in food and drink, so often I was the one who drew their tumblers and served their meals without any prompting. Despite Suzannah's conspicuous absence as the cornerstone of our establishment, our fine reputation persisted unabated, and the money continued to pour in.

Doc Brown kept his medical eye upon Suzannah and examined her every two weeks. He arranged for Mildred Lovejoy—who had given birth to thirteen healthy children of her own—to serve as midwife to Suzannah, a decision all of us endorsed enthusiastically.

When I devoted my full time in attending to Suzannah during her confinement, Dimmis became the proprietress of the tavern; and although we hired a couple of new hands to assist her, she worked tirelessly—starting the fires at five every morning, cooking with Fanny, serving all day and into the night, and supervising the final cleanup. Yet after working such long hours, she was as fresh at the end of the day as she was at the beginning . . . and I uttered a grateful prayer every night—thanking Mother for hiring Dimmis . . . and God for sparing her.

As the leaves donned their rich October colors, Suzannah's twentieth birthday was upon us. On the morning of that day, Fanny, Sam and Dimmis arrived to inform her of a special surprise—her sisters and their husbands had come from Boston to celebrate it with her. Right now, they were cooking a birthday feast, which would be followed by Fanny's "great cake" dripping with Mother's milk frosting.

When we went over to the Ellingwoods later that day, our noses were teased and tempted by the delicious aromas wafting in our direction. They started my mouth watering before we even reached the front door, and as such I couldn't wait to eat.

Once inside the parlor, Suzannah managed with some difficulty to hug her sisters and brothers-in-law, and then kiss them—a much easier task. The greetings over, everyone took a seat, since us locals were eager to hear about the latest doings in Boston.

Suzannah was given a place of honor in Sam's oversized armchair, and she nestled herself in it—queen for the day. Katharine and Sarah passed around a platter of crackers and cheese, and Sam served tea and mulled cider, perfect drinks for a brisk October day.

Fanny had no desire to let the political events of the day darken her family gathering, and thus, she encouraged her four older daughters to recount amusing moments from their girlhoods, particularly after Suzannah was born.

As the meal of smoked ham, baked potatoes, beans, bread, pumpkin pie and blueberries was served, Sarah recalled a time when she and Suzannah discovered Fanny's petticoats, pantaloons and bonnets in her wardrobe trunk. Suzannah, delighted by the find, dressed herself in several of the garments. Sarah decided to show off her little sister's "big girl" wardrobe on the streets of Boston—much to the amusement of passersby.

When Fanny noticed a small crowd tittering and laughing near her front door, she was mortified to discover—"Suzannah proudly modeling my petticoats before the entire city!" After Fanny retrieved her daughters, she scowled at them in disapproval. But apparently Suzannah's smiling eyes and innocent toothy grin totally forbade a more serious scolding.

Lydia's story came next. She told about when the minister of the Ellingwoods' church was invited to Sunday dinner. After the meal, while the servants were clearing the table, six-year-old Suzannah challenged the poor man with her jaw-dropping hypothesis: that God was a woman, not a man!

She based her argument upon the premise that women were the fairer sex; and as such, more thoughtful, analytical and logical than men, and thus considerably more advanced. She bolstered her theory by hypothesizing that in a sympathetic moment of weakness, God created Eve as a companion for Adam—and therefore didn't it make sense that God might indeed *be* a woman?

At last the time came for Fanny's cake to be served. Amidst all the chattering upon its arrival, I rose from my place and quietly withdrew into the parlor. From its concealing shadows I gazed wistfully into the dining room, wondering how many stories like that my parents could have shared; and if I'd had a sister or brother, what they would have said about me. As the sound of laughter suddenly exploded at the table, my bittersweet thought was, "How I *miss* my little family . . ."

But my smiling eyes now rested upon my extraordinary wife. She was so happy and vibrant. And as her laughter echoed in my sacred reverie, it was the same laughter she had at fifteen, but now it was richer; and because of her maturity and the depth that attended it, her beauty had become even more compelling. As such, because she grew so gracefully into each new role she encountered, it seemed it was her natural gift to do so. And now she carried our child, and so, along with Suzannah, our child and I had gotten a new family . . . *her* family. So despite my tragic personal losses, what I had gained was far more precious than anything I could have hoped for—on that night so long ago, when I was lonesome . . . and wished *only* for a new friend.

On the Saturday after Suzannah's birthday, Doc paid a visit with Mrs. Lovejoy to examine Suzannah in our chamber. After they had finished, he came downstairs and told me he wanted a word with me privately. Leaving Suzannah upstairs with Mrs. Lovejoy, we seated ourselves in the kitchen. After serving Doc a small tankard of beer mixed with rum, I asked, "Well, how are they faring?"

"From all indications the child is healthy and well, Jim, but I have concerns about Suzannah."

"She seems *fine* to me," I offered, wondering what he saw that I didn't, and also, to some extent, wanting to stifle a sense of alarm.

As he sipped his beer, Doc looked thoughtful for a few moments before venturing an explanation. "Well, Jim, as you know there can be grave dangers associated with childbearing—though you would never think so by looking at Mrs. Lovejoy's history!"

I laughed at his indelicate humor, but I knew he was serious.

After taking another swallow, Doc placed his tankard on the table. "We need to have a brief discussion about childbirth. So I'd like to tell you about your mother, and why she never had any more children after you were born."

"Mother never mentioned that to me, Doc—other than to express regret about my not having a brother or sister. Please tell me more."

"It was because she was so badly mangled when you were born. I was there, and I remember all too well that she damn near died. I never expected to tell you about it, and you were indeed fortunate to have her as long as you did. The upshot is, it's a miracle she didn't die when you were born." Pulling his chair closer, he added, "You were *breeched*."

"What does *that* mean?"

"It means you were *feet* first coming out of the womb, while most babes are born *head* first. The mother's pelvic muscles are configured to push the infant out smoothly and with little resistance—but only if it's head first."

"I see," I said thoughtfully, as I absorbed this new knowledge.

Doc continued, "During the final month of confinement, the babe will usually turn itself inside the womb, so its head is *down*, in preparation for birthing." He paused here to illustrate with his hands the act of turning. "You did not do that."

I was suddenly engulfed by a wave of guilt, as I sorely regretted that poor Mother had to suffer because I did not turn properly.

Doc noticed my reaction, and with a new note of levity added, "You were a *little* stubborn back then, but you are *much* worse now!"

We both laughed, and then he carried on with the demeanor of a war veteran recalling an old battle he barely survived.

"I could see your mother was pretty tore up giving birth to you—she nearly died from the loss of so much blood. Her uterus was so badly lacerated that it never had a chance to heal right. Consequently, I knew she would never have another child; and as I lay you upon her loving breast, I had to tell her that sorrowful news." Doc drank deeply from the tankard before he continued.

"But it mattered not to your parents, Jim, for they were thankful to have *you* as their only child—and yet *still* have each other. They took that secret to their graves, and I now lift it from the sepulchral dust to illustrate my point."

"And that is?" I inquired.

"Giving birth is a perilous enterprise. Death in childbirth is a pervasive fear that shadows the highlights of a woman's life: in marriage, in the conjugal act—and in bringing new life into the world.

A woman in Suzannah's state already *has* one foot in the grave if things go wrong. Or if fate is smiling upon her, and her doctor and midwife are skilled, she can *withdraw* that foot . . . until the next time."

"If there *is* a next time . . ." I murmured, feeling overburdened with guilt.

Doc stood and angrily gripping my chin with his thumb and fingers, sternly admonished, "Your mother was a God-fearing woman *and* a superb trader! She *prayed* all week from her sickbed, day and night . . . that *He* trade her next child for continued life with *this* one . . ." His eyes filled as his voice wavered and broke, ". . . it was a *damned good* trade!"

Realizing then how badly I was wanted, I humbly asked, "Is what you say true, Doc?"

Wiping his eyes as his passion subsided, Doc said softly, "I would *never* lie, Jim—and I know because I was the physician at her side that entire week." Doc leaned back, drained the rest of his beer and then finished his thought.

"So as I was saying, as a *man* you must learn to appreciate this: that despite the harrowing possibility of death through birth, the deep maternal feeling that Suzannah has, and your mother had and Mrs. Lovejoy had—makes them risk *everything* they have in this world . . . for the sake of their *child* . . . of such *strength* is their instinct to *love*."

Patting my shoulder, Doc rose and said, "Thanks for the drink, Jim. Now go upstairs and hold *close* that little mother-to-be."

Two weeks later, Doc and Mildred Lovejoy came again to examine Suzannah. They were especially concerned because she was so small and her child was so large. Doc wondered if she might be farther along to birthing than he previously thought.

"My fear is she will not pass a large head and shoulders through her pelvis . . ." he soberly admitted to me in the privacy of our parlor.

"Then again, Doc," I suggested, "Suzannah is so small to begin with that she just *looks* bigger because her child is now perhaps a tenth of her body weight."

"Indeed, there may be an illusory element in her apparent size, Jim; but I fear for her if the child gets much larger, that complications may arise."

"What kind of complications?" I asked, knowing nothing about birthing other than what we'd discussed two weeks earlier.

Raising his eyebrows, he said in more confidential tones, "Jim, you are six feet and two inches. Suzannah is four feet and ten inches—perhaps *eleven* on a good day. It stands to reason if she bore you a child, it would be *larger* rather than smaller. I don't know if her delicate frame can deliver a nine-pound child."

At that moment, Mrs. Lovejoy came downstairs and joined us in the parlor.

"What is your assessment, Mildred?" asked Doc, folding his hands over his weskit.

"She needs to birth soon, or I think she will be in danger," Mrs. Lovejoy said with obvious concern.

Doc leaned forward, looking directly at Mildred. "Let's gather everyone together who will help you, Mildred, and let's plan this out. I am not leaving this child to chance."

"Then I suggest we meet at your house at sundown this very day. What do you say, Doc?" she replied.

"Done; and at that time we'll discuss all possible options."

As Mildred rose and draped her shawl around her shoulders I said, "Thank you, Mildred, for all you have done on Suzannah's behalf."

"No need, Jim. I hope you don't mind my mentioning that I always found it *strange* that none of her sisters ever bore children. I believe there is that tendency with the Ellingwood girls."

"Suzannah told me once it was her secret grief not to bear children," I replied. "Since then, her sisters have opened their hearts to Suzannah, and told her that their childlessness was not for lack of trying . . ."

"I understand," she replied; "but there are many women who do not wish to find themselves in the condition I found myself in on *thirteen* occasions—mostly because they fear the danger and the pain . . ."

Doc glanced at me with a meaningful smile.

As I escorted Mildred to the door, she stopped and stood upon the threshold. After a moment, she turned around to us and confessed, "But I find it is *worth* it . . . because I *love* to be *loved* . . ."

"Mildred!" Doc protested, standing in disbelief. "Such impropriety! What would Osgood say?"

"That he is the *happiest* man in the world!" she barked back at him, and cackling with satisfaction, joyfully slammed the door.

I stared at the spot where she last stood, wondering if in fact Osgood *was* that happy. I could hardly believe that Mildred Lovejoy had the fiery libido my little Suzannah did . . . but she certainly had the children to prove it!

A Promise Broken

oc Brown descended the stairs slowly, taking cautious deliberate steps. Stopping on the bottom landing, he turned to face me with a solemn countenance. I anxiously had anticipated seeing and holding our child for the very first time, and so I rose to face him. He wordlessly raised a small bundle toward me—a little girl—asleep and totally at peace.

When I smiled at seeing her, Doc's eyes filled as he hoarsely croaked, "I'm so *sorry*, Jim. I *lost* her . . ."

I swooned at his words as the blood drained from my heart. I was instantly devastated, and doing all I could to suppress my tears, I approached him and the child. Laying my comforting hand upon the tiny bundle, I whispered, "Don't blame yourself, Doc, I'm sure you did all you could. Does Suzannah know?"

"I suspect she does, Jim, since it's so quiet up there. She will soon know if she doesn't already. She should not be alone when she wakes and hears no cry. Either way, you should be with her."

Wiping his eyes, Doc shook his head and bent to look wistfully at the small motionless face. With a cracked voice he lamented, "Of all the little girls I've delivered safely into this life, it had to be *hers* that wasn't. I can scarcely believe it."

I could think of nothing to say, so I kept silent.

"How was she to be called, Jim?" he asked as he handed her over to me.

"Fanny," I said sadly as I took her into my arms while feeling my heart break.

He looked at me and said, "You couldn't have chosen a better name . . . save Ainsley, of course."

I wept openly now, for the reality was that our little girl had died. Wiping my tears with the back of my hand in abject misery, I quietly added, "We agreed that our first daughter would be named for Fanny, our second for Ainsley."

Dabbing at his eyes with a handkerchief, Doc collapsed heavily into the rocker. He leaned his head back and closed his eyes.

Meanwhile, I kissed my child's forehead and tiny cheeks to find she was still warm. Then I murmured to her, "God bless your *dear* little soul. May you take your place in Heaven amongst His *best* and most precious angels."

I was now a childless father, and never lower in spirit, except when I wished to die. Suzannah saved me then, but now who was going to save *us*? As I gazed into our baby's face, all I could see was the image of Suzannah.

Doc opened his eyes and said brokenly, "I have delivered dozens of children, Jim—and my heart breaks at the thought of losing *any* one of them. But to lose *Suzannah's* firstborn . . ." He covered his face in shame as he lost control, his entire frame shaking with profound regret. "When your mother was still alive, I made her a promise just between the two of us—to deliver your *firstborn* after you were married, and retire after that. I'm too old for doctoring."

"You can't do that!" I protested. "Look at all the *good* you've done, all the *lives* you've saved, including mine *and* Suzannah's! I beg of you, Doc, do *not* end it here! Not only are you the finest of physicians, but you're also a healer of broken hearts. This was *not* your fault—you're not God, you're a *doctor*, and a damned *good* one!"

"But not good enough to save that precious child!" he spat out bitterly, pointing to the bundle in my arms. His voice tapering in resignation, he then sadly added, "I just don't understand it . . ."

I placed Fanny gently on the sofa and then knelt before Doc, clasping his arms and looking earnestly into his face. "Sometimes, Doc, heaven's ways are difficult for us to understand. I don't believe even the breath of God could have saved little Fanny."

Doc suddenly lifted his head and stared hard at my face.

"What's wrong?" I asked.

"*What* did you just say?" he said, sounding dumbfounded.

"I said not even the breath of God could . . ."

Before I could finish my sentence, he cut me off. "But *mine* could have, Jim. I believe that's *it*! Perhaps if I could have helped her breathe by giving her *my* breath to sustain her . . . she might have *lived* . . ." Then he broke down again and wept openly this time.

Not knowing what else I could say to relieve his pain and overwhelming guilt, I picked up Fanny and gently laid her in his arms. "Doc, can you ask Reverend Metcalf to bury her for us . . . next to her grandmother and great-grandparents?"

He rose, holding my poor babe close and said reassuringly, "Of course we will bury her for you. Now *you* need to get up there before Suzannah wakes! I will tend to Fanny, *you* tend to *her*!"

Before he donned his coat, Doc gave Fanny back to me. "I need to bring my bag out to my carriage first, so meanwhile you hold her, Jim. Give her a final prayer and a kiss."

Through eyes glistening with tears, I looked at her fingers and touched them gently. Even in death, how tiny and sweet they were! How perfectly her nails were formed, despite being so small. I drew her hand to my lips and whispered; "Dearest daughter of my love and life, may God and Grandma guide thee on thy heavenly journey. *Wait* for your papa and mama, and we shall meet *again*, little one. Ever remember that you were yearned for and loved, and may God help us heal our wounds, since He has taken you to a better place . . ."

Doc returned with a blanket from his carriage, and while he tenderly wrapped Fanny within it, I sat at a nearby table and wrote these lines.

Rest, sweet daughter, rest in peace,
Away from fear and noise,
Here thy earthly sorrows cease,
Now commence thy heavenly joys.

I handed the paper to Doc. "For her stone . . . with an angel, please . . ." and I could say no more.

Clutching the sheet with Fanny's epitaph, Doc read it through and then hugged me. "What you have written here is beautiful, Jim. May the comfort of God be yours."

And with that, he and our Fanny were gone.

A Broken Heart

fter Doc left, I stood morosely before the door wishing he hadn't. We were now only *two*, and still the most dreadful task lay before me—facing Suzannah *without* our child; and trying to instill in my unsuspecting wife, the courage to heal yet another wound to her golden heart.

As I turned toward the parlor to collect my thoughts, to my abject dismay, there, upon the stairway landing . . . *stood Suzannah!* She was motionless, a wordless living statue as she looked at me with dear imploring eyes. But Suzannah's face said it all—she had overheard us. She knew her baby was dead. She was a childless mother, and *nothing* could atone for that unmitigated grief.

Seeing her heart torn and crushed before me was unbearable, so I gently took her trembling hand, and with my sheltering arm, guided her into the parlor. She walked as if she were stuporous, taking the little baby steps she would never see.

I sat down in the rocker and beckoned her to snuzzle, but she resisted. I wondered how I could help her endure the painful torment swirling in her bosom? Her beautiful heart was finally broken, and my anguished soul cried out silently to God . . . because *I* did not know how to fix it.

Still unbeaten, she stood there—oh so brave, straight and proud . . . and finally, she shuffled closer to me. Staring into my face through birth-dampened tresses, her streaming eyes and shattered heart begged her silent but hopeless question . . . "Is she *really* dead?"

Overwhelmed with sympathy for my poor wife, I opened my arms to her and silently nodded. Only then, in total defeat, did she drop into my lap. Drawing my arms around her, we sobbed uncontrollably the wretched tears of loss for our innocent little Fanny . . . who was loved, wanted and cherished, and never had a chance to know it.

Recovering my poise in some small measure, I pressed Suzannah's hands to my heart and softly said, "Make your sorrow, *my* sorrow. I'm here for you, my love." Drawing her arms around my neck, I embraced her tiny form while stroking her damp stringy hair. We gazed at each other through pools of tears, and through them we kissed, first delicately and then with a hungry longing. Pushing her tangled hair from her brow, I gently pressed her to my heart and began to rock her tenderly.

Through a nearby window, the full moon shone fully upon us, and from the depths of my aching soul, to its beams I humbly whispered, "Dear God in Heaven, if thou art truly there, please help my poor wife . . . for she suffers from the loss of her child. Touch my angel with thy goodness, comfort and warmth; grant her healing and the miracle of another life. For if anyone deserves it, it is *she*, who suffers here before thee."

On hearing these words, Suzannah buried her face against my neck, and squeezing me in quiet desperation, her little frame shook with wracking sobs of heartrending loss. We rocked for countless hours while she cried in broken-hearted agony. Meanwhile, my own tears continued to flow as we mourned our little baby girl . . .who was the seed of our love, our souls and ourselves, and who was no longer with us . . . she was with God.

Once Upon a Dream

ildred Lovejoy was the first person to visit us the next day to offer solace. She explained that Suzannah had struggled valiantly to bring Fanny into the world, while Mildred's skills were tested almost beyond her endurance: eleven hours of agonizing labor preceded the birth.

Although Mildred received the child in what appeared to be good condition, Doc discovered there were problems with the babe's breathing, for her lungs were severely congested. Yet she cried and wailed normally, so Doc gave her to Suzannah to suckle at her breast. And there, Fanny nursed while Suzannah held her.

But within minutes, induced by blood loss and sheer exhaustion, Suzannah fell into a deep slumber. Fanny still lay at her breast, but difficulties with her breathing persisted. Doc kept on trying to clear her air passages, but whenever he seemed to make progress, the baby's lungs would fill again.

While Suzannah was blessedly asleep, Mildred, Fanny and Dimmis worked frantically to staunch her bleeding—which they finally did. It was during these few hours when Suzannah slept so peacefully, that our little Fanny slipped away to the next world.

At Doc's request, the tearful womenfolk left our home by the rear door, and I remained waiting until Doc came downstairs carrying the small bundle.

We closed the tavern during the period of our mourning. After Fanny's burial, Doc, Mildred and I met privately to discuss what might have caused the child's death. I hoped to learn something from them, perhaps for future reference when we might conceive again.

Mildred thought it was a form of infantile consumption, save the child was fat and healthy otherwise. Doc thought there was too much water with the child inside Suzannah, which caused the lungs to absorb too much fluid. He suggested that breathing into the lungs might work to clear the air passages—should it ever happen again.

During the weeks of Suzannah's convalescence, nearly every woman in Walker's Cove came to sit with her. Twenty-four hours a day they cared for her—holding her, taking her hand and pouring out their heart feelings to the heart feeler.

Some of these women never had children, many had lost children, and yet they all came with the same purpose of bringing love and support to my little wife. Some brought her meals while others did laundry for us. But in the end, it was Fanny, Dimmis, Mildred and Rhoda who remained by Suzannah's bed, all night every night, until she was well.

Three months later, Suzannah was strong enough to do light work, so we reopened the tavern at her request. It was then that I took Suzannah to Fanny's grave for the first time.

We walked in silence to the cemetery, but for support I kept her hand firmly in mine.

There, next to Mother's grave, was the small slate headstone bearing an angel. Beneath the angel were engraved the words "Our Beloved Fanny," followed by my poem.

Suzannah released my hand to kneel at Fanny's side. She stared at the headstone for a long time . . . and bending low, she gently kissed the angel. After that, she kissed her palm and placed it flat upon the grave, moving it slowly back and forth. I wondered if somehow she could "feel" Fanny . . . as she did with me through the door, and Mother during the shipwreck, and then again when she touched her portrait. Her hand finally stopped directly over Fanny's heart, and I choked back my pain as Suzannah, through a veil of sacred tears, spoke to her only daughter.

"*Fanny*, it's Mama . . . I have felt your life *inside* me . . . and I have comforted you at my breast. You are part of *me*, and I am part of *you* . . . and so we shall remain, until I see you in the next world. Remember who *loves* you evermore . . . my *dearest* little angel . . ."

Gently taking my hand, she rose unsteadily. Wiping her tears and taking a deep breath, she softly whimpered, "Let's go to the point . . . like the *old* days . . ."

It was her fondest dream to be a mother, to have three of us in our loving home. For me, it was starting a little family with the love of my life. Despite our high hopes and best efforts, our dreams came crashing down in heartbreak. But through the love and caring of friends and neighbors, Suzannah recovered from her birthing injuries. Her golden heart was mending with restored hope—for at *her* suggestion—we sat once again at our beloved Walker's Point.

As we were comforted by the gentle sea breezes, Suzannah took my hands and tenderly kissed them. Then looking deep into my eyes, she said with loving conviction, "This *will* pass, Jim . . . our hearts *will* heal . . . and we shall *begin* . . . once again . . ."

Inspired by her inner strength, I cradled her to my heart and tearfully whispered, "I *love* you, Suzannah . . . *God*, how I love you . . ."

No Ordinary Year

uzannah's determination to "begin again" was steadfast and true. By February of 1772, she had finally recovered her strength, her enthusiasm for life—and her lovely girlish figure. The characteristic spring in her step finally returned, and we resumed our daily routines in our busy tavern. I was pleased it remained as popular as ever, not only because of our high quality goods and services, but also because a sense of upheaval now permeated the colonies . . . and folks needed a place to congregate—and to vent.

Dimmis remained indispensable, and was responsible for so much new business, that we offered to make her a partner in the tavern. But she refused our offer, saying she preferred to keep her position as it was. Since we wanted to show our gratitude for everything she was to us, including her devotion to Suzannah during her recovery, we decided to make her another gift of 250 pieces of eight.

After we lost Fanny, our love grew stronger in every way—

During the evenings, just as in the "old days," we revived our rocking sessions. We would caress and kiss, feed each other custards and sometimes Suzannah read poetry aloud. If a particular line struck her fancy, she would often repeat it slowly in her gentle silvery voice . . . and I would listen with admiring eyes: upon her lips, upon her face, and finally upon her finger . . . bearing mother's wedding band.

We resumed our regular visits to Walker's Point and sat before the sunsets. We discussed Fanny and our new lives: agreeing that while the past belonged to God, the present was still ours. We discovered that memories did indeed preside over the past, but that *action* presided over the ever-changing present.

Our lovemaking became even more passionate than before. Every week, Suzannah would venture into Richardson's fields and gather up wildflowers. These she used to enliven our bedchamber and adorn her hair. It was as though she sought to recreate the Garden of Eden . . . by scattering flower petals all around our room. Their scent was so refreshing, that Suzannah would simply undress and lie naked on our bed. I would then cover her with cooling flower petals . . . and among them . . . we pursued our intimate journeys "to the heights."

Within the sanctuary of our wonderful marriage we traveled afar: building *new* air castles, and seeking health and prosperity for us, and for those we might bring into the world. Even though fate had extinguished our brightest dream, Suzannah and I were ever creating new ones . . . because much to our delight, she was with child once again.

THIS TIME, SUZANNAH curtailed her daily activities and she ate well—much better than before—for the sake of our baby. Doc and Mildred examined her regularly, and everything seemed to be going well as we progressed through the first few months. As her second child grew inside her, Suzannah's buoyant spirits perched her upon a cloud of maternal joy, from which she had no intention of coming down. She was always whispering endearments to the child, rubbing and petting her belly, reassuring the babe it was safe and they were one.

One warm night, as we prepared for sleep, Suzannah removed her clothes and climbed into bed. Rather than ask me to cover her with flower petals, she lay back and covered her breasts discreetly with her flowing hair, which now reached below her womanhood. Her provocative pose put me in mind of a demure maiden who had never before made love.

"Jim," she said, "would you be good enough to rub my belly?"

Thinking she wished to seduce me, I replied, "Of course, my darling, but why now?"

"Well, for one thing, it would soothe your little wife; but more than that, so our child will know the loving touch of her father."

After I finished hanging up my clothes and started washing my face, I suddenly realized what she had said. Astonished, I looked up from the basin and asked, "*Her?*"

"Her," she said firmly, her gray-blue eyes radiant with a mother's love.

"How do you know it's a her?"

Holding her belly in both hands, she smiled at me proudly. "*She* told me so."

I felt like a dolt for asking. Suzannah was indeed the heart feeler, and I *never* questioned what she "felt"—for she was *always* correct.

As I sat beside her on the bed and placed my hands softly on her belly, Suzannah gave a start. "*Jim*, your hands are *freezing*! You'll give Ainsley a chill!"

"*Ainsley?*" I repeated, incredulous that she had already named the child.

"Don't you remember? It's what we agreed upon. We *promised* each other Fanny would be the name of the first female child, and Ainsley that of the second."

"But darling, Fanny never lived, so shouldn't this child be called Fanny?"

Suzannah rose and deliberately sauntered to where I was sitting. She gently pushed me into the pillows and boldly pressed her naked body against mine. She then draped her hair over our faces, and giving me deep delicious kisses beneath its canopy . . . she suggestively fondled me. She could always make me *want* her at will.

As my manhood rose, she broke the kiss and suddenly purred, "My goodness . . . what is *this?*" After she moved down to investigate, she pressed me against her soft cheek and giggled. With sparkling eyes, she licked her lips in anticipation and finally whispered, "*Well*, darling, a promise is a *promise*."

Ainsley it was.

M*EANWHILE, AS UNREST* in the colonies grew apace, we had increasing difficulty obtaining certain supplies for our tavern. Suzannah and Dimmis frequented the wharf, hobnobbing with ships' captains in the hope of striking a deal to smuggle in some tea and rum, safely out of sight of tax collectors and British customs schooners, as was done in my grandfather's day. With boycots and blockades all along the coast, I wondered if Suzannah's prediction might come to pass—that murder and other injustices would breed hate, and then the demons of war would descend upon us.

With increasing frequency, our patrons were the bawlers and table-pounders. And as altercations broke out in Boston and Providence, every misfortune or misadventure—personal or otherwise— was blamed upon British soldiers, tax collectors, revenue schooners and the weakheaded king they served.

One morning, a crew of noisy sailors wandered into our tavern, all excitedly chattering about a band of Rhode Islanders . . . who had declared *war* upon the long abhorred British customs schooner, HMS *Gaspée*. Having driven her aground on a sandbar in Narraganett Bay, they boarded her and attacked the crew. News of the incident had spread through the colonies like wildfire, inciting a spirit of solidarity on behalf of the attackers in its wake.

As I helped Suzannah and Dimmis serve drinks amidst the roar of the crowd, I suddenly heard a familiar voice. As I looked around, my eyes soon came to rest on none other than Henry Wiggins! Unbidden, I drew a fresh tankard of Suzannah's flip—which I recalled he esteemed above all others—and I placed it on the table before him. Seeing the drink and then who brought it, he jumped up, took me by the shoulders and shook me like a rag doll.

"James Walker! *Damn!* How is my *favorite* tavern-keeper, and what have you been up to for the past two years? Let me have a look at you!" Apparently satisfied at what he saw, he pushed me away playfully and said, "Better yet, let me see that pretty *wife* of yours!"

Suzannah must have spotted Henry, because she was already at my side. Henry honored her with a bow, took her hand and kissed it before placing it back in mine.

"Hah! Heaven preserves its beauty tenfold!" he remarked while looking her over. "You haven't aged a *day*, Suzannah . . ."

To our surprise, she looked down and remained silent.

Henry, sensing something awkward was afoot, cleared his throat and lifted his tankard, holding it before her in a gesture of respect and admiration. "I am anxious, dear lady, to have the sweet nectar of Walker's Cove pass through my parched withered lips . . ."

And with that, he took a swig of the flip and rolled it around his tongue. Looking delighted, he smacked his lips and said, "Nectar of the gods and as sweet as *ever*, Suzannah Walker . . . like *you*, perhaps?"

Suzannah smiled up at Henry and said demurely, "It's a pleasure to see you again, Henry. Please sit down and rest awhile—and tell us of your adventures." Glancing at me, she added, "Jim can fill you in on what *we* have been doing around here."

After Dimmis brought me a tumbler of mulled cider, I invited Henry to join me in our parlor so we could hear ourselves talk. And so we retired to catch up on two years of news.

First I told him about Fanny, so he would understand Suzannah's earlier demeanor. He appeared downcast as I spoke, fingering the rim of his tankard.

"I'm frightfully sorry, Jim." He replied, "I didn't mean to hurt her with a compliment."

"She is *fine*, Henry—she is *very* strong," I replied, placing my hand over my heart to emphasize where her strength lay.

Nodding solemnly, he added, "Tell her privately for me, that *Henry Wiggins* sends his fondest wishes for her recovery . . . *and* continued good health." He lifted his drink before he added, "*Without* it, one hasn't much in this life. But she appears not to have aged one day since I saw her last, let alone show any sign of having suffered the rigors of losing a child . . . especially after a difficult birth."

He drained the tankard and placing it on the table, he smiled and said, "Yes, your Suzannah's a *remarkable* lady—you are a *fortunate* man, Jim."

"You have no idea *how* fortunate," I replied.

"Indeed, Jim, in these troubled times, you need to watch over and protect your precious wife, whom you love beyond all else."

"Is it *that* obvious?" I asked, feeling a flush steal across my face.

"It's all around you *both* . . . for the love in your eyes for each other, shines like a beacon to all but the most obtuse."

Henry stood, placed his strong hands upon my shoulders and whispered, "Yours is a marriage we sailors *dream* about . . . and I am *proud* to be among your associates, Jim. You're a *good* man."

"Thank you, Henry—but what do you mean by 'troubled times'?"

Suddenly Suzannah arrived with a tray of warm fritters dripping with frosting, and I could tell by Henry's face he had noticed her belly protruding under the tray.

"I thought these would make the troubled times a *little* easier to bear," she announced, all smiles.

"I remember how keen her hearing was the *last* time I was here!" Henry exclaimed, blushing with embarrassment.

Dimmis came in after her, bringing more flip and mulled cider, as well as some tea for Suzannah.

As we partook of the fritters, Suzannah sat in the rocker to rest for a few moments, while Henry replied to my question.

"I don't know exactly what you've heard in your tavern, but I am now captain and owner of the *Fortune Two*, a modified packet sloop. The first *Fortune* was lost to the British ship *Gaspée*, and therein lies the thorn in our side."

Suzannah placed her cup down and said, "Well, Henry, my hearty congratulations on your captaincy. How did this transpire in the midst of all the trouble we've heard about from Boston?"

"I'm leading into that, Suzannah, but first some background needs filling in. Have either of you heard of Sam Adams?"

"Sam Adams is one of the Sons of Liberty," I replied. "He sent me the letter about the British murdering my father outside the Green Dragon."

After looking askance, Henry whispered, "The *Sons* are the ones that burned the *Gaspée*—though it is *not* common knowledge."

Suzannah glanced at me warily and then at Henry. She rose to open the secretary and withdrew Sam Adams' letter, handing it to Henry.

After he read it, he handed it back to her. "So it's true then . . . they *are* murdering bastards."

Then, realizing what he'd said, he apologized profusely. "I'm *terribly* sorry, Suzannah, such *unseemly* language before a lady . . ."

"You needn't worry, Henry," she replied with an understanding smile. "We've heard much worse in the great room. Just ask Dimmis, who's heard such utterances as could turn a person's ears a bright shade of blue!"

"Well then, here's the *truth* of it." Henry said as he lit his pipe from the fire, and puffing contentedly, his eyes followed the smoke rings to the ceiling before he thoughtfully continued. "The *Gaspée* had a somewhat overzealous captain, William Dudingston by name, who delighted in boarding any vessel he saw fit, including the *Fortune*— my ship! Under the guise of enforcing customs laws—in the name of the king—he confiscated cargos, men, specie and ships. He and his greedy crew even raided the warehouses on the wharves, striking every town and ship 'twixt Narragansett Bay and Boston. He and his sailors beat our hapless crews bloody and removed them to Boston for trial."

After taking a deep draught of his flip, he bit hungrily into a plump fritter such that it's frosting stuck to his nose.

When Suzannah saw it there, she tried to stifle a giggle, whereupon Henry grew disconcerted and warned, "My *dear* Suzannah, such matters are of grave concern! After all, these are *your* countrymen whose rights and freedoms are being violated! Have you not noticed that Essex rum is nearly *impossible* to obtain these days?"

"Indeed it is," she agreed before hastening to add, "I'm sorry, Henry, but your *nose* . . ."

Touching his forefinger to his nose, Henry contemplated the large blob of milk frosting that stuck to it. Smiling at his folly, he said, "My apologies *again*, Suzannah. It seems I am *overfond* of your fritter."

"There's no need to apologize, Henry." Suzannah replied. Then giving him her sweetest smile, she added, "Please *do* continue."

Sighing, Henry licked his finger and thus continued, "So what happened? *Gaspée*'s raids upon cargos such as mine were strangling the profits of rum distilleries, leaving their owners nearly destitute—and it wasn't just rum they were confiscating. Yet Dudingston kept on with his damnable raids—until he became a focal point for the colonists' hostilities toward Britain."

"And that explains why we are having so much trouble getting rum," Suzannah observed.

"*Exactly!*" Henry exclaimed. "So here is what was planned; several prominent merchants of Providence—including John Brown, Abraham Whipple and Sam Adams—gathered at Sabin's Tavern for a secret meeting . . . and formed a local chapter of the Sons of Liberty. Since I too wanted payback, I *joined* them!"

Suzannah's eyes widened, as did mine . . . for here was a Son of Liberty, sitting before us in our *own* parlor! And Henry *knew* Sam Adams, who knew all about the murder of my father.

Suzannah was speechless, but I whispered, "You *are* a Son of Liberty, Henry?"

"At your *service*, James Walker. I was sent here by Adams himself!"

"He *remembered?*" was all I could gasp.

"Indeed, Jim, he *did!*" Henry replied, pointing to Adams' letter. "And he has no doubt you would gladly join our ranks."

I looked at Suzannah, who nodded her assent without a word.

"Done!" was my reply.

"Excellent!" crowed Henry. "Now, let us pretend this conversation did not take place, and I shall contact you at a later date regarding such matters."

He paused thoughtfully. "Now let me see . . . where was I? Oh yes, our plan was to lure the *Gaspée* into the shallow harbor of Namquid Point, hoping to hang her up on a sand bar. We all agreed that if the *Gaspeé* was out of commission, free and open trade would resume and we would all be the better for it.

"We let the word leak out that the packet sloop, *Hannah*—captained by my good friend and fellow smuggler, Benjamin Lindsey—would be transporting a shipment of contraband rum in the middle of the night."

After taking a long draw on his pipe, he continued. "Indeed, Jim, *Gaspée* took the bait and chased *Hannah* to Namquid Point where she ran aground. The stranded vessel could not free herself until the next high tide—because her draft was much *deeper* than the *Hannah's*. It was *then* that the Sons rowed out to the *Gaspée* under the cover of night, and set her afire. Some say the rum supplied as the agent for her destruction came from the stills of the perpetrators."

"*Hell, that wasn't a damned great use for good drinkin' rum!*" cracked like thunder from the parlor entrance, and I immediately recognized the gruff tone and hulking figure of Zeb Hawkes, leaning against the doorway, holding a tankard in his hand, no doubt courtesy of Dimmis. Then I watched in horror as Suzannah ran to Zeb, who scooped her up and nearly crushed her in a one armed bear hug, until she squeaked and he gently set her down.

"I ain't seen you since you was a little *girl!*" he bellowed, lightly pushing her away to get a better look at her. I then remembered it had been nearly seven years since Zeb moved the Ellingwoods in next door.

Turning her around as though she was a tiny ballerina, Zeb observed, "You're as *beautiful* as you can be, Suzannah." When he patted her on the head, she wrinkled her nose at him—just as she did when she was fifteen.

"Hah, still the cutest little nose . . . and now with a *child*, I see . . ."

When Suzannah suddenly looked stricken, Zeb laid a gentle hand on her shoulder and said, "I am very sorry about Fanny. I remember well the note you sent with an order last year . . . telling me of her tragic loss."

"We're going to have another girl—Ainsley," she declared with a proud smile.

Zeb nodded at Suzannah and then looked at me. "I'm happy to hear there will be another Ainsley in this tavern. Your mother meant a *lot* to me, Jim . . . and I will always miss her."

"So will I, Zeb. But what about our business—how will we survive all this upheaval?" Then I remembered my manners, adding, "By the way, this is our friend, Henry Wiggins, captain and owner of the *Fortune Two*."

After the two men engaged in a hearty handshake, Henry said, "If you can lend me a hand, Zeb, we can beat them *all*! As such, I actually came here to offer you all a chance for ownership shares in my new sloop *Fortune Two*, to finance her and bring my co-owners a tidy profit, for despite the British deviltries, free trade *must* go on, as you well know."

"Well by *God*!" Zeb bellowed, scratching his armpit to mimic removing an active insect. "Nothin' would suit me better than *ridding* myself of loyalist *vermin*." Then squashing the imaginary bug between his fingers, he let out a roar of glee while slapping our backs so hard we nearly choked.

After we'd recovered, Zeb, Henry, Suzannah and I discussed the terms of the ownership, and the upshot of our discussion was that Henry would own half, Zeb, one sixth, we would have three twelfths and we would purchase Dimmis one twelfth.

We all shook hands on it and Henry drew up an agreement that we all executed, and on behalf of all the new owners, Suzannah advanced the funds to Henry. After our business was concluded, we accepted the fresh tankards brought in from Dimmis, and as she left the room, I noticed Zeb follow her with his eyes.

Taking a long swallow and then turning to Suzannah, Zeb asked, "Who is the red haired one?"

"Dimmis Sexton," Suzannah replied. "Ainsley hired her to help us run the tavern just before she died, and she has been perfectly *wonderful*. Dimmis was the only one to survive the wreck of the *Sunrise* . . . that is why we bought her a share."

Nodding somberly, Zeb returned his gaze to the doorway where Dimmis had just exited, letting it remain there for several moments. When he turned around to Suzannah, he lifted his tankard in a toast: "Here's to you and Jim and Ainsley and Walker's Cove—it's damned good to be back!" Scratching the stubble on his chin, he thoughtfully asked, "What's it been . . . six years?"

"Nearly seven years!" I declared, recalling the events of that special morning . . . when Zeb and his crew took some refreshment in our old parlor . . . and I met a little angel in the house next door.

✦◎◈

We all returned to the great room, where Zeb, Henry and I took a table in the far corner near the fireplace. Once seated, Zeb's upper body towered over us all—and I thought perhaps he had grown taller. As I observed him, I noticed he was quietly observing Dimmis as she went about her work.

"Well, this place has seen a *lot* o' changes since *I* was here last!" he exclaimed.

It was then that Suzannah brought us three bowls of a rich moose stew. As she passed around the spoons she said, "This is Ainsley's recipe—one of the first she taught me."

Henry lifted his tankard in a salute to Suzannah, saying, "I thank you, dear hostess. It smells wonderful!"

Whereupon Zeb declared, "I *told* Ainsley if she opened it, they would come—and so they *have!*" Then holding his tankard up, to which we all joined ours together, he merrily asked, "It sure hasn't been no ordinary year, *has* it?"

What with Fanny's death, Suzannah's recovery and Ainsley on the way—and me now one of the Sons of Liberty—it certainly *hadn't* been an ordinary year.

"No it hasn't," I affirmed as I made a toast: "To our continued health, for this is but the *beginning*—God save the colonies!"

And we pledged ourselves to that . . . little knowing what lay ahead.

THE CONFESSION

hen dawn broke on Sunday, I left the house to wander among the creatures that frequent the shoreline in the morning. Suzannah usually joined me on these morning walks, but now that she was with child again, I discouraged her from any strenuous activity.

As I sauntered down to the beach, I stopped often to admire my surroundings. All of nature was awake and actively courting my senses . . . and how I wished Suzannah were with me . . . just to hold her close and share the beauty of this spring morning.

I looked forward to telling her about the birds that greeted my eye and ear: seagulls, plover, jays, yellow tails, finches and doves. I spotted several squirrels high up in our beech tree that barked at me angrily for encroaching upon their territory. In the background was the abiding sound and salty aroma of the rolling waves, breaking upon the rocks of Walker's Point, and lapping along the crescent beach below it to the south.

It seemed that nature was welcoming *me*, the solitary human who dared intrude upon her pristine innocence. As I stood there in its midst I thought, "May the day never come when nature fails to pleasure the heart of man—especially by its absence."

I stayed for a little while more, until I decided I'd been away from Suzannah long enough, and was desirous of her company and her morning kisses. On the way home, I met Noah Blake, a blacksmith who had come to Walker's Cove not long after the death of my father.

Noah was a tall willowy fellow, with a gaunt appearance . . . somewhat exaggerated because his clothes seemed too large for his body. Despite his scarecrow-like appearance, he was the cheeri-est man I ever knew. When I first met him in his new smithy, he pumped my hand furiously in greeting, as though we were long-lost boyhood friends.

One particular skill Noah brought to our little village was that of a wheelwright, so that an increasing number of wagons were brought in for repairs and refitting. Along with the wagons came their merchant owners—and more trade for Walker's Cove.

Noah's best customer by far was Jens, the boat builder. His needs were so great that Noah considered taking on a partner—and at least one apprentice—just to keep up with them. In fact, the over-all success of his business was making Noah the richest man in Walker's Cove.

"Greetings, James!" he shouted from across the street when he spotted me. He crossed over to my side and patting my shoulder affectionately, he happily confessed, "I have heard the delightful news about Suzannah, and I wish the best to the both of you."

"Why, thank you, Noah, I will be sure to tell my wife," I gra-ciously replied. "How is your Frances doing?"

"Oh, she is *very* large indeed. I suspect it may be a boy!"

"A boy, you think?" I said in surprise.

"Yes—perhaps *two* boys!" he exclaimed, indicating their girth by the way he circled his arms around his waist.

"You mean, *twins?*" I asked, startled by the idea. "Well, *that* would certainly solve your apprentice problem . . . and perhaps down the road they might even take up the forge hammer as your partners."

"Now that would be a dream come true!" Noah said, nodding enthusiastically. "By the way, has Suzannah had any sickness?" he asked.

"No, not yet," I replied. "But it is still a few months to her con-finement. She is being very careful since she is so small and delicate."

Noah looked thoughtful. "Small, yes . . . delicate, perhaps . . . but only in *appearance*. Frances says Suzannah has the heart of a *lioness*, and that she is very strong indeed!" He pointed to his heart to emphasize his meaning, and added, "You have the best known wife in Walker's Cove, Jim! Everyone hereabouts holds her in such high esteem—including my wife and myself, though we are relative newcomers."

It thrilled me to hear such compliments regarding my Suzannah. "Well, I'm flattered, Noah. But I think she is well liked for her cooking and tavern-keeping—after all, she *is* the keeper, just like my mother used to be."

"Yes, I've heard about the legendary Ainsley Rennsdale Walker! I understand she was also much beloved."

I looked down for a moment as I thought about Mother, and saw her face in my mind's eye.

Noah seemed to sense my feelings, because he interrupted my musings with a tap on my shoulder, saying, "Did you know my father used to trade with your mother? It was at the old Portsmouth schooner landing."

"I'm a little surprised to hear that, though I shouldn't be. Being a trader there and then here brought her into contact with so many different people."

Noah looked at me quizzically. "Why did she give it all up?"

"Why, she fell in love with my father and wanted her time back to raise a family," I replied, smiling. "But don't grieve the loss of Mother's talent—she taught Suzannah *everything* she knew before she died. So I would not try to strike up a bargain with Suzannah . . . unless you have several pairs of spare breeches."

Laughing heartily, Noah slapped his knee. "Well, I'll be *damned*! Beauty and brains too!"

"Indeed, Noah, I'm justly proud of Suzannah and not just because she's my wife! I promise to remember you to her."

"Please do!" Noah said breathlessly as he pumped my hand, and then he made off toward Thatcher's dry goods store.

When I came in the front door, I found Suzannah sitting on a stool, tending a kettle that was steaming vigorously in the fireplace of the great room. As she rose to kiss me, she inquired, "How was your walk without me?"

"It's never the same . . ." I answered before we kissed. "It was still beautiful, but not nearly as rewarding, for God's littlest angel was not with me."

"But her *heart* was—never forget that, dear husband." she cooed, flashing her incomparable smile.

I kissed her again and admired her beauty for a long moment. Being with child brought an extra measure of radiance to her face, just like the first time. It was then I remembered I had a message to deliver. "Noah Blake wishes to be remembered to you. He and Frances send their warm wishes for Ainsley."

Cradling her stomach lovingly, Suzannah said, "Tell them I'm grateful for their thoughts and wishes—next time you see him."

She went silent then and placed a finger in her mouth, looking thoughtful. "Oh, Jim," she exclaimed with some dismay, "Frances is *much* farther along in her confinement than I am—and she is to be in danger before me. It is *I* who should be wishing *them* God's blessings and happiness."

Feeling guilty myself for being so self-centered and not equally considerate of Noah's wife, I reaffirmed, "I'll make a point of seeing him tomorrow and telling him that, darling."

Taking my hand, Suzannah whispered, "I have a special guest in the parlor waiting for an audience."

"And who might that be?"

"Wait until you *see* who it is!" she said coyly. "I'm making some tea and buttered rum—would you like some?"

"No rum, thank you—but tea would be nice," I replied, planting another tender kiss on her sweet lips.

Threading her arms around my waist, she buried her face in my chest. "I missed you," she mumbled into my shirt. As I held her in my arms, I noticed her bosom was getting larger—or my arms were getting shorter. Her eyes sparkled with mischief as she whispered, "Can you please love me tonight? I'm getting bigger *everywhere* you know . . . we can *experiment* . . . like *last* time!"

"Of course!" I agreed, elated at the idea.

"Long and extra *tender?*" Came her sweet little response.

"Oh, yes," I whispered into her ear, while gently fingering her hair.

Pressing herself against me, she drew my head toward her gently parted lips, and as she received the warm kiss that awaited her, she lovingly moaned.

When she tried to pull away and I wouldn't let her, she broke the kiss, swallowed hard and urgently whispered, "Oh Jim, let's not start something now we cannot finish . . ."

"You have *iron* discipline!" I chided her in frustration.

"If we had no *guest* in our parlor, that iron would melt away before the flames of passion!" And after gently flicking her tongue in my ear, she whispered, ". . . so we'll just have to *wait* till later, darling."

With that, she busied herself preparing the drinks. Drawing a tankard down from the shelf, she filled it halfway with dark rum. She then added ground clove, cinnamon, a touch of molasses, a lump of butter and mixed in hot mulled cider up to the top.

Its irresistible aroma was indeed a selling point, as it even tempted me. Hot buttered rum was our big moneymaker—our specialty. Suzannah used the forty-year-old recipe Mother developed originally for the Mariner's Rest, and it was still a surefire winner.

Suzannah filled another tankard with smuggled tea and placed it in my hands saying, "Now, let's greet our guest."

When I stepped into the parlor, a tall wide figure stood at a window, staring out toward the Ellingwood house . . . it was Zeb Hawkes. With his hands clasped behind his back in an uncharacteristically thoughtful pose, he looked almost like a gentleman.

He turned around to face us as we entered, and his eyes lit up as he took the tankard Suzannah offered him.

After seating herself in the rocker, she said somewhat formally, "So, Zebulon Galletin Hawks . . . you have a *question* for us, that you would wish us to answer *yes* to—and you would like to ask it now."

After hearing *that*, my curiosity was piqued, so I sat on the sofa with my tea and crossed my legs, ready to listen.

Zeb sat down next to me, looking very ill at ease. He was perspiring heavily and the tankard trembled as he held it in his large hands.

Sipping her tea, Suzannah regarded Zeb over the rim of her cup. Then she leaned back in the rocker, stretching herself like a cat before a warm fire. With an adorable half smile, she searched his face with a focused intensity but said nothing, apparently waiting for him to broach *his* subject.

Finally, she decided to break the silence and speak first. "Perhaps, dear Zebulon, you might enlighten a girl's inquiring mind as to the nature of your new heart feelings . . . and the lovely maiden who inspires them?"

My jaw dropped and my mouth hung open. *What* maiden? The vagabond Zebulon Hawkes—singer of ribald songs, speaker of uncouth language, free-spirited smuggler and accomplished drinker— was in *love*, stricken by cupid's arrow? I couldn't believe the words of my own wife . . . yet knowing she had read his heart like an open book, I held my breath for what might come next.

Growing restless under Suzannah's knowing gaze, Zeb fidgeted before finally clearing his throat to reply. "I fancy *her* . . . she is the best cook that ever was. She has shown me great kindness . . . a thoughtfulness that warms me deep inside. She has smiling, happy eyes . . . she lights every pathway . . . and she is willing to show me how to live a good, productive and *virtuous* life, for *all* my remaining days."

Leaning toward Suzannah, he pressed on. "When I found it difficult to express my feelings to her, she told me that *some* feelings, however *deep*, need not find their way into words, but rather in actions and deeds."

I stared at Suzannah, thunderstruck! It seemed I was hearing about our *own* courtship, but from another heart with a different woman. My cheeks burned as I recalled how I struggled to say those things to Suzannah. And now here was Zeb, seeking advice and comfort from the selfsame heart.

Suzannah looked at me with moist eyes but said nothing. I knew that she too was remembering my struggles.

Zeb bowed his head as he continued. "She could *feel* my loneliness, Suzannah, and she told me that through *love*, I would be healed of my secret pain. She placed her hand on my heart and told me, 'Nevermore will there be loneliness, for it has no resting place here . . .'" Then he went silent.

"Zeb, old friend," Suzannah began, "it's wonderful that you are discovering *love*. You know how we all hear the falling rain, but never *hear* the falling snow? Life is like the rain—you know when you are *in* it, and you can *feel* it all around you. But *love* is like the newly fallen snow. It descends upon you silently, and suddenly— when you look at the same world—you find a new and *beautiful* world to behold . . . in the peace and sanctity of the human heart."

Suzannah paused to sip her tea and then fixed her eyes on Zeb's hopeful face, now riveted on hers as he hungrily took in every word she said.

"You were *made* to love, Zeb, we *all* are. You *want* to love her, but you have a sense of being totally alone and unsure in your quest. But you are *not* alone! All who feel love, and have ever done so, are with you in a common bond. The lives of many yet unborn, are profoundly affected by what your love does in the present. It has *always* been so . . ."

Suzannah leaned back in her rocker, settling herself more comfortably before she went on. "And so you come to ask *us* for the gift of the object of your affection. The awakening of true love has indeed begun for you, Zeb, but *we* are not the ones you must implore for that precious gift. You must ask *her*."

"So what must I *say* to make this come to pass?" Zeb asked, looking perplexed.

"You must look into the depths of her eyes and tell her—that you desire to be one with her in *everything*—in every breath of every day—in every word of every whisper—*in every* loving touch and kindred thought. Ask *her* to share this dream with you—now *and* into the next world."

Humbled by her words, Zeb rose shakily to his feet, looking at me sheepishly, then at Suzannah. "I want to have what *you* two have. So tell me, Suzannah, where does that come from?"

Suzannah looked up through the window at the sky while she formed her reply. "Reverend Metcalf says all love comes from God, Zeb. Love is an immortal creation that dwells in its purest form . . .

somewhere beyond earthly passions and struggles . . . in the safety of the human heart, *and* in the heart of Him who created us. Love defines His image . . . and is the sole reason He created us: our purpose, Zeb, is *to love* . . ."

"Yes," Zeb replied, while rising to nod his understanding and gratitude. "I have very deep feelings toward *her*—who I desire *more* than all else."

Burning with curiosity, I leaned forward to place my tankard on the table, and then casually asked, "So *who* is this girl who has captured your heart, Zeb?"

Kneeling before Suzannah and folding his hands upon her knees, Zeb bowed his head and hoarsely whispered, "Dimmis . . ."

TRANSITIONS

eb's affection for Dimmis at least partly explained why he had lately been seen more often in Walker's Cove. But since he was also one of those "traders" who sought to avoid the British customs tax, it wasn't too surprising he sought refuge here. And his covert deliveries of Essex rum to our tavern gave him more time to court his ladylove.

On many occasions, especially after certain tax collectors were tarred and feathered, Zeb would exile himself by arriving at our doorstep . . . laden with bottles and barrels. Here, he spent his time concocting potent distillations of unknown origin. Suzannah ruled against offering the resulting intoxicants to our patrons, lest—as Doc Brown warned—they putrefy their unsuspecting livers.

Henry Wiggins was also sighted more frequently in Walker's Cove these days, boarding quietly at our tavern. Since Henry had direct involvement in the burning of the *Gaspée*, it was a good guess that he'd want to remain out of the public eye for a time. So we became Henry's safe harbor too—and while ashore he delighted in joining Zeb in his experiments. Together they hoped to create a new brew unique to Walker's Tavern.

Since Zeb's confession, Suzannah and Dimmis could freely discuss the blossoming relationship. Like me, Suzannah had no hard evidence of it beforehand, and she was impressed not only with the fact they were courting, but how remarkably well they'd kept it from everyone—especially Rhoda Barrett.

During a warm day in August, while repairing a clock jack in our kitchen, I overheard them talking about it. Apparently, Dimmis didn't mind my presence there while she confided in Suzannah.

"What was your first impression of Zeb, before you got to know him?" Suzannah asked while vigorously drying her bean pot.

Dimmis stopped chopping carrots long enough to think about her answer. "Well, at first I thought him uncouth and not caring to improve his mind, his manners—or himself. So I felt it was high time *someone* told him to grow up and become a *man* . . . 'tis as simple as that!"

Looking askance at Suzannah to judge her reaction, she cautiously added, "'Tis nothing *less* gentle than I would say to a drunken fop at Sexton's."

It seemed she was minimizing the extent of her affections for Zeb; but before I could fully decide that, she turned to Suzannah and declared, "And when I said *that* to him—he *listened!*"

Pouring molasses and beans into her pot, Suzannah smiled and said, "For a *man*, Dimmis, that's the first step to a sound relationship with a woman. I would consider that a *very* good start."

From this point on, their conversation suddenly changed to Gaelic, so I knew they wished me not to overhear it. There was nothing about the language I understood—save that it was soft and beautiful—like the two lovely women I left chatting in the kitchen.

THAT NIGHT, AFTER we closed, Suzannah came upstairs when I was already in bed. My libidinous desires heightened as I watched her undress and finally hang her clothes next to mine. Sensing my longing, she displayed herself before me, loosening her hair and letting it tumble over her breasts and nearly to her womanhood. Rolling herself gently onto the bed—being mindful of her swollen stomach—she kissed me, saying, "I didn't *mean* to exclude your ears this afternoon, Jim." Pressing her enlarged breasts against my chest, she softly explained, "When Dimmis and I started speaking in Gaelic, you *must* understand a woman's desire for privacy in mixed company."

To let her know she was understood, I kissed the tip of her nose. Taking a handful of her hair, I drew it over us as we nestled against each other. Her soft skin and warm body enveloped me as she snuzzled comfortably in my arms.

Just as I was reveling in her womanly comforts, Suzannah blurted, "In case you were *wondering* what we talked about, Dimmis told me that Zeb came to her a few days after she ridiculed him, and asked her if she would teach him to be . . . uh . . . a *gentleman*."

I sat up in amazement. "Zeb? You must be *joking*!"

She shook her head no.

"He really *is* stricken then," I confirmed.

As she rubbed my back, she added, "Enough so that he cannot speak his heart."

Remembering I once suffered from the same affliction, I kissed her tenderly and asked, "So what do *we* do?"

"Nothing," she replied. "Since we heard his confession, I've seen subtle changes in Zeb's appearance, demeanor—and in particular—an absence of *cursing* in his speech. I think his association with Henry Wiggins does no harm, either."

"The transformative powers of *love* at work . . . but are you *sure* he hasn't been over-imbibing Essex rum, Suzannah?"

"Oh, I wouldn't say *that* exactly, but Zeb *does* have a need to . . . ah . . . *ascertain* the quality of our tavern's stock." She giggled and left it at that.

"Indeed, some of the concoctions Zeb and Henry have been mixing possess a resemblance to high explosives. But what if they do *taste* good, Suzannah? Shouldn't we at least ask our patrons for an *opinion* of a free sample?"

"Perhaps," she replied noncommittally.

"It might make us some money," I suggested. "Think about it— if only one of their new recipes is successful, it would be unique to *us* . . . like Mother's flip."

Returning to the subject of Zeb, I asked, "What *else* did Dimmis say?"

"She told Zeb all about her terrible life up until the wreck, and she made him swear never to ask her about it again, explaining that she needed to look *forward* in her life, as there was nothing to revere in her past, save her experience at working in a tavern."

Suzannah paused to sit up as best she could, leaning heavily on her elbow. "It has been two years and more since the wreck . . . and Dimmis is *lonely*, Jim. Not for companionship or friendship, but for *love*. She is older than either of us, and she fears being alone in her new life. She has had enough of loneliness."

Nodding my understanding, I added, "I must admit she *is* beautiful, Suzannah. I've never seen her likes. I can't imagine why men have chosen to ignore her."

"I'm her best friend and soul mate, Jim, and I can assure you that plenty of men admire her unique beauty and seek her out. But it's beauty of the heart *she* seeks, and we both know she can tell which men are genuine, and which are looking for a warm bedmate . . . why, your own mother was an expert at that!"

"As is the proprietress of our tavern!" I jibed, poking her playfully in the ribs.

After recovering from my tickling, she said, "Well, I plan to encourage both of them on the path they seem to have chosen already. But in the end, of course, it will be up to them."

As she lay in my arms gently pressing her hands upon her stomach, Suzannah sighed dreamily as she felt the baby move. "So here we are . . ."

While adding my hands to hers to rub her stomach, I looked directly into her enormous gray-blue eyes. How I *wanted* her now, and kissing her hungrily, I became inflamed with passion while I gathered her hair and draped it all around us.

Suzannah responded by fingering her hardened breasts, while pressing her womanhood against my erect member. Suddenly, with a moist and burning desire, she eagerly mounted me.

When I felt her soft upper limit, I gathered her to my heart, and embracing her there, my loving thrusts evoked her rhythmic moans of exceeding pleasure. As she ground herself upon me while kissing and nibbling my nipples, my impulse to explode inside her overtook me . . . and with each pulsating wave I gave her, I fiercely pulled her hair and moaned her name.

Now delirious with her own ecstasy, Suzannah raised her head, and gasping and groaning as she raked her nails across my chest, I felt those wonderful contracting waves from within her . . . pulling me into her as one. It was our first of many "trips to the heights" that night . . . and another unforgettable evening of erotic fantasies came true.

DURING THE WEEK that followed, Suzannah and Dimmis continued as co-workers in the tavern and confidantes in the kitchen. When Suzannah suggested to her that some of Zeb's experimental brews might be included on our menu, Dimmis agreed. She felt it would keep both Zeb and Henry out of trouble while they sought the "elixir of liberty."

With Henry off to the dock on some unspecified business one morning, Zeb and I moved his makeshift laboratory to a more spacious and congenial setting—in our old clock shop. Here, among the cabinets and shelves, we unpacked and inventoried his bottles and barrels of spirits. On my old workbench, I carefully arranged his tankards that he used for mixing.

Here, I paused to contemplate that far away day . . . when Suzannah first came to visit and cut a wheel on this very bench. That day seemed like yesterday, rather than nearly seven years ago . . . and I recalled a small packet of brass shavings sequestered in a safe place.

"Hmmm . . . what have we here?" asked Zeb, withdrawing a dusty packet from the top of one of the shelves. Turning it over, he read the faded handwriting aloud: "'August 3rd, 1765'—is this some sort of *vintage* date, Jim?" Hearing nothing from me, he inquired hopefully, "You and your father had a *still* back here?"

"No, Zeb," I answered curtly, snatching it out of his hands and opening it carefully. Feeling some remorse for being so brusque, as I handed it back to him, in a softer tone I added, "These are Suzannah's."

Zeb, looking at me quizzically, examined the tiny pile of brass shavings. "These belong to Suzannah?" he repeated, not quite understanding.

"Yes. She cut them with my clockmaker's file. I was teaching her how to make clock wheels on that day, right *here* on this bench— where we are now."

Suddenly it all came back . . . her sweet smile, the soft touch of her hand and her gentle voice. I felt a fluttering in my chest as I recalled Mother coming in, and standing beside Suzannah, she reminded us of the Ellingwoods' party. Gazing at the very section of floor where she'd stood, my heart wished she could be there *now*, and I comforted myself with the thought that perhaps she was.

"So this is what Dimmis calls a '*heart* treasure'?" Zeb asked, jolting me out of my reverie.

"Yes . . . *exactly* . . . this is a Suzannah heart treasure for me . . ."

Gently refolding the packet and placing it in my palm, Zeb softly added, "*Memories* can be heart treasures too, Jim." And he closed my fingers around it.

"Yes . . . they *can* be," I slowly replied, thinking of Mother, ". . . even dearer than those we can touch."

As I returned the packet to its rightful place, Zeb seemed lost in thought.

"Precious memories are stored in the heart, Jim. Some are good and some are better, but all are necessary . . . so we can reflect upon their truth. What truth did you *see* just now?"

I stared at Zeb in disbelief. I had never before heard such profundity expressed from one so coarse and indelicate; but then again, Dimmis was in his life now.

"I see two truths before me," I replied. "I realize how much I miss my mother—especially when places like this remind me of her memory. And I remember my Suzannah . . . she was but a sweet young *girl* back then, my new neighbor—but *Zeb*, how I *loved* her!"

I stopped to wipe my eyes before I continued. "The second truth is that *you* now recognize memories as heart treasures. I'm *happy* for you, Zeb. Dimmis is a *fine* woman, and she has been our salvation as a friend, *and* in the tavern."

"And *my* salvation from a rogue's life . . ." he added, wiping a tear from his cheek.

We heard an anxious knock at the door, interrupting our talk. "I'll see who it is. Finish setting up here, if you will. I won't be long."

When I opened the door, I was greeted by Fanny Ellingwood.

"Fanny, what a nice surprise to see you," I said as I embraced her and gave her a kiss.

It was then I noticed the concerned expression on her face. With a nervous edge to her voice, she urgently asked, "Have you seen Suzannah? Is she here?"

"No, Fanny, only Zeb and I are here. Suzannah and Dimmis should be in the tavern, working."

"They aren't there," Fanny snapped.

"So *who* is minding the tavern?" I asked, feeling the first stirrings of apprehension.

"*Henry Wiggins!*" Fanny retorted almost angrily.

"Henry Wig . . . Zeb, let's go!" I managed to blurt out despite my astonishment.

The three of us bolted into the kitchen through the back door. Making our way to the great room, we found Henry, frantically trying to fill the orders and then serve them himself.

"Where are the *girls*, Henry?" I asked him calmly, though incensed that he alone was running my tavern without my knowledge.

"I'm frightfully sorry, Jim, but Suzannah told me to do the *best* I could, and to get you when I had a free moment. But—by God— I haven't had a minute to spare!" Toweling off the overflow from three tankards, he rushed off to deliver them to a table.

As Zeb and I exchanged disbelieving glances, Henry returned with nine coppers and tossed them into a bowl beneath the counter.

"She went to get Doc Brown, Jim . . . and she was in a *hurry!*"

As soon as he said it, I wondered if Suzannah was about to give birth. It made sense, I thought, as Dimmis was at her side the first time—and Dimmis too was gone. Then I wondered why she would go to Doc's house, when Mildred and her helpmates would normally come here.

"Jim, would you please find out what's going on and let me know. I'll wait at home to hear from you," Fanny said. "But please, *don't forget* I'm waiting . . ."

As Fanny bustled out the door, Zeb shook his head and dryly observed, "These moments are *not* heart treasures . . ." Strapping on my apron I tersely replied, "No, they certainly are not, Zeb! Will *you* please go to Doc's and see what in hell happened to my wife! I shall be here—where *else*—waiting very anxiously . . ."

And Zeb was off like a shot.

Meanwhile, I hastened to give Henry some impromptu lessons in serving up food and drink over the next few hours. And despite my best efforts to remain composed, inside I was in an uproar—why would Suzannah and Dimmis disappear without a word to me? All I could think was that something terrible had happened to Ainsley, and she was Ainsley no more—which is another reason, besides attending to the tavern, I had to send Zeb in my stead.

Sick at heart the entire afternoon, I made drinks and prepared food while nervously watching the door. Henry, to his credit, did yeoman service as a tavern maid.

When Zeb finally returned with news, he slapped his massive hand on my shoulder and yelled, "By God, I finally *found* 'em!"

"Where *were* they?" I asked, nearly apoplectic with fear.

"Where they are *now*—at Sam's place."

"*Sam's* place? How is that possible if Fanny came *here* looking for them?"

"Well, Jim, it seems Suzannah heard Sam was taken very sick— but not from her mother. So she went directly to her father, sending Dimmis to fetch Doc to have a look at him. It seems Fanny had already left the house to come *here*, so they kind o' *missed* each other."

Bending down close to my ear, he rumbled hoarsely, "Things ain't so *good* over there, Jim. Both girls are *still* there. Oh, and Suzannah is fine and you do *not* have a daughter . . . *yet!*"

While I was very relieved that Suzannah was safe and well, this was the first I'd heard about any illness involving Sam. He was the same age as my father, and remembering my catastrophic reaction to my own father's death, I wondered how Suzannah would fare if she lost hers. But I hoped I was way ahead of myself in even thinking such a thing as that.

When we closed the tavern that night, Suzannah and Dimmis had still not returned. Henry retired to his guest chamber, and Zeb and I went to see Sam.

When we arrived, Fanny took us right up to see him. As we were climbing the stairs, Doc was coming down.

"Hold it there, Jim!" he warned, putting his palm out. "I want *no* visitors up here until I find out what's ailing Sam. Of course, Fanny, you can go in . . ."

So Zeb and I turned around and went downstairs to the parlor with Doc, making ourselves comfortable in Fanny's overstuffed chairs.

"So what's wrong, Doc? Is Sam *that* sick?" I asked.

"He's pretty bad," Doc mused. He leaned back and closed his eyes as he recounted Sam's symptoms. "He's got a fever, the sweats, a cough, pain in the belly and spots on the chest—red ones. Worst part is, Sam can't make it to the privy . . . and that makes things very messy."

"What do you think has laid him so low so quickly?" I asked, leaning forward to get his attention.

Before Doc could reply, Zeb interjected, "Dammit, Doc, Sam was *fine* two days ago—healthy as a horse he was!"

Doc didn't answer right away. "I'm uncertain about his condition. Maybe Sam has the flux, but it's the fever that's dangerous. Suzannah and Dimmis are constantly swabbing him down to keep him cool. He will need constant care, Jim. Maybe I can convince Mildred to come over and relieve Dimmis—that way at least you can have some help running the tavern."

"Fanny will care for him too," I reminded him.

"Fanny and Suzannah *should* care for Sam," Doc said with conviction.

With a pang, I remembered distinctly when I first met Suzannah, how she told me she wished to care for her parents in their old age. Now it was coming to pass, and I had been without her for nearly a day . . . and she was already sorely missed.

"We will take turns," Doc said, sounding invigorated by the idea, "just like we did during Suzannah's confinement. We will need extra hands for the daytime hours, but usually fevers worsen at night. Suzannah and Fanny will remain here at night, and I'll talk to Rhoda and Mildred now about helping out during the day."

After he packed up his case, Doc opened the door to leave, but turned to me with a very grave countenance. In low tones he soberly admitted, "My gut tells me he has *typhus*, but it's too early to tell. It's *deadly*, Jim—so do *not* tell the girls—I will bear that burden."

And closing the door, he left us in stunned silence.

The Long Summer Night

am's condition did not improve, so Suzannah remained at her father's side—and slept in her old room—for the next few weeks. News of Sam's illness brought visitors to our tavern and the Ellingwood home. The outpouring of love and support for Sam bolstered Zeb's observation: that a man never really knows who his true friends are . . . until he is at death's door. Despite all the care and concern lavished upon Sam, his fate was largely in the hands of God.

Dimmis worked in the kitchen, while Zeb and I served in the great room. Henry, flatly declaring he was not fitted to be a tavern-keeper, happily returned to sea.

Although not as charming as Suzannah and Dimmis—nor as pleasurable to look upon—Zeb and I made out after a fashion, and business carried on, albeit with unaccustomed difficulties occasioned by Sam's prolonged illness.

One evening after closing, Doc showed up looking haggard and tired. In the fire's flickering shadows I saw his eyes were watery and swollen. There were dark saggy pouches below them; giving him the appearance of someone who had not slept for a long time. Slumping heavily into a chair across from the fireplace, he placed his palms upon the table and merely sat, staring deeply into the fire. His hands involuntarily trembled and thumped against the tabletop, and every few minutes he would blink, open his mouth—and yet say nothing.

Witnessing Doc's condition, Zeb hoisted himself from behind a newly tapped barrel of rum. Clearing his throat, he hoarsely whispered, "Say, Jim, he don't *look* so good . . . maybe he's in a stupor on account of that *rum* I gave him yesterday. Maybe you better ask him—just in case I gotta leave suddenly."

"Nonsense—that's not it!" I exclaimed. "But he sure looks done in by *something*."

The kitchen door opened and Dimmis stepped out, silhouetted by the firelight as she regarded the tormented physician.

With a look of great compassion, she went to his side and draped her arm around his shoulders. Then looking toward Zeb, she tersely barked, "Can't you *see* his heart aches and his spirit is broken? Get him something to drink . . . *now!*"

Zeb and I watched wordlessly as she gently dabbed Doc's cheeks with her apron. Angered by our apparent paralysis, she hurled out the words, "*Men*—get to it!"

Finally, Zeb took the mulled cider from the flames and poured it into a tumbler. He laced it with two parts of rum, and after stirring the mixture he passed it to Dimmis, who pressed it gently into Doc's quivering hands.

She then knelt beside him to embrace his hands and steady them. The firelight illuminated her sympathetic face as she searched his features for a sign of acknowledgement. Seeing none, she tugged at his sleeve and softly inquired, "How does it go with *Sam*, Doc?"

Doc, silent and unmoving, continued to stare into the fire. As it hissed and spat in derision at his plight, he looked into Dimmis' upturned face, and took a long slow swallow as the tumbler trembled in his grasp. The beverage dribbled down his unshaven chin, and he still said nothing as he placed it shakily upon the table.

Doc sighed deeply and shifted his gaze to me, then to Zeb—and finally to the tall clock. Then a sudden rage seemed to overtake him. "How *fleeting* time is when you are alive . . . and how *eternal* it is when you are dead! Fixed is the term of life—and we shall all fall alike!" Then he added in a mournful tone, "I do *not* think I can save him—for the only promise of *life* I can give . . . is that it will end."

Addressing us all now, Doc said brokenly, "Tonight . . . I may have to bury . . . my *oldest* remaining friend . . . Sam Ellingwood."

Zeb and I simply stared at each other in disbelief, while Dimmis held Doc, gently rocking him as she would a troubled child. She could do no more for the man who had done so much for her.

Wanting desperately to say something meaningful, the swelling lump in my throat prohibited me from doing so . . . and as the thunking escapement of the tall clock pervaded the great room . . . I stood alone in choking silence . . . because I didn't know what to say.

AFTER A TWENTY-four-hour vigil, Doc had come to us to unburden himself about Sam. In the privacy of our empty tavern, he begged us never to tell the Ellingwoods of his profound distress.

After Dimmis nurtured him with her kindness, hot stew, bread and apple pie, Doc started coming back to himself. Since he was determined to be at Sam's side until he either recovered or died, Doc and Dimmis returned to Sam's chamber later that same night . . . and stayed through the following day.

My father in law was dying, and I could only wonder how Suzannah was faring under this terrible news, but dared not ask. She was still in her father's chamber, the helpless but ever loving daughter to the end . . . as was her youthful wish. I wondered if she would fulfill that wish . . . but secretly I prayed she wouldn't . . . so that Sam might live. But Doc was doing all he could, and now, only God knew the final answer.

SUNDAY MORNING DAWNED to a cloudless, bright blue sky. I'd always believed that sunshine brought light and life to all living things; and hoped that just for today, it might apply to Sam in particular . . . but still there was no sign of Suzannah, and no news from the Ellingwoods.

Zeb left early on my behalf to see if Fanny needed help. While I silently bore my frustration at not being able to free myself to render aid and support, my heart was ever with them. And as I busied myself with the endless chores at the tavern (that could only be done while it was closed), my angst for Suzannah and her father increased measurably . . . for I realized that Sam Ellingwood, my father's best friend, could be reuniting with him in the great beyond alongside mother.

A couple of hours later, Zeb returned with the news that Sam's condition was largely unchanged, and that Suzannah would fill me in later in the day, when she planned to return home.

She'd undoubtedly be exhausted and hungry when she arrived, so I thought I would make something that might tempt her appetite— keeping in mind she was eating for two. Flattening some dough that Dimmis had prepared and left to rise, I then rolled cinnamon and sugar into it, cutting the resulting log into slices of tiny cakes. These I laid upon a tin sheet greased with butter.

After stoking the fire and putting a kettle on for tea and another for porridge, I began to slice apples and strawberries. Arranging the pieces on a pewter plate, I placed it in the center of the table. My hope was that just seeing these treats attractively arrayed would stimulate her appetite.

When a gentle rap came from the front door, I went over to open it. There, I was greeted not by Suzannah, but by Rhoda Barrett.

"Welcome, Rhoda! To what do I owe this pleasure?"

She smiled broadly as she held up a large oval basket covered with a cloth. "I've brought some cooked ducks, roasted potatoes and warm bread for you and Suzannah. She needs to keep her strength up, not only because of Sam's illness, but also for the sake of the child."

As she handed me the basket, she looked up with hopeful eyes and added, "I hope she'll have appetite enough to eat . . . do you think she will like them?"

I was touched by Rhoda's concern and her generous gift. "I'm sure she will. And I know I speak for both of us when I say we're very grateful for your kindness."

Placing her hand over her heart, Rhoda smiled crookedly, and then said, "I pray all goes well with Sam and the little one . . ."

Then, as her eyes filled with tears, "I *feel* for Suzannah, who just dealt with one loss and now faces another . . . and then there's the child of course . . . I don't know how to help . . . so this is my little way to ease your burdens . . ."

She pulled a handkerchief from her pocket to dry the tears that clung to her face. Kissing her forehead, I gently took it from her and finished the job.

"I'll be sure to tell Suzannah how much you care. And no matter what happens, she will overcome it. She is strong and brave, and has a *very* resilient heart."

"I believe you," she sniffed, "it will bend . . . but never break . . ."

"That's right," I reassured her. "Suzannah is a *survivor*—I can tell you that from my *own* experience . . . Why don't you stay and have supper with us? She'll be home soon and I'm sure she'd welcome your company."

"Oh no, I wouldn't think of intruding upon your privacy, especially *now* . . . when she needs to save all her strength for her family."

"But I'm certain she would *love* to see you, if you would stay . . . at least for a short visit."

"Oh no, no, no . . ." she said, shaking her head and smiling again now. "I have some matters of my own to attend to. Jonathan will be returning home soon, so I must get things ready for him. Please, just remember me to her, and enjoy the food with my heartfelt wishes for Sam's welfare . . . and the child's."

As THE MILD afternoon air drifted sweetly through the windows, I began to set the table with plates and utensils. The food Rhoda brought was keeping warm in the oven, awaiting only Suzannah's arrival.

When she finally came home, she was exceedingly tired and preoccupied, surely thinking herself still beside her father's bed.

Seeking to relieve her of some of that burden, I pulled out her chair and said, "Please sit down and rest for a while, darling. Rhoda has made a nice supper for you."

As I set out the food, Suzannah said, "Rhoda has become a dear in her old age. I shall have to thank her."

Pushing her chair in, I said, "Yes, she has. And now let's partake of her generosity."

And thus, we shared our first meal together in some time. Suzannah ate very well, almost too well, for she consumed one whole duck and a part of another. She ate most of the bread herself and one potato soaked in duck drippings. She topped it off with tea, cinnamon rolls and sliced fruit.

During her second time with child, I marveled at Suzannah's seemingly endless capacity to eat. In my heart I was grateful, since this meant good things for the health of our baby; for despite all the trouble outside its mother, the child was doing very well within her.

I deliberately avoided discussing her father so she could enjoy her meal in peace. But now that she'd eaten and seemed more relaxed, it was time to broach the subject.

After clearing the table and pouring my tired little wife another cup of tea, I suggested we move to the parlor so we could talk together more comfortably on the sofa.

Once settled there I said, "Please tell me how your father is doing, Suzannah."

Valiantly holding back tears, she reported that his fever had risen and he wasn't breathing well that day. Doc was fearful about his survival come nightfall, so in preparation, he applied hot plasters soaked with boiled mint to open his lungs.

As she discussed her family's recent trials, I felt there was a new distance between us that I couldn't understand . . . as though she was confused about something.

Possibly sensing my concern, she finally said, "Jim, I've discovered that sorrow makes us children once again—regardless of our age—does it not?"

Lifting her chin with my forefinger to bring her face to mine, her misty eyes silently pleaded for comfort and encouragement. Indeed, she did seem like a child then, and my heart melted at her beseeching look for paternal reassurance.

I silently nodded my answer, and softly brushing her lips with mine, I gently stroked her hair while pressing her wordlessly to my heart. As I did so, the soft warm breeze touched us as it drifted through the open window, prompting me to suggest a walk to the point. The change of scene and fresh air might help to clear her head, and perhaps together, we could place her burdens in perspective.

I draped her shawl across her shoulders, and she took the blanket—and hand in hand we slowly walked past her father's house. I noted her longing look toward the right bedroom chamber . . . where Sam lay near death . . . and knew her heart was *there*, and not with me. I figured this is probably as it should be.

Part of old age is coping with its infirmaries, hopefully to the best of one's ability. Suzannah is a loving compassionate caregiver . . . the youngest daughter with the golden heart. Tonight—she stepped away from being the wife of James Walker—from being an expectant mother carrying his child—and once again became her father's loving daughter.

In his time of desperate need, I totally understood her position. The truth be told . . . I was proud to have her do so, for I knew where she would fly if tragedy struck . . . and I would await her with open arms.

Arriving at our favorite spot on Walker's Point, we settled ourselves comfortably on the blanket. As we sat and peacefully watched the setting sun, its fading glow illuminated Suzannah's face. There, I clearly saw the etched changes I'd noticed earlier: she had hardened her golden heart against the impending loss of her father.

As Suzannah stared forlornly at the flaming clouds, I wracked my brain for encouraging words of hope and support.

After a few moments, I began to gently stroke her hair; and softly kissing her ear, I tenderly whispered, "Suzannah, those who must *walk* alone, sometimes must *fall* alone . . . but my love is here to lift you *up* . . . and we shall walk on . . . *together*."

Suzannah turned from the orange clouds to look up into my face, her eyes swimming at my words. Although her tears trickled in little meandering trails, and her mouth trembled at holding back a cry—not a whimper escaped from my brave little wife.

Slowly closing her eyes with a soft flutter, she drew her knees up, and snuzzling under my sheltering arm, within moments, without a sound . . . she mercifully fell asleep.

Serenity

 s I held Suzannah, the waves murmured and hissed as they gently broke upon the rocks below. Knowing my angel needed sleep, I dared not move or breathe deeply, lest I awaken her. In the darkening sky, the moon slowly rose to nestle itself among the stars. As I looked aloft and pondered all that was before me . . . I silently asked God, "What sort of justice was this—that a girl so recently bereaved, should next suffer the loss of her father—just before the birth of his first grandchild?"

In the early morning, I woke to the cacophonous song of sea gulls. Stiff and numb from remaining in one position all night, I found my little wife still safely nestled in my arms, sound asleep.

I thought it remarkable that Suzannah didn't wake during the night. I supposed we must have been tired enough—or perhaps needed to feel *safe* enough—so we dared not leave the sanctuary of what we called "our little piece of heaven."

In the serenity of the early morning, I sat there watching as the squawking gulls dropped mussels and crabs on the rocks below. When the shells cracked open, they swooped down to breakfast on the exposed remains. What a contrast, I thought: using the simple tools nature provided, the gulls carried on in ignorant bliss . . . while the two humans were—or would be when Suzannah woke up—in anxious turmoil.

In the shallows, I saw two seals drag a large codfish up to the lower rocks, barking as others attempted to steal it. The argument was finally settled when a large bull seal heaved itself out of the water to snatch the prize for himself. As he waddled away with it, the shrill squawks of protest escalated, finally waking my Suzannah.

Slowly lifting her head, she looked around to get her bearings. I bent to kiss her forehead and stood to help her rise. As I tightened the blanket around her and pushed the hair from her face, ah, what a *look* of love she gave me! I felt her unspoken words as though she had written them in my heart.

Breaking the silence I said, "Good morning, my darling—did you sleep well?"

Threading her arms around my waist, she squeezed me, saying, "I had a *wonderful*, comforting pillow to sleep on, Jim. Thank you for staying here and letting me sleep."

"I'm happy to lend myself as your pillow anytime, Suzannah—you know that."

"Indeed I do, darling—but guess what?"

"What?"

"I have to *pee* . . ."

And while Suzannah crossed her legs and anxiously hopped in the crisp morning air—I desperately looked for a suitable outcropping, behind which she could hide and relieve herself. But I stopped when the sudden clopping of horses' hooves echoed above us and abruptly halted.

Together our attention was drawn to the top of the point, where we saw the tall willowy figure of Dimmis Sexton materialize, waving her arms and calling out our names to draw our attention. Then we practically held our breath as she announced, "Jim, bring Suzannah home and be quick about it. Sam's fever broke last night—and he wants to see her *right away*!" She pointed to a second horse she'd brought to save time.

As we rejoiced and hugged each other, I heard Suzannah whisper, "Thank thee, dear God, for saving my poor father . . . I am *ever* thy servant!"

She then kissed me, the first meaningful kiss we had in a long while. When she broke the kiss, she smiled that beautiful smile, and hand in hand we scampered up the rocks.

At the summit, Dimmis met us with a joyous hug, saying that Sam's fever broke at three in the morning, and his delirium had been gone by seven. His calls for the chamber pot lessened in urgency, and he was taking in small amounts of food as Doc had prescribed.

Apparently the urge to relieve herself had passed, since Suzannah immediately mounted the horse Dimmis had brought and pelted homeward without a word.

As we watched the small retreating figure on horseback, Dimmis said somberly, "The hand of death has been lifted, Jim . . . you can't imagine the *joy* in that house."

"Indeed, I *can*, Dimmis. Sam's time to leave us will come, but *not* today!"

I took her hand and guided her across the rocky ledges; then we climbed on her horse and headed home.

As we trotted along, Dimmis—elated by the turn of events—continued to talk about Sam's condition, reporting that he still had a long way to go before he would be fully recovered. But now, at least, Suzannah and Fanny would be free of their deathbed vigil and able to resume a more normal routine.

I felt a profound sense of relief at the news about Sam—for my own sake, and especially for my wife and our unborn child. In many ways I saw Father in Sam . . . especially after Suzannah and I were married, when his goodness and love were generously trained on me. Now I was determined to help him recover as best I could . . . and my loving wife would lead the way.

ONCE AT THE Ellingwoods', Dimmis and I were surprised to find that Suzannah's sisters had arrived from Boston in the interim. After receiving news of Sam's illness, it took them longer than they would have liked to arrange passage to Walker's Cove; but they were finally there and the timing was fortuitous.

We were all, of course, thrilled to see them—Fanny and Suzannah in particular. I couldn't help but be quietly relieved to know that caring for Sam would now be distributed among others, and not fall so heavily upon a few. And despite the solemn occasion that brought them home, their irrepressible high spirits lifted us all out of our doldrums.

After an exuberant exchange of greetings, I rushed upstairs to see Sam. For the first time in over a month, he was sitting up in bed, but he was so emaciated that I hardly recognized him.

Suzannah was already there, sitting next to him on the bed—wiping away her tears of happiness. As she cried openly, Sam's skeletal hand stretched to feebly stroke her hair, and placing his spindly arms around his youngest daughter, his look of gratitude spoke volumes hidden within his heart . . . and a happier union between father and daughter was rarely, if ever equaled.

When they had separated, he gazed steadily at his daughter's face. Then, in a weak voice trembling with emotion, he said, "I hear you and your mother are the guardian angels who saved my life . . . who never slept and were ever-vigilant day and night. Is that true?"

Moving closer to her father so she could touch his stubbled cheek as she spoke, Suzannah replied, "'Twas nothing but *love* that spared you, Father . . . *love* and many, *many* prayers from all who love you."

Sam smiled and patted his daughter's head as if she were three years old. "Well now, thanks to *you*, I'm still *here* . . . and I'm vertical, and I'm as hungry as a beast in the wilderness!"

At that very moment, Fanny came through the door carrying a large pewter tray laden with food. As she placed it on Sam's bedside table, I saw a large bowl filled to the brim with steaming venison stew, a plate of fresh-baked buttered bread, slices of pumpkin pie and two apple fritters.

It did our hearts good to watch Sam devour the venison stew, smacking his lips with pleasure and asking repeatedly that his water glass be refilled. Doc had emphasized to him the importance of replenishing the liquids he'd lost through his illness.

I believed that with the tender loving care he would receive, and the plentiful—and delectable—food coming his way, he would be plump and vigorous in no time.

After Suzannah and I had finished our visit with Sam, we relinquished our places so her sisters could spend the remaining evening with their father. As we withdrew from Sam's bedroom, their presence and chattering would undoubtedly go a long way toward restoring his good cheer. Indeed, their giggling made me imagine when they were all twelve years of age and younger . . . and I easily saw how much *fun* Sam could have had on a cold winter day, frolicking with all five girls before a roaring fire.

And so on that night of peaceful serenity, as Suzannah and I rocked in our rocker, we had much to be thankful for: Sam's triumph over death first and foremost, the wishes and prayers of our friends and neighbors, the unstinting labors from Dimmis and Zeb—who helped us preserve our livelihood during the long ordeal, and finally, Doc Brown's tireless ministrations and vigilance. Through *all* these efforts, Sam would now know the incomparable joy of meeting his first grandchild.

SUZANNAH'S PRESENT

fter the long weeks of gloom, Sam's recovery rejuvenated everyone. The weight we'd borne was lifted as Sam's emaciated frame gradually filled out and became strong again. Fanny made him drink at least one tumbler of milk every day, and Suzannah added cream to her fritter recipe. Soon Sam was teasing them—accusing them of fattening him up with turkey, ham and duck, and pies, cakes and fritters.

Nearly losing Sam that spring brought the family closer together. Thus, Suzannah's sisters remained in Walker's Cove all summer and into the fall for two reasons: to be near their father *and* to give back to Suzannah. They were mindful of the fact—and grateful—that although she was with child, she gave of herself selflessly and tirelessly to care for Sam when they were unable to be there.

As the child grew within her, Suzannah remained confined in the tavern kitchen, away from the daily demands of the great room. Dimmis and I took charge of running the tavern, and it helped that Dimmis was temporarily rooming upstairs now, to assist me and care for Suzannah when she gave birth.

Doc kept a watchful eye on Suzannah, as did Mildred. They examined her once a week and reassured us that everything was fine and the child was healthy. Ainsley evidently agreed, since she obliged their pokes and prodding by moving around inside Suzannah's belly—to the extent that we could *see* it—much to our delight and amusement!

All things considered, we felt blessed in being so well prepared for the arrival of our child. As fall slowly draped its colorful blanket over our little world, we were content. Sam was back in his shop, the tavern was busy and our cellar was fully stocked, save for the Essex rum. Suzannah had three barrels of it remaining in the cellar and we needed ten more.

Armed with ample money for the purchase, Zeb Hawkes had departed Walker's Cove to replenish our supplies. Essex rum had always been Mother's favorite; she claimed it was the most potent brand and had the best flavor. The well-known product of distilleries located in Essex county—it bore a heavy molasses taste that masked its strength and enhanced its aroma. It was *the* secret ingredient in Mother's hot buttered rum recipe, our most popular drink. It outsold flip and mulled cider, which Suzannah mixed with a gill of Essex rum "to warm the insides"—as she was fond of telling our patrons.

Octobɛʀ 18ᴛʜ ᴍᴀʀᴋᴇᴅ Suzannah's twenty-first birthday, and I wondered if my brothers-in-law would be able to join their wives in Walker's Cove to celebrate. I had written to ask them if they could manage to break away for a family party at our tavern, but I was still awaiting an answer.

One fine day, more than two weeks after I sent my inquiry, Osgood Lovejoy, carrying a fresh batch of letters, came in to drop one off and have a tumbler of rum to chase away the autumn chill. He wasn't alone in that desire; the tavern was already filled with noisy sailors in from the wharf, seeking the warmth of our fire and our refreshments.

"Pretty damned cold out there, Jim!" Osgood remarked, looking back toward the closed door. "Mebbe mix an extra *strong* one for me?" he asked with a sudden shiver as he placed a letter before me.

It was welcome news from Fay, reporting that the husbands planned to arrive together early on the Sunday morning of Suzannah's birthday.

"Free of charge, Osgood!" I barked from behind the rum barrels, greatly pleased to know we would have a full house for the celebration.

After setting down his drink, I sat beside him and asked, "So what's the news from the wharf these days?"

After taking a large swallow, Osgood gulped hard. "*Whoo!* My gosh, Jim, this here is nearly straight alcohol!"

"No, it isn't," I said, smiling at his reddened face. "It's Essex rum—six and a half months old. Problem is, Osgood, you are too used to weak and watery rum, to say nothing of rancid cider. You will not get any of that here!"

He grinned broadly and lifting his tumbler in appreciative toast, he smiled a toothy grin and replied, "Thank ye, Jim. By God, this is true firewater!"

An Irish sailor behind us commented loudly in a heavy brogue, "Nah, nah, dear sar . . . 'tis this stuff *we* call holy water!"

We turned around to see whom the voice belonged to, as he hoisted his drink and flashed us a gap-toothed smile.

"Aye, matey," he continued, "on our little isle o' green, such stuff as *this* can make tavern owners into kings!"

"I will tell my wife you said so," I said, laughing. "She will be pleased to hear of your high opinion of our recipe . . . though I don't think she would like to be a king . . . but a *queen* perhaps!"

"Your *wife*? She be the red-haired Mary over yonder?" he inquired, raising his eyebrows so they nearly disappeared beneath his cap.

"No, sir, that's *Dimmis*. She probably served you," I explained. "My wife is with child and working only in the kitchen now."

"Aye, is that a fact? Congratulations, sar!" he said, offering his hand as he introduced himself. "Seamus O'Brien at your service, master o' the schooner *Shannon* out o' Boston."

Giving his hand a hearty shake, I said, "It's good to meet you, Seamus. I'm James Walker, the keeper here. Welcome to Walker's Tavern."

Nodding affectionately at Osgood, I added, "My friend here is Osgood Lovejoy. He collects letters and packages from the wharf and delivers them hereabouts. He also makes and mends shoes, when he is not busy at home with his wife and *thirteen* children."

Osgood, all smiles, failed to notice my jibe at his libidinous habits and saw my introduction as a pure compliment—which in truth it was.

After shaking hands with Seamus, Osgood asked, "Are you the fellow with the violin on board?"

"No violin, but a squeezebox and pipes, *indeed*, sar! I dinna get ta play terribly often, ye see, as there's always so much work on board, and we shove off quickly after delivering our goods."

"And what goods did you deliver today?" I inquired casually, thinking they were probably headed for Eben's store.

"Twenty five barrels o' rum, four hogsheads o' flour, fifteen pounds o' salt, and twenty hundred board feet o' mahogany. Unloadin' now, and when the hold is empty, we load up with pure white oak from the old boatyard."

"The rum is probably ours," I said, thinking that Zeb's mission must have been successful.

Turning to Osgood, I remarked, "I didn't know Jens was in the *lumber* business, I thought he only built boats."

"I thought you knew, Jim . . ." Osgood said solemnly. "Jens felt so bad about what happened to your mother on one of *his* boats—that he decided to quit boatbuilding. Now he sells lumber from the king's pines and oaks—and makes better money doing that."

I felt a deep pang of regret on hearing that Jens, on account of Mother's death, gave up his long-cherished business. I wondered if Mother hadn't been the one who'd died in the wreck of the *Sunrise* . . .would he have still made the same decision?

"By the way, Jim, you asked me for news from the wharf," Osgood said, changing the subject. "Well, I heard there's a reward offered for the capture of those who burned the *Gaspée*. And when the perpetrators are caught, they're to be sent to England to stand trial."

"Sent to be *hanged* by the king, by *damn!*" Seamus bellowed, slamming his fist on the table . . . and thus began the evening table pounding sessions. Soon the rants of his sailors were embellished with a torrent of cursing that turned the air "blue"—as Dimmis was fond of saying.

Indeed, the *Gaspée* affair of last June was fresh in the mind of every sailor, and there was general agreement among them about what the British could do with their "damned, bloody, thieving, bastardly trials."

As more hot buttered rum and flip were distributed among the sailors, an enthusiastic bawling for placing the king's head on a pike permeated the great room. The heartiness with which they cursed the British and all things associated with them soon became deafening . . . and amidst all the cursing, drinking and table pounding, I wondered what Henry Wiggins and Sam Adams could accomplish . . . if Seamus and his crew *ever* joined the Sons of Liberty.

I turned out that it was our rum that had been aboard the *Shannon*. It was delivered to us on an overburdened wagon driven by Wheezer Hutchinson, who did a little of everything to make a living, but mostly farmed on land above the cove, across from the burial ground. I safely stowed the barrels of rum, flour and salt in the cellar with Wheezer's help, for which he gladly accepted five coppers and the promise of a plate of apple fritters on his next visit.

I headed toward the kitchen to inform Suzannah that our supplies had been replenished and stowed. When I entered the room, she was standing in a corner by the window, leaning heavily on a table with her head bowed in a peculiar fashion . . . and she was shaking all over.

I approached her with concern, and gently touching her shoulders I softly asked, "Are you sick, darling?"

She stepped away from the table, and on the floor where she had stood, was a large irregular puddle. Blushing, she looked up at me and whispered, "It's *time*, Jim . . . I'll get Dimmis. I believe Osgood is still in the great room, so you can tell him to go home and get Mildred."

"Don't *you* worry about that, my darling. I'll let Dimmis know, and Osgood too."

Despite my confidence at thinking we were prepared for the birth, I was unprepared for it happening at *this* particular moment, especially with the tavern open and packed to the gills. My thoughts were racing as I thought about the next step—going for Doc and Fanny, and perhaps Rhoda. But then I remembered that Suzannah's sisters were nearby, so we would have plenty of help right away.

I carried Suzannah up the back stairs in my arms, her dress and legs wet with birthing fluid. Settling her gently on the bed and placing pillows under her head, I kissed her tenderly several times. She smiled nervously as I fussed over her and moved the chamber pot close, in case she should need it.

I heard rapid steps on the rear stairs before Dimmis burst into the room, panting. "*Suzannah*, I saw the puddle on the floor and knew what had happened. I sent Osgood to get Mildred, Doc, Fanny and Lydia. I have towels and water that were intended for my cooking chores, but now they shall be used for *birthing!*"

After she gently prodded Suzannah's stomach, she declared, "The child is getting ready, Suzannah, she will be here very soon." Dimmis started undressing her then, but stopped suddenly to look up at me and bark, "Jim Walker, I believe you have a *tavern* to keep . . ."

After giving Suzannah another brief kiss, I went out on the landing to find Fanny and Lydia coming up the stairs, holding arm-fuls of towels.

As she passed me, Fanny said, "Don't worry, Jim. Doc and Mildred will be here soon. Just tend to your business and keep your noisy customers happy. You'll be a *father* soon enough!"

Returning to my duties, I stood alone in the kitchen feeling downcast, unwanted and totally lost. I gawked at all the pots and pans and ingredients that Suzannah and Dimmis had left behind, but I had no idea how to cook anything—except cinnamon rolls. So for the time being, I decided to simply serve drinks, and the food on hand that had already been cooked or didn't need to be.

I manned the great room alone, hoping the hours to closing would fly by. But in short order—to my great relief—Lydia Barrett came down from the borning room to help out, bringing news that Suzannah was fine, but the baby wasn't yet ready to be born. She said Mildred had estimated about ten hours hence.

After the *Shannon*'s crew left in time for the early evening tide, we closed the tavern. The wait for the birth was interminably long, and to pass the time, Lydia and I cleaned up the great room, set the tables and by eleven that night, everything was in good order.

I pressed her hands and kissed her forehead. "Thank you, Lydia—you are an angel."

"Speaking of *angels*, did you know that Suzannah was born on a *Sunday?*"

"God's day . . . why am I not surprised?" Before she could answer, I suggested we sit together by the fire . . . since we had a long wait before us.

Once we were settled, Lydia stretched her feet toward the flames and continued, "*Mother* was *also* born on a Sunday, Jim."

"*Both* of them?" I exclaimed.

Lydia nodded. "Mother and father always thought Suzannah was a *special* child, being born on the Sabbath like mother."

Staring into the flames, I remembered Sam telling me about Suzannah being "unique."

Lydia broke my pensive silence by adding, "Now it seems likely your daughter will be born on the Sabbath too."

"So they *are* angels . . ." I murmured, as my long-held belief was confirmed at last.

"I cannot say, Jim, but *three* successive generations of women born on the Sabbath . . . seems too coincidental *not* to have something in it of divine intervention."

"So, if all goes well, Ainsley will be born tomorrow—on Suzannah's *birthday*."

As it dawned on her that there were not one but two synchronisms, Lydia exclaimed, "How wondrous that is: not only the Sabbath, but her *birthday!*"

When I looked into her eyes, I saw she was as mystified at the odds as I was.

Lydia rose, and after placing two large cauldrons of water over the fire, she then resumed her seat. Leaning back in her chair, she closed her eyes and wistfully said, "Oh, that it were *me* in childbirth!"

Mildred once told me that none of the Ellingwood sisters had ever borne children. Although I hadn't given the matter much thought, I felt rather awkward at hearing Lydia's comment now . . . and didn't quite know what to say.

I watched her wordlessly, feeling a twinge of sorrow, as she sat back with her eyes closed, seemingly in fanciful reveries with her own child . . . the child she never had . . . and my heart wept at her maternal loneliness.

Suddenly, Lydia buried her face in her hands and began to cry. In a tremulous halting voice she lamented, "Of the five of us, only Suzannah has ever felt the presence of life growing within her body . . . that special sense of *fullness* only pending motherhood brings . . . and yet, alone in barren solitude, I ever weep for my unborn children . . ."

Remembering Suzannah's secret grief, I rose and draped a comforting arm about her shoulders. "Lydia, you are one of the finest people I've ever known, and I'm honored to have you as my sister. What has been denied you enables your heart to see truths that many cannot. Because of that, you are more sensitive, open, sympathetic and dear to all of us . . . *and* we love you dearly . . . child or no child."

She looked up at me, her gray-blue eyes still wet with bittersweet tears of failed hope. And yet, I saw in them that my words had given her comfort . . . and for the briefest moment, I envisioned Suzannah in her older years.

Lydia stood and then she kissed me. With that kiss I knew her secret grief would ever remain hidden . . . in the hearts of her unborn children. I kissed her cheeks and after holding her to my heart, in a voice still showing traces of her anguish, she tearfully whimpered, "You are the *finest* brother I never had . . ."

"Lydia! Lydia! We need the water!" were the words that woke me. I sat up abruptly to hear once more, "Lydia! We need the water!"

Lydia and I had fallen asleep in our chairs, aided no doubt by the roasting bed of coals beneath the cauldrons of water. It was Dimmis who bounded down the stairs and from the stairwell asked, "May we have the water *now*? Suzannah is birthing!"

Lydia sprang up from her chair while I took the first cauldron, and together we went upstairs. As I stood in the doorway, I could hear Mildred patiently asking Suzannah to "breathe three times and push again!" but I could see nothing of what was going on inside.

I could smell asafoetida, so I presumed Suzannah or someone else had to be revived. Doc came to the door and took the cauldron, and Lydia disappeared into the room. Fanny instructed me to return downstairs to await further news.

Sequestered in the great room, I could hear something of what was going on in the borning room above. Knowing I could become a father at any time, I practically held my breath as I waited—and watching the tall clock tick away the hours until then, I tried to guess when it would be.

A shriek from above startled me so that I nearly fell off my chair. Next came a sustained scream followed immediately by applause, the scrambling of feet and muffled female chatter—which I could not decipher.

"She's come!" I called out excitedly, as I ran to the stairs and bounded up to the second floor.

Knocking furiously on the door as the scrambling within continued, Lydia's voice rang out, "Please, Jim—give us a few minutes to clean up."

And so I waited, pacing back and forth . . . minutes seemed like hours, and I decided this event was a much greater test of nerves than getting married *ever* was. And then I heard it . . . a tiny birdlike cry . . . a repeating warble that told me that as of today— Sunday, October 18th, 1772, my wife's birthday—I was indeed a *father*.

The door finally opened and Lydia stood before me, smiling as though she had given birth herself—and in her heart, I think she did.

"Greetings, *Aunt* Lydia. Is Suzannah available?" I asked with feigned calm.

Her eyes filled at the words "Aunt Lydia," whereupon she curtseyed and replied, "Yes, and I want you to meet the newest member of our family . . . you, Jim, are the father of a *beautiful* baby girl . . ."

As my eyes filled with tears, I could only stand stock-still, staring at the bed. Finally, I whimpered, "A girl? A little *girl?*"

Taking my hand, Lydia led me to Suzannah, her face radiating joy as mother and daughter rested comfortably together.

My living angel had borne another, and when I bent to embrace my dear one with a tender kiss, she responded by opening her gray-blue eyes . . . and regarding me with a look of pure angelic bliss.

Fighting back tears, I whispered to her, "Happy birthday, Suzannah, my loving wife—and now a mother too. Without you, I would *never* have known this depth of love within my being." As I gently stroked her hair and caressed her cheek, I softly asked, "How can I ever *thank* you for this blessing?"

She said simply, "Love *us* . . . as you have *me.*"

Once Doc and Mildred satisfied themselves that all was well, they left the three of us alone. I sat in a chair next to my wife and our child, and we all drowsed for a time.

When darkness approached, a knock at the door woke us. When it opened, there before us was Fanny and Sam with their daughters—and their husbands, who had earlier arrived from Boston while we slept. Once inside the room, they all stood quietly and gaped at Suzannah and Ainsley.

Despite being tired and weak from the birthing experience, Suzannah mustered up enough strength to say, "I *thank* you for what you have done for us. My greatest birthday present—besides my little girl—is having my whole family *here. I love* you all very much."

Suzannah handed Ainsley to me, and I could feel the pleasing warmth of her tiny body against mine. I looked at this miracle of miracles, and planted light kisses on her forehead, each little cheek and the tip of her miniature nose, just like I often did for her mother. Then I whispered to my daughter, "Welcome *home*, Ainsley . . ."

Everyone proceeded in an orderly fashion to congratulate Suzannah and get a closer look at our child, who by then was nursing at her mother's breast. I could see them bonding as the babe suckled contentedly, while Suzannah kissed and fondled her tiny hands. It was then that I first noticed she had the same shade of golden hair, and the same gray-blue eyes as her mother.

When Suzannah was finished nursing, she handed the child to Fanny and softly said, "Take her, Mama, she is your *first* grandchild. How shall she be called?"

I was stunned by her words, for we had already agreed on her name, even before Fanny was born—and Suzannah herself had named her in the womb. But the look on Fanny's face told me I would be a brute to deny her this offer.

Looking rapturously at the sleeping babe in her arms, Fanny walked across the room into the moonlight. She glanced aloft through the window to its source . . . and remained pensive. Finally, with moistened eyes she softly said, "*Ainsley* . . . after my *dear*, lifelong friend in Heaven." Then while she and the child were bathed in moonlight, she whispered a heartfelt prayer. "May your namesake's loving grace fall upon you . . . and guide thy innocent heart evermore."

AFTER FANNY'S NAMING and benediction, everyone returned home knowing we needed our rest. As I sat alone, watching over my sleeping angels, the crisp evening air still seemed laden with divine moonlight. Wondering what Fanny saw when she looked out that window—I quietly went over to open it and investigete.

No wonder Fanny teared up . . . for it was Midnight Blue, and she made her wish for Ainsley . . . *both* of them.

I thought of Mother and how she would have rejoiced at witnessing the birth and naming of her first grandchild. But as Suzannah and Ainsley reposed in sweet slumber, bathed in moonlit grace . . . on this night of Midnight Blue . . . somehow . . . I knew Mother was watching.

GRATITUDE

uring her first six weeks of life, Ainsley slept very well and grew chubby on her mother's milk. Her cheeks puffed out such that she vaguely resembled a nut-stuffed squirrel . . . so we nicknamed her "Squirrely girly."

Her four aunts were constantly at her side, taking turns playing with her and attending to her needs. Their assistance enabled Suzannah to rest between feedings, as well as wash clothes and deal with aspects of our tavern business that were her specialties.

I was very fortunate to have the invaluable services of Dimmis and now Zeb too—who on the birth of Ainsley agreed to work with me full time in the tavern. While Dimmis usually stayed in the kitchen preparing meals, Zeb and I worked in the great room together. In the colder weather there were fewer sailors to serve, but more of our village folk came in to warm up, imbibe in a pint or two, and share news and gossip before returning home.

Keeping a tavern means being married to it, in some ways more than to a wife—especially when the wife is a partner in the business and now otherwise occupied. Because of Suzannah's absence, I worried constantly about Dimmis becoming overburdened. I asked Fanny, if she would be willing to assist Dimmis in the kitchen whenever she could spare the time, and thankfully, she readily agreed.

Since Zeb and I usually worked fourteen hours a day, I rarely saw my daughter except when she was sleeping—either early before the sun rose or long after it set. I did *hear* her from time to time, especially when she was hungry or needed her diaper changed. I wondered how my father managed to carry on with his two trades when I was Ainsley's age—and still spend time with me, or so he had told me. I decided that clockmaking and blacksmithing must have been far less demanding than keeping a tavern.

I especially looked forward to Sundays. They were now our family days, opening up a new world of wonders in the company of my infant child. Playing finger and toe games with Ainsley, and receiving her toothless smiles became my treasured escape from my endless work. It was always with great reluctance that I returned her to her cradle . . . because when Ainsley fell asleep, my fantasy world vanished. Thankfully, there were chance moments between Sundays when I would surreptitiously observe Suzannah and Ainsley playing together: little games such as "boop be doo" and "Where's Ainsley." With my dear wife's heart overflowing with maternal happiness during such moments, I was quietly moved to tears . . . and I hoped her loving influences would ever remain upon Ainsley's character.

That winter, despite the cold and snow, our home life was better and brighter than ever. Suzannah had given me the most precious of all gifts . . . fatherhood . . . and a beautiful child who was the image of her dear mother.

And on Christmas morning, while observing my girls playing before the warmth of our crackling fire, I sat contentedly in Sam's rocker—relishing their giggles and squeals. How it reminded me of how Father always quoted an old saying: that life is not measured by how many breaths you take, but by the moments that take your breath away . . .

THE YEAR 1773 began with making Dimmis a quarter owner, sharing in twenty-five percent of the tavern's profits and expenses. After turning down our previous offers, she finally accepted this one, probably because she and Zeb were now attached, and he was as nearly as committed to the tavern as she was.

In the spring of the year, Suzannah's sisters parted reluctantly from their treasured niece, and amidst many tearful hugs and kisses at the wharf, returned to Boston. Although their presence was sorely missed in Walker's Cove, life went on as usual albeit with a few modifications. When Zeb resumed his role of trader and set off to obtain sorely needed provisions, we hired Osgood's eldest daughter Amity to help me in the great room. And fortunately, with Sam's health greatly improved, Fanny was able to give even more generously of her time to assist Dimmis in the kitchen.

There was a lot of talk in our tavern about the new surge of political unrest in Boston over taxes and tea. Parliament had passed the Tea Act, claiming a three-penny per pound tax on tea arriving in the colonies. This gave the floundering East India Company a monopoly on the product, which they sold at wholesale prices only to their Tory cronies, leaving folks like us out in the cold. So the smuggling of British and Dutch teas became a cat-and-mouse game that Zeb Hawkes in particular relished above all else, except for the smuggling of Essex rum.

At the beginning of May, Dimmis received a letter with good news from Zeb; that some "trusted acquaintances" could arrange to have English tea smuggled directly into Walker's Cove at four pennies a pound *less* than the East India Company's wholesale price. This would allow us to serve it cheaply at the tavern *and* sell the excess covertly through Eben's store for less than any tea anywhere. We would all make a couple of pennies for every pound we bought, and the tea-drinking folks hereabouts would undoubtedly be gratefully silent.

Around this time, we began to see a lot more of Osgood Lovejoy in the tavern. It was partly because he enjoyed seeing his own daughter; but he was now delivering a greater abundance of mail these days from Suzannah's sisters, occasioned by the news from Boston in the wake of the Tea Act. As I read their letters, it struck me how little progress had been made since grandfather's time, when he separated himself from the crown's taxes and its incessant meddling in fair and open trade—nearly one hundred years ago!

In fact, the wisdom of grandfather's decision to leave Boston had even greater weight now, since Walker's Cove remained largely unaffected by the turmoil that currently plagued the major port cities. Sailors trundled into our tavern and over a few pints of flip, grog or buttered rum, pounded the tables and howled with delight as they told us that ships carrying English tea to New York and Philadelphia were promptly sent back to Britain. Or that in Charleston, the tea was unloaded and sat untouched on the docks for weeks until it finally rotted.

I HAD RESIGNED myself to a quiet uneventful afternoon in the tavern, when Zeb Hawkes suddenly barged through our tavern door, hauling two large kegs under his massive arms.

"Hell's own kitchen, Jim!" he roared, in a throwback to his former uncouth manners. "Where in hell is the damned *lady* of the house? I got some *business* to discuss!"

"She's right *here*!" Suzannah replied, standing in the kitchen doorway with Ainsley on her hip, the child gawking in wonder at everything around her.

As he slammed the two heavy kegs upon the bar, Zeb furtively whispered, "This here is a *secret* formula, Suzannah—and we don't want *anybody* to know about it until they drink it!" Slapping one of the kegs affectionately as though it were a maiden's backside, and, as an afterthought he bellowed, "Good for the *ladies* too!"

When he finally turned around to face Suzannah, he saw Ainsley, whereupon his tone of voice immediately softened. "Well, look who's here!" Zeb went over and gently poked his finger into Ainsley's cheek, inspiring a little laugh and a toothless grin from the delighted child.

"I'll be damned if she don't look more and more like her *mother*, because she sure as hell don't look like her *father*!"

"Good thing too!" I enthusiastically agreed, and just as I said it, I remembered Zeb and my father exchanging those same words about *me* about eight years ago . . . when the Ellingwoods were moving into the Whipple house.

Suzannah kissed Zeb on the cheek and handed Ainsley over to him, saying, "It's *Uncle Zeb's* turn to hold her for a while."

Clearly honored by the appellation, Zeb carefully took the child and nestled her in his massive arms. As Ainsley cooed at him and patted his face with her tiny hands, Zeb kissed her squirrelly cheek then fingered the silky golden hair. In a hoarse whisper he said, "That you have a long and beautiful life, little one, is the fondest wish of your uncle Zeb."

As if on cue, Ainsley sighed and touched Zeb's shoulder as though testing its strength. Then she promptly belched, hurling half-digested milk down the front of his coat, sending us all into gales of laughter—including Zeb.

With a reddening face, Suzannah hastily took Ainsley and placed her in my arms so that I might clean her up. Zeb hastily removed his coat as Suzannah prepared a wet cloth to clean it up.

"How was your trip?" Dimmis said as she came in from the kitchen, and without waiting for a reply gave Zeb a kiss—not on the cheek as we expected, but squarely upon the lips . . . and it was a long one.

Suzannah and I observed them appreciatively, exchanging gleeful smiles.

After they broke from their embrace, Dimmis said, "Sit and relax for a while, Zeb. *All* your girls are here to keep you company."

Zeb took a seat and motioned to me that he was again ready to play with the freshly restored Ainsley. I brought her over to him, and he took her and dandled her on his knee, bellowing, "Hey *ho*, little girl! Hey ho . . . you never looked better in your life, now that you are nice and tidy!" While she cooed and giggled, he laughed in turn at hearing the baby noises she made.

I suppressed the urge to warn Zeb about jostling Ainsley overmuch, lest she spit up more milk. Instead, I simply looked on as the innocence of childhood touched an older heart.

As she beheld the two at play, the wistful look in Dimmis' eyes told me everything about her joy in their reunion. Even after a relatively short absence, I could feel the power of her love as she took Ainsley from Zeb and embraced her with a kiss . . . a yearning *mother's* kiss.

Suzannah glanced at me meaningfully once again, and I, in turn, nodded my understanding: that Dimmis wanted to be settled for

good, and have a child with Zeb . . . and I hoped that for Dimmis'
sake, a marriage was clearly in the offing.

As Ainsley's needs changed so did Suzannah's routine, and she
gradually became more involved with the tavern again. It was only
natural then that Fanny's role as Ainsley's grandmother evolved
too. She would care for the child and keep her occupied all day,
reliving the motherhood of her youth. Sometimes she took Ainsley
home with her in the morning, allowing Suzannah and I to focus
entirely on the tavern, or spend some rare private time together,
either upstairs or at Walker's Point.

Suzannah found herself with more and more time to think
about varying our menu as Mother had originally planned to do.
She'd actively solicited her sisters' help in finding new recipes to
which we received an enthusiastic response, yielding more than our
usual quota of letters from Boston, each with recipes collected from
all corners of the thirteen colonies.

In the ensuing summer, Suzannah and Dimmis experimented
with several of these new dishes until they finally arrived at their
first official offering—coot stew; which was the only way to cook
coot. Upon tasting it for the first time, Zeb evinced a series of guf-
faws before making a suggestion to improve the dish. He said he
knew by heart a better recipe from Rhode Island:

> *Into a pot throw two sturdy building bricks and lay a bed*
> *of salt over them.*
> *Add the breasts of six freshly killed coot plus two gallons*
> *of water,*
> *Slowly parboil for twenty-four hours.*
> *Next day, when ready to eat, drain off the water,*
> *Throw away the coot and eat the bricks.*

Suzannah and Dimmis were *not* amused. While stifling the immediate impulse to laugh, I managed to maintain a serious expression

throughout. I certainly wouldn't mention that coot stew wasn't high on my list of favorites, either.

Things improved when we moved on to sample a few other recipes like Brunswick stew, rabbit stew and a southern colonial stew called Burgoo, which combined squirrel, chicken, salted pork and vegetables; though, as an unusually adaptable dish, its ingredients could include muskrat, porcupine, woodchuck and seal meat. Yet despite the occasional experiment with something previously untried, the mainstay of our summer menu was the most toothsome of readily available game birds—turkey, geese, pheasant, woodcock and pigeon—all easily taken on the marsh and in Richardson's fields.

Any discussion of Suzannah's culinary art would be incomplete without a mention of her fresh smoked eel, which I for one couldn't get enough of. She made it not too salty or fatty, yet the flesh was always firm and tender, with just the right amount of smoky flavor from curing it in Sam's smokehouse.

Most popular of all were Suzannah's chowders and creamed fish dishes, most especially her corn and fish chowder, which she called scrapple. It was a tavern favorite particularly during the colder months. But if there was an abundance of cod or haddock in the summer, she happily purchased it from the local fishermen to make creamed fish dishes, which became locally famous and sold briskly, no matter what the time of year.

AFTER NINETY DAYS of aging, Zeb was anxious to sample the new concoction he had brewed with the help of his fellow patriots, Henry Wiggins and Sam Adams. Adams himself was once a maltster who'd learned the trade at his family's malthouse on Purchase Street in Boston. During his recent trip there, Zeb had met with Adams while on Sons of Liberty business, and took the opportunity to solicit his advice about some of the finer points in bringing his custom-made brew to the next stage. Sam gladly shared his expertise with Zeb, especially when he heard that the beverage in question was destined for Walker's Tavern. The resulting two special kegs now awaited the final taste test.

Retrieving one barrel from the cellar, Zeb set it on the bar and anxiously removed the bung, unleashing a sustained hiss, followed by an enticing aroma I did not recognize.

"What's that I smell?" I asked as I seated myself next to him.

After he let the keg breathe for a few moments, Zeb tipped the barrel and spilled some of the contents into a tumbler. "This here is ginger, beer and rum all mixed together with some secret spices." He passed it to me, and casually leaning back in his chair, he watched as I carefully took the first sip.

Raising the drink to my lips, its pleasant rooty aroma urged me on . . . and it *was* delicious: I detected rum laced with vanilla and molasses, and it was mixed with beer that possessed a distinct bite of a ginger aftertaste.

"This is wonderful, Zeb!" I exclaimed before taking another deep draw.

Suzannah, emerging from the kitchen carrying a large bowl of custard, nearly dropped it at the sight of *me* with a tumbler to my lips. I seldom drank any of our spirits, for it was my habit not to indulge myself in consuming the profits. But this was a special occasion—plus the beverage was *irresistible*!

"I do *not* believe what I'm *seeing*!" Suzannah crowed with evident delight. "My dear husband, having a tumbler for *himself*! To what occasion do we owe *this* honor?"

I wiped my lips and said, "Well dear, this is Zeb's special brew . . . you *must* try it!"

Setting her bowl down on the bar, she took my empty tumbler and held it out so Zeb could fill it with some of his elixir.

She sipped it thoughtfully. "This is *very* rich and delicious . . ." As she drank some more, she nearly choked before adding, "and *powerful* too . . . *what* is in it?"

Zeb, obviously taking the question very seriously, sat up straight before he answered. "It's four parts Essex rum, mixed with molasses, ginger, small beer and spices—the same spices you use in your buttered rum and flip." He paused thoughtfully and then explained,

"Sam Adams, Henry and I—we kind of *invented* it. Henry and I worked together on the ingredients, and Sam helped mostly with the proportions."

When he glimpsed Suzannah's admiring look and afterglow, his face bore an expression of pride, as if the king had just knighted him.

"Why don't we let Dimmis try it?" Suzannah suggested, cooling her flushed face by fanning her hand.

Zeb reached for another tumbler while Suzannah went to fetch Dimmis from the kitchen.

When Dimmis appeared, Zeb handed her the drink, kissed her and said, "Two down, one to go . . . sweetheart, we're eager to hear what *you* think of my new brew."

Taking a cautious sniff of the beverage, Dimmis said firmly, "If this *tastes* as good as it *smells*, we can sell it this very day!"

THE TWO BARRELS of Zeb's ginger beer rum sold out in two days to Henry Wiggins' crew, who'd arrived shortly after it was first offered. It was such a resounding success that Zeb decided to go back to Boston and arrange for another batch—*twenty* barrels this time. He would leave almost immediately on the *Fortune Two*, since it was preparing to set sail the following day. He promised Henry a barrel from the new batch as the price of his passage—as well as a token of his appreciation for his help early on.

That morning Fanny came for Ainsley, and we loaded ourselves into the wagon—Suzannah and I snuggling in the front seat, while Dimmis and Zeb sat in the back with his trunk.

In route to the wharf, soft whispers of endearment floated up to us from behind. Suzannah poked me meaningfully and smiled, remembering when *our* love was fresh and new. As she gave me a particularly affectionate deep kiss, we were startled apart when Zeb suddenly roared, "Ya know, Jim, I bet we can make more damned money on ten barrels of ginger beer rum, than on all the smuggled tea from England!"

Because he had abruptly broken our kiss, I nodded my reluctant acknowledgement to Zeb, as Suzannah slid her eyes toward mine and suppressed occasional giggles . . . the meaning of which I couldn't quite discern.

Once we arrived and debarked from the wagon, we watched Dimmis' tearful parting as Zeb kissed her several times, and after embracing her to his heart, reluctantly boarded the *Fortune Two*.

As a pair of deck hands muscled Zeb's trunk into the hold, Henry Wiggins came ashore to greet us. After formally kissing each lady's hand, with a gentle nod toward Zeb he inquired of Dimmis, "Do I detect an *attachment* here, my dear lady?"

Dimmis' face turned as red as her hair as she glanced down and softly uttered, "Perhaps."

"No—no *perhaps* about it. I am the *captain*, and my job is to see *all* that happens around me . . . for that's how we stay alive and out of the hands of the British! I am honored Miss Sexton . . . for although Zebulon Hawkes might carry your heart away with him, I will ensure he cares for it well by keeping him out of harm's way."

Turning away, he headed back to the ship and was halfway up the gangway when he stopped suddenly to shout at me. "And *you too*, James Walker," he barked, pointing at the two women beside me, "you must take good care of *both* these precious ladies!"

Saluting my acknowledgement, I replied, "I will, Henry. Safe journey—I'll see you on your return, old friend!"

Henry returned the salute standing at the gunnels as the gangway was removed and the sails unfurled. As *Fortune Two* slowly drifted away, Zeb and Henry remained at the rail until the ship heaved to . . . and then they were gone.

When it was time to leave, Suzannah took Dimmis' hand and sweetly asked, "Shall we have a *private* talk, just the two of us?"

"Indeed," Dimmis replied softly, and without a word to me, with hushed whispers they walked hand in hand up the street toward the tavern—abandoning me, Winnie and the wagon: leaving me to endlessly speculate on what they were discussing.

⌒◎⌒

Winnie and I returned to the barn, and after leaving her with a few apples, I walked toward the house. When I passed the clock shop, now closed, I felt an inexplicable tug upon my heartstrings; so I quietly entered and stood alone in the stillness of a past life.

Looking wistfully at the bare walls and my old workbench, and finally at the dusty shelves, I imagined the scene without the progress of time: my father still in the back room with his depthing tools, and Mother still busy in our kitchen.

My heart ached as I recalled Father's words—even the sound of his voice—when Suzannah came to invite us to Sam's open house; and Mother was there too as he observed us at the bench, teasing about how he kept getting new apprentices, each more beautiful than any he'd had before.

Ah, the reveries of precious days gone by! I closed my eyes and my heart yearned for one more glance, one more word from either of my lost parents. But in return I was mocked by the penetrating silence. Indeed, how ironic—that the clockmaker could not turn back the hands of time—so the return of treasured loved ones could relieve life's terrible burdens. But against that, I was now a changed man . . . a better man with a beautiful wife and daughter. I also have the Ellingwoods, Zeb and Dimmis, and my friends in Walker's Cove and elsewhere. For this I had paid a heavy price; but life is delicate and precious, and such things of beauty and immense value are easily lost . . . unless forever treasured and well cared for. And keeping this in mind, my heart became content, and so I turned to leave.

While standing in the open doorway, I felt comforted by the warmth of the autumn sun as I took one last look . . . ah—this cherished place of my sacred past. And as the precious memories faded into the depths of my heart, I softly whispered, "Thank you, Mother and Father . . . how I *love* you and *miss* you . . . God keep you both . . ." And with a grateful tear, I quietly closed the door.

When I finally returned to the tavern, I found Suzannah and Dimmis serving food and drink to our patrons in the great room. I felt a pang of guilt for tarrying in the clock shop, but it was with a lighter heart and an inner smile that I leapt into the fray, and carried out the heavier trays for the women. As if on cue, a synchronous "thank you" rewarded my newly buoyed spirit.

Maybe it was the crisp chill air or the welcome heat from the fire in the great room, but I noticed that the longer I was tavern-keeper, the more I enjoyed sharing the fall season with our patrons and friends. Undoubtedly, our sense of camaraderie and the quality of our conversation was considerably enhanced by the sight and smells of apple fritters, pumpkin pie and Indian pudding—even without the irresistible aroma of ginger beer rum.

As the busy weeks passed, Dimmis still had no word from Zeb, and I began to wonder if we would ever see a shipment of his highly coveted brew. It seemed like we were missing out on the perfect opportunity to establish it as the new specialty of the house.

During the month of September, we barely had time to even discuss it, let alone write a letter to Zeb. We had no idea where he was, so how could we know where to direct it? As time went on, we all grew increasingly concerned that some misfortune might have befallen him. But we knew all we could do was wait for news and get on with our lives in the meantime.

When I had a spare moment away from the tavern, I spent it with Ainsley. Fanny knew of our eagerness to see her, so she brought her downstairs several times a day so we could play with her. Fanny had become our child's constant companion, so much so that she even cooked Sam's meals in our tavern kitchen, often alongside Suzannah and Dimmis. Fortunately, our attentions to Ainsley freed her at intervals to tend to her cooking without any distractions.

I would occasionally steal an hour or so for one of my favorite pursuits—visiting Richardson's fields with Ainsley. I talked to her there as we explored the riches of nature together. She loved to watch the finches chasing each other across the fading meadows, and the last butterflies flitting lazily among the fall wildflowers. Once, when she discovered a rabbit hiding beneath the thickets, she shrieked with delight, pointing as the animal hopped away from the noisy intruder.

Her infatuation with nature seemed to awaken a special consciousness in her, and I marveled at her facial expressions. Even though she couldn't talk yet, she made all kinds of sounds and gestures that enabled me to interpret her responses to everything around her—although there was no one better at seeing into her heart than her dear mother.

On one such day, as I carried her home from our walk, I wondered what we would do to celebrate the birthdays in October: it would be Suzannah's twenty-third and Ainsley's first—the second double celebration, although this year they would not fall upon a Sunday.

As we passed the shoreline, I noticed some grey driftwood scattered along the beach below, free of bark and beautifully polished from being constantly washed in the waves. Taking Ainsley's hand, we carefully stepped down to search among the dunes for several pieces to burn in our fireplace. Ainsley was so proud to carry her two twigs in "big girl" fashion . . . and thus flushed with enthusiasm, we headed home.

As we passed the old beech tree by the point, I noticed it was nearly bare of leaves. I stopped to examine my inscriptions in the bark, now a little higher than they were, and well scabbed after seven years. It seemed like only last week that I'd carved them with Suzannah at my side. I remembered too, those moments in that same spot when Suzannah was crushed with grief—because she was still childless—and she selflessly suggested that I seek another wife, one who could bear children. I was suddenly overcome with tears of gratitude at that memory—for here I was, holding our next generation in my arms.

Bringing Ainsley closer to my carvings, she touched them curiously with her forefinger. As she did, I kissed my fingers and placed them where her finger was, and said, "Ainsley, never forget this special tree . . . Mama and Papa shared much happiness and many tears beneath its sheltering arms. This makes it safe and sacred to *us*, and may it be so to *you* in times of joy and sorrow . . . for as long as life is . . ." And as we turned toward home, thinking of Suzannah's precious words, I then added, "Papa will show you Walker's Point . . . when you're a little older."

THE FIRE WAS burning brightly that night as the three of us sat in the parlor at tween time. Suzannah had placed a comforter across the floor to play peek-a-boo with Ainsley, while I went over the week's receipts and recorded them in my account book.

"Has Dimmis had *any* word from Zeb?" I asked, reminded of the lost revenue due to the lack of ginger beer rum in our tavern.

"No; and she's quite concerned that the British might have captured him, although she doesn't talk about it much."

"What do *you* think?" I asked hopefully, thinking that perhaps Suzannah's heart feelings had given her an inkling of his fate.

Suzannah looked thoughtful. "I feel he is fine, Jim—although it is not to his credit that he never writes to Dimmis to allay her fears, or express his affection for her. Zeb is clearly not fully a gentleman . . . yet."

"I trust your heart feelings, dear," I said in return, as I inwardly breathed a sigh of relief.

Suzannah rose to select some pieces of driftwood from the batch I'd brought home today. She added them to the fire and almost instantly, vivid multicolored flames burst from the twigs in a fluttering pattern of rainbows, safely contained within the fireplace.

Finished with the accounts, I moved to the rocker, where I sat and enjoyed the spectacle with a sense of contentment. In so many ways, I saw so much of her mother in Ainsley as she cooed, clapped her hands and pointed toward the flames—and then began to giggle in excitement as the colors swooped across the lengths of the driftwood . . . and suddenly, they magically disappeared. Suzannah fed another branch into the fire and the colorful light show resumed—much to Ainsley's delight.

Since our child had become foremost in our hearts and minds, and the tavern preoccupied us the rest of the time, Suzannah and I had little opportunity to pursue our love life. But at this moment I had a strong desire to snuzzle with her together in our rocker.

"It's been a long while, Suzannah," I observed while opening my arms to her, "since we've had any real time for ourselves . . . Ainsley keeps us so beautifully busy, we have few spare moments."

"Being a new papa isn't easy, is it, Jim?" she said, joining me in the rocker.

"No, but I would never have it otherwise . . ." I whispered, kissing her then gently pressing her head to my heart. As we rocked together silently, I stroked her hair, remembering those grand hopes and dreams I had as a youth . . . *all* had come to pass because of Suzannah. Indeed, in the chambers of our hearts we continue gathering memories and life stories, that someday would reveal to Ainsley a most remarkable past. I secretly hoped these would become *her* heart treasures too.

When I noticed that Ainsley had fallen asleep on the comforter, I kissed the top of Suzannah's head and whispered, "Someone is asleep, Suzannah."

Slowly rousing herself from *her* comfortable perch, Suzannah lifted our daughter off the comforter and lovingly tucked her in her cradle.

When she returned to me, we resumed our snuzzling while gently rocking in the chair. After a time, she looked up at me and whispered dreamily, "We have some spare moments now, Jim . . . do you *miss* me?"

"Oh, Suzannah, indeed I do!" I exclaimed, kissing her ardently.

Her lips opened to mine, and the passionate creature I experienced before Ainsley was born, materialized again with an erotic vengeance. Suzannah began to moan and whimper as I caressed her body with my hands and lips. With a sense of urgency, she broke away to step over to the fireplace, where she teasingly removed her clothes—letting them drop slowly to the floor. Never taking her eyes from mine, she stretched herself out naked on the warm comforter. Letting her hair flow gloriously along her side, she slowly fanned it back and forth across her womanhood. I was beside myself with excited desire—and I fully rose to her wiles. Pleased at my anxious response, she leaned upon a pillow, moistened her lips, and finally crooking her finger, in a breathless invitation she softly cooed, "Papa . . . come to mama . . ."

A Christmas Surprise

On October 18th, we went ahead and celebrated the birthdays of my wife and child, despite the fact that our hearts were somewhat heavy since we'd heard no word from Zeb—or Henry either, for that matter.

Suzannah finally decided it was high time to write Fay and her sisters to inquire about their whereabouts, suggesting her family quietly put the word out with the Sons of Liberty that they seemed to be missing. Suzannah mentioned Sam Adams in particular, since he had recently collaborated with Zeb on the first batch of ginger beer rum, and she knew it was likely he would consult him about the second batch.

As we waited on tenterhooks for word from Boston, Dimmis was the most troubled of all by Zeb's absence. So much so that Suzannah devised a strategy to quell her distress by arranging a welcome distraction. Every Saturday evening the two would make music together in the great room, much to the delight of our patrons: Suzannah on her pianoforte, Dimmis playing her violin.

News about our weekly entertainment spread quickly, and Walker's Tavern was soon crammed to the rafters on Saturday evenings. Now the local folk were drawn in not only for the food and drink, but also to enjoy the music, and when the rhythm was lively, a dance as well—particularly when the hot buttered rum flowed freely. As it happened, the crowds provided us with a valuable opportunity . . . to let it be known we were looking for any information on Zebulon Galletin Hawkes, or Henry Wiggins, captain of the *Fortune Two*. By this time, we were desperate for any clue at all.

Suzannah invited Dimmis over to have dinner with us every Sunday afternoon. After the meal, I would play with Ainsley while the women retired to the parlor for a private conversation. Dimmis did not hold back her pain, and Suzannah listened patiently; providing a great comfort to our dear and loyal friend. I often felt that it was her tender ministrations alone that carried Dimmis through each difficult day . . . with still no word from her sweetheart.

Meanwhile, despite our strenuous efforts, neither the townsfolk, or the captain and crew of every vessel that arrived at Walker's Cove, yielded any news of Zeb or Henry. Although Dimmis and I became ever more discouraged, we still held out hope, because Suzannah was still optimistic, as she felt it every day in her heart.

As fall rounded into winter, Suzannah, Dimmis and I discussed seeking another means of obtaining certain essentials . . . in particular, rum, since our supply was dwindling steadily and the tavern couldn't do without it.

One frosty afternoon, as Christmas drew near, I noticed three sailors at one of our tables, tending to their wassail and turkey pie. When I overheard the words "damned tax," I decided to approach them.

"Greetings, fellows," I said cheerfully. "Might I inquire about these 'taxes' you're talking about? I'd welcome *any* news you'd be willing to share."

One fellow with no upper teeth belched, while the other two laughed hysterically at their comrade's blatant rudeness.

Feeling somewhat insulted, I began to turn away, when one took my wrist with a vise-like grip, saying, "Hold *fast*, me young boyo . . . dinna go nowheres. We be from Boston, an' the boyos down 'ere are havin' a wee bit o' trouble, as we sees it."

Pulling out the fourth chair, I sat down with them. "I'm James Walker, the keeper here. I trust you're enjoying your refreshments? When you're done, be sure to have another round—on the house!"

My cordial approach produced immediate results, and as I felt their resistive barrier drop, one of them held up his tumbler. Smiling broadly and arching his eyebrows, he pleasantly said, "'Tis the best stuff since *George* was a gleam in 'is father's eye!"

"Or a *dewdrop* in 'is mum's arse!" one of his mates coarsely added, whereupon they all roared and vigorously pounded the table.

Here was a glimpse of what Dimmis and Suzannah had to bear from some of our more vulgar and vociferous patrons.

The toothless fellow stood, arched his neck upward toward the ceiling and belched—a long, drawn-out musical affair, at which his companions slapped each other on the back in ecstatic glee, and regarded him with an envious respect. The belcher I presumed was the leader of this trio of troglodytes.

I laughed heartily along with them to show I appreciated their ribald humor, before I asked once again, "So, my friends, what of these taxes in Boston?"

"It's the guv'ner, mate, 'e's a tosspot of the first order, an' a pissant to boot!"

"What's happened?" I asked, now listening intently.

"Three ships a sailed inta Boston 'arbor "ey did . . . as tho' they *owned* the bloody place, loaded wi' *tea* 'ey was . . . an nobody wanted to pay the *tax* on it!"

His friend piped in, "Aye, 'e's roight. So this man . . . ah . . . *Adams* . . ."

"*Sam* Adams?" I asked, cutting him off, my heart quickening.

"Aye, or as 'ey say, *Damn* Samuel Adams!"

"Carry on!" I said, holding my breath.

"'Ey 'ad a meetin' in . . . 'ere wuz it? At a *church*, by me soul . . . an' 'ere was *thousands* of 'em there!"

"Aye, and calling themselves the Body o' the People, 'ey did . . . and Adams was the leader . . ."

"So what did they do?" I asked, trying not to sound impatient because these fellows took *turns* telling the story—and ever so *slowly* at that.

"'ey said all the tea goes back to *Georgie*! din 'ey, Mick?"

"'At's ri', boyo John—back she goes!" Mick affirmed.

Mick continued the narrative while the other two drank and picked at their food.

"Ye see, James Walker, 'ere wasn't nobody goin' against the mob— 'twas mob rule! So 'ey ordered the owner, a bloke named Rotch, to beg a pass from the guv'ner to clear the ship for England—an' 'e says *no*. An' so ol' Rotch tells the people the guv'ner wants 'is taxes, so they rose up."

"Rose up?" I echoed.

"Aye . . . they went out ina middle o' the night . . . and *sacked* the ships! Tossed the bloody tea in the 'arbor 'ey did! Three hunnerd boxes an' more, it was!"

"For God's sake!" I exclaimed, shocked by such boldness of action against the monarchy.

Just then, Suzannah, who'd been standing nearby and overheard most of the conversation, came over to the table and addressed Mick, "Who tossed the tea?"

"The bastard Sons did it . . . 'ey surely *did*, miss . . . Sons o' Liberty . . . 'ey dinna want the bloody tea—or the *tax* on it—so they 'ad their *own* tea party!"

At the tail end of his comment, all three sailors laughed and howled, pounding the table, belching and breaking wind.

In the midst of their crude antics, Suzannah leaned over to whisper, "Jim, I think I know where Zeb has been . . ."

THAT NIGHT AFTER we closed the tavern, Suzannah retrieved her sisters' letters and read through them more carefully than she had before; this time with an eye out for the less personal, more political details. It was all there, she said, after she pieced all the bits together. It confirmed the truth of the sailors' account of the events that had recently transpired in Boston. And, in Lydia's most recent letter, which Osgood had delivered that very morning, she mentioned that Fay was to represent poor Francis Rotch, owner of the ship *Dartmouth*, whose cargo had been tossed overboard by the Sons.

From all that she'd learned, Suzannah concluded it was very likely that Sam Adams, Zeb and Henry were involved in this tea-dumping affair, since all three were Sons of Liberty.

After Suzannah tucked Ainsley into bed, I tossed a few logs into the parlor fireplace to warm ourselves while we rocked. Pulling the rocker nearer the fire, I sank down into the soft seat cushion, making myself comfortable while Suzannah, having wrapped herself snugly in a blanket, nestled sweetly in my lap. As I gently rocked, she leaned her head against my chest, staring dreamily into the flames. I stroked her golden brown tresses, and as they glinted and shimmered in the firelight, I realized my dear wife had become the embodiment of loveliness, family, heart and home. Overcome with how fortunate I was, I squeezed her tighter and placed endearing little kisses on her forehead, totally unprepared for the abrupt change to our quiet evening.

A soft, yet urgent tapping suddenly came from our front door. Suzannah looked up at me with an expression of concern.

"What are you feeling?" I asked her, sensing her heart had just felt a jolt.

She answered me with just one word, "Anger . . ."

Suzannah rose to answer the door, and I followed right behind her, in case there was trouble afoot.

When she opened the door, we were surprised to see Dimmis hurry past us into the parlor without a single word of greeting. As she stood shivering before the fire to warm up, she tersely hurled out, "Henry's ship just slid into the harbor, and I have come directly from there."

"In the pitch of night?" I asked, incredulous at the idea he would take such a chance.

"Well, if Henry pulls in here at all, there must be trouble," Suzannah said thoughtfully. "Walker's Cove is his safe haven. The fact that he arrived under the cloak of darkness means there is a grave situation at hand. Have you seen him, Dimmis?"

"No, not yet; but they will tie up very shortly . . . and I suspect Zeb is with him . . . and I'm so angry, I could eat nails and spit out tacks! I do *not* wish him in my presence, Suzannah, until you and I have spoken."

Drawing up another chair, Suzannah motioned Dimmis to sit in the rocker, while I took the kettle from the fire and prepared three cups of extra strong tea with a touch of rum.

Dimmis rocked herself slowly while she drank her tea, and seemed to grow calmer as she did so. Believing that her friend was now reasonably composed, Suzannah went to the kitchen and brought back a few freshly warmed fritters.

Dimmis took one and nibbled at it slowly while she stared mutely into the fire for a time. Finally, she said dolefully, "What shall I say to him?"

"Say what your heart *feels*, Dimmis," Suzannah replied. "But mind *how* you say it . . . often it's not the *words* that hurt, but the *way* they are said. Keep your heart open and listen to him . . ." But before she could continue, she was interrupted by a loud knock at the door.

Dimmis looked up at us, wide-eyed, and Suzannah whispered, "Stay *here* . . . and keep calm as best you can. I shall *not* let this get out of hand."

We hurried to the door, and I opened it to find Henry Wiggins standing before me in the falling snow. Behind him was the anxious chill-reddened face of Zebulon Hawkes.

"Come in, gentlemen—it's been a *long* time!" I said heartily. "We . . . ah . . . have been *expecting* you."

Henry bowed before Suzannah and kissed her hand, saying, "The pleasure is ever mine, Mrs. Walker!"

Zeb shambled in behind him, and brushing the snow off his coat, he sheepishly asked, "You folks seen Dimmis by any chance?"

Suzannah was about to respond, but before she could, Dimmis appeared in the parlor doorway, silhouetted by the firelight within. When he saw her, Zeb stepped forward with his arms outstretched to greet her. But as he approached, she delivered a resounding slap to his cheek that sounded like a pistol shot . . . and then all hell broke loose.

"Well, *God alive!*" shrieked Dimmis, her hands flailing at Zeb's face. While we looked on in stunned but sympathetic silence, she unloaded her frustration at Zeb. "Zebulon Galletin Hawkes! *What* is the *meaning* of your *silence* all these bloody months . . . with never a *word* or by your *leave* to me? Is it *too* damned much to write a *note*, or pass a few words to some drunken sailor that you are *well* and in *one* piece?"

She paused to catch her breath, and then thumped her fists upon his chest as she ranted at him in yet a higher shrill. "*I have been up all night for weeks* at a time, fearing you were *dead . . .* or perhaps lying in some Boston gutter, beaten and robbed—or perhaps even captured and keelhauled by the bloody British!

"I believed you would try and forget at least for a while, your drab and wretched past life of drunkenness and debauchery—and *think*, if that is possible, the way a *woman* thinks! To feel, or at least to *imagine* how a woman *feels*!" Pounding her chest she then shrieked, "To *remember* the woman who waits day and night for *you* . . . with no *word* . . . and no *hope* . . . but what poor Suzannah *feeds* into my aching *heart*."

As the tears streamed down her face, Dimmis looked pleadingly into Zeb's eyes and softly whimpered, "If you are *incapable* of this . . . then reassess, dear sir: which path in your life is the way to virtue!"

Zeb could not look at her for his shame. "Yes, ma'm," he replied softly, shuffling uncomfortably on his feet in the silence between her sobs.

At that moment, Henry broke the tense and hostile atmosphere. "*Perhaps*, ladies and gentlemen, an *explanation* is in order. Shall we retire to the parlor?"

I BROUGHT THE sofa closer to the fire against the chill air, and then carried in another round of hot tea laced with rum. Suzannah and Dimmis settled themselves on the sofa next to each other, and I joined them there after I served the tea. Henry and Zeb sat on a couple of chairs nearby.

After the drinks had partially restored our chastened spirits, Henry rose and standing before Dimmis, he bowed profusely and entered his plea. "You must forgive me, dear lady, for any foul dishonor lies upon *my* head, not that of Zebulon Hawkes!"

He took her hand and kissed it, and while her eyes brimmed with tears, he continued.

"To tear him from your heart would be an unjustifiable cruelty beyond measure for the offense given . . . for I offer myself to you as the responsible culprit." Kissing her hand again, he then resumed his seat and calmly offered, "But please allow me to explain what has transpired."

As Dimmis dabbed at her face with the handkerchief Suzannah offered, she meekly said, "Carry on then—I shall listen."

Suzannah patted Dimmis' hand in approval, and then clasped it gently to lend support.

"Very well then . . . here is the truth of it," Henry declared. "I say this for those in this room and *none* other—for the act is *done* and those perpetrators who performed it do *not* exist," adding emphatically, "*vanished* into the fog of night."

"Like *you* and the *Fortune Two?*" remarked Dimmis with a smirk.

Henry smiled wanly, but said nothing. Instead, he sat down, took up his cup and drank deeply from it before muttering, "I wish this were *straight* rum . . ."

"I could arrange that for you if only I could *ever* get my order in!" I said tersely, letting him know I had been put out by the long-delayed shipment of rum.

Henry nodded his understanding and said, "I presume you have heard of the troubles in Boston?"

"Yes, we have—but only recently," I affirmed.

"Well then, here are the details—we arrived in Boston two days after leaving Walker's Cove. With hard money in hand, Zeb and I paid a visit to Sam Adams. Strange to say, we received a rather chilly reception from Mrs. Adams, who claimed her husband had more important things to do than tending to a couple of fellows with a twenty-keg beer order.

"She ultimately granted us an audience, but only because we told her we were also Sons of Liberty. When she showed us in to Sam, he declined to discuss our order, explaining that the myriad of

Parliamentary Acts were getting much too intrusive on the people's lives and purses. He felt the only way Parliament would listen to its colonies would be through the power of the purse . . . that is to say, the people would make their discontent known by withholding as one body, all tax revenue from England . . . thus commanding attention.

"So, her husband was being asked to *do* something . . . to send a message to the king . . . not as Sam Adams, but as a *Son of Liberty!* Therefore, secrecy was of the highest order.

"Sam explained that sending any letters between the Sons about this plan bordered on insurrection, and hastily explained that as a leader of the Sons, he was up to his neck in danger, and could be hung or shot if his current plans were ever discovered. But when Zeb and I reminded him we *too* were Sons, he recruited us upon the spot—but not before swearing us to *absolute secrecy!*"

He rose and knelt before Dimmis, and bowing his head, he solemnly said, "We *gave* our sacred *oath*, Dimmis, and from that moment on—we ceased to exist for all who knew us—save our fellow Sons." Raising his head he softly continued. "I asked Mrs. Adams to write a letter to the tavern explaining our situation, but Sam forbade it. He said if the letter were ever intercepted, we would all be rounded up and shot like dogs in the street—and Walker's Cove would become a special target of the British."

Henry took Dimmis' free hand—and Suzannah's as well—and looking deep into their eyes, he boldly said, "Yes . . . *we* carried the letters for the Sons, *we* helped draw those thousands of people to the church to protest—aye—and *we* threw that *damned* tea into the *harbor* . . ."

Both women stared at him in stunned disbelief. Then Dimmis rose from the sofa and went over to Zeb, and sat in his lap without a word. She embraced him fervently as she uttered words of regret and endearment. Zeb in turn wrapped his enormous arms around her and cradled her as gently as he would a newborn babe.

But Henry wasn't quite done with his story, and so he pressed on. "Zeb and I are marked men, with prices on our heads. But for one glorious night, we were Indians with painted faces . . . and the powers that be will never know our true identities—for the oath is *sacred* to all Sons."

He then turned to Dimmis and reiterated, "Understand that Zeb was a hero, he offered to *die* for what he believed in . . . and one of the two things he truly believes in, dear lady . . . is *you.*"

Dimmis hugged Zeb once again, kissing him ardently and then nuzzling her cheek into his neck, her blue eyes glittering in the firelight

"Well, Henry," I declared, offering him my hand, "I guess you have been busy . . . but I cannot imagine doing *what!*"

He shook my hand warmly, reassured that his secret was forever safe in our house.

Feeling it was time to change the subject and lighten the atmosphere so fraught with emotion, I reminded the group, "It's Christmas in three days . . ." It was then I noticed Suzannah's absence—until she reappeared from the kitchen a minute later bearing a tray with pumpkin pie, and a bottle of smuggled brandy.

I poured the precious liquor into five crystal glasses, the same ones that had last been used by Fanny, Sam and my parents on that long-ago day . . . during the first Christmas after the Ellingwoods' return to Walker's Cove.

As I handed out the brandy, I toasted Henry and Zeb, "Well done, men! To *God* and our *colonies!*"

Raising his glass and giving Dimmis an affectionate squeeze, Zeb nobly added, "To true friends and *truer* women . . ."

"Aye . . ." Henry agreed, joining Zeb in his toast, "for in *them* . . . lies the true strength of men . . ."

THE RISING STORM

uring that winter of 1774, Henry placed the *Fortune Two* under his first mate's command in order to keep a low profile in the aftermath of the Boston tea party. He and Zeb remained through Christmas, lodging in our guest rooms, sharing stories of their recent adventures, and helping around the tavern.

Zeb was clearly overjoyed to be home again in Walker's Cove with Dimmis. For Christmas, he presented us with twenty-*five* barrels of ginger beer rum *and* ten gallons of Essex rum. For Dimmis there were three new dresses from one of Charleston's finest shops, and a bolt of their best linen.

Henry surprised us all when he gave Suzannah a bag of twenty gold sovereigns as a belated wedding gift. These were courtesy of a Boston tax collector, whose house had been ransacked by "parties unknown." Suzannah accepted them gratefully with heartfelt thanks, delivering a kiss on the cheek of our dashing captain.

On Sundays, I took Suzannah and Ainsley for sleigh rides, exploring every nook and cranny of our town, including our beloved Walker's Point. There, I would tie up Winnie at the old beech tree, and carry Ainsley, all bundled up, to the point. Despite the cold, the three of us would enjoy each other's company as we wiled away the afternoon, playing and exploring under the winter sun. Now that Ainsley could walk and speak a few words, it was ever more thrilling to witness her joyous participation in our lives. It made me feel young again just to share her happiness . . . and the family time we spent together became the highlight of my every day.

AFTER SUZANNAH RECEIVED some disturbing letters from her sisters, the five of us decided to meet over a Sunday dinner to discuss the affairs in Boston, and how they might affect our lives—both personally and with regard to the tavern.

Because of the tea party, and then, in March, the destruction of another shipment of tea from London by Bostonians, Lydia wrote that Hutchinson—the royal governor—was stewing over the considerable loss of revenue. He had asked Fay to represent the case against those responsible, but her husband refused, wanting to thwart the crown's ability to recover damages for the lost tea and the unpaid taxes. When an infuriated Hutchinson "officially assigned" him the case, Fay respectfully declined "the honor," claiming he was "permanently indisposed in the bowels, and thus could not perform at the standard to which the governor had become accustomed." To avoid any further harassment, Fay was seriously considering the idea of quietly withdrawing to Walker's Cove with Lydia—and remaining there indefinitely, but when a royal edict came down to Fay, who felt threatened if he did not comply . . . intestinal fermentation suddenly became a very comforting ally.

Lydia also warned that under no circumstances should Henry and Zeb return to Boston, despite the fact that nobody yet had a clue as to *who* threw the tea in the harbor, save the "wild savages" who could not be identified—even by eyewitnesses. So for the moment, Henry and Zeb were safe from prosecution for participating in that action; but as smugglers, they were still at great risk anywhere around Boston harbor.

While finishing our pumpkin pie and custards, Suzannah read aloud excerpts from Sarah's more recent letter, which focused on the British parliament's enactment of what the patriots had dubbed the Intolerable Acts. These were viewed as punishment for the Boston tea party. Her account made clear that the political and financial cost of these punitive measures on the people of Massachusetts was great.

> *These so-called Intolerable Acts are just what they say they*
> *are . . . among the worst are the Massachusetts Government Act,*

Suzannah lowered the letter as Zeb grumbled, "No God damned,
cob-swiping, piss ant Tory governor is gonna tell *me* what to do! By
God, I'll stuff him down his own damned privy . . . *head first!*"

"*Zeb!*" exclaimed Dimmis, dismayed at his thoughtless lapse into
crudeness.

"Sorry, Dimmis, I *forgot* . . ." he sheepishly replied and resuming
his spoon, quietly ate his custard.

Suzannah continued reading, and as she read, Henry looked as
though butter would not melt in his mouth.

Henry finally jumped to his feet—his neck veins bulging as
though they would explode. Ferociously pounding the table, he
vehemently declared, "This is a damned *outrage* . . . absolutely
intolerable! Boston is a key port of entry—why in God's name will
they punish *all* for the sins of a few? Even the misbegotten Tory

merchants will be ruined! That damned king will cut off his nose to spite his own face!"

Stalking to the fireplace, he nervously paced before it as though to wear a path in the floor. "Such idiocy *befuddles* the imagination!" he fumed, kicking at the flames in frustration. "By God, we are going to South Carolina to trade. To hell with them and their damnable *intolerable acts!*"

Coming back to the table he ordered, "Zeb, get down to the wharf and roust up the crew. We need supplies, and as God is my judge, we're going to get 'em . . . even if I have to *shoot* my way into Charleston harbor!"

Suzannah rose and stood before Henry. "There is a unique opportunity here, Henry, not only for merchants like us, but for the colonies as well."

His expression softened as he looked down at her. "What do you mean by *that*, my dear lady?"

Sliding her eyes to the table, Suzannah confidently replied, "Have a seat and I shall explain myself, Captain."

I poured a fresh tumbler of buttered rum for Henry, who sat and sipped—quieted at last. As Suzannah began, he listened while staring mournfully into the fire.

"You see, Henry, a closed harbor will force dramatic price increases for essential goods. We could take Jens' lumber and our hard money, and exchange them in South Carolina for goods that Boston needs. Using Walker's Cove as our base, we could arrange to have Wheezer Hutchinson transport them to certain relay points just *outside* of Boston. They will never be looking for wagons from the north and west, Henry . . . they will be looking for *ships from the east!*"

As she touched Henry's arm sympathetically, she added, "It will be an arduous task to accomplish, but what is *not* arduous these days?"

Looking up, Henry smiled at Suzannah and then expanded on her idea. "And I can make new contacts in Charleston, opening up new avenues of commerce for the *fine* tavern at Walker's Cove!" Rubbing his chin with his fingers, he then mused, "By Boston harbor being closed to merchant shipping, Wheezer Hutchinson will likely see his earnings increase tenfold. Now, who will tell *him* that?"

"*I* will!" Suzannah replied, "and my father can build him the heavy wagons to haul the stores—and luckily, we have a wheelwright living here, Noah Blake. There will be hard money and hard goods all around, and much more *of* it!"

"How much money do you think you can make, Suzannah?" I asked, a little concerned about her sudden flash of avarice.

"It's *not* about the money, Jim—" she cried, "it's about the ability to trade freely, without the bullying restraints of the British!" Looking deadly serious she then added, "Any time I can poke the king in the eye through the power of the purse, I certainly intend to *do* so!"

"Damned well said, young lady!" Henry bellowed, standing to warmly embrace her shoulders. "You'll make one hell of a *daughter* of liberty! Why, if we had a hundred women who thought as you do, we could send the king's troops back to England without further ado!"

Just at that moment Dimmis strolled in from the kitchen, and leaning upon the doorframe, she crossed her arms and boldly stated, "Now you need only ninety *eight* . . ."

Suzannah, enthused by Dimmis' resolve, flashed her beautiful smile at Henry, triumphantly crossed her own arms, and perkily nodded . . . and although she was serious, she was *so* adorable I couldn't wait to hug her.

THE NEXT STEP was to enlist the help of Sam, Wheezer and Noah Blake in our plan, so we arranged a gathering a few nights later at the tavern. After some discussion, it was agreed that Sam and Noah would build three heavy freight wagons in time for Henry's first return voyage from South Carolina. Wheezer would haul the smuggled goods from Walker's Cove to a Son of Liberty headquarters—located just outside Roxbury, where they would be "quietly distributed" among the local merchants.

In a week's time, Henry had the *Fortune Two* completely outfitted and ready to sail. Two days later, her hold was replete with
lumber from Jens' sawmill. In Henry's cabin a small chest of hard
money resided that included Suzannah's gold and Dimmis' Spanish
silver.

On the night before departure, we settled up our shares. Then
Suzannah reviewed her "secret code" with Henry, a system she'd
carefully worked out for them to use for all their correspondence—
in case by chance it fell into the wrong hands.

The following day, the five of us rode to the wharf and bid
Henry and Zeb a fond farewell before the *Fortune Two* pulled away.
The leave-taking was an especially difficult and tearful one for
Dimmis—and we noticed that Zeb seemed to fight back some tears
of his own.

MAY WAS A favorite month for Suzannah and me. It was never hot,
never cold, but mostly sunny and breezy. While Dimmis and Fanny
minded Ainsley and the tavern, we walked to the point nearly every
evening . . . just to talk, cuddle and watch the sunsets.

After nine years of knowing her and nearly five years of marriage, I was more in love with Suzannah than ever before. Still
a wildly passionate and uninhibited lover, she was also a nurturing and loving mother. She always found the time and energy for
"heart matters" that pertained to *all* of us. She was also the shrewd
proprietress of our tavern, possessed of a seemingly endless capacity
for patience *and* stamina. More than anything or anyone else, she
made our good life possible.

Never had I realized how thankless, yet so vital a woman's role
was in making a home a *complete* home. As such, I placed Suzannah above all else in my life . . . until our baby was born. Yet
through Ainsley, our love never diminished or faded, but matured
and deepened.

Indeed, as the world around us seemed ever more in the grip of
turmoil and uncertainty, because of Suzannah's gentle and faithful
presence, our kindred souls blended firmly together . . . and through

her wonderful sensual fantasies, we found comfort and relief from life's endless stress.

As the summer months approached, the news from Boston grew more distressing. It seemed that Parliament and the governor were fiercely determined to break the people and their collective will. In one letter, Katharine wrote of the steady emergence of a dark spirit of rebellion that these heinous actions inspired.

> *There is something mighty strange about the anger that readily surfaces when our liberties are taken away . . . A brooding hatred of the King's despicable acts wells up in the hearts of the people, who are so contemptuously hurled aside in such a thoughtless manner . . .*

After I read Lydia's heartbreaking account of how General Thomas Gage, the commander of British forces in the colonies, had replaced the hapless Hutchinson as royal governor, I realized it meant that for all intents and purposes, martial law had been imposed on the people of Boston. Gage, she said, showed a ". . . total disrespect for God's laws, and a plainly arrogant reproach for the truth of English common law." Poor Fay had to spend weeks on end in court, condemning the injustice and the shabby treatment his clients received from the crown—all to no avail.

I wondered why the king and his minions were so heartbreakingly pig headed. Why would they *not* listen to what their former countrymen were attempting to say? But then again, considering the monarchy's callous apathy, prejudice, and antagonism toward its colonies, it seemed clear that they didn't *want* to listen.

My heart ached for Suzannah and her sisters, and trying to shine a ray of hope on their bitter turmoil . . . I suggested that her sisters and their husbands—like her parents—might return to their old home in Walker's Cove . . . and live freely in peace.

Early in November, Osgood Lovejoy made Dimmis' day brighter when he brought her a letter from Zeb. After reading it, she told Suzannah and me that it contained mostly amorous sentiments and little about his present activities—but mentioned that he'd closed with the curious phrase, "A golden future awaits us all . . ."

Soon thereafter, Suzannah received a letter from Henry—the first coded letter so far, which signaled it was probably of significance to our new trading arrangement. Suzannah translated the code aloud so I could record the actual message on a sheet of paper. It yielded the following revelation.

In early fall, the Continental Congress—the new governing body of the colonies comprised of delegates from each—had convened in Philadelphia to affirm the rights of the colonists to life, liberty and property. It challenged the legitimacy of the crown's Intolerable Acts, and petitioned the king to that effect. The body also created the Continental Association for the purpose of enforcing a boycott on British goods if the king did not repeal them. Henry noted that Sam Adams and the Sons of Liberty were actively promoting the ban through the Committees of Correspondence in every town throughout the colonies.

Suzannah paused to look up at me and exclaim, "Jim, we can make a fortune! We have a ship—the *Fortune Two*—and if her hold is overflowing with stocks of banned goods, Wheezer can haul them all to Roxbury in the freight wagons . . . think of the profits *everyone* can make!"

I didn't have to think about it to know she was right. In fact, I secretly hoped that Zeb and Henry would load up on the most desirable essential goods while they were in South Carolina. If there was a conflict to come, and it looked ever more likely, I wanted us to be awash in hard money, so we would want for nothing and be secure.

Finally, Suzannah reached the end of Henry's message, where his last coded words were, "Home for Christmas."

It was nearly Christmas again—and much snow had fallen in plenty of time for the occasion. I wondered if Zeb and Henry would return in time to celebrate the holiday with us. Suzannah had invited her parents and Dimmis for Christmas dinner, and if the *Fortune Two* arrived by then, the more, the merrier.

I wondered what the king would do to punish the colonies for the boycott. It was still early on, yet visiting ships were already fewer and nights in the tavern quieter. It was difficult to learn more about what had transpired since Henry's coded missive. Fewer ships meant that letters posted from Boston took much longer to arrive—awaiting a kind brave soul to carry them on what were now hazardous journeys. Now that letters came to Walker's Cove only sporadically from volunteers on foot or horseback, it seemed like the world as we knew it . . . was coming to a halt.

When Eben Thatcher complained to Suzannah that supplies were becoming difficult to obtain, she implemented a voluntary policy of frugality when using what were now considered limited resources. Since hard money had practically disappeared, she bartered with our customers for their food and drink.

Finally, when necessities were so scarce that it had become the talk of the town, one evening, Suzannah convened a meeting at our home. She invited Rhoda, Mildred, Fanny and several other women of her close acquaintance. That night, I heard them discuss how they might do without certain essential items in their homes and kitchens.

Suzannah's answer was calm and reassuring. "Ladies, you would be *amazed* at what you can do without if you don't *have* it"; she then took their hands in a comforting embrace and softly added, "We will *share* what we have to make do—and we'll get through this *together*."

I was struck with a feeling of pride as I heard my sweet wife offer comfort and guidance to her friends. With her nimble mind, goodwill and courage, she often found simple solutions to what seemed like limitless challenges . . . and because she shared her resourcefulness with our entire village—she became more admired than ever.

☙◉❧

ONCE THE WINTER gales had set in with exceptional violence, I had to haul firewood twice a day for our tavern kitchen. On particularly gloomy days, a dense heavy rain accompanied by a thick fog saturated the frozen snow. These sloppy conditions chilled my bones worse than any snowstorm.

One such morning shortly before Christmas day, as I returned with a new load of wood, I heard an unexpected commotion in our great room, as though a large group of sailors had suddenly arrived and settled at the tables.

When I poked my head in to see who was there, I was astonished to find Henry, Zeb, Dimmis and Suzannah, seated comfortably together at a table before the crackling fireplace. Everyone's tumblers were full, and in the center of the table was a heaping plate of freshly smoked eel.

Clapping my hands in delight, I asked, "Might the *keeper* join this happy gathering?"

Henry and Zeb stood, and I embraced each of them for a long moment. To have my dear friends safe at home for Christmas, sitting at my table with plentiful food and drink, was a great blessing to me . . . and it lightened my mood considerably.

"So, Jim, what have you been doing these many months?" Zeb asked, casually refilling his tumbler with buttered rum.

"Good heavens, Zeb!" crowed Henry, with a humorous twinkle in his eye. "I would venture he hasn't been as busy as *we* have!"

"Where's your crew, Henry?" I asked, noting that none were present.

"Back in South Carolina," Henry said with sudden seriousness, "which brings me to my plans for the future—as I see them."

"Carry on, Henry—but first, please have some," I said, indicating the plate of eel. I speared a large piece and chewed it, savoring the smoky taste, while Suzannah placed a tumbler of buttered rum before me.

Waving away the offer of eel, Henry declared, "With all due respect to Suzannah, I don't relish touching anything that is . . . ah . . . *serpentine* in nature."

Suzannah nodded her understanding, saying, "Perhaps some nice warm scrapple instead, Henry? It's perfect on a day such as this one!"

"Now *that* sounds far more appealing! Thank you, dear lady."

Henry stood and bowed to Suzannah as she went off to get the scrapple. As Henry seated himself once again, his face suddenly darkened with a rising anger. Placing his hands flat upon the table before him, he drummed his fingers and then sternly announced, "Jim, a firestorm is rising! Soon—very soon, my dear friend—it shall be upon us . . . and we'll be awash in blood, heartbreak and agonies yet unimagined!"

I stopped chewing and swallowed my eel—I wanted no more, for my appetite had just been stolen.

"We are at the brink of conflict with our own mother country. It's *inevitable*, Jim! We need to wrest control of the colonies from the hands of Parliament—*and* the king!"

"My God, man!" I cried out in disbelief. "Are you out of your mind?"

With a cold eye and a rigid stare, Henry hissed, "Let me tell you what's been going on—since in your sequestered little world of Walker's Cove, you don't have the *faintest* notion of the dangers that are imminent. This is a storm that will swallow you whole. If you don't prepare for it, James Walker, you and yours will surely perish! Ignore my words at your own damned peril, but please . . . think of your wife and daughter!"

I could only sit there in stunned silence.

As Suzannah placed a bowl of hot scrapple before Henry and handed him a spoon, she remarked, "It all sounds very serious, Henry . . . I couldn't help but overhear you from the kitchen."

"Please sit down and listen to me, my dear Suzannah. What I'm telling all of you will have a profound effect upon our lives, and we shall *never* be the same . . ."

Suzannah sat quietly as Zeb raised his eyebrows and nodded toward Henry's bowl. "Are you gonna *eat* that scrapple or what?" he said, looking hopeful.

"*Zebulon Hawkes!*" cried Dimmis in dismay, "How can you possibly think of your *stomach* at a time like *this?*"

Henry smiled cordially, and pushing the bowl toward Zeb, simply said, "Waste not . . . *want* not."

As he picked up the spoon, Zeb added, "Listen, folks . . . there will soon come a time when we will sorely regret not eating this scrapple—because we won't have *anything* to eat."

At that moment, I had no idea how prophetic Zeb's words would become.

As Zeb relished his scrapple, Henry rose and paced restlessly before the enormous fireplace—his chin sunken on his chest and his hands clasped behind his back. His attitude and demeanor suggested that of a general, greatly overburdened with responsibility; and turning such that his figure was darkly silhouetted against the walls, he began sharing his thoughts.

"When we were holed up in South Carolina, I found trade there quite favorable indeed, and we have all profited quite handsomely," he uttered calmly enough. "I will disclose those details later. I happened to meet a man there of considerable wealth, talent and vigor in a tavern of some repute. He knew far more than the average fellow, particularly about the doings of the British troops, and where those doings are taking place—and by whom.

"As a fellow trader, captain of his own vessel and owner of several more, we were in instant agreement over the cause of free trade without royal entanglements—like the taxes and regulations imposed that restrict every move we make. We also agreed that earning a copper these days through such enterprises as ours is nigh on impossible without smuggling. Keeping ahead of these tiresome taxes, port restrictions and choking regulations has—ah—accelerated our *nighttime* proclivities . . . shall we say."

"Damned right on *that* one!" grumbled Zeb with his spoon in midair. Pointing it toward Henry, he added, "This man keeps me *awake* all night . . . thinks I'm some damned sailor and gives me hell's own time, too! By God, if I was meant to stay up all night, He'd a made me a damned owl!"

"*Indeed!*" Henry replied quite sharply, "but at least an *owl* can readily see his opportunities at night, and silently strike at will to maximize his gains. However, let us not spoil our night with the unfortunate details of your languishing skills as a third watch sailor . . . so let's focus upon what's to come.

Henry stopped pacing and returned to his seat. Before resuming his narrative, he gave Zeb a fond pat on the back. "Sorry, my boy, I meant no disrespect in remarking on your abilities aboard ship; for a landlubber you do just fine . . . all things considered."

"None taken," Zeb replied, finishing the last of his scrapple and then holding the bowl up for more.

While Suzannah left for the kitchen to refill it, Henry remained silent, waiting for her to return. When she did, he hunched up to the table and waved us closer. We all listened intently as he spoke in nearly a whisper that could barely be heard above the moaning gales. Outside, the storm had worsened, and the rain fell heavily.

"As I was saying, this gentleman and I shared information, supplementing each other's knowledge and experience to gain a more complete picture—and this is what we believe will come. We all know the colonies have been long suffering with fear and oppression under the rule of His Majesty's governors, particularly Massachusetts. As you *also* know, it was just a few years ago that British soldiers bespattered the streets of Boston with our countrymen's brains before the customhouse . . ." And looking at Suzannah he added pointedly, "Ah . . .for want of *words*, I believe."

"Before that, there were uprisings between the Loyalists and those who were *not* loyal. Why, my dear Suzannah, your own father was such a victim . . . as your sisters are now."

She quietly nodded her assent.

"Similar incidents took place all over the colonies in general, but *particularly* in the northeast, fueled by the various punitive measures that Parliament, in their jangled discordant wisdom, thrust upon us! Their lofty hope was to recover some measure of control over colonial trade by edicts from the crown. They wanted their pound of flesh, and intended to take it from the top of our hard-earned money pile. But it wasn't rightfully theirs and never could be . . . no matter how many damned, worthless, restrictive acts they threw at us . . . until we say—enough is *enough*!

"So we *strike*, to assert our freedom—and they strike back! And so we strike *again*, and *again* . . . like the serpent I'm so loath to touch! Our problem is that we are not striking back *collectively*!

There are thirteen colonies, each one wrestling with their own issues involving the crown; but think what would happen if the colonies *united* to become one—and so strike with a much *greater* poison?"

"War . . ." Suzannah said, lowering her head onto her folded hands. "I have *foreseen* it!" She tried to choke back tears as she hid her face, while Dimmis embraced her and took her hand.

"She *has* foreseen it, Henry!" I confirmed, searching his face for any shred of redeeming hope. "The entire tavern heard her, including *you*! That was the day her sister wrote of the massacre in Boston."

"Indeed!" Henry said softly. "I *was* there and she *did* foresee it! I was on the *Palladium* then." Setting his tumbler down, he added, "But the good news is that this process of unification has already begun in the form of the new congress and their Continental Association—as I wrote you in my coded letter.

"During the trade bans we have now, guidelines were established for a strict but voluntary policy among merchants, ship owners and agents abroad . . . so that there may be no profiteering from the collective misery of our people. Local committees of inspection will monitor trade to ensure compliance to these self-imposed restrictions. Those who violate that pledge will receive a friendly visit from the Sons of Liberty—to *remind* them of their obligation."

"There go our freight wagons." Suzannah said with a sigh of resignation.

"And there go our profits . . ." Zeb groaned, as he finished up his second helping of scrapple.

As the fire snapped and hissed from the rain falling through the chimney, I felt my spirits fall at the combined effect of Henry's pronouncements and Suzannah's evident sorrow. Finally, I summoned the courage to broach the question the others were *thinking*, but dared not ask. "What will be the final consequence if the colonies go to war with England?"

Henry's expression reflected traces of doubt and confusion, but there was nothing of either when after a pause, he answered in a brittle voice, "Liberty . . . or Death . . ."

enry's assessment left us stunned, as if we all had awak-ened from the same ghastly nightmare. Suzannah ex-cused herself to bring us hot mulled cider from the kitchen, while I, having a profound dislike for Henry's Death option, soberly commented, "I remain hopeful for Liberty, as I have seen enough death in my life."

Zeb cleared his throat and bluntly added, "Well, Jim, I prefer *liberty* also . . . hell, I better sit closer to that parlor fire with Dimmis . . . *especially* if they'll take away my liberty to do so!"

Suzannah brought a tray of mugs into the parlor, steaming with her aromatic mulled cider, and following her, we each took one and sat down to contemplate our fate.

Dimmis and Zeb settled into the smaller sofa, sitting so close together they were practically one. Henry sat in the rocker, gliding back and forth, staring into his mug, deeply immersed in thought.

I sat on the other sofa, and there, Suzannah joined me, cuddling beneath my arm and leaning into me with more urgency than usual. Despite holding her tightly to my side, I was haunted by an impen-etrable fear—that war would be upon us before we could brace for it. And thus we all remained amid an uncomfortable silence . . . a silence broken only by the crackling logs and the pensive sipping of mulled cider.

Suzannah repeatedly wrapped her hair twixt her fingers, and nervously releasing it, finally broke the echoes of the wailing winds, "So what are we to *do*, Henry?"

Stopping the rocker, Henry rose to once again pace before the fire. "I believe we should hold tight until more information is at hand. There is little that vindicates the dishonor foisted upon the colonies at the moment, other than what the Sons have personally accomplished. But there is *more* that can be done toward that end . . . and to achieve our liberty in the process. Meanwhile, sinister forces are still at work—especially in Boston."

Henry suddenly stomped his boot on the floor before the fire, "*Damn* it to hell, we need so much . . . to be successful in any enterprise against these . . . these . . . *incidents!*"

"*Incidents!*" exploded Zeb, as he stood up, nearly toppling Dimmis to the floor. "I guess they sure in hell *are* incidents . . . *murdering* the citizens in the streets, *taxing* everything in sight, *seizing* our ships and cargo, *threatening* our womenfolk, and bringing their damned, pigeon toed, parrot brained generals into Boston . . . to *take over* everybody's life . . . by boarding their misbegotten troops in private *homes! I'll* say they're incidents, by God!"

Breathing heavily after his comments, Zeb reached for his rum and drank deeply.

Henry, calm as could be, thoughtfully quipped, "We will need a *navy*, Zeb."

Choking on his rum, Zeb whooped and coughed as he sputtered out, "Well . . . *Hell's* own *kitchen*, Henry, I'll just damn well reach into my *pocket* . . . and pull one *out* for you . . . or better *yet*, they grow on *trees* don't they? By God, let's just go into this *nice* winter rainstorm . . . and *pick* us a mighty *fine* one! *Nothin'* but the *best* for *us!*"

Either not seeing Zeb's sarcasm or choosing to ignore it, Henry continued his thinking aloud. "*Ah*, my good friend, although I do indeed appreciate your sentiments of being hearty for our cause, we must however, begin at the *beginning!* That means a *navy* that will need men, foodstuffs, ordinance and vessels . . . indeed . . . *vessels!*

Then Henry slowly turned toward us and raising one finger, he triumphantly announced, "*We* have one such vessel—the *Fortune Two*—and I know where to find three more."

Henry now began to pace, unleashing his thoughts in rapid succession. "A good navy is an absolute necessity for the colonies, because the British control all lines of communication by sea—the absence of letters from Suzannah's sisters is ample proof of that! And with their substantial armada, they can block every port along the eastern coast and use them to land many more troops, crushing us before we even begin to rally our own forces!"

He stopped momentarily and then his voice rang out with excitement. "We must start by seeking a few good men—men of character, men of business, whose minds are particularly sharp. Men who possess the motivation and discipline to drive themselves *and* lead their men into war, no matter how overwhelming the odds are against them. For the good of our great and noble cause, such men as I describe will ensure our victory. And I happen to know a man who would meet the challenge with spirited enthusiasm!"

With a guffaw of cynicism, Zeb asked, "And pray tell, who in hell would *that* be?"

Taking up his mug of cider, Henry raised it toward us and pleasantly announced, "We need not go to hell, Zeb. We need only have a little chat with my new friend, Mr. Benedict Arnold, the gentleman I met at the tavern in South Carolina."

Having had his say, Henry resumed his seat in the rocker. "My dear Zebulon," he said, "whatever became of that special bottle I brought with me here?"

"I left it in the kitchen," Zeb volunteered. "I thought we would try it tonight and see if it's a worthy blend."

"Let's do that!" Henry replied, rubbing his hands together vigorously in anticipation. "In view of recent developments, perhaps we could all use something to comfort our restless souls."

Zeb fetched the bottle and brought it into the parlor; he slowly worked the wax and cork out of the top, and then sniffed loudly at the opening. When the intensity of the effluvium assailed his unsuspecting nostrils, he took a step back. "Damn!" he exclaimed, holding the dark brown bottle at arm's length. "It smells like burnt feathers and whale oil . . ."

When he poured a small amount into his empty tumbler, the liquid was as clear as water, and not as appealing to the eye as the rich amber liquid we were expecting. After sipping it skeptically,

Zeb smacked his lips and declared, "Jim, you *gotta* try this! I never tasted the like in my life, and I've been drinking a *long* time."

After he poured some into my waiting tumbler, I noticed an unusually strong aroma. It had a very pleasant taste, and because of the beverage's heavy viscosity, it's benign taste lingered for some time after it was swallowed. Because of its gentle nature, I thought it would be enjoyable to Suzannah and Dimmis.

Zeb then poured some for Dimmis, Suzannah and Henry.

Feeling positively aglow, I asked Henry, "Where did you get it?"

"From a merchant in South Carolina who told me it originated in the hills of ancient Rome . . . and that it has been distilled there for *centuries*. Unique, is it not?"

Sipping slowly from her tumbler, her eyes bright with intoxication, Suzannah murmured, "Indeed!"

During the ensuing hours our mood mellowed as we sipped and savored our drinks, and engaged in small talk. But when I rose to throw more logs on the fire, I was struck by a sudden bout of dizziness that sent my head spinning, followed by a sudden wave of unsteadiness. As I leaned heavily against the wall, I fell into a dismal state of lassitude, accompanied by a dry mouth, a swollen tongue and an insatiable thirst. The taste and aroma of the liquor still penetrated my senses, lingering like a toxic perfume—and then my vision blurred.

Suzannah rose to take my arm in assistance, although she too was unsteady on her feet. Leaning on her as lightly as I could, we stumbled back to the sofa.

I tried to speak, but my words emerged in an incoherent jumble.

Dimmis leaned toward me to gently ask, "Why, James Walker, are you *drunk?*"

"Perhapsh . . . a little . . ." was all I could manage.

"*Fascinating* . . ." she uttered. Then she turned to Suzannah. "Are *you* drunk too?"

"No," she replied sweetly, and holding tightly to my arm and looking into my eyes, she added, "But I *am* tipsy . . . and *very* ready!"

When Henry tried to stand, he stumbled over his feet and crashed into the fireplace tools, sending them clattering in all directions. "Why *Henry*, you *too* are drunk?" Dimmis inquired. His wobbly knees refused to support his weight, and so he collapsed on the floor in a rumpled heap, grasping feebly at the air for support.

Suzannah began to laugh. Her little girl laugh was infectious, and soon we were all laughing with her until tears of mirth rolled down our cheeks.

Poor Henry remained on the floor, apparently resigned to stay there for the time being, as he struggled to form a sentence: "I beliebe I am . . . incapa . . . incapackateted . . . bloody Hell, Wig-gish . . .Wigginsh is bloody *drunk* . . . 'e ish!" A few moments later he was snoring noisily.

Dimmis got up to place a cushion beneath his head, and retrieved a blanket from the closet to cover him against the cold.

Deciding that the meeting was over, Suzannah's hands were now probing around the area of my belt, which had the effect of raising my interest in her intentions—and I felt the soporific effect of the liquor begin to fade.

Bidding Dimmis and Zeb goodnight, we stood up unsteadily and staggered up the stairs together to our chamber. There, Suzannah immediately removed our clothes and pulled me urgently onto the bed. Despite having no fire in our chamber fireplace, something in that bottle had set *her* on fire!

She was on top of me in an instant, and had me ready in a heartbeat. No matter how often I warned her that our guests would overhear our shrieks and moans, she persisted with her fabu-lous advances. She wanted the freedom to completely let go, she explained, which led to the noisiest, most reckless and thrilling night of our entire married life . . . and I would never forget it—or the elixir that ignited her desires with such a passionate urgency.

THE RAYS OF the early morning sun entered our chamber window, crept along the width of the floor and stole into my bed. It nes-tled on my pillow and stroked me with its warmth, so that still half-asleep and half-sober, I thought it was Suzannah petting me. When I noticed the empty pillow beside me, I knew she had already risen.

As I recalled our exhilarating—and exhausting—night of unbridled passion, I wondered how she had managed to rise so early, and I was curious to see how she was faring after our nocturnal deviltries. Stepping cautiously down the stairs, I heard snippets of conversation coming from the kitchen. I realized it was Sam and Suzannah and Dimmis speaking in low tones.

When I entered, Suzannah turned to me and said, "Please keep your voice down, Jim. The *boys* are still sleeping."

Dimmis nodded toward the parlor where I saw Henry and Zeb, each asleep on one of the sofas.

As I sat down next to Suzannah, she gave me an especially warm and lingering kiss. Dimmis placed a hot loaf of cinnamon bread before me, and a hot cup of spiced cider to ward off the morning chill.

Noticing the bottle of Roman elixir on the table, I picked it up to check its contents. It was empty. Because every muscle in my body ached, I had a profound respect for the now vanished liquid, and concluded from Suzannah's extraordinary display of passion, that the tales of ancient Roman orgies were perhaps true—especially if *this* spirituous nectar was involved.

"Potent little *drink* was it not?" Dimmis remarked with a blush . . . and I knew that she'd overheard the sounds of our lovemaking.

Before I could utter a word, Suzannah beamed a knowing smile at me and joyously replied, "Yes—and *very* pleasing!" She then gustily exhaled the word "*Ten!*" to emphasize her satisfaction. I didn't know whether she was referring to the liquor's quality, or counting her "trips to the heights" from last night.

Sam, now eyeing the bottle with great interest innocently asked, "Ten *what*? Perhaps Fanny and I should try this fabulous spirit!"

Choking on my cider, as it ran up my nasal passages and out my nostrils, I frantically jumped for a kitchen towel to aid my distress . . . and laugh at the results, should Fanny ever react the same way Suzannah did.

Resuming my seat, Suzannah joyfully slid her eyes aloft and firmly declared, "That was the *best* drink I've ever had, and after it came the best *night* of my marriage!"

"Really?" Sam asked skeptically, lifting the empty bottle and sniffing suspiciously at the top. "I would think the best night of your marriage was your wedding night."

I choked on the cinnamon bread at his innocent remark, and thus coughing up cider and bread, I stumbled and staggered off into the parlor to hide my embarrassment. As I did so, I heard Sam ask Suzannah, "I wonder what's *wrong* with your husband?"

Through watery eyes of laughter, Suzannah kissed her father's cheek and sweetly replied, "Absolutely nothing, Father . . . my husband is *perfectly* healthy!"

MY NOISY ENTRANCE into the parlor woke Henry and Zeb. After looking around groggily to remind themselves of where they were, the two managed to stand up without help and shambled into the kitchen.

After they seated themselves, Dimmis said to them cheerfully, "Good *morning*, gentlemen—and how are we feeling this morning?" Then she gave each a plate and placed a large platter with ham, loaves of cinnamon bread and a tub of butter on the table.

Henry, indicating the bottle on the table cautiously replied, "Very well, my dear lady . . . *remarkably* well, considering the potency of that most dangerous spirit." He then picked it up, sniffed at the opening and declared, "I believe henceforth we need to treat this Roman elixir with the respect it deserves—for it possesses latent qualities that might . . . ah . . . under the proper circumstances with appropriate company of course, produce results that are . . . shall we say . . . quite startling!"

A female voice murmured, "*I'll* say!"

Nobody was certain as to whose voice it was, but having witnessed its libidinous effects, the meaning was unmistakable.

Zeb then agreed. "That's hot stuff! I drank a mere half pint of it, and I dimly recollect doing something under its influence that I'd never have done sober!"

I'll never utter another word on the matter—but despite not being in full possession of my faculties right then, I could *swear* it was Dimmis' voice I heard and *not* Suzannah's!

"And how may I serve you *today?*" asked Dimmis, flashing a mischievous smirk at Zeb.

"Oh . . . just be yourself, my dear—but you certainly know how to liven up my otherwise drab existence," he replied. As she slipped a mug of spiced cider into his hands and placed another into in Henry's, Zeb smiled up at his benefactress and affectionately patted her backside.

After a slightly awkward silence, especially on Sam's part, Suzannah deftly turned the conversation to the previous night's discussion.

"Henry, what about the gentleman you spoke of last night . . . Benedict Arnold? I was telling Father what you said, and he was curious to hear more about this person you want to ally yourself with."

After dabbing his lips with his napkin, Henry enthusiastically said, "I've been following his activities with considerable interest since we met. He is a masterful merchant sea captain and possesses a keen mind of the highest order. His agents are numerous and splendidly organized, as is Arnold himself. He is a man of remarkable clarity, ability and discretion, and can turn a common piece of eight into a gold sovereign in short order. In other words, he is someone of considerable ingenuity from whom I can definitely learn a lesson or two."

After drawing out his pipe, he stuffed it with tobacco as he continued. "He paces about through life with a restless fever of suppressed energy . . . a man who does not scuttle about, but presses directly toward his goals with a lucid methodology that seems to yield bountiful results, each and . . . ."

He was interrupted in midsentence by a knock at the door. When I opened it, Osgood Lovejoy stood before me with a letter— for Henry! I invited him in, gave him a copper and offered him some breakfast, which he gratefully accepted.

Meanwhile, Henry lit his pipe, opened his letter and read it to himself, as the rest of us chatted with Osgood.

"Hear this, hear *this!*" exclaimed Henry, and we all became silent as he read aloud:

To Captain Wiggins, master, Fortune Two:

As I make no doubt in your being hearty in the cause to free commerce from the oppressive burdens now imposed by the King, I should take it as a particular favor if you would have the goodness to call upon me as soon as convenience permits at the tavern of our first meeting.

If, dear sir, lingering doubts persist as to the viability of free trade at sea, might I suggest you suffer not from the quaintest delusions, as your sentiment does you credit.

As this must be left in the competent hands of men whose affairs depend upon ships at sea, I trust you will keep this in strictest confidence, as I am your humble servant,

B. Arnold.

Henry lowered the letter and placed it in the center of the table for all to see.

"We would be rich if I had his foresight!" Henry declared. He smiled and patted my shoulder, adding, "It must be this tavern, Jim. No sooner than one speaks of Providence . . . and she comes calling. No sooner than we utter Arnold's *name*, and he wishes to share his vision!"

In response, I merely looked over at Suzannah and smiled proudly.

Henry stood and addressed Zeb. "Will you accompany me back to South Carolina? I believe we have a meeting to attend."

Zeb glanced at Dimmis, who quickly nodded her assent.

"Good!" crowed Henry. Then, after resuming his seat and his pipe, with an air of confidence he tapped the letter on the table and said, "Arnold has certainly started something here, though clubbing the ship owners into believing it will be pretty wearing. But if anyone can do it, Benedict Arnold can!"

THE DRUMS OF WAR

After Christmas, Henry and Zeb left for South Carolina to meet with Benedict Arnold, fortunate to miss the frigid weather that soon enveloped us. As usual, our tavern became the gathering place for our townsfolk, wherein before our warm fire, they sought a few of life's little pleasures: companionship, a pint, and piping hot food served fresh from our kitchen.

Sometimes, when Suzannah could be spared from her usual chores, she would play the pianoforte softly in the background—while our patrons sat on either side of the fire: some with pipes in hand, others with eyes half-closed, discoursing upon their favorite subjects amid large blue clouds of tobacco smoke.

But lately, all too often, a less than convivial atmosphere would prevail when conversations turned to the subject of British rule—or Parliament's appalling lack of competence. Heated arguments ensued when opinions were expressed that derived from rumor or hearsay, rather than from facts of the actual events. Suzannah and I felt that simmering discontent, and it was a sign that the colonists' lives had become rife with anxiety, exacerbated by a growing awareness that crossing swords with the British was inevitable.

On a freezing afternoon in early March of 1775, Suzannah received a disturbing letter from Sarah. In it, she noted that Parliament declared Massachusetts to be in a state of open rebellion against the crown . . . and authorized British soldiers to shoot suspected rebels on sight.

News was rare in Walker's Cove these days, and Suzannah was often the recipient—whether from her sisters' letters, Henry and Zeb, or the sailors who frequented our tavern. Not surprisingly, many folks were accustomed to stopping by our tavern to ask her if there were any new developments. So, once the word was out about Sarah's most recent letter, the following day we were thronged with visitors, clamoring for confirmation of the rumors they'd heard.

Sympathetic to their concerns, at the first opportune moment, Suzannah stood on a chair and faced the crowd, ringing Mother's bell to silence the room. It quieted immediately and then she began to read aloud from Sarah's letter verbatim.

> *General Gage was directed to use whatever force was necessary to hunt down the perpetrators of the Massachusetts rebellion, and take them into custody. As such, it was deemed by Lord North's administration that any resistance that might be met from the Massachusetts militia would surely not be formidable.*
>
> *What an insult to our people! Such a contemptuous attitude inspires an atmosphere conducive to violence against those who oppress us in such a wretched, callous manner!*
>
> *Although I am desperate with fear, and perhaps nearing mortal terror for my life, I shall not be trampled upon like some despised serpent in the dirt—for the fires of sedition have spread through the colonies, and we are slowly becoming one in a common cause . . . to take up arms against the powers trying to crush us.*
>
> *It is said that General Gage's primary targets are Samuel Adams and John Hancock; and both men have since left Boston for parts unknown, so they might carry on their activities and thwart the objectives Lord North has set upon the general and his troops.*
>
> *Remember that from this day forward, our lives have taken a turn so that our liberty, which we hold dear, is the supreme focal point in this grim tragedy. I cannot tell you with certainty what the outcome shall be, save that the drums of war will roll across this land . . . and if God is with us . . . we shall not be the intended victims.*

Suzannah lowered the letter, and sitting down in the chair without a word, she placed it on the table. With an air of sorrow, she leaned back with moistened eyes to gaze wistfully into the fire.

Sarah's letter was a foreshadowing of what was to come—and we all knew it.

The tavern was absolutely silent as we stared at each other in stunned resignation. As the crackling fire broke the gloomy silence, the loud ticking of the tall clock marked the inevitable passage of precious seconds . . . as they marched relentlessly forward . . . away from the life we once knew . . . and toward the hour of war.

THE TALL LANKY form of Noah Blake extricated itself slowly from his chair to approach Suzannah. "I'm heading on home, Suzannah. This troubling news makes me fearful for my wife and children."

All eyes turned toward Noah, for he had uttered the very thought that lay unsaid in every heart.

Then he added, "I feel rather sick inside, but it's nothing to do with your food or drink. What shall I leave for payment?"

Suzannah rose from her chair to face Noah and softly replied, "*Hope* . . . that's what we need most right now."

Noah nodded his understanding and prepared to leave, first bundling himself up against the cold. As he opened the door and stood in its shadow, he turned and longingly searched the silent faces of his neighbors. Perhaps he was seeking an answer of some kind in their expressions, or memorizing for future reference, a tableau of things as they were . . . before the onslaught of hardship and war. Whatever his reason, the look of deep sorrow on his sensitive features foreshadowed many sleepless nights to come—not only for him—but for us all.

OUR PATRONS WERE unusually quiet as they left the tavern that night, doubtless contemplating what would become of the colonies if His Majesty's troops imposed martial law—and how it would affect our lives and our means to earn a living. At that moment, I felt fortunate indeed that we had gone back into the tavern business.

Clock production had stopped dead for lack of brass, lead, imported tools, dials and other parts necessary to clockmaking; and nowadays pig iron was nearly impossible to obtain even through smuggling—and without pig iron, a blacksmith couldn't create anything at his forge.

That night, Suzannah and I lay in our bed with Ainsley nestled between us. But our play was eclipsed by our overshadowing worry over how our little girl would be affected . . . *if* we were to face financial hardship. After Ainsley fell asleep, we talked long into the night . . . about how much foresight, conscious or otherwise, Mother had shown in reopening the tavern; for had she not done so, how much sooner might we have become destitute?

We soon had actual reasons for concern, nevertheless, since early in May there was a sudden and inexplicable drop in business at the tavern. First the visits from ships' crews, traders and travelers dwindled to practically nothing—for not a single vessel had docked at Walker's Cove since late March. Overland travelers were still in evidence for a while, but soon they were few. And then the locals came in less.

In late May, Wheezer Hutchinson arrived with a wagonload of sorely needed supplies from Boston. Among them were a few barrels of Essex rum and some ginger beer rum—courtesy of our smuggling cohorts among the Sons of Liberty. Wheezer also brought a long letter addressed to Suzannah from Henry Wiggins. Once she opened it and saw it was coded, she immediately withdrew to her secretary in the parlor to translate it.

As I was wrestling a barrel of ginger beer rum into its carriage behind the bar, Suzannah came running into the great room screaming, "Jim, the British troops have marched to Lexington looking for Adams and Hancock!"

The seven patrons who were present looked up in alarm, and rose from their places when Suzannah began to cry.

When I approached her, I was taken back when she suddenly blurted, "When they *got* to Lexington . . . my *God*, Jim . . . they *fired* on us . . . and they *killed* some of our *people!*"

Embracing my little wife to comfort her, she slowly wrapped her arms around my waist and continued weeping. While gently rubbing her back, I heard an ominous male voice utter, "She's finally come . . ."

Indeed . . . the drums of war had finally arrived, and the first blood had been spilled. Despite Sarah's brave declaration of defiance, the blood that soaked the gentle grasses of Lexington green . . . was *ours*.

The March to Concord

iping away her tears, Suzannah gradually regained her composure. Then fingering her hair, she looked up at me and warned, "There is *more* to this letter, Jim."

I considered how serious the contents of Henry's letter were so far, so I said, "Why don't we all sit down together," motioning to our patrons too, "to absorb the facts in their entirety," I offered a free round of their choice, as I felt we all needed something to help us calm ourselves.

From the kitchen, Dimmis had heard Suzannah's cry, and came in to see what was afoot. She helped us combine three tables into one so we could all sit together. I served the drinks as Suzannah took up her translated notes and read them aloud.

> *The British troops re-formed, and with their fifes shrilling and their drums beating, let out a victorious huzzah and set off for Concord. Upon their arrival they proceeded to sack the houses, barns and taverns, and in the process, the blacksmith shop and Concord courthouse were burned.*
>
> *Militia from the neighboring towns were summoned and met the light companies of British regulars, whereupon musket fire was exchanged with casualties on both sides. Many of the British officers were wounded and out of the fight.*

Suzannah paused to glance around at our faces, only to see all eyes riveted upon her. Drawing a deep breath, she continued.

> *The British column became confused without its officers and retreated in disarray. Thus the militia began picking them off*

from the cover of trees, houses, walls and fences. In the woods they peppered the British with sniper fire, shooting them until a British relief force arrived at Lexington. There, a large brigade of fresh regulars escorted the remaining British survivors back to Cambridge.

All had not been avenged, however; for new companies of militia from outlying farms and woods responded to the general alarm—and the British column was further decimated by militia crossfire and fierce hand-to-hand combat—Indian style—with the quick viciousness of hatchet, club and knife, against slow muskets and cumbersome bayonets.

The British, inexperienced in this type of battle, lost heavily to the militia, but during their retreat, there remained sufficient able-bodied soldiers who looted and pillaged our houses, ruthlessly attacking mothers and their children, and sometimes killing them out of brutal frustration . . ."

Suzannah's voice cracked with emotion as she lowered the letter, and through streaming tears, sobbed out the final line: ". . . and the *floors* of their loving homes . . . were *soaked* with their own blood . . ."

Looking helplessly about her, she choked, wiped her eyes and finally whimpered, "*Dear God*, we shall never be the same . . ."

I KNEW SUZANNAH feared such a fate for Ainsley. The distressing thought of such acute misfortune made me reflect upon my own character. What would I do if I, like the brave souls of Lexington and Concord, were called upon to serve the cause of liberty? Would I respond with the burning instinct to protect those who were dearest to my heart?

While I pondered this weighty matter, the group of patrons quietly rose and left for home—undoubtedly to give us privacy and share what they'd learned with their families and neighbors.

I embraced Suzannah to dab her tears; then whispered, "What else does Henry say, darling?"

Suzannah took a few minutes to compose herself and then picked up her notes to resume reading.

> *They are forming an army, paying six shillings a day per soldier, and putting Benedict Arnold in charge of a secret mission to capture Fort Ticonderoga. They plan to seize the cannons from there and transport them to Boston for a siege against the British.*
>
> *I will commit myself, Zeb and the Fortune Two to assist Benedict Arnold, my vessel to be used as a privateer as he sees fit—whether at sea or on the lakes. Any bounty taken shall be sold for the greater good of the colonies, with profits to be divided among us, and the crew.*
>
> *Since I find the direct approach the most satisfactory, I trust your assent will be given in full support for this matter, as will Dimmis'. Should we perish in this great enterprise, my dear Suzannah, my share shall go to Ainsley, and Zeb's to Dimmis. My solicitor has papers instructing him accordingly, and I remain confident of your friendship and your enthusiasm for our cause.*

Placing the letter down, Suzannah softly said, seemingly to herself more so than to me or Dimmis, "A privateer . . ."

As the summer months passed, business remained slow, but Suzannah received periodic deliveries of Spanish pieces of eight and British sovereigns; the proceeds from the sale of Henry's prizes taken at sea, and sold for our benefit as part-owners of the *Fortune Two*. The coins invariably arrived in kegs of nails, hidden in small wooden boxes underneath the loose nails—just in case the "nails" came under scrutiny.

We continued to receive letters from Henry and Suzannah's sisters, facilitated by the Committees of Correspondence—and Zeb, who had become one of their most trusted letter carriers. Deciding he'd had enough of being a sailor, he wrote us to say he wished to remain "on terra firma, riding a horsa higha"—as he put it. Needless to say, Dimmis was overjoyed at his decision.

In July, Suzannah, wishing to escape her tavern duties for an afternoon, took Ainsley into Richardson's fields to harvest blackberries for a batch of tarts and fritters she planned to bake.

Dimmis and I stayed behind to work the tavern until Wheezer Hutchinson stopped by to deliver a keg of nails, and a letter from Katharine.

"You building something *big*, Jim?" asked Wheezer, setting the keg on the table with a loud thump.

"No, Wheezer, I get them for Sam. He can't secure as low a price as I can," I replied matter-of-factly.

Apparently satisfied with my answer, he accepted my five coppers, whereupon I retired to the rocker to read Katharine's letter. Since we'd only had a small trickle of business that day, I could afford to leave the tavern solely in Dimmis' capable hands.

Katharine wrote that, in May, Arnold had indeed taken Fort Ticonderoga, little aided by the ostensible leader of the effort, the boorish Ethan Allen. Allen was a noisy Vermonter who continually tried to challenge or usurp Arnold's command, and required special treatment for his militia unit—known as the Green Mountain Boys. Katharine described them as drunken louts of dubious integrity, who were more interested in stealing land and possessions from New Yorkers, than in the cause of liberty or the greater good.

Despite his troubles with Allen, she said, "we" were off to a proper start—as Arnold had made good on his promise to take Ticonderoga. Henry Knox would escort the artillery they'd captured—including the cannons—back to Boston, where, as Katharine also reported, Henry Wiggins had delivered 1,100 barrels of precious gunpowder seized from the British. These would be distributed by the colonial militia for use in the cannons, as well as in their muskets and pistols.

From all I could glean, it seemed as if the Arnold-Wiggins alliance was, so far, producing exceptional results . . . and that kept the hapless British out of step . . . ever behind the quick tactical thinking and strategic vision that these two men shared in such abundance.

Resting my head against the back of the rocker, I closed my eyes, grateful for our safety and the news about these small but not insignificant victories . . . and pressing Katharine's letter to my heart, I fell asleep.

I WAS STARTLED awake by the sound of the door to the great room banging open with a crash, followed by a loud rumbling and the uneven tread of stumbling feet.

I hastily made my way into the room, where I found Dimmis standing alone in the shadows, wide eyed and her mouth agape with disbelief. Following her gaze, I saw the struggling form of Zeb Hawkes, bent over and hastily collecting runaway kegs of nails and righting several barrels of ginger beer rum.

Finally, he stood and murmured apologetically, "Sorry to have made such a commotion, Dimmis, my dear. I thought only to stop by for a spell, I have some interesting . . ."

Zeb never got to finish, because Dimmis was upon him in an instant, whimpering while smothering his face with grateful kisses.

Swinging her round and round, her brilliant red hair flying, Zeb declared, "You're the *best* damned thing I've held since I left here with Henry—seven long months ago!"

"Well Zeb, you certainly are a sight for sore eyes!" I said, rubbing the sleep from my face. "When you wrote and told us you'd signed on with the Committees of Correspondence, we expected a visit from you sooner than this."

"Well . . . be that as it may, it's good to see you too, Jim! Did I catch you sleeping in the rocker again?" he asked laughing, and linking arms with Dimmis, he guided her to a table before the fireplace. She laughed delightedly as he pulled out a chair for her and bid her sit, saying, "Damned shame you are so *beautiful* . . ." and kissing her deeply while threading his fingers through her locks, he then added. "Sometimes I feel undeserving—having you in my life and in my heart—you're *that* special!"

Dimmis answered with a kiss as passionate as any I'd shared with Suzannah. It did my heart good to see that their relationship had endured amid all the uncertainty that surrounded us.

Finally, Zeb broke away from Dimmis just long enough to pour us each a tumbler of ginger beer rum.

Once the three of us were settled in our chairs, I began to share some of the contents of Katharine's letter—until the door opened and there were Ainsley and Suzannah back from their walk, laden with pails of blackberries.

Once they spotted Zeb, they raced toward him, shrieking his name, and he enveloped them both in a big bear hug. "Well, well, well—let me look at this little *grownup* girl! By God, you are gonna be *taller* than your mama, I do believe!"

"I want to be the *tallest*, Uncle Zeb!" she responded excitedly, standing on tiptoe to plant a kiss on one heavily whiskered cheek.

Bending low to wrap an arm around her waist, Zeb threaded his fingers into her golden hair and whispered into her ear loud enough so Suzannah could hear, "You keep listening to your mama, and you will be the *tallest*, maybe even *taller* than your grandma Walker!" Then he reached into his coat pocket to retrieve a cylindrical object wrapped in paper and held it out to her.

"Oooohhhh!" came a squeal of delight from Ainsley, who took it and examined it closely, feeling its shape with her fingers.

Zeb explained, "Those are *snickerdoodles*—just for you!"

Ainsley looked up at her mother, seeking her approval to accept the gift, whereupon Suzannah nodded.

"Thank you, Uncle Zeb!" Ainsley chirped as she perched on a nearby chair to unwrap the package. After she slowly opened the paper, she took the first cookie off the top and put the rest aside. She carefully bit off a small piece, and as she chewed, her face lit up with a delightful smile as she savored its unique and pleasing taste.

"Those come from the Pennsylvania colony," Zeb explained. Then he added, in a rather pedantic tone, "Snickerdoodles are *not* to be confused with 'Yankee Doodle,' the tune the British sing to scorn our patriots. They're made from cream and flour, enlivened with sugar, nutmeg, cinnamon, nuts and dried fruit . . . Now, may I have one of those, Ainsley?"

After giving one to Zeb, she offered the third one to Dimmis, saying, "Will you have a tea party with me, Aunt Dimmis?"

Upon seeing the wistful look on Dimmis' face as she accepted the cookie, Suzannah's eyes moistened when Dimmis softly whispered, "I shall be *honored* to have a tea party with *you*, Miss Ainsley!" Sensing that Zeb had weighty matters to discuss, she beckoned the child to her and said, "Let's go to the kitchen and brew a fresh pot of tea—just for *us*—and bring the rest of those *snickerdoodles* with you!"

Holding her cookies tightly in one hand, Ainsley grabbed Dimmis' hand with her other, and the two withdrew to the kitchen.

Watching them leave, I reflected on how Dimmis was Ainsley's favorite "aunt," even more favored than her real aunts because of her daily presence in the child's life. Dimmis received as much love from Ainsley as she gave, and perhaps even a little more. She was the perfect recipient for Dimmis' starving affections . . . for, like her mother, she was very easy to love—and returned that love tenfold.

This train of thought led me to wonder what was taking Zeb so long in asking for Dimmis' hand in marriage. But I wasn't about to broach the subject just then, since after his long absence we had other matters to discuss.

"Well, now," I asked Zeb, "can you tell us about your adventures?"

After sipping his ginger beer rum thoughtfully, instead of answering my question, he looked almost furtively at Suzannah as he said, "You got the seven kegs of coins I sent?"

Nodding, Suzannah rose to retrieve her account book and returned momentarily. "Here are the totals so far, broken down by share—but these figures don't include today's delivery. Henry's share is 867 pounds, yours is 289 pounds, our share is 435 pounds, and Dimmis' share is 145 pounds—all rounded up."

"You know about my share going to Dimmis?" Zeb asked.

"Yes, I know, Zeb; but I would rather it *not* go to Dimmis, as I want you to stay *alive*—and enjoy it *with* her."

Looking directly into her eyes, Zeb softly replied, "You touch me deeply, Suzannah . . . you are the very soul of kindness and generosity."

Startled and impressed by his newfound eloquence, I softly added, "Well *said*, Zeb!" I was pleased his association with Dimmis and Henry was gradually elevating him to the level of a gentleman—an impressive contrast from the unrefined bumpkin I first met some ten years ago.

After eating his snickerdoodle, Zeb embarked on an account of his recent exploits.

"Henry and I met with Arnold, and he was enthusiastic about Henry's plan to make the *Fortune Two* a privateer. It would be the first ship in Arnold's navy, so to speak. While Arnold would leave for New York to take Fort Ticonderoga from the British, Henry was to patrol the waters off Massachusetts and seize any British or Loyalist ship in the name of the colonies and the Continental Congress. Those are the folks whose names you've already heard mentioned, like John Hancock, John Adams and George Washington.

"Hancock, he is presiding over the group. They are drawing up a petition to give directly to the king . . . in the hope he will intervene with Parliament on behalf of the colonies, since we have no representation of any kind."

"Taxation without representation . . ." Dimmis muttered as she joined us at the table, having tucked Ainsley in for the night.

"That's right, Dimmis—we have no say in how they govern. Many of the delegates want a complete break with England no matter what the cost, while others wish to avoid war and remain affiliated with the crown as long as we are treated as fellow citizens . . ."

Interrupting Zeb, Suzannah stood and vehemently stamping her foot on the floor, bitterly cried, "How in God's name can we be *fellow citizens*, when the streets and houses of Lexington and Concord are stained with the *blood* of our fellow patriots?"

"We cannot remain thus," Zeb replied solemnly. "Arnold says Parliament is hopelessly inept at running the colonies, and the king is even worse. We *must* break away . . . for good . . ."

Suzannah quieted visibly after that, and resuming her seat, let Zeb continue.

"Now, *here* is the latest," Zeb said after finishing his drink and lowering his voice to lend a confidential air. "The cannons that Arnold captured are being dug out of the ruins of Ticonderoga, and Henry Knox will be transporting them from there to Boston . . . to drive the British out.

"To that same end, there was a skirmish on Breed's Hill last month. The colonists drove the world's finest army of 10,000 men to sustain losses of over 1,000 men killed or wounded, while we retreated into the hills to fight another day."

"A *thousand* men?" gasped Dimmis, her hand pressed to her throat.

"Indeed, and we lost about half that number out of 2,000. I heard that the fighting was so intense that our soldiers were using nails, rocks, dirt or anything else they could stuff into their muskets for ammunition. This is why privateers are so important—we must have that ball and powder!"

Zeb paused to pour himself another tumbler of ginger beer rum before resuming his narrative.

"George Washington was appointed Commander-in-Chief by the congress, and just this month took command of the Continental Army. He is outside Boston, where the siege has been ongoing, as you know.

"Meanwhile, our friend Henry, along with Captain James Mugford, took the HMS *Hope* as a prize in Boston harbor, and with it came over 1,000 barrels of powder and 1,000 muskets—complete with 50,000 balls. That got us each 1,000 pounds sterling in yonder kegs."

"My *heavens*, Zeb!" gasped Suzannah, staring in amazement at the kegs sitting on the table across the room. "How much did you sell the spoils for?" she asked cautiously.

"Hell, we *gave* 'em to the Continental Army!" he exclaimed, and pointing to the kegs added, "Those are the *specie* barrels that we found in the hold, underneath the decking to the bilge. Not one damned nail in *those* kegs!"

Dimmis rose and went over to the table to lift one of the kegs. She struggled to raise it about an inch, and then dropped it down with a thud because of its weight. Written on the lid was "1000."

"Well, I reckon we ought to see what we got here between us," Zeb declared as he went and stood next to Dimmis. Pulling out a knife to pry off the lid of the keg she'd been handling, after a few prods it came away. Dimmis' eyes widened as she exclaimed, "Dear God, Zeb, that's *gold*—not silver!"

"Well, no *wonder* they were so damned heavy," he remarked. "Maybe *this* one contains silver . . ." he conjectured as he loosened the lid of another keg.

But it too was full of gold sovereigns . . . 1,000 of them, to be exact.

Dimmis dipped her hand into the mass of gold coins and came up with a handful, enjoying how they glittered as they caught the light, and how they jangled agreeably as she let them drop back into the barrel.

"They must have been intended as pay for the British troops in Boston," Zeb speculated, as he opened another. Again, he was rewarded with flashes of lustrous gold. He picked up one coin and held it to the firelight, squinting at the newly minted image of George III.

After thrusting the coin in his pocket, he patted it affection-ately and happily mused, "George, you never did anything so right in your whole damned life . . . until now!"

"My *God*, Zeb . . .we have *ten* of these kegs," Suzannah shrieked, unable to contain her excitement. "We are *rich* beyond our dreams!"

"Well, that might be, little lady. But, mind you, I suggest we bury these kegs in your cellar and keep 'em full and by . . . just in case . . . after all, hard money is king of the world!"

After indicating her agreement, Suzannah poured us each a tum-bler of her famous flip, and holding hers aloft, she declared, "*To Henry Wiggins!*"

Joining in her toast, we raised our tumblers and repeated "To Henry Wiggins—*Huzzah!*"

SUZANNAH AND DIMMIS surprised us by having already prepared a large quantity of smoked sausages, beans and baked potatoes, which they served in the great room before the comforting fire. There was much laughter and more storytelling as we dined heartily, celebrating our good fortune, for indeed, the gold granted us freedom from want—and thus lightened life's burdens—at least for the moment.

Now that we were financially secure, it seemed like the perfect opportunity for Zeb to propose to Dimmis. I planned to discuss the matter in private with Suzannah later on, since I wanted to suggest that she encourage Zeb to finally ask for her hand. But after the pumpkin pie was served, I thought I might have been pre-empted when Zeb stood up to make an announcement.

"Since we are now secure in hard money for the rest of our lives," he said, "I feel compelled to tell you all that I have decided to accompany Benedict Arnold on a secret mission—to take the British-occupied city of Quebec."

Dimmis was stunned . . . and bowing her head, she remained downcast and said nothing.

Observing her reaction, Suzannah glared at Zeb and hotly scorned, "What in hell are you talking about!"

Zeb shuffled uneasily and tried begging her off, but Suzannah insisted by tersely demanding, "Please *explain*, Zeb!"

He looked down at the floor, his gaze unable to meet hers or that of poor Dimmis. "Arnold entrusted me to recruit soldiers for a surprise attack on Quebec—and I feel it's only right to do my part. Working for the committee and delivering letters just isn't enough."

Dimmis rose and then stood stock-still. With silent tears rolling down her cheeks, she looked at Zeb with the expression of a little girl lost. Grief-stricken on her behalf because she had to endure yet another separation . . . and they still weren't married; I knew that if Zeb did not survive his mission, she would be left alone—her love lost—and her best dreams finally beaten.

ANOTHER PARTING

eb stood before her, apparently unable to speak. While his lips moved but uttered not a sound, he shot furtive glances first at Suzannah and then at Dimmis . . . searching for a scrap of encouragement or support. Finding none, he stretched to his full height of over six-and-a-half feet, cleared his throat, and spoke to Dimmis as though Suzannah and I weren't present.

"In the face of insurmountable obstacles, Dimmis, *you* have made me the man that I am; a *gentleman.* Your painstaking efforts have given me a chance to finally speak to you with an eloquence that is worthy of your character. During all our time together, you have been the tireless embodiment of tenderness, virtue and truth—and you deserve boundless praise for your remarkable patience with me.

"I loved you from the moment I saw you . . . when you first served Henry and me in this very room. I *love* you like no other . . . and I must defend and protect that love against *anything* that could bring us harm."

Walking to the window and gazing out to sea, Zeb murmured just loud enough to be heard, "There is an *enemy* out there that is seeking to destroy our lives and our love—and I *cannot* accept that Providence has delivered such to be our fate . . . and so, I am temporarily called to a higher cause—to earn our freedom and then to preserve it, to preserve *you* . . . to preserve *us.*"

When Zeb turned around, he saw that Dimmis was looking directly at him. Her features had softened into an expression of dawning comprehension and acceptance. Seizing the opportunity, he approached her and gently caressing her shoulders, he bravely proclaimed, "I now stand humbly before you, Dimmis Sexton, your *servant*—an uncouth creature to be sure, now totally reproved. Aye, I have *not* been the most ardent or attentive suitor, particularly since all this devilment transpired. But I have no wish to *ever again* leave you in a dreadful state of uncertainty—or with *any* regrets for the time and love you have given me."

Stepping back with both hands toward her in a pleading gesture, he then continued. "And so, the one thing I desire before leaving this earth—or this *room*—is that you grant me your hand in marriage to be ever as one . . . and nevermore shall our hearts be parted . . ."

Moved to tears, I sat and held my breath, waiting for Dimmis' reply. When I looked at Suzannah, her mouth was open and silent tears were running down her cheeks. Never before had we been so privy to the inner longings of other hearts—and it was beautiful to behold.

Dimmis, her face streaked with tears, approached Zeb and gently took his hands while he searched her eyes for any sign of acceptance.

As she caressed his cheeks with trembling hands, Dimmis steadily returned his gaze before she finally spoke. "Dearest Zeb, you have the gift of silent strength . . . that I draw from you . . . and you in turn draw from me. Although we may be companions of the doomed, to the end I shall *ever* be your wife. Zebulon Galletin Hawkes, I give myself to you—for myself is all I have to give. But the love in my heart is greater than the universe, and my universe is now *yours*."

Her moist cheeks reflected the moonlight as Zeb picked her up and held her tightly to his heart. Rejoicing in each other's arms, little did they notice the watery eyed married couple holding hands at the table behind them. And so, we rose to embrace them, and all wept with joy at the prospect of Dimmis and Zeb finally becoming one.

After much animated discussion about the pending marriage, we resumed our seats at the table, while Zeb shared details about Arnold's planned expedition to Quebec.

"We're to leave in September from Cambridge," he said, "following Lieutenant Montresor's map of 1761. Arnold expects we should arrive in Quebec within twenty days—and then we *get* 'em!"

"Why Quebec?" Dimmis asked.

Trying to suppress an edge of impatience in his voice, Zeb explained, "Arnold and Washington are convinced that the British want to isolate the northeastern colonies, and both men know that *nothing* gets by the fortress at Quebec. If *we* held it, there's no way the damned British could ever sail down the Hudson to New York, and cut us off"; then he added: "As Henry once said, the northeastern colonies are the head of the serpent, and the British *know* if they sever the head, the others shall quickly die.

"Arnold does not want them to have that chance, which is why he asked me to assist him. Henry will remain at sea to thwart the blockades, and commandeer any vessel he sees as a threat to the colonies, or an obstacle to free trade."

Zeb leaned back in his chair, thinking the subject was done, but Dimmis had another question. "What happens if they *do* cut us off?"

"Oh hell, nothin' *much*!" Zeb bellowed, sounding like his old self. "We just get shot dead in the streets, no better'n no worse'n them poor bastards down in Lexington!"

Then, folding his arms and fluttering his eyes, he mimicked a distressingly high, sanctimonious British accent, "Then they march over our bloody bullet-perforated bodies and hurry home to have tea and crumpets at four!"

As Dimmis nodded her understanding, Zeb added, "And *I* don't want that to happen! Not while I'm *alive*, by God!" Then he gently kissed his finger and pressing it to Dimmis' lips, softly added, "Come to think of it, I don't want it to happen if I'm *dead*, either."

Zeb's reasoning sounded so convincing that I asked Suzannah, "Would it be a hardship for you if I volunteered to go with Zeb?"

Suzannah looked distressed but said nothing at first, and fortunately, Zeb spoke before she could.

"Jim, you need to stay *here*—at least for the time being—to ensure the protection of our three girls. Once I return from Quebec—that will be the time for us to reconsider the matter."

Suzannah looked relieved, and Dimmis' face seemed to reflect pride in Zeb's good judgment.

Zeb stood up and went over to one of the open kegs to withdraw a fistful of gold sovereigns, depositing them into one of his capacious pockets. "Never underestimate what hard money can buy in an army," he remarked. "I just want to be prepared . . . call it road gold, if you will. Suzannah, you can deduct this from my share—if you would be so kind."

Turning to me he said, "Don't forget, Jim, you should get those kegs buried in a good hiding place, since as long as we have hard money, we will want for *nothing*!" And as an afterthought, he gently patted the girls' heads and subtly added, "No matter *who* wins . . ."

There was a temporary lull in the conversation as Dimmis smiled up at Zeb. It was a smile of temerity and effeminacy . . . when a woman knows her man's love is unconditionally hers . . . and now, she had found that special strength in that deep sacred bond—that only love could bring.

As Zeb sat down, Dimmis served him another sausage, and I confidently sipped my flip. Looking at the kegs of gold and wondering how wealthy we were, a sudden knock interrupted my musings. When we looked toward the door, we saw it stood partly open. Silhouetted against the darkness was a lone male figure entering the great room, his face obscured despite the flickering firelight.

His steady controlled footsteps echoed off the pine floorboards as he approached our table, and then stopped short. "Dear me, I hesitate asking you to concern yourselves with such a *trifling* visitor as myself . . . but are you usually so casually aloof to all your patrons?"

Suzannah suddenly gasped, and jumped up to fly squealing into the waiting arms of Henry Wiggins, showering his face with kisses.

Henry, laughing heartily while swinging Suzannah around, neatly placed her in my arms, declaring, "I daresay *this* belongs to *you*, my good fellow!"

As soon as Henry had released Suzannah, it was Dimmis' turn to bestow more affectionate kisses on our old friend, who embraced her warmly in return.

"Ah! What a *splendid* greeting!" he said appreciatively. "Here I *am*, folks—fresh from my privateering adventures of audacity and romance!"

After Henry took a seat at our table, I brought him a tankard of flip, while Suzannah disappeared into the kitchen. When she returned, it was with a large plate of sausages and baked beans, and a large chunk of warm bread spread with salted butter.

Henry, a devotee of Suzannah's cooking, clapped his hands in gleeful anticipation as she placed the heaping plate before him. Looking around at us, he joyfully remarked, "I am *sorry* to find you all so remarkably *unmoved* by my arrival!" Which sent us into gales of laughter.

Henry speared half a sausage, loaded it with beans, and then forked the entire wedge into his mouth. Smiling blissfully as he chewed, he noted, "My *dear* Suzannah, if there are such meals as this in heaven, then I am obliged to get *there* the minute I leave this world!"

He then took a deep drink of the flip, and placing the tumbler down, again complimented, "When it comes to the matter of *flip*, Suzannah, there are many untrustworthy palates that narrowly interpret the *facts* of what they taste . . . *mine* is not one of them . . . my dear lady, *yours* is *still* the most *incomparable* flip in the colonies!"

Suzannah clapped delightedly like Ainsley would . . . nodding her approval at being declared purveyor of the finest flip anywhere. "Let us not neglect your *own* contribution to our tavern's fame . . . *ginger beer rum!*" she replied.

We all gave a hearty cheer in response, singling Henry out for his efforts with Zeb to invent our signature drink. As Henry ate his dinner, he filled us in on his latest activities—all the latest news, and we listened intently, not uttering a word lest we interrupt him and lose a single detail.

When he was finishing up the last morsel of food on his plate, Suzannah said, "So tell us news of Arnold, Henry. Zeb has just informed us he has agreed to assist him in his expedition to Quebec."

Henry's face suddenly darkened. "I have been entrusted with delivering *this* to James Otis, Jr., while accompanying Zeb to Cambridge in the process." Reaching into his coat, he withdrew a letter, and carefully unfolding it, read it to us.

My compliments, Mr. Otis,

I beg leave to observe I have had intimation given me, that some persons had determined to apply to you and the Provincial Congress, to injure me in your esteem by misrepresenting matters of fact.

I know of no other motive they can have, only my refusing them commission for the very simple reason that I did not think them qualified.

However, gentlemen, I have the satisfaction of imagining I am employed by gentlemen of such good judgment that my conduct shall not be condemned until I have had the opportunity of being heard.

I am in haste, yours,

B. Arnold

Zeb leaned toward Henry and growled, "Sounds like someone is trying to steal the minister's breeches, Henry! Who in hell are the *persons* crying out to their *mamas*? Maybe we ought to go over there and stuff them up their own chimneys . . . or better yet, down their own privies!"

Henry casually waved him off. "Oh Zeb, there are malcontents such as these in *every* army! Such men of bogus elegance and spurious philosophy are like *fleas* and *vermin*: they are indeed pesky and bothersome . . . but like flea bites, if they are allowed to fester and remain untreated, these singular affairs can become grotesque boils of irritation . . . which can cost a good man of leadership his commission . . . and possibly his soul . . .”

“*Or* his breeches!” Zeb added.

Henry folded the letter and replacing it in his pocket, he continued, “These three men are spewing unjustifiable slurs of contemptible pettiness, mostly figments of imagination and hearsay evidence against a brilliant tactical leader, to whom they are egregiously ill-disposed.”

“That’s because Arnold damned well knows the difference between *horse droppings* and pumpkin *pie!*” Zeb bellowed.

Dimmis bowed her head in embarrassment at Zeb’s vulgarity, but her half-smile betrayed a secret pride in his instinctive candor that left no holds barred.

Turning to me, Henry said, “You will *not* be pleased to learn, Jim, that *one* of them, James Easton, is a *tavern*-keeper.”

“Why hell’s bells, Henry, that is an insult to *all* tavern-keepers—especially the Walkers!” Zeb observed.

“James Easton would *not* be insulted, even if you told him his rum was watered down and his bread was populated with perambulating weevils—which they *are!*”

“Goddamned, misbegotten, lily-livered, bug serving, cob swiping *skunk!*” Zeb roared, as he pounded the table.

“*Zebulon Hawkes!*” cried Dimmis, as she stood to protest his admirable profanity, but Zeb continued his rant.

“This bastard has the *same* first name as Jim! By God, they better not *call* him Jim, or I will come down there and carve his damned gizzard out . . . then toss it into Lake Champlain with no further ado . . . and then *suddenly*, he will cease to be a problem for Arnold!”

Rising to stand beside the fire, Zeb pulled his knife to examine its sharpness. While calmly thumbing its blade, he gently asked, “So who are the others, Henry?”

“John Brown and Ethan Allen . . .” Henry replied.

“John Brown . . . *John Brown?*” Zeb echoed. After a pause, he then bellowed, “What God damned gutless creature in hell’s bowels has a name like *that* attached to it?”

But before Henry could explain further, I suggested we all retire to the parlor, where we could be more comfortable as we heard him out.

Henry chose the rocker, and after seating himself there he lit his pipe, while we arranged our chairs so we could gather around him.

As undulating curls of smoke drifted toward the ceiling and fireplace, he rocked silently at first, then picked up where he left off . . .

"The answer to your question, Zeb, is that John Brown is a very dry and pedantic creature! Worthless as he is, he once worked in a law office belonging to Arnold's cousin in Rhode Island—rum country. Due to his incompetence, he was . . . ah . . . summarily dismissed shall we say, and ever since, he's had an axe to grind with the Arnold family—blaming *them* for his dismal failures, which of course is total *rubbish!*"

After pausing to again draw from his pipe, Henry sent a perfect circle of smoke toward the fireplace . . . and after we all smiled in admiration as it magically dissipated, he then continued, "Brown is a charming man of mercurial temperament who speaks convincingly to congress of talents he does not possess—to conceal the truth of his life's unremarkable affairs—in the interests of his own abominable misplaced patriotism, of course!"

Sounds like a *gizzard* case to *me*! Zeb declared. "Now who in hell is Allen?"

I then added, "Katharine wrote in one of her recent letters that Ethan Allen and his men were rakehells and braggarts; and Allen does not believe in Arnold's right to command. She says he challenges Arnold at every turn while in the field, nearly causing Arnold disastrous results during engagements."

Leaning back in the rocker, Henry mused for a few moments with his eyes closed. "Indeed, Jim, I believe Allen to be a man of dubious integrity, with an *amazing* capacity for pomposity and insubordination. Possessing a painfully disingenuous nobility, he is a *loose*-thinking man, who, I am told when once in his cups, engaged in a *furious* battle with an elderly seagull—and *lost!*"

We all roared with laughter, causing Henry to bolt upright in the rocker, popeyed at our reaction. "Why, *surely* I'm not being *scoffed* at?" Henry inquired.

Suzannah waved to reassure him. "No, no, dear Henry. It should be perfectly apparent that we are laughing at the folly of Ethan Allen . . . and his inconsequential skills at fighting . . . ah . . . *birds!*"

Dimmis, also suppressing a laugh added, "Either that, or perhaps you merely possess a scintillating, lively imagination . . . of a far superior and entertaining quality!"

Visibly impressed by Dimmis' refined and intellectual comment, Henry, looking distressed, got up from the rocker and stood near the fireplace, apparently seeking consolation more than warmth. "Oh, how I wish that were *true*, my dear Dimmis!" He knocked the ashes from the bowl of his pipe and stared dolefully into the fire.

Dimmis softly inquired then, "Why are you so upset, Henry? I can see it plainly."

Henry sighed, snapping the end off his pipe and placing the remainder in his pocket. "It is Arnold's confounding *letter* . . . not so much for what it *says*—but for what it *represents*. Can you see that?"

Looking around earnestly at our faces, Henry explained, "It is *not* with dignity that I bear this letter for one so brilliant, for what this letter indicates is that there are many Browns, Allens and Eastons out there: men of small minds—revolting individuals who have been overlooked for promotion due to their lack of acumen, tactical foresight, or general knowledge of military affairs! Indeed, men like Arnold and Washington will ever be plagued by unceremonious pests such as these—*grotesque* little men with *dull* minds— who are *poisoned* by the jealousy they feel for their superior officers."

"Why do *you* fear them, Henry?" Suzannah asked.

Henry resumed his seat in the rocker, and as he glided, he tapped the letter. "*This* is when they are most dangerous and destructive, Suzannah. As the war grows in intensity, they accost their leaders with *politics*, using ambiguously worded accusations based upon their own imaginings. Yet such churlish assaults upon one's character must be defended, recanted, or called out in a duel—lest they be *believed* by delegates of the congress—consuming precious time, when defeating the common enemy should be paramount."

"Why would they *believe* this nonsense?" Suzannah asked, pointing at the letter.

"Ah, my dear Suzannah, I have *seen* them in operation! In politics it is *who* you know that breeds success, not *what* you know. And such success is usually *not* for the benefit of the general good, but results in a host of unintended and often *malicious* consequences . . . that typically harm everyone *except* the instigator of such actions. To my way of thinking, the average congressional politician who is misguided or misinformed—is *exceedingly* dangerous. Many are gullible as sea gulls and have as little gray matter to work with! As such, incompetently elected and informed public servants can do more damage with one arm tied behind his back, than an entire British regiment could ever *hope* to do."

When Zeb mumbled from the back of the room something about checking up on congressional gizzards, I knew that if the two of them had their way, Arnold and Washington would be in charge of military affairs, and not the politicians of Allen, Brown and Easton.

Henry was silent for a long while thereafter, brooding over the letter he had to deliver to James Otis. I felt terrible that Arnold's time and resources were diverted to defend himself against such baseless attacks.

Mercifully, Suzannah chose that moment to suggest we all move back into the great room, where she would serve some hot tea, fritters and pumpkin bread, the prospect of which lightened our collective mood considerably.

We enjoyed our refreshments as Henry filled us in further about Arnold's endeavors. The man had personally paid in excess of 1,388 pounds from his own pocket to outfit and provision his militia. This he did because delegates of the congress would not, or could not appropriate the money for his purposes. Thus Arnold funded the defense of the colonies by capturing Crown Point from the British—a vital strategic holding near Ticonderoga.

Pondering the kegs of specie sitting idly by on the table, I suggested, "Perhaps, Henry, we should contribute some of this money to Arnold or Washington. Surely they cannot afford to personally finance a war from their own fortunes."

"Ah, but Jim, such sacrifices are what make these men *patriots*. We have given so much more than money—contributing arms, powder, ships and food. Indeed, we have *all* done our part—including putting our families and livelihoods at risk to support the cause at any cost!"

Suddenly, we heard a rapping at the front door. Henry turned from the table and called out, "Enter, Seamus!"

It was Seamus O'Brien—master of the schooner *Shannon*—whom I'd first met around the time Ainsley was born. As he approached, I added another chair to our table as Henry said, "Seamus, this is James Walker and his wife Suzannah."

Turning to greet Suzannah, Seamus took her hand and kissed it. "Aye, neow . . . how I remember you, sweet maid! 'Tis a face *loovely* as yourn tha can make a mahn give up 'is meat, potatas and spirit liquor . . . and live on *tarnips* between thirtee day fasts!"

Turning to me he said, "Hansome boyo o' yon spirits ye be . . . *king* o' rum, ye are. Be damned to me soul if yur na' the same!"

Although I didn't *quite* understand him, I remembered him well from our last meeting—and his intense dislike for all things British. As I warmly shook his hand, I wondered if he was now shipping with Henry.

As if he'd heard my unspoken question, Henry explained, "Seamus was captain of the *Shannon* out of Boston, which was taken by the *Gaspée* under horrible circumstances. Let's just say he squeezed through a rusty scupper and managed to escape with his life . . . which is more than the remaining members of his crew can boast."

After Seamus gave a somber nod, Henry added, "His narrow escape from that British vessel of iniquity increased his dislike of the crown tenfold—Seamus being a native of *Ireland*."

At hearing that, Suzannah's eyes widened in surprise and she began conversing with Seamus in Gaelic. Whereupon the coarse man who stood before us responded in lilting tones in his native tongue.

It didn't take Dimmis long to join the conversation already in progress . . . asking Seamus a question only half of those present could understand.

His lengthy reply made her gasp as she was moved to tears. And when he had finished speaking, she encircled him in her arms and held him to her heart, crying softly between gentle Gaelic phrases.

Zeb, visibly agitated over all this familiarity with a total stranger, finally spoke up. "*Say,* what's going on here? You all act like this is *old home week* or something. And what is this secret talk about, anyway? By God, I may not like him, but it's only the damned King's English I speak and understand!"

Dimmis, releasing Seamus, wiped her eyes and turned to Zeb. As she reached up to touch his cheek affectionately, she explained, "It *is* old home week, Zeb. Seamus here, he's from the village my mother was born in. His *father* is my *mother's* younger brother . . . *we are cousins!*"

Her pronouncement was greeted by a stunned silence, until Dimmis and Seamus continued their exchange in Gaelic, and Suzannah translated for our benefit.

"According to Seamus, her mother is from the little hamlet of *Ballybay,* Ireland. Their common grandparents had died young so that the two children were separated. Seamus' father remained in Ballybay, while his older sister—Dimmis' mother—was sent to work in parts unknown as a tavern maid. The family never heard from her again. For the first time in her life, thanks to Seamus, her *only* living relative, Dimmis knows something about her roots."

Zeb looked apprehensive, as though anticipating an unwelcome event.

When Suzannah noticed his expression, she took him aside and spoke reassuringly to his fears. "Zeb, Dimmis' heart is with *you,* and ever *shall* be. Your love is *safe* . . . and *her* life is now complete. You should be happy for her . . . celebrate her heritage *with* her."

I nodded to Zeb and added, "Suzannah is *always* correct in matters of the heart, Zeb—*you* know that!"

Dimmis and Seamus chatted on in Gaelic, she taking notes on his ramblings about Ballybay and their family's colorful heritage. With each page she filled she grew more animated, and I noticed a new glint of pride in her eyes—for she had been made whole by finally knowing her ancestry.

Then I went off to the parlor and returned with six crystal glasses and the old bottle of wine—the wedding gift for my parents from Sam's father. It was nearly empty, but I couldn't think of a better occasion to finish it off than this one—Dimmis' betrothal *and* the chance encounter with her first cousin, Seamus.

I set down the glasses and poured equal amounts into each until the bottle was empty. Then I announced jubilantly, "To Dimmis and Zeb!" and in an aside to Henry and Seamus, "Tonight, before your arrival, they were *betrothed!*"

Looking pleasantly surprised, Henry crowed, "My, my, my, I *always* like to know when love is promised for a lifetime! Indeed, from such promises we harvest those special opportunities to move forward in grace, hopefully for the greater good of man and God." Then addressing me, "Might I be permitted to say a few words too?"

I nodded to indicate he should proceed.

Holding his glass aloft, Henry declared, "To your love—Dimmis and Zeb—may it ever reside in your hearts and be immune to my incoherent ramblings, but *never* from my heartfelt good wishes! And to Dimmis *again*—for discovering your roots and your long lost cousin, and the knowledge, dear lady, that you are no longer a solitary worldling . . . for you are now blessed with a family—besides the Walkers, of course!"

Henry nodded my way and raising my glass, I looked steadily into Dimmis' eyes, "On this night, your life departs from its stormy past—and into the present of new found love and great promise. May *all* your dreams come true . . . and may your heart ever be proud of who you have been, who you have become, and who you shall *be* . . . the wonderful and lovely Dimmis . . . *wife* of Zebulon Hawkes!"

After three joyous huzzahs, we drank the last of my parents' rich aromatic liquor. That which had brought so much pleasure to so many people for so many years, was now gone . . . but it was a most worthy parting.

In the early hours of morning, it was Henry who finally broke up our gathering. He stood up and stretched, saying, "Well, ladies and gentlemen, it is time for me to bid you all a fond farewell. His voice broke as he wistfully added, "I do not know *when*—or even *if*—we shall ever gather again, but I pray that the fates will allow us to share more joyful occasions like this one—that I was *honored* to share with you tonight . . ."

Brushing a tear from his eye, he finally announced, "Now, my dearest friends, the tide awaits . . . Zeb, Seamus, are you ready?"

With heavy hearts we accompanied our friends to the wharf just before sunrise. Seamus led the way, while Dimmis and Zeb followed on either side of Henry. Suzannah and I trailed behind them. Fanny and Sam would soon follow in the wagon with Ainsley after we were gone.

As we approached the *Fortune Two*, she looked very different from the modified packet sloop she'd been heretofore. She was now a snow brig, rigged for speed with enlarged snow sails, and her sides were now bristling with the muzzles of eighteen cannons, lending her the appearance of a brigantine. Contributing to that impression were the pikes and muskets lined up along her standing rigging.

As we approached the gangway, Henry proudly declared, "She is as *fast* as ever . . . perhaps a little *faster*, now that her sticks have been trimmed!"

Her deck was swarming with sailors who Henry had not brought with him to the tavern. But then he reminded us that he demanded strict discipline from his crew; and since his visit was on the *order* of Benedict Arnold himself, it was *not* to be regarded as shore leave.

Henry invited us on board for a tour. He pointed out that there was nothing of commercial value in the hold, only barrels of powder, cannonballs, hammocks and a galley kitchen. I found myself gawking at the wondrous details of this brigantine of battle, while Suzannah seemed just as impressed. At one point, she exclaimed in amazement, "Just think, Jim, we *own* a part of *all this!*"

"*Indeed,* you do!" replied Henry. "After all, you and Jim were instrumental in the development of our partnership—and your active participation in her ownership is vital. In fact, were it not bad luck to rename a vessel, I would call her *Suzannah's Pride* in her present configuration." He took Suzannah's hand and kissing it, he suggested, "When you go ashore, take a good look under her bowsprit . . . you may *like* what you see . . ."

After hearing that, Suzannah couldn't contain her curiosity even for a minute. She hurried us to the main deck, then off the ship and onto the wharf. We skirted the length of the *Fortune Two* to get a better view of her bowsprit, where two sailors were working in preparation for departure. She abruptly halted, staring ahead without a sound.

Following her gaze, I saw it—and couldn't believe what I was seeing. For beautifully nestled below the bowsprit and gracing the prow of the *Fortune Two*, was a superbly carved and painted figurehead—of my own Suzannah!

It was her likeness in all respects, with a glowing complexion, gray-blue eyes—and light brown hair with a golden sheen . . . and it flowed gracefully to either side of the prow. She wore a loosely fitting dress, meticulously sculpted so that it seemed to be fluttering in the wind—when in reality it wasn't moving at all.

Most striking, however, was her pose. She held a Grecian victory wreath in one hand, lifting it out toward the waters ahead, with another one tucked at her waist, tightly held and at the ready.

The final glory was the gilded ribbon that was threaded through her hair: Pure gold hammered to the thickness of a leaf was inlaid into the carved ribbon.

With her eyes still riveted on the magnificent sculpture, without a word, Suzannah took my hand and gave it a loving squeeze. "I'm speechless, Jim . . . absolutely speechless, to be so honored."

Stooping to kiss her tenderly, I whispered, "Henry couldn't have chosen a more exquisite and deserving subject . . ."

She kissed me again, and while caressing me in her needful little way, "Mama, *there* you are!" rang out from a sweet familiar voice.

As we turned around, we saw Ainsley racing toward us across the wharf, with Fanny and Sam close behind her. I picked her up and tossed her into the air, eliciting squeals of joy. As I caught her coming down, I heard Suzannah warn, "Jim, please be mindful of her delicacy! Remember, she *is* just a *child!*"

But I couldn't resist doing it again, and was amply rewarded with another display of childish delight—much to her mother's displeasure. As Ainsley hugged me elatedly, Suzannah crossed her arms and tersely declared, "Sometimes I think I have *two* children . . . *neither* of whom is very *mindful* these days!"

Perched on my shoulders, Ainsley noticed the figurehead, and pointing at it she sweetly asked, "Papa, is that *Mama?*"

"It certainly *is*, little one," said Sam's voice from behind us. "That's what we brought you here to see."

Suzannah embraced her parents and excitedly asked, "Have you *ever* seen anything so *beautiful?*"

"Why yes, I *have!*" replied Sam, much to Suzannah's surprise.

"And *what* could be more beautiful than *that* work of art, Father?" she asked, pointing at the figurehead.

Looking down at his feet, Sam cleared his throat and taking Fanny's hand, sheepishly replied, "Why, the *original*, of course!"

Suzannah whimpered at his endearing response, and kissing her father she humbly asked, "Do you know who did the carving, Father, or where Henry had it done?"

"Well . . . ah . . . it was me—*I* carved it," Sam said modestly while threading his arm around Fanny's waist.

Suzannah's jaw dropped, while Sam explained, "Henry needed a figurehead and I needed the business—so he commissioned *me* to do it. After all, Suzannah, who knows you better than your old father?"

Suzannah embraced both her parents and they spoke together in hushed tones of endearment. Sam's work was indeed that of a great master, and Sam was very proud of his youngest daughter's place, both in life—and under the bowsprit.

Admiring the grand figurehead, we pointed out to each other the intricacies that enhanced its beauty—just in case one of us missed them.

Suddenly there was a scrambling on the deck of the brig, and as the sails were hoisted, Dimmis came running down the retreating gangway, her dress hiked up to her knees.

Arriving breathlessly to nestle among us, in wide-eyed amazement she watched Suzannah's figurehead slowly pay out toward open sea.

Henry, now dashingly attired in his uniform and cocked hat, suddenly appeared at the gunnel. He bowed and waved goodbye and was joined by Zeb and Seamus, who did likewise.

As we watched the *Fortune Two* depart, we waved back and cheered as she finally hove to—and as her stern receded into the distant horizon, I coughed to mask the bittersweet tears that clouded my vision . . . because the most endearing sight of that parting was Ainsley, waving and squealing, "Good *bye* Uncle Zeb! Good *bye* Uncle Henry . . . we *love* you!"

CHRISTMAS RECRUITS

Along with the departure of the *Fortune Two* went pieces of ourselves—a feeling that was particularly true for Dimmis. That night, as we sat disconsolate before the parlor fire, imagining what was to come, Suzannah noticed the etched concern on Dimmis' face. Taking her dear friend's hand, she spoke for both of us when she said, "Keep everything full and by, Dimmis . . . he is in good hands. We do *not* wish you to remain at the Thatchers' while Zeb is away. You know you have a home and a family *here*, should you choose to accept it." Looking into Dimmis' eyes, Suzannah softly confessed, "In my *heart*, Dimmis, you *are* my *sister*. And my home would feel more complete if you were living here with us—and that would make your adoring niece very happy too."

Dimmis smiled through her tears and nodded her agreement. "Thank you . . . I love you all very much too. It already feels like my true home." And kissing Suzannah's cheek, they embraced each other, and thus it was decided that Dimmis would live with us . . . at least until Zeb returned; and if the unthinkable ever happened, she would still have a family and a home to call her own.

As winter approached, there was little news and virtually no activity at the wharf. Life was hard for our tradesmen. That summer many had turned to the soil, some to animal husbandry, and others to fishing and bartering to make ends meet. Others had joined the Continental Army simply because they could find no other way to survive.

There were many nights when Suzannah and I went to bed ridden with guilt—knowing that untold riches lay buried in our cellar, which had to be withheld from our friends and neighbors in need. Against that, there was no easy way to buy goods to even give away—unless we traveled to Boston to make our purchases, since payment in gold would surely attract British attention.

But as time went on, we couldn't sit idly by and watch others suffer hardship without offering some form of aid. Finally, we could stand it no longer, and Suzannah came up with a plan. She would hire Wheezer to drive her to Boston periodically to visit her sisters, where the five of them would discreetly exchange a few of our sovereigns for silver and copper coins. Through this method, we became, in essence, the trading post for Walker's Cove, exchanging modest coinage for our neighbors' goods and services. Every so often we passed along a few to those in dire need, calling it a loan to quell their reluctance to accept it outright.

AFTER THE FIRST snowfall, our tavern became the place where sharing problems and solutions was soon the primary activity. Listening to the misfortunes of others made us feel ever more blessed to be in the position we were in—even without the gold. In a spirit of gratitude, Suzannah announced that there would be a Christmas feast at Walker's Tavern on the Sunday before Christmas, and that *all* the townsfolk were welcome to celebrate with us—to eat, drink and enjoy some lively music.

Excited at the prospect, Suzannah, Dimmis and Fanny wasted no time in getting started. They made a concerted effort to purchase as much as they could from the locals, using the coins exchanged in Boston—and when they had finished their purchasing, the final menu consisted of roast pig, roast mutton, fresh bread with plenty of butter, scrapple, baked beans, hasty pudding, rich custard, apple pie, pumpkin bread, Indian pudding, whipped syllabub, Suzannah's flip and of course our signature drink—ginger beer rum. After all the expenses were tallied, Suzannah and I gave thanks to the hapless British—for donating their gold to sustain our worthy endeavor.

AFTER WHAT SEEMED like an endless period of preparation, the day of the feast finally arrived. By midday, despite the bitter cold, every seat in our great room was taken, and despite the recent tribulations, everyone's spirits were infused with goodwill and Christmas cheer.

While the blazing logs crackled upon our giant hearth, the women scurried around the great room serving up the victuals. I in turn enjoyed passing out beverages and engaging in conversations with my fellow villagers. The topics varied: from innocent ramblings about numerous wants to lamenting days gone by. But in every story there was a common truth—that in the face of a pending war, great risks had to be taken so we could move forward and reestablish our livelihoods.

As evening approached, Suzannah and Dimmis took a break to play music together before an eager audience. Whenever the tune they chose was a Christmas carol, all voices in the room broke into song to accompany them.

I'd returned to the kitchen to fetch a fresh barrel of ginger beer rum, when a sharp banging at the door startled me. I froze, thinking the British had found out about our gold and tracked us down. I feared our fate had finally come to claim us.

Suzannah and Dimmis began to play another carol, and as everyone joined in, I wondered what to do next. The door suddenly burst open, sending a cascade of snow onto the floor, and Zeb Hawkes stood in the doorway bellowing in frustration, "*Damn it to hell*, Jim, you ever gonna *answer* your damned *door*? Didn't you *hear* me? It's *cold* out there . . . who did you *think* I was, some damned lily-livered, red-coated, rat-assed, *lobsterback*, or something?"

As he headed straight for the fire to warm himself, I closed the door and annoyed by his fearsome and coarse entrance, I tersely asked, "For God's sake, Zeb, what are you doing *here*? I thought you were with Arnold!"

"I *was* with Arnold, Jim—only he sent me back on a new mission. He's still up in Canada, maybe even in Quebec by now, enjoying a pipe and a flagon of brandy over a nice warm fire like this one!"

"What *is* this new mission?" I asked, curiosity burning away my patience.

Zeb, indicating the carolers singing in the great room, said in low tones, "We can't talk here. Let's go out to the stable."

Reluctantly, I threw on my coat and lighting a pierced tin lantern, I left our warm kitchen to follow Zeb into the frigid darkness. But once we arrived at the stable, Zeb decided we were still too close to the tavern, and that the smithy—being more distant— would be safer. So we trudged on until we reached our next destination where, despite the shelter, the cold was bone chilling.

"So, Zeb, what is this all about?" I asked, my teeth starting to chatter.

"Look here," Zeb said, drawing out a letter from the recesses of his great coat, and after reverently unfolding it, presented it to me.

Holding up the lantern, I could barely make out the signature at the bottom—G. *Washington*—and I couldn't read the contents due to its poor light.

"I can't make it out, Zeb, what does it say," I asked, giving it back to him.

Reciting from memory, he said, "It gives me the rightful duty to recruit, coerce and otherwise cajole any and all able-bodied men not gainfully occupied to join the army in the interest of their future."

Then, after refolding the letter and sliding it into a pocket big enough to hold a suckling pig, he added, "Jim, I gotta take those boys you got in there. Most of 'em are doing nothing except biding their time until spring. I'm authorized to promise five cows as payment to anyone who comes with me."

"Are things that *bad* for the army that you must forcibly enlist recruits?" I asked.

"They're *worse* than that!" he growled, rubbing the stubble of his beard. "Most of Arnold's men took sick in the damned wilderness on the way to Quebec and had to be left behind. The only reason I'm here is because Arnold needs to keep the damned British delayed up north for the winter . . . and that requires *more men*! But not all of them will be heading north, as you will soon find out."

I'd had enough of the cold so I suggested we go back inside to see how the order from Washington would be greeted.

When we got to the door, Zeb whispered hoarsely, "Now Jim, there are folks in there who don't understand the situation, so let *me* do the talking. But you can introduce me . . ."

I nodded my understanding and as Zeb grabbed the door's handle, I firmly added, "Remember, these are *our* friends! This is *my* home and *our* business . . . so *no* violence, Zeb!"

"Naw, not a chance of that!" he murmured, and threw back the latch.

WE ENTERED THE great room side by side, met by a welcome blast of warm air permeated by the sweet aromas of burning spruce, buttered rum and mulled cider. Suzannah's pianoforte and Dimmis' violin could be heard behind the roaring din of another carol—wretchedly sung by good-natured carolers, some of dubious sobriety and talent.

Zeb slammed the door shut so hard it sounded like a pistol shot, and the merriment suddenly turned to a deafening silence. The fire crackled on, and Suzannah sat ramrod straight in her seat, staring openmouthed in our direction. Lowering her bow and violin, Dimmis also looked on in disbelief, while our guests followed their gazes toward the door.

Someone belched and another broke wind. Amused titterings rose among the crowd, and because the wind breaking seemed to put everyone at ease, the right moment to introduce Zeb had come.

"Folks, you all know who *this* is," I began, pointing to Zeb. "He has a message for us from George Washington, the commander-in-chief of the Continental Army."

A loud rumbling and hissing broke the silence as Dimmis thrust a redhot poker into a tankard of flip, which she brought over to Zeb. He gave her a knowing wink as he took it, a grateful expression on his face.

He drained the contents in seven gulps and bellowed, "Whoooo! By *God*, if we could drink this stuff and take a nap near the British camp, we could beat hell out of those damned red-coated weasels just by *breathing* while we sleep!" Then in a more somber tone he added, "But please, listen . . . *all* of you!"

Retrieving his letter, Zeb held it up against the wall next to a mirrored wall sconce. Wielding his hunting knife, he pierced the paper and affixed it to the wall as if posting a notice. Then he turned to his spellbound audience, and while pacing back and forth, he firmly addressed them.

"You know who I am and what I do for a living. The fancy signature on the bottom of that letter is that of General Washington himself—yessir, it *is*! It says he has invested me with the authority to round up, coerce and bribe any and all able-bodied men to join the Continental Army, to help him dispatch the lobsterbacks—*back* to where they came from! Hell, he says you get to camp out with all the *food* you can eat—*and* you'll be paid *five* cows each and one fine new musket for your services!" To drive his point home, Zeb enthusiastically added, "Why by God, there's even free *rum* for you in *this* army!"

Feet shuffled and tankards landed on wooden surfaces; otherwise the room was silent.

Zeb, sensing indifference, scowled and his voice now rose to a shout. "Look, I know it is *Christmas* and all . . . but if you want to have *more* Christmases, you'd better come with me *to get this job done!*"

"But this is not our fight!" Wheezer Hutchinson protested. "I got a home, a wife and children I gotta tend!"

"Me too!" echoed Josiah Poole.

Zeb, his face ablaze with anger, stepped over to Wheezer, grabbed his right ear and roared into it, "Now, you listen to *me*, Wheezer Hutchinson. If these red-coated British bastards get up here, they are going to *hang* you and then *stuff* your *miserable spindly carcass* up your own damned chimney! Then they will let loose their damned Indian friends on your *wife and children* and they will proceed to *disembowel* the lot—*hang* their gizzards out to dry, *bespatter* their brains upon the trees, and *eat* their livers! Then the *Hessians* get what's left! Do you want *that* for your family, you weaselly *rat?*"

Wheezer stumbled for words, but yelped in pain as Zeb grabbed his left ear, and nose-to-nose roared into Wheezer's face so spittle covered his cheeks, "Are you telling me you *ain't* gonna come? Why, so help me *God,* I'll take your gizzard out *right this minute,* and save the Indians the trouble!"

Slamming Wheezer upon a table, Zeb began pawing at Wheezer's clothes. "No, no—oh God, no—don't hurt me, Zeb!" Wheezer wailed, flailing helplessly at Zeb's massive arms.

Zeb lifted Wheezer back to vertical, planting him so forcefully on his feet that his teeth clacked. "So—you're coming *along* then?" Zeb thundered.

"Yes, I will come, I will come!" Wheezer whimpered, his face totally drained of color.

Zeb whirled around and looked at Josiah Poole so fiercely that he sat down in his chair as though he'd been pushed. "And what shape is *your* gizzard in?" Zeb growled.

"Fine—it's fine. I'm going too . . ." Josiah said quickly, as Wheezer fled back to his table.

Zeb stepped back to survey the others and calmly stated, "That's *two* now, so how 'bout the *rest* of you boys? If you got a problem like Wheezer here, speak up! I am Doctor Liberty and I can remove anything that ails you: weak hearts, small gizzards, lazy livers—or anything else!"

When he was answered by silence, Zeb returned to the door and calmly announced: "Good—very good, gentlemen! You've got *five hours* to get your guns, powder, balls, clothes and shoes! We'll meet at Doc Brown's barn, and then we'll come back here and get Jim." As Dimmis refilled his tankard, he added, "And we'll all have one more drink on General George before we leave!"

After Suzannah, Dimmis and I refilled every tankard and mug to the brim, Zeb held up his drink and toasted the room, "*Merry Christmas,* gentlemen, you are now in the Continental Army!" Then, seemingly satisfied, he linked arms with Dimmis, who wanted to show him her new living quarters in our home.

Once he was gone, Ezekiah Wilford approached me to meekly ask, "Jim, the British are using *Indians* agin' us?"

"That's what I've heard," I replied. "Zeb says Jonas Baker ran into some bad ones while on the Arnold campaign."

"*Damn!*" he exclaimed, eyes widening in surprise. "Them savages, do they *really* eat *people* livers?"

"I heard they do, according to the Merritts of Portsmouth . . . or maybe it was the hearts," I added, just to extinguish doubt.

"Damn!" Ezekiah declared. "We better not let 'em get to our womenfolk."

"No, definitely *not*," I agreed with a tone of finality.

"We must take some sort of action agin' 'em," Ezekiah said soberly as he stepped over to view Zeb's letter.

Pulling Zeb's knife out of the wall, I gave Ezekiah the letter to read and pass around to the others, who began to cluster around us.

Noah Blake piped up next, "Jim, do you *really* think they would come up this way?"

Thumbing the sharp edge of Zeb's knife, and remembering his zeal for removing gizzards, I finally replied, "Well, Noah, I would hate to think what would happen—if they *ever* did."

THE TALISMAN

fter my remark to Noah, the lingering effects of Christmas carols and spirituous liquors seemed suddenly neutralized . . . and the soft rumble of serious conversation permeated the room.

Standing on a chair before the fireplace, I rang Mother's bell and announced: "I suggest all you men return home now with your families, and prepare to meet at Doc's *on time* as Zeb instructed. So please finish up your food and drinks now, and remember that despite the short notice, we have a long night ahead."

"'Nuff said!" barked Josiah Poole, and as he and Wheezer gathered their families, he slapped Wheezer's back and pleasantly urged, "*C'mon* Wheezer . . . and bring your damned gizzard!"

As the door closed behind the last of them, an inexplicable sadness crept over me—along with the gloomy thought that this Christmas might indeed have been our last. These were my friends and neighbors. We worked together and helped each other when times got hard. Now we would find ourselves in the Continental Army, where there were no guarantees of survival. God only knew when or *if* we would ever get the cows, muskets and rum we'd been promised in the letter.

As I wiped down the tables, fearful thoughts raced through my mind. "What if some of us are *killed*? How could I bear to watch my neighbors murdered at the hands of the British who—despite what Zeb claimed—were not an imminent threat to Walker's Cove?"

Feeling a sudden flash of anger for having such a cowardly attitude, I threw down my towel and headed into the borning room. There I donned my utility belt, knife, powder horns, hatchet, pistol and possibles bag. I then went upstairs to pack the essential items and clothing I needed to survive the weather; and finally, I would take the musket hanging in our chamber.

As I pondered leaving my loved ones, possibly forever, I felt frightened, anxious and saddened. Knowing that just the sight of her alone would calm my inner turmoil, I decided to visit Ainsley. After tiptoeing into her chamber, the shimmering moonlight revealed her sleeping form, casting an ethereal halo over her golden hair. "Our little gift from God" was my only thought as I stood gazing at her, overcome with love.

Kneeling beside her, I gently pulled the cover back, and stroking her wavy curls, I lovingly whispered, "Without *you* and *your mama*, I would never have discovered the deepest meaning of love. How I love you . . . *both* of you. May God's blessing be upon us and keep us all safe." I kissed her cheek, and tucking her blanket up beneath her chin . . . through welling tears I quietly pulled back.

As I stood in her doorway adjusting my accoutrements of war, I stared back at our cherished daughter, so thankful she was blissfully unaware of her yearning father. I thought how war, evil, hardship and worry are *not* part of a child's world, nor should they *ever* be. "Oh, to be *you!*" I whispered forlornly, and wiping my eyes in agonized worry, I silently left the room . . . and the sanctity of a beautiful innocent heart.

WHEN I ENTERED our bedroom, I lit a fire and began to pack. I changed into my heavy buckskins for protection on my wintry journey. While I was searching through the extra clothing we stored in our spare chamber, I heard the sounds of Suzannah and Dimmis still hard at work cleaning up the great room. Shortly thereafter, Dimmis and Zeb left to visit the Thatchers.

I was back in our chamber when the clock struck ten bells and I heard Suzannah coming up the stairs. Her footfalls were slow and hesitant . . . so I knew she was feeling as burdened as I was.

She came in and poked at the fire, forcing a smile. "It will be very cold tonight . . . I'll find your hunting blanket, some extra stockings and some warmer shoes."

I went to embrace her, but she quickly turned away with a tell-tale sniff, putting on a brave air as she busied herself finding these items.

When I lowered my musket from the wall, she suddenly pleaded, "You *must* be careful so you can return . . . to *both* of us who will miss you terribly."

As she turned her face toward mine, I gently lifted her chin to kiss her, and saw that her eyes were filled with tears. The sight of her dear face tore at my heart, and all I could do was kneel before her and whisper, "My *dear* Suzannah . . ." And after tenderly kissing her, I stroked her hair and pressed my cheek to her heart. When I stood, she crushed her body to mine, and sobbing, she nuzzled her face to my chest and choked on her words: "I *love* you . . . so *much*! I'm *so* frightened, Jim . . . our love . . . Ainsley . . . our tavern . . . this war has cast a shadow of uncertainty onto *all*."

I began to rock her in my arms and softly said, "Suzannah, my darling, take heart and be brave. Through all the uncertainty we have our love as a *family* to carry us through. While I'm away I'll have *your* love, and *that* I shall carry with me wherever I go." Then I softly confided, "If my final hour should come, do not weep for me: for having had you and Ainsley, I've had *all* the happiness that life can hold."

We remained locked in our embrace for a long time, sharing tears, and then more kisses and caresses.

Suzannah gradually released me, and then slowly backed away, her tear stained cheeks glowing in the firelight. Reaching for her sewing table, she retrieved a pair of scissors. She removed her hair-pins and freed her tresses so they cascaded across her shoulders and down her back. She was so lovely that I was half-mad with desire for her.

Sensing that desire, she looked at me seductively, and gathering a ten-inch length of her hair, she cut it off. Using a length of heavy thread, she bound it into a firm three-inch circle; one half inch thick. Next, she strung it on a strand of leather to make a necklace. Looking at me with adoring eyes, she then opened my shirt, kissed the circle of hair and placed the necklace around my neck. She adjusted it so the ring hung directly over my heart, and it still felt warm as it lay against my skin—and suddenly—I felt calmer, less fearful . . . and *safe*.

While tenderly pressing the ring of hair to my heart, Suzannah half-cried and half-whispered a sacred oath. "This ring is *me*—keep me next to your heart—for I'm your guardian angel, your wife, your lover and the mother of your child. This talisman of my love will protect you and ensure your return—safe and well." She then kissed the ring one last time, and lovingly patted it in place. Looking deep into my eyes and running her palm along my cheek, she tearfully whispered, "Always remember, James Walker . . . what awaits you *here* . . ."

"I will!" I said breathlessly, my heart pounding at the strength of her love and the depth of her tenderness. Embracing her cheeks, I kissed her warmly and deeply.

I took her hand then and pressed it against the talisman, and placing mine over hers, I made a solemn pledge. "I shall have you with me at all times and in all places. Although every day may lengthen the distance between us, we are still together in spirit. Dearest Suzannah . . . I *shall* come back . . . I *swear* it to you."

Suzannah began to tremble and slipped her arms around my waist. I picked her up and kissed her passionately, but when I set her down, she suddenly removed my shirt and then opened her dress to her waist. Her nipples were already hard, and as she rubbed her breasts, I removed my buckskins. Dropping her dress to the floor, she jumped up and wrapped her legs around my waist, and her arms around my neck. When she felt my instant arousal, she licked her lips, smiled and breathlessly whispered, "We only have an hour, darling . . . let's not waste it . . ."

WE WERE LIKE demons possessed, and Suzannah made every minute of that hour count. Such was her passion and noise, I feared we would wake Ainsley, so Suzannah suggested we carry on in the far corner bedroom, which we did until we were totally spent. Finally, we lay naked in bed, stroking each other with soft reassuring caresses . . . until we heard a knock on the front door below.

"It must be Zeb and Dimmis!" I shouted, leaping from the bed in a frenzy to get dressed.

We dashed back to our chamber where we threw on our clothes, and after Suzannah fingered her hair in place, she smiled her beautiful smile, and holding hands, we headed down the stairs.

We met Zeb just as he strolled in, covered with a thick layer of fresh snow. Brushing himself off before the fire, he apologetically announced, "Sorry for the intrusion, Jim, Dimmis is still visiting the Thatchers, but there has been a small *delay* . . . Osgood needs more time to . . . ah . . . be with his *wife*, then we'll be around to get you."

Glancing at Suzannah, I suggestively raised my eyebrows, and she signaled me back with her knowing smile. We both knew that had it not been Osgood holding things up, it would surely have been *us*.

"I also came to collect General George's letter," he added. Then in a confidential tone he hoarsely whispered, "Seems I forgot about the letter . . . what with Osgood's romantic *activity* going on."

"It's right here, Zeb," I replied, as I fetched it for him, suppressing a laugh about Osgood. "Sorry about the tear, but it was *your* knife that did it."

"No matter . . ." he said as he stuffed it into his great coat. "Orders are orders and his official signature is still intact!"

As he gazed at the clock, he mumbled something under his breath about Osgood wearing out Mildred, or perhaps it was *she* wearing out Osgood. Then as he stroked his beard, he absently wondered aloud, "How *do* they get so much *scrogging* done with all those *children* around? Beats hell out of me! No privacy in *that* house!"

"Well, *that* certainly doesn't stop *those* two!" Suzannah chimed in.

"Well, I *never*!" I exclaimed, looking directly at Suzannah, who should be the *last* one to remark on anyone's overactive libido. Before I could answer her comment, she blew me a kiss and with a hoydenish titter, disappeared into the kitchen.

Instead, I turned to Zeb and suggested he allow Osgood another hour.

"I will give him *three*!" he replied. "We'll be better off leaving *after* the womenfolk are exhausted and sleeping . . . then the men can depart in a peaceable manner, with their minds at rest."

"I'll see you in about three hours then," I replied. And with that settled, I escorted Zeb to the door.

I went to fetch Suzannah from the kitchen, where she had already started her preparations for the following day's business, scant though it might be with so many of us gone.

Wanting to ensure I'd left nothing out of my pack, I asked her to accompany me upstairs for a final check. She found a few items I'd overlooked and then we tidied up the bedrooms.

Since I was tired and wished a nap before Zeb and Dimmis returned, I sat on the bed and closed my eyes in fatigue. Suzannah sat beside me, and leaning her head against my arm, she quietly asked, "Can we just snuzzle under the comforter for the time we have left?"

I put out the candle and we lay back on the pillows and pulled the comforter over us. We held each other tightly in the darkness, and after a few moments, she rolled on top of me, letting her hair hang over our faces. Beneath its floral canopy she opened my shirt and laid her cheek upon my talisman. From time to time she would raise her head, and after she kissed my "heart" through its opening, we exchanged tender kisses of devoted love. Each of those kisses, combined with her loving embrace, the talisman, and her hair wrapped around us, made me feel *totally* safe . . . and as I gently stroked her back, we both fell asleep.

WHEN I AWOKE, I left my darling still nestled in the comforter without disturbing her sleep. I was relieved that she would miss my actual departure since it would only bring her sorrow—as it would me too.

As I crept softly down the stairs, the house itself seemed to slumber, and I memorized a few details to take with me for solace later on: a blanket hung from a chair-back, Ainsley's wooden top she had left behind on the kitchen table, the lingering scent of apple fritters . . . all precious memories of home.

I went to the chimney vault where we kept our ready supply of hard money, and retrieved some pieces of eight for myself, leaving behind the considerable quantity of gold coins for Suzannah's use. She would need them to keep the tavern supplied with provisions.

When I returned to the great room, I checked the time to see it was 12:40. Zeb and Dimmis would be arriving soon.

Looking around, I again drank in the familiar scene—the portrait of Mother, Suzannah's pianoforte—wondering if I would ever see it all again. I touched the talisman around my neck for reassurance, but at that moment I was overwhelmed with dread at leaving my home, my cherished wife, and my precious child.

Opening the front door, I strapped on my pack, grabbed my musket and stepped out into the freshly fallen snow. Greeted by the still white silence of the winter landscape, I asked myself, "What am I doing?" I looked up and surveyed the stars, which are always extraordinarily bright after a snowfall, and continued to ponder my uncertain fate: "I'm putting everything at risk for a cause that may prove to be a great enterprise—or a cataclysmic failure. My life might be taken from me! What would happen to Suzannah and Ainsley if I died?"

As I stood alone waiting in the biting cold, more dismal thoughts crowded my mind, and I wondered if we would be hung if we were ever captured. We, who were hastily assembled and poorly equipped, were going into battle against the world's finest army and navy. Fortunately, my miserable thoughts were interrupted by the sound of footsteps crunching snow as they approached. It was Zeb Hawkes and his band of Christmas recruits.

They came up to the hitching rail, and stopped to check their accoutrements, while Zeb sauntered over to me.

"Where is Dimmis?" I asked, wondering why she did not return home.

"She is staying with the Thatchers tonight . . ." and clearing his throat, he leaned to me and softly added, ". . . to give you and Suzannah privacy . . ."

Placing his ham-like hand on my shoulder and gazing directly into my eyes, he said, "You look *worried*, Jim."

"Well . . . that's because I *am* worried."

"What about?"

"*Everything!*" I said, choking back my tears.

"*Listen*, Jim . . ." he whispered hoarsely, "everything will be here when you get back. "Every*thing* and every*body!*" Then he added, "These folks out yonder are having the same damned thoughts and feelings as *you*, by God! You all wouldn't be *human* if you didn't."

Leaning closer once again, he said reassuringly, "*I* know how you feel, Jim. We *both* have a reason to come *home* . . . so let's go and get this damned thing *done!*"

And draping his arm securely around my shoulders, we headed off into the snow.

Zeb's Letter

espite the intense cold, we were fortunate there was no wind as we trudged down the street toward the wharf. When we passed the beech tree that marked the path to Walker's Point, I recalled the special moments I spent there with my dear girls. As pangs of regret pierced my heart, again I asked myself, "How could you leave them . . . to possibly never return?"

Approaching the wharf, we saw the dim silhouette of *Fortune Two* waiting in the harbor. Several large bateaux were tied at the wharf, ready to shuttle us over to board her. By the moonlight, Zeb helped the men clamber into the bateaux; and while they were getting settled, I was comforted knowing that Henry would be our captain.

As I gazed mournfully toward home, pressing my talisman to my heart, I envisioned my two sleeping angels . . . my sanctum sanctorum . . . how *lost* I would be without them . . . without *her* . . .

"C'mon Jim! Get the hell over here, we got a *boat* to catch!" Zeb ordered from the wharf; and somehow ignoring the wetness upon my cheeks, I sighed, blew a kiss, and finally turned away.

Once aboard the *Fortune Two*, we discovered there were already dozens of recruits below, sipping mulled cider and spiced rum, and playing games upon makeshift tables of powder kegs. We noticed a palpable warmth generated by the crowd of bodies that greeted us, and they made us feel welcome as comrades-in-arms.

The frigid temperature on land was more moderate at sea, and so calm was the evening, that in my solitary mood, the bow area beckoned me for quiet reflection. I withdrew from my mates and made my way to stand at the bowsprit, thinking of my girls . . . when I remembered that here before me was the carving of my own Suzannah . . . guiding our way, just as she does in life. Reaching down to gently touch her hair, it hadn't the warm comfort of the original.

I watched the ship float on in silence, save for the gentle whisper of the breeze filtering through her sails. As the bow made its way gracefully through the water, it was as though heaven itself was parting the waves before us—hastening our journey—but to what end? Pressing my talisman, I felt my fate open before me once more, just as it did when Death so cruelly touched my life.

But to die would be impossible—for I could not leave Suzannah and Ainsley alone. Thus, I was determined to survive whatever might befall me, and prayed that the fates would allow it. Suddenly I sensed a presence beside me—a towering silhouette that could only belong to my dear friend, Zeb Hawkes.

"What are you doing out here, Jim?" he asked gently, putting his musket down beside him. "Are you thinking about the same thing I am?"

Feeling a tear fall, I simply nodded my agreement—ashamed at being so transparent.

"I can tell by your look," Zeb added as he removed his hat and looked skyward at the stars. "God's universe . . . makes me feel so damned *insignificant*. So much bigger than we . . . is He . . ." and his voice dropped off into silence.

"I never *once* heard you mention that you believe in a supreme being," I remarked in surprise.

"Well . . . that's true . . ." he said hesitantly; "but there's something about the specter of death drawing nearer—that makes me realize how insignificant man's doings *are* . . . in the grand expanse of the universe."

This time I was struck dumb by his eloquence.

So in silence we stood, contemplating the stars and listening to the waves. The sails flapped in unison, the ropes gently patted their masts, and the wooden beams creaked and groaned rhythmically below us. "*Take heart . . . take heart,*" they seemed to say, as though the spirit of the ship was speaking to us.

Zeb broke the spell. "You're worried about the *girls*, aren't you?"

"Yes, I am, Zeb. I feel so *helpless* right now."

"Me too!" he agreed, "me too . . . But they *will* be safe, Jim—you know Suzannah is a *strong* woman," and tapping his chest, he added, "I mean *here* as well . . . no matter what, she will be *fine*. And you're a good man, and you've provided a fine foundation for her to carry on without you."

"Where did you learn about insignificance, the universe and foundations, Zeb? I know Dimmis played a part, but the changes in you and the way you express yourself these days . . . well, they seem to go deeper and deeper . . ."

"It's from that preacher feller down below! You see, Jim, we've been talking philosophy and he's been educating me . . . helping me put my inner feelings into fancy words."

"Philosophy indeed!" I exclaimed, caught off-guard by his answer.

Zeb fished through his array of pockets—cursing—until he finally produced a piece of parchment inked with a beautiful script. Looking me straight in the eyes he said, "Jim, I need to entrust this document to you, being that I am in love and all. Will you please see that Dimmis gets this . . . should anything happen to me?" Holding it out to me he added, "Tell me if you think it's the right thing to say . . . you know a lot about woman stuff."

I took the paper, and opening it in the moonlight, I decided to read it aloud so Zeb could judge for himself.

My own Dimmis,

As we sail into our unknown destiny, I thought I would set down a few lines to you, lest I should not return to Walker's Cove. I feel compelled to write them so that through our closest friend, Jim Walker, my comforting words might stay your sorrow if I am no more.

*My dearest faithful wife, I shall not rend thy heart by
recounting my past sins and the sufferings I caused you . . . nay,
I ask for thy forgiveness and pray that upon delivery of this letter,
you maintain your strength and poise upon its arrival . . . and
never castigate its noble bearer, for he bears me a sacred trust.*

*Should I not return, I implore you to not wed again hastily,
and to seek guidance from Suzannah and Jim—they are your
family and they love you. Above all else, let the purity of love
sanctify thy next union, as it has ours.*

*Please remember, dear wife, while the hand of God closes our
eyes in Death, it is the soul that sees evermore. And so, would that
I could know when your time comes, my spirit shall return from
my world to cradle thine . . . and peacefully guide thee home . . .
into my heart forever.*

*War is fraught with the unknown and makes life itself uncertain.
The hour may come when I shall breathe no more of this life . . .
and if it comes, although I am not worthy to utter its divine sound,
your name shall be upon my lips.*

*Through your love and infinite patience, I have been, and
always shall be, freed from those chains of ignorance and the
painful mediocrity that shackled my youth.*

*Dimmis, how I secretly adored you . . . and into the dust you
could have cast my unworthy offering of love—but you did not.
Never did you trifle with my hopes, or make void your promises.
My life with you is a beautiful dream come true. Your love and
character have made your unworthy suitor a better man than he
ever could have been without you . . . and I am proud to be . . .*

> *Your ever-loving husband to the end,*
> *Zebulon Galletin Hawkes*

"It's the most *beautiful* thing I've ever read, Zeb . . . and I had
no idea you were *married!*"

As he explained, his eyes clouded over with tears. "We were
married in *secret*, Jim . . . by Henry, on this very ship. That's why
he was wearing his uniform that day we were to shove off—and

remember how Dimmis was late getting off the ship?" He paused to allow me to recollect the scene. "But if the worst comes to pass, Jim, I would be most grateful if you would deliver this to Dimmis for me."

"Of course, Zeb. You can count on me."

For the second time in his adult life, Zebulon Galletin Hawkes wept openly. I hugged him and whispered, "Well done, Zeb! She is a *fine* lady—and *beautiful* too!"

"I'm thankful for her every day of my life," he said, nearly squeezing the air out of me with his strength. Then, pulling back, he confessed, "I would never wish any man by my side this night . . . save you or Henry Wiggins. Friends for life?"

"For as long as life is," I said, remembering Suzannah's sacred vow.

On this final night before entering the crucible of war, we rejoiced in Zeb's marriage, but worried about our girls . . . and late into the night we comforted each other . . . fully realizing that only the Fates knew our future.

Sullivan's Island

rom the frozen north, we sailed south to warmer seas that blessed us with sunshine and mild breezes. In the course of our first full week at sea, Zeb and I spent several pleasant evenings with Henry in his cabin, chatting about our "good old days," which in truth were not yet old. But since the preoccupations of war had overwhelmed the colonies, it seemed like a decade had passed since we first partnered with Henry to buy the *Fortune Two* . . . instead of three years ago.

Each night before I turned in, I stood alone at the bow, murmuring to Suzannah's figurehead, willing myself to believe she could hear me. Then I contemplated the stars as I clasped my talisman and prayed my family was safe—and that war would not come to their doorstep, as Zeb had intimated.

One balmy night as we dined in Henry's cabin, he helped to allay my fears about their safety—at least momentarily. "My dear Jim, rest assured the British have much larger fish to catch than a few minnows safely nestled in Walker's Cove . . . which is as *far* from the king's mind as the dark side of the moon."

Henry poured us some rum and after handing us our glasses, he raised his to ours and continued, "The coming battles the king will have to engage in will be fought all over the colonies, gentlemen . . . in Boston, New York, Quebec, Ticonderoga, the Hudson river . . . and especially *here* on the open *sea* . . . where death is quick and alone for *both* sides . . . and trust me gentlemen, when you die at *sea* . . . nobody hears you scream . . ."

After he uttered those macabre words—my sense of panic returned. They were so uncharacteristic of Henry—yet from his life's experience at sea, he spoke of death as though it might become a daily event in our lives. In my uncomfortable silence, I looked downward and pressed my talisman, while Zeb coughed dryly and said nothing.

Sensing our palpable anxiety, Henry lowered his glass and continued, "Let's face it, my good friends, we are at the precipice of a *long* and *bloody* war. It may take as long as a decade to shed our yoke of servitude to the king. Why just recently a pamphlet was circulated by one brave soul, arguing the case for the colonies to become separate entities—entirely independent from the monarchy."

Henry paused as he rose to retrieve a booklet that he tossed on the table. "I picked up this incendiary little item in Philadelphia, Jim—have a look at it. It was published anonymously, but rumor has it that the author is one Thomas Paine. If widely read, it will inflame the desires of all but those with absolutely *no* common sense."

When I opened it, the title page read:

COMMON SENSE:
ADDRESSED TO THE
INHABITANTS
OF
AMERICA,
On the following interesting
SUBJECTS.

I. Of the Origin and Design of Government in general, with concise Remarks on the English Constitution.
II. Of Monarchy and Hereditary Succession.
III. Thoughts on the perfect State of American Affairs.
IV. Of the present Ability of America, with some miscellaneous Reflections

Written by an ENGLISHMAN.

Man knows no Master save creating HEAVEN,
Or those whom choice and common good ordain.
THOMSON.

"I see that Paine's name is not on the title page, but that of 'an Englishman' . . . for fear of retribution no doubt," I said.

"No doubt, indeed, Jim. After all, treason is a serious crime," Henry affirmed.

Thumbing randomly to a page, I read a passage aloud. "Most wise men in their private sentiments, have ever treated hereditary right with contempt; yet it is one of those evils which, when once established, is not easily removed; many submit from fear, others from superstition, and the more powerful part shares with the king the plunder of the rest . . ."

"Exactly!" Henry declared, pounding his fist on the table. "You chose a *brilliant* passage, dear boy!"

The sound reminded me of the tavern and home, while the words I'd read seemed to bolster my decision to participate in the war—that in doing so I was doing right by my family. To wrestle free from this wrongheaded rule by a king, who by a mere stroke of fortune was born into the crown to become master of his universe— and *ours*. Whether he was deserving of our subjugation or not, we were *his* to do exactly as he wished.

Zeb quietly nursed his rum as I continued to read other portions. The text took shape as a brilliant yet simple fusion of ideas drawn from history, philosophy and religion. For me, the author brought forward the realization that for those with *any* common sense, our destiny was *not* to be sheep—to be exploited for the good of the few—but to be an independent people with equal rights for all, just as God had intended.

After finishing the pamphlet, amidst the groaning of the ship's timbers I sat quietly and contemplated these new ideas. And then it occurred to me that I knew nothing about our mission, and so I asked, "Where exactly are we headed, Henry?"

"We're on our way to South Carolina to build a fort on Sullivan's Island. While the British forces are encamped up north for the winter, we anticipate that they'll attempt a campaign in the *south!*" Leaning forward and furrowing his brows, Henry added, "We cannot grant *any* advantage to them . . . our greatest enemy right now is *time* . . . because we *have* none."

Henry stood and began to pace with his hands locked behind his back, as was his habit when thinking. He continued, "But nature might *grant* us some time, as the British *hate* a winter campaign. They are not accustomed to the harsh conditions we normally endure up north. As Arnold says, their fatal weakness is being too used to the *comforts* of life.

Henry finished his rum, and leaning on the table with his palms, he suddenly declared, "Gentlemen, our greatest weapon up north is *surprise* . . . whilst they enjoy their toddies and mutton by their cozy winter campfires, we will stealthily go *around* 'em, *through* 'em and *over* 'em in the frozen grip of the night . . . when Arnold takes Quebec!"

Henry sat again before he continued. "Meanwhile, in the south we will build a fort on Sullivan's Island—and they will be so totally *flummoxed* at the rapidity and diversity of our movements—they will not know whether they are on sea, foot or horseback!"

"Well *Hell's bells*, Henry!" exclaimed Zeb, "They ain't gonna be on horseback any damned way—they will be on *ships!*" He pulled out his knife absently and began fingering the blade.

"Yes, they *will* be on ships, my good friend," Henry agreed. "While they're camped up north in the winter, the British will be *desperate* to muster support among the Loyalists in the south in order to establish a foothold there. But," he warned, "We *cannot* permit them to land *anywhere* in the south—at *any* cost!"

He stood up then and began his nervous pacing again. "Which is why *we* are needed to construct a fort, to fend off any British advance to the south."

"Where would they try to establish a foothold, Henry?" I asked.

"Why, *Charleston!*" he said instantly. Seeing my look of confusion, he added,

"Charleston is where Zeb and I first met Arnold. It's the major seaport and center of trade for the southern colonies—and it's still open. If the British want to end any hope of colonial independence in the south, their seizure of Charleston would do quite nicely."

Returning his knife to its sheath, Zeb bitterly objected, "So it looks to me like we ain't gonna fight *anybody* except the bugs and the vermin!"

"No, Zeb—not yet . . ."

And as Henry turned his hourglass over on the table, he watched morosely as the sand trickled through its waist. Then, nodding to Zeb, he somberly added, "But our *time* is coming . . ."

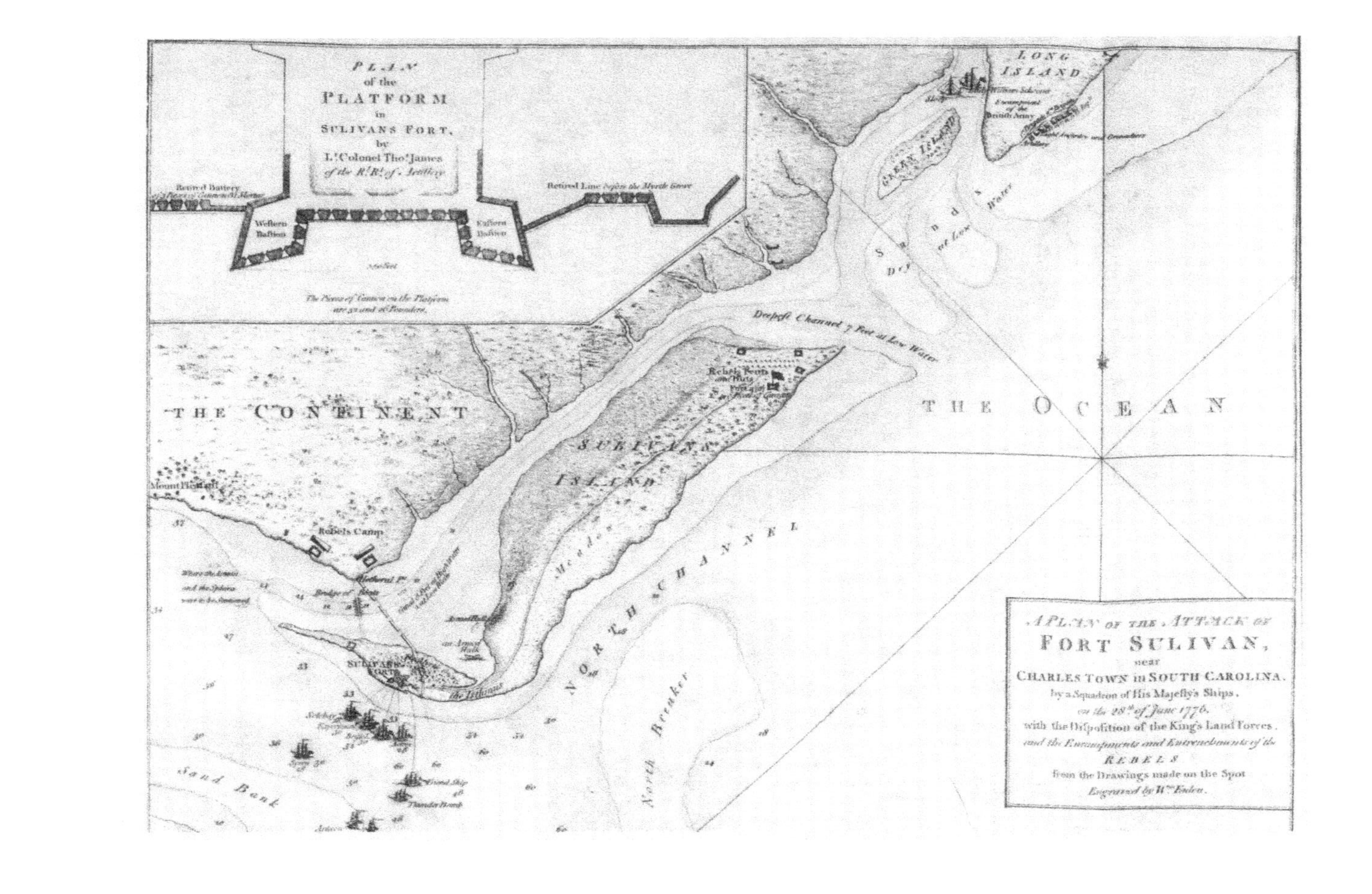

PLAN of the PLATFORM in SULIVANS FORT, by Lt. Colonel Thos James of the Rl. Regt. of Artillery
Retired Battery
Western Bastion
Eastern Bastion
Retired Line before the North Grove
The Pieces of Cannon on the Platform are 32 and 16 Pounders.
LONG ISLAND
GREEN ISLAND
THE OCEAN
THE CONTINENT
SULIVAN ISLAND
Deepest Channel 7 Feet at Low Water
Rebels Fort and Huts
Sands Dry at Low Water
NORTH CHANNEL
North Breaker
Sand Bank
Meadow
Mount Pleasant
Rebels Camp
SULIVANS FORT
the Isthmus
A PLAN OF THE ATTACK OF
FORT SULIVAN,
near
CHARLES TOWN in SOUTH CAROLINA.
by a Squadron of His Majesty's Ships,
on the 28th of June 1776,
with the Disposition of the King's Land Forces,
and the Encampments and Entrenchments of the
REBELS
from the Drawings made on the Spot
Engraved by Wm. Faden.

Sullivan's Island is a comma-shaped island about three miles long and half a mile wide. It sits at the entrance of Charleston harbor, nestled among several other islands—Long Island, Green Island, Hog Island, and James Island—which collectively form a protective cluster before Charleston itself.

As we sailed through the northern channel, Henry, Zeb and I stood at the gunnels, observing Sullivan Island and its barren sandy windswept features . . . with nothing but palmetto trees and scrub growth dotting its sandy landscape.

"Damnedest misbegotten place as I ever *saw*!" grumbled Zeb as he squinted to starboard.

"Indeed!" Henry replied, stretching his telescope to have a closer look. "I cannot disagree with your valid summation of this turgid sandpit of an island. But if you look ahead, you can see there is no chance of a vessel getting through this channel—*if* a fort is located at *that* point!" indicating the tip of the comma's base with the eyepiece of his telescope.

While we scanned our destination, we heard soundings being taken and recorded by the mate and another crewmember.

"We need to establish the depth," Henry explained, "so we can lure an English ship of the line to ground herself in the shoals." Then, pointing to the south, "There are rumored to be large sand-banks just below dead low tide—which for our purposes are better weapons than an entire deck of eighteen-pounders. In fact, a rea-sonably well-constructed garrison at this location, equipped with twelve- or eighteen-pounders, could blow any ship heading toward Charleston out of the water—or at least force it to the inside chan-nel, where once run aground, it could be shot to pieces from the two shorelines."

As we drifted toward the island, there was a noticeable flurry of activity onshore. Then a signal cannon was fired, and Henry gave the order to answer it with two affirmative shots. We dropped anchor between the island and the mainland, and soon thereafter a dozen longboats rowed out to greet us.

The *Fortune Two* remained offshore while the longboats ferried us over the shoals to Sullivan's Island. Our contingent would be under the command of Colonel William Moultrie, who would greet us there. Afterward, Henry would resume his patrol, seeking bounty and attempting to thwart any British ship he sighted.

As we gathered our packs, I took Henry aside. "I pray to see your safe return, Henry."

Henry sighed and said in low tones, "Jim, if Providence is on our side and God wills it, we shall meet again in this world. But if this should *not* come to pass, *know* that you are loved and dearly marked in this voyager's heart . . . for you and Suzannah are part of my being . . . and no matter what end may find us, I am well satisfied on that account."

Then he leaned over to pat the figurehead and affectionately added, "*She* will guide us, Jim—and *she* will bring us home— *together* . . ."

We embraced as the men boarded the longboats, and when we parted, I felt a painful vacancy in my heart . . . for despite Henry's faith in Suzannah, I feared for him—and for us all.

As our longboats scraped the sandy shore; a small knot of men came to greet us, including William Moultrie. He was clearly the leader of the group, as the rest stood behind him, peering at us as if observing a strange breed of insects. A kind-looking man in his forties with a serene countenance, one would never have guessed he had been an Indian fighter. He carried himself with dignity and he was impeccably dressed, especially considering the occasion. His breeches were neatly tucked into his boots and his weskit was in good order—as were his coat and epaulettes, which marked him as a colonel.

He saluted formally and addressed me first. "I am Colonel William Moultrie of the 2nd South Carolina Regiment. Welcome to Sullivan's Island, gentlemen. Might I ask your name and rank, sir?"

"I am James Walker from Walker's Cove, tavern-keeper and blacksmith . . . and this man is Zebulon Hawkes, my partner."

Zeb saluted clumsily and gruffly added, "We have no rank, Colonel, but Captain Henry Wiggins said to tell you we're here as volunteers for the Continental Army . . . to help you build a fort." He turned to look around, and dubiously pointing toward the dunes overlooking the beach, he hopefully added, "Over *yonder*, perhaps?"

"Perhaps!" Colonel Moultrie replied with a smile. Then slapping his hands together enthusiastically, he said, "We're mighty glad to have you here, gentlemen! We need every pair of hands we can get! And who are these others?"

Turning toward the group, I first introduced our cohorts from Walker's Cove, and when I was done, I motioned the remaining men to come forward and state their names—and ranks, if they had one. As they did so, a secretary behind Colonel Moultrie scribbled the information into a ponderous ledger book. When he was finished, he issued a roll call to confirm the information he'd collected.

Colonel Moultrie saluted us and returned to his duties, then the secretary led us to a secluded area behind the beach, where a dense growth of spindly palmetto trees provided shelter from the relentless heat of the sun. It was there we discovered that Moultrie's men were far greater in number than we'd hitherto seen. They were from South Carolina, North Carolina and Virginia, and among them were infantry regiments, rifle regiments and independent artillery companies, expert in the placement and firing of cannons.

I was contemplating the collective expertise of these comrades, when a thin man with a bobbing Adam's apple approached me. "Are you James Walker?"

"Yes, I am," I replied.

He politely saluted and said, "Sergeant William Jasper, sir . . ."

I saluted in return. "I'm glad to meet you, Sergeant Jasper. Are you my superior officer?"

"Doubt it all to hell . . ." he casually muttered. "But Colonel Moultrie would like to see you and the big feller in his quarters."

Looking toward Zeb, I shouted, "Hey *big* feller—we are *wanted!*"

Zeb stood—towering over everyone—and slapping his hands in delight, humorously declared, "Well, it's about damned time! I was getting *bored* all of a sudden . . ."

Jasper led the way to a large hut built from palmetto logs. Standing off to one side of the entrance without a door, he motioned us inside. In the gloom broken by a crude opening in the opposite wall, we observed Colonel Moultrie scratching out a letter on a makeshift table. He looked up briefly, and waving his quill to acknowledge our presence, he brightly said, "Please have a seat, gentlemen. I'll be right with you."

Zeb looked all around, fidgeting nervously. Following his gaze, I noticed there wasn't a chair in sight. We exchanged resigned glances and stood waiting as Colonel Moultrie continued writing, unaware of our predicament.

When he finished his letter, he stood to greet us, and noticing our chair-less state, with profuse apologies, he heartily exclaimed, "*Oh!* Please forgive me gentlemen, forgive me—*my* error," and he called out, "Jasper?"

Sergeant Jasper poked his head in as Colonel Moultrie asked, "The *chairs*, William, are they nearby?"

Within seconds, two men came in with two palmetto trunks and stood them on end.

Colonel Moultrie thanked them and then turned to us. "Please, gentlemen . . . *now* you may *sit*."

I must say that I would have given anything to donate the crudest of chairs to the colonel's cabin—for I noticed that he himself was also perched on a palmetto trunk behind his table . . . which itself was constructed of palmetto wood.

As Colonel Moultrie paced to and fro across the hut, he seemed to think aloud, "I have a great need for you, Mr. Walker. A blacksmith is a scarce commodity and a highly valuable asset to *any* army, so I wish to keep you safe from harm or capture. Your skills will be put to good use building our fort."

"When will we start?" I asked.

"My plans are preliminary at the moment, but by tomorrow I shall have them all sorted out . . . This fort—and the methods of fighting we learned from the Indians—may force the British to reevaluate their entire concept of warfare!"

Eager to know more, I asked, "How is that, sir?"

"We hit them and *run* . . . we do *not* stand thirty yards apart in open fields with muskets trained upon their lines, and then exchange volleys that expose our men to open slaughter. Why, in '61—the Cherokee War—those Cherokee were the *finest* warriors I ever saw! A man would indeed be a fool not to learn from *them* the art of inflicting maximum damage on the enemy, while suffering the fewest number of casualties.

"So we fight the *Indian* way: we hide behind trees, bushes, logs, rocks, structures of all kinds, and we use *rifles*, which use *half* the powder, *half* the ball and can shoot a man in the *heart* at one hundred yards! A Brown Bess has but a *quarter* of that accuracy! For close combat we rely on hatchets and knives instead of pistols. A pistol is but *one shot* and then it's done—a hatchet and knife can be thrown from a great distance, well beyond the accuracy of any pistol, and *kill* its target. As long as they are skillfully thrown, they can put men out of action, be retrieved and used again."

Moultrie returned to his desk, and drawing an enormous knife from his belt, he held out a sheet of paper to the air and slit it in half with ease. Looking at Zeb, he soberly added, "In close combat, even *big* men will shrink from a knife . . ."

The observation made Zeb squirm uncomfortably, but I wasn't sure whether it was because he agreed with that statement—or worse, wanted to challenge it.

Moultrie, oblivious to Zeb's reaction, pressed on: "When we fight the British *Indian* style, their officers will never know what hit them! And if we target the *officers*—we send their troops into total disarray, which means we pick them off with rifles from a distance— and thus we curtail our losses—and soon there will be no more British soldiers left to fight!"

"Wouldn't targeting their officers be unseemly?" I asked, knowing how formal the British army was in its rigid chain of command.

"Not in the *least!*" Moultrie exclaimed, pounding his table, which made almost no sound due to the softness of the palmetto wood. Looking at his fist in frustration, he added, "This damned *wood* . . . it hardly deserves the *name* . . . it's like a sea sponge with as little strength . . . But at least it's very pliable and easy to build with, *and* we are overrun with it around here."

Resuming his seat, he continued, "Which brings me to our main objective—using this miserable wood to build a fort that will stand up to heavy British man o' war firepower." Pointing at me he said, "Walker, you said you're a blacksmith and I need *saws*—as many as you can make. Can you do this for me if I get you everything you need for a forge?"

"Yes, sir," I replied, "and perhaps coarse-tooth saws will work better on soft wood such as this palmetto."

"Good! I will need at least fifteen two-man saws. And perhaps some drills for wooden spikes, because palmetto will never hold a damned nail. Do you require help in setting up a smithy?"

"Yes, sir," I replied, placing a hand on Zeb's shoulder. "I can use *Zeb*—we have worked together before in my smithy back home."

"I'm glad to hear it. So let's get to it, Walker. See Sergeant Jasper for the men and materials you need, and get started immediately . . . and remember that time is against us!"

Before we left Moultrie's hut, I made Sergeant Jasper a list of the supplies I needed and told him the minimum number of men. He promised to leave for Charleston forthwith.

As we followed one of Jasper's aides to the site of the proposed smithy, Zeb jabbed me in the ribs and complained vehemently about my volunteering him. "Damn it, Jim—I *never* was a black-smith and you *know* it! What's the idea of dragging me into your private hell?"

I smiled and replied evenly, "I decided it would keep *us* together and *you* out of trouble."

Before he had a chance to reply, the aide stopped to show us around the proposed blacksmith site, which consisted of a mountain of bricks, an almost equal quantity of fieldstone, and scattered heaps of rusting scrap pig iron.

"*What* trouble?" Zeb asked, once the aide was out of earshot.

I nodded toward the palmetto groves. "Did you notice those fellows back there who had only one eye?"

Shaking his head no, Zeb turned back to look where I had indicated, and saw that several men wore eye patches, exhibiting only their one good eye.

I told him that I'd learned from Henry—just before we parted— that these were mostly Virginians. As a group, they were tall and willowy men of rude simplicity in their ways, but were renowned as being fearless—with total disregard for the consequences of their actions. Among them was a marked talent for scooping an eye out of its socket with remarkable dexterity and swiftness. Furthermore, Henry said if scooping out an eye did not suffice—they were very quick to fall upon their deadly rifles, their hatchets or their knives.

Zeb, cautiously observing the behavior of the "one eyed Joes" as they were called, gave me a wry smile and nodded, saying, "Come to think of it, Jim, I guess I *do* have some experience in the smithy . . . starting right *now*! So what do you need me to do?"

Reflections

March 1776
Sullivan's Island

My Suzannah,

How I wish you could see these beautiful mornings here; how the birds sing to greet the waking dawn; how the sun makes its way across the pastel sky, chasing the wispy clouds as they scurry above me!

Dearest angel . . . although I'm away from you, I feel you around and within me, your faithful Love crowds my senses and comforts my soul . . .

So often I fall into sweet reveries and build air castles around you and our darling daughter, who are not beside me, but safely nestled in my heart. How is our beautiful little Ainsley? Our sweet little child, with the charming smile and silvery laugh! So much like her mamma is she who occupies my heart!

How I miss both pairs of wondrous gray-blue eyes, drawing strength and purpose—and a sense of belonging from their gaze. How I miss snuzzling you both in bed, an arm around each—we three as one! How I miss the tickles, pokes, prods and pestering!

Give my kisses to Ainsley, and snuzzle her for me . . .

Love evermore,
Your James
Sullivan's Forge

P.S. Direct letters to me in care of Colonel William Moultrie, Army at Charleston, South Carolina.

Sullivan's Forge

ithin a week, Zeb and I had laid a fieldstone perimeter for an open front U-shaped forge. Mortar was hard to find, so mixing mud and crushed seashells, we managed to anchor the fieldstones for a stable foundation. The three sides of the forge would be constructed of notched palmetto logs, saddled together with wooden pins soaked in water. We moved the bricks to the rear center, where we would use them to build a raised hearth.

The open front faced south, allowing in plenty of light and a cooling breeze while we worked. Every other day, Colonel Moultrie would stop by to assess our progress, offering encouragement and praise for building a forge—so vital to the construction of his fortress.

Two weeks later, the colonel paid us a visit to inform us that Jasper had managed to acquire nearly every item on my list; and that the goods were on boats already heading across the channel to be delivered.

Sure enough, they arrived about an hour later. When I unpacked the crates, I found an anvil of good bounce, accompanied by matching hardie and pritchel tools. In addition, there were hammers, sledges, tongs, a vice, files—and much to my surprise—a bellows and hood assembly for our hearth. But even more remarkable than those were the hundreds of pounds of scrap pig iron and several bags of lime, which we sorely needed to make mortar for the raised-brick hearth. The lime we immediately mixed with sand and water, and we wasted no time in building our hearth.

By the middle of March, our forge shed was finished. The hood and bellows were in place, and the hearth was ready for firing. My tools were hung in their places ready for use, and we awaited only the hardwood for making the charcoal that would fuel it. When it came, we marveled at the vast quantities of maple, hickory, birch and oak they'd brought us, and appreciated their Herculean efforts in getting it to the island without complaint.

Zeb worked incessantly at my side. In addition to pumping the bellows, quenching and annealing, we pounded the pig iron together to form our first saw blades. With two hammers ringing constantly, we turned out three saw blades a day. Once they were forged, Zeb would sharpen the teeth with files, and finally attach them to bucking cradles. With these, the palmetto trees would be felled, to provide the logs to build the fortress.

When Zeb and I finished the first three saws, we carried them to Colonel Moultrie's hut. There, we proudly offered him these *first* products from our forge for his inspection.

The saws pleased him greatly, and as he handed them over to Jasper, he ordered, "Jasper, here are the *fine* results from the forge *everyone* said was *impossible* to build . . . now . . . *cut* the palmettos down!"

"How many, sir?" the sergeant asked meekly.

"*All* of them—cut them *all* down! Then drag them over to the point. There are more saws coming, so keep the men moving—we have no time to spare!"

Turning to me, he said, "*Walker*, I need to get as many of these saws as you can make in a week. After that, we will also need smaller saws for the pegs, and sharp hatchets to trim 'em with! By God, we will get this fort built and give 'em hell!"

I acknowledged his order with a snappy, "*Yes, sir!*" and turned to leave. But then he shouted unexpectedly, "*Walker!*"

"Yes, sir?"

Approaching me with an outstretched hand, Colonel Moultrie took mine and shook it firmly in appreciation. "Thank you, Jim." He quietly added, "You're a damned good blacksmith! In fact, you are so good at making something out of so little, I have no doubt you can make anything out of nothing at all!"

Not wishing to have to prove his belief, I murmured a modest, "Thank you, sir."

He saluted me and commanded, "Back to the forge, soldier!"

Clad in our leather aprons and breeches, Zeb and I pounded continuously for the next ten days. During that time we turned out sixteen additional saws for the tree crews. After that, we turned our attention to small saws, hatchet heads—and finally—a few long knives for the men who had none.

The wood pit that provided our charcoal burned and smoked villainously day and night, and I feared it might signal our activities to the British. When I expressed my concern to Colonel Moultrie, he said the charcoal was desperately needed for our makeshift forge, and without the forge, there could be *no* fort for defense—and thus, we should carry on with our work.

The only relief from our ceaseless labor was our evening swim, when Zeb and I would wade into the warm waters of the ocean to wash away the day's dirt and sweat. It rejuvenated us just enough so that we could drag ourselves to bed and pass out from exhaustion.

But each night when I lay down to sleep, my arms and legs would spasmodically twitch and quiver from overwork, such that Zeb feared I was afflicted with a palsy of some kind and might die.

I reassured him that it was happening because I hadn't worked a smithy since I was a boy, and that my arms and legs would eventually strengthen in response to the stress. I would become more muscular, with intensely defined vascularity, which would herald my newfound vitality.

Despite all this, without Suzannah, I felt like a miserable drone, mindlessly hammering every day. As I incessantly labored, I wondered if she'd received my first letter. Although I fell into bed each night holding her precious talisman, I couldn't dwell on her sweetness and comforting presence. I could think of nothing but sleep . . . and what we had to hammer the following morning.

Where is God?

March 17, 1776

My dearest James,

I am overjoyed at having a letter from you—and an address I can write to—at long last. It is very comforting for me to know you are well and stationed in a congenial climate.

I've been spilling over with news to tell you—from far, from my sisters' letters, and near, since the war not only came to our doorstep, but stepped inside.

Generals Arnold and Montgomery have failed in Canada, having been soundly defeated attempting to take the garrison at Quebec. General Arnold was shot in the thigh, but word is that he lives. General Greene evidently has been captured by the enemy, and was taken inside the gates of Quebec. General Montgomery is dead, having been shot twice through his thighs, and once through the head.

The army under Arnold's command has been split in two: the sick and the well. Before the attack, many of the sick remained in the wilderness under Colonel Roger Enos. Because of the bitter cold, many of them have been dispatched by any desperate means available from an isolated encampment called Norridgewock, to the nearest places dispensing shelter and medical care. Because of Doc Brown, one such place is Walker's Cove.

Every day, sick men under Enos' command stagger in from the sub-zero cold. It is so frigid here that the new arrivals are in a wretched state when finally brought before Doc Brown, who mournfully concedes they are literally upon Death's door . . . our door.

It is heartbreaking to see Doc struggle to perform what few ministrations he can. He is mostly alone in his task, with Dimmis and I his nurses . . . for what little aid and encouragement we can provide to bolster his heroic spirit.

Smallpox and consumption are rampant among those sent to us for care, but more often to die. At times some of the womenfolk stop by to help us, but several have gone away with infections or sick from exposure to the more contagious ailments. Fate has indeed been fickle in the case of many of them . . . for some have died as their reward for offering care to the war's sorriest victims. Among them were Lavinia Bates, Emma Watson and our dear Rhoda Barrett . . . all gave unselfishly of themselves to render aid, administer medicine, and lend a tender hand to comfort the soldiers.

Our tavern, our once beautiful home . . . is now a makeshift hospital of Death, where Doc does the best he can. He is aging rapidly and becoming wearier, tasked with the ceaseless burden of being the only physician within 70 miles. With few medicines to offer, the men suffer terribly. Doc must often resort to horrible amputations of legs and arms, as many have gangrene, and the blood of his patients now stain the once joyous floors of our tavern.

Worse yet, Doc's worst enemies, Mr. Headache and his wife, Mrs. Fever, plague many of these wretched men with their company, as well as dysentery, which makes the sufferer wish for death as much as life. Others are here with the rheumatism from the cold, thus making the joints and connections so painful that Doc may as well tear the sockets out of their tortured joints and have done with them. It seems the array of various aches pains and afflictions keep all our patients in desperate want of laudanum, which is in very short supply.

Men without shoes have such thoroughly frozen flesh on their feet, their toes readily snap off if pressured.

I cannot describe the extent of my own agonized suffering, and the silent depression of my spirit in tending these hopeless creatures.

Whilst they suffer in our great room and guest chambers, in our kitchen we make shrouds for their corpses, since God comes to claim so many. In my heart and my conscience, I inwardly rejoice at the end of their sufferings: for Death turns agony into sweet release . . . and *provides passage to a better place. Meanwhile, Father keeps the frozen corpses in his barn, waiting for ships to come and bear them home.*

Through God's graces, Doc, Dimmis and I are so far mercifully spared their terrible afflictions . . . but I fear my heart has hardened, for I have become frightened, particularly for Ainsley. So I have given her to Father and Mother for safekeeping, away from her miserable home.

During these long suffering nights, I feel wicked as I bolt my chamber door against their piteous groans . . . and without you, I cry myself into a restless sleep. And so alone—racked with guilt ridden sobs—I ask God each and every night, "What good could ever come of all this misery?"

There are many agonies . . . and very few raptures here . . . may God protect us all . . . and you . . .

This, from your little wife who loves and misses you,

Ever your Suzannah

Courage

March 30, 1776

My dearest Suzannah,

The sorrowful duty to which you so willingly attend moves me deeply. How I wish I could sit and weep with you . . . rock you and caress you to renew your burdened spirit. For those at death's door, you are the living angel that comforts their wretched souls in their journey toward the inevitable end.

How many fatherless children are now left behind? How many husbandless wives must press forward in life, totally alone? May God guide you in your choices . . . and may He provide you the spiritual and physical means to afford comfort and succor to those poor, miserable souls who have sacrificed themselves to a noble cause. The hopeful outcome of their suffering, however ghastly, will bring a great gain to our earthly existence—and the generations that come after us— as a free people.

Dear wife, heed my words. Stay brave and true . . . for you are the one fixed point in a changing age that gives every life you touch comfort and hope. Should we be successful in this noble enterprise, our earthly reward will be freedom from British rule evermore . . . and we shall forge our own path to our own destiny.

And now dear heart, let me tell you how much I yearn for you each and every day. My memories and dreams of you cast delicious spells that abolish time and space, and make the surrounding world dissolve like summer mist upon the sea.

{ 553 }

At night when I clutch your talisman to my heart, know that your name upon my lips is like a comforting balm. In my dreams, I feel great waves of your love wash over me . . . and envelop me in that divine cocoon of your sweet soul and soft heavenly embrace.

Suzannah, you are and have always been the best wife and my only angel . . . and ever will be. Remember me to our little Ainsley and kiss her for me. Tell her how her father loves her, and wishes to hold her to his heart.

With Love evermore and untold,
Your husband James

Island Life

Culinary shortcomings are legendary in army camps, and ours was no exception. On most nights, squirrel or fish was generally served slopped over stale dry biscuits, with an occasional garnish of clams, possum, salted sea gull, stringy bear meat or long dead turkey. But I knew that to carry on as the island's blacksmiths, Zeb and I needed a rich hardy meat to nourish us—so we would have enough strength to haul the heavy ingots of pig iron and to wield hammers and sledges for hours on end.

After our evening meal, the men from Walker's Cove would gather before the fire to write letters destined for home or to swap stories about the past day's activities. Invariably, their conversations would always turn to food . . . and Zeb would be the target of their good-natured resentment. They would chide him constantly for promising food the army couldn't deliver, and for the unappetizing cuisine they were now stuck with. And then there was the rum he had promised too—or rather, the appalling *lack* of it within a twenty mile-radius of Sullivan's Island. Each mention of that rum, (which now according to rumors lay beneath the island sands just waiting to be discovered), brought snickers and knee slaps from volunteers who always promised to dig for it . . . next year.

When Zeb and I were alone, I shared the contents of Suzannah's letter with him, and cautioned him not to tell our Walker's Cove compatriots about Arnold's defeat at Quebec or the dire conditions at home. I knew they'd hear the news soon enough, either officially or unofficially—but I didn't want it coming from me.

Despite their endless toil as loggers and many complaints about the poor food and lack of rum, my friends were still in very good spirits. One day as I sat among them while we rested, I heard

Wheezer Hutchinson engaged in an argument about the proper way to construct a bean hole.

"Jim, we need your opinion!" he demanded fiercely. Then, pointing at me he added, "Now *here* is the man whose wife is the *best* cook in Walker's Cove, so surely *he* knows how Suzannah does it!" Looking at me hopefully, he said, "Go *ahead*, Jim, tell 'em how *she* does it!"

Taking the end of a palm frond, in the sand I traced a large circle and explained, "Well, to tell you the truth, Wheezer, Suzannah no longer uses bean holes, she uses an *oven*! But my mother once told me that *she* used bean holes every so often—especially for large gatherings at the tavern, before she had brick ovens."

Pointing to the center of the circle I continued, "Father would dig her a deep bean hole of perhaps three feet in diameter. He would line its bottom and sides with wood, the harder the better, and let it burn until the wood was reduced to a hot bed of coals. Mother's bean kettle was brought to the spot . . . I recall it was a well-seasoned five-gallon kettle, with a very heavy lid."

Abner Blatchford interrupted to anxiously inquire, "Did she *parboil* the beans beforehand, Jim?"

"Yes, she did, Abner—two *days* beforehand."

"I *told* you so!" Wheezer bellowed, jumping up to emphasize his point. "You gotta *parboil* 'em, Abner—two *days* ahead no less—not just dump 'em in the kettle willy-nilly!" Turning to me, he asked, "And how did she *make* 'em, Jim?"

"She would pull several pounds of salt pork into chunks, cut up a couple of eye-watering onions, and ready a quart of molasses—and all this went into her kettle. Lastly, she poured the parboiled beans into the kettle—water and all."

"Water and *all?*" Abner echoed.

"Why yes, Abner," I said, puzzled by his question. "In any case, the kettle was brought to the bean hole—by which time the bed of coals were ready to heat it—and it was carefully nestled there. Father would make sure the heat was sealed in by raking the coals around the kettle and over its lid, and then covered the entire bean hole with loose dirt. It was left to simmer all night and well into the following day."

"No *wonder* your damned beans rattled on the plate, Abner!" chided Wheezer. "You didn't put *water* in the kettle! Nor did you *parboil* 'em! So never invite me to *your* house for a bean supper . . . I might be *poisoned*!"

We all laughed heartily, although I did feel badly about Abner's failed attempt at baking beans. He was, after all, a widower who'd made a valiant effort to cook by himself. But after Suzannah and I opened the tavern, he made it his habit to eat there. Suzannah—who knew he was lonely *and* lacked culinary skills—usually charged him nothing more than the pleasure of a good conversation.

Pressing my talisman, I reflected on Suzannah's kindness and generosity, which had made Abner's solitary life a little easier—especially considering he was now on this dangerous adventure. As the men continued to scoff at his feeble efforts to bake beans, I knew how it felt to be alone in the world—for without his sweet wife's seraphic smile and abiding presence, Abner had lost so much more in his life—than just baked beans.

In addition to my evening plunge in the ocean with Zeb, I took another solitary one in the morning. As I did, I developed a growing appreciation for the lush verdancy of South Carolina's pristine shoreline. It was pleasing to simply walk about, enjoying the gentle morning breezes that greeted me before my day of labor. How lovely it was too to feel the sensation of the soft warm sand between my toes. It was all in such marked contrast to the ice-encrusted, boulder-strewn shores of Walker's Cove, and I sorely wished Suzannah were here to share it with me, and make love under the palmettos.

I gave the wish more serious consideration when I discovered that there were numerous women on Sullivan's Island, known as "camp followers." These were usually soldiers' wives who wished to remain near their husbands despite the dangers of battle. I began formulating a plan to bring Suzannah down here with me, but eventually Colonel Moultrie banished the camp followers, claiming they were too much of a distraction. They were all escorted to the mainland when the construction of the fort began.

Oddly enough, it seemed that Zeb had disappeared with them, so I assumed he had volunteered as an escort. While I knew he was tired of being badgered and teased about the food and the non-existent rum, I was seriously concerned about what he was up to, and why he left me alone in the smithy without any warning.

One morning, when I wanted to observe firsthand how well our forged tools were holding up, I decided to approach Colonel Moultrie while he was overseeing the delivery of palmetto logs to the site of the projected fort. Not wishing him to think I had abandoned my forge, I wore my leather apron and carried a pair of well-burned pincers so he would assume I was merely taking a rest from my work.

"I presume all is going according to plan, Colonel?"

"Ah, Jim Walker . . . my best blacksmith! I hope I find *you* well today?"

I coughed and apologetically replied, "Well sir . . . I am your *only* blacksmith . . . and yes, I *am* well."

We watched silently as men and oxen were hauling the palmetto logs, which were naturally uniform in diameter. They were being arranged to form a double wall, approximately five hundred feet long and about twenty feet apart.

"Am I to understand you will make two walls, sir?" I inquired, not able to visualize his concept.

"Ah . . . the infernal palmetto!" he announced, apparently to the wind. Then addressing me directly, "It's a blessing *and* a curse. In some ways it's a superior wood, for its consistent diameter saves us the work of trimming each one to size. It also resists the pestilential sea worms, and does not splinter easily. Many of the men boil the terminal buds for food—a bitter plate, but just as nourishing as any sea gull, I presume . . ."

Then, abruptly, he broke off. "Jasper!" he yelled, "The rear wall is not equidistant from the first wall. They must be *equidistant* because the gun platforms and parapets will be built upon them! Use the chains to measure!"

After a distant acknowledgement from Jasper, he turned back to me. "Hmmm . . . where was I? Ah, yes . . . the palmetto fruit is fleshy and dark, and seems to attract many creatures that the men shoot for food—raccoons, turkeys, gulls and many other sorts of birds. As you can see for yourself, Jim, the very fact that so many grow upon the shores would indicate they are a hardy breed of palm, and very pliable against the wind, lest they be ripped out of the sand."

Turning to see Jasper realigning the twin sets of logs, he commented absently, "Good man, Jasper! We *will* build this fort *yet*, by damn!"

Then, suddenly alert to my presence once more, he said, "My apologies, Jim. You were asking about the *design*, were you not?"

"Yes, sir."

"The plan is to have *two* walls, but they are not *separate*—they will be joined as one."

Noticing my confusion, he stooped to grab a handful of sand, and letting it trickle through his fingers, he said, "The walls will be joined with *this*!"

"*Sand?*" I asked incredulously.

"Yes, sand," Moultrie calmly replied. Squinting toward the south, the colonel started to explain his reasoning. "Jim, we have more sand around here than any other material. The palmetto logs are very pliable and so is the sand. When cannonballs are fired and hit a palmetto log backed by sand, they will do little or no damage. Their energy is dissipated in the logs first, and then into the sand, and thus our little fortress can withstand quite a pounding and still remain in the fight."

He added, for clarification, an opposite scenario. "When a cannonball hits the rigid hull of a ship—unless it's constructed of the stoutest material or supported by the ribs of the ship—the wooden hull *must* give way."

Placing his hand upon my shoulder, he confided, "We have but thirty-one cannon, Jim, and we need to gain all the advantage we can muster. Having such a fortress as this one will keep us in the fight. Hell, we can even retrieve the spent British shot from the sand and send them back—with far more devastating results.

"Our shots must be well placed . . . but I believe we can do it. And you, my *only* blacksmith, might then be spared the experience of inspecting the interior of a British prison ship."

His explanations made good sense and his faith seemed boundless. I decided that Colonel Moultrie was making the best use of what nature provided—for the Continental Army hadn't the funds at its disposal to build enormous fortresses like the one in Quebec. But it did possess men with vision and a passionate devotion to their cause. They alone could, in the colonel's mind, be the great equalizer.

When I returned to my forge, I continued hammering out hatchets, small saws and knives for the men who worked endlessly on the fort from dawn to dusk. As they toiled, small detachments of men brought tools to the forge to be sharpened and repaired. These tasks kept me working at a furious pace—and I became even more resentful over Zeb's sudden disappearance.

⤙◉⤚

During one predawn morning, I was awakened by a loud rumbling voice coming from somewhere in the distance. As I sat up to listen more intently, I heard it again . . . broken verses of song drifting and tumbling on the morning breeze . . . something about wenches, rum and ale.

The gritty tone was indeed familiar, and I rose to scan the western horizon. Far in the distance, an enormous four-wheeled over-burdened oxcart trundled laboriously across the expanse of white sand—with Zebulon Galletin Hawkes tottering precariously in its seat. Pulled by twenty stoutly built oxen harnessed to the front, a single cow could be seen tethered to its rear.

As my heart beat with joy and relief at the sight of him, I raced toward him across the sand. Slowing the wagon's pace, he stood up and waved me on, bellowing, "Hey, *Jim*, look here at what *I* got! Come and see these *goodies* . . ." But when he looked down, with a new expression of distress on his face, he added, "and some *not* so goodies!"

Not knowing whether to feel joy or anger—since he *had* abandoned me—for a moment I was both. Zeb's cart was heavily laden with coveted treasures: barrels of salt pork and salted beef, dried beans, rum, molasses, and a quantity of fresh vegetables including potatoes, along with some cooking utensils we lacked. He also had gunpowder and pig iron—and from the looks of it, a thousand yards of heavy rope.

"Where in God's name did you get all these supplies, Zeb?"

"Well, Jim, there was this *farmer* . . . and he kind o' ran into a *problem* . . ."

"What *sort* of problem?" I asked, expecting a tall tale to cover mischievous deeds of ill-gotten gains.

Rolling his eyes skyward, he said, "Well, the problem was he decided all of a sudden that he was a *Tory*! Hell's bells, Jim, knowing that Colonel Moultrie would appreciate any and all donations to his cause, and knowing how difficult it is to be a Tory hereabouts, this one was duly granted relief from his burdensome farm . . . and was suddenly covered with honey . . . and then someone found some feathers . . . and this Tory suddenly found himself stuck to the top of a horse that knew the way to Canada . . . where he came from—the *horse* that is . . .”

Looking deeper into the cart, I spotted dozens of eggs nestled in straw-lined buckets, and a dozen more broken on the seat of the cart—residing in an ever-widening pool of gelatinous goo, punctuated liberally with crushed shells.

I let out a sigh and shook my head, as I realized that there was undeniable evidence in support of Zeb’s story. When I sauntered off to inspect the cow, I saw it was branded with the king’s mark—a broad arrow.

“Zeb, this is a *British* cow!” I wailed in distress. “It belongs to the damned king, and we will have to return it!”

Zeb immediately jumped down from his seat and spat out, “Now, *you* just wait a damned minute here, James Walker. This godforsaken cow doesn’t know it belonged to that fatheaded, cob-swiping, misbegotten *king*! Nor does she give two cow pies as to whose *fingers* squeeze her teats, or on whose *table* her milk is served!”

His boisterous imprecations suddenly caused the cow to relieve herself, dropping a moist, hay-prickled pie squarely upon my bare foot—whereupon it quickly sought its own level between my toes, diffusing its warm effluvium to assail our nostrils with its ineffable stench.

Flabbergasted and at a loss for words, I merely stared open-mouthed at my freshly encased foot.

Zeb, oblivious to my dismay, stooped to probe the cow’s udder, feeling tenderly of its girth. “*Damn* it, Jim, *now* you’ve done it! Look at her poor udder—all swollen *up*! Now you’ve made her nervous and fretty . . . because she hears a puling nanny goat behind her that wants to take her *back to the British*!”

Still speechless with wonder, I watched as he affectionately patted the cow’s backside. “Now,” he grumbled to me, “I suggest you get your foot *out* of that cow pie, and stop your vacuous *bleating*.” Then, after thrusting a bucket into my hands, he ordered, “And for God’s sake, take her to the forge and *milk* her!”

Shaking his head in disbelief, he rummaged around in the cart, adding, "I got some *rum* in here somewhere that will help you relax, and make you more amenable to *teat*-squeezing!"

THE ARRIVAL OF Zeb's booty made Colonel Moultrie's day. But the news he delivered that had come from the Tory farmer implied another message: that the goods had been stockpiled for eventual delivery to the British commissary, who would be arriving by ship—as predicted by Henry—to occupy the port of Charleston. In other words, it meant we were running out of time—the British admiralty was on its way.

The cow was quickly named Mehitable, after the wife of one of the Virginians, who was reputed to be a very large but affectionate woman. We made butter from Mehitable's milk, which we mixed with molasses and rum, to produce a makeshift version of hot buttered rum.

Mealtimes, instead of being dreaded, were now welcome, thanks to Zeb's contributions. The kinds of creations found in more civilized kitchens enhanced our island life. They included a variety of stews, soups, hasty pudding—and even pots of baked beans made just like Mother's.

When the barrels of rum were broken out, so effusive were Colonel Moultrie's grateful compliments, I thought Zeb would never cease telling his story of how Sullivan's Island was spared from culinary disgrace—by his feat of daring against the British king.

The newly acquired oxen meant additional loads of palmetto logs could be brought to the fortress each day, and the progress on it grew apace. With the British on the way, the hauling of sand and palmetto logs was now given top priority. Zeb and I were assigned a yoke of oxen and asked to participate in hauling palmetto logs to the fortress. This pleasantly spared us from working at the forge—and the endless tedium of creating the same tools day after day.

Seemingly, the combination of better food and buttered rum had transformed the motivation level of some workers, who went from indolent to industrious.

Zeb's oxcart was used to haul sand from the dunes into the void between the two palmetto walls. When the sand reached a depth of ten feet, gun platforms—also made from palmetto—were lashed together with wooden spikes and laid across its width. They compressed the sand beneath to form a solid wall that was nearly twenty feet thick.

After weeks of ceaseless hard labor, the seaward wall was finally completed. Its ends were turned rearward to form an inner palisade that would hold men, gunpowder and cannon fodder.

As the fortress took shape, the cannon were mounted on their platforms with their muzzles pointing seaward, and we felt a growing sense of pride and accomplishment. We had done what others said was impossible—we had built a fortress out of nothing but palmettos and sand, and armed it with volunteers and a few undersized cannons—in a hopeful attempt to turn away the world's most powerful navy.

Companionship

April 27, 1776

My dearest Suzannah,

You are a sweet vision in my dreams, bending o'er the waters of life, gently dipping your hands into their softness, then cooling my tired brow with thy loving touch . . . and calming my heart . . . for suddenly, I am home.

O my dearest little wife, the want of your companionship and soothing ministrations urges me to leave this isolated place; for there is nothing here for me but constant, unremitting labor . . . so why am I away? And yet the gentle warm breezes remind me of you! I only wish they could bring me home, so I could feel you in my arms once more!

I thank God for our true hearts . . . for they stave off my grief and loneliness without you. Somehow I sense your presence in the moonlight, and rejoice when it bathes me in the solitude of night. Your precious talisman ever comforts me . . . . it is my spring of tranquility on this island of despair.

Soon the British shall arrive to take Charleston, and our southern campaign shall begin. But Colonel Moultrie is a man of courage and decency, and because of him; we are living in good conditions. Meanwhile, Zeb has managed to plunder a local Tory, and freed from his possessions, which have been donated to the Continental Army, he is obliged to find shelter and sustenance elsewhere. As a consequence, our food has much improved.

In this temperate weather we all enjoy the ocean waters to bathe . . . which saves us from the unpleasant sights and smells we might otherwise be forced to tolerate in each other.

Suzannah, before we engage the British, I must press upon you the testament of my soul . . . and remember to keep this unto yours . . . for if the moment comes when I lose my resolve or human dignity, I will stop and reassess what values and purpose God has assigned to my burden.

I fear that many of our friends will never live to see the spring. I pray this unutterable fear will not come to pass. There are so many lives dear to us here, and they, through events yet to come; may have already slipped beyond our powerless grasp.

I fear warfare . . . in dreams I have looked into the fiery eyes of Death . . . and I have an abject fear of him . . . for he is ready to strike me down and rob my soul from you, Ainsley and God.

And so dear wife, I shall rest my heart upon yours, and it aches with the need to hear Ainsley's childish prattle and her girlish giggles, which sound so like her mother's. I want to press both of you to my heart and never let you go.

Send me a letter with loving thoughts from home, and stay with me, my living angel.

May God bless you and Ainsley, and keep you safe.

Your adoring husband

THE HEART OF SUZANNAH

May 17, 1776

My dearest Jim,

It is ever so late, and I'm very tired, but wanted you to know how heartwarming it is to read how much you love your little family, who is here for you always!

How I love receiving your letters . . . and during these lonesome nights, I read them over and over in bed . . . then press them to my heart because they were once in your hands. Each and every night, I pray for your safe return!

Here, to the good, we have saved nearly 117 soldiers through our untiring efforts. Against that, sixty-three men and boys have died in our home.

A few of Colonel Enos' men yet remain, but shall go home within a fortnight. Despite the winter months surrounded by death and the need for Doc's dreadful surgeries, Dimmis and I shall remake a wretched field hospital into our loving home once again.

Father and Mother ask for you and wish me to remember them to you. They still have Ainsley with them—she now occupies my old chamber. It seems a lifetime ago that I slept there, and yet our own daughter now rests her head upon my pillow, where you and I have rested. How I ache for you to sleep beside me again!

Lately, a general weariness has overtaken me, probably because of tending to the incessant needs of the sick and wounded. Or perhaps it's simply a tinge of rheumatism. In spite of it, dear Jim, if it were possible, I would gladly come there and fly away with you—away from earthly cares into the golden glow of the sunset . . . and then vanish into infinity . . . to protect and love you every moment thereafter. We would be forgotten in this world, but I know we would be happy . . . for we would belong for all eternity to each other, and to God.

Remember, my dear husband, all we are and ever shall be, depends upon us finding Love within ourselves, and then ourselves within Love. Darling, you have found my Love within you, and no one can ever take that away. May its warmth sustain you . . . and carry you safely back to my arms.

This from the heart of your loving wife . . .

Suzannah

The Past and the Present

In late March of 1776, John Rutledge was elected president of South Carolina's General Assembly, which formed the backbone of the revolutionary government that hired Colonel Moultrie. It was Rutledge in conjunction with Moultrie, Arnold and Henry, who had conceived the idea of building a fortress on Sullivan's Island—as a preemptive defense against the British plan to wage a winter campaign in the south.

Meanwhile, the Continental Congress, in its infinite wisdom, had appointed Charles Lee, a former British officer discontented with the king's army, as general to assist in the southern defense effort. Lee's command in Charleston extended to the South Carolina troops, who were originally under Rutledge and Moultrie. The men that found themselves under General Lee's command disliked his brash bombastic manner and mercenary nature. It was generally believed that he sought a higher post within the ranks of the Continental Army—even replacing General Washington was thought to be within the realm of his ambitions, by fair means or foul.

To Colonel Moultrie's mind, achieving this goal implied the devious use of politics, rather than sound military principles and leadership—as I discovered one day when I went to see him in his hut.

"*Typical* British officer!" were the words hurled at me as I entered. "*Always* thinking of the capacity of his breeches' *pockets*, or plotting his advancement above all *others*!"

Having no idea this would be the topic of our discussion when he invited me to meet with him, I remained silent as he raged on.

Waving a letter in my face, he said, "That damned fool is coming here to inspect *my* fortress! What in hell does a *British* soldier know about *fortress* building? For God's sake, he was with *Braddock* when they were slaughtered in the forests twenty-one years ago! Washington was Braddock's advisor and he suggested they fight the *Indian* way—behind trees, from the cover of forests or rock formations . . . But, *no*! Lee and Orme advised Braddock to carry on in battle formation, as the French-led Indians would *never* rattle the king's troops while in battle formation!"

Throwing the letter on the palmetto table and drawing his knife, he violently threw it through its center and stared at it, breathing heavily as it quivered.

He then approached me, clutched my shirt, and seething in anger, contemptuously hissed, "So Braddock *ignored* Washington's advice and chose *Lee's* instead—and *paid* for that choice with his miserable overconfident *life*!"

He stopped for a moment, and releasing me, he calmed down before resuming his harangue—this time, seemingly from a dark memory in his past, "Well, my dear Mr. Walker, twenty-one *years* a man makes, but *not* if you are *Charles Lee*. Washington is the only *man* of the two, possessing the requisite common sense and wisdom due a man! By God, during that disastrous affair, *Washington's* coat was pierced by four bullets—*and* he had at least *two* horses shot out from underneath him! Why, to add insult to injury, I believe it was Washington who carried the mortally wounded Braddock off the field—*after* he was sick abed for two weeks!"

He then returned to his desk, removed his knife and examined its blade while uttering in slow deliberation, "Fewer than three hundred French and Indian fighters were in those woods, yet they *decimated* Braddock's *glorious* troops—some 1,300—were laid *waste* in that forest. All because of the poor judgment exercised by *two* men—Robert Orme and Charles Lee—and the *stupidity* of another, Edward Braddock!"

I knew that Colonel Moultrie, based on his firsthand experience as an Indian fighter, firmly believed in the methods of stealth combat, and wanted to apply them in any battle with the British on

Sullivan's Island. As such, I witnessed how it greatly displeased him that Charles Lee was now in command of our fortress—and our lives.

But as I pressed my talisman, the smoldering determination in Colonel Moultrie's expression assured me that under *his* command, the same fate would not befall *us*.

Remembering my presence, he beamed an apologetic smile in my direction. His anger seemed to vanish as quickly as it came. Then, shaking my hand, he added, "I did not mean to *frighten* you, old friend. But in *war*, when incompetence triumphs over skill and strategy, I find it quite troubling . . . *especially* when the lives of those under my command are at stake."

"If General Lee doesn't inspire confidence in a true Indian fighter like yourself, then I have good reason to be frightened."

"Don't be, Jim. You can count on me," he said firmly, waving Lee out of our lives with a flick of his hand.

Turning away to a corner of his hut, he came back with a dark blue bundle. "I asked you here today because I need your advice, Jim. I value the opinion of my one and only blacksmith."

"Yes, sir?" I said, feeling honored by his words.

He shook out the bundle so that a flag of dark blue velvet cloth unfurled—revealing a solitary crescent of brilliant white that stood out starkly against the deep blue background. The crescent, located in the upper corner of the flag, was embroidered with the word LIBERTY in the same blue as the background.

"What do you think, Jim . . . for the fortress?"

"The one word says it all," I said with a grin. "They will have *no* trouble seeing it, sir—either from the sea, or from inside the fortress."

Raising his eyebrows, with a pleading voice he asked, " But, Jim, does it *inspire?*"

"I think it *does*, sir. After all, that's why we're *here* Colonel . . . for *liberty* . . ." As I stroked the soft velvet fabric, a wave of homesickness washed over me . . . and I wistfully added, "I know Suzannah would *love* this color—*and* this fabric—*indeed* she would. I'm sure she would approve of the design as well—and the *message*, of course!"

"I'm *delighted* to hear such things, Jim . . . I know from my own experience that a good woman's touch blesses all things."

Suzannah's face suddenly flashed before me—how I *missed* her! And yet, here was a man whose heart treasured a woman's abiding presence—and the tender touch of her delicate hand—as much as I did. Indeed, from his last remark I surmised that back at Colonel Moultrie's home, a beloved wife dwelled—and I also knew from his grateful expression, that it was *she* who made the flag.

I hastily wiped away my tears while Moultrie patted my shoulder and softly commented, "I didn't realize the flag was *that* inspirational . . ."

Then he took the flag and called out to Jasper, who entered immediately and saluted smartly. Handing the flag to the incredulous Jasper, Moultrie declared, "William, we have a *flag* for our fortress, so please devise a mast and fly this high, where it will be the most visible. I want to remind our men what they are fighting for—and let the British *know* what is at stake."

"Yes, *sir!*" Jasper replied enthusiastically, and left smiling broadly.

Colonel Moultrie resumed his desk and sharply ordered, "*Dismissed*, Mr. Walker!" and began to organize his papers. Seeing the top one reminded him of General Lee's impending visit, he frowned. Sensing his irritation, I quietly turned to leave, but as I approached the door, he startled me by softly announcing, "Oh, Jim . . . I would *love* to meet your Suzannah someday . . ."

Distant drums announcing the arrival of General Charles Lee and his entourage woke us in the early morning. From the other sounds that reached my ears, I gathered he was already on the island and before I set to work with my oxen, I would have a look at this survivor of Braddock's misadventure.

The commotion drew me toward Colonel Moultrie's hut, and as I situated myself nearby, I watched the haughty looking Charles Lee stride regally toward Moultrie's doorway. His uniform was well worn but his face had a smooth complexion with a light ruddiness to his cheeks. His eyes rode high above a long, aristocratic nose. Although he wore no wig, his slightly graying hair was slovenly clubbed, leaving him with a distinctly unfinished appearance for one of his rank.

As his aide remained outside the doorway of the hut, General Lee leaned toward him and tersely commented, "Let us see how they explain their latest failures . . . remain here . . ." The aide saluted and remained in position outside the doorway.

I couldn't hear much of their exchange, save that it was peppered with uncommonly emphatic utterances—until the two emerged together and went on to view the fortress.

That was my cue to resume my work, which was hauling more palmetto logs toward the unfinished north wall with one of the large jack sleds we'd built for a smoother journey over the sand. At our launch site, while Abner Blatchford cinched the rope to secure twelve freshly cut palmetto logs to my sled, he asked, "Jim, is that *Lee* over yonder?"

"Yes it is, Abner." When I saw a look of concern cross his face, I clapped him on his shoulder and humorously added, ". . . and I doubt he will criticize you for your cooking!"

Looking dubiously in Lee's direction, Abner added, "No, Jim, it's not my cooking I'm worried about . . . he wants us to *abandon* the fort!"

"What makes you think such a thing?" I asked in disbelief.

Abner just looked at me sadly and without a word, slowly shook his head. Then, indicating my sled, he advised, "Before you haul this off, you should probably check in first with Colonel Moultrie . . . since we may just be wasting our time on this . . ."

In view of the endless hours of labor we had all contributed, I was enraged by this sudden turn of events. I decided I wanted to hear *firsthand* the order to abandon the fortress.

As I came upon Lee and Moultrie, I observed a heated argument in progress. Lee was complaining bitterly about the fort's unfinished state, blaming Moultrie for his failure to secure a strategic point so vital to the defense effort.

When I heard the former British soldier berate the colonel in front of the men, I felt sickened. "I will say once again, Colonel Moultrie, that this entire fortress should be torn down. It is nothing but a *slaughter* pen . . . for the *sheep* you intend to lead astray here. Do you *really* believe this slapdash structure . . . constructed with such flimsy commonplace materials . . . can actually withstand an assault by a British ship of the line . . . firing a broadside of thirty-six-pound shot?"

"I believe so, sir," came Moultrie's firm reply.

Lee crowed loudly and derisively, throwing his head back to emphasize his distressing spectacle—and trying not to laugh, he mawkishly asked, "And *what*, my dear Colonel Moultrie, has you laboring under *that* delusion?"

"A knowledge of the palmettos, the uses of sand, along with a little science . . . my father was a physician, you know."

"Indeed he *was*!" Lee scornfully responded, "Then I suggest you have *him* here when the admiralty arrives, to tend to your maimed flock—*after* they knock down those worthless walls and overrun your hapless compatriots!"

Lee stepped back from Moultrie and observed the men busy at work. Turning back to Moultrie, he delivered one final derisive cut to the colonel's pride. "This fortress is nothing but a colossal *blunder* . . . a blunder that would be *laughable* if the consequences were not so *lamentable*!"

Lee turned away from Moultrie and stalked in my direction, nearly colliding with me as he did. Shoving me aside roughly, he said, "Pardon me, soldier . . . you can be the *first* to know that you need a *new* commander!"

Observing the encounter, Colonel Moultrie rushed forward and confronted Lee, blocking his path so he was obliged to listen. "General Lee, with all due respect, sir, I resent and reject your underhanded attempts to remove me from my command, granted me by the South Carolina General Assembly!"

Seething, Lee spat back into Moultrie's face, "*You*, sir, are a person without *property, perception or even* good taste . . . you're nothing but a cheap . . . a cheap, heathen *Indian* fighter! I need a career *soldier* to properly build and command a fortress—and *you*, sir, shall be discharged *forthwith*!"

As General Lee stalked off to the boat that would take him across the channel, Colonel Moultrie defiantly shouted after him, "Well General Lee, allow me to inform you, *sir*—it takes *brains*, *foresight* and strategic *planning* to see a potential failing—*sir*—and take the appropriate measures to *prevent* it from coming to pass— *sir*—unlike *your* actions twenty-one years ago with Braddock—*sir*!"

He paused for breath and as he shook his fist, he added, "Your opinion be damned, *sir*! I am *still* in charge of this fortress—*sir*—and I *defy* you to remove *me*—from *my* duty . . . to *my* men . . . and to *my* country!"

His defiant words rang in my ears as I watched General Lee, never missing his stride, walk away and board his boat. While I observed them rowing back across the channel, I tried to sort out what I'd witnessed in terms of what our next move would be.

Colonel Moultrie came to stand beside me, and after following Lee's progress across the channel, he tersely commented, "There is more menace in *his* shortsightedness than in all the British soldiers of the admiralty—that *man* is the very model of an ignorant English aristocrat that typically *buys* his commission . . . and *that* is the truth of it, my good friend!"

Looking into his face, I soberly asked, "Well sir, in light of his threats, shall we still carry on with our work to build the fort?"

"Without question!" Moultrie exclaimed, as he turned to gaze at his flag, now unfurled over the seaward wall, flanked by two cannons. Breathing deeply of the salt air, he exhaled gustily and declared proudly, "We are *not* abandoning this fortress, and I will see that man in *hell* before we do!"

Turning to slap me on the back as though for a deed well done, he smiled jovially and shouted, "*Carry on*, Mr. Walker!"

The Admiralty and the Fortress

olonel Moultrie wrote to John Rutledge of General Lee's visit and about his obstreperous attempts to undermine his command, as well as his order to abandon the fortress. Reminding him of Braddock's fate on following Lee's advice some twenty years before, Colonel Moultrie requested to be relieved of his duty to serve under him.

A few days later, in his written reply, Rutledge informed Moultrie that he was to obey Lee's commands . . . *except* that of abandoning the fortress; which was to be finished and defended at all costs.

I learned all this from Moultrie himself, since he seemed to enjoy chatting with his "one and only blacksmith"—as he liked to call me. I felt privileged to be one of his closest advisors, albeit in an unofficial capacity, since I wasn't qualified to provide any advice on military affairs. Rather, we usually talked of personal matters, and in particular, about our homes and families.

I grew to respect and admire him, for like my father, Moultrie was clear-sighted and levelheaded. He seemed particularly well suited to his job, and like the best military commanders, his ability to make snap decisions in the face of changing circumstances, always proved to be correct.

While I attended a briefing in Moultrie's hut about the completion of the north wall, Abner Blatchford rushed in uninvited and breathlessly addressed the colonel. "A boat, sir, a *boat*, near the north wall . . . *redcoats* aboard! Better have a look, sir . . ."

Colonel Moultrie sprang up and snatching his telescope, said, "Lead the way, soldier!"

We hurried to the north wall, where—from behind the palmetto logs—the colonel observed the boat's movements for a long while. "It's a *scout* boat!" he whispered to us.

Peering over the logs, we could see the vessel carefully nosing its way around the shoreline of Long Island, the one adjacent to ours—about a hundred yards distant.

Colonel Moultrie finally turned away from the boat, collapsed his telescope and announced. "Well, men, where there's a *boat*, there are *ships* . . . and we need to find *them* before they find *us*! Abner, tell Sergeant Jasper to arm and dispatch all the men to their posts. Then tell him to get three nine-pounders and two twenty-four pounders down here—*right away!*"

Again stretching his telescope to observe the progress of the scout boat, he absently commented, "There will be more of these little boats . . . but a well-placed nine-pounder should easily *sink* a scout boat . . . *and* hopefully take out a few men in the process—*hah*—the challenge is *on!*"

We all remained silent and alert while the scout boat continued surveying the shoals of Long Island. In a few days' time, by posting three watches of eight hours each, we finally spotted the billowed sails of nine men-of-war, drifting slowly into Five Fathom Hole. Having successfully averted the sandbars, they dropped their anchors and settled in without a single shot fired from us.

Two of these magnificent ships were equipped with fifty guns each—the *Bristol*, their flagship, and the *Experiment*. The other seven—the *Syren*, *Sphinx*, *Actaeon*, *Active*, *Solebay*, *Thunder* and *Friendship*—carried lighter armament. At day's end, a total of three hundred British cannons yawned lazily at our defiant little fortress . . . proudly displaying its blue flag and our measly thirty-one guns.

"How ironic," I thought, "that a man-of-war should be named *Friendship*. After all, it was here to *kill* us." Despite Colonel Moultrie's confidence: with a British gun ratio of ten to our one, this fleet would reduce our fortress to kindling with their first volley.

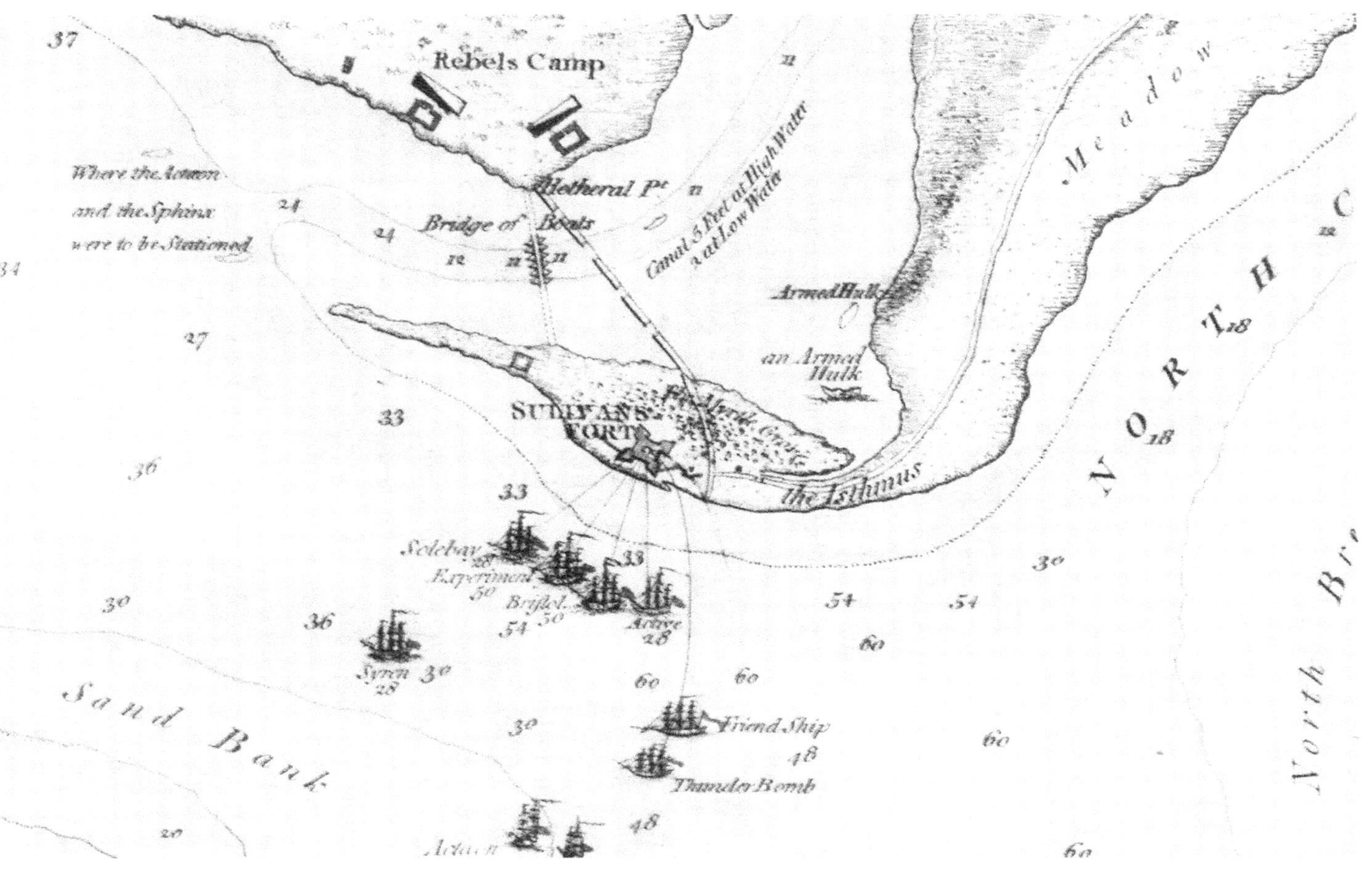

Rebels Camp
Where the Action
and the Sphinx
were to be Stationed
Hetheral Pt
Bridge of Boats
Canal 5 Feet at High Water
2 at Low Water
Meadow
Armed Hulk
an Armed Hulk
NORTH C
North Br
the Isthmus
SULIVANS FORT
Sand Bank
Solebay
Experiment
Bristol
Active
Syren
Friend Ship
Thunder Bomb
Acteon

My mouth suddenly went dry as I nervously fingered Suzannah's talisman—for the penetrating fear in my stomach warned—I might *never* see her again.

THE SUN RELENTLESSLY scorched us as we watched anxiously for activity aboard the vessels. Although I stared at them for hours, I was lost in thought . . . that here will be my grave . . . far from those I love in Walker's Cove. My only consolation was that at least I would die among some of my friends and neighbors.

Meanwhile, construction on the north wall continued at a feverish pace, with supplies laid into the central area of the fortress. Cannonballs were distributed to each artillery crew with the warning that if a shot was to be fired, it must hit something British—no exceptions. Because we had to remain at our posts . . . except for nature's calling . . . hard tack, pemmican, jerky and water were our fare for many days. We now slept within the fortress, made no fires, took no baths, and every eight hours another shift went on watch.

Early the next morning, Colonel Moultrie came to our parapet with a small group of Virginians. "These are the finest sharpshooters of our lot!" he announced. "I want them in position so they can pick off any targets they see onboard those ships: British officers strolling on the decks, for instance . . . or better yet, a nice British *general*—or even a handsome *admiral!*"

A few snickers went up as the men repositioned themselves to allow the Virginians a clear view of their targets.

Zeb and I were familiar with their rifles, having had occasion to repair them from time to time. They were unusually long, the barrels alone exceeding forty-six inches. I knew that with a steady rest, these rifles could hit an area the size of a squirrel's head at a hundred yards.

Once all his sharpshooters were in place, Colonel Moultrie returned to his hut to dispatch a message to Charleston for General Lee, informing him of the British arrival. Despite their contentious differences, I was impressed with how easily Colonel Moultrie followed strict military protocol when it came to General Lee. Although the odds were against us, I was confident that the colonel was still the best commander for Sullivan's Island . . . and that somehow, he would lead our way to victory.

Because of its vulnerability, Colonel Moultrie stationed over seven hundred men at the unfinished north wall. He was convinced that because of its perceived weakness, it would be the target of the initial British advance. Zeb and I were among those assigned there, and we entrenched ourselves for better cover against potential British fire. Here, we watched and waited until early one morning when Wheezer Hutchinson rushed up to us, whispering, "Another boat has been spotted and it's headed this way!"

Three of the Virginians rose to look across the river where they saw a boat slowly making its way toward us. They reported that there were very few men in the boat, which was odd, considering the hundreds of soldiers that were landing on Long Island. So we surmised it was another scout boat, just as Colonel Moultrie had predicted.

I hadn't long to think about it because a series of sharp cracks emanated from the Virginians' long rifles . . . they had fired over the scout boat as a warning. As they were reloading for another volley, the boat kept advancing toward us. After taking careful aim, one of them fired, and the white bow flag flipped into the air and fell into the water. At the second crack, an oarsman's hat flew off and he collapsed head first into the boat. The vessel suddenly hove to, and resembling a wounded water bug, with spasmodic sweeps of its oars, it skittered back to Long Island. As we silently watched it retreat, our three sharpshooters were gleefully slapping their knees, while exchanging remarks about how terrible the last shot was— for the target was much too *large*!

Looking out to where the flag remained floating in the water, I judged the distance to be *at least* eighty yards. I now regarded the Virginians with a newfound respect: there was some kind of magic in their long rifles and the skills they possessed—such as cutting a flag's mast in two with a single ball from such a distance. I truly admired those beautiful rifles . . . their construction, their gracefulness, and having witnessed firsthand the damage they inflicted at great distances, I was relieved that such exquisite weapons and skilled marksmen—were on *our* side.

HAVING HEARD THE shooting, Moultrie and Jasper soon came pelting toward us across the sand. Breathing heavily from the exertion, Moultrie demanded, "What in hell is all the *shooting* about, Walker?"

"A boat approached us, sir," I said evenly, "and the Virginians shot at it." I pointed to the white flag, now sinking below the surface. "They shot the mast in two, Colonel, from up *there*—and hit one of the oarsmen too."

"Is that so?" Moultrie said thoughtfully. "Jasper, get the shooters' story. I'll need to report the initial action." Then he turned to me: "*Walker*, you come with me!"

As we made our way to the beach, Moultrie pointed to the spot the flag had formerly occupied and bitterly complained, "*Damn it*, Jim—that was a *truce* flag . . . a symbol of respect and civility during warfare . . . under which *complete quarter* is given to the bearer, *regardless* of circumstances!"

He turned to look me straight in the eyes as he added, "They had something to *say*, Jim, and perhaps now we shall never know what it was—thanks to those possum shooters up there." Standing at the water's edge and training his gaze back to the north wall, he shook his head in amazement. "*Remarkable* skill to shoot as they did from such a distance! I hope to turn them loose on the decks of those ships very soon."

"I didn't know that the flag signified anything, Colonel, but I do now . . . thanks to you." I said, but added "And I too was impressed with their marksmanship, sir."

Moultrie turned to scrutinize the Virginians talking to Jasper. "Jim, it's always educational to examine the field of battle after every engagement, no matter how small. Win or lose, there is much to be learned from such observations. It's what makes a good commander." He paused a moment before he asked, "Was the oarsman *killed?*"

"I think not, sir, but it was difficult to see from so far away. I *did* see him collapse into the boat though . . ."

Colonel Moultrie pulled out his telescope, and peered through it toward the Long Island shore. After a time, he handed it to me, and said with marked satisfaction, "Take a look, Jim . . . I suspect he will *not* be taking his afternoon tea."

Focusing upon the shore, I saw a knot of men bearing a covered body out of the boat and up the beach, finally disappearing with it into the palmettos.

As I gave the telescope back to Moultrie, he said in somber tones, "Well, in any case, they have their answer."

ON THE FOLLOWING day, another boat flying a white flag cautiously made its way toward our north wall. This time Colonel Moultrie was there to receive them. The small band of men, led by an officer, delivered a proclamation from Commanding General Henry Clinton, calling for us to lay down our arms and surrender the fortress.

As Moultrie read the message, heavy drums echoed from across the river. It was soon followed by the sight of thousands of soldiers appearing at the shoreline, turning it red with the color of their uniforms. Lining up in such numbers was apparently intended to intimidate the colonel to the point of surrendering.

Ignoring the entire display of sight and sound, Moultrie calmly handed the proclamation back to the British officer, bowed and replied, "Please convey my sincere compliments to General Clinton, but also be informed that having already refused to relinquish my fortress to my *own* commanding general, I respectfully submit that I shall *not* relinquish it to *yours!*"

"I will tell him, sir," the officer said firmly as he saluted the colonel. Then he returned to the boat with his men, and they rowed back across the river.

Watching their progress, Moultrie muttered, "And now the challenge shall truly begin."

When the boat landed, the drummers resumed their beat, and more British soldiers gathered at the shore—they were now several layers deep. All of a sudden the drum cadence changed and the first row of soldiers began wading into the river.

"*Surely they will not attempt to ford the river!*" Moultrie exclaimed, bringing his telescope to his eye. With a lamenting sigh, he handed it to me and said, "What a *waste* of young life!"

Through it I could see the first wave of soldiers had waded less than halfway across the river . . . then they began to struggle, and amid frantic wails for help, quickly dropped out of sight. As the soldiers lost their footing, their muskets were lost, and the surface of the river roiled with the thrashing of red arms and white legs. Although they struggled to swim, the current sucked them down, carrying them toward the anchored warships. After shedding their packs and accouterments, they finally rose to the surface, gasping and clawing desperately at the water.

The drum beat changed, and the second and third rows of soldiers stood down as the half-drowned survivors, choking and coughing, managed to drag themselves to shore. It seemed the order had been given to finally abort the mission.

As I returned the telescope to Moultrie, he tersely commented, "We would have *picked* them off . . . like *fish* in a *barrel* . . ." Collapsing his telescope and finally turning away, he firmly added, "There will be no further movements today for the British!" And as usual, the colonel was correct.

AFTER SEVERAL DAYS of heavy rain, Zeb became increasingly restless, often waking before sunrise and foraging for something to eat that wasn't salted. On this particular morning, he declared his tongue was so swollen it felt like a salted cod, and his lips were cracked and shrunken from the lack of rum passing over them.

"You got that letter to Dimmis?" he asked, looking over at me hopefully.

"Indeed, I do," I replied, just coming awake myself. "It's safely hidden with Suzannah's letters."

"Why do you want to *hide* it, Jim? After today you may *need* it. Not only that, but what happens if *you* get killed and I don't?"

"In that case, you'll have no need for it, and it will simply remain hidden."

A massive concussion ended our conversation abruptly, as we all scrambled for our arms and reported to our posts.

Colonel Moultrie was already out of his hut and headed toward the fortress. His knife and hatchet were at his waist, and he held a long rifle in his left hand. Flapping against his side were a possibles bag and two powder horns. Scampering up the steps to the seaward parapet, he trained his telescope on the British fleet.

After some moments, he called down to us as we gathered below the gun platforms. "That was nothing but a signal shot, men, but keep *alert*, for the challenge is *on*! I want the Virginians up here— *now*! Colonel Thompson, I need you at the north wall to protect our rear from movements on Long Island! Lieutenant Sumter, take our flank battery, and under *no* circumstances let anything get by! Walker, I need you and Zeb to help with these twenty-four-pounders—so come on up."

Stationing ourselves between the two twenty-four-pounders, our orders were to load, reload, and assist the gunnery officer in aiming and aligning two of our largest cannons. Looking out the port and over the muzzle of one, I could see it was trained upon the largest man-o-war, the flagship *Bristol.*

The ground crew began passing up powder, round shot, wads and swabs to us, and finally, several loads of bar and chain shot; the latter being a somewhat lethal combination of two iron balls tied together with a bar or chain, which when fired, ripped away masts, rigging and sails—and an occasional human torso—if it was unfortunate enough to be in its path.

There was movement among the ships as anchors were weighed, and longboats were dispatched from the Long Island shore. These had quickly formed a flotilla that was heading steadily toward our north wall. Each vessel was fully loaded with soldiers, whose muskets and bayonets gleamed malevolently in the morning sun. The challenge was indeed—as Colonel Moultrie was fond of saying—"at hand."

All activity ceased momentarily, when Colonel Moultrie sharply announced. "Men, the *Sphinx*, *Syren* and *Actaeon* are *moving*! Lieutenant Sumter—send one across their bows! We need to force them onto the sandbars. Should they flank us, we will be *severely* compromised!"

The flank crews sprang into action as the ships rounded the southern front of our fortress. Just as their sails unfurled a little fuller, two shots boomed forth from our flank stations, both splashing down before the lead ship. At the same moment, the *Bristol*, *Experiment* and *Solebay* began to pull closer to our seaward wall.

Zeb and I were at the ready when Colonel Moultrie ordered, "Steady, boys . . . steady . . . lead *ship—fire*! Our cannons belched, and the parapet shook violently. As they kicked back nearly three feet, the recoil ropes whipped and sang within their restraints. I went deaf instantly from the horrific noise as smoke drifted back through the ports, enveloping us in a thick choking haze.

Despite the ringing in my ears, I could hear Colonel Moultrie's next command: "*Swab! Reload chain, and ready!*"

After a quick swab, I shoved down the next powder charge. Zeb rammed the chain shot home, and we yanked and pulled the cannon back into position once more. As we secured the recoil ropes, the gunnery officer leveled the muzzle once again, just in time to hear Colonel Moultrie yell, "*Fire! And be damned quick about it!*"

Again the guns roared, and our little fortress shook as though in fear; and for the briefest moment I heard a hellish wailing above us, as the *Bristol* answered by unleashing a full broadside in a staccato burst. Smoke puffs emanated from bow to stern as the flagship delivered a devastating broadside, engulfing itself behind white smoke.

Amidst the shots screaming overhead, we could hear thunderous thumping sounds all along our seawall. Colonel Moultrie shouted a huzzah, declaring, "*Keep firing, boys!* By God, she cannot harm us—their shots are being smothered or repelled! Fire at will and keep 'em coming! Take the damned rigging! Take the damned rigging! They are helpless without it. Forget the hull shots! *Get the damned rigging!*"

The cannons at the north wall had erupted, and the Virginians were firing fierce volleys at the approaching longboats. It pleased me to witness their deadly accuracy—for our withering rifle fire quickly decimated their ranks. The men who were hit pitched over the sides at awkward angles. Inside the vessels, panic and chaos ensued as the deadly volleys continued from over one hundred yards away—well beyond the range of the British muskets. Many of the boats exploded into splinters from the direct hits of the cannons, sending soldiers flying into the air and water.

As I loaded more chain shot, five Virginians lined up beside me, and as their rifles spat fire toward the *Bristol*, I followed its progress. After an eerie delay, men suddenly fell from the topsails and rigging, tumbled in midair, and finally slammed onto the deck with sickening thuds.

While the Virginians withdrew to reload, we hoisted our cannon back into position, and with a touch of the match rope, another chain shot screamed its way toward the *Bristol*.

Sweating furiously with the efforts to reload and position our guns, I barely noticed that our flank side had exploded again with continuous fire. With our targets on the river in total disarray, the British were not in position to rake our flank, as had been their intent. From the looks of their yaw and tangled rigging, they were firmly grounded, as Colonel Moultrie had hoped. And now, the Virginians were shooting them to pieces.

As the heavy shot aimed at our fortress from the *Bristol* and the *Experiment* reached their target, the morass of sand and palmettos absorbed their energy—as our wise colonel had predicted. In return, we kept firing chain shot, not with rapidity, but with surgical accuracy.

Zeb and I kept loading until our muscles screamed for mercy—yet because our lives were at stake, we fought on—finding within ourselves that 'final reserve' that wills survival when all other powers have failed.

Colonel Moultrie watched the action through his telescope, cheering us on: "Great shot! Now let's tear up a mast if we can! By God, there is an *officer* on the foredeck, a little to the right, boys . . . and then we will have him!"

As Zeb muscled the cannon to the right and I secured its recoil ropes, the cannon roared. Through the smoke I saw splinters fly upward from the foredeck, and to my amazement—though my ears were ringing—I heard Moultrie declare, "By God! You got him . . . *you got him! He is down!*" Turning around to slap each of us on the back, he screamed delightedly above the din, "Grand *shooting,* boys . . . *he's lost his breeches!*"

At that moment, my jubilation at his compliment made me realize that we were holding firm—despite the efforts of the world's most powerful navy to destroy us.

DESPITE HAVING INFLICTED heavy damage on the *Bristol* and the *Experiment,* they were not yet out of action, and our powder supply was dwindling. Chain shot consumed more cannon powder than round shot, so by afternoon we used only rifle fire to pepper the decks . . . in order to save our precious powder. Colonel Moultrie hoped this measure might get us through until nightfall, after which we would decide how to carry on with what little powder we had left.

Since the *Bristol* could still maneuver, she responded to the abatement of cannon fire by drifting ever closer to our seaward wall for a kill. Then she continuously bombarded our fortress with thunderous solid shot, wailing grapeshot and screaming chain shot . . . in a desperate attempt to either breach our wall—or somehow murder us within it.

As we waited helplessly within, the capacity of the British powder magazines seemed to be endless. As they unmercifully raked our fortress, it seemed their purpose was well served—because now we began to lose men.

When Sergeant Jasper arrived to inform Colonel Moultrie of our mounting casualties, our gunnery officer suddenly dropped to the platform, his face riddled with grapeshot. Then our flag, which had been mounted above the seaward parapet, suddenly came tumbling down, its mast shattered and splintered beyond repair. Next to it landed the body of a Virginian, shot dead in mid-aim.

Through the din of the constant bombardment and the whistling of ordnance above our heads, Jasper stood below me stock-still, staring in disbelief at the Virginian's body. Colonel Moultrie had long since gone to the north flank, to ensure the destruction of the British ships that were grounded in the river.

Our seaward cannons were now silent. Without powder and someone who knew how to properly aim them, they were worthless. As Zeb and I stood in petrified silence wondering what to do, the men inside the fortress began to notice our flag was gone. With dampened spirits they began to lay down their arms. Worse, Moultrie was not present to buoy them.

Sergeant Jasper, apparently shaken out of his stupor, grasped the situation. Without a word, he picked up the Virginian's rifle, and after deftly tying the flag onto its lengthy barrel, clambered up the parapet. Facing the men in the center of the fortress, he waved the rifle frantically by its butt, and the flag fluttered to life once more.

Soon after, Colonel Moultrie could be seen racing toward the ladder and scrambling up the parapet. Spotting the muskets on the ground, he bellowed, "We are not done, boys—*we are not done!*" Brandishing his knife in the air he defiantly added, "We are still here . . . and by God, if they knock our fortress down, we shall fight to the death behind its tumbled logs!" Then, pointing his knife toward Jasper waving the remounted flag, he said, "Buck up, men—*here* is the symbol of your courage and *our* destiny . . . so let us fight *on*—and be *damned* to them in *Hell!*"

The men let out a rousing huzzah and began to take up their arms—when suddenly from behind us, out to seaward, we heard sharp staccato bursts of heavy cannon fire.

Following so close upon such a stirring scene, I feared that we might now face our final undoing. Zeb shoved the cannon away from its port so we could see. To my utter amazement, there was no smoke to be seen from the *Bristol* or the *Experiment*.

Another series of rapid discharges came to us—the echoes of canny, well-paced firings, unlike the ragged fire the British were now mustering against us.

As Colonel Moultrie looked searchingly beyond the parapet, he demanded, "What in hell do you think is going on out there, Walker?"

Again, a staccato firing of heavy cannons pierced the air, and as I gazed toward the *Experiment*, her rigging in the mizzenmast suddenly flew apart, and it then collapsed—but she was not fired upon from our fortress—it was from *seaward*. In response to this sudden attack from a new direction, the two ships ignored our fortress and began to fire their seaward guns.

Colonel Moultrie strained to see the action through his telescope, while barking out orders. "I want all twenty-four-pounders on this parapet—*now*! And to hell with the powder! We are going to blow these bastards out of the water! By God, someone is *attacking* them on their seaward side!"

Now only rifle fire was returned from our north wall, and through superhuman effort, the two remaining twenty-four-pounders were heaved and lifted to the forward parapet. All remaining gunnery officers were called to man them, thus abandoning the smaller guns.

As Colonel Moultrie watched anxiously, the steady firing at sea continued, answered by sputtering shots from the two crippled ships. Our remaining barrels of powder, chain shot and solid shot were brought forward, and once again we fired at them.

The colonel was pleased when he saw holes open in the *Bristol*'s hull. Turning toward us as we heaved our guns back into position, he commanded, "Keep it *going*, boys, until your powder is out! We have a *hell* of an *ally* out there—and they are *very good* shots!"

As we fired, the gun platform rumbled and shook worse than before, and I feared the four twenty-four-pounders were far too heavy for our sand supported parapets. As we frantically reloaded, the constant fire from those seaward broadsides continued unabated, tearing apart the *Bristol* and the *Experiment*. Suddenly, as the last echoes of our cannon fire faded into silence, Zeb leaned forward, squinting through the smoke. After a moment, he slowly grumbled, "*What* in *hell?*"

Moultrie handed him the telescope so he could see for himself, and as Zeb peered into it, he trained it on a swiftly moving vessel as she raked a broadside across Bristol's shattered bow. When Bristol's foremast collapsed into her upper topsail, he bellowed exuberantly, "Sons of *Belial!* It's the *Fortune Two!* It's the mother-loving, god-damned misbegotten *Fortune Two!*"

Elegy

dropped my swab, and leaving my post to get a better view to seaward, as the smoke cleared away, I saw it was indeed the *Fortune Two*! Cracking full canvass before onshore winds, she was going fast—*very fast*—and she swept around the hulking men-of-war like a nimble dog chasing wounded quails, tormenting them with devastating broadsides at every pass.

The two British vessels were severely crippled, and their crews frantically tried to haul their anchors as the *Fortune Two*, deftly tacking around them in figure-eight patterns, sprayed their decks with withering grapeshot. Their answering fire was far too slow and erratic to even catch her wind . . . and as she raced across the *Bristol*'s starboard, she released a high volley into her tops.

We watched awestruck as the *Bristol*'s main mast collapsed, and crashed into her aft mast topgallant. Meanwhile, listing heavily, the *Sphinx* and the *Syren*—two of the three ships that had run aground on the uncharted sandbars—finally managed to withdraw; but the *Actaeon*, hopelessly stranded, was abandoned. From this spectacle no other conclusion could be drawn but that the British were done.

The men raced over to the parapet, waving their guns and hats, and as the *Fortune Two* passed and re passed before us—they continued their chorus of huzzahs to greet her and cheer her on.

For me, there were solitary tears amid the joy of victory. As her majestic figurehead rose and fell in a graceful rhythm—so free and spirited above the waves, my own spirits were soaring, and I felt I would never come down—for this was my first sight of Suzannah since I'd left home—and she looked more *beautiful* than ever.

As the day wore on, the British guns remained silent—the fleet had withdrawn out of range. Just before dusk, General Lee arrived to see how we, and the fortress had fared. Powder-stained, lacerated, stinking, unkempt and exhausted—in no condition to withstand scrutiny—we nevertheless assembled dutifully before Colonel Moultrie's hut. We stood proudly at attention to greet the man who brazenly declared our fortress and commander—were total failures.

Colonel Moultrie emerged from his hut and saluted Lee with all the respect due a superior officer—although, in my opinion, all he deserved was a sharp slap across his arrogant face.

"I see you have things well in *hand*, Colonel!" Lee remarked gleefully as he observed the bodies of the dead being gathered nearby. Surveying those of us who had survived, he added, "I see you have no further need for me here, Colonel, so as you were . . . and I shall expect your full report in Charleston, in due course."

Moultrie saluted him and said, "*Yes*, sir, *thank* you, sir!" and turning on his heel, headed back to his hut.

After taking a few steps, "*Colonel Moultrie!*" rang out in Lee's brittle voice.

"Yes, sir?" the colonel answered, turning to face Lee.

Lee approached him and said in low tones, "Colonel, what a self-centered, miserable, unproductive *bastard* I have been."

The two men silently regarded each other until Moultrie said loud enough for all to hear, "Then perhaps this *unexpected* victory— will *remove* that apparent stain upon your character, *sir*."

And with that, the colonel saluted one last time—and returned to his hut.

Just before dawn, Zeb woke me up to tell me that the British had departed during the night, after setting the *Actaeon* on fire. He was going out with a small crew to salvage what they could, and informed me that Moultrie wanted to see me in his hut after sunrise. Before we parted, we speculated on the present whereabouts of the *Fortune Two*, and wondered if we would soon see Henry.

Not wishing to be late I stayed awake, and after Zeb had gone, I went to bathe in the warm waters off Sullivan's Island. It was there that I had my first glimpse of the exterior of our beleaguered fortress. Spent cannonballs littered the beach. Our palmetto walls were heavily scarred by chain and grapeshot. There were many large holes where logs had become dislodged by cannonballs that found their way between them. Piles of sand had thus trickled out through the holes, forming little ramps of various heights all along our sea-ward wall. But despite all the visible destruction, I smiled when I saw our flag—newly mounted—waving unscathed over our fortress.

I felt *proud* as I reflected on that flag . . . for it had been made by a woman "whose touch blessed all things" as the colonel said—and yesterday—her touch blessed *us*, inspiring victory when there was none. Indeed, I was satisfied with what we had done—for despite being outmanned, outgunned, ill equipped and undermined by our own commanding general—*we* had turned away the world's most *powerful* navy; and in so doing, we were one step closer to securing our liberty.

"Ah, Walker!" was the enthusiastic greeting I received as I stood in Colonel Moultrie's doorway. "Please, come *in* . . . and how *is* my one and only blacksmith on this first day of victory?"

Not yet knowing what to say, I silently approached his desk to find him scribbling furiously, deftly dipping his quill into the ink-well without even looking. What struck me most was how calm and lucid he seemed, especially after a fearfully tense day on which he had attained a victory of heroic proportions.

Seating myself on one of the palmetto logs, I watched him silently as he carried on as though I wasn't there.

Finally, he broke the silence. "Twelve men lost and twenty-five wounded," he said, not looking up. "You'll be happy to know that *none* were Walker's Cove men!"

"I'm glad to hear that, sir," I said, feeling blessed on behalf of my townsfolk.

Moultrie lay his quill down, blotted the paper, folded it and handed it to me. "Jim, I'm eternally grateful to you and your friends for your outstanding service under my command—and I shall sorely miss the pleasure of *your* company."

Looking at him in surprise, I couldn't get the question out before he answered: "These are your discharge orders, Jim. Your mission here is finished, and you and the rest of the Walker's Cove contingent are needed in New York, where there are more battles to be won. You'll return on the *Fortune Two* with Henry Wiggins."

"New York?" I asked, nearly suffocating with emotion . . . because I would be nearer Suzannah.

"You think of *her,* do you not?" he asked, placing a gentle hand upon my shoulder.

Looking down, I replied, "Yes sir, I do."

"So do *I!*" he replied.

Looking up in surprise at him, he raised his brows and continued, "And why should I *not* think of her . . . for indeed, I *met* her yesterday!"

Seeing the confused look upon my face, he softly added, "Come, come, Jim . . . from the looks on your face yesterday, I could instantly tell—the figurehead on the *Fortune Two*—is your *Suzannah* . . . is she not?"

Looking up at him and seeing the graciousness in his eyes, I softly replied, "Yes, sir—carved and gilded by her father."

Taking my hand and pressing it warmly, he earnestly said, "Not sir—just *William*—and yes, she *is* everything I *thought* she would be. Thank you for sharing her, Jim, now Henry is waiting for you in Charleston. The ship is undergoing a major refitting, but in a few more weeks you will be heading closer to home. It is the best I can do for the man who has done so much for me."

I could not speak, but merely embraced him as I would my own father.

After we broke apart, Moultrie returned to his desk, dabbed an eye with his finger and firmly announced, "Dis—*missed!*"

CHARLESTON

he next day, we found ourselves gathered at the far end of the Charleston dock. As I looked down its entire length, I was overwhelmed by the astounding maritime activity that greeted me. It made such a contrast from where we'd just been, making it seem as though our battle at Sullivan's Island was a mere figment of the imagination.

Throngs of fashionably dressed people were everywhere, strolling along the great length of Charleston's dock. Flitting between and around them were carriages of well-dressed dandies and their ladies, hurrying to unknown destinations. Overburdened wagons stumbled and creaked their way toward the appropriate vessels, to transfer goods to or from distant places.

On our left were dozens of bowsprits, their majestic lengths regally protruding above the street, dwarfing carriages and curious onlookers alike. To our right, magnificent buildings—many being four storeys in height, towered along the entire length of the dock, save for one church that was even higher. Closer to ground level as far as the eye could see were taverns and inns, and sprinkled among them, silversmiths, shoemakers, wigmakers, barbers and cabinetmakers.

As Zeb surveyed the forest of masts and bowsprits before us, he absently declared, "This damned place sure has *changed* since Henry and *I* were last here . . . there were *never* this many ships tied up at the same time . . ." And gesturing toward the thick haze of ropes and spars, he dolefully complained, ". . . especially like *this*. How in hell are we going to find Henry and the *Fortune Two?*"

I had no answer for him as I too surveyed the dozens of barques, brigs, brigantines, topsail schooners and full-rigged ships that clustered at the dock—but Wheezer Hutchinson did.

"Well, Zeb, I heard the colonel say that Henry was boarding at Dillon's on Broad Street."

"Broad Street, *hell!*" Zeb spat out. "*Damn it*, Wheezer, these are *all* broad streets around here! By God, if you can't say something more *useful*, I will stuff you through the nearest hawsehole—and they can use you for oakum!"

As we walked along Dock Street, I noticed the many Negroes who were carrying heavy bundles and tools from place to place, or loading and unloading the huge freight wagons. Although they weren't shackled, I surmised—from what I'd heard back home—that many were apparently slaves, or perhaps indentured servants. If so, I felt these Charleston merchants perhaps lived a somewhat coddled lifestyle through the tireless efforts of these colored men—who labored with little thanks or no reward.

I was interrupted in my musings by a sudden tug on my shirt. It was Abner nodding in the direction of a stevedore, suggesting we ask him for the address of Dillon's tavern.

The stevedore in question was supervising the unloading of a ship, scribbling a record of the contents in his ledger. As we approached, we heard him call out to the teamster receiving the load, "Twelve hundred and twenty hogsheads of rice; two hundred eighty-four tierces of small beer, fifty-eight barrels of rum, twenty-five kegs of nails! That's the entire load . . . so, off with you and see you next trip!"

The man doffed his cap before he hauled away the remaining kegs of nails. Pulled by four horses, his wagon had wheels as tall as I was, while the bed had unusually high sides and a very thick bottom. It was built to haul loads far more ponderous than anything I'd ever seen delivered to Walker's Cove.

Turning to face us, the stevedore clapped his ledger book shut, slightly bowed and kindly asked, "Gentlemen . . . of what service might I be to you? Forgive me, but I dare say that you look like lost puppies!"

Zeb, ever ready for a challenge after Sullivan' Island, stepped up and declared, "*Listen*, mister—we ain't *lost*—we are *mislocated!*"

Since Zeb towered over the stevedore, there was no resistance to his brusque definition of our circumstance. Instead, a pleasant smile came upon the stevedore's face. Respectfully tapping his forehead in a half salute to Zeb, he replied, "Very well my good man, then perhaps I might *relocate* you, if that is your ardent desire."

Seemingly apoplectic, Zeb suddenly bellowed, "My ardent *desire*? What in hell kind of talk is *that* for a man?"

"Why, it's called being a *gentleman*, sir! Allow me to introduce myself . . . I am Henry Colburn Whittenhandler—at your service. And *you* are?"

"*Zebulon Galletin Hawkes!*" I answered, stepping in to defuse any misunderstanding. "My name is James Walker, sir, and we're from Walker's Cove—but more recently, from Sullivan's Island."

"Ah . . . Walker's Cove! Now, is that not a *coincidence!*" he said, lifting his brows in surprise. "You have, no doubt, made the acquaintance of Henry *Wiggins*, master of the beautiful snow brig *Fortune Two*, who has been known to frequent Walker's Cove from time to time?"

"That's our man!" Zeb broke in—"so you *know* Henry Wiggins?"

"*Everybody* knows Henry Wiggins," Whittenhandler replied. "It was his brilliant maneuvering and gunnery that took down two of the king's ships off Sullivan's Island. When the *Fortune Two* returned here to be refitted, she was greeted by hordes of people shouting huzzahs until she berthed. Such good news traveled fast!"

Biting his lip, he added, "She was shot up pretty bad, she was— but her figurehead came through it unscathed, because, I'm told, she was agile as a cat, and as I saw for myself, beautiful to boot!"

Zeb guffawed and thrusting out his thumb toward me, said, "You might like to know that figurehead is of his *wife*—Suzannah Walker!"

"Then I know I was bereft all my life of the true definition of beauty until now," Whittenhandler replied, taking my hand and shaking it warmly. "You, Mr. Walker, are a most *fortunate* soul to be married to such an inspirational and *exquisite* woman."

Embarrassed by his lavish compliments, I could only answer, "Well, I do feel blessed by my good fortune. Suzannah and I are part-owners of the *Fortune Two*—as is Zeb here."

"In that case, I'm delighted to meet the other victors of Sullivan's Island! It is indeed unfortunate that nobody hereabouts is interested in rendering aid to our cause—these ships have been languishing here for weeks waiting to depart."

Indicating the tangled spars and masts, he added, "They remain huddled here together because their owners are afraid they'd be taken by the British otherwise. It's highly unusual to see such a clustering of vessels within our bastions; but for the past month, most are reluctant to ship out. Now that the British fleet has withdrawn to lick its wounds, I'm sure *some* will finally be on their way . . ."

"Lick their wounds, *hell!*" Zeb interjected. "They got more than wounds—two of their ships barely *floated* after the *Fortune Two* pounded hell out of 'em! By God, they even left one behind on fire in the shoals, but we managed to get powder and shot out of her before she exploded."

Deciding it was time to move along, I said, "Mr. Whittenhandler, we are looking for Dillon's on Broad Street . . . and can you tell us where the *Fortune Two* is berthed as well."

"Please call me Henry, Jim," he said, prefacing his directions. "Broad Street intersects Dock Street at the corner down there to your right. Dillon's is about halfway up on the left."

Pointing straight ahead, he added, "At the end of this pier you will find Granville's Bastion. The *Fortune Two* is there." Then his face broke out in a broad grin as he whispered, "You'll have no trouble finding her, Jim—just look for your *wife!*"

Shaking hands, I thanked him. After we parted, while walking away I looked back to see him reopen his ledger book—and brightly hail the next ship to confirm its cargo to be unloaded.

As I observed his demeanor, his kindness and gentility were similar to that of Colonel Moultrie's—and I began to think that perhaps Charleston was the kindest place in the colonies—that is, except for Walker's Cove.

Leaving Charleston

Charleston, July 4, 1776

My dearest Suzannah,

Nearer to home we shall soon be, for a victory and honorable discharge from Colonel Moultrie returns us to New York, where we will serve under General Washington. Henry will carry us there as soon as the Fortune Two is refitted. You should have seen her in action, Suzannah, so thrilling and majestic . . . and yet through the smoke and noise, all I could see was your lovely figurehead . . . such a welcome sight for lonely eyes!

As I write this letter, I see you now, peeking demurely at me from beyond my window. Although fashioned from wood, how real your likeness seems: your lovely creamy skin tinged with a touch of rouge, your deep and soulful eyes captivating mine, the trace of a sweet smile that ever graces your lips, as though you hold a secret and will never tell.

Dear angel of mine, I wonder what are those secrets your heart holds as I sit here, mesmerized by your beauty . . . how is it not possible to fall in love with you all over again? I am the moth, Suzannah . . . you are the flame . . . and though I would willingly sacrifice myself to your heavenly incandescence, I could ever say it would be worth it . . . just for that sweet but fatal reward.

How I love you, miss you and wish you were here: just to feel the comfort of your hand in mine, to hear your soft voice . . . to see your kindred glance conveying Love's blessings upon its unworthy recipient.

Indeed, your love is a treasure I carry home, where I may once again feel the loving touch of God's best and loveliest angel.

Kiss Ainsley for me, and remember me to your parents and our friends.

I shall write again from New York.

Ever your loving husband,
James

A Declaration

Wednesday, July 17, 1776

My dearest Suzannah,

I take long walks around Charleston wishing you were by my side, knowing it can't yet be. So I decided to share some of my observations with you, in the hope I might tempt you to return with me to visit this fascinating city.

While lodging at the George Tavern, I've noticed that folks here are generally more genteel and refined than those at home, but I've discovered these qualities have little substance, for the attainment of a higher station in life here, rests solely upon slavery and the cultivation of rice.

It seems that all masters of the various trades own slaves to operate them. Lately, these masters are anxious to cash out of their trades and purchase farmland to grow rice, which is the most profitable commodity in Charleston. I have yet to meet a poor rice farmer; and despite their success in bringing culture and refinement into their society, their dependence upon slavery to fuel their businesses, is Charleston's one great failing. As such, the value of honest labor and the appreciation of success that goes with it, become irretrievably lost.

The second interesting thing for you to know is that women here in their own right, own and operate many of the taverns and inns— separate and independent of a husband's powers and earnings. So, my dear, although Mother was the owner of our tavern, as you are today, it would appear that she is not the first woman to hold that position.

In the early years of the last century, a female tavern-keeper was allowed by law to guard her wealth and keep her income separate from *her husband. If a woman was single and then later married, her business and property were protected by law when brought into the marriage.*

The unmarried ladies among them are sole traders, known as "feme sole" in the eyes of the law. They are granted an official license by South Carolina to carry on their business just as you do, and are granted prenuptial rights and remedies should their marriage fail, or their husband turn out to be unscrupulous.

Charleston has wonderful shops filled with beautiful dresses I'd love to see you wear. Highly skilled seamstresses with keen business acumen own most of these establishments, and the competition between fashion, style and price is quite fierce. This results in dresses of astonishing detail and quality . . . the dresses Zeb brought Dimmis last year can give you some idea of what I mean. I hear they are in demand all over the colonies, even in New York and Philadelphia.

My dear wife, while I was writing this letter to you, Zeb brought me a broadside; the title is, "In Congress, July 4th, 1776. A Declaration by the Representatives of the UNITED STATES OF AMERICA, in General Congress Assembled . . ." *And here are the words of its declaration:*

> "When in the Course of human Events, it becomes necessary for one People to dissolve the Political Bands which have connected them with another, and to assume among the Powers of the Earth, the separate and equal Station to which the Laws of Nature and Nature's God entitle them, a decent Respect to the Opinions of Mankind requires that they should declare the causes which impel them to the Separation."

The rest of it cites the multitude of reasons why this separation must occur. I will bring this to Henry immediately, for perhaps we have broken free of the bonds that have held colonial trade prisoner for so many months. If the war is over—I might hold your precious heart to mine very soon.

In haste my darling—we're off to New York!

Ever your loving husband,
James

Mystic Voyage

o, my dear James," Henry crowed as he handed me a tumbler of brandy, "What do you think of my new . . . ah . . . *accommodations?*"

After admiring his smartly decorated uniform and the finely wrought wooden panels of his newly restored cabin, I said, "The *Fortune Two* looks magnificent, Henry—better than new."

"Thank you, dear friend, but remember this vessel belongs to you and your wife as well." Lifting his brandy to make a toast, he declared, "To *Suzannah* . . . may Providence guide her namesake to success and freedom's shores—wherever they may be!"

I swallowed hard and repeated, "Her *namesake?*"

"Why, yes! The *Fortune Two* was so extensively rebuilt that we decided to *rename* her as well!" Deeply bowing while swishing his commander's hat in a grand manner, he humbly announced, "So, Jim . . . welcome aboard *Suzannah's Pride.*"

"*Suzannah's Pride?*" I hesitantly repeated, overcome with astonishment.

"It's the very least I can do for her, who has done so much for *us!*" Henry leaned on his captain's desk, and raising his brows, cautiously asked, "*Think* about it, Jim . . . where in the world would we be, *without* Suzannah?"

Remembering her arrival at Walker's Cove and how she had magically touched us all, I somberly replied, "*Nowhere . . .*"

"*Precisely!*" Henry affirmed enthusiastically. "Someday, Jim, in the wilderness of old age, when my memory is failing and my mind is sluggish, I will still hear her sweet friendly voice—counseling us on life's complications, big and small . . .

"As such, my boy, I'm happy to think it is *Suzannah's Pride* that will carry us closer to Walker's Cove—where her namesake resides."

"You have bestowed a worthy honor on her, Henry, and I thank you for that," I said sincerely, relieved to have found my voice at last.

He refilled our tumblers, saying, "Now, Jim, about your time on Sullivan's Island—what did you make of General Charles Lee?"

After taking a mouthful of brandy and letting it flow smoothly down my gullet, I said, "From my perspective—and Colonel Moultrie's perspective—not much *good.*"

"Indeed!" Henry exclaimed, lifting his brows and leaning back in his magnificent captain's chair. After draining his brandy, he continued. "Let me tell you, the Sons in Philadelphia have heard Continental army officers claim that General Lee is a thoroughly unpleasant scoundrel, a cunning and diabolical man whose innards are riddled with poisonous envy—particularly of General Washington."

"Colonel Moultrie says that based upon his advice to Braddock, Lee is incompetent, a typical British officer, full of fraud and corruption, hoping to buy his way to the top . . . like so many others . . . and I witnessed Lee's reprehensible behavior toward the colonel firsthand . . . and he seems to be everything you say." I replied.

"You're both *entirely* correct!" Henry declared, folding his hands on his stomach and starting to twiddle his thumbs. He seemed in a state of considerable agitation until he finally shot up to his full height and shouted, "It's damnably unfortunate that he's on *our* side . . . for now, at least."

I nodded in silent agreement.

Resuming his seat, Henry said, "You seem rather subdued . . . especially for someone who has just achieved a major victory. Perhaps you haven't heard the extent of it, Jim, but the news is all over Charleston, you know."

"Yes, I heard a little from a stevedore on the Charleston dock."

"Well, my boy, here is the whole story; our side lost twelve men and twenty-five were wounded—but *you* fellows in the *fortress*— shot up an *admiral!*"

"I had no idea of his rank!" I nearly shouted in surprise, remembering the officer we targeted.

Henry, motioning for me to sit, elaborated. "Indeed . . . *someone* in that little sand hut sent a twenty-four-pound ball into the *Bristol's* starboard quarterdeck. It bounced around very nicely, but it could *not* figure out *where* to land! So it tore open a wound on Admiral Parker's *thigh*, crashed into the *gunnels*, sending a shard into his *knee*, and then whizzed across the *backside* of his neatly tailored breeches . . . leaving his entire *rear* . . . of the British *fleet*, of course . . . *exposed!*"

After I asked, "Were his linens—a—*clean?*" We hooted and slapped ourselves mirthfully for some time, enjoying the spectacle in our imaginations, until we calmed down enough so Henry could refresh our brandies. Then we toasted our good fortune and victory.

After a couple of swallows, Henry recited more statistics. "The Admiralty lost sixty-four men, one hundred and sixty-one were wounded, and seven went missing. The *Bristol* took seventy hits, Jim—*seventy!* She is fortunate to be *afloat*, I would say."

"I'm certain that many of those hits were from *your* guns, Henry. We could see your devastating broadsides from the fort." I stood then to toast Henry, adding, "History may never record it; but the *Fortune Two*—under Henry Wiggins, master—is *truly* responsible for our victory at Sullivan's Island."

Nodding his appreciation, Henry asked, "And what makes you so certain of this, Jim?"

Laying my hand affectionately on his shoulder, I softly confessed, "We were *finished*, Henry! We were *out* of powder and shot . . . with only *rifles* to bear." And taking his other shoulder, I gently squeezed them while giving him the unspoken truth: "Had you not arrived *precisely* when you *did*, Henry, the British would have *destroyed* us . . . and Charleston would now be occupied by the *redcoats!*"

Henry, his face drained of color, looked up and murmured, "And Suzannah would be a widow . . ."

Henry's remark hit me hard, and as I fingered my talisman in gratitude, it seemed that our miraculous victory was indeed aided by a divine hand. Anxious to change the subject, I said, "Tell me about New York, Henry."

"While you were building sand forts and shooting the breeches off admirals, Washington drove the British out of Boston in March. He moved his army to New York, where it lies in wait for the Howe brothers to descend upon it. It seems that the British are more riled up than ever by our declaration of independence."

With an exaggerated tone of sarcasm, I said, "Of course, the king will miss his tax money *and* his tyranny over our daily lives."

"Jim, you cannot imagine how *difficult* it is to wean a power-hungry ruler off the *teat* of absolute rule . . . and as such, we need to finish the break and become our own republic."

As I thought about men like General Lee vying for power and position, I added, "*If* we can manage to keep it, Henry."

He said nothing, but nodded in agreement.

"Do you know what the plan is and who will be in charge of our mission in New York?"

Rolling his eyes upward while fingering his cheek, Henry said thoughtfully, "As far as I know, we will join the nearly ten thousand troops of the Continental Army who are already there."

"Ten *thousand!*" I repeated in astonishment. "I didn't know there were ten thousand *people* in all the colonies!"

"Washington needs *thirty* thousand men if he is to succeed against the Howe brothers, Jim. While he is in dire need of *everything*, he especially needs good scouts with good horses. And because you and Zeb have horses, he'll want you both to be his eyes and ears—to keep track of what the Howe brothers are doing every moment!"

He paused to offer me a wedge of pemmican, before he continued. "You'll be pleased to know that our next destination will be Walker's Cove, where we'll retrieve the horses for you and Zeb. We'll anchor there for a day or two so you and your cohorts can spend some time with your families. From there, we *must* get to

New York—without meeting up with the Howe brothers along the way."

I was totally dumbfounded by the news that we would soon be back in Walker's Cove. I was overjoyed at the prospect . . . and told Henry so. When I had my wits about me again, I finally remembered to ask him the question that was on my mind.

"You keep mentioning the Howe brothers, Henry—but who in hell *are* the Howe brothers?"

"Let me tell you about them, Jim." Henry began while easing himself into his chair. Taking a wedge of pemmican, he offered me a wedge, and then he continued. "Vice Admiral Richard Howe, who is older brother to Sir William Howe, believes there can be reconciliation between the colonies and the king. He's in full charge of the British navy, a portion of which you defeated at Sullivan's Island. Brother William is in charge of the army, and both are headed for New York. It is estimated their combined troop count will exceed thirty thousand men . . . or perhaps a trifle under *forty* thousand—if the truth be known."

Aghast, I sat up and stopped chewing. "My God!" And speechless at this staggering number, I brooded upon our fate against such odds.

Henry leaned toward me and wearing a grave countenance, added soberly, "The Howe brothers are, despite being British, superb tactical officers of unexcelled competence—every bit as good as Washington or Arnold. Neither will shrink from a fight—and like all brothers in war, they watch each other's backs."

Henry paused for a moment to pour me a mug of cider, and then continued. "Washington will be challenged, because William Howe knows the methods of Indian fighting, Jim, and he is *not* afraid to employ it if he is actively commanding on the battlefield."

Well, where else would he be?" I asked, still wondering how we could stand against such overwhelming numbers.

Henry stood and flicking his finger triumphantly, brightly answered, "With Mrs. *Loring*, of course . . . Howe is thought to be infatuated with Mrs. Betsey Loring, the Sultana. She is the wife of one of the most worthless of Tory soldiers, who consented to sell her *services* to the British for tuppence ha'penny—*and* favorable treatment by the army. William Howe's infatuation for this blonde-headed vixen is sure to weaken his judgment in military affairs."

After taking another bite of the pemmican and a sip of cider, I asked, "What makes you think so, Henry?"

"A woman can be a severe distraction in the military, especially a cunning little poppet as she is, using the skills of a common strumpet to lead a man into thinking with the wrong *head* . . . if you catch my drift. But if Howe brings her to New York, it may be to *our* advantage, since she is rumored to be a spy for the colonial cause . . . but from the salacious ditties *I* have heard, such altruism on our part is perhaps misplaced." Then he added, "Despite Sir William's frivolities, as a commander he will still be a *force* to be reckoned with, Jim. Mark my words, this will be a battle for the ages."

"Considering the four to one advantage they have, I wouldn't think so . . ." I said mournfully.

"Normally, I would agree with that conclusion. But the British have a tendency to underestimate the resourcefulness and determination of men like Washington, Arnold and Knox."

Remembering Suzannah's letter about Arnold's failure in Quebec, I decided to confirm her information regarding the northern army. "Back in March, Suzannah wrote that Arnold's army had suffered defeat in Quebec. Was her information accurate?"

Sighing heavily, Henry replied, "I'm sorry to confirm that our troops fared poorly in Canada, Jim—and yes, Montgomery was killed and Arnold was badly wounded. Many officers were taken into Quebec and held as prisoners by the British, while the survivors of Arnold's army remain out of action."

Remembering more details from the letter, I probed further. "Suzannah said half the army was disabled by smallpox, dysentery and consumption. Colonel Enos, who stayed behind to attend to those poor wretches, eventually released them into the wilderness after their enlistments expired. Many died of exposure seeking medical care wherever they could, and those who didn't, staggered into places like Walker's Cove—half dead."

Overcome with emotion, I clutched Henry's forearm. "The damned war has hit *home*, Henry! Our tavern . . . my *home* . . . became a *hospital*, where Doc was forced to resort to horrible, mutilating surgeries, while for my poor wife, death became a daily event. Finally, there was little that Doc, Suzannah, Dimmis and the other womenfolk could do to *help* those poor men. Suzannah said three of our good friends—Emma Watson, Lavinia Bates, and Rhoda Barrett—*died* from the contagious diseases they'd contracted just by *caring* for them—by trying to cure the incurable . . . you remember them, don't you?"

Henry nodded and said solemnly, "Their loving efforts . . . and those of *thousands* yet to come . . . shall remain forever buried beneath the altar of freedom . . ."

I stared at him mutely and was further saddened by the idea that so much sacrifice lay ahead, for up to now I mistakenly believed that with the issuance of the declaration, the war would soon be over . . . but clearly, this was only the beginning.

Sensing my melancholy, Henry placed his hand upon my shoulder sympathetically. "Jim, we are all the instruments of our own destiny. We all *want* freedom. We only need to have the eyes to *see* it . . . and the heart to *reach* for it. Knowing it may come at a *very* heavy price . . . it is our lot as individuals to decide . . . if that cost is too much to bear."

I pondered the wisdom of Henry's words. Despite the setbacks in Canada and back home, we were at a crossroads in our time of separation from England. Which of us would make the correct decision to fight . . . and in doing so, possibly pay the ultimate price?

Looking into the sincere eyes of Henry Wiggins, I pledged myself to our cause, "No matter what the outcome, I look forward to the day when this war will have nothing but the past to live on—but *not* this day . . ."

We stood and embraced as brothers, and with that embrace, I resigned myself to extract from the fearsome quagmire of war, the freedom to make a better life for those I loved . . . and I prayed I would survive to see its glorious fulfillment.

DESPITE HENRY'S INSISTENCE that we bunk in his quarters, Zeb and I refused. Although we were part owners of *Suzannah's Pride*, we chose not to exploit our status, but rather share a seaman's life with our friends and neighbors, thus promoting our sense of brotherhood.

Every evening belowdecks, we exchanged stories about our families, our trades and our experiences on Sullivan's Island. We also speculated on what changes would face us upon our arrival in New York—after an eagerly anticipated visit home. We also talked about how wonderfully refreshing it was to be on the open sea. Not only for the invigorating salt air and warm sunshine, but also because we slept so soundly in our hammocks . . . being gently rocked by the rolling motion of the ship.

The following afternoon, Henry invited me once again to his cabin. He declared that being captain was a lonely job, and his want for female companionship became greatest when he was at sea. "That is the most difficult aspect of being master," he elaborated, offering me a pemmican wedge and a small tumbler of spiced cider. "Too bad it's not ginger beer rum, my dear friend—but beggars can't be choosy!" Then turning to raise his tumbler toward the northwest, he made a toast: "To friendship and *love* . . ."

"To friendship and love, indeed!" I echoed.

Henry sat down and motioned for me to sit too. "It's true that being master of a vessel is extraordinarily exhilarating, and yet it's the *loneliest* damned job in the world . . . what a *hell* of a dichotomy, my good friend!"

Surprised and curious, I said, "What makes you say that, Henry? I didn't know you felt that way."

Placing a hand over his heart, he asked, "Jim, do you never get *lonely*? Do you not *miss* Suzannah . . . Ainsley . . . Dimmis . . . home?"

"Yes, Henry, my heart aches for them every night . . ."

Henry interjected, "I don't mean just missing the *people*—but your *life*."

"Well," I said slowly, allowing my thoughts to gather, "I feel they *are* my life."

Henry rose to open his cabin window and stared wistfully out to sea. After sighing heavily, he spoke as though recalling a distant dream. "Although I am laden with gold, with each passing year I suffer from the emptiness of what life truly should be . . . *besides* the promise of death. At *my* age, Jim, I should be *sharing* my life with someone . . . a *wife* to love and return to. As the time grows nearer for my body to yield to spirit, I focus far less upon the *vanities* of this life. My own battered hulk longs for a twin of *soul* and *heart* . . . so we may subsist on the joy we bring to each other—and thus, though our eyes be dimmed and our steps be feeble, we shall drift together—toward the ultimate safe haven that awaits us."

Henry returned to sit at the table, and taking my hand, he pressed it gently. "Jim, your wife and child bless your hearth; and there they patiently wait because their hearts are centered on the same place yours is . . . and that is called *home.*

"I have spent my *entire* life at sea, never knowing a home. Aye, I have *chosen* this life, and it prevented me from experiencing what you have had . . . a home . . . and a life with your family. As it is, Jim, you, Suzannah and Ainsley have richened my life . . . just by living yours and welcoming me into it. From you I have learned its true value . . . and when this war ends, I *hope* to spend my final years in Walker's Cove . . . with you, and a soul mate that *loves* me.

The silent moisture in his eyes affirmed his suppressed yearning, and touching his cheek to stop the progress of a wayward tear, Henry added, "Indeed James, we *must* be prepared for Death, for he knocks indiscriminately upon any door . . . but should my hope ever come to pass, I shall open my door . . . and *welcome* him."

ALL THE DIAMONDS

n a quiet sultry pre dawn morning, under bare poles, *Suzannah's Pride* drifted slowly into the harbor of Walker's Cove. As she quietly settled into its shallow waters, Zeb and I anxiously monitored the slow descent of a newly built longboat. We were home for the first time in months, and this boat would carry us ashore.

Wedging himself between us, Henry jovially asked, "So . . . my good friends are going *ashore* on this fine summer morning, eh?"

Looking dubiously at the teetering longboat, Zeb sarcastically offered, "Yeah, Henry—if that damned boat don't sink with us *in* it!"

"Now Zeb!" Henry soothingly replied, "A better boat for your journey home was never more stoutly built—after *all* my good man, you *own* it!"

Backing away from Henry and planting his fists upon his hips, Zeb demanded, "Why in hell do I keep *ownin'* stuff I don't *know* about?"

Henry, placing a comforting arm about Zeb's shoulder, patiently explained, "Zebulon Galletin Hawkes, you are part *owner* of this vessel—and as such, you rely upon *my* sound judgment as her *master*, to purchase and invest your assets wisely—to use them efficiently, and *maximize* any profits we might share through doing so."

Escorting Zeb toward a Jacob's ladder being thrown over the side for our descent to the longboat, Henry then added, "I believe buried safely in the cellar of Jim's tavern, a vast return on your investment in this vessel awaits your pleasure . . . as does an even *more* valuable asset . . . your lovely red headed *wife!*"

Zeb, now quietly contemplating his reunion with Dimmis, smiled salaciously and said nothing.

Poking Zeb in the chest, Henry then suggested, "As Captain, I now order you to row yourself ashore in *your* boat, and take *your* wife into *your* arms, and show her *your* true heart—and *never mind* the quibbling nature of what you *own* or do *not* own . . . it is what you *love* that is *most* precious . . ."

Patting Zeb on his massive shoulder, Henry then ordered, "Now get your bloody ass ashore, sailor, and give Dimmis my highest regards!"

Zeb carefully climbed down the rope ladder while I remained on deck, waiting for him to free the rope. While waiting, I turned to bid Henry farewell, but he'd gone forward to view the silhouette of Walker's Cove beneath the sunrise. As I stepped onto the ladder, I heard Henry breathe deeply of the air and mutter, "Damned *fine* place, Walker's Cove . . . far away from all the *hell* in the world . . ."

WHEN WE WERE both safely aboard, we rowed rapidly toward the wharf. The harbor was empty of other vessels, and as we approached the town, I saw no obvious changes—save there were no signs of commercial activity. Other than a few gulls overhead dropping shellfish on the wharf, there were no welcoming arms or sweet smiles to greet us . . . and the emptiness was palpable and disheartening.

So we hastened to secure the longboat, and after trotting up the familiar road toward home, we soon found ourselves standing awkwardly before the tavern door.

My racing heartbeat and the lump in my throat signaled that behind this door, lay the entire reason for my existence—and this would be the first reunion with my family since winter.

While I was reluctant to knock at such an early hour, Zeb, having felt he'd waited long enough for *his* homecoming, reached around me to rap softly on the door.

Silence pervaded, and when the door slowly opened with a screeching protest of the hinges, I knew that it hadn't been opened for a long while. Its opening yielded a view into the cavernous gloom within . . . and like a disembodied spirit, Dimmis' figure loomed out of the darkness.

She looked worn and thin, as though she had labored endlessly without proper nourishment. As the morning light flooded her eyes, she peered blindly at the two shadows that greeted her—until she put her hand up to shield them.

As her eyes widened with the dawning realization that her husband was standing before her, Dimmis finally managed, "Am I *seeing* things?"

"Yup . . . *two* of them to be exact . . ." Zeb replied humorously, and unable to restrain himself any longer, he grabbed her and cradled her in his arms. She wept with joy and threw her arms around him. As they held each other in a long desperate embrace, they shared many tears, ardent kisses and murmurings of love.

Although I enjoyed their affections, it occurred to me to ask if I could enter my own home. Breaking her kisses long enough to apologize for her lack of propriety, Dimmis invited us in.

Once inside, I saw the reason for the darkness—no fires had yet been kindled. The windows were still shuttered from within, keeping the house dark for sleeping. When I glanced up at the tall clock, by the light from the open doorway I saw it read 5:43.

The tables and chairs of the great room were gone, it being totally void of anything, save numerous dark stains upon the floorboards. Remembering what Suzannah had written about Doc's surgeries, I presumed these were the bloodstains of the poor fellows who spent agonizing days here—until many of them died . . .

As if she'd read my mind, Dimmis interrupted my thoughts. "It was here that we had the hospital, Jim. We tried *so* hard to save them—it was so *cruel* what they had to endure—and we felt so *helpless*. We have *tried* to remove the stains—to make this a *home* and a *tavern* once again—but there was so much *blood* . . . and choking with tears, she finally cried, "Oh *God* forgive us!" . . . and buried her face in Zeb's chest. There, in total despondency, she sobbed while Zeb tried to comfort her, holding her close and gently stroking her hair.

Indicating to Zeb he should carry Dimmis to the parlor, I went ahead to hastily kindle a fire. After I had it roaring in short order, I dragged the sofa in front of it, and motioned to Zeb to sit with her there. This he did, cuddling her in his lap before the crackling flames.

Through streaming tears, she looked up so pleadingly into Zeb's face, that I was deeply moved by her pain. Softly stroking her long red hair while kissing her dampened cheeks, he then reassured her with a profound sincerity. "Dimmis, your eyes are full of tragedy that I shall never see, and because nobody can ever see what you have seen, those secrets—the horrors of this war—shall ever remain with you."

He then took her hand and tenderly kissing it, he delicately pressed it to his heart—and looking deep into her searching eyes, he confessed, "I too have seen such terrible things in this war . . . and bearing these scars together, we shall go *forward* . . . and *love* each other all the more."

I was proud to see what a passionate and caring gentleman he had become, and while he continued to whisper encouraging words to Dimmis, I desperately ached to hold Suzannah.

I went into the kitchen expecting to find her, and was crushed to discover she was not there. Noticing a pitcher of cider and a plate of apple fritters on the kitchen table, and thinking to comfort Dimmis, I brought them to the parlor and placed them near the sofa. Again, Dimmis seemed to glean my thoughts and answered my unasked question.

"Suzannah took Ainsley for an early morning walk . . . I think they are in Richardson's fields—or perhaps at the seashore. Suzannah had a small basket for . . ."

I was gone before she finished her sentence.

ALTHOUGH I RACED toward the shore, I was certain that I hadn't missed my wife and daughter along the way. When I was near enough to hear the churning waves, I looked toward Walker's Point, where we'd spent so much precious time together. I instantly recalled the serene beauty and healing power of its sunsets—how they gave us so much hope when there was none, and so much happiness—simply because we were together.

As I walked along the coastline, I beheld two distant figures—one stooping to pick up something from the sand, and the other whirling and dancing in and out of the water like a tiny shorebird. Bits of delightful squeals reached me in the drifting wind . . . and as tears flooded my eyes, I carefully approached them.

As they walked hand in hand, Suzannah with her basket of shells and Ainsley searching for new ones, my delicate perceptions of family flooded my heart.

Suddenly, Ainsley darted into the water and pointed down, begging her mother to add the shell to their basket.

When Suzannah turned to pick it up, I beheld her loveliness for the first time in months: her radiant face, her dainty figure, and her wavy gleaming hair nearly falling to the sand as she stooped. My heart fluttered and ached for this beautiful woman before me.

Ainsley, who saw my shadow, raised her hand to shade her eyes and suddenly blurted, "Papa's here—*Papa's here!*" as she tugged at her mother's dress. Then she jumped up and came running toward me, screeching, "Papa! Papa!" Never before had I heard such a sweet sound as that little voice right then.

Catching her as she flew into my arms, I twirled her around and tossed her high in the air and she shrieked with every toss. When I caught her for the fifth time, I nestled her upon my hip and finally turned toward Suzannah.

Standing like a statue, her lower lip quivering, she suddenly dropped her basket into the shallows; and splashing toward me with open arms, she tearfully whimpered, "My dear *God* . . ." before screaming, "*Jim!*"

She collided with me with such force that we all landed together in the shallow water, embracing each other as we fell. Thoroughly soaked, all were crying as we kissed each other's faces, hair and lips. Hands were clutched, hugs were everywhere, fingers ran through hair, and laughing, kissing and crying with happiness and relief, we joyously frolicked and splashed in the sandy water . . . because I was finally *home* . . .

AFTER OUR TEARFUL reunion on the beach, we withdrew to Walker's Point to dry out. While Ainsley explored the tidal pools, Suzannah and I settled in our usual spot, facing due west. Between burning kisses of unrequited desire and whispered confidences, we made plans to quell the fires of our long-denied passion. Suzannah admitted she needed *total* release, and such was her long suppressed urgency to make love, she now threatened to cross the boundaries of propriety to do it.

Such talk after our long absence made me crave her, and had Ainsley not been present, I would have taken Suzannah right where she sat . . . and I know she wouldn't give a damn if anyone saw us.

But instead I merely held her, for nothing felt as good right now—as the comforting warmth of feeling her safely nestled in my arms.

Suzannah turned our conversation to her traumatic experiences of tending the men in our hospital. She included the more lurid details of Doc's mutilating surgeries, and how the animals came in the night . . . to steal the severed body parts. I listened carefully and held her tight as she told about the monstrous disposition of bodies . . . knowing she had waited a long time to share what she'd suffered. It wrenched my heart to hear of her pain, but I admired her strength and selflessness in the face of a terrible ordeal—that *nothing* in her life had prepared her for.

In the early afternoon, the three of us returned home. Dimmis and Zeb were waiting to discuss their ideas for a homecoming celebration at the tavern . . . the first since we left for the war. They would invite the crew and soldiers aboard *Suzannah's Pride*, as well as all the locals and their families who wished to attend. Since the Walker's Cove contingent would soon be off to New York—we decided to have it on the following evening.

Preparations were soon underway. Arrangements were made to refurnish the great room with its accustomed tables and chairs, which had to be brought over from Sam's work shed where they had been stored. Suzannah and Dimmis were planning the menu, with cooking to begin the next morning.

Zeb and I rowed back out to *Suzannah's Pride* and notified all aboard that they were invited for a celebration on the morrow—of good food, good drink, good music and good company. Not surprisingly, our invitation was greeted with a chorus of huzzahs, with one notable exception.

When we went to see Henry, we found he wasn't his usual hearty and expansive self. He explained he was feeling unusually tired and a bit unwell. We immediately suggested that he come back with us to the tavern, where he could stay overnight, and offered to fetch Doc Brown for him.

But he refused, saying that he didn't think his ailment warranted all that fuss; he preferred to stay behind in his cabin until he was recovered enough to resume his post.

When we protested, he reassured us that all he needed was rest, and told us to drink up his share of the rum. We felt reassured by his last remark, as it sounded more like the Henry we knew and loved.

As we rowed back to shore, Zeb and I talked about how good it felt to be home—and for the briefest moment, it even felt like old times. But against that, even though we were the same *people*, we felt intangibly different. What had the war done to us? It had changed our souls . . . and although we still experienced love and happiness, they were constantly overshadowed by the conflict to come . . . and our pressing need to leave our loved ones.

When we arrived at the tavern, we were greeted by the sweet sound of Suzannah's pianoforte. Zeb went to the kitchen while I lingered in the doorway to listen. Peeking inside, I was astonished to see Suzannah *and* Ainsley sitting together at the pianoforte. Ainsley was slowly playing the keys, and as I approached, they began to sing a soft lullaby.

Their duet was so endearing, a swelling lump came to my throat . . . and while Ainsley played, I fondly remembered her toddler years: when she and Suzannah shared stories, knitted together, and especially learned and explored music together. My daughter was growing up; learning so much about the wonderful things in life from her gifted mother—and because of the war—I was missing all of it.

After finishing their song and applauding each other, they rose and Suzannah smiled proudly at her daughter and warmly kissed her cheek. Then she patted her behind and told her to get ready for bed, saying she would soon be up to tuck her in.

As Ainsley scrambled upstairs, Suzannah came over to me, and tucking a teasing finger beneath my chin, she gently pressed my lips with a soft openmouthed kiss. Moaning hungrily as I returned her warmth in kind, she broke the kiss and whispered. "I shall tend to *you*, shortly . . . *after* I tuck our daughter in for the night."

Anticipating her desires, I distracted myself by going to the kitchen to discuss with Dimmis, the final details about the homecoming meal tomorrow evening. When all was settled, I climbed upstairs in my stockings to quietly observe my growing daughter. Peeking into Ainsley's bedchamber, I found the bed blanket partially drawn, with a bed warmer's handle jutting from its opening. Suzannah was sitting in Mother's rocker reading to her daughter, now snuggled in her lap.

In my heart I knew that this was an oft-repeated scene in their lives, one they both looked forward to at the conclusion of every day. By adhering to this ritual and sharing her most-beloved stories, Suzannah believed she was inspiring her daughter—not only with a love of books, but with the highest ideals of her own girlhood.

Admiring the bond between Suzannah and my dearest child, I felt her wellbeing was in the best of hands. And as I watched Suzannah remove the bed warmer, the reflection of her loving face in its brass could never be mistaken . . . and because of her devoted attention to Ainsley, although I thought it impossible—I now loved Suzannah more than ever.

It was barely light out when Suzannah came downstairs, and Fanny had arrived for her nightly sitting with Ainsley. Suzannah took my hand and a blanket—and led me out the door and down to Walker's Point. In the dusk we skipped along like children, abandoning our cares and shedding the heaviness of the world. Now, the world was *us*.

On Walker's Point we found our favorite spot, which during my absence, Suzannah named Sunset Rock. After we sat, she deeply inhaled the salty air and asked, "Don't you wish you could live *forever*, Jim? Every time I smell this fresh invigorating air, I think I could, darling."

I kissed her and whispered in her ear, "I would only do so angel . . . if *you* were with me."

Squeezing my hand, she kissed it and softly asked, "So you *are* still in love with your little wife, Jim?"

Drawing her close, I gently caressed her hair, releasing a heavenly floral scent. Never was anything more dear to me—and *safe*—than *my* Suzannah.

But my loving gestures weren't answer enough. Again she looked at me and between the crashing of the waves, she repeated, "Are you still in love with your little wife?"

With moistened eyes, I gazed into hers and merely asked, "What does your *heart* say?"

"It says that through shadows and darkness, our love will endure and ever grow stronger. It's growing stronger even now—I can feel it."

"Your heart feelings are as true as ever, my darling . . . and yes, it *is* growing. When I saw you with Ainsley tonight, I felt a new depth to our love, which we share through *her*."

Nodding her understanding, Suzannah added, "She has grown so much, Jim, and imagine—she is already in her *fifth* year!"

Regretting my absence from her life, I reluctantly asked, "Do you think she missed me, Suzannah?"

"She asks for you *every* day. She misses you and your tossing her into the air . . . she misses being *held* . . . by her strong loving father."

I pressed her hand in gratitude, relieved to know that despite my daughter's tender age, I was still important in her life, and worthy of being missed . . .

My thoughts were interrupted when Suzannah suddenly commanded: "Follow me!"

We carefully removed our shoes and taking our blanket, she led me down toward the beach. The summer breeze was coming off the water, where whitecaps rolled and hissed noisily onto the shore. Here she laid her blanket where the waves couldn't reach us, and taking my hand, we walked in the shallows to observe the full moon rising. It shone with a penetrating brilliance beyond anything

I'd seen before—and had I not known better, it seemed as though Suzannah had arranged for it herself.

I let her hand go and focused on the moon for several long minutes . . . and realized that tonight might very well be—a Midnight Blue.

When I turned to suggest this exciting possibility to Suzannah, she was standing in the shallows, covered in nothing but moonlight. She was fondling her erect nipples with one hand and her womanhood with the other.

As the breeze gently carried her hair in sensuous flowing waves, I gawked in mute admiration at my love goddess. Her wanton behavior never ceased to amaze me, and as the moonlight highlighted her spectacular figure, she licked her parted lips and sweetly asked, "What are you *waiting* for, Jim . . . Christmas?"

Removing my clothes, I staggered toward her, letting them drop where they would. When I stood before her, I noticed that my manhood had arrived before I did.

Looking up at me with an amused smile, she took it in her hands, and drawing them up and down its length, she softly cooed. "My, my . . . what have we *here?*" Taking my hand and pressing it between her breasts, she softly asked, "Can you feel my heart beating?"

Dumbstruck with desire, "*Yes . . .*" was all I could manage.

"It holds the love that's forever yours—the flame that burns between us, has waited *far* too long . . ." She took my other hand and placing it on her womanhood, held it there tightly. I felt her heat and knew she had a throbbing need, for her moisture was at the ready.

Looking up with eyes closed, she whispered barely audible above the gentle breakers, "A moment lost can never be again, so let's not lose any more . . . take me gently, darling—let us be as one . . ."

Suzannah drew me toward her and clasped her arms about my neck, lifting her body to straddle me by hooking her legs around my waist. With a sharp gasp, she fitted herself onto me, drawing me completely inside. Upon the very instant of my penetration to her soft limit, she thrashed, quivered and moaned in her first "trip to the heights."

So shaken was I by the intensity of her passion, I lost my balance and we fell into the water. Although the current carried us to deeper shoals, Suzannah held onto me, thus maintaining our connection; and when I found my footing once again, we shared deep kisses while my slow thrusting underwater—caused her to climax again and again.

We continued our night of exotic lovemaking under Midnight Blue: in the sand, in the marsh grass, and back in the water. Suzannah's one rule was that whenever I had a climax, she would lead me back to the shallows, and there she used her incredible skills to re invogorate me. Sometimes she would not stop when I was ready, boldly declaring she wanted me above as well as below. I could only give in . . . and as she effortlessly worked, she acknowledged my exploding gratitude with a loving moan of acceptance.

When we found ourselves glistening from our passion, we took advantage of the cooling water for breaks. We swam blissfully under the moonlight, chasing one another, kissing under the water, splashing each other in water fights, and after a truce was finally called, we finished our lovemaking adventures on the most ordinary of places . . . our blanket.

This Midnight Blue became the most memorable of my life. Not because of my wife's uninhibited desires, or the pleasures of my family's reunion. It was because Susannah had wished upon it for the first time in her life—her wish being that I would return to her from the war—safe and sound. And if her wish was granted, she said . . . her life would be complete.

WE WOKE VERY late the following morning—naked and wrapped in each other's arms, cocooned within Suzannah's blanket.

After planting a sweet kiss on my lips, Suzannah set out to find her clothes, which were a few feet distant from the blanket. As she started buttoning her dress, I looked at her blankly and asked, "Where are *my* clothes?"

"Where you *left* them," she answered brightly, smoothing her dress.

Still wrapped in the blanket, I had just begun to search for my clothes when I tripped over a long piece of driftwood. I picked it up and wrote "James & Suzannah" in the sand, and added the word "forever" beneath it. I smiled at the thought that heaven for me— would be spending forever with my little wife . . . for she was more precious than life itself.

Suddenly hearing Suzannah's infectious laugh, I saw her standing in the center of the beach, her hands over her mouth desperately attempting to stifle the sound.

I called out, "Why are you laughing, darling?"

She stopped giggling long enough to say, "The emperor has no clothes!" and proceeded to titter endlessly afterward.

As the color drained from my face, I realized what she meant. We had spent our night of passion during low tide. But the tide had since come in and carried away my clothes on its way out again.

When I looked at her in dismay, she pointed up toward Walker's Point. "Don't worry, Jim, at least you have your *shoes!*"

Following her gaze, I saw that my shoes still rested on Sunset Rock, where we'd sat yesterday, high up on Walker's Point.

Suzannah approached me, and fishing for my hand through the blanket, took it and tenderly kissed it. "Don't worry, Jim," she said, "I'll help you get home . . ."

I gratefully squeezed her hand, and while scouting out an easy path to my shoes, a hoarse bellowing of my name came from Walker's Point above. It was none other than Zeb Hawkes, frantically waving for us to come up.

Turning away from Suzannah to glance once more for my clothes, I felt crushed when I didn't see them. But what I *did* see—was that the tide had washed away my lover's scratching in the sand—merely leaving the word "James."

As we approached the point, Zeb placed his hands on his waist and chided, "Where in hell have *you* two been? We got *work* to do, and Fanny says that you and Suzannah went to the point last night and never returned!"

As we stood before him, he noticed Suzannah's tangled and matted hair, flecked with sea hay and grains of sand, and then my lack of clothing. "God*damn* you two!" he grumbled, "Can't you *ever* leave each other *alone?*"

Suzannah stamped her foot in anger to castigate him in turn. "Are *you* trying to tell me that you and Dimmis didn't loosen the bed ropes last night?"

"By God, Suzannah, where we go there *aren't* any damned bed ropes!" he roared back. "Dimmis is too damned *noisy*. Our bed is hay in a rick!"

"So you took her in a *rick?*" Suzannah repeated incredulously.

"That's right, all night long . . ." Zeb replied with a knowing smirk.

Breaking into a broad grin, Suzannah patted his shoulder and said, "Well done, Zeb . . . now where was this rick?"

"Richardson's fields . . . there are *lots* of 'em out there," he said, adding proudly, "We went from one to another . . . and ended up together in the *stream* down below—now *that* was something to experience!"

Sliding her eyes toward mine, Suzannah nodded, winked her eye, and merely smiled.

Wearing only my shoes and the blanket, I rode home on Zeb's horse, which he'd purchased that day from Richardson to take to New York. This saved me from prying eyes and embarrassing questions. My concern had been that tongues would wag about Suzannah and I being as libidinous as Mildred and Osgood.

When we arrived, the tavern was a beehive of activity. Dimmis seemed to be everywhere at once, darting in and out of the kitchen while instructing the men who would arrange the furniture in the great room. When Suzannah arrived, she begged for her help in the kitchen as soon as possible, adding there were many other matters they needed to attend to as well.

Despite our long night of great exertion and little sleep, after washing ourselves beneath the barrel, we were as fresh as daisies and ready to work.

Zeb and I hauled furniture to the great room all afternoon, and when everything was finally in place, the stains of suffering were eclipsed by the reemergence of our familiar surroundings—soon to be a scene of celebration. As Suzannah stood by to judge the end result, she nodded her approval, declaring that things were looking more like "our good old days."

After Zeb and I brought up the spirits from the cellar, the womenfolk took over and decided we were "getting underfoot." So Zeb was glad to go off and rest for a while, while Suzannah suggested I take Ainsley to Richardson's fields for a long walk. Overjoyed at the prospect of spending time alone with my daughter, I readily assented.

Suzannah went upstairs to fetch Ainsley, who came down resplendent in her blue dress and white bonnet—the epitome of childhood innocence. Taking my hand, she squealed excitedly, "Papa and I are going to find flowers and *butterflies!*"

Kneeling to give Ainsley a kiss on the cheek, Suzannah hugged her and said, "Well now, since you are a *big* girl, you must show Papa where nature lives. Have a good time and when you return we will have *snickerdoodles!* I love you, sweetheart. Now take Papa's hand and do not *lose* him."

Ainsley, nodding to her mother, said resolutely, "I shall keep him full and by, Mama, and return him to you in good *order!*"

Astonished by her choice of words, I asked, "*Where* did you learn such talk as *that?*"

With an adorable wink, she replied evenly, "Why, from grandpa *Sam*, of course! That's how he talks to me *all* the time."

Suzannah's eyes filled, and as she gazed lovingly into mine, I could do nothing but kiss the dear lips that need not have spoken.

IN MY ABSENCE, Richardson's fields had become more overgrown than I last remembered it. Wading through the ocean of flowers,

Ainsley chattered away like a little magpie, following the erratic flights of butterflies, and showing me all the different wildflowers she knew by name. When she came upon an especially colorful patch, she sat down in the grass and patted the spot beside her, saying, "Papa, will you sit with me and look at these ones?"

I was delighted to simply sit and watch her as she delicately handled them, examining them in detail and sharing with me what her mother had taught her.

"There's things in here that make *new* flowers . . ." she explained, carefully parting the petals to point out the parts. "This is a stamen, this is a sepal, and way inside—that little bell-shaped thing—that is the ovary . . ."

When she looked up at me to ensure I understood her, I saw in her face—and her gray-blue eyes—the image of her mother. I also observed her long yellow hair was turning the same shade of golden brown as Suzannah's.

As Ainsley chatted on, her busy little hands went from flower to flower—and although each one was different, she knew all the parts and where they were located.

Suddenly she stopped talking, and stood up to indicate a point farther down the field. "Papa, those are Mama's *favorite* flowers—can I show you?"

"Of course, sweetheart, lead me there."

As she took my hand, I nearly wept at her sweet endearing ways.

Stopping before a large cluster of pink and white flowers, she said, "These are *Mama's* flowers . . . and she likes them so much, she puts them in her hair. They smell nice too!"

She picked one and smelled it, and then held it up for me to smell too. "These are called *carnations*, Papa. They are the *oldest* flower in the bible. It says when Jesus carried his cross, His mama cried and pink carnations grew where her tears fell. Mama says they mean a mama's undying love."

I had never heard the story before, but I quietly replied, "Yes, sweetheart, I believe that's true."

She gave me a toothy grin of satisfaction and added, "The *white* ones are purity . . . Papa, what is purity?"

"*You* are purity . . ." I answered, as my eyes filled at her innocence. I knelt down, and kissing her cheek and running my fingers through her hair, I softly added, "Ainsley, you and Mama are the purest, most loving people I have ever known . . . and your grandma Ainsley was the same . . ."

I looked away, and dabbing my tears, I wished that Mother could be here to see this beautiful child . . . her amazing grand daughter.

When I turned to Ainsley once again, a butterfly fluttered down and landed on my nose.

Ainsley's eyes opened wide in excitement as she quietly said, "She *loves* you!"

"*She?* It's a *she?* And she *loves* me? How do you know all *that?*" I whispered, being careful not to scare it off.

Ainsley, looking thoughtfully at the butterfly, finally lowered her eyes and said, "I don't *know*, Papa . . . I just *feel* it . . . *here.*"

She was pointing to her heart.

Stunned at this revelation, I quietly uttered, "My God—another heart feeler . . ."

Ainsley, unable to contain herself any longer, gently placed a finger to my nose so the butterfly could crawl onto it. As she held it before her face, she carefully examined its geometric patterns of black and gold. Then she looked up at me and firmly said, "Mama says the heart always feels the truth and knows the way home . . ."

Shaken out of my daze, I affirmed, "Yes, Ainsley, Mama's *right*— she knows all about these things. Never forget that Mama is extra special, as are *you*, my dear one."

Standing tall, Ainsley lowered her finger to a pink carnation so the butterfly could perch there. Her face brightened as she asked, "Can we pick some carnations for Mama's hair?"

Pressing her to my heart, I whimpered, "Let's pick some for *both* of you!"

Agus Paidir o Mo Chroi
(A Prayer from My Heart)

t was dusk when Ainsley and I got back to the tavern. From outside, we could hear music and voices that reminded me of old times. Once inside the door, we found the great room thronged with people—and I was pleased so many had come. Zeb was serving at the bar and everyone was enjoying the music: in the corner, Suzannah was playing her piano-forte, Dimmis her violin and Seamus O'Brien his squeezebox.

Seamus' presence came as a complete surprise to me, since I had no idea he was in town. I later learned that he had lost his second schooner *Fairwind* when the British seized her in February near Cape Ann, and that arrangements had been made for him to once again join Henry's crew. He would be going aboard *Suzannah's Pride* that very night.

I stood Ainsley on a chair so she could get a better view. After the trio finished an old Celtic tune, Suzannah rose from her bench to come forward and face her audience. As Dimmis and Seamus remained behind her, awaiting their cue, I whispered to Ainsley, "Mama is going to *sing* . . . !"

Just as Ainsley nodded, Suzannah launched into a song; with her eyes closed in a dreamlike state, she seemed transported to another land. The song was in Gaelic, a lullaby that was both serene and comforting. Her beautiful warbling trill thrilled me as she sang . . . and the exquisite purity of her voice sent chills down my spine. While I listened to my little songbird of a wife, an unstop-pable wave of loving pride washed over me . . . never could I ask for a better homecoming than this.

When Dimmis joined her voice to Suzannah's, I felt their hearts were together in the same enchanted place. They sang in perfect pitch and harmony, and the audience swayed gracefully in their seats to the rhythm of their song.

After a few stanzas, Dimmis picked up her violin to accompany Suzannah, who continued to sing solo. Her soft comforting voice, combined with the plaintive tones of the violin, made my eyes water with tears of remembrance . . . for this was the same Gaelic tune she sang to me in the church . . . just after we had first met. Despite few of us understanding Gaelic, the sheer emotion of the music gripped the entire room; and in the hushed silence . . . many hearts that had never wept to the songs of Gaelic beauty, compelled cheeks to glisten with streams of silent tears.

When the song ended, Suzannah and Dimmis lovingly embraced. It was a memorable moment for all—for through the magic touch of their music, the war was now forgotten—especially after Ainsley chirped, "Mama is singing about *heart* feelings . . ."

FIRST THE TUMBLERS were refilled and then the food was served while the music continued in the background. The songs were a mixture of tunes that began slowly and morphed into waltzes, and finally into quickfingered dandies that were down right infectious to hear. On one quick song in particular, the pace of the pianoforte and violin suddenly quickened, and Seamus began to sing. His rowdy sharp staccato was so rousing that nearly everyone started clapping to the music. The crowd's enthusiasm inspired Dimmis to begin playing at a frenzied pace, and the atmosphere became an elixir of release—for some of the men stood, clapped, hooted and screamed in time to her burning strings.

They danced around the tables, taking any female hand available— and the blistering pace flew on with such fancy finger-work, that we stopped dancing and simply held our collective breath as we watched. The piece ended abruptly, and everyone rose to give the musicians a standing ovation . . . and kept chanting for more . . .

Our celebration went on past midnight; with Dimmis and Seamus singing what I would call the fast songs: whereas Suzannah sang those that were ethereal and emotional—which highlighted the delicacy of her enchanting voice.

After the tavern emptied out, Dimmis came over to me with Zeb in tow.

"I would call this a roarin' success, would you not?" she breathlessly asked.

Rising to kiss her, I said, "Indeed, I would! What an expereience!" and embraced her gratefully. "Thank you, Dimmis, you have given Walker's Cove a joyous time . . . and for one *glorious* night, we were our old selves again."

"Well, Ireland has a rich heritage of song, unique among all music." She replied. "I believe Ireland's long sad history of want and passionate conflict is what inspired it—as *our* conflict has inspired me!" Nodding in Seamus' direction as he headed for the door, she tearfully added, "I hope everyone *loved* the music . . . the music of my *homeland* . . ."

I nodded in admiration of her sensitivity. "That was an energetic performance you gave us, Dimmis. How long can you keep playing and singing like *that?*"

"When God says I must leave, I'll sing my last . . . and surely there will be a roarin' good time when I get to heaven!"

Seamus, who must have overheard our conversation, was still standing in the doorway. Addressing his cousin, he softly said, "Sphoken like a true Celtic lass, by God! An' may ye get to heaven three minutes afore God knows you're *dead*, little cousin. An' by the Jesus, I'll *meet* ye there . . . Meantime, safe home to you all . . ." and quietly leaving for *Suzannah's Pride*, he gently closed the door.

Taking her arm, Zeb escorted Dimmis toward the door, and when he turned to bid us goodbye, I asked, "Aren't you two staying here?"

Zeb seemed to hesitate at first, but then he suggestively cleared his throat and admitted, "There's a full moon tonight, Jim. And my *wife* wants to see Richardson's fields by moonlight."

Reading his meaning clearly, I warned, "Well, be careful of *hayricks*—they're so easy to fall *into*, you know . . . good night and God bless!"

After they left, I thought of them frolicking in the hay, and noting her sudden approval of hayricks, I hoped Suzannah was not feeling experimental tonight.

I then went upstairs to look in on Ainsley, and found Suzannah in Mother's rocker once again, singing her daughter to sleep—with another Gaelic lullaby. Earlier in the evening, I'd wondered if Ainsley understood what Suzannah's songs were about—and now I knew. Evidently, she was a prodigy like her mother, and *had* inherited her heart feelings as well. She didn't fully understand them yet, but fortunately, Suzannah was aware and could guide her in their workings.

I wondered if Katharine's husband, Francis, would one day also serve as Ainsley's tutor, and give her the benefit of his Harvard education as he'd done for Suzannah. With her knowledge of flora and fauna, Ainsley was well on her way to being an exceptional pupil.

As I stood outside the door regarding my dear ones, my spirits plummeted at the thought of returning to war. My heart ached as I reflected on how my absence would affect them: Ainsley enjoyed my company and needed me at home to enrich her life. I knew that Suzannah missed me emotionally, spiritually and physically—and, at times, her longings felt visceral. I was ashamed to admit that as much as I had missed her—she missed me more—because of what she'd suffered while nursing the sick and dying men in our tavern.

Fearful of death, I closed my eyes and slumped to the floor. I tried to envision us in our old age, and through tearful images I saw myself; still stroking her long gray hair, kissing her tired wrinkled brow, and caressing her toil-worn hands. Then I whimpered at the thought of her growing old without me.

Suzannah was my dream come true, and because *our* dream had begotten Ainsley, and knowing that a horrible war still lay ahead, I determined that dreams are *still* more precious than gold . . . or even freedom.

⁂

THE SOUND OF dainty steps interrupted my reverie . . . and looking up, Suzannah stood before me, holding out her hand.

"Let's go to the point." She firmly announced, looking straight into my eyes. "We need to talk."

With my stomach in knots, I wiped my tears and knew she was serious; and this was one time I wished she *was* feeling experimental.

I took her hand, whereupon she kissed it and quietly said, "You know Jim, there are times when you might look back to steal yourself away from reality . . . but you are *wrong* in doing what your heart is feeling . . ."

"What do you mean, Suzannah?" I meekly asked, knowing she *knew* what I was feeling.

She merely kissed me. Not with a passionate "take me" kiss, but an understanding kiss—the kind that made me feel better—because that was her way.

As we came downstairs, Fanny had arrived to sit for Ainsley, and had settled into the rocker. As we left for the point, she waved and gave us a cheery, "Have fun on the point!" as we passed by her and closed the door.

Little did she know how reluctant I felt about our trip tonight.

The moon illuminated our path to the point. After arranging her blanket on Sunset Rock, Suzannah faced me, took my hands and pressed them to her heart. Then she gently kissed me with a kiss that spoke of angelic origins . . . and with a great deal of tenderness, I returned it in equal measure.

As we sat locked in our embrace, the moonlight reflected off the water, illuminating our faces and urging us to bear our souls—both to God—and to each other.

"I love you, Jim, more than life itself. I would give my life for you or Ainsley . . . and I know you love us the same." Looking up at me, her soulful eyes probed my very heart. As I touched my forehead to hers, she softly continued, "What you were feeling back there was not *right*, Jim. I *saw* the expression on your face as you stood in the doorway . . . and I *felt* what you were feeling . . . and you are being selfish and narrow in your reasoning."

"But I'm so *torn*, Suzannah," I protested. "I don't *know* what's ahead or what it will lead to. And the thought of leaving you and Ainsley—possibly *never* to return—is *unbearable* to me!"

Caressing my cheek with her palm, she softly replied, "If you don't know where you're going, my dearest, *any* road will take you there—and you will end up *nowhere*. I don't want that for *you*, for *me*, or for *Ainsley*."

All I could do was tear up in frustration.

Leaning forward, she softly kissed them all away, and gently pressing her fingers to her lips, she placed them over my heart. "Your trouble is now my trouble, so let me try to help you, Jim. Let's choose a road *together*, where we have a destination that is *worthy* of our supreme sacrifice."

I nodded quietly.

"You have your orders from General Washington, who expects you and Zeb to retrieve your horses and report back to him as scouts. So *that* is what you should be doing. I *know* how much you love us, and how much you'd rather *stay*. But, darling—think what will become of *us* if we fail to break away from England," she implored.

She kissed me again. This time she opened her lips and I savored her comfortable penetrating warmth. After slowly breaking the kiss, she then continued. "More than I care for myself, I care for *you*, and especially our *daughter*. Think about the *life* she will have if we remain subjects of the crown. This war is not for *our* benefit, Jim—it's for *her*, and the generations that will come after her. *Our* time matters *not*, but I do *not* wish to go out of this world subservient to a weak-headed king! I want my daughter to be *free*. And if it was humanly possible, I would be at your side: guiding you, encouraging you, defending you, saving you . . . and *loving* you . . . all the while." She ended with a whimper, which soon became an uncontrollable stream of sobbing.

Gathering her in my arms, I gently rocked her while pondering her meaning. Our strong desire to remain together had to be overruled by more pressing matters. Yes, the war was our one and only chance for independence from the British. If the monarchy prevailed at this point, those of us who were soldiers would be shot or imprisoned, which was a fate worse than death since it came with the knowledge of failure. We had to think beyond the immediate moment to Ainsley's future—and that of generations to come.

When Suzannah finally quieted and raised her face to mine, I kissed each cheek, then her forehead, her chin—and finally her nose.

She giggled. "Can you do that again, please?"

As the breakers rolled and hissed on the rocks below, I happily complied. When I finished, she smiled as she placed her hand upon my heart, and held it there.

I recalled this gesture from our younger days—and now, as then, I sat and waited patiently for her to speak, my eyes riveted to her face.

"Many lives will be shattered and much hope will be lost," she said solemnly. "But out of war's darkness shall come the bright light of freedom. Do not fear the reaper, Jim—he seeks *others*. Meanwhile, my love shall remain warm and sweet, and *yours* when you return."

I smiled and removed her hand to kiss her soft palm and press it to my cheek. "Suzannah, should the weight of war depress me into hell's depths, I have *you* to lift me away . . . and carry me into your little heaven—I *truly* believe that, you know."

Laying her head upon my shoulder, she reassured me once more. "I know you'll be out there *somewhere*, and I shall *ever* be with you—in the talisman you wear . . . and in the shelter of your heart."

I lifted her chin tenderly, and as her eyes begged for comfort, her lips slowly parted . . . and into them I whispered my fondest desire, "Suzannah . . . I wish to *God* there was more time to enjoy the purity of your soul . . . is it possible for *any* man to love his wife more than I love you? Can you *feel* that, darling?"

One long ardent kiss later, she gently whispered, "Look into my heart, Jim, and *find* your answer."

Then she stood up and removed her dress. I was instantly stimulated by her total lack of under clothing. Straddling herself across my stomach, I felt the heat of her womanhood as she softly begged, "Jim, I *need* you, I *want* you . . . *now* . . . *here*, on this rock where we've always shared our deepest feelings. Let us *sanctify* this spot . . . *Sunset Rock* . . . on Walker's Point . . . our *own* little piece of heaven . . ."

With that I quickly undressed and no sooner had I comfortably reclined, than she lowered herself upon me. Rather than making love aggressively, she merely leaned forward, pressing her warm breasts into my chest. She then slowly draped her arms around my waist and remained absolutely still.

The breeze fingered her hair, scattering it it across her back and over her bottom. I placed my hands under it and slowly rubbed her back: first in little circles, then up and down, and finally side-to-side, repeating the pattern over and over to the timing of the waves.

She looked up at me with those wonderful eyes and pleaded, "Darling, can we just stay joined . . . and sleep *here* tonight? Mother knows we will not return . . . until morning."

Never surprised at her planning, I whispered, "Whatever your heart desires angel." And carefully securing my arms behind her waist, I began to rub her bottom.

She moaned delightfully and whispered, "I miss your bottom rubs, Jim . . . please don't stop . . . it's *so* relaxing . . ."

As I continued, she periodically adjusted her hips, ensuring a gentle stimulation that kept us together. She made me relax so much that I was drifting into sleep when suddenly, Suzannah gasped and her arms quickly tightened around me. Within her, intense contractions enveloped my manhood in perfect rhythm to her gasping. They worked me like a slow exotic dream . . . and while pressing herself deeper, her enveloping pulsations quickly accepted my lengthy burning response.

As she wished, we remained joined and naked while embracing as one. Bathed in moonlight on the altar of our hearts, I continued to rub her bottom while Suzannah slept. Tonight we were in desperate need for emotional shelter, and I was grateful to my wife for her quiet night of gentle love . . . and also to God—for in *my* unworthy arms—she found the comforting love she so desperately sought.

I was awakened by the sound of gulls squawking, and the constant clatter of shellfish being dropped on the rocks from above. Feeling a weight on my stomach, I looked down to see a naked and still sleeping Suzannah. Despite the morning breeze floating her hair into my face, I kept still, so as not to wake her.

Judging from the position of the sun, I reckoned it was about nine, and that the morning routine at the tavern was probably underway. Someone would soon be out looking for us, and we were in no condition to be seen by eyes other than our own.

With a growing sense of urgency, I slowly rubbed Suzannah's back, hoping to waken her gently, which I did.

She groaned and finally opened her eyes and squinted at her surroundings. "Don't we need to go *home*, darling?" she asked, groggily.

"Yes, my love, we do . . ." I said, and as I hastily began to don my clothes, Suzannah simply threw her dress over her head, and she was ready.

Still, we were reluctant to leave; so we continued to sit in our fully sanctified spot. As we watched the seagulls have their breakfast, I wrapped my arm across her shoulder, and drawing her tightly against me, she took my other hand and stroked it with her thumb.

Looking adorably at me from her little nest, she nibbled at my fingers and we shared more tender kisses.

We recalled the magic moments of our brief reunion: the caresses, kisses, and the comforts and thrills of our lovemaking, and most of all . . . the healing we gave to each other's souls.

Finally, Suzannah gently took my hand and sweetly whispered, "Let's take the *long* way home . . ."

During the short time I was home, Suzannah and I became as connected as a man and wife could ever be. Of all the things we ever did during our marriage, as bold or inappropriate as they seemed, within the sanctity of our love, it was ever beautiful in addition to being fun. No matter what we did with or to one another, it was done as the ultimate expression and acceptance of undying love.

Indeed, because we have physical limitations on this earth, our conjugal adventures became outward expressions of our inward spiritual grace. Suzannah would never admit it, but I know that if it were possible, she would wish our ethereal souls to intertwine; to blend and remain as one . . . forever and ever . . . such is the depth of her priceless love.

THAT NIGHT THE Walkers and the Hawkes dined together, since Zeb and I were expected onboard *Suzannah's Pride* the following morning.

Henry was fully recovered from his illness. It was a cause of regret for us all that it had laid him low during our brief time in Walker's Cove—although it gave us a little more precious time here ourselves than we'd have had otherwise.

Despite Suzannah's loving guidance in preparing me for my departure, I still felt a strong resistance to it. I didn't have much of an appetite either. I felt that Zeb shared my discomfort, and little was said by either of us during dinner—despite the best efforts of our wives to create a loving and supportive atmosphere.

While I struggled to eat my dinner, I couldn't take my eyes off my beautiful Suzannah. She now wore her pink and white dress— the same one she'd worn on the day we were betrothed. With Ainsley's freshly picked flowers woven into her cascading hair, her beautiful smile and soft loving eyes made her the portrait of angelhood—and I was leaving her—and the wonderful world she carefully built around me.

When my eyes weren't on Suzannah, they were on our little Ainsley, who was wearing flowers in *her* hair—"just like Mama." As I reveled in her sweetness and smiles, I silently repeated to myself, "This war is for *her*—and then *hers*, and then *theirs*."

I memorized these images of my wife and child, while treasuring every moment of their presence. Knowing that I might witness many horrors in battles yet to come, no matter where the war took me, I was comforted in knowing their hearts would follow mine.

Once dinner was done, Zeb and I retired to the parlor, where I lit a small fire and Zeb moved the sofa before it. Dimmis poured tumblers of mulled cider, while Suzannah brought in a plate of snickerdoodles and molasses cookies.

Here we shared our last night together. Dimmis and Zeb nestled in the sofa, while Suzannah and I cuddled in our favorite rocker, with Ainsley fitting snugly in her mother's lap.

The evening faded away, taking us ever closer to the moment of departure. Other than the bells of the clock, the only sound was the crackle of the fire. As I gently rocked, the moonlight drifted on its journey, coming to rest upon Ainsley's face, now graced with innocent slumber.

Suzannah was drifting into sleep, but was still conscious of my kisses and whispered words. "Good night, my dearest angels . . . Papa loves you *both* . . ." In answer, she pressed her face into the warmth of my neck and kissed me there. After gently nestling into its crook, she smiled, and without opening her eyes, fell sound asleep.

Placing my arms around them, I locked my fingers to secure a hug for three. I then lay my head against Ainsley's flowers—and while inhaling their delicate fragrance—I instantly joined her in slumber.

SOMETHING BRILLIANT PENETRATED my eyelids, forcing me to avert my face; but no matter where I turned, it was inescapable. Opening my eyes, I realized the morning sun was blazing a path through the window. If that hadn't awakened me, the aroma of sausages and fritters that made my mouth water furiously, certainly would have.

I had little appetite last night when my spirits were low, but this morning I was absolutely ravenous. But since Suzannah and Ainsley were still sound asleep in my lap, I made no attempt to move.

Dimmis appeared from the kitchen, kissed my cheek and whispered, "Good morning, Jim—breakfast is ready . . ." With a giggle she added, "We are giving you and Zeb a *fine* send-off! *Our* men will be the happiest in the army . . . with their hearts full of *love* and their stomachs full of *good* food. So, hurry in when you can." And with that, she kissed me again and returned to the kitchen.

Suzannah must have heard her, because she twisted toward the window, knocking my empty tumbler to the floor with a clatter.

The sudden sound awakened Ainsley, who opened her sleepy eyes and happily chirped, "Papa, I smell *punkin* bread!"

After Ainsley's feet met the floor, Suzannah was right behind her, saying, "Pumpkin bread requires clean faces and hands—so off we go to the kitchen to wash . . ."

Emerging from the rocker, I stood near the open window and inhaled deeply of the invigorating salt air . . . the last I would have at home for some time. When I felt a sudden tugging at my breeches, I looked down and saw a sweet little girl with gray-blue eyes and a captivating smile.

"Papa, Mama says breakfast is ready in the kitchen."

I stood at attention, saluted my little darling and replied, "Yes, Miss Walker! *Aye* Miss Walker! Consider me *there*, Miss Walker!

Saluting me back, she bravely ordered, "Carry *on* then, Papa!" and proudly marched into the kitchen, the most important person in Walker's Cove.

ZEB AND I both ate as though we hadn't eaten in weeks. I think our wives were stupefied at seeing how often we replenished the heaping mounds of food on our plates. Even Ainsley looked on in wide-eyed speechless wonder. While we were truly hungry, an endless breakfast also served to delay our departure—at least for a little while longer. It was Suzannah who finally suggested it was time we got going. The ship was waiting only for us . . . and the tide was turning.

Once the horses were packed, and we checked our pistols, knives, muskets and bags, we had no further reason to tarry.

Dimmis went to Zeb and placed five gold sovereigns in his greatcoat, and Suzannah followed suit by giving me the same.

"A parting gift from our wives?" I quipped, tossing them playfully from hand to hand—until I saw the look on Suzannah's face—a look that I'd never seen before.

Pressing my cheek with her gentle palm, she gazed deeply into my eyes and softly said, "*Cuimhnigh i gconai,* Jim . . . *tu go a ghra mo chroi . . . mo anam . . . mo ghra . . . lo deo . . .*"

I knew it was Gaelic, but to me it was angel talk, straight from heaven. Shaking my head in speechless emotion, I embraced her tiny form, lifting her up and pressing her tightly to my heart.

Resting her cheek upon my shoulder, Suzannah tearfully whispered, "It means . . . always remember, Jim, you are the love of my heart . . . my soul . . . *my* love . . . *forever.*"

"You are the most *beautiful* creature God ever created . . ." I choked out, while fighting my tears. She then softly added, "If you have restless stirrings or haunted dreams, think of *me,* lover . . . and remember that when the leaves fall, we shall *then* be reunited . . ."

I put her down reluctantly, and when I did, she smiled and kissed me tenderly, adding, "I shall await your return . . ."

As we shared our last moments of parting, so were Dimmis and Zeb. She too placed her palm upon his cheek and softly spoke from her heart in Gaelic: "*An rud a lionas mo tsun . . . lionann se mo chroi . . . lo deo.*"

Zeb merely stared at his wife, clearly enchanted by everything he heard. She kissed him deeply and finally breaking the kiss, she softly continued, "It means . . . what fills my *eyes* . . . fills my *heart . . . forever.*"

Zeb cleared his throat, choking back tears until he finally managed, "While we are gone, Dimmis, will the music still play? Will our wedding song still be sung?"

She embraced him, and pressing her cheek to his chest, she softly answered, "Every night until you return, heaven shall hear your name. In my heart it shall remain, where our love shall ever be remembered . . . and *yes* . . . our song shall ever be sung . . ."

While Zeb and Dimmis engaged in lengthy tearful kisses, I lifted Suzannah up once again. Without a sound, she immediately clamped her arms around my neck, and locked her legs around my waist. She held me with such strength that I could feel the beating of her heart. We prolonged our final goodbye kiss . . . and when I finally tried to break away, she tightened her grip . . . she would *not* let me go.

Suzannah's unspoken message was very clear: *I* was her entire world. And while nearly crushing her in my loving embrace . . . I thanked God the time for miracles had not passed.

The Charm of Elsewhere

As we trotted along in the morning sun, Zeb sang one of his ribald songs about bringing on the wenches, the rum and the ale. The ancient battle song brought a smile to my face, because it reminded me of our tavern in days gone by; when sailors raised their tumblers and swayed while bellowing—

> *Bring, bring, bring on the wenches,*
> *Bring on the rum and the ale,*
> *Bring, bring, bring on the wenches,*
> *Tomorrow we fight in the dale.*
> *Hail, hail, hail all ye ladies,*
> *Hail all ye ladies of fun,*
> *Bring, bring, bring on the wenches,*
> *Tomorrow our lives will be done!*

When Zeb began peppering his verses with references to some very unbridled acts that sounded familiar to me, I asked him about them. He freely admitted that he and Dimmis had no inhibitions, and they did what they wanted with no regrets—and for all he cared, tomorrow his life *could* be done.

I smiled to myself—for I suspected Suzannah had been sharing some of her exotic secrets with Dimmis—although, come to think of it—since the Roman elixir, they might have been *pooling* their ideas.

W E ARRIVED AT the wharf, where *Suzannah's Pride* was secured and waiting just for us. Soon we were greeted by the welcome sight of a hale and hearty Henry Wiggins, leaning contentedly over the gunnels. He observed Zeb with some amusement as he watched him trying to handle his horse, Slumber—so named because he always seemed to be on the verge of sleeping, even while in motion.

"It's mostly his damned eyes!" Zeb complained bitterly. "Half the time I don't know if he's awake or asleep . . . he's got lazy eyelids and they just don't open *up* right!"

From above us Henry remarked, "Well, my good friend, it seems he *did* get you here after all, *despite* his drowsy nature. Come aboard, gentlemen, and I will have Seamus tend to your mounts."

Henry invited us to his cabin, which was permeated with the heavenly aroma of spiced rum. After pouring us each a tumbler, he raised his own in the air for a toast. "To my good friends and partners . . . may fortune smile upon us all!"

We lifted ours to Henry in turn, and drank to our good fortune.

Lowering his drink, Henry said in a more somber tone, "There's a slight addendum to our original mission, which I had to keep secret until now. In the hold of *Suzannah's Pride* are seventy-three barrels of smuggled gunpowder that are to be delivered to General Israel Putnam. They were received under the cover of night while the ship was anchored in Walker's Cove—it was only partly true that my sickness was what kept me here. We will unload those—as well as your precious selves—at our destination. Between the two, I believe our good General Washington should have all he needs to secure the city of New York against the brothers Howe."

W E WERE FORTUNATE that the seas were calm on our first day out. One night, when the weather was especially warm and pleasant, I decided to sleep on deck. The ship's constant rhythm relaxed me, finally lulling me into a dream world. As Suzannah's figurehead led the way by slicing the waters ahead, my memories drifted into dreams of home—to the intoxicating joy I felt spending precious time with Suzannah and Ainsley . . .

My dream ended abruptly when my name was called repeatedly, and I slowly came awake. Out of the foggy darkness rose a demon with eyes aglow and flames in his hand. Rubbing my eyes vigorously, I looked again to see Seamus O'Brien standing before me, holding a pierced-tin lantern. Its dissipated light infused his face with a yellowish hue, giving it a macabre, unworldly appearance.

"Jim lad, ye be snoring so damned loud . . . but I'd a never woke ye, lest the divil was on our tail . . ."

I stood up quietly, and while Seamus blew out the lantern's candle, he whispered, "There be British *bastards* over yonder . . . and misbegotten *Hessians* all 'round us too, by God—be damned to hell's privy if they ain't! I can *smell* 'em, I can!"

"How is that possible, Seamus? Can you show me?"

Moving forward carefully through the heavy mist to the forestaysail, we found Henry with his telescope stretched toward starboard, straining to see through the fog. As we approached, he signaled us to be silent with a quick finger to his lips. After a few more moments of intense peering, he finally whispered, "We are amidst the *entire* British fleet! God knows how we managed *that* . . . but *here* we are. I can barely see the outlines of some of the full-rigged vessels. Some are ships of the line, and as we passed through them, I counted *twenty* frigates. This is not a fleet, Jim—it's a goddamned *armada*! Possibly twelve hundred guns!"

The shroud of fog, combined with the low profile of *Suzannah's Pride*, were all that kept us from being discovered—and blown out of the water! Meanwhile, after lengthy observation, Henry determined the fleet was dragging sea anchors to maintain position, and if we unfurled but one foresail, we might glide through it unnoticed.

Seamus, leaning over the port gunnels to listen, detected faint guttural tones he confirmed were Hessian voices. Off to starboard, he heard the dull clanking of heavy iron hoops against thick timbers of mast, which indicated that whatever was out there was *big*—and unaware of our presence.

Henry, striding along the deck in his stocking feet, advised the crew in hushed tones to remove their boots, and to quietly secure anything that could possibly make noise.

When removing my own boots, Henry came upon me so stealthily that he gave me a fright.

"I've done everything I can to ensure silence onboard." He whispered. "But if we're discovered, Jim, I make *no* doubt that we will make that discovery as *costly* as possible—by taking as many of their vessels to the gates of hell *with* us!"

As the crew stood motionless but ready at their stations and their guns, Henry whispered to Seamus, "Open the foremast topsail *only* . . . and be damned *quiet* about it!"

Two men in stocking feet crept up the mast and unfurled the sail without a sound, and let it slowly inch down until it was full. The fog was so dense the sail was nearly indistinguishable to us on deck, which satisfied Henry that it could not be seen by an enemy watch.

After some moments the sail caught a mere wisp of air, yet it responded by billowing to the point when we felt a discernable tug. Then it went flat, but after a few minutes began to fill again. This repeated catching of oceanic sighs began to have results . . . and we inched forward at an agonizing pace, with no wake whatsoever.

From all sides of *Suzannah's Pride*, our watering eyes peered unrelentingly into the swirling mists of fog . . . boring into the murky distance for any discernable shape, and alert to any tell-tale sound that might reveal our position to the vessels around us. We remained so silent we could overhear conversations aboard the enemy ships, many of which were jovial in nature. Using the voices as reference points, we plotted the locations of the surrounding vessels, and despite the conviviality of the disembodied voices; they didn't mask the murderous intent that would surely rise if we were discovered.

As we silently slipped away unseen by the British ships of the line, the volatility of man's nature confounded me as being par-adoxical. A close brush with death can clear the mind of many things . . . but the inconsistencies in a man's behavior during war—was the most illogical pattern I ever found in nature.

THE FOLLOWING MORNING revealed the British sails to be far astern, and we were finally safe from danger. Henry ordered all sheets to the wind, and his voice conveyed a deep sense of urgency. With all canvas cracked, *Suzannah's Pride* immediately began to porpoise, pulling nearly seventeen knots.

As I watched her figurehead rise and fall, I pressed my talisman while thanking her in a whisper—for once again I believed she'd delivered us from certain death.

Satisfied that she was full and by, Henry waved to Seamus and ordered, "Steady as she goes, first mate!" Then he headed toward his cabin and motioned me to follow.

He went directly to his window to watch our trailing wake. "Yes, nearly *seventeen*," he affirmed, clicking his tongue in satisfaction. Slapping the nearest support beam, he added, "*Suzannah's Pride* . . . she's in a *hurry* . . . and *well* she *should* be!"

Seating himself at his desk, he took paper and quill and began to scratch away, but not before telling me to sit too.

A few minutes passed and then he paused to address me. "For a neophyte, you have probably seen more than any experienced scout in Washington's army, Jim. The general will need to know what we, by the luck of Providence, have just seen and heard. He has no concept of what is heading his way, and I believe the only advantage we have—if one can reasonably call it an *advantage*—is knowing what is coming to *kill* us! Especially the Hessians," he added pointedly, "who have a fearsome reputation of showing no quarter to any foe."

Henry continued to write until he stopped to pin a separate paper to his letter. He explained that it contained his observations of the types of British ships and their approximate numbers, as best as he could determine them under conditions of such poor visibility.

Folding the papers, he sealed them with wax and handed them to me, saying, "Jim, we can easily outrun these heavy ships of the line, but Washington can't—it is certain death for our side if he is not prepared for what's coming. It is *imperative* that you get this information to him as quickly as possible!"

After that he stood and with his hands clenched behind his back, and head pressed forward in grave concern, he started pacing restlessly amid the confines of his cabin. Suddenly he stopped to share his train of thought.

"The most useful service I can render is to deliver the smuggled gunpowder in a timely fashion, as well as you and Zeb with this urgent warning. It might give the general an extra day to prepare, which is little enough, God knows, but it is all I can do."

He returned to his chair to pour himself a small measure of brandy. I sat in silence, watching the brandy rock within the glass. As I felt a knot of anxiety form in the pit of my stomach, all I could think about was how desperately I wanted to be home with my wife and child.

Because every minute counted, the following night we continued pressing full ahead. Henry strode the decks all night and whenever he sensed us slowing, he would bark, "*Thousands* of lives are at stake—*work her*! I want every *knot* and *partial* knot . . . make her *strain* . . . *push* her to her limit, by God!"

There was enough moonlight to navigate by, without curtailing speed. After Henry took his readings, he estimated that we would arrive in New York by early morning—a full day and a half before the British.

THAT NIGHT AS I lay in my hammock down below, I was tense and wakeful, unable to sleep for the first time in days. Sensing I was being watched, I turned to my right and saw Zeb lying sideways in his hammock, wide-eyed and sleepless as well.

"Thinking about home?" I casually asked amid the chorus of snores around us.

Zeb sat up. "I was thinking about the hayricks . . ." he murmured, "and how comfortable they were to sleep in . . . and do *other* things in. The strong smell of the hay remains with me and ever will—because of *Dimmis*, I suppose."

Smiling at his description, I replied, "I would think *so*, Zeb. After all, without the association with the woman of your dreams, there's nothing special or attractive at all about hay—unless you're a horse."

"What's your favorite spot with Suzannah?" he asked, sounding genuinely curious.

"Walker's Point," I said without hesitation.

"What makes it so special?"

"It's *our* place . . . Suzannah even gave our spot a name . . . Sunset Rock . . . it's where we go to sit and watch the sunsets—and while we do, we always share our deepest thoughts, desires and troubles—and even our sorrows that are often too heavy to bear alone."

"It sounds like you've been going down there for a long time."

"After Suzannah moved into the Whipple house, we took our very first walk together to Walker's Point—after I fell asleep in her father's rocker during their housewarming party. We've been taking walks there ever since, as often as we can. What's your favorite place with Dimmis?"

Closing his eyes, Zeb sighed and thoughtfully answered, "I find our evenings of quiet companionship to be the most gratifying, Jim—lying together on the sofa, with a fire blazing away in the hearth, reassuring each other we're not alone in this damned cruel world. Being Dimmis' husband sure as hell nurtures my pride!"

Zeb paused to gather his thoughts. "I love the way she responds to my every touch, especially when we're out in Richardson's fields. The beauty of her eyes and her silky red hair make me wish I were home to see her. But now I just recalled our beautiful lovemaking in slow lingering reveries . . . until reality seeps in—that I'm in this damned misbegotten war, away from my one true love, never knowing when I'll see her again. After it took us so long to find each other, we are forced to be apart. But I keep her in my heart . . . and I believe she is my angel of hope . . ."

Patting his shoulder affectionately, I lay back in my hammock and simply replied, "Welcome to the *joys* of married life, Zeb . . ." and pressing my talisman to my heart, I promptly fell asleep.

THE FOLLOWING MORNING I awoke to an unexpected stillness—there was no motion aboard *Suzannah's Pride*. Suddenly I realized we were docked and tied. I awakened Zeb, and we hastily gathered our guns and packs and made our way topside. There we discovered we were tied to a wharf perhaps three times the size of ours at home, on which our horses patiently awaited us.

From the bow we heard Henry's reassuring voice. "Good morning and welcome to Gowans Cove, gentlemen!"

Gowans was a very busy place, full of meandering soldiers, but in particular, we noticed various stenches that assaulted our nostrils: the air was permeated with the combined odors of rotting flesh, burnt hair, excrement and tarred rope.

Soldiers in various degrees of shabbiness roamed about like mindless ants, hauling supplies and buckets of water, and stacking our barrels of gunpowder on large sturdy wagons. Others were attempting to form unified ranks, while marching disjointedly under officers who looked as slovenly as the men they commanded. The entire area was dotted with small huts: leprous little enclosures hastily thrown upon bare earth, where the inhabitants dwelled amid malodorous squalor.

Zeb's first bellowing words echoed my own thoughts. "What in hell's own privy can smell as *bad* as *this* putrid army smells?" Then, loud enough to be heard far below, he called out, "Smells like a cow's *backside . . . after* she gave birth!"

A few of the soldiers looked up at Zeb and turning to face him, they made obscene hand gestures—and then promptly relieved themselves where they stood—waving their streams to and fro as though to taunt him.

Enfuriated, Zeb mounted the gunnels and hanging onto a rope, roared back, "By *God*, you *dung*-beetled, *piss*-brained, *rump-swabbing titmice*—don't make me come down there and *find* you . . . because if I *do*, I will take your damned little *shortcomings* and ram 'em up your *snouts* so they stick out of your eye sockets. Then you'll look like the weasely little snake-eyed *dickheads* you really *are!*"

Hearing the commotion, Henry hurried over to Zeb and calmly advised, "Now listen, my boy, come on *down* from there and save your venom for the British fellows behind us. After all, *they* are the enemy!"

Zeb climbed down and stood on deck, wiping his forehead before pointing to the encampment below. "Damn it to *hell*, Henry, I already *met* our damned enemy—and he is *us!* How will we *ever* win *any* damned war with *these* misbegotten self-indulgent, undisciplined, sorry excuses for *soldiers* in our midst? By God, they ain't even normal *folks!*"

Impressed by his crude assessment of our circumstances, I stared at Henry, expecting an encouraging response . . . but he said nothing . . . and now Zeb's concerns were also mine.

AFTER A LONG ride past the woody Heights of Guana—where our ragged troops had formed a line of defense—Zeb and I arrived at a hut situated in the rear, surrounded by soldiers in clean, well-tailored uniforms who looked more worthy of their station.

Leaning forward over Winnie's neck, I asked one of them if General Washington was headquartered near here.

"What is your business with him?" he brusquely challenged, looking us over with a contemptuous face that said, "What could *these* two possibly want to discuss with General Washington?"

Before I could answer, Zeb dismounted from Slumber, and standing a foot taller than the soldier, lifted him up by his lapels and whispered, "We are his *scouts* and we been doing some *scouting* . . . and we got a *report* to give him and *no one else*. So if you want your bony-assed *backside* to *survive* the next few days of the British onslaught, I suggest you let George know we are here!"

Calmly placing the soldier down as though he weighed nothing, Zeb patted his head. "Now—go on and tell him we're *here!*"

As the soldier turned to enter the hut, Zeb looked at me apologetically. "Dimmis would approve . . . I was a *nice* man—wasn't I?"

I had no chance to reply since two other soldiers came forward to relieve us of our knives, pistols and muskets. A third beckoned us to enter, and we did.

Inside, we beheld a distinguished-looking gentleman wearing tan breeches, a tan weskit and a deep blue coat with a tan lining. Under his coat he wore a white shirt, bound tightly at the neck and ruffled at the wrists. A gold epaulette adorned each shoulder. A tricorn hat with a medallion on one side rested on a nearby table.

He was nearly as tall as Zeb, with strong sloping shoulders and a muscular torso. His hair was brown, touched with wisps of gray. He'd apparently suffered a bout of smallpox in his youth, since his face was pitted with old scars. Most interesting however were his eyes, for they were a comforting gray-blue that reminded me of Suzannah's. He looked tremendously vigorous for a man of his age, and bore a noble countenance that bespoke of a splendid reputation . . . and I regarded him as the very soul of respectability.

So *this* was General Washington.

It was up to one of us to speak, so I decided to break the silence. "Good morning, sir. We are reporting for duty as scouts, and we've brought our horses with us. I'm James Walker, and this is my friend and colleague, Zebulon Galletin Hawkes. We come from Walker's Cove, although we were last stationed on Sullivan's Island."

He saluted me with a stiff smile and said, "Welcome, Mr. Walker and Mr. Hawkes. I understand that Henry Wiggins brought you."

"Yes sir, he did—as well as the powder being unloaded at Gowans Cove," I replied, returning his salute.

Zeb then muttered into my ear, "Seems like Henry's name sure as hell gets *around*, don't it?"

"Pardon me?" Asked the general, leaning forward to better hear.

Diverting Zeb's remark, I quickly placed Henry's letter upon the table, and pointing to it I explained, "That's Henry's report on the British fleet, sir. We managed to sail through it on our way down . . . they will probably arrive here in about two days . . ."

I watched as the general broke the seal on the letter and sat down to read it. Then he regarded me with a puzzled expression. "You say you sailed *through* the fleet? How so without discovery?"

"There was a terrible fog, sir, and that's how we found ourselves among them. Henry says there are *hundreds* of British ships headed here."

Washington examined Henry's diagram and exclaimed, "Three to four hundred *more* ships of the line? *Impossible!*"

"Because of the fog, they were dragging sea anchors to keep together," I explained. "We were so close we overheard dozens of conversations among the crew members, some of them Hessians— we could tell by their language. They wouldn't lie to each other regarding their own armada, sir."

"There is already a significant British presence on Staten Island—how did you slip by them?" Washington asked.

"The same way we slipped past the fleet, I suppose—in the darkness of night, running silent, blanketed by fog. We were asleep when we landed, sir, so I don't know much beyond that."

"Where is your ship now, Mr. Walker?"

"I believe she will be headed north after all the powder has been delivered at Gowans Cove."

"Too late for that, she is probably long gone by now . . ." Washington mused, apparently dismissing the possibility of meeting with Henry to glean more details. "You will be valuable to me as scouts, and bringing your own horses makes it all the better. It is unfortunate that so few around here are willing to render aid to our cause—so I humbly thank you for your efforts."

He stood and pointed to a map of the Heights of Guana tacked to the wall. "*Here* is what I need you to do." Sweeping his finger from the heights to the sea, he said, "I would like you to scout the entire area around Yellow Hook, New Utrecht and Gravesend—up to and including the shorelines they border. From there you can observe British activities on Staten Island, and report the sighting of *anything* that flies British colors, *anything!* I need to *verify* what Henry says is true."

"What do we do if what Henry says *is* true?" Zeb asked earnestly.

"You can *pray*—and then report back to me, *immediately!*"

General Washington had one of his aides write our orders: in sum, that we should have complete autonomy to move freely about the entire encampment on his behalf, in order to collect whatever pertinent information we could for the strategic benefit of the Continental Army.

After the aide finished, the general read it, signed it and handed it to Zeb. He next presented us with a telescope for the purpose of monitoring activities at a safe distance, and finally begging his leave, sent us on our way.

THE ROAD TO RUIN

rom the Heights of Guana, a lofty wooded point a hundred feet above the shoreline, regiments of the Continental Army could command the roads and high ground that led toward the city of New York. It was from these lowlands that the British were expected to begin their campaign to capture it.

Zeb and I chose to station ourselves on a rolling knoll overgrown with tall grass, where we could hide and feed our horses. It oversaw the entire Gravesend shoreline and overlooked the Narrows toward Staten Island, as well as the open sea to our left and the mouth of the Hudson to our right.

After surveying all the islands around Oyster Bay through the telescope, Zeb concluded, "You know, Jim, we don't have enough damned men to cover all these misbegotten islands. The British are sitting pretty on Staten Island, enjoying their afternoon tea and crumpets, while Washington is trying to figure out how to spread his thin, ragged, undisciplined forces even *thinner* to defend 'em. Hell, Jim, they're gonna walk right *through* us!"

Scouring the shoreline of Staten Island through the telescope, I had to reluctantly agree.

Considering the British were trying to separate New York from the other colonies, they certainly were biding their time—no doubt believing we were no match for the king's armada, which would soon arrive.

"Add to it that their leaders are the famous *Howe* brothers, Zeb. Remember what Henry said about them? Master tacticians, the finest in the civilized world!"

NEWARK BAY
Barren Neck
OYSTER BAY
Gallows
Bedloes Id
Govenors I. occupy'd by the Hessians after the Battle.
Brookland or Brooklyn
Red Hook
Gen. Putnams Camp
The Lines
Q
Bedford
Oyster Island cover'd at High Water
Reebuck during the Battle
Bergen Point
Robins Reef
Gowans Cove
The Heights of Guana
Constable Hook
THE KILLS
The Americans
Dutch Church
Ducksberry Pt
Yellow Hook
The Heights of
The Americans
Flatbush
Castle Town
Doyles Ferry
P
Narrows Ferry
Position of the British Army
TEN ISLAND
New Utrecht
Narrows
Vandeventers Pt
Richmond
Gravesend

Taking the telescope from me to gaze across the Narrows at the British camp, Zeb softly replied, "*Listen*, Jim . . . there's *nothing* civilized about bastards *killing* folks deader 'n hell . . . *especially* when those killed are outnumbered three to one!"

I plucked a piece of grass that had gone to seed, and placing it in my mouth, chewed on it nervously as Zeb continued.

"What a damned *box* to be caught in: if they swarm up over us, Washington will have *plenty* to worry about—that damned army of ours will scatter and run as soon as Howe breaks wind, *either* of 'em, by God! I'd lay odds that the pissers of Gowans Cove would *die of fright*, before they would pick up a *real* gun to shoot! I feel *sorry* for George . . . having to do battle against such overwhelming odds."

Collapsing the telescope, he turned toward me looking downcast . . . and reverting to his old self, he looked me in the eyes and soberly admitted, "Jim, I ain't gonna mince any God damned words . . . but as our Virginian friends would say—a victory against *these* odds—is a *long* shot."

THE FOLLOWING DAY, using the knoll as a rendezvous point, we rode in opposite directions: Zeb toward Yellow Hook, and I toward Gravesend. We would explore the coastline and compile our findings, and if we had anything to report, we would ride to Washington's headquarters immediately with the details.

Along my route, I occasionally encountered Loyalists who inhabited the shore settlements and farms. When asked, I feigned sympathy for their cause, and confirmed that the armada would likely arrive the next day. In turn, I was informed that together the lords Howe commanded forty thousand British and Hessian troops, which would indeed make short work of the fewer than fifteen thousand "sniveling" Continentals.

Wondering if Zeb had found similar results during his search, I returned to our knoll to await his arrival. Leaving Winnie to graze in the luxuriant meadow, I sat for a while and chewed thoughtfully on pemmican and hard tack, chasing them down with water. When finished, I lay in the grass to watch the clouds drift across the sky. I was wondering if Suzannah could see the same clouds from Walker's Cove, when I heard the distant echo of cannon fire.

I scrambled to my feet and stretching the telescope, I anxiously peered through it to see a large ship of the line entering the Narrows, headed for Staten Island . . . and she was flying English colors. Since the smoke was still dispersing from her bow port, I knew the shot was from her signal cannon.

My heart began to race as another ship rounded the Narrows, heading in the same direction, followed by another and another; all at full sail, as their towering masts exposed them to the strong headwinds of the Narrows. Every vessel I saw bristled with cannons lined up in multiple rows along their sides.

Panic-stricken and feeling helpless, all I could do was watch the spectacle unfolding before me. Interspersed with the warships were troop carriers laden with soldiers. Although I attempted to count the number of vessels, I had no hope of doing so. The fear that was pressing my heart overwhelmed my ability to focus or think rationally, so that I lost count after forty.

Off to my rear I heard the sound of a horse snorting, and knew it had to be Zeb.

He flopped down next to me, breathing heavily and whispered, "I don't need to tell you the damned British fleet has arrived—*look* at 'em, by God . . . there's *hundreds* of 'em!"

Looking alarmed, he added, "We *must* get to Washington, Jim. He hasn't a chance against *this*!"

"I agree, Zeb, but let's see how many ships come in before we make our report."

Taking turns with the telescope, we kept a diligent watch. As the afternoon wore on, hundreds of ships anchored in the Narrows, forming a virtual forest of masts between us, and the shore of Staten Island. Indeed, their density was so thick that we could no longer *see* it—and sick at heart, we decided to make our report sooner rather than later.

As we stood before him, Washington asked, "Gentlemen, my aide informed me that you have something important to report?"

"Yes, sir," I said. "In addition to finding loyalists scattered throughout the lowlands who are anxious to do away with us—the British fleet has arrived at Staten Island, sir—and is amassing in the Narrows."

"Now, tell me, gentlemen—what are their numbers?"

Zeb and I hesitated to answer and looked at each other in distress.

"Come, come gentlemen, tempus fugit . . . lives are at stake . . ." Washington added as he stepped aside to draw his hand across the map of the islands. "Show me on the map then, perhaps we may get a better sense of our plight."

"Yes sir," I replied, ". . . a plight it *is*, sir."

Drawing my finger from the Narrows before Staten Island, across the mouth of Oyster Bay, and all the way to New York City, I said, "Zeb counted 318 *so far*. Most are anchored in the Narrows between Gravesend and Staten Island. We have seen hundreds of longboats and flatboats ferrying men and supplies there."

"318 vessels?" he repeated. "Are you *certain* of your count?" he asked, furrowing his brow in doubt.

Stepping up to the table, Zeb emphatically pounded it, startling the general and bellowed, "He's damned *right*, General! By God, I counted every damned *one* of 'em—*twice*! I counted over seven hundred cannons on those floating fortresses, most of 'em three-deckers . . . and I'll bet those are the thirty-six-pounders we've been hearin' about, too!"

Allowing himself a moment or two to quiet down, Zeb softly added, "Sorry, sir, I just mean to say that with forty thousand men and ships armed with thirty-six-pounders—they sure in hell ain't here to play *draughts*, sir!"

Nodding his understanding, Washington turned to me. "What about you, Mr. Walker, how many men would *you* say, have landed on Staten Island?"

"I concur with Zeb's numbers . . . as I heard the same counts from the loyalists; but that perhaps ten thousand Hessians are included in Zeb's count," I said carefully.

Washington stood and holding his chin, silently contemplated the map, his darting eyes betraying active tactical considerations being weighed.

Then he turned around abruptly and called out for his horse to be brought, indicating that we should accompany him. "I intend to witness the gathering place firsthand, so I can properly draw up a plan of defense . . . or escape." he explained.

Thinking him out of his reasoning for leaving the safety of his headquarters, Zeb and I left to mount our horses and wait for the general to join us, but no sooner than we were mounted, then Washington came up to us from behind the hut at nearly a full gallop.

Pulling his spirited gray horse up short before us, Washington ordered, "Now, gentlemen, show me where they are!"

We made off for the Gravesend point, and as we pelted through the scattered encampments and tall grasses, I wondered which one of those thousands of enemy soldiers had a musket ball with my name on it.

SAFELY ENSCONCED ON our knoll, Washington lay prone in a bed of grass observing the activities of the British through his telescope. The time seemed interminable before he finally rose and brushed off the dried grass from his uniform.

"An astute job well done, gentlemen—your information has proved quite valuable. From what I can tell, I believe our enemy will attack New York directly, but we may have an opportunity to stage a diversion if they come ashore at Gravesend. I shall consult with Greene and Reed to reach a consensus about what to do."

Looking back toward Staten Island and the thousands of flat-boats, galleys and longboats tied and waiting, he added quietly, "If there is *anything* to be done against such odds . . ."

"Do you wish us to remain here, General?" I asked, wondering if we would be reassigned.

"Yes, I do, Walker—you must alert me at the *first* sign of any British movement! Take your fastest horse and bring me word *immediately!*"

We followed behind the general as he approached his mount, awaiting further orders. Once he was seated, he saluted, saying, "You have been my eyes and ears, gentlemen, and I pray you continue to be. I am very grateful for your service. Remember this: you have brought our cause one step closer on its long journey to fulfillment—and one step farther away from tyranny."

As he rode off toward his headquarters, Zeb looked thoughtful. "I wonder if he is as good as Moultrie . . . he's rather standoffish, isn't he?"

With a sinking heart, I gazed at the spectacle of hundreds of British masts below us. "Washington is evidently not a man of many words, Zeb . . . but he *is* the best hope of a troubled, turbulent and deluded army."

By early evening, we suddenly heard drumbeats behind and below us. Looking down with our telescope, we saw a regiment of Pennsylvania riflemen marching toward the shoreline below.

We reckoned that Washington had already started bracing his paltry defenses with these skilled marksmen, who were rumored to be on a par with the Virginians. Their firearms—as artful as they were utilitarian—were famous too, fashioned by gifted artisans from Lancaster and Dauphin counties.

As I watched them set up their camps in the marshes along the shore, I was confident that if the British made a move, these men could pick them off from great distances—like the Virginians did at Sullivan's Island. But I feared that the sheer numbers of British regulars would overwhelm their ability to swab their bores, reload and fire fast enough to significantly diminish their ranks.

Zeb and I settled into our grass beds, while we looked out at the glorious evening sky.

"What if they come ashore, Jim . . . do you think we will *survive* all this?"

I chose among the stars—the one that appeared brightest to me—and clutching my talisman, I answered, "It's not a question of *if*, Zeb—it's a question of *when* . . . but fear not the reaper, Zeb, he seeks *others* . . ."

He smiled. "Now that sounds *exactly* like something Suzannah would say . . ."

I took first watch, and while I observed what seemed like thousands of fires dotting Staten Island, I thought about Suzannah. For some reason, she felt farther away from me than ever before—as if I'd been abandoned. When I turned to tell Zeb about my feelings of distress, I realized he was already asleep.

Shaking my head in frustration, I wondered how he could sleep with the potential of death all around us; but then again, *I* had assured him not to fear the reaper, just as Suzannah had assured me. Listening to the crickets and watching the fireflies, I kissed my talisman and prayed softly—that of all Suzannah's predictions, I hoped *that* one would prove correct.

THE LOUD CRACK of rifle fire woke me in the predawn morning. I had fallen asleep at my post, and fumbling to get the telescope in position, I saw an enormous flotilla of flatboats, longboats and galleys inching their way toward Gravesend shore.

A thudding sound beside me signified that Zeb was awake, and rubbing his eyes to see better, he whispered hoarsely, "*Sons* of Belial . . . here they *come!*"

We watched the rising sun glittering off polished buttons, buckles, barrels and bayonets. The oars glistened with every stroke as the boats, packed with untold thousands of soldiers, slowly pressed closer.

I panicked and said, "You must go, Zeb, and tell Washington they're coming—*now!*"

"You gonna stay here, Jim?" he asked looking worried, as he saddled up Slumber.

"Yes, I'll wait until the last possible moment, and then I'll report my final observations to Washington. Be careful, Zeb."

"You too. I'll see you at headquarters then," Zeb said, mounting Slumber and gazing down at the endless flotilla of death inching toward us.

"Yes, God willing . . ."

As he rode off, with the telescope, I followed his swift progress across the flat marshlands that led north toward Yellow Hook. I marveled at how much speed Slumber had in him. After riding at such a blistering pace, I was certain that Zeb would never again complain about his horse's somnambulism.

Returning my attention to the shore, I pressed my talisman and prayed I would see him again before the navy of "Black Dick" swallowed us whole. As the first wave of the flotilla landed on the shores below, the Pennsylvanians were outmanned by perhaps five to one. As they pulled back toward the Heights of Guana, they picked off what regulars they could.

As the numbers of British increased, they advanced on the Pennsylvanians, who began to retreat back across the flatlands. While doing so, they plundered the Tory farms, burning them and slaughtering their livestock. They wanted to leave nothing behind that the British could use—nothing but smoke and ruin.

By midday, the British flotilla had made three trips to Gravesend shore, and now a sea of redcoats were forming massive brigades of hale and hearty regulars, who quickly made their way up from the landing area toward the northern marshes. "No hard tack for *these* soldiers," I mused.

On their fourth trip across, heavy cannons were unloaded from the flatboats with teams of horses—dragoon horses with bobbed tails, manicured manes and pistols strapped to their saddles. Their *horses* received better care than our highest generals did.

There was no doubt that these troops, who lacked for nothing, had come to destroy us—and I helplessly wondered how could our little band of Yankee Doodle soldiers—untrained, undisciplined, underfed, under-equipped and vastly outnumbered, could ever make a credible stand against *this* . . . the most formidable and deadly force ever assembled?

The vessels kept coming, this time carrying Hessians by the thousands: battalions of grenadiers, light infantry and foot soldiers. The next wave of landings consisted of artillery pieces mounted on well-appointed carriages, pulled by teams of sturdy horses.

By dusk, with my mind overloaded with information, and my heart squeezed with desperation, I collapsed the telescope, shouldered my water, mounted Winnie and rode at a mad clip back to headquarters.

Upon my arrival there, I learned that Washington was engaged in the field, dividing his troops into numerous subsections. I couldn't imagine how these smaller divisions could ever stand against the juggernaut gathering on Gravesend's shores.

An aide to Washington scribbled assiduously as I dictated what I had seen; and when he was finished, he looked up at me expectantly. "Is that all, sir?"

Staring in disbelief at this pie-faced lad, I retorted, "My *God*, man—isn't that *enough?*" He signed and folded the paper, saying, "May God help us all!"

The words "*God* ain't got a *damned* thing to do with it!" rumbled from behind us, and I turned to face Zeb. Embracing him, I felt saved and relieved as we warmly patted each other's back.

Turning to address the aide, he said, "You better ride out and give that letter to the general right away." Pointing to me, he added, "Jim here is under strict orders to report his findings *directly* and *immediately* to Washington—not some interpreter of the facts. So hurry along, son, get on your horse and *find* 'im . . . otherwise we'll be finding your gizzard alongside the road tomorrow!"

As the aide bolted from the hut and galloped away, Zeb followed his progress with a skeptical expression on his face, as he grumbled, "*Damn* it to hell, Jim, I just don't trust *anyone* in this bug-infested army!" Then guiding my shoulder, he reassuringly added. "Come along with me—we've been assigned to Sullivan's division."

"Sullivan's division? Is *this* Sullivan related in some way to the island?"

"Damned if I know, old friend, but we at least we've got *horses*. There is a steep craggy hill to climb, and most of these poor bastards got only their feet!"

As Zeb shouldered a wooden canteen of water, I heard a distinct clink, and hollow slosh that indicated a bottle was on his person.

"What's that?" I calmly asked,

"What's what?" he replied, feigning perplexity and straightening his great coat.

"The sound of a *bottle* . . ." I said with distain.

"*What* bottle?" Zeb said innocently.

After that, I lost patience with him. "Damn it, Zeb, I'm a *tavern-keeper* . . . and I know the sound of a damned *bottle* when I *hear* it—especially a half-*empty* one!"

Raising his eyes in surprise, he then confessed, "Oh . . . you must mean *this* bottle!" Fishing it out of one of his voluminous pockets, he proudly held it up so I could read the label.

"Where did you get it?" I asked. "Spirits are rare and expensive these days."

Without a word, Zeb pulled the cork and offered me a drink.

Sniffing at the opening, I wondered if it was the Roman elixir Henry had brought us on that memorable evening, that now seemed so long ago. But no, it smelled nothing like it—indeed, it had practically no odor at all.

"Take a good swig of it, Jim." Zeb suggested. "I figure if we ever get back home, we can sell this stuff . . . *if* I can find out where it came from."

"You don't know where it *came* from?" I asked, taking a cautious sip. It had a pleasant lingering flavor that was delicate and uncommonly smooth, so I took another. My face and ears began to redden as it heated up my innards. It was *so* strong that I thought it might even be a more powerful intoxicant than Essex rum—but I didn't want to test my theory by drinking more of it.

"Where did you get this, Zeb?" I asked again as I handed him back the bottle.

He took it from me and replaced the cork. "Will you promise never to tell anyone?"

Knowing now that this was an underhanded acquisition, I then promised. "I shall never tell—but I'll kill you later if I find out you stole it!"

"Now Jim, I *never* steal *anything* anymore—save in time of *war!*"

"But *where* did you get it?" I repeated, impatient with his stalling.

"I kind of *borrowed* it . . . for the *duration*, you understand. He won't miss them at all."

"*Them?*" I echoed, incredulous. "So where did you get *them?*"

Finally pulling an unopened bottle from the recesses of another pocket, with a broad grin and darting eyes, he furtively whispered, "From General Washington's *liquor* chest . . ."

THE VIOLENT POUNDING in my head afterward revealed this was no ordinary spirit. Although it did not urge any libidinous desires, it did soothe my nerves and rendered me some moments of welcome tranquility. That helped explain why the liquor was in Washington's possession, since he probably used it to temporarily remove himself from the trials of war—which seemed, under the present circumstances, reasonably valid.

As we trotted toward the Heights of Guana, the spirit's effects quickly wore off. Upon our arrival at its base, we saw men with broken limbs and severe head wounds being carried in stretchers, or lowered by ropes down the sheer bluffs for transport to our field hospital. The rescue itself required herculean efforts from its participants.

Building this redoubt was a hazardous undertaking, perhaps as hazardous to life and limb as were the British themselves. As we passed by these wounded men, I admired their iron-willed determination in the face of such an onerous task. They put me in mind of Colonel Moultrie's pronouncement: that he would prefer a hundred dedicated men under his command, than a thousand who weren't.

Finally arriving at the heights, we were met by a nervous lieutenant named Morris Murphy, whom we were told, was ordered to finish the defense bulwarks after General Greene became ill. When he introduced himself to us, I noticed a lilting accent similar to Seamus O'Brien's.

"Are you from Ireland?" I asked.

"Aye, sir. I came here in 1740 from Cork, and I wish to God I were there now . . ."

Seeing the distress in his face, I asked, "Why so fearful, Lieutenant? Surely you must know it's the nature of a soldier's lot?"

"My wife Dorothy is a titled British lady. When we wed in Cork, I was accused of being a British sympathizer, so we came here for a new life. But now, once more, I am accused of the same thing just because she is British. I must take care to protect my babes and darling wife from the likes of Colonel James Grant."

"Never heard of *him*!" Zeb declared while wiping his hands as though ridding himself of Grant. "Sure as hell hope he ain't as *infested* with lice as the *rest* of this bug ridden army!"

"He's not even on *our* side," Murphy explained. "He's a *British* officer who has openly vowed to *geld* every rebel he can get his hands on . . . our men are *fearful* of his promise . . ."

Zeb's knife suddenly appeared out of nowhere, and holding its massive blade before Murphy's face, he swore an oath. "Well, Lieutenant, he's gonna have to geld *me* before he ever gets to fresh-faced fellers like *you*! Why by God, after I toss his own oysters to the bottom of Oyster Bay . . . then maybe I'll tend to their little *companion* . . . that will just be hangin' around with nothin' to do . . ."

Encouraged, Murphy smiled and seemed to relax in the face of Zeb's avowed solidarity. "Come along with me, gentlemen, and I will show you around," Murphy said, then quickly added, "Did I hear that you are *Washington*'s scouts?"

From the front barricade we saw our soldiers stationed across the broad plains below us, while General Putnam's troops—consisting of about six thousand men—were behind us. There were three main roads that led through the heights: Gowanus Road to our right,

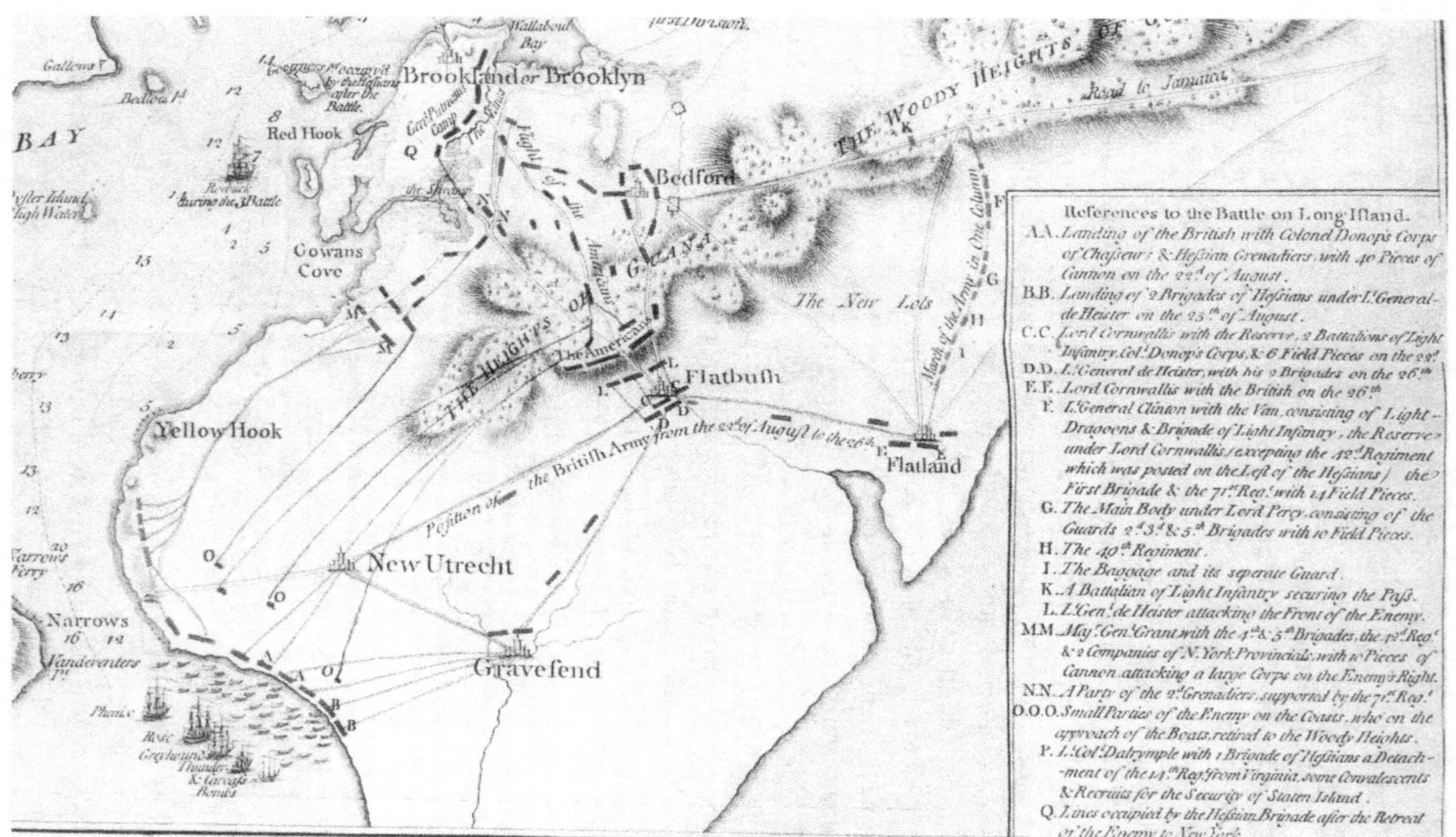
References to the Battle on Long Island.
A.A. Landing of the British with Colonel Donop's Corps of Chasseurs & Hessian Grenadiers, with 40 Pieces of Cannon on the 22.d of August.
B.B. Landing of 2 Brigades of Hessians under L.t General de Heister on the 25.th of August.
C.C. Lord Cornwallis with the Reserve, 2 Battalions of Light Infantry, Col.l Donop's Corps, & 6 Field Pieces on the 22.d
D.D. L.t General de Heister, with his 2 Brigades on the 26.th
E.E. Lord Cornwallis with the British on the 26.th
F. L.t General Clinton with the Van, consisting of Light Dragoons & Brigade of Light Infantry, the Reserve under Lord Cornwallis, excepting the 42.d Regiment which was posted on the Left of the Hessians) the First Brigade & the 71.st Reg.t with 14 Field Pieces.
G. The Main Body under Lord Percy, consisting of the Guards 2.d 3.d & 5.th Brigades with 10 Field Pieces.
H. The 40.th Regiment.
I. The Baggage and its seperate Guard.
K. A Battalion of Light Infantry securing the Pass.
L. L.t Gen.l de Heister attacking the Front of the Enemy.
M.M. Maj.r Gen.l Grant with the 4.th & 5.th Brigades, the 12.d Reg.t & 2 Companies of N. York Provincials, with 10 Pieces of Cannon attacking a large Corps on the Enemy's Right.
N.N. A Party of the 2.d Grenadiers, supported by the 71.st Reg.t
O.O.O. Small Parties of the Enemy on the Coasts, who on the approach of the Boats, retired to the Woody Heights.
P. L.t Col.l Dalrymple with 1 Brigade of Hessians a Detachment of the 14.th Reg.t from Virginia, some Convalescents & Recruits for the Security of Staten Island.
Q. Lines occupied by the Hessian Brigade after the Retreat of the Enemy to New York.

Brookland or Brooklyn
Bedford
THE WOODY HEIGHTS
Road to Jamaica
BAY
Gallows I.
Bedlos I.
Red Hook
Oyster Island High Water
Red Duck during the Battle
Gowans Cove
Yellow Hook
THE HEIGHTS OF GUANA
The New Lots
Flatbush
Flatland
March of the Army in One Column
Position of the British Army from the 22.d of August to the 26.th
The Americans
Flight of the Americans
the Lines
Cap.t Putnam's Camp
Wallaboud Bay
New Utrecht
Gravesend
Narrows
Narrows Ferry
Vanderventer's P.t
Phenix
Rose
Greyhound
Thunder & Carcass Bombs

defended by General Stirling, the Flatbush Road, centrally located and defended by General Sullivan, and the Bedford Road to our left, also defended by Sullivan.

Lieutenant Murphy asked us if the British attack was imminent, since the construction of our defenses had been nearly constant since his arrival nearly two months earlier. I told him that they had indeed landed, and we would likely see action within a few days. Nodding, he indicated he was pleased the works were as complete as they could be.

As the sky started to darken, we prepared to head out toward the easterly side of the redoubt. Our orders were to patrol on horseback all the paths and roads that led to the heights—to ensure there would be no "surprises," as to our defenses being flanked, or worse yet, being attacked from the rear. We were to report anything directly to Lieutenant Murphy.

THE NEXT MORNING, I was awakened by shots fired south of us. I shook Zeb and whispered, "I heard *gunfire* to the south—we must investigate its source *immediately!*"

In no time we saddled up, and rode at a full gallop in the direction of the shooting. Breaking through the overgrowth, and onto the Gowanus Road, we were met by troops running toward us—*our* troops.

As the men raced by us, Zeb bellowed out, "Where in hell are *you* all runnin' to?"

One slowed his pace just long enough to call back, "They're *here*! They're *here*! They've got Major Burd and most of our men. I ain't runnin' *to* anything, I'm runnin' *from* the British!"

As the last of the men passed us, another yelled out, "We all gonna be kilt to *dead* we are . . . lessen we git outta here . . ." and kept on running.

Zeb sat astride Slumber watching the dust settle from the soldiers' panicked flight. Then he expectorated voluminously in their direction and grumbled, "I swear, I'm gonna find me one of those misbegotten weasels and carve out his worthless gizzard—if he ever *lives* that long!"

"Let's find out what caused his gizzard to turn tail and run," I added, sharing his disgust.

As we trotted along the road, it wasn't long before we came to an inn, whose sign indicated it was called the Red Lion. In the adjacent clearing we saw a group of British soldiers, possibly a scouting party consisting of about twenty men. We dismounted quietly and took cover behind some bushes, while we overheard an animated conversation between one of the officers and a local. The local had an arm raised, pointing toward an area to our left, while the officer was nodding in assent—but to what?

"I *met* that feller," Zeb whispered, "he's a damned Tory farmer from behind the pass over yonder . . ."

"*What* pass?" I asked, cutting him off in midsentence.

"*Jamaica* Pass . . . it's beside his farm," Zeb said.

Once the knot of soldiers withdrew into the tavern, I said, "Take me to Jamaica Pass, Zeb. Let's see where in hell it goes . . . and then we must report all this to Murphy."

Once we were back on our horses and well out of earshot of the inn, Zeb told me he'd originally encountered the pass, and the Tory farmer, on his first scouting trip. At that time, he hadn't seen any point in riding it, because it was unimproved all the way to the end, but this time we did.

After several hours of clambering around fallen trees, breaking through low growing scrub, skirting around immovable boulders and stubborn brush, we finally came upon—*our own camp*!

We departed immediately to inform Murphy of our findings, but we were stopped in our tracks by the sudden sound of drumbeats, accompanied by the music of a brass band.

As all of us in the general area rushed to the forward bulwarks, we saw below a sea of Hessian soldiers, swinging along toward us in formation, flanked by redcoats on the left and right, backed up by carriages with heavy cannons in tow. And then the barrage began, with gunfire and furious hand-to-hand combat.

As we watched our men below engage the heavily armed Hessions on the plain, war cries and a sudden spattering of musket fire came from behind us. When I turned to glance back, I saw that the British had already sent a column of regulars up the unguarded Jamaica Pass, and were now flooding in behind us, fanning out among our men. As Zeb feared a few days before, we were now boxed in, with no place to go other than into the river . . .

"My *God*, Zeb!" I cried. "It's too *late* to guard Jamaica Pass! They have flanked us—we are *undone!*"

HELL'S GATE

With Zeb leading the way, the two of us rode off at a frenzied pace until we reached the top of a heavily wooded hillock; then we dismounted and surveyed the battle.

I was wracked with tremors of fear, since even from this distance, we could hear bodies being pierced by musket balls. Our ragged untrained troops were being hacked to pieces in their futile attempt to escape . . . and the sight and sounds of their suffering was unbearable.

A dark choking pall hung over the swarming battlefield, and like the foul breath from Hell's gate, its putrid stench strangled us with an unrelenting grip. The horrific images of blood soaked earth beneath mutilated corpses made every moment a living nightmare. One hapless British soldier suddenly looked in disbelief at a two-inch exit hole in his stomach: blood burbling from the opening as though from a miniature volcano. Sinking to his knees, another ball took away the front half of his skull, and the faceless body crumpled to the ground . . . the hands spasmodically grasping at air to save what they could not.

"*Damn* it, Jim . . . this is Hell's gate—and everybody is tryin' to get in!" Zeb growled, as we watched the carnage continue.

From the left side of our hillock, I spotted Lieutenant Murphy, an enormous cutlass in hand, charging a British soldier. Realizing he was outmatched, the redcoat threw his musket to the ground in a gesture of surrender. Undeterred, Murphy let out a thunderous roar as he swung the cutlass in a great arc, severing the head of the poor fellow. The headless corpse took one step back—still upright—while torrents of blood darkened his uniform. Another man came from behind and violently kicked the corpse's back, toppling it to the ground. There it remained splayed in a widening crimson pool beside its head.

Murphy stomped off and was immediately joined by three of our regulars. All four charged into a knot of Hessians, thrusting and stabbing with bayonets in furious close combat. A Hessian body fell, dropping its musket. Murphy grabbed it, and using it as a lance, skewered the remaining two men with such passionate vengeance, that the gun ran completely through the first man up to its lock, while impaling the second so thoroughly, he was front to back with the first.

"There's Abner Blatchford!" bellowed Zeb, pointing to a small cluster of men who stood to Murphy's right.

When I looked, it was indeed Abner I saw with two other familiar-looking men, possibly Wheezer Hutchinson and Josiah Poole. They were desperately trying to load their muskets while engaged in hand-to-hand combat with a swarm of redcoats.

The next second I watched in horror as a British soldier—who looked no more than sixteen—fired his musket straight into Abner's eye, unleashing a spray of bone, brains and blood all over Wheezer. Josiah swung his musket like a club, knocking the young redcoat to the ground, whereupon Wheezer was instantly upon him with a knife, hacking away at his chest. The redcoat's anguished wails softened when Wheezer delivered a final thrust.

Amid cries of suffering and screams of the dying, were the ceaseless screeching and whizzing sounds of musket balls, nails and grapeshot. But in the desperate effort to keep pace with the demonic fighting, most of the loads were never rammed properly, thus rendering the firepower worthless.

My only thought was that there, but for the grace of God, could be James Walker, participating in this scene from hell's worst nightmare. I was distracted then by the groan that emerged from Zeb as he watched Josiah being lanced with five British bayonets, and then pitchforked over Wheezer's head.

"Damn you to *hell*, you mutton-guzzling bastards! You killed Josiah! You killed *Josiah*!" Zeb howled while violently shaking his fist. "Goddamn you red-coated, misbegotten sons of Belial . . . you squatting spawn of hell's putrid loins!"

Nobody heard.

The British dragoons came thundering down from the left end of the hillock, pistols ablaze, shooting at anything that moved. We saw Wheezer run toward them with his musket swinging. The butt met the lead horse's head with a meaty crunch. The horse collapsed, pitching the rider face first onto the ground.

Grabbing a pistol from the poor beast's saddle, Wheezer rammed it into the rider's mouth, smashing his teeth. Then he cocked the hammer and pulled the trigger, whereupon the rider's face became shreds of red pulp, clinging tenuously to the remnants of his brain stem.

As our soldiers began to flee from the battlefield, sixty of Pennsylvania's riflemen formed two lines, thirty behind thirty. The front row stood at attention and fired their rifles into the charging cavalry. A dozen horses went down, throwing their riders to the ground with sickening thuds, and clattering of accoutrements. While the second group of thirty stood and fired, the first line knelt to reload. Again, dragoons and horses went down.

Suddenly, a commanding voice rose above the din, and I saw it was General Stirling, who was ordering every available man to mass behind the two lines of riflemen. Within seconds, four more lines were formed, and all those with a musket or rifle joined in firing into the ranks of those dauntless dragoons.

Stirling, like a demon possessed, paced behind the lines and tirelessly commanded, "Fire! Stoop! Load! Fire! Stoop! Load! Fire! Stoop! Load!"

As he did, more horses died and more men died. Hell was now here—compressed into this one unholy spot.

"By God, I'm gonna get a *piece* of those bastards!" Zeb roared, as he picked up his musket, gnashed his teeth and hissed as though to frighten the spirit of death to another place. Feeling the dark prospect of an instant death because my friends were dead, I hesitated to join him.

Sensing my trepidation, he firmly gripped my shoulders and shook me angrily. "What *in hell*, James! Wheezer and Josiah have just shown us they got more gizzard so far than *either one of us* . . . you wanna live *forever*? Now *you* listen to *me*!"

For emphasis, he held my chin in a vise-like grip. "If we don't kick these sons o' bitches *outta* here, we won't *have* any damned home or families left to *live* for! Wheezer and Josiah were our *neighbors* . . . and they just sacrificed themselves for *our* cause. By God, if we don't fight for our homes like *they* did, these redcoats will hunt down every last *one* of us and *shoot* us as spies and rebels! You *know* what they call us—*traitorous rabble*! Besides, Suzannah said *not* to fear the reaper . . ."

Zeb's tough impassioned plea was true, so I pressed my talisman, cocked my musket, and slapping him on the back, I bravely announced, "Let's go *get* 'em, Zeb!"

We ran at top speed onto the field of death, and in the midst of all the devilment, although my lungs screamed for air, and the din of battle rendered me nearly deaf, we joined the melee by lining up behind Pennsylvania's riflemen.

Suddenly I heard a grinding thump, and the soldier standing before me grunted and fell back into my arms. "Ah cain't stand . . . none mah laigs feel nothin'," he mumbled as I laid him gently on the ground.

When I stepped around to examine him, to my horror I saw that one leg was severed at the hip, and his pelvis was exposed through a ragged gaping hole.

As he looked with curiosity at where his leg used to be, he innocently asked, "Do this mean what ah think it do?"

"Yes," I solemnly answered, though for my life, I don't know how he heard me.

"Keep mah rihfle safe fum 'ese folks . . . mah brother John made it . . . back in '61."

"Sure," I replied on the verge of tears. "I'll keep it *safe* . . ."

The shooting, screaming and dying continued around us as he feebly placed the beautiful rifle in my hands. Closing my fingers around the barrel, he patted them lightly and said, "Semty grains she takes, no more . . . goin' possum huntin' . . . tomorrah . . ." His lifeless hand dropped to the bloody ground, where only seconds before he'd stood, so alive and strong.

Checking to see that the rifle was loaded, I stood up to shoot, only to find myself staring straight into the face of a Hessian officer. His eyes were inflamed with hatred as he raised his sword to strike me down.

My heart pounded in great heaving beats as I instinctively raised the rifle, placing it at right angles to his downward swing. His blade struck the barrel with such force, that I fell backward into a sitting position. As he again raised his sword for my deathblow, I aimed at his chest and pulled the trigger. Just as the sword came down, the ball tore into his throat . . . spraying me with the warm sticky fluid that gave him life.

Scrambling to my feet and snatching the Pennsylvanian's ball pouch from his body, I proceeded to reload, and looking around for Zeb, I spotted him wading fearlessly into a knot of redcoats, swinging a sword—no doubt taken from one of his conquests. Body parts fell all around him as he hacked and chopped his way through the throng, bellowing something about bastards.

The salty soot and smoke of gunpowder settled over the battle-field like a creeping fog of death—rendering horrific glimpses of the continuing nightmarish struggle. My momentary reverie ended when a severed arm bounced violently off my chest, and landed at my feet—it had a red sleeve. Choking down my bile so I might concentrate on staying alive, I raised my rifle toward the oncoming horde of British soldiers and fired. A redcoat dropped to the ground.

But wave upon wave of His Majesty's regulars continued to engulf us, finally rendering our attempts at resistance useless. The Hessians continued their slaughter by pursuing our men into the heights and marshes—and bayoneting them against trees and in the soggy bogs. Those who weren't bayoneted were forcibly drowned, and only a lucky few managed to escape.

Quickly reloading, I stood again and raised my rifle, only to discover that Zeb had disappeared. Waving the smoke aside, I looked about frantically in all directions—Zeb was gone. My dear friend was gone—and now Dimmis was a widow.

I began to fire furiously at anything Hessian or in a red coat, wishing them all in hell. Reloading as quickly as I could, I fired again, again and again. With Zeb's loss, my soul descended into the dark crucible of war—and my hatred and unrequited anger knew no bounds. I became an unholy demon: condemned and doomed as a lost soul that even Beelzebub himself would not take, for fear of reprisal.

My fevered brain turned numb to all my surroundings . . . and as the faceless reaper of death waded in to overtake my soul . . . I ceased to be—James Walker.

FROM BEING FIRED continuously, the barrel of the coveted rifle became so hot it burned my hands—but *still* I fired. I fired for Wheezer. I fired for Josiah. I fired for Zeb. I fired for Abner. I fired for Suzannah and I fired for Dimmis.

As I murdered relentlessly, my tortured soul cried out from its very depths for God's forgiveness. It pleaded for an end to this purgatory in hell. Between anguished sobs, I shouted Suzannah's name over and over, hoping it would bring me solace. Still, I loaded and fired—and still, red-coated sons of English mothers went down.

Blisters formed on my hands and fingers from the burning barrel. Feeling alone in my own private corner of hell, not knowing when or how it would all end, my stomach flopped in endless churnings— and then I finally vomited.

Leaning on my rifle for support, I contemplated my noxious pool of vomit until—with a resounding splat—a man's body fell into it.

He flopped and gasped for air, while his bloody hands clutched his throat.

It was another Pennsylvanian. As I bent down to render him aid, his hands came away. To my horror, I saw that his throat had been laid open by a sword. His windpipe was severed—with the end sticking straight out at me, making repellent sucking sounds. As I silently wailed damnations and cursed myself for being unable to help, his mouth formed but two words: "*Shoot me.*"

I stood, aimed my rifle at his chest and cocked the lock, whereupon he weakly guided the muzzle to his forehead and nodded. Screaming as though God had driven a nail through my head, I pulled the trigger—his head exploded and he suffered no more.

I leaned upon the rifle to once again purge my stomach, and while recovering from the sickness of my own horror; I heard the bark of unfamiliar syllables behind me. Wearily, I turned around to see a Hessian lunge . . . then all went black.

AFTERMATH

❦ 683 ❧

he memory of trees rustling softly under summer's gentle breath, calls to me of us . . . joyously walking through wildflowers hand in hand. We are totally alone to express our love unfettered. The sun blankets us in light and warmth as I enfold you in my loving embrace. I press you gently against an apple tree, and pluck one of its dainty blossoms. Pressing it to my lips, I place it tenderly in your hair. Your lips then part expectantly . . . and I caress them with a dreamy kiss that is sweeter than heaven . . . Oh, God how I love you, Suzannah . . .

Abruptly, my dream life ended . . . and I became dimly aware of an overpowering stench, and a warm wetness covering my face. As my eyes fluttered open, I beheld a fuzzy image of *something* frightening coming at me. From what I could make out, it was large, brown and had fire-breathing nostrils, but no eyes to see. When I was finally able to focus, the creature was already at my face—nuzzling and licking it . . . and it was *Winnie!*

While she snuffled around my neck and shoulders, I came more fully awake . . . and with a crushing sense of disappointment, I realized I was *not* in Richardson's fields with Suzannah . . . but lying on the field of battle.

After nibbling at me for a while, Winnie suddenly grabbed my sleeve and tugged on it as if urging me to rise. But when I tried to raise myself by leaning on an elbow, a searing pain in my side made me cry out—so I immediately had to lie down again.

As I explored the area around my ribs, my right hand came away covered with fresh blood. Staring at it for several minutes in disbelief, I tried to remember what had happened to me—and as memory returned, I recalled being attacked by the Hessian.

Groaning in pain, I forced myself to sit upright—and finally struggled to my feet. Although I was unsteady, I leaned heavily against Winnie for support and slowly surveyed the battlefield. Only then did I see the horrors of what had transpired. This was a scene of total devastation. As far as my eyes could see, Winnie and I were the only living creatures among acres of grotesque corpses—human and horse.

The armies had moved on, apparently leaving the dead to rot where they'd fallen. Thrust into the air at odd angles, stiffened arms and legs resisted gravity. Horribly contorted faces were frozen with whatever final agony had befallen their owners: a cry for help, for God, for a mother, for pain . . . or for death.

Flies buzzed in and out of distorted mouths and nostrils. Ants and beetles freely perambulated inside open wounds. Many of the dead had lost their bowels; and the resultant effluent added its vile existence to the choking stench of blood-soaked earth and decaying flesh.

When one thinks of battle, it is usually in terms of victory or defeat. In my hazy mind, however, I realized the most repellant outcome of battle is that the human body is mutilated beyond ugliness; so it personifies a denizen of hell—a faceless, soulless, otherworldly creature—that only lives in our worst nightmares.

In the distance, foxes and an occasional wolverine prowled among the bodies for a quick picking of man flesh, while crows and ravens picked at the eye sockets. Shooing a crow from the bloated face of a corpse beside me, its departure revealed a yellow liquid slowly oozing from the corpse's deflated eye.

Overcome with repugnance, I wretched violently, and as I did, I once again felt the searing pain deep in my side—and there was new blood seeping from the wound near my ribs. I was in trouble and had to staunch the bleeding.

As I searched among the corpses for a reasonably clean shirt to salvage for a bandage, a young corpse with a hand stiffly raised, beckoned me to join him in the afterlife: to march in death beside the other dead heroes. I stared at him vacuously, wondering if he had a wife like Suzannah at home, or perhaps a little daughter like Ainsley—who would never see him again in this world. For a moment, I felt in the grip of despair, for like my bleeding wound, the instinct for survival seemed to drain out of me. Suddenly—the world didn't matter anymore—only the sweetness of eternal rest.

But I was soon overwhelmed with guilt about leaving Suzannah and Ainsley behind, so I resumed the task at hand: I *had* to stop the blood loss that was clouding my thoughts and making me ever weaker. I needed to remove the shirt—not an easy task in my condition—while I still could. Since he'd been shot in the chest, I hoped that the ball had stuck in his chest cavity, since that would afford me a large and clean swath of cloth at the back.

Rolling him over, a torrent of protesting flies buzzed around me, furious that their meal had been disturbed. Fortunately for me, all the blood was at the front, so the cloth was clean. Pulling out my knife, I cut a large square from the shirt, and then cut one of the legs of his breeches lengthwise. Placing the shirt cloth to my wound, I then tied the leg wrap around my waist to secure it there.

The enormous energy I expended on this undertaking left me feeling faint once again. Using the Pennsylvanian's rifle as a support to mount Winnie, I struggled upward, feeling a sharp stabbing pain from my wound that was agonizing. The effort had me gasping for air in quick tiny breaths, and although I struggled valiantly, I barely seemed to have my wits about me.

Desperate for air and groaning from searing pain, my brain whirled as I weakly flopped on Winnie's neck, resting my cheek upon her mane. Weakly patting her neck, I barely whispered, "Home, Winnie . . . *Home* . . ." and once again, I drifted into darkness . . .

As I floated in and out of the purgatory of consciousness, my tortured brain became aware of unceasing interruptions . . . including that of a gentle human voice, mumbling on in a vague fashion . . . until I was dulled into a stupor by its sheer emptiness. As the voice droned on and on, somehow within its unintelligable echoes, I caught snippets of words, but still, their meaning was empty . . . and once again, I fell into a fevered darkness . . .

Spectral images haunted my soul . . . dark demonic reminders of war: the sound of drums, the booming echoes of cannons, the cracks of rifle fire, the sickening images of steel biting into human flesh; the screams, the smells, the contorted bodies—and blood soaked earth. Flashbacks of myself murdering my fellow men . . . merely to ensure that I survived to kill again, led me to the darkest side of hell . . . where the demons of war rose up to take me.

Grasping my arms with skeletal hands possessing vise like power, they judged me guilty and had come for my soul. Dragging me kicking and screaming into Lucifer's fires, I thrashed in vain to escape their grasp— but was powerless to do so.

From the flames rose the unholy being, Lucifer . . . a ghoulish red giant posessing an enormous head, crowned with irregular shaped horns and pointed ears. A sharp nose distorted his red, wart filled face: wherein crawled white slimy worms, chewing bloody trails within his cheeks . . . and raising their putrefied heads, they mocked me with high-pitched squeals.

His hideous eyes possessed vertical serpentine irises of gold, centered with black vertical slits that bore no end to their depth or darkness . . . and most frightening of all . . . was his triumphant brittle laugh . . . a scarcastic unworldly sound that burst my ears with its insidious malevolence.

As he lowered a clawed hand to rip the soul from my heart, he stopped abruptly and looked beyond me into the distance.

Turning to follow his gaze, my soul leapt with joy . . . for in the distance, walking toward us . . . was my guardian angel, Suzannah. Surrounded by a divine energy radiating the only light in Lucifer's eternal darkness, I ran toward her, desperately calling her name and begging her to chase the demons away.

But her light grew dimmer as more demons rushed forward to overtake her, and with deafening shrieks, they drove my angel back. Somehow, through strength that she alone could give me, I broke free of my demons and ran toward her . . .

As I approached Suzannah, she urgently thrust out her hands for me to grasp. I was inches away, and as I desperately stretched to grab them, my feet were suddenly held fast by the same force that had gripped my arms . . . and now, mocked by Lucifer's sinister laugh, I was completely helpless . . . and thus bound, the skeletal demons dragged me back. And as my angel faded into the darkness, I screamed my final defiant rebuke toward the ultimate soul taker . . . a long, agonizing, "Nnnoooooo . . ."

"Soldier, are you dreaming?" were the words I heard as an indistinct image hovered above me. I was gasping for breath from my Luciferian nightmare when, suddenly, a cool wet cloth was gently drawn across my burning face. This welcome act soothed my forehead, cheeks and cracked lips. Then an unseen hand lifted my head to help me sip from a cup of water, and its welcoming trickle moistened my parched mouth and throat.

As my head was returned to a pillow, my breathing gradually slowed, and although I still couldn't see clearly, I perceived a female figure seated beside me.

I stared at her in mute delirium, trying to see her clearly when she softly said, "You nearly perished, young man, and you are gravely wounded. We have given you some water, and we'll feed you in due course. Meanwhile, is there anything else you need?"

Mustering all my strength, I merely croaked, "A bedpan . . . please?"

I must have fallen asleep for a time, because when I next opened my eyes, a pleasant looking older man was standing beside my bed. With a kindly face that reminded me of Reverend Metcalf, he drew a chair to my bedside, sat down, and offered his hand, "You have quite a horse, young fellow . . . she brought you all the way here from the lower plains—nearly eight miles."

Sitting up to take his hand, a searing pain knifed through the wound in my side, causing me to immediately collapse and clutch it.

"*Easy*, son," he said gently, patting my shoulder. "As my wife said, you have been *gravely* wounded. She wasn't certain you would survive . . . particularly since you slept so fitfully."

At that moment, a woman with striking hazel eyes and a lush mane of gray hair entered the room.

"This is my wife, Thankful," the man explained. "She was the one who found you and brought you here, and has been nursing you for nearly two weeks. I am Obediah—Reverend Obediah Walker."

He rose then and retrieved my rifle from a corner of the room. Holding it before me, he asked, "Are you in Washington's army?"

"Yes," I said absently, marveling at the remarkable coincidence of our sharing the name Walker.

"We weren't sure what side you were on . . . until we found *this*," Thankful said, pointing to the rifle, "and then we knew . . ."

Addressing Obediah, I said, "You say your name is Walker. Who is your grandfather?"

"My grandfather's name was William, and he had several sons, one of whom was Thomas, my father."

The comforting manner in which he spoke of his people made me relax. "My family name is Walker too—I'm James Walker . . . of Walker's Cove. My grandfather was Richard and my father was James. I have a wife and a daughter—Suzannah and Ainsley, who was named after my mother."

"Walker's Cove . . . yes . . . founded by Richard. But do you know who your *great* grandfather was?"

Shaking my head in ignorance, Reverend Walker grinned broadly and declared, "I believe your great grandfather was *my* grandfather, *William Walker*. So you can rest easy now, son, you are with family here—both God's . . . and your *own*."

I stared at him in wide-eyed disbelief, incredulous at my good fortune.

"Indeed, James," Obediah explained, ". . . among your great grandfather's many children, were two impetuous little boys, Thomas and Richard. Thomas remained in England to become a distinguished cleric, while his renegade younger brother Richard, sought the green fields of the New World and its unfettered opportunities."

Thankful left the room at this point and returned moments later with a bowl of thick creamy soup, made from potatoes, pork scraps, carrots, corn and milk. Placing the bowl in my hands, she then handed me a spoon, saying, "You have a cousin . . . Nathaniel, our son. Like you, he is serving in the colonial army under General Washington."

"I'd very much like to meet him one day," I said, adding, "I was a scout for Washington, and before that, I served at Sullivan's Island. Where am I now?"

"You are in Newtown, a little north of Brookland Heights, which some now call Brooklyn Heights. I'm the county minister, with congregations here and in neighboring Flushing and Whitestone."

After a thoughtful pause, he soberly continued, "We've learned that Washington suffered a terrible defeat in the battle you just fought. It's said that over nine hundred soldiers were killed or wounded, and over a thousand were captured . . . making it a decisive victory for Howe, I'm sorry to say."

"All for the want of words . . ." I sighed, thinking of Lydia's prophetic letter from what seemed like ages ago. After a silence of pondering the enormity of our loss, I added, "We were trying to inform General Sullivan that Jamaica Pass was unprotected. We were looking for him when the British regulars flooded in from that very area, straight into our rear—and *that* was our undoing. Had we found him sooner, the outcome might have been very different."

Repentant for not being as quick and efficient as I *could* have been, I contemplated momentarily what *might* have been. Had Zeb mentioned the pass the day it was found, Sullivan could have fortified it. But for want of timely words, hundreds of our own now lay dead; including my friends and Zeb . . . and here was I—as close to death as I could be.

Remembering my feverish visions of Lucifer, I instinctively reached for my talisman, which miraculously, still remained.

"I know a woman's blessing when I see one," said Thankful, her eyes alight as she beamed a warm smile at me. "That is your wife's hair . . . *she* made that for you, didn't she?"

"Yes, she did," I answered, amazed at her perception.

"While we treated your wounds and washed your body clean, I was careful with it and let it remain. Such gifts of love are more valuable than gold to those who treasure them."

She was amazing to hear. In many ways she reminded me of Mother, and I wondered if she was a heart feeler, for surely she showed the signs. As I ate my soup, she shared more details about my injuries while dabbing at my wounds.

"Obed was in Whitestone when your horse arrived. You were stabbed twice—deeply—in the same area; and although I couldn't help you on the inside, I sewed up your entry wounds as best I could. Thereafter, all I could do was sponge water to your lips and clean your wounds every day. Your injuries were so severe and you'd lost so much blood . . . that I truly feared you would die, young cousin. They are mostly dry now, but healing on your *inside* will take much longer. You are welcome to remain here—and with God's help, you shall recover."

As she rose to leave, she murmured with a knowing smile, "By all rights, you should be *dead* . . . isn't it *wonderful* to have a guardian angel?"

As THE DAYS passed, I would wonder sometimes what Thankful meant by "guardian angel." I wasn't sure if she was referring to herself, to Suzannah—or a random guardian angel from heaven. At all events, I improved very slowly; and despite my best efforts to rise, I remained confined to my bed.

Every week I gained a little more strength and movement in my upper body; but my insides still gave me such pain that I didn't push myself . . . lest something inside burst or reopen from the strain.

Obed visited with me frequently, and we chatted congenially night after night. Sometimes we discussed our Walker ancestors of old England. At other times, he brought news of the war and we discussed what it meant to each of us, and our families. Whatever he said, he always spoke from his heart. He was a sensitive man, seeming to know my longings without needing to ask.

Finally, on one freezing December morning he asked me if I should like to write a letter. He offered to post it with a friend who was travelling to Boston, since he knew it could be delivered there to Fay and Lydia—and thence to Suzannah.

Because of the war, letters were scarce and often went astray; so before I sealed mine, I pressed it to my talisman for good fortune, and kissed the seal . . . because I knew my darling's fingers would open it.

In January 1777, I received my first letter from Suzannah since we'd parted in August. I was overjoyed to learn that everyone was well and that Zeb wasn't dead. He had written to Dimmis after the battle, informing her he'd survived intact; and now he "scouted" food for the army—mainly by plundering Tory farms throughout New Jersey.

Suzannah said she felt a "disturbance" of her heart in August— similar to what she'd experienced when Mother died. But her faith remained unshaken, even after Zeb reported me missing in a letter to Dimmis—because she had foreseen that death would seek others, but not me.

She told me that Dimmis would inform Zeb in her next letter that I was alive and healing from my wounds. Also, she was grateful that through sheer serendipity—or Winnie's sixth sense—I had found a temporary home with Walker relatives! Winnie knew she couldn't take me *all the way* home, but she got close enough.

Thereafter, Suzannah devoted the most space to Ainsley—how she was spending her time; and how she missed being thrown in the air, as "Grandpa was now too feeble to toss a 'big' girl of 53 pounds." It thrilled me to read about Ainsley's antics, and I was especially touched by Suzannah's comment of how much she loved motherhood . . . and her only source of distress was that I wasn't home with them.

At the bottom of her final page, there was a large **X** where Suzannah had placed her kiss—and I noticed the paper beneath it was wrinkled by moisture, now long dried. She wrote that she placed a special kiss there to carry me forward, ". . . *in brave assurance that your girls—all three of them—await your return.*"

While gently pressing that water stained **X** to my own cracked lips, tears of homesickness rolled . . . *especially* when I read her endearing farewell: "*Goodbye, my darling . . . with love forever and untold . . . your Suzannah.*"

Guardian angel indeed . . .

SOLITARY WORLD

Once having lived there, Walker's Cove can lay claim to your affections by nestling itself forever in your heart. So it was that throughout my lengthy convalescence, I felt the irresistible pull of home.

Suzannah would have none of it though, declaring in her letters that Washington needed me more than she did—but *only* for military reasons, she added; otherwise, if it were in her power, she would have me home tomorrow.

Her descriptions of her "desires d'amour" made me even *more* anxious to return. Worse yet, her passionate details of what she *would* do after my recovery, burned the pages of my letters with such ardor, I felt obliged to keep them hidden, lest Obed and Thankful think I had married a reckless harlot.

By spring, the pain in my insides had diminished considerably. Cousin Obed suggested I try to rebuild my strength by easing into tasks that required using my weakest area—the abdominal muscles below my ribs on the right side of my body.

To that end, he introduced me to an elderly farmer named Caleb Loring, so that I might volunteer to help him with his chores. He readily embraced the idea, and for the first time in six months, I started using my body again—for milking cows, feeding chickens, currying horses and shoveling manure.

Finding myself with a renewed feeling of purpose and self-worth, by summer my strength had improved such that I could handle a new and more demanding task: pitching hay onto a rick. I went about it slowly and methodically; and every forkful that I pressed onto that rick reminded me of Zeb and Dimmis, and brought a constant smile to my face. Caleb never understood how someone could perform such tedious work with a constant smile . . . but I could never tell him why.

In the early evenings, I practiced using my Pennsylvania long rifle. While experimenting with powder loads, ball diameters and patching materials, I became so accurate, that within a month's time, I could place five offhand shots within the area of a teacup at one hundred yards. I was, as the Virginians were fond of saying, a "long shot"—and very proud of it!

Finally, I felt confident enough to leave my cousins and rejoin Washington's army. I was strong enough physically—but did I have the emotional will to make the painful break?

ON A HOT July morning, I forced myself to pack up my belongings and get ready to leave. Once satisfied with the organization of my bundles, I brought them with me into the parlor. There, cousin Obed was sitting at his desk, scratching out notes for Sunday's sermon, his bible close at hand.

Rising to greet me as he always did, when he observed my bundles, he sadly asked, "The time has *come*—hasn't it?"

I looked down, and sensing my melancholy as I choked back tears, he softly added, "'Tis God's justice, my boy, that by a divine hand . . . you were led here to be healed and live among your kin."

Clutching my arms, he firmly said, "I am proud to say that your time with us has made us better people . . . at least in God's eyes. You are so much like my son, Nathaniel. Both of you possess a noble countenance and a fine character. Now *you* are a son to me . . . and I know that if you were Nathaniel's older brother, he would look up to you and be as proud of you as *I* am."

We both sat down, and gathering my thoughts I finally replied, "Obediah, words alone cannot express the extent of my gratitude to you and your wife. Suzannah and I both know you have saved my life . . . and we want to somehow repay you for all you've done for me—and my family."

Handing him the five sovereigns and cupping his fingers around them, I added, "It's but little to offer in exchange for a *life*—but it's all I have. I'll be forever grateful I found you. I shall look for Nathaniel, and tell him of our relationship. You are the first relatives I have ever known, other than Suzannah's family. In heaven, my parents are smiling at your kindness and generosity to their son."

Pressing his hands within mine, I hastened to add, "After all this is over, no matter what the outcome, I should like to have you and Thankful—and Nathaniel—meet Suzannah and Ainsley. We own the tavern in Walker's Cove, where we serve good food and drink. We often have music, singing, and sometimes duos with pianoforte and violin. We would love you to come and be our guests . . . after all, you are *family* . . ."

"We'll *plan* on that . . ." came from behind me, as Thankful wrapped her arms around my shoulders. How wonderful it felt . . . for it reminded me of Mother's embrace, and once again I felt deeply touched by a mother's unforgettable love.

In Obediah and Thankful, I saw what my parents would have been like had they lived to be older. My only regret was that they never had the opportunity to meet these dear cousins while living.

And so, amid an abundance of hugs, kisses and tears, I regretfully left my Walker relatives. As Winnie wound down the path leading south, I turned to gaze once more upon these two endearing people: one with his hand raised in blessing, and the other anxiously fluttering her apron. As I waved a heartfelt farewell, a wayward tear stole down my cheek . . . for it wasn't the leaving that made my heart ache . . . it was wondering if I would ever see them again.

WINNIE KEPT HER pace as I followed the sun's course across the sky, while the little country roads seemed unending. When we finally settled down that night to sleep under the stars, I longed for Suzannah. I wanted her so much that I *begged* the stars to transport me home. Knowing that couldn't happen, I pulled out my talisman and kissed it, fondling the lock of her hair and entwining it around my fingers. Then pressing it to my heart, I closed my eyes and its softness lulled me to sleep.

When we resumed our trek south the next morning, I came upon scattered farms and villages. Desirous of steering clear of Tories, I kept to the trails, stopping only once: to ask the driver of a passing wagon for the way to New Jersey.

As we went along, I saw no sign of either army, and wondered if the war had ended during my convalescence. From what cousin Obed had heard from his neighbors, the theatre of war had moved south to New Jersey—or possibly into Pennsylvania. Considering that Zeb's job was plundering Tory farms in New Jersey, I reckoned the armies must be camped somewhere in that vicinity. So Winnie and I proceeded to head in a southwesterly direction.

As we were passing beneath the shady canopy of some bull pines, a shot suddenly barked from the woods, spooking Winnie to rear up and throw me down. As Winnie dashed off with my rifle, I rolled into the tall grass, drew my knife and lay completely still. My nostrils flared as my heart rate soared and pounded as though every beat should be its last. There is no greater human fear than that of being hunted—*especially* by man, who is the ultimate hunter—*and* the ultimate game.

Waiting in readiness for whatever might come next; a loud rustling in the bushes across the road was followed by a meaty thump. Suddenly, from the same bushes emanated a familiar sounding bellow, "Now what in *hell* you wanna do *that* for? *Give* me that damned musket . . . you're as *nervous* as a whore in church . . . now *go* on over and see if he's still alive!"

I could hardly believe my ears—but it was the unmistakable bellow of Zeb Hawkes!

As the stranger was heading in my direction, I called out, "Zeb? Zeb Hawkes? Is that *you*?"

Abruptly, the man halted and turned around, clearly waiting for a response.

Another rustling in the bushes produced a knot of men that emerged and joined the stranger, muskets at the ready. At their front, strode the grand figure of Zebulon Galletin Hawkes, grinning from ear to ear once he saw me rise from the tall grass.

While brushing off the dust from my clothes, I declared in my best Henry Wiggins manner, "Is *this* the sort of greeting an old friend gets from another after such a lengthy *absence?*"

THE NEWS THAT I'd survived the battle hadn't yet reached Zeb, so his reaction at seeing me was even more exuberant than mine at seeing him. After a joyous embrace, he pulled away first to examine me more closely, and I saw an expression on his face of grateful relief. "You're thinner than I remember, but at least you ain't *dead!*"

Suddenly, we heard the clip-clop of hooves approaching, and all heads turned as Winnie sauntered over to me. I patted her affectionately as I said, "Zeb, I was as close to death as I dare to get, and I don't recommend it much."

"Where'd you get wounded?" he asked, seeing no apparent defects.

Lifting my shirt, the welted abdominal scars below my ribs told my story.

"Looks like somebody stabbed you with a bayonet . . . more than once," he remarked, looking distressed.

"It was a Hessian . . . and he wanted to make sure I died," I said, looking down as I replayed the scene in my imagination—my last memory of the war.

Zeb's men stepped toward me to have a look at my scars, and glance at me admiringly before I pulled my shirt down.

"These gentlemen are my new recruits," Zeb announced proudly. "Today I'm trainin' 'em to be scouts—per the general's orders."

As they looked at him expectantly, he barked, "Attention, men!"

They all stood up straight and looked alert.

Pointing to me, he said, "This is James Walker of Walker's Cove—same town as me. Jim, this is John Titcomb, Josiah Boynton, Joshua Adams, Caleb Dean, Samuel Moody . . . and this young feller here is Nathaniel Walker—no relation, I presume?"

Speechless with astonishment, as I gazed into that face of youthful innocence, I saw my own boyhood there, for Nathaniel looked to be all of seventeen years. I thought about my own life at that age . . . the thrill of meeting Suzannah and falling in love . . . That was the kind of life-changing event my cousin should be experiencing—*not* the horror and deprivations of war.

"Good afternoon, men," I said calmly, "I'm pleased to meet you all. But I'm sure you'll understand that it's a special pleasure for me to meet my cousin, Nathaniel."

I held out my hand to shake his, and with a look of wide-eyed surprise, he took it and pressed it warmly as I explained, "Your father is my father's cousin. Our great grandfathers are one and the same: William Walker."

His fresh-faced smile made me wish we were at his home or mine . . . so we could bond together as the sole children of cousinly fathers—but there was no changing our present circumstances.

"Your parents saved my life, Nathaniel—I've been living with them for the past nine months. I was badly wounded last August, and left your home only two weeks ago. Your parents asked me to remember them to you if we happened to meet up with each other."

Zeb handed Nathaniel a discharged musket declaring, "Well now, ain't that just *grand*! You damned near killed your own *cousin*!" Then turning to me, he scolded, "And *you* nearly got killed for the *second* time in a year!" Slapping Nathaniel's back, he roared jovially. "Nice shootin', Nat! Damned good thing you're still a *pup*!"

Draping my arm about Nathaniel's shoulder, I drew him closer, saying, "Unlike my good friend, Zeb, here, I'm very grateful that you *missed*, dear cousin!" And offering him my long rifle, I said, "I'll teach you to shoot properly . . . with *this*!"

Looking at me with affection, he replied, "I shall look forward to that, cousin Jim."

Nathaniel took his place among his fellows, and I led Winnie on foot as Zeb and I talked as we headed back to camp. He reiterated how heartsick he felt about not knowing my whereabouts, or whether I was alive or dead. He also described our army's dire engagement at Trenton, and the somewhat hopeful ones at

Hubbardton, Walloomsac—and most recently at Brandywine Creek. In turn, I informed Zeb of all the news I'd had from Suzannah about life on the home front.

As the September sun basked us in its warmth, I turned back to see Nathaniel marching in stride with the others, and a brotherly pride welled up inside me. It was a new and welcome feeling, and patting my talisman in gratitude—I wondered if Suzannah had something to do with these *remarkable* coincidences.

General Washington looked incredulous when Zeb brought me to see him.

"I'm thankful to see you are still alive, Scout Walker," he said evenly, as his eyes were drawn to my rifle, and he inspected it with great interest. "I trust you are sufficiently recovered to resume service?" he inquired, raising his brows quizzically.

"I am, sir. I've heard things have gone poorly, sir. Is that so?"

"First, I thank you for your service once more; and for what it's worth, I prefer not to bore you with any ephemeral drivel about this war—now—how are your wife and daughter?"

What a shining manifestation of character amidst such dire circumstances—for here was the besieged commanding general of our poor army, taking precious time to ask after my wife and daughter.

Honored and touched at his asking, while their images filled my heart, from my eyes I brushed aside the involuntary moisture and replied, "Thank you for asking, sir, they are well and look forward to my return, sir . . . that is, *after* the war, sir . . ."

Washington affectionately patted my shoulder and returned to his desk. Seemingly reading my thoughts, he said, "Scout Walker, war is a very cruel mistress. You will find that in war, even the best and finest men are naught but shadows—merely flitting about attempting to achieve a constructive end to all of *this*. Indeed, through our numerous defeats or setbacks, our souls have become ravaged, and so, during our darkest hours, they sink to hell's bottom . . . whilst the waves of death, rage and anger, swell mightily above us . . . drowning us in absolute despair."

Standing at his full height, he took a deep breath, and raising his voice, he encouragingly continued, "But we shall all rise *above* that, for within our being burns the *fire* of righteous independence . . . and that fire shall continue to burn and smolder . . . to catch with *others*. In unity of spirit, belief and cause, *we* shall find the strength to go forward . . . to be a *free* and *indivisible* nation . . . so help me *God*."

His words resonated within my soul, moving me so deeply; I had never been so proud or inspired in my entire life . . . except when I married Suzannah.

ZEB AND I were assigned to General Arnold's left wing division as scouts. The new recruits, including Nathaniel, went to generals Lincoln on the right wing and Gates in the center. I was glad that Nathaniel was with Gates because he held field command; thus I felt he would be safer there.

Because of my skill with the rifle, I was ordered to report to Colonel Daniel Morgan, commander of the 11th Virginia Regiment. Zeb, under protest, was ordered to report to Henry Dearborn's light infantry unit. Although we would not be serving together, Dearborn was under Morgan's command, so Zeb would still be nearby.

From Washington's headquarters I was led by a soft-spoken Virginian named Silas Tate to a large open shelter, similar to the forge I had built on Sullivan Island. There, I met the hard scrabbled man known as the "Old Waggoner"—Daniel Morgan himself.

Morgan's aide, a man who called himself Lewis, was stationed outside the shelter. He had a singular reptilian look about his face, quite fearsome, such that it cast a foreboding countenance to all who saw it. As I approached the shelter, he stared at me with unblinking eyes and imperiously demanded, "What is your business here, soldier?" I handed him my orders from headquarters, which he read and then sourly commanded, "Follow me, Walker."

Lewis led me inside and announced to Morgan, "Soldier Walker, sir . . ." and giving me a sneer, sarcastically added, "reporting for *duty*, sir."

Morgan took the orders from Lewis and perused the contents without even looking at me. "It says here you can *shoot*, but how *good* are you?"

"Well I . . ."

Jumping up to glare at me, he rapidly fired off a hostile question, "Can you load and shoot six times in sixty seconds and pierce a tin cup at sixty paces, all while running through a broken corn-field, son?"

"I don't know, sir . . ."

"By *God!*" Morgan bellowed, and contemptuously hurling my orders back at Lewis, he screamed, "When are those lily-livered, teat-sucking, political rump-sniffers going to send me some god-damned men who can *shoot?*"

Turning away from Lewis to face me, he slammed his fist on his table and wailed, "All they send me are *babes* and puling *nanny* goats, all just weaned from the *teat*. I'm sick to *death* of 'em—yeah, *stinkers* like *you*, son. I have no damned use for you in Virginia's 11th!"

Feeling mortified and disheartened, I simply stood there, unable to speak.

Walking around me, Morgan glared at me as if I were a repellent slug. "You look like the best part of you was left at *home*, son." Then he sneered, "Maybe you ought to get *back* there and *grow* a pair, then come back to *me* when you find 'em betwixt those *misbegotten* thighs o' your'n! This is a *man's* army, son. This is a *man's* regiment. This is a man's *war!*"

I pulled up my shirt and showed him my wounds.

Turning away, he muttered, "*Sheeiit*, son . . . that ain't *nothin'* . . ." and after ordering Lewis out, he removed his coat and shirt. Then he turned to reveal his back, which had evidently been torn to shreds. Every inch of skin was covered with deep lacerations that had healed to angry red welts.

"*That* I got from the British *cat!*" he declared. "For punching a mealymouthed officer, whose only qualification to *command*, was that his mother was being screwed by the right son of a bitch!"

As he donned his shirt, he murmured, "I enjoyed every lash . . ." When fully attired again, he added, "I was in the French and Indian *war*, son . . . not only was I *flogged*, but I took an Indian ball to the mouth and lost half my damned teeth in the process. War ain't *pretty*, son—we just got back from Quebec, and I got a *score* to settle with the British—*all* of 'em!"

Sitting behind his table, he sighed heavily and then asked, "So, tell me, son . . . what in hell *can* you do?"

Freeman's Farm

Freeman's Farm, September 17, 1777

My dearest Suzannah,

I am well and in good health, and suffer but little from my wounds, now completely healed over.

I sorely miss you and Ainsley, and want more than anything to be back home.

I have been assigned to a division where I am not wanted, in the command of a cruel, hard-nosed taskmaster named Daniel Morgan. He sets lofty standards for his men, and your husband does not meet them, mostly because I'm not a full-blooded trained Virginia rifleman.

Zeb is with Dearborn's light infantry . . . can you imagine anything droller than Zeb as an infantryman? That said, he has managed to find two cows that are being well used by the army for milk, and will perhaps find themselves upon army dinner plates before very long.

Freeman's farm belonged to a Tory named John Freeman, who abandoned it when he fled to Canada for safety. I believe Zeb's cows were once Freeman's strays left to wander.

There are numerous skirmishes with the British, as we constantly hear rifle fire. Many British scouting parties are sneaking around hereabouts, and I've heard rumors that General Burgoyne is coming down here from the north. We are set to engage him on our fortified territory called Bemis Heights.

What about you, Suzannah? I hunger for news from you soon, darling. You know how precious your letters are to me.

I feel somehow as if I have squandered our affections by being the one who had to leave. How neglected you must feel without me at home . . . to care for you, love you, caress you—and to be with you and our sweet daughter.

But your silence leaves me helpless to know your feelings, so I blame myself for your lack of letters. And on nights like this one, plagued with doubt, I lie awake clutching your talisman . . . and feeling afraid.

My dearest Suzannah, history shall never reveal the unintended disruption this war inflicts upon its innocent victims. I pray that we are not among them.

Good night, dearest angel . . . kiss Ainsley for me . . . my heart loves you with no bounds.

Your loving husband,
Jim

The Chase

he upshot of my demeaning interview with Morgan was that I was a scout once more, and not a rifleman. He continued to treat me in a callous manner, and I chafed under his abuse on a daily basis. Needless to say, when I rode out with Winnie each day to patrol our camp's perimeter, I felt vastly relieved to get away from him.

It was my job to be on the lookout for British scouting parties. They usually sought information about our defenses and the strength of our numbers. Ironically, it was deserters from our side and disgruntled soldiers whose terms of enlistment had expired, who were often the major informants. My orders were to arrest and return to Morgan anyone caught outside our borders, and to shoot those who resisted right where they stood. But I had no intention of shooting any man who willingly pitchforked himself into this war.

My solitary patrols with Winnie gave me plenty of time to think about home; but what should have been a good thing made me sick with worry . . . for it had been a very long while since I'd heard from Suzannah. I wondered if the war had stopped her letters—or worse yet, *she* did. I resolved to seek out Dearborn's camp at the first available opportunity, and ask Zeb how long it had been since he'd heard from Dimmis.

As I approached Dearborn's encampment, I was challenged by an amiable sentry whose name was Ephraim Larcom. He knew who Zeb was, and escorting me into their camp, he shared details about it.

"This is my fahm," he said proudly, arcing his arm toward a rolling hill on our left. "I built that shed up theah," he added, indicating a ramshackle building nearby, made of logs, mud and tree branches. "They's Zeb's cows an' sheeps out yondah. I gots 'leven children home."

"What kind of work do you do?" I inquired, smiling at the idea that he might be a shoemaker like Osgood.

Ephraim looked thoughtful and scratching the stubble on his chin he answered. "I'm a fahma, a weava, a shoemaka, a furria, a wheelwright, an' a docta—though I know nuthin' 'bout any of 'em but the doin'." And then, looking straight into my eyes he added, "And when it cain't be helped, a damned good solja . . ."

Pointing to a large knot of tents where men were milling about, he said, "Zeb be in *theah* somewheah . . . jes look around . . . he's big—*really* big!"

I thanked him and proceeded into their midst. The men I observed were not well dressed. Most lacked shoes and their clothes were so threadbare, that one could imagine reading a broadsheet through them. Many carried muskets that looked so old and decrepit that they might have belonged to their owners merely by right of salvage.

I wondered how effective Dearborn's infantry could be, consisting of soldiers who hadn't the basic necessities, let alone the skills to match the illustrious troops I observed at Gravesend. The sight of this motley crew depressed my spirits even further, for I knew they would never stand a chance against the world's finest army.

As I made my way through the throng of scarecrow infantrymen, I tried to keep my distance from those who looked the sickliest. I was accustomed to doing the same among my own regiment, since I'd recently learned that nearly half their number was plagued with illness.

Suddenly, I heard a distant voice bellow about "moving a cow's backside" from Ephraim's sorry excuse for a barn, and saw a tall figure emerge, stooping low to avoid the overhang of its entrance. It was Zeb. After dashing across the meadow and up the hill, I called out his name.

"By God, if it ain't ole Jim Walker!" Zeb exclaimed when he saw me. He embraced me warmly and slapped my back so hard he winded me.

"This here is Jenny the cow . . ." he said as he turned and slapped its rump so hard, it sounded like a pistol shot. "Move *aside*, Jenny, my old friend *Jim* is here . . . will you give some milk for our noble guest?" Zeb kneeled as he placed a bucket below the cow's udder and hollered, "Now *give*, damn you!" and began massaging the teats.

"To hell with the cows, Zeb . . . have you heard from Dimmis recently? Do you have any news from home?" I said, trying not to sound too apprehensive.

"No, nothing since we left New York," Zeb replied calmly. But when he saw the look of alarm on my face, he added, "What in hell is the damned burr you got under your saddle, Jim?"

"Zeb, I haven't had a letter from Suzannah since before I left the Walkers. I keep writing her, but I've received no reply. I was wondering if it's because of the war."

"Yeah, it's the damned *war* all right!" he retorted. "And what makes it worse is the longer men go with nothing to do, not hearing from loved ones is ever more detrimental to their morale! So they saunter about, getting into all manner of mischief. Unlike *me*, some have lost their desire for industry *and* their sobriety, thus rendering themselves useless under *anyone's* command!"

Spitting contemptuously, Zeb launched into a cruder tirade. "Why, does this damned infantry keep giving me *infant* tasks to do, like marching in line for days on end? These bastards keep marching me in circles goin' nowhere, and also made me the head *teat*-squeezer for the whole damned regiment!

"Well, I'm tellin' *you*, Jim, I'm damned *tired* of marchin' nowhere and squeezing *teats* that ain't a woman's! Ole Jenny and my other cow Penny have imprints of my hands on their teats from my squeezing 'em so damned much. By God, Jim, I want to be a *scout*! At least Washington *appreciated* us. Dearborn couldn't give a damned piss upriver about *me*, or anything I do!"

"Well, Morgan hates *me* and he lets me know it every day. He wouldn't even consider me for a rifleman, but at least I'm a scout so I can get away from his miserable self. Perhaps I can help get you get away from your teats . . . if I convince Dearborn you were once a valued scout of Washington's."

No sooner had I said it, than a man in brown leather clothing, better dressed than most soldiers hereabouts, came charging up the hill on horseback. As he dismounted, he stood before us and breathlessly asked, "Are either one of you scouts?"

We both answered "yes" simultaneously, causing him to look askance at us and curtly demand, "For *whom?*"

Again, Zeb and I answered together, "Washington."

Lowering his jaw in frustration and confusion, he paused to weigh our answers. Finally, he ordered, "Then come with me and be snappy about it!"

We were led to a tent much larger than the others in the bevy. There we met a neatly dressed man with a noble countenance. He was clean-shaven and his eyes were bright with a lively intelligence.

"Good morning, gentlemen. I am Major Henry Dearborn of the 3rd New Hampshire regiment. And you are . . .?"

Saluting him, I replied, "I am scout James Walker, and this is scout Zeb Hawkes. We are both from Walker's Cove, sir."

Breaking out in a broad grin, Dearborn informally asked, "Do either of you happen to know Henry *Wiggins* by chance?"

Speechless with astonishment, Zeb and I merely stared at each other, then I spoke up. "Yes, sir, we are good friends and business partners with Henry Wiggins. We own a ship together . . . that is, if he still has it."

"Oh, indeed he *does* . . . she is called *Suzannah's Pride*—" Dearborn enthusiastically affirmed. "She is famous for her actions during the Parker defeat at Fort Moultrie."

"Fort Moultrie?" I repeated.

"Indeed! Colonel Moultrie and his men fought so valiantly against the British, that the fort he built on Sullivan's Island was named in his honor. But Moultrie, nonetheless, gave the lion's share of credit to Henry and the crew of *Suzannah's Pride*."

My heart swelled with pride, while Zeb cleared his throat in an unsuccessful attempt to mask the tears in his eyes. We were part of history, as was *Suzannah's Pride*.

Touching his lip thoughtfully, Dearborn added, "In fact, I believe Henry's ship has captured over three *thousand* barrels of powder from British supply ships, which were delivered to our army *intact*. Someday I hope to see this sleek little craft . . . fast as the *wind*, I hear . . ."

All I could do was smile and affirm, "Yes, sir."

"Now, let's get to the task at hand, gentlemen. We have it on good authority that the British are particularly active hereabouts, and we'd like you to find out anything you can—either by observation, or better yet, by what you *hear*. We need you to scout the perimeter of their camp, and I would prefer this be done under cover of night, when your risk of exposure is relatively minimal."

He paused before he added, almost as an afterthought, "Do you have your own horses?"

"Yes, sir—we *definitely* got horses!" Zeb replied and then softly added, "Sir, can I ask you a *personal* question . . . off the record?"

Dearborn nodded, and Zeb then inquired, "How come you are so *different* than some of these other hard assed commanders? I get *tired* of pulling cow teats and marching in circles! I should be shooting heads off British regulars, or better yet, as Moultrie would say, off British *officers*."

"You *know* Moultrie?" asked Dearborn, raising his eyebrows with alacrity and expectation.

"Naw, we just *heard* about him." Zeb replied, casually waving Moultrie off. He then coughed heartily and loudly added, "Damned good *commander*, though."

IN THE WEE hours of the morning, Zeb and I tied our horses to a tree on the edge of the woods, just outside the British encampment. Proceeding stealthily on foot, we stole across an open field blanketed with high grasses, and finally settled into a large thicket, well hidden from view.

We observed a colorful sight—fires flickering everywhere around the tents, while sentries stood silhouetted against the firelight, guarding clusters of horses and wagons. Amid the silence of the night, we heard the echoes of voices on the wind, exchanging greetings or snippets of conversation about battle plans. Like the voices from the ships we heard in the fog at sea, again, there were ghastly murderers before us. Although I did not know them, their wives or children, my urge to kill them weighed heavily upon my conscience.

Suddenly we heard the snap of a branch, not far from our hideout.

Zeb hushed me to silence and whispered, "What in hell was *that?*"

"*Wer da geht?*" a voice called out from our right . . . and again, "*WER DA GEHT?*" this time accompanied by a loud click.

As we looked into each other's eyes, Zeb retrieved his knife and slipping it under his sleeve, rose slowly to face a Hessian soldier with his musket lowered, cocked and ready, his bayonet aimed at Zeb's stomach.

"*Hier—hier kommen!*" the soldier shouted, shaking his bayonet threateningly, waving it first at Zeb and then at me.

I was distracted with the irresistible fascination of his uniform and language as my inner anxieties overtook me. The combination of us being discovered and knowing they gave no quarter, made me tremble for my life. Indeed, through the auspices of this Hessian soldier, we were facing the end of our days.

Soon, his fellow Hessians approached us from the edge of the forest. In the fading darkness, their orderly formations and sheer numbers certainly spelled our doom.

As they approached, I trembled as I whispered, "What should we do, Zeb?"

"Don't worry, Jim. They'll have to go through *me* to get to you!"

It was easy now for me to regret everything I'd done to get myself into this war. I should have gone back home, even if it *was* against Suzannah's wishes.

Seemingly Zeb had read my mind, because he softly said, "We ain't dead *yet*, Jim. Remember, we got *womenfolk* to care for."

As the soldiers drew closer, I saw Zeb's arm thrust forward as he buried the knife into the Hessian's chest. At the same instant his musket fired, and the others now came running.

"*Run*, Jim!" Zeb shouted, pulling out his pistol. "Run like *hell*, and don't *dare* look back!"

I took off as though shot out of a cannon. Zeb was right behind me. He stopped once to fire his pistol, and then caught up to me as the Hessians now gave chase, yelling and shooting, thus alerting the entire British camp.

Hearing the distant rumble of wagons being whirled into defensive positions, we scurried on, stumbling over the rough uneven surface into brambles and then into thorny hedges where a rabbit wouldn't run. I relentlessly hacked at them with my knife to clear a way . . . a way to freedom, and another chance at life.

The hedges viciously hacked back . . . by resisting our desperate effort. They slashed our hands and faces, needled our legs and unmercifully stabbed the bottoms of our feet, despite our shoes.

Shots were fired from behind us, and the balls flew by with brain piercing whines, tearing at our clothing and searing our skin. Yet on we went through the endless thickets and briars. Suddenly I saw in the distance two large and familiar shapes. When I whistled, I heard the sound of thrashing. It was Winnie responding by pulling at her moorings, with Slumber right beside her. Instantly, I knew we were saved.

Zeb and I hopped onto our horses and immediately they carried us away. Thundering through the night in the darkeness, Winnie and Slumber ran like they never ran before. While the screams and whirs of musket balls faded among the protesting Hessian shouts, I was certain they were damning *us* and all our soldiers straight to hell—furious that they hadn't helped us get there.

Ephraim Larcom met us at Dearborn's camp just as the sun rose. Once he saw our sorry state, he asked, "What in *tarnation* happened to *you* two? You get tangled up with a lactatin' *she bar* or somethin'?"

Saying nothing, Zeb trotted on to the medical tent. Looking down at him I simply stated, "We ran into some pretty mean Hessians out yonder, Eph . . . will you tell Dearborn they got Hessians off to our right flank? *Lots* of 'em?"

I gave Winnie a nudge and we headed off to join Zeb. There was a small fire before the medical tent, but it provided little more warmth than a firefly. When I gave up and went inside, I encountered a long line of men awaiting care, while an effluvium of genital stench and unwashed backsides nearly suffocated me. I thought I was about ready to pass out, when two orderlies brought us large buckets filled with heated water and lightly soiled rags to clean ourselves up.

When Zeb and I removed our clothes, we were dismayed to discover how battered our bodies were from our mad dash to escape. But we were both grateful too, since we couldn't fail to realize the alternative would have been far worse.

The doctor examined our wounds with fumbling bony fingers and reassured us that despite our pain and suffering, they were all of a transient nature. Amidst the cluttered gloom, we soaked our sore legs and feet and bandaged the worst of the open wounds that were still oozing.

As Zeb and I were dressing, I heard the repellent voice of Daniel Morgan as he entered the tent. He stood before me, scrutinizing my visible bruises, lacerations, and bloodstained bandages.

"Sheeeiiit, I send you on a *scouting* mission and you come back looking like a goddamned Hessian *harlot* got the best of you!"

"In fact, *we* . . ." I said, indicating Zeb, who was standing next to me, "despite being surrounded by Hessian soldiers, managed to *kill* one and escape with our lives."

"So you didn't get much scouting done for all your damage, did you, son?" Morgan said flatly.

"Well, sir, I did determine that the British have plenty of Hessians aiding them. They were on the right flank, and apparently in a separate camp of their own."

"But did you see anything in the *British* camp?" he asked in his highly offensive manner.

"Yes, sir, there were numerous supply wagons, teams of horses and field cannons, all guarded by sentries. I believe the Hessians were patrolling the outside perimeter, while the British kept watch over the interior."

Morgan nodded, saying, "Good—*very* good, Walker. On another subject, what do you know of blacksmithing?"

"I'm a trained blacksmith, sir."

"Can you make muskets or rifles? Can you repair 'em?" he asked expectantly.

"Yes, sir, if I had the proper forge, iron and help. Someone would have to help me, like Zeb here . . . we worked together in a forge, on Sullivan's Island. Who would make the stocks?"

"We already have the stocks, but we need locks and barrels—*rifled* barrels! The best of the British officers are little more than title-bearing creatures of privilege. Most know little or nothing of tactical warfare." Laughing heartily, Morgan added, "With a decent *rifle*, we can kill 'em from one hundred yards or more!"

Then he turned abruptly, went over to the flap and drawing it aside, inhaled deeply of the fresh air. Once he was done, he came back to me and bellowed, "*Hah, Walker!* It will be like shooting squirrels out of a damned tree—and we will come to little harm. Report to my quarters when you two have finished here! By God, we might make you *blacksmiths* Virginians yet—and *riflemen* to boot!"

"Yes, sir," I replied enthusiastically, so glad to see the back of him.

After he was gone, Zeb cleared his throat with a sound like a rusty anchor chain passing through a hawsehole. As the entire group of sick men looked on in wonder, Zeb smiled sheepishly and admitted, "Well, Jim, blacksmithing ain't so bad . . . after all, we both could be *dead!*"

IN SHORT ORDER, we arrived at Morgan's headquarters, and he escorted us to a superior smithy that lacked for nothing. It even had a rifling bench against the far wall, stretching nearly nine feet.

It was well stocked with worms, cutters, guides and braces. In the corner, weapons in various states of disrepair lay in several stacks.

Morgan left us to carry on, but ordered us to give him a progress report by evening.

Ignoring the discomfort of our injuries, we carefully inventoried the tools, to ensure we had everything we needed, especially important were a wide variety of small files, so I could do lock work. Zeb would weld the barrels together, as he was strong and tireless with a three-pound mallet. He could also straighten them after they were welded.

In a few hours' time, we were satisfied we had everything we needed to begin work the following day. So that night we reported to Morgan and told him so, and his response was uncharacteristically civil.

We got to the smithy before dawn broke, since I wanted to fire up early enough to have a hot bed of coals by midmorning. I assigned Zeb the task of disassembling the broken firearms, while I focused on repairing them. Most had broken flies, sears and springs, and were easy to fix. Within a week, we had all the damaged guns out of the shop and back into service.

Each night I returned to my bed so exhausted, that as I drifted into sleep, I fondly remembered Mother's favorite rhyme: "Man's work is sun to sun, but woman's work is never done." How I wished to tell her that man's work is never done either—especially if he is at war.

An Angel's Cry

October 8, 1777

My dearest husband,

I haven't written till now because I wanted to spare you the news
of my illness. For the past eight months, a persistent cough has been
my constant companion. At first, I thought nothing of it—that it
would soon pass. When it lingered, Dimmis reminded me that the
steady decline of the soldiers we nursed, began with the same symptoms
as mine. She wasn't trying to alarm me, but she felt I might neglect
myself otherwise.

During your recovery at the Walker's, a coughing spell caused me
such distress that I was compelled to cover my mouth with a towel.
Upon removing it, bright stains of blood covered its surface. I became
frightened, so Dimmis immediately summoned Doc.

His diagnosis was consumption, and he said there is little hope of
my recovery.

And so, my love, although these words may hurt, I cannot
withhold them any longer . . . my life's summer is drawing to a
close . . . for with every day that passes, I float farther from the shore
of our dreams—and without you, not even sunsets at Walker's Point
soothe my restless anxiety.

Because my death shall be slow and fickle, Doc has removed
Ainsley to my mother's house, as he fears for her also. How this breaks
my heart for our little girl . . . and for myself. She is the dearest and
most comforting thing I can embrace to feel your gentle presence.

Many are the nights I wake up shaking with fear . . . and pray God to deliver me from my trial, even though such deliverance can only increase the distance between us. But remember, my dearest husband, as I do, we are always together in spirit.

This arduous war may break our bodies, but never our hearts. Oh Jim, if there was a way I could find you, I surely would. Indeed, I am so desperate I would walk into the very depths of hell to find you. But while my hope for your imminent return fades, I sit alone on the point and find refuge in His spirit and in your love.

Long are the shadows that fall upon your living flower . . . as she fades into the coming darkness. Soon my weakness will show, yet I shall seal my heart against the fear of dying alone. Should I so die, I still hold within me the unending grace of your love, and the everlasting comfort of your devotion.

Last night I dreamed I was alone by a darkened fountain, and beheld you as a fluttering dove. It spoke with your voice, and reached into my soul and said you loved me still . . .

Oh Jim . . . dwell on me in your heart and carry me across the dark waters—far from my solitary distress—so that in your arms I might find the joy of sweet surrender. Until then, I shall hold on hope—for to inhale the breath of your tender kiss—is the dying wish of your loving wife,

Suzannah.

Breaking Away

After reading Suzannah's letter over and over again, hoping against hope there was something in it I misunderstood, I finally realized that my worst fears had come to pass. Now the long silences made sense: Suzannah and Dimmis wanted to spare us the horrible news their loving hearts had to deliver!

As I held the precious letter to my heart, pressing it to my talisman, I could almost *feel* her life force ebbing, and I became desperate to return home. The cold gray cast of the morning sky increased the depth of my depression, while a singular thought seeped from my heart into my brain—my life was slowly ending—yet I was still *alive*.

Indeed, considering the cruel fate that awaited my Suzannah, I was determined to see Morgan and *demand* a discharge—although at that moment I was debilitated by weakness. As heartache seared across my chest, my stomach was so hollow, it felt like my insides were missing. My hands trembled and shook, as the very idea of confronting Morgan profoundly unnerved me.

Zeb had left early for the smithy to fire up. So not wishing to drag him into my private hell, I went directly to Morgan's quarters to beg entry. There I met Lewis, the same aide who witnessed my disasterous induction into Morgan's command. After I requested an audience with Morgan, he escorted me toward the shelter. His reptilian eyes turned sinister as he motioned me in, and as I passed, he laughed derisively and resumed his post.

Morgan was seated at his desk, examining what looked to be a map. I could see the markings for the Hessians and British camps, just as we had described them. I realized then that he'd taken our findings seriously and recorded the information we'd given him. Knowing that I'd provided this valuable service helped bolster my resolve for this confrontation.

I saluted him first, and said, "Sir, I must request a leave."

"You sick, Walker?" he inquired, not looking up.

"No, sir, I am well. It's my *wife* . . . *she* is sick."

Morgan finally lifted his head and looked me in the eyes. "And you would like to go home and take *care* of her? Is *that* what you're saying, Walker?"

"Yes, sir."

Morgan stood to his full height, and suddenly barked, "What is it with you puling nanny goats . . . that you need to go home for the same godforsaken reason . . . that amounts to a hill of sheeiiit in a flowerbed?"

As he stepped in front of me, he started pacing. "I have 578 men in my division, and of those, only 374 are *active*—the others are *sick*, or so they *say*. They don't ask for or get any leave because, by God, they are here to *fight*! So you come along, and whine to *me*, that because of your *wife*, *you've* got to run home!"

Morgan shook his head and sarcastically added, "What do you think I *am*, Walker? Do you take me for a damned fool? Your motive is hardly unique or credible, and I'll be damned if I know what it truly is, but I think in the face of coming engagements, your liver has turned *yellow* and you want *out*!"

"That's not *true*!" I vehemently retorted, placing Suzannah's letter upon his desk. "Read *her own words*, sir; and then I beg you to reconsider your position—*sir*!"

Morgan took up the letter, and my stomach wretched at the thought of him even *touching* something Suzannah had touched. I felt her purity being violated as he fingered it roughly, squinting to read the pleading message from a dying wife.

After a few moments, he tossed it back and flatly declared. "You *dare* present me with *this*, while I cannot spare a single *man*? Walker, *half* my command is *out* of action and so is half this damned *army*!

I *cannot* let you go! We need *every* able-bodied man for the conflict to *come*."

I wanted to choke the life out of him, but I was no match for his strength. At all events I would probably be shot if I lay a finger on him—no matter what the outcome.

Finally, in a fit of despair and frustration I blurted out, "You, sir, are a crass, uncultured, unfeeling, heartless, witless ass!"

Striding up to me and standing such that his chin nearly touched mine, he bellowed, "Why you goddamned sniveling, impertinent little *worm*! Don't you *dare* shovel your caterwauling excuses at *me*! Men like you will do *anything* to avoid confrontation with impending danger!"

"How *dare* you treat this with such *disrespect*!" I shouted back at him, holding up Suzannah's letter between us like a protective shield. "Will the loss of *one man* make such a *difference* to this army, sir?" I asked, attempting to reason with this monstrous beast. "It's not as if I have contributed *nothing* in my time as a soldier. I have selflessly given much already, including *that* . . ." I said, pointing to the map.

Morgan's hot breath was redolent with offensive odors as he continued his maniacal tirade. "I still find your *infatuation* with your *paramour* rather *excessive*, Walker! Although she is unwell, the fact still remains that I am *shorthanded* going into this next engagement. I *do* expect to see a singular change in your attitude right *now*, Walker . . . because I need *every* last goddamned man."

He paused and then angrily hissed, "After that battle, you can do whatever *you* damned well *please*, for all I care. But until *then*, *I* am still in command—and this discussion is *closed*, soldier! Your request is denied! Now *get* back to your damned smithy and do *something* to *help* this *godforsaken* army!"

Turning toward the opening he yelled, "*Lewis*, get your ass in here!"

Lewis came in and stood silently while saluting, after which Morgan acknowledged his salute. Pointing at me, he then asked, "Do *you* really think he means what he says, Lewis?"

Lewis, whose reptilian jaw muscles throbbed continuously, hesitated and finally said, "That letter is a ruse, sir—we are short handed as it is! I say enough with this endless palavering, sir."

Seething with rage, I saluted Morgan, and as I stormed out past Lewis, I heard Morgan rumble, "Lewis, I *detest* these damned people of *feeling*—they are the most abominable of mortals because they take everything so damned *seriously!*"

INSIDE MY TENT, I paced like a caged animal. My fixation on returning home became an unnatural force that completely overwhelmed me . . . driving me by pure instinct—to desperately hold in my arms during her fatal illness . . . the one I loved more than life.

My teeth chattered as I again lost control of my nerves. Shuffling and muttering, I stormed about within the tent, and with my mind in chaos, I considered my options of a way to escape.

The tent flap suddenly folded back and Zeb lumbered in. "What in hell happened to *you*, Jim? Pull yourself together, man—you look like you're about to be *hanged!*"

Without a word, I handed him Suzannah's letter. As he read it, he looked increasingly downcast and fell silent for a time.

"I'm so *sorry*, Jim . . . I can hardly believe it. Tell me what to do," he said softly.

"*Morgan* didn't believe it either! He will *not* grant me leave to help her die. She will die *alone*, Zeb! I *cannot* let her go out of this world without me at her side."

Shaking his head in disgust, Zeb kicked the dirt as he blurted, "Why that goddamned, head-bustin', liver-carvin', cob-swipin' son of *Belial!*"

Despite my anger, I smiled at the predictability of Zeb's reaction—its familiarity was comforting—because at least *he* was normal.

"You ain't thinkin' of *desertin'*, are you?" Zeb said carefully, with a look of deep concern.

"I don't know *what* to do!" I cried out in frustration. "All I know is that every moment I delay . . . is a moment closer to her death . . ."

Choking back tears, I added, "I have fought and nearly *died* for this *cause* of ours. But no matter how grand it may be, Zeb, as God is my witness, I will *not* let my poor wife wither away and *die alone* without me at her side!"

Without waiting to hear Zeb's reply, I took the letter, left the tent and headed out to get Winnie.

WARMED BY THE fire outside his headquarters, I waited nearly the entire night before General Washington could finally see me. While I sat there idle, I read Suzannah's letter repeatedly, while the imagery of our lives floated before me in fine detail. I refused to believe that they were merely treasures of the past . . . and now, there would be no more to come. I still held hope that Doc's diagnosis was wrong, that she had a terrible cold, and if only I could be at her side, she would fully recover. After all, our love had conquered everything fate had thrown against us . . . but now, could the sweet innocence of a dreamer's hope do likewise?

"The general will see you now," shook me from my musings. Indeed, it felt disorienting to return to the present, because for the briefest moment—I had forgotten where I was or why I came.

I soon found myself standing humbly before the familiar desk of General Washington. As the flickering shadows from his desk lanterns danced upon my face, a shuffling occurred from behind the wall, and the general finally stepped in.

"Good morning, Scout Walker," he said, sounding pleased to see me. With a slight bow, he smiled and extended his hand to shake mine. "My aide-de-camp says you have a matter of great importance to discuss with me. How may I be of service to you?"

On the verge of tears, I couldn't speak, but merely handed him Suzannah's heartrending letter.

As he read it, I watched his eyes as they crossed the page, taking in the delicately written sorrow . . . and saw them droop as he placed the letter on his desk.

Looking at me gravely, the general said in low tones, "It grieves me to hear of such sorrow, expressed so poignantly, so bravely. Your wife is frightened . . . and she needs you. Are you going to her?"

"I cannot *go* to her, sir! Colonel Morgan will not *release* me because of the shortage of men. In refusing me, he condemns her to a solitary death, a cruelty beyond bearing. I cannot fathom his unwillingness to let me return home to ease her final days."

In desperation, I added, "With all due respect, sir, what he's doing is *evil*."

Washington looked thoughtful before he replied. "Son, Colonel Morgan is a great and capable soldier. He is also a friend of mine. He is *not* an evil man . . . he is a *warrior* . . . and *true* warriors know *little* of the human heart and its affairs. As such, they have no frame of reference to judge a case such as yours."

The general rose from his desk and softly asked, "Walker, may I divert a brief moment—to *share* with you some little things that life has taught me about the heart?"

His voice was so soothing, and wanting to hear more of this man's inner self, I simply nodded in veneration.

"Heartbreaking struggles occur in many more places than on the battlefield, Mr. Walker. Most occur in the human heart . . . *far* from where one can outwardly determine an inward defeat . . . or a victory. In my youth, I twice proposed to a young maiden I *dearly* loved, and I was twice rejected . . . I can *relate* to sorrow, Mr. Walker.

Turning away, he approached a small sideboard and removed two glasses. From a chest below it, he lifted a crystal decanter containing an amber liquid. While he poured two drinks, he continued, "In general, Mr. Walker, if one casts aside the false mantles of propriety, manners and societal behavior, the essence of a man's soul is all that remains. Seldom do we ever encounter the fabric of our true selves. We *think* we know ourselves, but do we *really*?"

The clinking of the crystal stopper in the decanter sounded pleasing. He then confessed, "I've had but *two experiences* in my entire life that dragged my essence forth . . . to lay it *bare*, exposing it to those around me, *despite* my intentions to protect it. For me, the *first* of these experiences was *war*. I was *tested* during battle, and my true nature was exposed at the instantaneous moment of truth . . . when a musket was *aimed* at me, or a bayonet *thrust* at me, or a *sword* descended toward my neck . . . *all* brought about that flashing moment of realization that: *This is who I am . . . and am I worthy of survival?*"

Turning toward me, he leaned against the sideboard to add, "And the decision is made *within* a heartbeat . . . to instinctively *fight*, or perish. It is *then* that good men become desperately evil. Evil men become benevolent. Brave men are sometimes reduced to cowards, and cowards sometimes rise to the occasion . . . becoming great soldiers who fear *nothing*."

"Nearly *all* men can stand such tests of adversity, Mr. Walker . . . I have done it . . . *you* have done it . . . the fact that you are here, *proves* it. But if you truly wish to test the strength and purity of a man's soul and character . . . you grant him *love*."

Bringing the glasses, he then came before me and softly added, "Ever remember the road to Hell is laid with good intentions. As such, despite what Colonel Morgan *wants*, *I* have decided that under careful consideration of the facts presented in your case, the individual *need* must take precedence."

I stood up and stared at him then, struggling to absorb the meaning of his words.

Washington handed me a glass, and held his up to me. "You have a *kind* and generous soul, Mr. Walker. Now, go *home* . . . and *tend* to your ailing wife."

I could barely contain my joy. "Thank you, sir, I will!" I said with as much gravity as I could muster.

Then the two of us drank together.

After we finished our drinks, the general returned to his chair. He placed a sheet of paper in front of him, and dipping his quill, began scratching away.

Having time to reflect on what he'd said, I finally asked, "Sir, you said there were *two* experiences in your life that revealed your true self . . . the first was *war* . . . but what was the *other*, if I may ask?"

Handing me my discharge orders, Washington smiled benevolently, and raising his brows, he softly whispered, "*Marriage . . .*"

General Washington's discharge included the provision that Zeb was to accompany me home. It granted us unfettered passage through the colonies, unmolested by any colonial militias who might question our allegiance, or force us into their ranks.

When I returned to our tent, Zeb wasn't there, so I checked the smithy, and found him welding rifle barrels, sweating profusely and in no mood for conversation.

"By the sons of *Beelzebub*, where in hell have you *been*, Jim?"

"I went to see General Washington. I had to wait all night for him," I said as I held up his orders.

"Does that mean we can go home without Morgan's permission?" he asked hopefully, laying down the barrel and mallet.

"Yes, it *does*, Zeb . . . he was everything that Morgan was not," I softly replied.

Removing his apron and donning his great coat, Zeb solemnly added, "Slumber is tied up over yonder by our tent . . . so let's get outta here."

Walking toward our tent we encountered Lewis, Morgan's repugnant aide-de-camp, who casually demanded, "Here *here*! Where are *you* two going? Why aren't you at your *smithy*? I shall *report* this to Colonel Morgan, and he will deal with you *severely*!

Zeb strode up to him and immediately punched him in the face, bursting his nose. Lewis staggered back, cupping his hands to catch the blood. Taking Lewis by the collar, Zeb dragged him behind the row of tents and began to rant, "Listen *here* you throne sniffing *rump swab*, I've had *enough* of you and your back stabbing antics! When a woman writes her husband to say she's *dyin'*, by God she ain't writin' a story for her *children* . . . and she sure in hell ain't *lyin'*! So next time somebody's wife tells her husband she's *dyin'*, mebbe you will *listen* a little *harder*—and keep your butt sniffing *nose* out of Morgan's ass!

Lifting Lewis high into the air, Zeb tossed him into the camp's open latrine, which swallowed him whole. Washing the blood from his hands in a nearby water bucket, Zeb finally added, "We ain't *part* of this damned army any longer, Lewis! So you have a damned good time stewing about it in the poo hole!"

Lewis thrashed and spluttered as a few men came to watch him struggle in the effluent—but not *one* rendered any aid.

Seeing that Lewis' fate was in good order, Zeb mounted Slumber and as we rode out of camp, he sang out, "*Bring, bring, bring on the wenches* . . ." Suddenly he stopped, and leaning toward me he confidentially rumbled, "You know, Jim, I hope we never have to look upon that lizard faced bastard ever *again* . . . he *lied* about Suzannah's letter . . . and the one thing I can't *stand* in life . . . is a lizard faced, concave chested, *rump* swabbin' *liar*."

The World Between

hen we finally arrived, our poor horses were bespattered with mud and nearly overcome with exhaustion. We entered the tavern immediately and Dimmis was the first to see us.

"Thank *God* you have *come*!" she said, choking back her tears.

I grabbed her arms and gasped hoarsely, "*Where is she?*"

"Upstairs in your bedchamber! *Jim*. The end is near . . ."

Without waiting to hear another word, I pelted up the stairs two at a time, calling out, "Suzannah! Suzannah! I'm *here*, Suzannah!"

When I reached the threshold of the door, I stood there panting to catch my breath. I looked into the room and beheld my beautiful Suzannah . . . lying motionless upon our bed. A solitary white carnation rested upon her breast, her delicate hands holding its stem. Her still luxurious hair had been carefully combed, and then crowned with a garland of pink and white carnations . . . she always wore them on special occasions.

My heart ached to see her so fearfully thin and wasted . . . but that dear face—oh, what loveliness *still*! Reverentially approaching my sleeping darling, I noticed her breathing was shallow and labored, but still, she looked peaceful and serene.

I tenderly removed her coverlet, and choked at the sight . . . for she was wearing her wedding dress. Dimmis' halting voice behind me explained, "Suzannah was *sure* you would come in time . . . and her final wish was that you would see her as your loving *bride* . . . *not* as a consumptive ruin . . ."

My voice cracked as I heard myself utter, "It's just like *her* to think of *me*—at the very hour of her passing . . ." And like a knight before his lady, I knelt at her bedside, and placing my hand upon her heart, I sadly whispered, "My *dear* Suzannah . . ."

"She was awake yesterday morning and desperately tried to hold on." Dimmis said solemnly. "But Doc says she fell into this dark sleep . . . the sleep of the world between . . . that knows no awakening."

I nodded, as she started sobbing and retreated downstairs.

I got up then, and reaching below her emaciated form, in silent tears I gently lifted her from the bed. The wedding dress hid the wasted husk that once was, is still, and always shall be, my reason for living. She seemed to weigh even less than Ainsley, who thankfully remained at the Ellingwood home, sheltered from witnessing her mother's decline.

I carried Suzannah downstairs to her father's rocker, where I gently sat. While I cradled us together in the same way she'd always loved, the wedding dress flowed gracefully over its arms and onto the floor.

Although her face was stark white, her hair remained as gleaming and soft as it had ever been. But her *eyes* . . . the loving pathways to her heart and healing soul . . . were now closed to my world.

While I sat rocking my adored wife of eight years and gazed into her dear face, I remembered the many times she had loved me . . . how her eyes looked so deeply into mine, how her lips felt as they covered me with thousands of kisses, how her arms felt as they clasped me tightly in her loving embrace . . .

But when I remembered that day of our first meeting . . . and her beautiful inviting smile; my heart burned from grief, anger and frustration. My old enemy, resentment, and its poisonous tears poured from my soul, and fell upon Suzannah's face.

I prayed to Mother's spirit for solace . . . and then asked God to guide my lost soul . . .

Kissing Suzannah's face everywhere, I tenderly whispered her name, begging her to awaken for just one moment . . . so she would know that I'd returned for her.

I was answered by deathly silence.

In panic, I gazed into the shadows of the lowering sun, and in heartbroken agony I finally wailed, "Oh, God in Heaven, if you are a God of *anything*, give me a *sign* she *knows* I'm here! She was *my life*! *Why* do you *take* her from me! If you need a soul, take *me* instead—take *me*!"

In a fit of desperation to capture any divine power I could, I tore my sacred talisman from my neck and pressed it to her heart. While I held it there, in broken voiced pleadings I begged, "In the name of *God*, Suzannah . . . *please* come *back* to me!"

Again, tomblike silence.

As I rocked her, I quietly prayed: "Dear God, if you are any-where, I beseech thee to hear me . . . do not *do* this to me . . . *not again*! She was my guardian angel by *your* good graces. She was all that remained in my life . . . after *you* took my parents . . ."

When I gently kissed her still lips, my tears rolled down her cheeks, and finally settled in the corners of her mouth.

Sam and Fanny silently came into the parlor, along with Dimmis and Zeb. There they stood, holding hands in unison, and softly prayed.

Upon seeing their quiet, loving support, I took a lock of Suzan-nah's hair, kissed it and dabbed my tears from her face, when she suddenly *coughed*! A wheezing, wracking unmistakable cough!

Encouraged, I shook her, imploring, "*Suzannah*! Suzannah! *Wake up*! It's *Jim*! Dearest angel, I am *here* . . . and I cannot live without you *knowing*!"

I waited for what seemed like an eternity, but there was no response, not even a hint of another cough.

But I couldn't give up. Pressing the talisman into her chest once more, again I tearfully implored, "*Suzannah*, for the love of *God*, I am *begging* you . . . from this world to the world between . . . please come *back* to me . . . It's *Jim*! It's *Jim*!"

Again, my helpless tears fell into her hair, and slowly rolled onto her carnations.

Plucking a wet carnation from her hair, I put it to her lips while desperately pleading, "I am *here* angel, just as you predicted . . . *please* remember, darling . . . you said when the leaves fall . . . we shall be reunited . . ."

No response.

I lifted my face toward heaven and wailed to God once more in seething anger, "*Please*, dear God in *heaven*, grant me *one more minute* of her love! Please grant this . . . or I *swear* I shall never darken a church door again! Through her entire *life*, she was the perfect embodiment of *goodness* and *love* . . . You *owe* her something for *that* at least, *damn* you!"

Silence.

In a final fit of defiant blasphemy, I raged on at God: "*Then damn you to hell! She was your masterpiece! Yet you have taken her! Are you listening? If you will not listen, then there is no heaven, and THERE IS NO GOD!*"

I was finished: I had nothing left.

With repentant sobs of hopeless defeat, I finally lay my cheek to hers . . . and as I clung to her hair, I sobbed to her golden heart, "*Oh, my love* . . . my *soul* is dying with you . . . I can feel it ebbing away with yours . . ."

Just then, a wave of inexplicable warmth enveloped me . . . for through the parlor window came a brilliant orange light . . . and once again, Suzannah coughed.

As its brilliant beams touched Suzannah's face, her eyes suddenly opened!

"Praise God, praise *God* . . ." echoed from Sam, Fanny, Zeb and Dimmis—and were followed by thumpings of their knees upon the floor as they stared reverently at Suzannah.

Her eyes were open, but gone was the glow of life . . . she was already halfway through the world between . . . and *I* could not help her.

Caressing her face, I kissed her and softly asked, "Suzannah? Suzannah? Darling, can you *hear* me?"

She answered in a ghostly distant whisper, "Jim . . . is that *you*? I cannot . . . *see* you . . ."

My throat ached as I choked out, "*Yes*, my God, Suzannah . . . it's *me* . . . I have *come* to be with you, angel."

I retrieved the talisman and pressing it lightly into her palm, I gently closed her fingers around it. She clenched it feebly and held it to her heart . . . and then she *smiled* . . . oh, that beautiful reassuring smile! She knew! She *knew* I was there!

"Darling . . . oh, *darling* . . ." I anxiously whimpered as my tears, like my soul, fell in broken pieces upon her sightless face.

"Jim, your presence comforts me . . . but your mother . . . beckons me . . ."

"*NO!*" I screamed in desperation. "Do *not* go to her—*please*, Suzannah!"

She tried to lift her head, but hadn't the strength to do so. "Hold me . . . Jim," she whispered weakly. "Rock . . . me . . ."

And so I rocked her, while gently kissing her forehead, her lips, her cheeks and her hair.

She gave a sudden rasping cough, and as the consumptive fluid choked her, a series of deep repeated hacks left her gasping for short breaths of air.

I was frightened. I was losing her! She was passing!

With the next cough, a trickle of viscous blood started from her mouth . . . so I held her even closer and kissed her bloodstained lips. And she returned my kiss with all the strength and love she could finally muster . . .

While stroking her cheek, in a halting whisper I cried out from the depths of my broken heart, "God, how I *love* you, Suzannah . . . my *love* . . . my *life* . . . my *blessed angel!*"

Her eyes welled with sightless tears as between short gasps for air, she whispered, "God will protect you . . . as will I . . . my dearest husband . . . but you *must* let me go . . ."

On the verge of insanity I cried out, "Suzannah . . . no . . .*no* . . ."

Came the holy reply, "*Yes* . . . sweet death . . . Jim . . . I love you . . . so . . . mu . . ."

Her mouth opened once more to speak, but was silent . . . and with that, the talisman dropped to the floor, her dying head relaxed, and my loving wife breathed no more.

The sun was now gone, my love was now grief . . . and its name was Death.

I MUST HAVE fallen asleep with Suzannah in my arms, because my next experience of consciousness was the embrace of a comforting arm around my shoulder.

It was Sam Ellingwood.

I raised my head, and upon seeing Suzannah's hair clinging to my tear dampened face, he softly brushed it aside with a father's loving touch . . . and kissed my forehead.

Kneeling down to gaze reverently at Suzannah, he arranged her hair and longingly kissed her cheek. Then, without a word, he rose and left the room, leaving us alone in the darkness.

I continued to rock my Suzannah as I watched the moon-light inch its way through the parlor window . . . until it graced the lifeless face of God's newest angel. My only thought was how delighted Suzannah would be with the particular brilliance of this full moon . . . for once again . . . it was Midnight Blue.

Feeling resigned and repentant at last, I longingly gazed at the heavens and easily spotted my first star. But instead of *wishing* upon Midnight Blue, I murmured a grateful prayer of thanks to God . . . for granting me those final moments of her love . . . for upon reflection, it was indeed a *miracle*, and only Suzannah could have ever done it.

An Angel's Message

n the light of Midnight Blue, with Suzannah still in my arms, I laid my cheek to her silent heart. After lifting her hair to cover my face, from beneath its sheltering softness, I murmured urgent prayers for divine guidance.

Once again here was death . . . the death of my marriage, my love and my home life. Yet against death I still had Ainsley, Suzannah's precious gift—a living heart treasure, blessed with her mother's beauty and warmth. Suzannah would wish me to carry on for myself and for Ainsley. But as I promised her long ago, there would never be a second wife . . . for the beauty of marriage now lay in my arms—and there would never be better.

As my mind wandered in helpless confusion, I suddenly felt a presence in the room and saw Dimmis at the door. I sat up and nodded for her to come forward. She kissed my cheek, and quietly placing a gentle hand on my back, she softly whispered, "Jim, I found this under Suzannah's pillow . . . it's for you."

Looking up at her quizzically, I asked, "How do you know? What is it?"

"It's a letter she wrote on her deathbed. Oh Jim," her voice suddenly cracked, then tapered off in sobs. "What a piteous sight . . . she was so *feeble* and *shaky* . . . but she was determined to make it her last act—while she still had the strength.

Dimmis knelt to stroke Suzannah's hair, and then longingly kissed her cheek. With silent tears she placed the sealed letter upon Suzannah's heart . . . as though she was making an offering to God. She wiped her tears and softly added, "I'll leave you now . . . so you can treasure her final heart feelings . . ."

Opening the letter, I saw in the moonlight the familiar but now unsteady script of my beloved.

My dearest James,

My heart is breaking because your living flower is dying without you, and I am helpless to stop the advancing curtain of death. Somehow, if God will permit it, I will send you my love from beyond the grave. I shall watch and wait for you . . . remember that love never dies . . . only the flesh.

Do you remember how I always said I was your guardian angel? Now, very soon, I shall more truly fulfill that honor. So when shadows fall and day is done, look up into heaven's stars and you shall find me . . . think of me, dear husband, and I shall be there to guide your heart.

I promise when your time comes, I shall find you, and lead you into His world, a paradise where our love, happiness and tranquility shall be everlasting. So, my loving husband, do not fear for me, and keep in mind that our parting now . . . is only temporary . . .

A final kiss here, darling: **X** *. . . it looks small, but it's so big in my heart.*

As I fly to memory . . .

I remain your loving and devoted wife,
Suzannah

Numb with grief, I pressed her precious letter to my heart, draped her hair back over my head, and cried myself to sleep.

From the Heart

 woke to a bright and sunny October day, a jarring contrast with the circumstances of my real world. I still remained in our rocker with the love of my life nestled in my arms. Aye, so it was *not* an endless nightmare after all . . . yet despite my final sleep with Suzannah, I felt exhausted and totally drained.

Sadly gazing upon her face, with a trembling finger I tidied the still seeping blood that remained upon her lips . . . sacred blood from our final kiss . . . as she bravely left her beautiful life behind.

Remembering father's private act with mother, I reverently placed my blood stained finger into my mouth, closed my eyes, and lovingly savored the remaining essence of her beautiful short life . . . she would now ever be a part of me . . . unto my death.

Again rocking her, through longing tears I stared at her portrait next to mother's in the great room, and as I cried in abject silence, I contemplated how to carry on without her. It seemed not fair to blithely go about as though she was on a visit to shortly return.

The silence was deafening.

"And now we are two . . ." I said aloud, laying my head back to ponder our future. How like father I sounded!

A sturdy knock came from the door, and when it opened, Sam and Doc entered my house of sorrow, to reverently stand before me. With tearful pleading eyes, all I could say was, "That I could dream myself into *her* world . . . though I should never awaken . . . just to take her in my arms once more . . . and *feel* her love!"

And then I broke down, sobbing inconsolably.

Without a word, Doc lifted Suzannah out of my arms and placed her on the sofa. Then Sam helped me to rise, since by now I had lost all feeling in my legs. The two of them supported me as they guided me into the kitchen, and we all took seats around the table.

Leaning forward, Sam placed his hand upon mine, and squeezing it, reassuringly said, "Jim, Doc thinks you should come to live with *us* for a while . . . at least until after the burial."

I said nothing, but nodded my assent.

"I made her a special coffin, Jim . . . it was at *her* request. While you were at war, she knew she was dying . . . and wished to see it before she passed."

"Did she?" was all I could say.

"You cannot imagine how difficult it was . . ." Sam's voice broke then, as he tried unsuccessfully to choke back tears, "to create a *coffin* . . . to *bury* my own daughter . . . my *youngest* daughter!"

It was the first time I ever saw him cry. I could not imagine what strength it must have taken as a final act of love . . . to build a coffin for his still-living child . . . knowing she would sleep forever within it.

A LITTLE WHILE later, Reverend Metcalf joined us in the kitchen, first offering his condolences to Sam, and then—as I stood to greet him—pressing me to his heart.

"I cannot fully express the *depth* of my sorrow at your loss, Jim. It is a tragedy for all of us who love Suzannah . . ."

As we broke apart, I said, "Thank you, Reverend . . . and God bless you for being here." My heart leapt to hear him speak of her that way, for it reminded me that she was precious to so many in our community. The notion inspired me with the urge to write a eulogy in her honor—not for me alone—but for all the folks who loved her.

"Jim," he said, "I do not wish to be indelicate, but we have arranged the coffin in Sam's parlor, and it's ready to receive our Suzannah . . . whenever *you* decide the time is right . . ."

I teared up at him calling her "our" Suzannah. Thinking it best not to wait, the four of us carried Suzannah's body over to the Ellingwood's home.

Her coffin lay in the parlor, and it had to be the high point of Sam's artistry: a gleaming masterpiece of solid mahogany, inlaid with beautiful white panels of curly maple. These in turn, were inlaid with highly figured rosewood. Such was its breathtaking elegance; it seemed tragic to bury it in the ground.

In short, it was a beautiful frame designed to hold our Suzannah. We gently lay her within it, and she was never so beautiful.

It took me by surprise when Suzannah's sisters came into the parlor, and without a single word, took me into their sheltering arms. How comforting it felt to be surrounded and held by them. After spending some time in their company, Ainsley came bounding down the stairs, and upon seeing the coffin and her mother lying within, she slowly approached it and softly announced, "Mama is an *angel* now . . ."

Lydia kneeled before her and giving Ainsley a hug, she softly asked, "Now how do you know *that*, little one?"

As all four sisters stepped back to hear her reply, Ainsley looked up at Lydia with wide eyed innocence, and happily confessed, "Mama *told* me . . . last *night* . . . right *here* . . ."

She was pointing to her heart . . .

Sam informed me that arrangements for the funeral had already been made, and it would be in two days. So there was much I had to do.

While Suzannah was being prepared for burial, Dimmis and I cleaned the tavern and closed its doors to business until further notice . . . that is—until I could bring myself to move forward and resume my life—without Suzannah.

We were not prepared for the crowds who came to see Suzannah. As she lay in repose in her coffin at the Ellingwoods, friends, neighbors, traders and merchants . . . *all* came to honor her and waited hours in line to do so.

I remained with the Ellingwoods, and Fanny insisted that I stay in Suzannah's old room and sleep in her bed. She said she wished this for me so that I would be as "close to her as I could be in this world." Having planted that thought, I found it particularly sweet to sleep in the bedchamber of her youth, and rest my cheek upon her pillow.

The time passed in a whirlwind of activity, and the day of the funeral arrived.

Doc arrived in his surrey to drive me to church. The pallbearers loaded Suzannah's coffin into the back of a wagon, now dressed as a hearse. The short ride to the church put me in mind of the time when I first heard her—singing in Gaelic and playing so beautifully at the organ.

At my request, the service was to be short and sweet—like Suzannah herself. After Reverend Metcalf's homily, there would be a humble thank you from me, and thusly from Suzannah, to the village we loved so well.

After everyone filed into the church, Doc, Sam, Reverend Metcalf and I bore Suzannah to the front, resting her on a platform there.

I sat in the front left-hand box, with Doc, Sam and Fanny. Suzannah's sisters and their husbands sat behind us. I was lost in a world of my own . . . reviewing the notes for my eulogy while the organ piped a sweet lullaby. I wondered if Suzannah could somehow see or hear this panoply in her honor, and thus ease her heavenly burdens, if there were any.

When the music ended, Reverend Metcalf stepped up to the pulpit and began his sermon.

"I am unhappy at the occasion, but happy to see all of you here—to share the love in your hearts for Suzannah and Jim Walker. I think I speak for us all when I say, that the loss of our Suzannah is the most untimely loss this village has ever sustained. Here before us lies the earthly remains of a gentle and loving spirit so unique— that finding the words to do her justice—is a most difficult task . . . but I shall *try*."

After pausing to inhale deeply, he continued. "Suzannah Elling- wood Walker was a beacon in our lives . . . a steady quiet light, ever guiding us to grace and goodness. She touched many hearts to show us what is beautiful and true."

The reverend stepped down and then over to the coffin to kneel beside it. He lovingly placed his hands upon it as he "spoke" to Suzannah.

"Suzannah . . . *dearest* child of God, we all felt blessed by your loving spirit. You came among us with a quiet and gentle tenderness . . . that enveloped us . . . like a comforting summer breeze."

He then stood, and placing his hand over the area of her heart, he continued. "The beauty of nature was your soul . . . you breathed it, revered it, and gave it to us all . . . through love, hospitality, caring for the sick and wounded, and even playing our organ in this church. And so, we now humbly say our reluctant goodbyes to you . . . gentle creature of God . . . and undoubtedly, His newest angel."

Reverend Metcalf's voice suddenly wavered, as he fought back tears. "How *I* will *miss* you, dear child! That *God* shall ever keep thee in the warmest corner of His heart . . . is the loving and final wish of your humble pastor . . . Amen!"

As the reverend rose and dabbed at his eyes, snuffling could be heard throughout the congregation. When he returned to the pulpit, he announced in an unsteady voice, "And now, Jim Walker wants to honor his and *our* Suzannah."

Still agonizing over what to say as I stepped up to the pulpit, I stuffed the notes in my pocket and decided for *her* sake—to simply speak from my *heart*—just as the reverend did.

Bravely gazing across the tear stained faces of the congregation, I looked aloft and lovingly whispered, "*For you darling!*" and so began.

"Thank you, Reverend Metcalf—and thank you *all* for being here today."

"Suzannah was so many things to so many people: a devoted wife, mother, daughter, sister and friend. She was also my guardian angel, and I am alive today *only* because of *her.* She possessed a heart of gold *and* a sterling character . . . because the qualities of beauty, peace and piety flourished under the influence of her generous spirit. She was God's little masterpiece.

"Ever since her arrival in Walker's Cove, Suzannah has unselfishly been our friend. Not even five feet tall, she helped carry us *all* through some *very* difficult times—uniting us so we might have the strength to survive adversity—as well as the horrors of war."

Gesturing toward her coffin, I choked up, but still managed to go on. "Suzannah lays before us in this little coffin of wood . . . the queen of hearts. As my wife, Suzannah was sacred to me . . . she was truly my gift from God. She could weave a spell of enchantment and make all the hard things in life disappear.

"Her sweet smile and tender love lifted our hearts . . . and when I was at war without her, her endearing letters always warmed my heart with cozy scenes of home. When she sang while playing her pianoforte in our tavern, or the organ in this church, the purity of her voice moved the souls of those who heard it . . . and were brought to tears by its ethereal beauty.

"You all know us . . . and you all know about the losses I've suffered in my life: my mother, my father and our firstborn, Fanny. But there is no grief so bitter as that of losing my Suzannah.

"Her soul has now gone to Heaven, where existence is ethereal and eternal . . . a place far greater than we can possibly imagine. I believe we shall love again in her world, *beyond* the narrow confines of the grave. Meanwhile, as we all move forward in this life, perhaps we will *see* her warm smile in the sunlight, and *feel* her quiet love in the moonlight, and ever remember her gentle demeanor and sweetness. I was privileged to be the recipient of her divine and selfless love, to live in her heavenly sacred domain . . . so warm, comforting and fleeting . . . as was her virtuous life. Suzannah once told me that as long as someone is kept in your heart, they are never really dead. And just like with everything else she ever told me . . . I truly believe her . . . and I hope you do too . . ."

I returned to my box with silent tears and her name upon my lips. While the organ started up again, Reverend Metcalf blessed us, and announced that the coffin would now be carried out, and everyone should follow thereafter.

Draping a comforting arm about me, Doc whispered, "Wait for me here, Jim. I'll come back for you. Let 'em all out first . . ."

I nodded, and then shivered as I realized that the service was suddenly over.

The Gathering

s I hoisted myself into Doc's surrey, I silently blessed him for tending to my family with such care all these years. He had delivered my father, myself, and Ainsley—and nearly all the Walker's Cove babies. He'd also had the unfortunate task of pronouncing many of them dead, including his own. During those dark, dark days after my parents died, he'd saved me. For what purpose I wondered . . . now that Suzannah is being put to rest.

Doc cracked his whip and in silence, we headed to the graveyard. As we trundled along, I thought about what lay ahead for Ainsley and me. Death is forever, but life goes on. Our lives as we knew them was over, but Ainsley is my living treasure given by Suzannah, which I can still hold and love . . . but it was Suzannah's beautiful *soul* I would truly miss, and shall never have again . . . for that now belonged to God.

I noticed tears running down Doc's aged cheeks, and yet, he drove on, saying nothing. Despite Suzannah's absence, I could still sense heart feelings, and I *knew* Doc wished he had died before we had to bury Suzannah.

"Are you all right, Doc?" I asked.

"Hell, no!" he replied, sniffing loudly.

"I'm *so* sorry," I said sadly, at that moment feeling worse for him than for myself.

"Jim?"

"Yes, Doc?"

Looking at me with watery eyes, he sniffed again and said, "You were *right* back there—she was indeed God's little masterpiece."

"Yes, I know she was . . ." I whispered, and choking on my tears, I bitterly lamented, "And there will *never* be another like her!"

"No, there won't." he sadly confirmed, and we rode on in silence the rest of the way.

WHEN WE ARRIVED at the graveyard and pulled up beside the empty hearse, we alighted, with Doc leading the way. As I followed him, I realized the path he had taken was not the right one.

"Doc, *this* isn't the way to the grave."

"No, it's not," he said evenly, and kept walking ahead.

"I don't understand. Where are we going, Doc?"

"Please allow me to tend to a little business up here before we go on. It won't take but a minute, Jim."

"Sure, Doc. I'm not really eager to bury her anyhow."

"Neither am I, son," he replied with a smile, "neither am I . . ."

We trudged from the lower graves toward the top of the hill, and at the summit were two enormous beech trees. Each had a heavily gnarled trunk about five feet in diameter. As we approached the trees, I noticed a small white edifice sheltered below them. It was shaped like a miniature church, complete with Doric columns on either side of the entryway.

Doc halted, and as his eyes brimmed with tears, he pointed his cane toward the little church and said, "Take a look, Jim."

He stayed behind, and as I slowly walked toward the little church, I noticed engraving above its entrance, and approaching the door, I discovered it was not a church, but a mausoleum. It was fashioned from pure-white polished marble, and standing on a granite foundation, it commanded a magnificent view of Walker's Point nestled far below. I also noticed that the entrance was facing west—*precisely* west.

As I read the engraving on the right side of the doorway, I felt my knees weaken. It read thus:

Suzannah Ellingwood Walker
Beloved Wife of James Walker
Born October 18, 1751
Died October 23, 1777

The rest of the space was blank, for that time when I would join her there. On the left side, I saw the following inscription:

Your friends from life,
Remember thy name;
The love in our hearts,
Whispers the same.
We pray God above,
To treasure thy love,
All wishing to see,
His angels with thee.

Her short life was Love

GIVEN BY THE FOLKS OF WALKER'S COVE

I was thunderstruck. It was like a monument to God . . . but it was *hers* . . . and all I could do was keep walking around it, over and over again . . . admiring everything about this testament to Suzannah: the purity of its beauty, the perfection of the site, and most of all, the tribute inscribed for all the ages by those who had given it.

Doc, hobbling up to me, placed his arm around my shoulder and squeezed it. "Well, Jim, how do you like it?"

Through my grateful tears, I stammered, "Doc, it's beautiful . . . just *beautiful*. How . . ." But choked with so much emotion, I could no longer speak.

"We tried to make it a piece of heaven on earth," he said modestly.

The sun was setting, and as its rays angled toward the mausoleum, I walked to the lee side of the hill . . . to gaze in sweet memory upon the point she loved so well. Once there, I fell to my knees, brushing aside cascading tears: before me was Suzannah's wooden coffin—now nested within a casket of polished marble, ready for the trip to her new home.

But more than that, every living soul in Walker's Cove was here—here to honor *her*. I saw Zeb and Dimmis, Steve and Phoebe Abbot, the Merrill brothers, the Barretts, the Lovejoys, the Johnsons, the Lanes, the Woodburys, the Lorings, the Rices and all the Ellingwoods, including all four sisters and their husbands—and my darling Ainsley too!

My brothers-in-law came forward bearing the marble casket and placed it on a scaffold before the mausoleum. The lid was lifted and Sam Ellingwood, placing his arm around my shoulders, escorted me over to peer at the slumbering face of God's newest angel.

I was surprised, and not for the first time, by how beautiful she looked after her sickness. Suzannah, her eyes closed, forever reposing in her wedding dress, with the pink and white carnations in her hair . . . was *still* my darling bride.

I gave one final kiss to her sacred lips and whispered, " "I love you, angel . . ."

Then I stood, and asked Doc and Sam to cover her up, for the sun would soon be gone.

"Not yet, Jim . . ." Sam said. "Watch . . ."

As the sun began to dip beyond the horizon, a glow of iridescent sunlight fell upon my darling Suzannah, fully lighting the way into the deepest part of the mausoleum, from the back wall to the entrance . . . and thence to Walker's Point.

"Remarkable!" I whispered in astonishment.

"You see, Jim," Sam explained, "we oriented the mausoleum such that the sun would do this . . . light her path to glory each and every day . . . forever."

And everyone came up to me, one by one, to embrace me and place a wildflower in her coffin. Suzannah, who asked for nothing in life, received an outpouring of love, respect, honor and eternal remembrance on this day of her burial.

As the crowd gathered around the mausoleum, her little marble casket was carried inside and set upon the altar bearing her name. Finally, the marble lid was fitted into its groove.

On the opposite wall, there was an empty altar bearing my name, where I would rest beside her.

The sun was just about gone, and the tomb was getting dark. After everybody filed out, I kissed the side of her casket where her precious head lay, and softly whispered, "Good night my only wife . . . God keep your golden heart . . . and I shall await your coming . . ."

I stood, and after reverently kissing the casket top, I wiped my eyes and finally turned away. As I left the mausoleum, I halted at the entrance to longingly look back . . . and slowly . . . with aching resignation . . . I closed the Iron Gate upon my dear wife.

After the sexton locked it with a tear in his eye, without a word he handed me the key.

I took it, and finally turning to breathe deeply of the salt-laden air, I gazed upon the magnificent panorama of Walker's Point. From here, she would enjoy the ocean, the rocks and especially the sunsets she loved so well. And while the light of God illuminated her path, she would ever build her air castles—my heart could *feel* it—for she truly *was* His masterpiece . . . and we were *all* grateful to have her.

A Day Without Rain
(*FROM* Jim's Diary)

October 18, 1786

My dearest Suzannah,

Today is your thirty-fifth birthday. I have just visited your little home, and kissed the dear white casket that enshrines your golden heart. It has been nine long years since I last kissed you, and in my heart it is raining.

My dear Suzannah, I feel old before my time . . . yet I have no fear of time. No matter how much rain there is, I know you are with me . . . watching . . . waiting . . . ever my guardian angel.

When the evenings deepen into soft spectral shadows, my thoughts and prayers are all about you, softening my entry into the endless nights without you.

I am here, while you are there in His world. From such a distance, I cannot contrive a better way to love you. My solitary prayers always have meaning . . . but they have the deepest meaning when my heart is lonely and troubled, or when grief is strong upon me from suffering the day's heartbreak without you.

Suzannah, what a sad painful vacancy dwells within my heart, when you, who have loved me and left nothing undone for my happiness, are away . . . for without you I am nowhere . . .

But look, my loving angel!

Our little Ainsley has become the very image of her beautiful mother! Oh, that you could see her! You have come back to me through her face and figure—but she is especially like you in her heart.

She is now fourteen . . . that magic age I well remember, and hold ever so dear; for I see you in her dainty little step, her sweet caring smile, and hear you in her silvery voice! The chestnut hair with a golden sheen . . . and those eyes! God blesses me—for all I see is you!

Her love for her father knows no bounds . . . she does all she can to be the flower of our home, and as such, brings radiant joy to your husband's lonely heart.

Ah! What heavenly rewards! My loving wife, I am falling in love all over again! Shame on me!

Be proud, my guardian angel! What we have wrought in this child of "God's littlest angel" is a faithful copy of the wondrous original. Someday she will go forth to sow her love and spirit amongst those who have yet to know her.

On a beautiful fall morning early last month, a sturdy knock came at the door. Our little Ainsley went to it, and upon opening it, beheld Jonathan Barrett . . . and his handsome young son, Edwin—a good, kind, strapping lad of seventeen years.

Of course, I was delighted to see Jonathan after all these years! But Suzannah! When Ainsley's eyes met Edwin's, I saw in his face that same look I had so long ago! He was mesmerized, totally smitten, and his first words to Ainsley were, "Are you an angel?" And as God is my witness, Suzannah . . . with a broad grin, her reply was, "Not yet!"

How that moment illuminated my heart! How well I remember that sacred day of our first meeting! Oh, what precious moments I relived upon hearing those words exchanged!

Jonathan is moving back to Walker's Cove, and plans to remain here till the end of his days.

Edwin wishes to be a clockmaker's apprentice; and so, after many visits filled with youthful prattle and enquiries, Edwin and Ainsley have found much happy, common ground together.

My darling angel . . . perhaps our love carries forward to the next generation, for today, whilst Jonathan and I revisited our boyhood together, Edwin and Ainsley went off to the point.

Ah, my dearest Suzannah! How the circle of life bestows upon us repeated blessings . . . and now the circle begins anew . . . but that is another story . . . for another time . . .

Evermore your husband,
Jim

End Notes

For those readers who are unfamiliar with our ancestors' customs and possessions during our country's formative years, I offer these few notes to aid your understanding of colonial life as referred to in Walker's Cove.

AIR CASTLES—A common term of Colonial and Victorian times that referred to what we call "day dreams" in modern life.

ATTACHED/ATTACHMENTS—The colonial equivalent of going steady, or in the state of being betrothed.

BEAN HOLE—A large half spherical hole dug in the earth in preparation to make baked beans. The hole was then filled with hardwood, the fire lit, and when the wood was reduced to glowing bed of coals, the prepared bean pot was produced and nestled in the glowing embers. The whole was covered with the remaining coals and buried with loose earth and left to bake overnight. The following day, the pot was unearthed and the beans enjoyed.

BUNDLING—Bundling was the colonial custom of attached/betrothed young men and women, wherein they were permitted to sleep in the same bed, fully clothed so they could snuggle together. Many times they were separated by a "bundling board" which was a wide pine plank set between them to keep them separate.

Although the intent was to maintain purity and character for the young folk involved, the practice was altruistic at best, and disastrous at worst.

Many times tavern maids were paid by tavern customers to bundle with them, or more . . .

CLOCK JACK—A meat roasting spit driven by a weight driven clock mechanism that rotated the spit before the fire. Many were custom fitted to the fireplace openings, and in later versions were spring driven. See illustration below.

COOT—The incomparable indigestible Atlantic shore sea duck; generally dark colored, they are difficult to shoot, more difficult to cook, and damned near impossible to eat, let alone to digest.

CONFINEMENT—Refers to the short period of time when a pregnant colonial woman became too "noticeable" to be seen in public. This term in Victorian years became associated with the few days shortly before birth, and the birth process itself.

FLIP—A mild popular beverage in Colonial times which was based upon beer, mixed with rum, brown sugar, molasses and dried pumpkin. Many taverns also kept a bowl of "flip sweetener" as an option, which consisted of cream, sugar, and eggs, well beaten together. The mixture was stirred with a red-hot poker, kept clean for that purpose.

Suzananh made her flip with the sweetener included, as opposed to being a separate option, and of course, the Essex rum made it extra potent.

HARD MONEY—Coins made of copper, silver or gold. Thus they were "hard" metal and always held intrinsic value, and thus the trust of those using them in commerce and trade.

JACK SLED—A low slung simple sled used for hauling immense heavy loads. See illustration below.

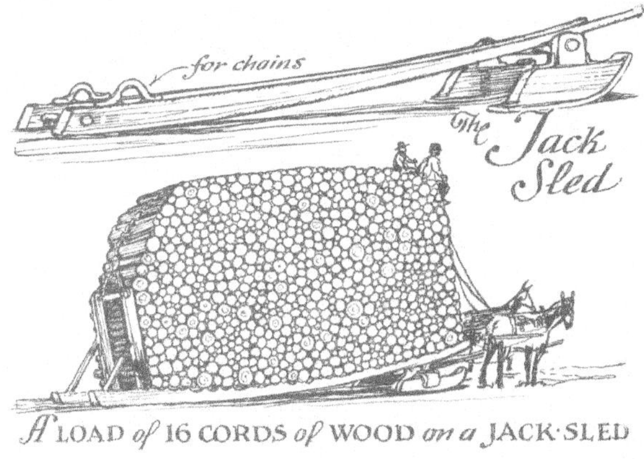

A LOAD of 16 CORDS of WOOD on a JACK·SLED

MOVEMENT—This illustration below is the style of movement that Suzannah examined in the Walker clock shop.

NIDDY NODDY—A yarn gathering device to keep it from being tangled as it was spun on the spinning wheel. See illustration below.

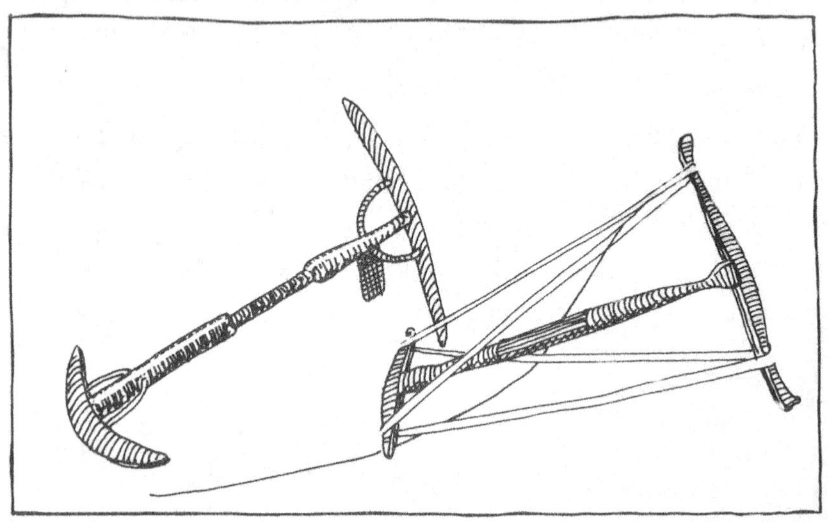

"Niddy-noddy, two heads and one body."

PEMMICAN—Originally a Native American ready to eat, high energy food, consisting of dried meats, (dried beef, buffalo, venison, squirrel, turkey, etc.) mixed with whatever berries might be had locally, (blueberries, cranberries, cherries, strawberries, etc.) in a beef or bear fat and dried.

Pemmican lasted for months and could be eaten any time and virtually any place.

POSSIBLES BAG—A small over the shoulder bag used to carry supplies for shooting and survival; such as lead balls, cloth patches, grease, gun flints, vent picks, cleaning jags, fire flint strikers and tinder for lighting fires.

SMALL BEER—A cheaper beer sold in colonial taverns that had little or no alcohol content.

SPANISH MILLED DOLLAR/PIECE OF EIGHT—The Spanish milled dollar was the world currency of its time. It also was the standard definition of "hard money" accepted throughout the world.

The American dollar coin, first produced in 1794, was a direct descendant of the famous "piece of eight." See illustration below.

SYLLABUB—A drink made primarily of heavy cream, which is whipped to a froth and curdled by a mixture of wine, cider or other popular local flavors, and served (spooned) over a base drink of wine, rum, or beer beneath it in a tumbler, glass or mug.

Suzannah's Chestnuts

One pound of chestnuts
6 TBS brown sugar
1 Cup of dark molasses rum (80–100 proof)

Dissolve sugar into rum and set aside.

Slice a large X into the chestnuts (to the meat) and roast in tin for 30 minutes over medium fire. (Or bake in oven at 325)

Remove chestnuts and peel them as they cool.

Stir the peeled chestnuts into the rum and sugar mixture, ensuring they are well covered and soaked.

Ignite the rum, and serve hot as flambé.

www.ingramcontent.com/pod-product-compliance
Lightning Source LLC
Chambersburg PA
CBHW070728120726
47910CB00001B/14